76

Shadbolt, Maurice.
    Strangers and journeys. New York, St. Martin's Press
[c1972]

    636 p. 22 cm. $10.00

    I. Title.

PZ4.S5235St 3
[PR9639.3.S5]

Strangers and
Journeys

MAURICE SHADBOLT

Strangers and Journeys

ST. MARTIN'S PRESS
NEW YORK

Acknowledgments are due to the editors of The New Yorker, Landfall *and* Otago Review '63 *for portions of this novel which originally appeared in different form in their magazines; also to Victor Gollancz (London) and Atheneum Publishers (New York) for portions of this book first used as short stories.*

St. Martin's Press
175 Fifth Avenue
New York, N.Y. 10010

Affiliated Publishers:
Macmillan & Company, Limited, London
—also at Bombay, Calcutta, Madras and Melbourne

The Erewhonians say that we are drawn through life backwards; or again, that we go onwards into the future as into a dark corridor. Time walks beside us and flings back shutters as we advance; but the light thus given often dazzles us, and deepens the darkness which is in front . . . They say at other times that the future and the past are as a panorama upon two rollers; that which is on the roller of the future unwraps itself on to the roller of the past . . . The same hand has painted the whole picture, and the incidents vary little — rivers, woods, plains, mountains, towns and peoples, love, sorrow and death.

— SAMUEL BUTLER

A country made for angels, not for men.

— JAMES K. BAXTER

To Frank Shadbolt, Kevin Ireland, Barry Mitcalfe, Dick Scott, Eric McCormick, Ian Cross, Colin McCahon, Michael Smither and Barbara Magner for their share of this journey. Also to the memory of Renato Amato, who journeyed always as a stranger.

Contents

Preludes

Paris, 1959

THE CAB DROPPED him at the Place Pigalle. The air was mild with September. Rain, earlier that evening, had left a melancholy shine on street and pavement. Lights flashing and jiggling advertised strip-tease cellars, hamburgers, Cinzano. The noisy crowd rippled sluggish each side of the street. Prostitutes formed ranks up side alleys. Some drunken American servicemen haggled angrily with a cab-driver.

Ian felt lost: it was his first time in this part of Paris. He had crossed the Seine only twice since he settled in his room off Odeon. He hadn't hurried his sight-seeing. He liked to take in one part of the city at a time, gently. This sudden surge was as brutal as a blow. Evidently this was the Paris the tourists purchased. Along Clichy he saw the neon windmill of the Moulin Rouge.

He floundered along with the crowd for a time, without an idea of how or where he should begin his search. At one point, outside a cafe which rang with the jazz of a negro band, the crowd banked up, spreading out across the street.

He stopped, as curious as the rest. At the centre of the crowd there was modest commotion. Then he saw the reason. A man had clambered out of a first-floor window, swaying perilously above the awning of the cafe, in pursuit of an escaped bird, a canary. Apparently he had been trying to entice the bird back into his room, back into its cage. Now he was going after it.

The canary sat jauntily on a stone projection. It even sang a note or two.

The crowd grew silent. In the background traffic hooted and grumbled.

The man inched his way across the face of the building, toward the canary. He tried to whistle reassuringly, to calm the bird. But the bird ignored him. Then he was near enough to grab it. He extended his arm, his hand, his fingers – then faltered. The canary fluttered out of reach.

There was a sigh of disappointment from the thickening crowd – a long, low, sibilant expulsion of breath.

'He'll never get it,' murmured a woman. 'He'll never get it now.'

'Never,' agreed a man.

'And it will die,' she said.

'Yes,' he said. 'It will die.'

But the man above the cafe did not give up. The canary had settled on a windowsill. He picked his way gently and quietly toward it, at times swaying out from the building again. The crowd was even quieter.

This time he pounced with success. He caught the bird firmly with both hands. There was a roar of pleasure, and then applause from the crowd. In that first moment of elation, though, the man lost his footing. A woman screamed as he lurched out and fell across the cafe awning. There was a ripping sound and he plummeted through the awning to the pavement. For a moment he lay there seemingly injured. But then he rose briskly, unhurt.

The applause began again.

With his two hands still fastened about the bird, the man made a prizefighter's gesture of victory toward the crowd. Then his expression changed to dismay. He opened his hands slowly. The bird lay limp. Evidently he had crushed it in his fall. It was already quite lifeless.

And the proprietor of the cafe was asking him to explain the damage to the awning.

'It's dead,' mourned the woman near Ian. 'They've killed it.'

'It's dead,' said the man beside her, 'and there is nothing we can do. Come along now, my love.'

The crowd dispersed quietly; Ian was again adrift. A short way along the street some prostitutes were wrangling with a man who wished to park his car on their beat.

He was getting nowhere. He tried to recall what Thompson, the American student, had told him: 'Off the Place Pigalle. In one of the bars. You might find him there – if he is the guy you're looking for. What does he call himself again?'

'Tim Livingstone.'

'That sounds right. I've seen him around there once or twice,

14

about three months ago. Ask around. You might strike him there somewhere.'

Off the Place Pigalle. In one of the bars.

He circled the place, trying to decide on a side street to start. He was snared briefly by a lottery-seller with cap and very thin lips who offered him a special exhibition – two men or two women or even, if he so preferred, a man and a woman. Escaping, Ian found he had chosen a side street, one with a great many bars. He selected one at random, went in and bought a beer. The place was crowded with Americans and girls. One girl, sitting next to him at the bar, slid her hand gently across his knee while he sipped his drink.

He smiled. 'Thanks,' he said. 'But I haven't the money.'

'If you haven't the money,' she replied gaily, 'you can't have the love.'

'No,' he agreed. 'I can't have the love.'

'Sad,' she said. 'Sad for the love.'

'Yes. Sad for most things.'

Her hand remained affectionate on his knee. 'I like you,' she announced. 'I could arrange a special price for the love.' She smiled. 'And some very special love.'

'Thanks all the same,' he said, 'but I'll buy you a drink.' Her good humour was pleasant.

'Aren't you here for the love?' she asked.

'Not really. No.'

This puzzled her. 'Then why do you come?'

'I'm looking for someone. A friend.'

'And she is not here? Sad.'

'Not she. He.'

'Ah,' she said. 'Like that. And you look so much a man.'

'No,' he said. 'Not like that.'

'Who is this one?'

'Perhaps you might know him. I think he is known about here.'

'Young or old?'

'Young.'

'His name?'

'Tim Livingstone.'

'An American?'

'No. Not American.'

'Hah. Then English.'

15

'Nor English. From the other side of the world.'

'A *colon,* yes?'

'In a way. From a place called New Zealand.'

'Of that I've heard. Australia? I have met one Australian man.'

'No. Not even Australia. Still further.'

'But that would be the end of the world,' she said, incredulous. 'Almost nowhere.'

'Indeed,' he said. 'Almost.' He paused. 'And you haven't heard of this man?'

'Not here. No. How could I forget a man from almost nowhere? He would be one always to remember.'

'Possibly,' Ian agreed.

'But then I am not long here. I am from Toulouse. Others may know of this one.' She called out to other women along the bar, asking if they knew of someone by the name Tim Livingstone.

Some thought they knew; others weren't sure. Certainly he didn't frequent this bar often, if at all. Ian should try one of the other bars.

He finished his beer and slid off his stool. The girl caught at his arm. 'Remember, if you are here again. Yvette from Toulouse.'

'Of course. Yvette from Toulouse.'

'I hope you find your friend.'

'Thank you, Yvette.'

As he left the bar, he heard her calling out: 'No use. No money. He was sad for a friend from almost nowhere.' There was laughter. Not like that, he repeated to himself silently; not like that, exactly.

He selected another bar and went inside. He stayed briefly; he merely looked around. It was a bar much like the other, with no familiar face, and there seemed no point in buying a beer.

Then he tried another bar, and another.

An hour or two later he felt ready to give up. Did he still care so much? He was no longer sure. The chances were that if he stayed in Paris he would strike Tim Livingstone sooner or later, one side of the Seine or the other. Thompson might have been wrong anyway; it might not have been Tim he had seen in Montmartre. An unlikely place to find Tim in any case. He would surely have been allergic to this atmosphere. Or should have been. Ian could not imagine finding him here.

16

He was in a long and narrow, dimly-lit street which he expected might cut back at an oblique angle towards the Place Pigalle. It was deserted; his footsteps echoed crisply. A sign at the end of the street, AMERICAN BAR, shed a faint orange light over the cobbles. The damp was gone from the ground, the smell of rain from the evening. He genuinely felt like a drink now.

He pushed into the place. Unlike the other bars, mirrored and bright, this one was lit in subdued fashion. Red shaded lamps; faint faces in rosy pools. It was difficult to see at first. He bought his beer and found an empty table; he was glad, for a moment, to relax and cease his search.

An old man, a yard or two away, was explaining something very patiently to a young girl. They talked in Spanish. There was this possibility, the man said, and that. This and that. Any number of possibilities. What did she think?

The girl didn't know, evidently.

Ian tried to make up his mind about them. Father and daughter? Uncle and niece? The girl, anyway, looked bored. She was attractive, perhaps no more than eighteen, and well dressed. The man hardly appeared good company. This possibility, and that.

He was losing interest. The beer was cold and pleasantly sharp. He decided, in the end, that he was simply witnessing another business transaction. That, or something like it. The girl had a wry and cheeky twist to her mouth whenever she talked, which was seldom. Once or twice she looked across at Ian, sitting alone. It might have been a frankly commercial appraisal, or just straying sexual curiosity. He was not sure he cared to meet her eye. On the whole Yvette from Toulouse would have been less of a problem, and certainly less committing an interest. And perhaps he preferred invisibility, as ghostly voyeur. (Did that lottery-seller, offering diverse performances, have an instinct for a good customer?) Certainly he felt, at this time, in this place, insubstantial enough. The third time the girl caught his eye – she was quite slow, and doubtless deliberate this time – he shifted his gaze.

And with a thump of the heart he was solid again, quite tight in his flesh, though he had soon to remind himself that he was still in Paris, and not half a world away. For he was, in fact, looking at someone not ten feet removed. And not years distant; as near as now. He was looking at Tim Livingstone half

17

anonymous in untidy beard and finally not really caring to believe it.

He made, though, no immediate move.

Wellington, 1919

THE AFTERNOON SUN is bright on raw hills and a still harbour. On Thorndon railway station platform drunken soldiers sing of a Madamoiselle from Armentieres. A train is ready to depart; there is a hissing of steam and a ringing of bells. A late-comer, tall, with lean face and prominent nose, hurries along the platform and jumps aboard a second-class carriage. He slams his small suitcase into the rack above a vacant seat and sits beside a short man of tanned, sturdy appearance. Both are young, no more than thirty. Both are fresh to civilian clothes, for different reasons.

The train gives a jolt and begins to pull out of Wellington; they seem to look back upon that city with no regret. After a time they begin conversation. The tall one – call him William Freeman – is reticent at first. He has reason; he has become accustomed to reticence. But it is by no means natural to him. He is just out of jail. There he conversed lengthily and often intensely with himself, but seldom with others. The short one – call him Edward Livingstone, or Ned as others might – is bluntly, rather clumsily friendly. This isn't in character either. Before the war he was quiet and retiring, and content enough with loneliness. The war made that self inconvenient, and he shelved it for the duration. He borrowed the boisterous and gregarious character of some of his comrades, enough to suffice, and not with any remarkable success. He saw Gallipoli and he saw the Somme. He also once, on a fortnight's leave, saw London but of that city he has small memory. Soon he will remember very little of the last four years, and even that will be more than enough. He finds it difficult to credit that he is really sitting here, in a new cheap suit, with a padded seat under his bum, on his way home, alive and almost intact; he finds it difficult to credit that he is, after all, much as he was. It could be dream. To believe it he needs the sound of his own voice. And also someone to take his existence for granted.

18

'You going far?' he asks the man beside him.

'Auckland,' is the reply. 'All the way.'

'Great place.' He does not really believe this, but he says it; he has heard it said.

'It's a city.'

This statement of fact puzzles Ned Livingstone. There is nothing to discuss, certainly nothing to argue. It does not strike him that the stranger beside him might, in some way, be as uneasy as himself.

'I hear this 'flu has been bad up there. People dying.'

'Bad everywhere.'

This too was beyond argument.

'I had a spell of it myself, in Trentham camp, before they let me out. You just out too?'

'Out of where?'

'The army. I thought you might be.'

'Not out of the army. Not me.'

'You didn't miss nothing.'

'No?'

'No. Most of the time it was like – ' He falters, and is lost. He can no longer say, if he ever could. His tender sense of reality seems again in peril. 'Like what they all say about it,' he attempts.

'You didn't like it?'

'I did what they told me.'

'See much fighting?'

'Enough.' Then, 'A bloody abattoir, it was. Dangling guts and raw steaks and bleeding livers.' He feels swift, unaccountable anger. He has never felt this before. He will probably never feel like this again. And he senses sympathy. 'My mates,' he adds.

'What for?'

He has not really asked that before, either; he has been too grateful for surviving. He is surprised, then, to receive so quick an answer.

'To make the rich richer and the poor poorer. Like all wars.'

Perhaps too quick. Ned Livingstone is dubious. But also troubled. 'You reckon?' he says, almost off-hand.

'I don't reckon; I know. And they'll have their wars so long as the workers are stupid enough to let them.'

'Who will?'

'The capitalist classes. The ones who collect the dividends.'

'You reckon?' he says again. It is, this time, all he can say.

19

It is too large, too terrible a thought. He cannot reject it wholly, no more than he can accept it. It remains an irritation in a sensitive place. And the man beside him looks normal, no crank. He goes on talking, frighteningly reasonable. About the capitalists, the war, the workers.

'What about Russia?' he asks at last. Out of some cloudy memory he thinks that this question may have some relevance. He hopes so because he wishes, before this stranger, not to appear a fool.

'There the workers got sense. They put a stop to the war. Kicked out the Czar and his generals and made their own government. That's why the capitalists, the British, the French, the Americans, are out to crush them. Because they can't be allowed to get away with it, see.'

'You seem,' Ned Livingstone observes gently, 'to know a lot about it.'

'I've had plenty of time to study these things, the last two years. Guest of the government.'

'Oh,' says Ned Livingstone. 'Like that.'

'Yes. Like that. Not so bad. They feed you, at least.'

'What were you in for?'

'Sedition, they called it. Disloyalty. Agitation against the war. Some would of liked us hung.'

Ned Livingstone is now uneasy, he isn't sure why. He wishes now that he had not asked. Better just to listen to this man, by way of passing time, without the ultimate issue made so plain. But now he knows.

'Many like you?' he asks.

'A few. They let a union band play for us outside the jail gate for Christmas. Nice. We weren't forgotten.'

'What are you going to do now?' Ned Livingstone means, of course, what kind of work; it is a sociable question.

'Now? We're going to keep up the fight, of course.'

The fight? Ned Livingstone has for some months thought the fight over and done, and twelve thousand miles behind. This is a new and unpleasant thought too. Wherever the new fighting is likely to be, he means this time to place himself at a great distance from it. Because he knows exactly where he is going, which he imagines is more than this stranger does. And exactly what he means to do. The only fighting he plans is for himself. But that is different. It is between himself and the land he took, but never farmed, before the war. It is different because there is no hate. He found hate once, it was difficult to find it, and he did not like it. Because his sleep now is seldom free of dreams of death. Because he is no longer clean. He remembers two things. The sound of a bayonet, a queerly distinct sound, as it enters a uniformed human body. The sound of a gutted man crying for mother. That was when hate mated obscenely with guilt, and his dreams began.

So he is silent, and obscurely threatened. It is not that he dislikes the stranger. It is just that he is uncomfortable. Better, sometimes, not to understand.

'It'll take time,' the stranger is saying. 'Years, maybe. People take time to learn. But there'll come a day – ' He pauses, momentarily lost in some vision. Ned Livingstone cannot share it. He cannot even begin to see, and is not sure he wants to.

Hunched forward in his seat, he feels an old misery return. It is, he imagines, a very private misery, quite unique to himself. It is the misery inflicted by a world in which things are never quite what they seem.

'Here,' the stranger says. 'Everywhere. That day will come.'

He might have been, with Ned at his side, about to signal start of battle.

Then Ned, with a warm rush of relief, remembers his land again; he has never been so grateful for it before. It seems even to give him strength to be a match for the man beside him. Does this man know of the slight sucking sound a bayonet makes as it withdraws from a still living human body? He thinks not. Otherwise the man would not talk so easy.

Now he leans forward in his seat to see out the window of the train. He is not exactly ignoring the stranger. He is simply trying to prolong his moment of pleasure, and at the same time conceal it; he could have quite choked with excitement. He has not often allowed himself to think about it for years now, and not thinking about it became habit. And now, incredibly, the land is almost within reach again.

Grassland, flat and rich, flanks the rushing train. The hard hills are behind, or pushed tall in the distance. He does not envy the owners of these prospering farms. He constructs no vision of his own future. He sees struggle, of course. But after all he does not aim to possess fat sheep, fatter cattle, glossy acres. He aims to possess himself again.

'Great green country,' he says. Making conversation of his own.

21

'Yes,' says the stranger. Whose moment has gone.

'Different to my part,' says Ned Livingstone, gaining confidence. 'No rich river-flat up there. All rough limestone country, and clay.'

'You a farmer?'

'That's right. Just getting started when I had to pull out.'

'You'll be glad to be back, then.'

'I am.'

He understates it. Those split, wired fence-posts passing in precise formation beyond the carriage window – there was a time when he could have taken one in his hands, in a flare of homesickness, and kissed it. Regardless of splinters.

Over there they had hedges and stone walls; and tight villages and narrow lanes. Everything tidy, unless war ripped the guts out of it. But never the same. It was all too neat for a man to make a real start. Everything had been done before.

'And I've still got my land,' he adds. 'It's good to be back, all right. You know,' he continues, trembling on the edge of his own thought, 'what I reckon? I reckon this country's still small enough for the small man to have a chance.'

But he cannot say what he means. No more, perhaps, than the other can. Who only says, 'We all learn.'

They read, doze, buy meat pies at station refreshment rooms, and carry thick china cups of tea back to their seats. Night begins to soften the stark ridges of the countryside through which they are passing; the last of sunset stains the wide rivers. Dim lights flicker on in the carriage. Their conversations grow easier, more companionable. Sometimes they even find something to laugh about. The train hammers up the rugged island. Across tussock desert where snowdrifts shine in moonlight, past whitened volcanoes, through tunnels and over viaducts, and round a great spiral cut into mountain.

Sometime in the morning, in the darkened carriage, Ned Livingstone stirs from sleep at the guard's call. He pulls on his jacket, fetches down his suitcase from the rack. His acquaintance awakes.

'You here already?' he says.

'Yes. Home. Next stop.'

The train has begun to slow.

'Well,' says the stranger, 'good luck.'

'To you too.'

And they are sincere. For they are both, on their separate

22

journeys, more vulnerable than they will likely be again. In some way they have touched each other, or met themselves. Anyway the liking was there, in the end, if not the sympathy. And they would not exchange.

So they shake hands, tightly, as the train halts. Beyond the carriage window is a feebly-lit station. Beyond that a dark, sleeping town. Ned Livingstone plunges down the aisle, out of the carriage, into the frosty night.

They will never really meet again, at least not as themselves.

Part One

Fathers

One:

TOWARDS THE END OF WAIATARUA VALLEY IS A NARROW GORGE. Beyond the gorge, with its crazily stacked limestone castles, the valley opens out again. There was a muddy track through the gorge, by the edge of the river. Toe toe and flax grew abundant alongside the river.

Before the war settlement sped up the valley as far as the gorge. Then it stopped, waiting for someone to go beyond. For there was clearly enough land beyond the gorge, in a hollow beneath tall hills, for one or perhaps two farms. But there were disadvantages. The distance from town, for one thing. The muddy track through the gorge, for another. And the land beyond was heavily timbered. There were strands of totara and tangles of supplejack; it was large land with large growth and dense places where light entered feebly and man perhaps never. Some of the bigger trees had been felled and dragged by bullocks through the gorge, thus creating the muddy track, by a company which later went bankrupt. Otherwise the land was untouched.

So it waited, and went cheap.

Ned Livingstone was the first at that end of the valley. He took his possessions up from town, past already tidy farms, and through the gorge. That was the last anyone saw of him for a while. He vanished into the wilderness with his horse and dray. On the dray, along with a couple of split suitcases, were axe, pick, shovel, slasher and rifle. People expected him back in disgust.

For there were some who said he'd been sold a pup. A musical pup. He in turn insisted he'd bought it for a song. Though he did make mention of a mortgage.

When he did return, down through the gorge, it was with his

horse and empty dray. He went to town to provision up. That was all. He did not look disgusted. He looked tired.

The next thing, there was another company dragging logs through the gorge. He had sold off some of his felled timber.

People hadn't expected much of him because he was a townie. Though he didn't look soft. After a while they had respect for him. So he began to have neighbours. That was when they learned he wasn't strictly a townie. He came from a farm up north, where his father had gone broke on the gumfields, trying to farm that hard and bitter land. Ned left school to dig gum while his father went broke. There were few amber nuggets left then, Dalmatian diggers having been much too thorough in that area, certainly not enough to save his father. So they walked off the land and went to town, to Auckland, where failure and dreams alike could be contained in wooden boxes, rank after peeling rank, ugly and quite inflammable. Since Ned didn't drink or gallivant, he saved money. Or rather, he had money. He hadn't really seen money he could call his own before.

Now he had it. Jingling into his pockets, rustling into his bank. Until he had enough. He wanted another start. He didn't want to walk asphalt streets to work and spend his life looking out his narrow bedroom window at board fences and drying underwear. He didn't want to feel cluttered and bossed. Even at home he was bossed, by a father turned cranky with age. His father was too old for a new start, too tired, and put all his hope on losing racehorses.

So Ned, when he had the money, struck off south for a new start. He was still young and very strong. He stopped off in a small town, only a few years past a trading post, where the railway had just gone through and he heard there might be land cheap. The name of this town was Te Ika or The Fish. Some Maori once having caught a fish of remarkable size there, possibly. Though the fish were quite modest now. Or it may have been that something about the place, some limestone outcrop on one of the hills perhaps, had a curious fish shape. Te Ika lay in the widest part of the Waipa valley, in country which until lately had still been wild and forbidden to white men. The river looped through the town and sometimes flooded. The main street was a collection of sheds and shops strung beside the railway, with a school at one end and a Maori meeting house at the other. The street itself was a dust-storm in summer and a bog in winter, with bullock teams and sometimes whooping Maoris on horseback.

Ned didn't rush into buying. He took a job as navvy on the railway, helping to clear the slips of clay and papa rock which still often engulfed the line. That was how he came to be known, at first, as a townie. Then he found his land at the end of the Waiatarua valley and the neighbours came. The women with home-baked cake and gentle curiosity, the men with advice and yarns.

They found he had built a whare. A one-room shack of roughly-split timber. He had cleared the bush around, to let the sunlight in, and planted vegetables in a neat garden. These surprise visitors, with cake and yarns, usually found Ned busy somewhere. Chopping or burning or digging. And dressed in black singlet, torn trousers and thick muddy boots. With a dirty hat askew on his head, looking rather forgotten.

They didn't stay long, the visitors. Ned didn't have much to offer in the way of hospitality apart from a billy of tea and a couple of chipped mugs. They wanted, of course, an exchange of visits. It was the neighbourly thing. Ned should come to dinner, one Sunday perhaps, after church. Then they remembered Ned hadn't been seen at church. They told him he would be welcome there.

Ned was embarrassed and silent. He didn't say he wanted no part of church, and had no business to do with God, having inherited a cantankerous Irish streak. It would have been unneighbourly.

Sometimes he went to some Sunday dinner, though, even if he didn't always know what to do with his big hands. Ned was a good listener, men agreed, if inclined at times to be a moody bugger.

And Ned toiled up beyond the gorge. Splitting and hammering and clearing. He was putting in his first fences and growing his first grass when Tom Jackson came riding up the gorge with the war. The Kaiser was already in Belgium, and the old country calling for men.

Ned, who in Auckland once joined the territorials for want of something better, was soon off to war with lemon-squeezer hat and puttees bound tight around his legs. He had less to leave than most; he had hardly begun.

When he returned, four years later, he made his way back up the Waiatarua valley in the early winter dark. Lights were on in

29

the farmhouses and there was no one to notice him – or, if noticing, to identify him. It was a week or more before some neighbours knew Ned Livingstone was back up there beyond the gorge.

That first morning was fine, with frost. He heard running water and birds.

He untangled himself from his blankets and climbed stiff from the floor where he had fallen tired the night before. He padded across creaking floor boards and opened the door. And breathed. Sunlight flared on the trees. The air was so magically solid and bright; the cold seemed to crackle in his lungs.

Scrub and fern, chalky with frost, had grown back up to the whare. It concealed his first, incomplete fences. It buried the garden. Except that here and there potatoes grew wild.

And the whare? Having survived four winters it was not in bad shape, considering. The crudely cut weatherboards still looked tough, prepared for worse weather, like the man. Paintless, resilient, a square box as functional as a fist. But the interior was changed beyond plausibility. The one window was dim with dirt, and thickly webbed. The tin chimney was holed with rust. Scavenging bush-rats had found a home, leaving litters of paper and filth. Everything had the damp and mould of returning bush.

He could hardly feel outrage. There was surprise in the rough hills, in the shiny green of the winter trees. In the metallic applause of water rushing over the stones in the creek. In the chilly blue sky above his acres. And there was something hard in his throat.

He relieved himself, leaving stain on the frost, a steaming signature of title. Filing at a blunt axe, rust against rust, reddish dust covered his hands. When the axe was something like keen, he began to chop wood. The crisp sounds rang against the trees like warning shots. There was a quivering of leaf and a fluttering of birds. And echoes back from the hills. Upon their flanks the sound grew puny; and their giant limestone outcrops remained indifferent against the sky.

The wood at which he chopped was from a heap he had built before the war. Now the logs were white and half rotten, tumbled by storm into long weeds. He split some for kindling. Then he carried an armload inside. In the long, wide fireplace, backed by sods, he prepared the fire carefully on scraps of old newspaper.

30

He struck a match and lit the paper. The first thin flame explored the damp wood and drew back trembling, a nervous lover. He encouraged it. He blew. He fed it more paper. Now the flame was eager. It snapped and leapt. It shrivelled the split wood. With sputtering sighs, tiny spurts of blue and yellow, the fire raced. An acrid smoke spun and gusted, uncertain of its direction, quite baffled, then lifted swiftly up through the tin chimney. The whare knew warmth again.

Ned felt satisfaction then. He fetched more wood and made the fire huge. Then he took a tin billy, freshly purchased from a Te Ika store, gleaming and with the price still marked in red chalk, down to the creek. The water ran icy through his thick, cautious fingers. He dipped once, experimentally, and then began with system to splash his face and arms. Until his flesh tingled, growing numb and one with the land's winter. He had forgotten soap, which would have intruded. And towel, which might have cheated the chill. The cold ebbed slowly from his grainy flesh as he rose. Then he rinsed and filled the billy and left the creek. The immaculate water slopped back and forward in the billy, shedding silver drops as he walked. Then he stopped and listened.

Up the creek, not far, a bird chimed. Once, twice, and again. A gentle sound, with some poignance.

He got back to the whare. Inside the fire roared now, and spat. He hung the billy on an iron bar above the blaze. As the new shine of the billy darkened so the water bubbled. Into the water he threw a handful of tea, for a brew-up. With a knife he sharpened a stick into a spear. He skewered sausages, toasted them until their flesh split and bubbled in the heat. The heat was thick now, and everywhere, drying out the whare. The sweat sprang out on his face as the sausages grew dark.

Later he sat on the step of his whare and ate and drank. An agreeable heat kindled in his gut. The day was warming too; frost steamed from the fern as shadows grew shorter and sun rose higher.

There was much to be done, of course: it could wait. For he was content to sit and breathe. To drink a decent brew of tea, and roll and smoke a cigarette, and enjoy the sun on his solid flesh. He had anticipated this moment for so long he had even grown afraid of it. And now it fell into his lap, shimmering. There were even some things he could not have expected, like the way the scrub was shot through with tiny glittering webs the

31

spiders had spun. He wanted the moment to last as long as he could. But there was a limit, as always.

Later that morning he swept and scrubbed the floor of the whare, while the fire blazed. He hammered up a new bunk. Soon the place was almost decent.

He began to think of food again. While mutton and potatoes boiled in the billy he spent time outside sorting and arranging his tools, sharpening his slasher, resharpening his axe. He stood these tokens, along with the grubber, by the door of the whare.

Yet after he had eaten he did not touch them. He wanted his first day of work, which would arrive soon enough, to be complete in itself; today was his last to take things easy. Perhaps he also sought again something of his morning moment. He did not know. Anyway, sitting on the step after lunch, he grew restless and impatient for his work to begin: an itch in his body.

He walked to relieve it. His legs took him across the derelict garden, along the bank of the creek. There were young willows he had planted to hold the bank in time of flood. They had grown enormously, but now were empty of leaf.

Here the creek swerved around a limestone bluff feathered with pale toe toe, and greened with stubborn treefern. Further up the creek were stepping stones to the other bank. He made his way carefully across, looking down into the clear water. He saw an eel snake away downstream; and caught the flash of a small trout.

Once over the creek, he began to climb. The winter sun was still soft on his skin. Through dense fern he made his way up to a point above the limestone bluff. From there he could see clear across his valley, his whare in the foreground; there was little other mark of man to be seen.

His heart still toiled within his ribs after his climb; but this pulse would have raced anyway. He could see, and imagine. There was this to be done, and that. From here he could see bright acres not yet cleared and sown with grass. From here he could see house and outbuildings not yet built. But he could also see, as surely as the contours of the valley, the possible shapes of his life.

A bullet might have punctured him on the beach at Gallipoli, allowing his life to bleed out. A shell might have shattered him in France, plastering his brain and bone into the mud. He might have found himself, once, on the wrong end of a bayonet. Any of these things, and more. Yet he lived, and could wonder now. He could see his life mean something here; and his death. For that he would die here, one day, he could not doubt; he could not afford to doubt. There had been more than enough madness. It was time things made sense.

And then things did make sense, or seem to, more than he bargained for. Afterwards all he could remember, exactly, was the sun on his face, the smoke drifting from his cigarette; the rest was to hard to hold. But everything, as if melting in dream, seemed to become one; the valley became the world, and he became the valley. And at the moment he might have gone further, known more, the landscape dissembled, broke up into its separate parts; and he was sitting alone on a hard rock.

He sat there, though, for a long time after. The sun sank toward the western hills. He tried to resurrect the vision, but without success. Not even when the sunset flared with spurt after spurt of fading colour. Other visions might have ridden there and he would not have seen. The colour of the upper hills mellowed from red to pale lemon and the air grew cool, the frost already gathering in the shadows.

He could not, and did not, expect another day like it.

The next morning was dull and he woke to the racket of rain on his iron roof. It rained all that day and for two days after. The creek grew high and muddy.

On the fourth day he began work. He worked through until the eighth day, when he resumed his regular weekly trips to town to provision up. That was when some saw Ned Livingstone for the first time. He hacked his way through winter into spring. And near the end of spring came the first burn-off. The fires began to roar against the hills.

Two:

AUCKLAND WAS NOT, HE SUPPOSED, ANY GREAT SHAKES OF A city; he had never really thought it much of a place. But it was there, and all he had for a start. In any case there was no real profit for him in attempting to unravel reason from its motley main street, with stone facades and electric wires and rackety trams; or the warehouses and factories and wooden acres of housing beyond. People lived there, on this lumpy limb of land between two harbours, and some called it home. It was hardly for him to argue it away. If it wasn't home to him, it was the next best thing; he had to have people, and wouldn't get anywhere without them. Auckland had people.

And it was really not much changed, unlike himself; he saw it through tighter eyes. There were still uniforms in the streets, and people talked of the influenza. This, though declining, was still a good subject; death was always something to share with neighbour or stranger. The coffins had been stacked six high on the railway platform near the city cemetery, at the worst.

He took a room over the hill from Queen Street, near enough to the centre, and found a casual job on the waterfront. He walked the streets alone. He was so long and lean he might at times have looked frightening. He could never get clothes to fit, for some reason. The sleeves slipped too far up the arm, or the trousers lifted too far above the ankles. His awkward frame should have filled out, but never had. It was not for want of eating. He ate in quantity every evening at a Dalmatian grill shop near the wharves. The Dalmatian was a fat, sweaty man who liked to joke with his customers in bad English. His bad English was part of the joke, always. It added something comic to the most indifferent stories; he often said it would not pay him to talk good. He made his money, enough to buy his business,

34

digging kauri gum in the north before the war. His name was
Rude, and his customers could make what they liked of it, and
did.

There was one customer, though, with whom he did not joke.
This one who came, ate, and went away without expression. He
did not complain if the fish was off, the steak tough, or the chips
cold. He fed whatever happened on his plate into his mechanical
mouth, as if it were of no importance. He left no stains on the
cloth, spilled no sauce. His plate was always left clean. He paid
his money and never made drunken issue of the change.

On the whole singular among Rude's customers. Soon there
was seldom a night when Rude did not watch that long back
move out of his shop without some wonder; he felt he might
have been missing something important, which would explain.
He even wished, for his own peace of mind, that the man
would complain about something. Perhaps he was some kind of
sex maniac who prowled the streets after dark; the thought gave
Rude an exciting chill. But the man always went as wordless as
he came; and his feet rang along empty asphalt as he walked.
There were few people about in the evenings now. Pubs closed
at six, a wartime measure which persisted. No one knew why,
exactly, but there were other questions to be asked.

The trouble was he did not know where to begin.

He looked for people. He did quite a bit of that, for a while.
They were scattered and gone, sometimes dead. The bookshop
where he had once bought his literature, the works of Marx
and Daniel de Leon, was closed and boarded up. There was
some sort of factory drumming away behind the boards, in
triumph or mockery.

There were those, people he had once known, who avoided
him for reasons they knew best. Evidently jail had given him
more than just a pale complexion. For these people he might
have been carrier of some past plague. They scurried past in
the crowded street, eyes down. They had homes no doubt, and
families and jobs. There was one who stopped, one who was
now respectably in Parliament, and could patronize. He was
obviously not to be trusted.

And eventually there was another. Charlie Higgins, a perky
little man, veteran of the Waihi strike and ex-I.W.W. He had
ridden freights in America, put explosive under factories,
escaped a lynch mob.

'There are some of us who meet,' said Charlie. 'And talk. In a room off Grafton. Once a week, on Wednesdays.'

So this was the revolution now. Once a week, on Wednesdays.

'We have discussions,' said Charlie. 'On many subjects. Including the works of Lenin. And the programme of the Bolsheviks, which we have just received.'

While the Bolsheviks fought and died, their blood bright on the Siberian snow.

'We mean to spread the word,' Charlie went on. 'But first there is need for organization.'

'To talk?' asked William Freeman.

'We must begin,' said Charlie. 'Somewhere. There is need to talk, to clear our minds. The world has changed, for one thing. The war has come and gone. There is need to adapt.'

Like the one now in Parliament; he had adapted. William Freeman was suspicious of adaption. Yet his suspicion fell short of Charlie. He had once, in the past, felt he might safely trust his life to Charlie. And so far had no cause to believe himself wrong.

'True,' Charlie continued, 'there are some who would like just to talk. Within safe walls. It is sometimes cosy to be among those of the same opinion, as we all know.'

He would still like to think Charlie no fool. In the 1913 wharf strike, when specials rode horseback up Queen Street, he saw tiny Charlie duck under flailing batons, like a dangerous little bird, to drag two specials from their saddles and hammer them half-dead with his fists. While blood sprayed from his own broken head. Charlie knew his way around.

'You must come,' insisted Charlie. 'We need experience in the new struggle. There is not so much of that around. We need fighters as well as dreamers.'

There was also the Charlie who had known Joe Hill, the I.W.W. balladeer now dead before a firing squad in Utah, and could sing his songs.

'You will be there then, Bill,' Charlie concluded. 'Next Wednesday.'

And they drank on it, though William Freeman was not much given to the drink. It did no harm in moderation, but sometimes clouded issues. It made it easier, for example, to forgive a man who could talk revolution and yet enter Parliament; or, if not forgive, at least to understand. Yet drinking with Charlie opened places in his mind long shut. He talked until his

36

mouth ran dry, and needed more moistening. So the coins rattled across the bar and Charlie chuckled. He even found humour in jail at last, since Charlie had jail stories of his own. He had survived the jails of at least three countries. Since the time, as a slum orphan, he had shipped out from London's Tilbury docks to the United States and there deserted. He knew his way around, all right.

'This Lenin,' Charlie said. 'He has some interesting things to say.'

As much of the world was discovering. It was said that even Big Bill Haywood, leader of the I.W.W. was going to Moscow. There to learn something, perhaps.

'And our old mate Jack Donovan is in Parliament now,' Charlie said.

The one William Freeman had seen. Jack Donovan had run wild in 1913, calling for arson and assassination, and had to be restrained.

'The seats are well padded down there,' Charlie observed. 'He can dance on the grave of capitalism, like he always said, in comfort. And the money, they say, is not bad. At least it comes regular.'

This was more than Charlie could say. He was still in and out of jobs. More often out than in, because of bosses. Charlie was forty now, and looked the kind of dry and timid man who should have been buried in a large family. But he was neither, and had never married, though he knew the girls.

Unlike Bill Freeman, whom Charlie studied. A good woman, he thought, wouldn't hurt young Bill. At least twenty five, and likely never been kissed. He had first known Bill as young and shy. The shyness might have gone, along with much of his youth, but a rather unnerving coldness remained. The fact was, though, that any man just out of jail needed warming up. Perhaps that was it. It was surprising what even a few beers, and a bit of chat, could do for young Bill. Charlie managed, soon, to spring a laugh or two from him, and that was improvement. Laughter, Charlie believed, was a precious weapon in the class war. If you couldn't see the funny side, sometimes, you could go under.

Anyway he had Bill laughing.

On the Wednesday there was the meeting. In the chair was a short tough French Canadian with a Chaplin moustache. There were others foreign. A Serb, a couple of Danes, three Americans strongly I.W.W. Also a few immigrant Irish, and some other faces familiar to Bill Freeman from the past, in strikes and socialist agitation. A willowy young man with trembling hands gave a short lecture in a soft voice. He discussed socialist theory up to the turn of the century, while his notes rustled violently, and then sat down in haste; he might have stopped perplexingly in mid-sentence, or at least on a question mark, so solid was the silence following. After a time there was coughing and shuffling. There was supposed to be debate.

Then Charlie stood.

'It seems,' he said presently, taking his time, 'that there are two kinds among us. Those who would think, and those who would do. True, there is room for both. But the world was never changed by thinking alone. No more than it was made different by blind doing. There must be balance, this is true. But my feeling at the moment is we are getting heavy arses with our thinking.'

The applause came from the Americans and from the Serb, who was not sure he understood.

'I would suggest in conclusion, mister chairman, that we take our finger out – and that, if we don't, we rest our arses elsewhere of a Wednesday night.' Charlie spoke with passion enough. Then he sat down, with a wink for Bill.

'Has the speaker intention of putting a formal motion before the meeting?' asked the chairman.

It was Charlie's moment, but again he took his time. 'If you want it polite, and I am not much good at that, I propose we start to talk about making a revolutionary organization on the Bolshevik lines. Since it seems to work. If we aren't here to do that, we are here to do sweet bugger all.'

It was not clear.

'We don't know enough,' a Scotsman grunted from a corner.

'We know that some can do it,' Charlie replied. 'So why not us? These Russians are making a fair fist of it. I am not suggesting the capitalists will collapse at the first blast of our trumpet. But we can start to give the bastards a run for their money. Have we got the guts to begin, mister chairman?'

There was no reply. Perhaps he was too far ahead.

'Look at it this way,' Charlie went on. 'Right now capitalism might be splitting down the middle, the way Marx predicted.

And what are we doing? We are sitting around, a lot of dozy pricks, like ladies at a church social.'

'Hear hear,' said Bill Freeman, who was surprised at the sound of his public voice; it had grown strange with disuse. He rose as Charlie sat and eyes were suddenly, and disconcertingly, upon him instead. 'Hear hear,' he repeated more firmly, discovering strength and some anger. 'This is getting nowhere.'

This was safe enough, to begin, while he found his measure. 'In Hungary, if I am to believe the papers, there are comrades dying,' he added, 'in a white terror. In Germany also, the Spartacists. Not to speak of the Bolsheviks in Russia. While we talk here, cosy, men are dying for what we are supposed to believe. Dying. And we talk. Jesus, can't you see? Can't you?'

Perhaps some could. Even Charlie looked surprised.

There was also a Swede at the meeting. A blond giant with huge golden moustache. He rose, one hand on hip, one arm aloft, in heroic stance.

'Action,' he announced, 'is our need. Action. Sabotage. Destruction. These things. Or else we are but playing like children. To put injustice in its grave we must hate like men. And kill, if necessary. Until capitalism is chaos. And from the chaos will come our kingdom.'

He continued to stand, breathing fiercely; his moustache quivered.

'The hell with kingdoms,' Charlie said. 'We're finishing with them.'

Yet that there was appeal in the simplicity of this giant, no one would deny.

'It is,' continued the Swede, 'time for the deed.'

'And time to know,' Charlie interjected, 'how much the police are paying you to be here tonight.'

This released the new tension; there was some ragged laughter. The Swede was isolated, but did not understand it yet. He stood waiting, perhaps for allies.

So it seemed, after Charlie's thrust, that Bill Freeman would have to use the sledgehammer. 'I have,' he said, rising, 'only this to say. We have had agent provocateurs with us before. And we will have them again. Let there be no mistake. Beware the enemies always in our ranks. That is all I have to say. I do not point the finger at anyone.'

But he did, surely. The Swede seemed or pretended not to

understand. And stood blinking. He was slow to sit down.

'I would suggest,' said the chairman, 'that we leave the question before us open until our next meeting. That will give us more time for thought. Can I have someone move in that direction?'

It was moved, and seconded. Bill Freeman and Charlie Higgins were voted down.

That was their last Wednesday meeting. They would have to get on with it themselves, if they could. Charlie joined Bill Freeman in hiring himself out for labour on the waterfront's auction block. The bosses had the whip in the port now, hiring and firing how they liked since the union was broken. They had to make their moves quietly. And there, when they got jobs, they not only worked the ships. They also picked up certain literature which some seamen had begun to smuggle into the country. They distributed it among other men who fronted up on the auction block, and sometimes more widely. And in connection with this literature, much of it headed with hammer and sickle, they were questioned by an unusually courteous detective and then arrested. In court, charged with spreading seditious utterances, they each received thirty days' jail. There was no future for them on the auction block now, and they afterwards travelled south together, to work in the mines, and otherwise do all that was necessary with their lives.

Three:

LATE IN SUMMER, AFTER A BURN-OFF, NED LIVINGSTONE ARRIVED
back at his whare with a blackened face. The sun was low in the
sky; he was about to wash himself in the creek and cool the
thirst in his throat. He had no reason to expect a visitor that
day, but there was a stranger sitting outside the whare. A thin
wizened little man, quite gnomic, who looked entirely at ease.
He had a swag resting beside him: a sugar bag fastened with
rope which he could swing over his shoulder as he trudged. His
dusty trousers were tied above his boots with string. A wide-
brimmed hat sat crookedly on his head. Yet he was complete
with tie, even if his suit was nondescript. The trousers did not
match with the jacket, and his waistcoat was vaguely checkered.
A gold watchchain hung looped across his buttoned belly. He
greeted Ned companionably, as if he were expected and had
no need to explain.

'I seen you up there, and all that smoke,' he said. 'But I
didn't come up. I was shagged from the walking. I walked all
the way from town. She's a fair stroll, up here.'

Ned could agree, confused.

'But it's nice enough country, up this valley. Things is looking
green enough. You get the rain.'

'We get the rain, all right,' Ned said. In spring he sometimes
thought it would never bloody stop.

'Still, you don't look as if you're doing too bad.' The stranger
gave Ned's land a critical gaze. 'You been clearing off long?'

'Six months. Near enough.' Ned no longer counted before
the war. It might never have been; only the war had been.

'You're doing all right, mate.'

'I just do my best with what I got.' He paused. 'And that's

not much.' He had begun to wonder about this talkative swaggie and what he was after.

'The name's Nick Bell,' said the stranger, evidently deciding his moment had come. He rose and took a bony grip on Ned's hand. 'I was just passing through this way.'

'This way?' Ned was perplexed. The track led through the gorge only to his farm, or the land which would be his farm. It was no route to anywhere. Unless to nowhere, that wild bush country beyond his land. It might have held the bones of extinct birds and long-dead Maoris, though no one knew.

'I mean this district. I was just passing through. When I asked round for work, they said you was up here. A joker called Ned Livingstone, they said, just back from the war and getting started again. They reckoned you might want help. Looks like they was right.'

'I don't know about work,' Ned said quickly. 'I'm by myself here.'

'I can see that. What you mean is, you like it by yourself. You want to keep it that way.'

'I don't know about that,' Ned said, though he did. Or thought he did.

'Fair enough, mate. I like a man who knows his mind.' The old man hoisted his swag. 'Like I said, it was a nice stroll.'

'Besides,' Ned added, 'I got no money for labour. I'm just making out, the way things are. Sorry. But you don't have to go yet.'

'It's a long way back to town before dark,' the old man said. 'Not that I mind sleeping on the road. I'm used to that.'

Ned could guess.

'I can fix you up a bunk for the night. And some tucker. And a yarn or two wouldn't hurt me.' Ned didn't mind a yarn now and then, with almost anyone, to break up his week. 'Sorry you walked all this way for nothing. But I can't let you shoot through without bed and tucker. I can't do that.' His racing words tumbled clumsily into sentences; it was near enough a week since he had talked to someone else, and then only a disgruntled neighbour. 'The least I can do. Hang on a minute and I'll clean up and swing the billy.'

'I'm always a starter for a brew,' said the older man. He dropped his swag, sat down, and began to scrape out his pipe.

After Ned had washed and made tea they sat talking for a

42

time. Nick was a great one for stories of places he'd been, people he'd known. He told them with a pretty fair sort of style.

Soon the day was darkening. Ned went out to milk his still solitary cow and Nick followed, talking. Later Ned got the tucker cooking. It was stew and spud, like most nights, and Nick seemed to think it a fair enough binder when he ate. 'I'd take you on as a cook any time,' he announced, after, filling his pipe.

Ned now felt it time to explain his situation. 'I'm living here pretty light, like,' he said. 'What I mean is, I'm just scraping through. I grow what I can, and if I want fresh meat I'd just as soon go off and shoot wild pig or goat. Or venison, if I got the time to chase the deer. I'd take on help if I could pay for it. But I can't.'

'That's all right, son,' Nick replied. 'Don't bother yourself talking. We'll be all right.'

We? Ned was baffled.

'What I mean is,' Nick said, sitting comfortable with his feet up on a box, 'I got not much use for the money. When I got it I only piss it away in some boozer. It's only tucker I need to keep me going, and a place to flop at nights. Then I'm all right.' He slapped his stomach. Smoke swayed up each side of his smile as he got his pipe alight. 'I often think I'd be better off without the money altogether. In me day the money's landed me in enough trouble. Into the cooler, more than once. I got a weakness for the bottle, boy, I don't mind telling you. It's best I'm away from it. Once I'm among it, I'm in trouble again. Like my old man, so they tell me. The booze killed him, more or less. The booze and the Maoris.'

'The Maoris?' Ned didn't see the connection.

'They say he shot one Maori too many for his land up the Waikato way. Or that's the story I heard. I was too young to remember. And it was all on account of the booze.'

Ned saw it coming, another yarn. So he had to listen.

'He did his share of shooting in the wars, all right. And got his land from the grateful government. The trouble was when the booze confused him he didn't know where to stop. He might of had the idea he'd get more land. No telling what the booze does to a man's brain. The shooting was pretty well over then, except for pot-shotting back in the hills, but one day he found

43

a Maori hiking across his land like the bugger still owned it. The old man was addled by the drink, they say, and shot this Maori. Who recovered nicely, after a month or two, and came back to shoot the old man. They never caught the Maori. He took to the bush. And the bullet played hell with the old man's digestion. That's what killed him, the booze and the Maoris.'

The story had a point somewhere, Ned felt, if only he could find it. But it seemed to drift away like Nick's pipe-smoke. Nick's yarns largely turned out to be like that. Everything explained, yet still inexplicable. He would have liked time to smooth out each yarn carefully, like a crinkled map, and think about it; and see what he could not see. The trouble was that Nick's yarns connected, one to the other, like wagons behind a smoky loco-motive. He was well on his way, now, into the evils of drink. Tantalizing himself, perhaps, and enjoying it. The drink, and some pugilism, had landed Nick in the cooler for a month, breaking rock. The accommodation, Nick said, hadn't been the best, but the booze was sweated out of him.

'And there was,' said Nick, 'this joker waiting for me when I got out. With his horse and wagon, all ready to start. A strange joker, tall, with burning eyes. Greek, some said, or Spanish or Portuguese. His name was Don Buck, mostly called the Don. A kind of king he was, with a nice little kingdom just north of the city. The jail knew him, and half the drunks around. He collected the drunks like he'd collect provisions, when they'd done their time inside. And he took us back up to his kingdom. It was a stretch of gumland, still being worked out. He'd work us all week, digging gum, and pay in kind with booze on Saturday night. Saturday night and most of Sunday the camp would roar. The police wouldn't mind, on account of the Don not allowing anyone outside the camp. We was all there in one place hurting no one but ourselves. I tell you, son, some of them up there thought it was a great bloody paradise. Booze for free, fights without the cooler after, and women whenever the Don could fetch them. But not for me, son. Not for me. I saw hell there, boy. Hell. Hairy men foaming at the mouth, clutching each other, and naked women with madness in their eyes. That's what it was like, Saturday night and Sunday. Sometimes it still comes back to me in nightmares and I wake up sweating. Nothing you can tell me about hell, boy. I been there. As for that Don, I couldn't get out quick enough. Because

44

those cloven hooves was there, for sure, in the boots he wore. I knew they was. I could smell the brimstone and hear the dead souls screaming.'

Nick's eyes ignited then. They might have burned with the very fires.

'When I got back among decent men it didn't take much for the Salvation Army to sort me out. I got down on my knees for Our Lord Jesus Christ. I think he understands and forgives my little sins since. I'm not really such a bad bugger. Not like some.'

Ned Livingstone was obscurely moved, and uncomfortable. The flames flapped weakly in the fireplace, and the silence seemed all at once to move in from the hills and bush. Though now and then a morepork cried feebly, quite distant. His lonelier fears might for once have been perceptible in his face, even if the other did not see.

Nick Bell knocked out his pipe, and began to refill it. 'So don't talk to me about money, son, or the lack. I didn't walk up here today for the money. Perhaps for my soul, boy, but not for the money. The road to hell is paved with money.'

Ned, who had nothing much against money, began to feel harassed. There was also the threat of a lecture, and he had no wish to be offered salvation on his young knees. He had to save himself, so far as he was able, on the two good feet he had been given. There was kneeling men, he supposed, and standing men. A God with half a brain, if there was One, would prefer standing men. But what of a God with no brain at all? This had sometimes seemed more likely when he looked out from the trenches at the men fly-blown on the wire. He could still imagine he could smell them, without much effort. Hell? Ned had been there and back. This old Nick knew nothing.

But Nick didn't persist. He didn't lecture.

'No, son, it's not the money. The truth is I like the looks of you. You look a clean living young joker. I don't mind staying to help. Just so long as me belly's full, and I got a bunk. I'm still handy with an axe. In me young days I swung an axe all up and down this country. I can garden, and help with the cooking. I can still do pretty near anything.'

'Well,' Ned said, still slow with doubt, 'all right. But I feel bad about the money. I mean, not paying. It's up to you.'

He still wasn't sure he liked the idea. He supposed, though, he could get on with the old man all right, so long as he didn't make too much of getting down on his knees. Ned would very quick have a gutsful of that. The best thing might be to keep the old bugger busy.

'Then it's settled,' Nick said. 'I'll stay and help you out.' For the second time that day he pushed his hand out towards Ned. 'Let's shake on it.'

Nick's hand, if ancient, was well tested and still wiry. Ned, after all, could find himself beginning to like the idea. A man might go queer on his own.

'If you keep me off the booze, son, you'll be doing me a kindness. So don't say more about the money. Some have it, some don't. We don't. And we can help each other out. No harm in that, is there?'

'No,' Ned agreed. It stood to reason, almost.

And Nick was already yarning again, before Ned had time to adjust. He'd known some strange people, some real dags, in his day. And he'd known the country too, it seemed, from end to end. He had seen the great mountains and rivers and glaciers of the south, and prospected vainly for gold in the silent fiords. He claimed to have made the most of a Maori girl or two in the places where the earth was still young and warm and steaming. And he'd cut his way into wild, strange places, according to his tale, where almost nothing had happened since the world was born. He had shovelled dirt for new roads, hammered spikes into railway sleepers, and rafted giant kauri logs down miles of river.

After a time his talk wandered off into the high country of the south, where he once trapped rabbits on a lonely sheep station. The mail and the booze arrived up there once a month, by wagon across fords and through a mountain pass. The rabbiters and shepherds descended on the homestead that day, from their outlying shanties. There were sometimes fatalities in the enthusiasm of bringing the booze and mail through to the station. Not to speak of the fatalities, or near fatalities, when the booze arrived. They usually cut it out in a day, and went four weeks dry. The D.Ts were common. There was, for example, Nick's mate Con. Con was a youngish man, inclined to the depressive side after mail days. One morning Nick found him out picking blackberries. The interesting thing was that while Con picked and ate blackberries with one hand, he used the other to saw at his throat with a rusty piece of tin. It was a

46

queer sight, altogether. The juice of the blackberries dripped down his chin and mingled with the blood from his throat. Though he had made some progress, he hadn't sawed deep enough to hear the angels carolling. Nick took him back to the station, cleaned off the blackberry and the blood, bandaged his tattered throat, and put him to bed. It turned out that the booze wasn't entirely the cause of Con's condition. There was a girl, who lived down the valley in the first township out of the station, with whom Con imagined himself much in love. Her letters made him hit the booze harder and harder on mail days; there was apparently something unsatisfying, perhaps evasive, about the letters she wrote. Con normally lived in a hut, with a mate, ten miles out from the station. They were often not seen, he and his mate, for a week or sometimes a month at a time. One mail day they didn't turn up. When the hut was visited they found two dead men. Con had evidently shot his mate, then shot himself. For the shotgun lay across Con's near headless corpse. It was known that Con had a suspicion that his mate, on a visit down the valley, had fooled with his girl in the course of delivering a message from Con. Nonsense, of course; his mate wasn't a day under sixty and no oil painting. But up there on the plateau, with only tussock and sheep and mountains, Con had much time to brood on what he imagined his mate had been up to. And one day he reached for the shotgun.

'I had the job of putting them together for a decent Christian burial,' Nick said. 'But the ground was still frozen hard, and we never did get the hole deeper than three feet. So we heaped up rock over them, and hunted up some twisted old matagauri for a cross. The worst thing was, it could of been me I was burying. I mean, I could of just as easy been up there with Con. I could of just as easy been struck down for a sin I didn't have the pleasure of. So I've counted each day since as a gift from the Almighty, you see.'

Ned didn't, quite. He thought about a clumsy cairn of stones, topped with crooked cross, in a bleak place under tall white mountains. He was trying to arrange this to his satisfaction, but then Nick began to moralize.

'So you see,' he said, 'it's not only the booze that brings a man to grief. It's the women too. Dear God, the women. They was brought into this world to make a man suffer and burn.'

Nick, though, appeared to take it very personally.

47

And Ned, faintly troubled, considered the empty places in his life.

After a time they brewed a last billy of tea, and went to their bunks. Ned lay awake, his brain restless, for some time as he listened to the wheezing sound of another sleeper in his whare. The night was different, almost to the touch. It was like rain after drought. He had a mate.

Nick didn't turn out too expert with an axe. Three days after he arrived he sliced into his leg and, after Ned had carefully disinfected and bandaged the wound, was in bed a week. Afterwards Nick was left mostly to the easier work. He pottered around in the garden and cooked meals. He helped with the burning off, though, and sometimes made gestures of slashing the lighter scrub.

Ned's land began to open up like a slow green flower, charred at the edges. After the rain of winter and early spring, the earth gave up a thick shining growth of grass where the ash had been. They got on with the fencing and Ned brought in his first dozen cows to graze. He was set on the cows now. Before the war he had intended running sheep in this almost shut-off hollow he could nearly call his own. But the way things were, with enough level pasture and butterfat prices up again, it seemed cows might be a fair proposition after all. Besides there was a busy dairy factory operating down in Te Ika now, and a truck came grinding up the Waiatarua valley, every morning early, to pick up the cream cans. After spring, when Ned had improved the route and made the track a passable sort of road, the truck came all the way up the valley, through the gorge; and Ned began to get his first cream cheques.

At first Ned and Nick had to milk in the open, which was a bastard when it rained, but before summer was out they knocked up a cowshed, and then another shed adjoining where they installed the cream separator. After morning milking they sluiced down the shed and scalded the separator and hauled the cans of cream by sledge down to the roadside.

Within two years of his return Ned Livingstone ran near enough to sixty cows. Neighbours said it was a bloody wonder, it just showed you. Ned, after all, had got the fag-end of the land along the Waiatarua valley, shut in there beyond the gorge.

48

Only a bastard for work would have made a go of it. And it was true, so far as work was concerned, Ned was a bloody terror. After three years Ned's cream cheques were fat enough for a man to start thinking ahead.

Four:

The coast, as it called itself, was a place for rain, beer and coal, almost to extravagance. There had also been gold in the fast rivers which rode from the white mountains. But the gold now lay locked in distant bank vaults and blighted towns were vanishing back into the bush. There was also, of course, a still earlier time, when only dragons of legend and thin defeated tribes inhabited this slender length of lowland. Stronger tribes had come from the north, to gather the greenstone which lay thick in the rivers, and to harvest slaves. The Coast had never been in on a win. Now they took the coal away.

There were still the mountains, though, in dense dozens above the bush, sometimes pushing peaks almost to the sea, and throwing off glaciers. There were the mountains, and the icy winds off them, and the heavy rains they trapped, and there was the creepered rain forest and the crashing sea; and there were the places where men felled timber, or dug for coal, because there was not much else.

It was a place where beer served best to wash the taste of coal away, and the pubs obliged after the legal hour while the police looked elsewhere. A man could seem to get the coal out of his system, if not altogether from his lungs. The beer helped, all right, down on the Coast.

The Party, now it had begun, did the best it could here. The Party was strong in the unions then, its comrades scattered evenly among the wooden houses of the little mining towns. And the Coast was pretty well the Party. Of course there were others, up in the cities, like the cranks Charlie Higgins and Bill Freeman had seen in Auckland, who claimed Party cards too. But they didn't amount to much. Down on the Coast they had the workers' paper and the Party executive. When the

50

Party spoke, the Coast listened. Elsewhere the Party might not have existed, except when the police jailed someone. But then everyone on the Coast belonged to everyone else. It was the way things were, under the mountains.

Charlie Higgins and Bill Freeman shared what they had. What they had was a leaky old whare, hard up against the bush, across the river from the mining township. And their wages from the pit. They pooled this, after they had given a share to the Party. They were both active. One of their responsibilities was seamen. Of a Saturday afternoon they would travel down to the port where the coal ships were loaded. They would chat the seamen up, sell the workers' paper, and pass around the hat for the Party. If necessary, and for Bill Freeman it had to be necessary, Charlie not caring one way or the other, they would hit the booze with the seamen. Of course there were some solid comrades on the ships already. It was just that, being seamen, they tended to be unreliable. They needed nudging along, even if they talked well enough. After all, seamen had brought the I.W.W. to the Coast before the war, and afterwards the first words of Lenin to the international working class. Often, Saturday nights and seamen being what they were, Charlie and Bill didn't make it home to their whare. They found bunks on a ship, or in the back shed of a pub.

Charlie, an old deck hand himself, reckoned you had to play along with seamen. Bill didn't always approve of the playing along. You lost sight, he said, of the point of the thing. But Charlie said it did no one, and certainly not Bill, any harm to loosen up now and then. You couldn't cope with people unless you enjoyed them, and a few beers. Charlie had been elected president of their local union branch, because of his popularity among the miners. Bill, on the other hand, was secretary of the Party branch. Bill was always on the Party line, all right, even if he couldn't seem to get it across. He didn't have the knack yet, Charlie said. He had to learn to crack a smile with his Marx, and not take himself so serious.

Their fourth winter, Charlie went down with pneumonia. Bill nursed him before he was taken to hospital, and after he came back. A rattling cough persisted. It was clear he couldn't take much more of the pit. It was convenient, then, that with the Party pushing Charlie was elected to more important posts in the miners' union, which took him out of the pits, if on smaller pay. He was soon on the national executive of the union, an organizer. He travelled from pit to pit, listening to problems, arguing the toss with the management. He had the knack of dealing very reasonably with the bosses, and generally getting what he wanted in the end. It was no use, he told Bill, ranting at the bastards and calling them for what they were, the way Bill might of done; the bastards only ranted back, and a man would get nowhere. Charlie was soon a large man in the unions. Bill was still good on the line, though. He put things straight in the articles he wrote, in stiff block letters, for the workers' paper whenever there was confusion among comrades. And went down the pit every day.

'You work it your way,' Charlie said, 'and I'll work it mine. You deal with the line, I deal with people. I find people a bloody sight easier, sometimes.'

This was in a pub, where they had arranged to meet. They didn't see so much of each other these days. Charlie had shifted down to the port, and was often elsewhere. Bill stayed on in their old whare alone for a month or two, then shifted right into the mining township. He boarded with the family of a schoolteacher comrade. This comrade, whose name was Campbell, was a pretty wordy customer; Bill had never quite got the hang of him. He was chairman of Bill's Party branch, and made a fair fist of it, with Bill's prompting.

'Yes,' Charlie said, 'I find people a bloody sight easier.'

Bill was alert to meanings.

'I don't get you,' he said, trying to bring it to a head.

'All this stuff in the abstract. I never got along with it too well for long. I mean I like to see some result for what I do. We can talk for years, Bill, but that don't bring the revolution no nearer. But in the union I can see results, all right. Even if it's only another penny an hour.'

'But that's education,' Bill said. 'The masses become educated in the struggle for better conditions.'

'Yes,' Charlie said. 'I know the line, all right. Even if I'm slow catching up sometimes. But all the same, it's results. You get me? Results. It's something you can see. A lot of this talk is farting into the wind. I farted a lot into the wind in me day, but I never raised much of a stink.'

'I wouldn't say that,' Bill argued, though unsure what he would say. He was confused by recalling the Charlie of the I.W.W. But where had that got to, in the end? To Big Bill Haywood, now dead in Russia, buried with honours in the

52

Kremlin wall. Well, that was fitting. The international workers'
movement was different now, toughening under a thicker skin.
It had more than just an ideology, and a plan. It had a country,
one sixth of the world. 'You got to talk, sometimes, to know
where you're going. Otherwise we might go nowhere, just
anarchists again. And back where we begun.'

Charlie saw a different Bill Freeman now, different from the
young Bill he had found walking lonely in Auckland after the
war, who wanted less talk and action quick. This Bill had
become lost in long meetings, murky with tobacco smoke, and
in the sound of his own voice. And in reports, literature, contacts
and directives, as if the machinery ticking over was the point.
Charlie realized now he was glad to escape that business.
Charlie was changing too.

'All I'm saying is people are easier,' he insisted. 'Maybe you
got to compromise here and there – '

'Compromise?' Bill said. This time there was no mistaking the
meaning. The thin end of the wedge, the way he saw it.

'What I mean is,' Charlie continued, 'when you work with
people, not ideas of people, there's got to be a bit of give and
take. You can't get things all your own way.'

'You can't compromise on fundamentals,' Bill argued.

'There's a hell of a sight more to the world than fundamentals.
I can tell you that, Bill. Now take the bosses, the way I
handle them. There's got to be give and take. Otherwise we'd
never get anywhere. And the union would strike itself out of
business. Then where would we be? You could say, Bill, I was
compromising on fundamentals when I give something to the
boss to get an agreement. Or settle for half I ask for. You could
say that, Bill. But that's the way life is.'

'And what way is that?' Bill asked.

'It's what is possible,' Charlie answered.

Bill wasn't sure. He was disturbed.

'So you,' he said finally, 'are happy with what is possible.'

'Not happy with it. Making the best of it.'

'I see.' Again he was silent. 'So where, Charlie, will that get
us?'

'Look, Bill, we won't argue. You haven't told me about yourself. How's the new digs? And that girl?'

'What girl?' Bill asked. Though he knew perfectly well.

'The one in your house. The schoolteacher's daughter.'

'She's all right. So far as I know.' She was a dumpy little

53

creature, this daughter of the schoolteacher comrade, and often went for walks by herself in the bush. And wrote verse, or so Bill had been given to understand. She was about twenty, and quiet.

'It struck me you might hit it off all right there. I been expecting something to happen. Or are you too slow?'

Bill had nothing to say. Charlie had him off balance. The truth was he had hardly spoken to the girl since he had taken a room in the schoolteacher's house. She was not an easy girl to speak to. Not that he tried much.

'You could do a lot worse, Bill,' Charlie suggested. 'That's all I'll say. Because I can see it's not for me to say more.'

Shortly afterwards they parted. Bill, that night, looked uneasily across the dinner table at the schoolteacher's daughter. For he still seemed off balance, quite vulnerable. And the schoolteacher's daughter, whose name was Peggy, seldom lifted her eyes from the meal she had cooked. True, he had suffered this unease before, but without giving it much thought. It seemed, now, he would have to.

After the meal she carried dishes out to the kitchen. Often, at this stage of an evening, unless there was a meeting somewhere, Bill found himself trapped by the fireplace with the schoolteacher, and his growling stomach and smelly pipe. The schoolteacher enjoyed lengthily circling discussions with Bill on what attitudes the Party should take, for example, to social democrats and other reformists who sold out short of revolution. That night, particularly after his meeting with Charlie Higgins, which left him irritable, Bill wasn't inclined towards discussion. Instead he acted as one of the family and helped with the dishes in the kitchen.

With the schoolteacher's daughter he came clumsily to the point. 'This poetry you write,' he said. 'I would like to have a read of it sometime.'

There might have been worse ways to begin.

Her eyes were on the dishes turning in the soapy froth. 'I didn't know you were interested in that kind of thing, Mr Freeman,' she said. She was still quite formal.

'I am interested in literature generally,' Bill said. 'I have a high regard for some writers. I have read Jack London, Henry Lawson and some Gorki. I am interested in it especially as it reflects the aspirations of the working class.'

54

'I am not sure,' she said, 'that my poetry reflects anything of the sort. Except myself.'

'All the same,' he insisted, 'I would like to have a read of it sometime.'

'And it is religious,' she added. 'At times there is mention of God.'

'It is difficult,' he offered, 'for some people to accept the scientific view. I understand that.'

But he didn't, quite.

Brisk at her work, she clinked dishes out of the sink. It was difficult to tell if she was joking. Or trying, perhaps, to intimidate.

'Do I surprise you?' she asked. 'About God? I think I do. You see, it is only a name for what is unknown. For the mystery upon which a poem ponders. God is most convenient for a poet. Sometimes God can be called Nature, or other names. Sometimes I use the names of the Maori gods. Tane, for example who was god of the forest, or Tangaroa who was god of the sea.'

This was confusing.

'I do not think,' she finished, 'that you would care for my poems, particularly.'

'I think you are shy about showing them.'

'I am careful,' she agreed. 'Some find it easy to laugh.'

'I wouldn't laugh,' he promised.

'All the same.'

'Yes. I see. I'm just interested. That's all. I thought I would just say I was interested.'

It all became, suddenly, too clear. She was silent.

'I am not always too good at saying what I mean,' he went on, in quick apology. 'I try hard, but I often make mistakes.'

It seemed to hang, this mistake, like a bright balloon between them. She remained silent, with her bruise.

'I am really interested in the poetry.' He had to take the risk, now, of making it worse. 'I was not just saying that for something to say.'

He could even begin to believe this himself.

'You do not go out much,' he persisted, 'I notice. Except by yourself.'

It was a relief, perhaps also for her, when he discovered he could say something new; his heavy boots might have found firmer ground in some swamp.

'There is not much. I mean, to go out to. There are the

dances. But I am not much of a dancer.' She was not prepared to chance looking at him directly as she spoke. 'And there are the moving pictures. But I cannot say I care for them a great deal.'

'We are alike, then,' he said uncertainly. 'In some respects.'

Again it was up to him to make the issue clear. His tongue threatened to fidget endlessly in his dry mouth.

'I see you walking,' he observed in the end.

'I have my own two feet,' she said. 'They are good for walking.'

It was perhaps as near sarcasm as she could or would ever get. But she might just have been restless beneath, for all he knew.

'I mean by yourself,' he expanded. 'Up into the hills, in summer.'

'There are interesting places,' she said. 'Back in the hills. Lonely places. Where men who looked for gold have been. And I have found greenstone. Places where Maoris have been. Those places are there, if one cares to look. And there are deer which scatter through the bush. Little fawns.'

It seemed she had wilfully stripped all surface away, to show herself free, if he cared to look. For she did raise her eyes to him now. They were bright, defiant eyes. He would need time to read them right.

'I have never had the time, for some reason,' he confessed. 'To look for those places. But I would be interested in looking.'

'You would?' The disbelief was plain.

He might have said: I would do anything. But he did not; he felt a prisoner in his bitter flesh. And the disbelief hung there, between them.

'I would not laugh,' he said. 'I am not even as hard as I look. I have never had time to be much else. Much else than what I am, I mean.'

This time he seemed to surprise her. Perhaps it was the honesty.

'Not that I am complaining,' he added. 'I have not had a bad life. For what it is worth.'

And what was it worth, life? At the worst times, awake in the night, he did not know. If it was only what was possible, then life was not worth much. He knew that, if Charlie didn't. Perhaps Charlie no longer looked at stars in a bright sky, and imagined man rising tall towards them.

The dishes were washed, dried and stacked away. They

56

lingered, the pair of them, quite amiable now, undisturbed in the kitchen.

'Perhaps in summer,' she said. 'I could show you things. We could make a picnic.'

'I would be glad.' He could not say how glad.

'We will see,' she went on. 'It is not always so easy for me to get away from the house, at times.' For her mother, Mrs Campbell, was an invalid who now left the business of house-keeping mainly to her daughter. There was an older child, a son. He had cleared off to the city, away from the Coast, and had been in trouble for something obscure. Though said to have been a brilliant boy, he was now never mentioned in the school-teacher's house. After this disappointment his parents had gone to separate refuges, one in the Party, the other in bed. Peggy, who was seldom heard to complain, was left to hold the house together. Perhaps she thought of her brother. There was no way of telling.

Bill Freeman, faintly giddy with his success, had no excuse to remain longer in the kitchen. He left Peggy and proceeded to his usual chair by the fireplace, where he could consider Party tactics with his branch chairman. Mr Campbell would talk until the mantel clock chimed ten, then knock the ashes from his pipe and go to bed. Peggy was the one thing un-predictable in that household, though Bill could quite easily never have known. He could sweat to think.

Summer came. It was a hot summer for the Coast. The skies were bright and cloudless; the rain stopped. Rivers thinned, after the long thaw, small creeks dried up and the glaciers melted back. Fires flashed now and then from the hillsides behind the towns.

Five:

NICK STOOD OUTSIDE THE WHARE, MOCKERED UP TO THE nines, his feet moving impatiently in the dust. They had risen an hour earlier than usual that morning, to get the milking over and done, for it was the day of the Te Ika show. The gold watch-chain, swinging across Nick's waistcoat, caught the light. A hat tilted rakishly on the old man's head.

'She'll be another scorcher, boy,' he announced, when Ned emerged at last from the whare.

Indeed the sun was warm in the sky already.

They approached the Ford. Ned had bought it the year before out of his cream cheques. Second hand, at a reasonable price. The thing was he would have to make do with his whare a little longer, but now he could make a quick run down into Te Ika whenever he liked. Ned worked the wheel of the Ford much as he might use a rein on a recalcitrant horse. He discovered it didn't pay to give the vehicle too much head. And he had difficulty with the gears, which sometimes seemed absent minded, or just unwilling. In winter he stalled the Ford often enough on muddy roads. He ran it into ditches, and once half into the river, before he got the hang.

The engine, when Ned gave a crank, kicked off in lively fashion, not grumbling at all, and they rolled across Ned's land and then out of the gorge, the sun bright and breeze fresh on their faces.

They passed the Fletcher place, the Jackson place, the Boswell place. Most farmers in the Waiatarua valley had milked and set out for the show already. On each side of the road the tamed land, manacled by wire fences, flowed green up to the foothills. On sharper slopes the pasture collapsed patchily

58

among stumps, tangles of dead wood, and forlorn cabbage trees. Sometimes the last pasture simply dipped out of sight, in some hollow, and the forest rose beyond. There were still idiosyncratic scatters of bush in deep little gullies. Higher hills, back farms, were often cleared entirely, streaked with fresh erosion and freckled with sheep. The lowland was mostly dairy country, the square wooden farmhouses almost always nudged by cowsheds. The river, growing sluggish, wandered between thick willows. The Ford rattled across wooden bridges and thumped down on to the dirt road again.

'Look after yourself today, Nick,' Ned said casually. 'We must keep you off the grog. No Mother Murphy's.'

Mother Murphy ran a boarding house in the town, and a sly-grog shop on the side. Nick had made her acquaintance early. A bloody wicked place, he said, where a decent man wouldn't be seen dead. Nick should have known. For he had been found there often enough, as near death as made no difference, with only Ned to care and take him home. Mother Murphy was the risk in taking Nick down to Te Ika. If he ever went missing, Ned knew where to find him.

'No Mother Murphy's,' Ned repeated, though without much hope.

Nick made a deep sound in his throat. It could have been agreement. It could also have been an apology in advance.

'All right,' he said at length. He was supposed to say something.

'We don't want to spoil the day,' Ned argued. 'Not one like this.'

For the day was brilliant, the sky clear and vast. Soon they would see the coloured banners fluttering above the show-grounds. There would be displays, sideshows, and the rodeo.

Te Ika began to grow around them. The first shabby houses, with unpainted wood and rusty iron, were merely something the town had left behind as its centre jerkily shifted. There were the remains of timber mills, with sterile hills of sawdust, and Maori children playing among the debris. Then the houses tightened into ranks, with squares of lawn and tidy shrubs, among flowerbeds and clipped hedges, each side of the road. They were coloured cream and red, with corrugated rooftops, usually modest with lace and lowered blinds. Here and there a church ruled, with a wooden spire.

They jolted across the railway track into the main street. A

59

school stood deserted behind fast rising poplars. The main street was wide and crowded with traffic. Shops multiplied, with verandahs strutting out above the new asphalt pavement. General stores and auction marts, drapers and bakers and Chinese fruiterers. It was a town of substance now, no one would argue. It could still surprise Ned. In less than his lifetime it had sprouted and grown among fern and forest. The railway station, a long low building of sooty red, stood to one side of the street; beyond were criss-crossing iron tracks, bulky sheds, and rakes of wagons. A shunting engine steamed and clanged. It might have been any day.

But a banner slung across the street, with streaky blue lettering, advertised the day of the annual show. And the town clock, still atop some makeshift scaffolding, told almost the hour.

The traffic thickened on the way to the showgrounds, cars and horses, wagons and walkers. On a narrow bridge across the river the movement choked; there were shouts, laughs, sometimes snapping voices, and growling gears. Then there was release, and excitement, and the tents on the showgrounds rising like white winter peaks above the dust.

Ned found a park for the car, and they followed the crowd through the gates, paying their entrance money. 'And remember, Nick,' Ned warned, 'no buggering off today.'

Nick's eyes were bright in his wrinkled face. He followed Ned like a child at heel. There were the agricultural displays first, where Ned was interested in the milking machines. He asked shrewd questions. Nick's patience, though, soon wandered. There were people from most places around, for fifty miles or more. There were big lonely men, looking lost, from backblock farms, and small crumpled women with bonnets. There were bearded old men, tanned dark as Maoris, from upland sheep farms. And more sunless faces from mines and forests and timber mills. There were hearty business people from Te Ika, and Maoris with flax kits of food.

When Ned had the milking machines and their salesmen sorted out, they moved on to the noisier parts of the show. In front of one of the sideshows Ned met Jack Crimmins. Ned once worked with Jack on the railways gangs, and even in those boozy gangs Jack was said to be rough as guts. But that was before the war, when Te Ika was just getting started, and Ned too, and Jack was now middle-aged. He had some land himself

60

now, he told Ned, up Waikato way. And he wasn't doing too bad. It had been pretty ropy land, mostly swamp, but he dug drains.

'And this is my girl Nance,' Jack said.

Nance might have been twenty, and was awkward and thin. But she could smile, as if on instruction, to show good teeth and a dimple. Ned could easily not have noticed her rough complexion.

'Nance helps on the farm,' said Jack. 'I tell you, Ned, kids can make life easier.'

Ned said he supposed they could.

'Got any yourself yet, Ned?' Jack asked, with a heavy slap on the shoulder.

Ned said he wasn't married yet.

'Like that,' Jack said. 'Still looking for the right sheila?'

Ned said he might be. 'There was the war,' he added. 'And I been getting started. This is Nick, who helps.'

Nick and Jack shook hands. And the girl Nance Crimmins studied her feet. Her feet were shod in tough, dusty leather.

'The longer you leave it,' Jack warned, 'the harder it gets. And besides a man could bloody do for himself, in the end, with his own cooking.'

'I'm all right,' Ned said. 'I get along. And Nick here makes a fair fist of the cooking.'

'How's that land?' Jack asked.

'Coming along,' Ned said. 'We're still in the old whare.'

'Time you built, then,' Jack insisted, evidently not knowing when to leave a subject alone. 'You got to build a cage to catch a bird.'

Nick shuffled and Nance blinked. She seemed unwilling to forget her shapeless shoes.

'Nance and me got a ride down with a neighbour,' Jack explained. 'A treat for her, like, and a chance for me to see the old village again. What are you doing with yourselves now?'

Ned, it turned out, wasn't doing anything in particular. So they moved to the show-ring where there was a parade of calves. The calves had been judged, the ribbons awarded, and the farm children walked solemn beside their sleek pets. Nance seemed to come alive.

'I think that one there should have won,' she said, pointing. Her voice, heard for the first time, was slow and pleasant enough. 'It is a shame.'

61

'Which one?' Jack said. He grinned at Ned, demonstrating patience with his daughter. 'Which one, Nance?'

'The little boy with fair hair,' she said. 'And the gumboots. His calf has no ribbon. And he looks so proud and sad.' She might even have wept, Ned thought, if there had not been strangers.

'You are looking at the kid, Nance, not the beast,' Jack answered. 'The ribbons are for the calves, not the kids.' Jack turned to Ned and Nick. 'Nance here has a thing about kids. I think she will drop a fair few sprogs, once she starts, if I know my Nance. She will make a good mother. And wife, for some fellow.'

He might have been parading Nance in the ring, with or without ribbon. It embarrassed Ned, who preferred at that moment not to look at the girl.

'You must come up and see our place sometime, Ned,' added Jack, never subtle. 'Perhaps when the cows have dried off. We could have a go at pig-shooting up on Pirongia.'

Now the ponies were parading.

Jack asked was Ned in for the rodeo later.

'No,' Ned answered shortly. 'It's not my style, much.'

Jack said Ned still looked young and strong enough.

'There are the cows to milk tonight,' answered Ned, beginning to feel pestered. 'How much use would I be with a broken leg?'

Then Jack said he would of been a starter, if he wasn't past it now. In his young days, it seemed, he had been game for most things.

Ned announced abruptly, 'There are some things I haven't seen. Some displays. I think I'll take a wander round.'

'We might see you later,' Jack said. 'And perhaps we can have another yarn. I think Nance and me will have a gander at the shearing competition for a while.'

Nick appeared interested in the shearing too.

'Then you stick with Jack,' Ned said. 'And we can all meet up when the rodeo starts.'

They arranged this, and Ned went off alone. He felt great relief, by himself in the crowd, free of doggy Nick, and Jack Crimmins' needling. He was sorry, though, for that girl Nance.

He was jostled back along sideshow alley, where the crowds were dense. There were games, hoop-la, darts, and shooting. A wall of death, and a boxing kangaroo. Kids hurtling on a merry-go-round. He stopped finally outside a tent where a girl, in some

62

sort of baggy transparent costume, swayed in a dance. She was foreign-looking, like some of the women he had seen in France, and a thick strip of flesh across her belly was bare. A speiler announced that this harem dancer was giving but a sample view of what went on inside the tent, for one shilling only.

The girl's face was attractive all right, but her smile seemed paralysed. She was slight and dark haired. She looked lost up there, before the palm trees painted on canvas, and her body went through indifferent motions as a breeze ballooned her gauzy costume. Her eyes were almost as fixed as her smile. She might have been drunk or bored or frightened. Frightened, perhaps, of remaining up there before the painted trees forever, above the dusty crowds and sticky kids with candy floss. Ned found it hard to move his eyes from the bared strip of flesh across her middle. He could almost feel that flesh silken beneath his blunt fingers. Her small bare feet slapped listlessly back and forward.

'Rescued from the princes and sultans of the mysterious East,' announced the sweaty speiler. 'And now here for your entertainment, the harem girls without their eunuchs. Only for you.'

They might possibly have still needed rescue even if they came from no further away than Auckland. Or Sydney, perhaps. The speiler had an Australian accent.

With others Ned paid money and found himself in the tepid gloom of a tent which might have contained mystery, though it seemed unlikely. The platform for the performance was only the back of a truck mockered up with some paper-mache palm trees, rather sad looking.

There was impatient shuffling and coughing within the tent. The air grew smoky. Those who had paid a shilling were mostly men not so unlike Ned. Perhaps they too had seen that silken flesh, though their wonder might not have been as gentle.

Music began, on a scratchy phonograph. Cymbals and bells and whiny sounds. The fat speiler, mounting the back of the truck, asked them all to imagine minarets in the sunset, the sultans feasting, and the door of the harem at last opening. The man next to Ned, who seemed a bit itchy, muttered that a shilling was a hell of a lot to pay for your own imagination.

The speiler jumped aside, and six girls scrambled up on the back of the truck. One was the girl Ned had seen outside the tent. It was not difficult to see why she had been on display. She was quite the most attractive of the six. One or two were downright scrawny.

They went through their clumsy, teasing dance and one tripped and almost fell from the truck. Their uncertain line reformed in time to the scratchy music. Their arms waved and their feet moved. And soon their audience was still. The girls did not need to do very much. It might have been enough, in the end, if they simply stood. It did not matter if they had names like Dorothy or Amy. They were real enough, and the money had been paid. Even the grumbler next to Ned was not heard to complain. There were twelve legs, twelve arms, and six smiles. And six identically bare midriffs. All at once the music died, the girls bowed and waved and it seemed the show was over. They could hear the speiler beginning again outside.

Some of the men felt cheated then. For it was an end without an end. The trees were paper mache, after all, and the girls really not much more. Without the music they were each alone, and uncomfortable, in their flesh. Their shillings had bought no more than a mirage, though some would pay again. They filed from the tent into the sunlight, which offered no relief. Splinters of sharp colour pierced their eyes. The sound of children was a meaningless jangle.

Ned Livingstone, though, held what he felt tightly to himself. He enjoyed his wonder. And he did not feel cheated, perhaps because he had not expected a great deal. His lust was not of the kind to turn outward in anger. And besides he would almost have been content just to touch that flesh. So that it did not matter. He could still look at the thick legs of country girls, of whom he was again aware. Nor, in this awakening, could he regret his body, which he propelled through the crowd on two strong legs. The noise flailed round him, yet did not bruise. The sunlight touched him, yet did not sting.

There was still the rodeo, of course. And the arrangement to meet.

But there was only Nance Crimmins waiting as arranged, quite alone. Ned approached her with care. 'Your father and Nick,' he said, clearing his throat. 'Are they coming?'

'I couldn't be sure,' she answered. 'They went off, him and Nick.'

'Off?' He was slow to understand.

'Nick and Dad was talking. And Nick said there was nothing like a show for working up a thirst. And Dad said by God Nick had something there. Nick said he knew just the place. So they left me here, and told me to wait. I been waiting half an hour. And then you come along, just now. I seen nobody I know all the time. And I got no money, even.'

It was pathetic. She had been promised a treat.

'You think they'll be long?' she asked. Her gaze was nervous on Ned.

'Hard to say,' he shrugged. 'But I think I know where I can find them.'

'You do?' Relief steadied her face. At times, at a certain angle, she might have looked pretty. 'Should we go looking?'

That could have been even more pathetic.

'They'll turn up again,' Ned said, and hoped it might be true. 'No sense waiting here, though. You haven't seen much yet.'

'No,' she agreed in a colourless voice. 'But I got no money.'

'Well, my pockets are fairly full,' Ned exaggerated. 'We might as well walk around for a bit.'

So they went through the sideshows and munched waffles and watermelon and rode on the merry go round and looked down into the wall of death, where the motor cycles roared monotonously. Nance enjoyed the boxing kangaroo and the house of mirrors. Her eyes were often huge with surprise. Ned could imagine she didn't have much of a life, not with an old man like Jack Crimmins. Jack likely wouldn't even let her out to country dances.

Then Ned tossed some balls, in a game of skill, and won a prize, a doll for Nance.

'Look,' said Nance. 'Isn't it lovely? A little gypsy doll. See. With ribbons and shiny sequins on the dress. And see. A little tambourine. In its hand. A tiny little tambourine. Is it really mine?'

'Of course,' Ned answered.

'To keep?'

'To keep.' He had to smile.

'And listen,' she said, holding the doll towards him and shaking it. 'Listen.'

'What?' He strained to hear, through the din around them.

'Can't you hear? That tambourine. It even makes a little sound.'

Ned thought he heard, in the end. But he was really more taken by her pleasure in the thing.

'I have never,' she said breathless, 'got nothing like this before. Never nothing so nice.'

He might just have made her a gift of the world. And she held on to the doll tight, as if it might be grabbed away from her. Just like a kid; it was like Ned taking a kid around. He wondered then what he might be like, really, with a kid of his own. A boy, say. A boy he could love and look after and teach. His imagination swiftly gave such a child an existence. The idea became so real he felt dazed. He might just have dropped a weighted line to the deep of his need. At once he felt empty, or at least incomplete, as if he had not even begun. He was limp with the thought.

And there was Nance beside him, hugging her gypsy doll, with sequins and little tambourine.

'It's terrible,' Nance said. 'And sad. To think of it – all this for only one day.' She looked around her as if the crowd was already dispersing, the tents collapsing; as if the noise and laughter had already gone like a fire doused with water. Perhaps she was oppressed by impermanence. 'Just for only one day.'

Ned took her arm and steered her through the crowd.

'There can be a lot in a day,' he said merely. He was not sure what he meant.

She smiled, though.

'Tomorrow,' she said, 'I will be back on the farm. Milking. And carrying buckets.'

It was evidently not a matter for particular regret. It was a matter of fact.

'I will have to be thinking about that myself pretty soon,' Ned replied. 'The time is getting on.'

Their lives, after all, knew the same boundaries. Could he suggest, though, that there might be more to the thing than just milking, and carrying buckets? He was not sure he was up to arguing the thing. Once he wanted to possess himself, and that seemed the point. But now he was possessed by his pastures.

At least it sounded as if he understood.

'And the way things are going,' he added, 'it looks like I might be milking in the dark tonight, and without Nick to help.'

'We should go looking,' she said suddenly, reminded.

66

'No hurry,' he insisted. 'There is the rodeo yet, we haven't seen.'

'I'd forgot the rodeo,' she said. 'I'd forgot all about it, with so much else.'

'We could have a gander for a bit. And then go after Nick and your Dad.'

'It'll be all right, you think?'

Her meaning was unclear. If she meant would her father be all right, then that depended on whether Jack Crimmins as booze artist could compete with Nick. It was very likely. So he did not answer.

'Come on,' he said. 'Let's go.'

The crowd was thick at the rodeo. And the dust stormed from under demented hooves as bodies crashed and voices roared. There were cash prizes, five pounds a time, for the men who stayed longest in each round of the competition. Ned and Nance Crimmins took seats, at a bob each, in a rough temporary stand, where they had a decent view. Most of the riders did not last five seconds. They were dumped heavily into the dust while their mounts careered away. One after another they tried, and failed. For failure was inevitable, and accepted. Success was impossible, never expected. It was simply a question of how long a man could hang on, a matter of time. Some hung on longer than others, that was all it amounted to. This possibly proved something, it was hard to tell. For the youngest and fittest were often first to go. And some of the older riders were resilient enough to come out for more.

The first aid men were busy. There had been two broken limbs, one cleanly snapped, and diverse bruises and abrasions.

'I would have a shot,' Ned said, 'but for the cows.'

'It is just as well,' Nance observed. 'You might get hurt.'

This was poor comfort. Ned grew restless on his hard seat and fidgeted. The horses skidded, hammering their hooves and shedding their riders. The crowd applauded the felled men impartially. Here, if nowhere else, the watchers were realistic about failure.

'And hardly worth a fiver,' she added.

She might have been mocking, but wasn't. For what he might find down there, in the dust, on a heaving animal, was hardly to be measured by a blue bit of money. Even if he found only that he could still own himself, if he liked. That seemed important now. He could no longer take it on trust.

67

Bugger the cows, he thought. I am free if I like.

It was not exactly revolt. It was an effort, rather. He rose with decision, if still bewildered. And the girl took his arm.

'No,' she said, quick. 'Please. You don't have to, just to show me.'

He had not thought of this, though it could be another reason. Even the real reason, if she liked.

'I believe you can do it,' she went on. 'So you don't have to show me. Anyhow I couldn't watch.'

'Why not?' he asked, perplexed.

'Because,' she said shyly, 'I would be afraid for you.' Her hand was anxious on his arm. 'Excuse me,' she finished, 'I am not much good at saying things.'

The idea that someone, even this possibly irrelevant girl, might for once tremble for his safety was not without appeal either. Muscle bulked in his arm as he clenched and un-clenched a fist.

'I will only have one shot,' he said, as if this were in dispute. 'Don't worry. It'll all be quick.'

So he left the stand and paid an entrance fee for the chance of breaking his neck or earning a fiver. And presently he was poised above a penned horse. At a signal he dropped on to the back of the beast and grabbed the rein. He hugged the frantic and sweaty animal tight, to make himself part of it. It was all quite simple, it seemed, a matter of hanging on. His legs and arms were iron leeches. And the restrained, cramped beast tried to rear.

Then a gate opened and they were out in the ring.

His bones seemed to clatter with the impact. He was aware of little but the jolting, murderous uproar beneath him. The sky swung and jerked, and the face-lined fence careered like a carousel. It was only, he had to tell himself again, a question of hanging on. He lifted, and perilously swayed, and then he was clenched to the beast again. He tried to give himself to its motion, but there was nothing definite, or predictable, to which he might accede. He had, instead, a volcano of caprice. He could be sure only that it would not last. His strength was flimsy and ephemeral against this immense tide of bone and muscle. He could smell sweat and dung and dust and had no fear, because there was not the time. There was only hanging on. There was only survival. All his life might have been in

68

those exploding seconds. Now the horse was in full cry, rearing and plunging and twisting. It was not something to control. It was not even anything to fight. It was just a matter of going with it to the end. He was at the brink, almost understanding at last, almost at one with all the knowledge he might ever have, when he was suddenly separate. The sky toppled and the earth slammed into his face.

Hands were scrabbling at him. People were helping him over the fence. His back was slapped, his shoulders pounded, in comfort or congratulation, it was not clear. There was blood in his mouth, thickened with dust. There was a burning at the centre of his head where lightning might have struck, if he could remember.

Nance was there tearful, somewhere in front of his eyes, quite clumsy with relief. Voices roared against his eardrums abruptly, and as suddenly vanished. He gathered he had stayed on his horse something near thirty seconds, which seemed fair enough, and at the same time absurd. He had also, as last rider, taken that round of the competition. So he had won a fiver, if nothing else. Someone asked would he be in for the final round.

'No,' he answered. 'I have bloody done my dash.' And he moved off with Nance, the money in his numb hand. Behind his back those who knew Ned Livingstone, from up the Waiatarua, said he had always been a pretty moody sod anyway. Others said he might be concussed, which would explain. For it was quite unnatural, they said, the way he took hold of that fiver without even a grin. And who was that sheila with him?

Nance was dabbing at his face, with a moistened handkerchief, while she talked. She was talking a great deal. That was his general impression.

'It was the hooves,' she explained, 'that scared me. They went close by your head. And the horse was rearing like it wanted to finish you off.'

'I didn't notice,' he said. It was an effort to listen.

'I wasn't so scared,' she insisted, 'when you was actually on the horse. Because it didn't look like you was ever going to let go. Or fall off.'

But he had, of course. And he had a fiver as consolation. It could have been worse.

'I wasn't going to look,' she reminded him. 'But I did. And I am glad that I did.'

Because, it was understood, she would remember.

'Jesus,' he confessed, 'I am properly stuffed.'

They had walked in no particular direction. They were clear of the tents, of penned animals and sideshows. There was grass beneath their feet. And in this corner of the showgrounds were shady pines and macrocarpa.

'Then you must sit and rest,' Nance announced. 'Over here, out of the sun. Until you feel better.'

She had his arm, and was guiding him gently. She was a practical enough girl, not the sort to irritate. They sat on the grass, in the pleasant shade. Away in the dusty distance the wood-chopping contest rang like gunfire.

The shock began to ebb from his body. He might have been bruised here and there, but not so painfully. His teeth had torn out some bit of flesh inside his mouth. He had not come off bad, considering. And there was the money, of which he might make the best. If he liked he could parcel everything inside the money. Perhaps he would, in time.

Soon he wasn't shaky at all. He felt quite peaceful, stretched out on the grass, with Nance quiet beside him. He thought he might like this girl, down to her funny shoes, because she offered no problem. Then he saw the gypsy doll, which he had almost forgotten, sitting where Nance had arranged it on the grass, like a little live thing between them. He laughed, picked it up, and gave it to Nance. She laughed too, for some reason.

'So you enjoyed yourself today,' he said. It appeared a reasonable conclusion.

'I wish,' she said, 'I could say. How much, I mean.' She was nervous again, and shy. 'Because of you.' She looked at her doll rather than at Ned.

'You get off the farm often?' he asked. He could imagine the Crimmins farm was a pretty dreary place for a girl. He mightn't have seen the farm, but he knew Jack Crimmins. Jack was always quick with his fists. He was the sort to bash his kids into shape, when they slacked. And she certainly had a beaten look when her father was near.

'Not very often. And when I do, with Dad, he gets off with someone. Like that Nick today. And then there is trouble, usually, and I have to manage Dad home.'

He didn't doubt she managed. She had to.

'I think we should go looking soon,' she added. 'If it is all right with you. The time's getting on. And Dad and me have to meet this neighbour at five who will run us back.'

'All right,' Ned agreed. 'We will go looking now.'

They retrieved the Ford and drove across the river into the old, cramped part of town where Mother Murphy prospered. Her establishment was a survival from the time when Irish navvies had pushed the railway through. Since Te Ika was still a dry town, without a pub because of the Maoris and a treaty signed with them, there was still room for a sly-grogger to have a fair sort of whack. That was, provided she was not arrested more than twice a year. Business people, and wealthier farmers, were not to be seen drinking there, however; they did the thing more or less legal, and joined a club with heavily curtained windows.

'You better wait in here,' Ned said when he had parked the car at a suitably discreet distance from Mother Murphy's. When Nance looked askance, he added, 'You'd be better off here.'

Himself too; he would sooner not go through with it again.

No one answered his knock. The noise roared out at him as he opened the door. It was like a lot of lunatics, on holiday from straightjackets, in a public lavatory. The floors were puddled with beer in which cigarette butts drifted. Ned started forcing his way through a dense arrangement of shoulders and arses. Then a big red-headed man, watery about the mouth, collided with him. In panic, it seemed.

'The buggers are after me,' the man cried. 'The buggers are killing me.'

Ned never saw who.

And the big red-head tripped and fell so that he lay half way out the front door, gasping and then vomiting.

Ned tried to press into the house again. Show day was Mother Murphy's big day. But she wasn't to be seen, nor did anyone appear to be watching for the police. Old Maori women with black head-scarves and blue tattoos on their chins sat calm in corners, in all the commotion. There were timber workers and shepherds and fencers in town for the day, and permanent customers like the railway gangmen. One or two were splashed with blood already. And Ned found himself crunching across the broken glass one fight had left behind. A fat woman with sagging breasts ducked out of one room, and into another, half undressed.

71

He found Nick first, stinking drunk, and jammed behind a sofa. Someone had evidently put the old man there out of the way. He made gurgling sounds in his throat, and then muttered, when Ned tried to revive him. So Ned left him and went to look for Jack Crimmins, who might help. Jack, though, was more difficult to find. Ned tracked through room after room, a stranger in that wilderness, until he found Jack hidden behind bodies in an alcove. He had a lumpy sort of woman on his knee. She wore a feathered hat, silk stockings and black slip, and not much else.

'Bugger me,' said Jack, 'if it's not me old mate Ned Livingstone.' He hiccuped and said to the woman, 'Ned and me was on the railways once. Till today I hadn't seen the bastard in years. And you know what he's been an gone an done? He's shagged off with my daughter. That's what the bastard's been an gone an done.'

'Jack,' said Ned, 'there is the question of Nick. He is shickered behind a sofa, and needs lifting. There is also Nance. She is outside in the car, waiting.'

'Now give me the guts of it,' Jack said. 'Have you, or have you not, been looking after my girl?'

'Yes,' Ned said. 'I been looking after her.'

The lumpy sort of woman did not seem to care, much.

'She's a good girl,' Jack announced.

It did not seem quite relevant. There was a fight thickening in some other part of the house, and walls were battered. Bottles smashed and women screamed.

'Well, then,' Ned said, trying for words suitable to the occasion, 'your good girl is still good, Jack. She is waiting outside in the car.'

'An I been on the booze all day,' Jack said. 'That mate of yours, Nick, is a hard case. An I am bloody crook in the guts on account of him. I been coming right. Haven't I, Mabel?'

Mabel, in her feathered hat, did not appear to know.

'I been coming right,' Jack went on, 'thanks to Mabel. She has kept me off the grog, these last two hours. Mabel's a wonder, she is.' And he slapped Mabel's substantial rump, as if to prove it.

'I'm worried about Nick,' Ned persisted. 'On account of I have to get him back to the farm and get on with the milking. And there is Nance. She says there is a neighbour who will be running you back at five.'

72

'Why don't you get on the grog, Ned? Put some lead in your pencil. The hell with the neighbours. The buggers are always prying.'

'They are waiting,' Ned said, quite hopeless, 'to take you and Nance back.'

'Your trouble,' Jack said, 'is you worry too fucking much. Now what is the use of it? I ask you. And what do I want to go back for, when there is a girl like Mabel here?'

Mabel, who doubtless had been a girl once, smiled vaguely. The bottles still smashed somewhere.

Ned thought with regret that he might have been longer sitting on the grass with Nance, in the shade of the pines. Or he might, better still, have been back on his farm, leaning on the gate and rolling a smoke after the cows were milked, with the astute hills, as they darkened, only mildly puzzling.

But he was not elsewhere. He was here on two feet, his arms useless, his mouth empty of pleading. In another room lay Nick, drunk. And out in the car Nance waited. In front of him was a man stupid with the booze. And a dim kind of woman with big buttocks. He was tired and pretty near fed up. Somehow, from all these facts, he had to fashion something. It was beyond him; he could not seem to start. So he stood.

'Your mate is a sad sort of customer,' said Mabel to Jack Crimmins. 'Don't he ever smile?'

'Ned? Ned's all right. Ned's trouble is he never got any fun out of life. Isn't that right, Ned?'

And Ned, whose hands were sometimes gentle with new calves, did not know. Give him a patch of bush, no matter how thick, and he could clear it.

'I won five quid in the rodeo, Jack,' he announced. It was something to say.

But Jack, who had decided to nuzzle Mabel's neck, did not seem to hear. Ned, impatient now, grabbed his shoulder.

'I can carry Nick out,' he went on. 'But what can I do with Nance?' This time he spoke louder.

'Nance? You can marry her, Ned. That's what you can do. She needs kids, boy. Like you need food. The law says I can't do nothing about that myself.' Jack seemed to think this a joke. 'And,' he added, 'I got other kids coming along to help with the cows. Kids to burn. Too many to feed. So I don't need Nance so bad now. You'd be on to a good thing there, Ned, and no mistake. And before your balls go rusty.'

Ned was beginning to feel tainted by this place. 'I mean,' he tried again, 'Nance is out in the car waiting. What can I do with her, Jack?'

'I could explain it, Ned, but there is a fucking lady present.' Jack grinned and Mabel giggled. 'Bugger me, it don't look like you're ever going to leave me alone. Come on then. We'll get Nick out to the car and see Nance right. Excuse me, Mabel. I might see you show day next year.'

Mabel did not seem to mind an annual encounter. She lifted herself from Jack's knee and then fitted snug into the seat he vacated, already beginning to look around again.

They went back through the house to fetch Nick. Lifting Nick was difficult. They had first to move the sofa behind which he lay. In moving the sofa they dislodged a couple of drunks who turned nasty. Some beer was spilt, quite unforgivable. One of the drunks fluttered a fist. Jack Crimmins, who was in the mood, responded with some vigour and greater accuracy and the drunk pitched sideways on the floor. When the other drunk took his place Jack hit him, then began to batter him down, with rising enthusiasm. The fight grew like a number of slowly flowering explosions. Then bodies ricocheted from wall to wall. Jack Crimmins did most of the fighting, using beside his fists a chair and a bottle, and frequently his feet. Ned was more concerned about protecting Nick, still prone, from trampling boots. On occasion, though, it was necessary to protect himself too. And Nick, altogether unaware, just groaned and mumbled.

'Get them in the balls, Ned,' Jack advised, 'or the bastards will be all over us.' He grunted, as he fought, like a man on the end of a pit-saw.

With perseverance he eventually cleared a way out, and they shouldered Nick from the house. They could see Nance still waiting in the Ford.

'Roll on next year,' Jack said. And a flung bottle dropped just a little short of them, smashing on the footpath.

Nick revived slightly when they dumped him in the back of the Ford. His feet kicked feebly as he slid and fell between the seats. His arms also made vaguely violent protest.

'No,' was all he said. 'No no.'

'Nance girl,' said Jack Crimmins, 'you better sit on me knee. And we'll leave Nick to fight it out with the back seat. He always get like this, Ned?'

'Now and then,' Ned conceded.

'No,' Nick said. 'No no.' There was considerable thumping behind them.

'Sometimes,' Ned continued conversationally, when he had cranked the car, 'he gets the idea there's a big dago devil picking him up and taking him away. A fellow with cloven hooves, he reckons, and gets him confused with me.'

'No,' Nick said. 'No no.' The thumping grew weaker and more sporadic.

'I can't tell him different,' Ned added. 'It was just a joker he used to work for.'

They were arranged, at least, and ready to start. 'Where can I drop you?' he asked Jack and Nance.

'Outside the post office was where we arranged to meet after the show,' Jack said. 'If the miserable buggers are still waiting for us. You never met worse neighbours than mine, Ned. They ask me and Nance down for the day, and then it turns out I have to pay for the petrol. And they'll still expect me to say thank you. How are your neighbours?'

'Not so bad,' said Ned, who seldom saw them.

The miserable buggers, though, were still waiting as arranged outside the post office. Jack and Nance clambered out of the Ford. Nick had gone quiet, fought to a finish, in the back.

'We're easy to find,' Jack said. 'Nip up, Ned, and see us any time.'

Nance was quiet. She looked intensely at the ground. Jack put his arm around her, with his boozy smile.

'I think our Nance would be glad to see you too, Ned,' Jack added.

It was obvious enough.

Jack's neighbours hooted impatiently. 'So don't forget,' Jack insisted. 'Come up.'

'All right,' Ned promised. 'I just might.'

With that Nance looked up from the ground at last, and slowly smiled. 'I am glad,' she said, clutching the doll he had given her, 'that I saw you in the rodeo.'

Ned was confused by the weakness he felt, and his foot was clumsy on the clutch; he grated the gears of the Ford as he started back for the farm. He even forgot Nick in the back. He drove fast, bouncing through ruts. Even so, his land was too long to arrive.

Once home, though, he remembered Nick. He tumbled the

old man into the whare, down on a bunk, and got no protest. Then he hurried to get the cows milked. Though some of the herd was drying, it was still a long milk. He finished well into the dark, and there was a quarter-moon in the sky and moreporks calling. He carried a lantern from the cowshed back to the whare, and large shadows loped among the trees on the other side of the creek. The whare was dark; Nick had evidently not woken. The feeble moonlight showed the hills in ragged silhouette. The darkness might have been a thing of the land, its native colour.

And his bruises had grown harder to carry. He was ready to call quits with the day.

There was a noise near the whare. And as Ned approached he saw the door stood open. He also saw, in the light of his lantern, the glint of an upswung axe.

He ducked, probably just in time, and the axe chopped down into the earth. It was Nick, of course, with the axe. And now swearing. And already raising the axe to swing again.

'Nick,' Ned said gently.

Nick swung. This time Ned was well clear. He should have known from experience not to leave anything lethal around, not after Nick had visited Mother Murphy's.

'Nick,' he repeated quietly.

He swung again. Ned retreated a yard or two from each swing, the lantern still joggling in his hand. Nick's eyes were huge, catching the light.

'You smell of hell,' he breathed. 'You smell of bloody hell. You think you got me now.'

'It's only me,' Ned suggested. 'Only me, Ned, and we been to the show.'

Nick declined to believe it. He plunged at Ned, with the axe held high. Ned stepped aside, pretty quick, and Nick hurtled past. The axe buried itself in some part of the whare.

'Think you can take me alive?' Nick raged, detaching the axe. 'You got another think coming. Fuck off. And wait till a man's decently dead.'

The old bugger might really do for me, Ned allowed himself to think at last. These things happened, after all, on lonely farms. Nick himself had told stories. He could, he supposed, take off for an hour or two, in hope Nick would come right. But the old man could do himself damage with those wild swings.

76

If Ned vanished he would likely offer violence to some tree, miss, and slice half a leg off.

'Give me the axe,' Ned said. It was time to be logical.

The proposition appeared to stun Nick for a moment, then to enrage him. 'You think I'm mad?' he asked in a high, cracking voice. 'I got your number this time, boyo.'

At least he appeared to hear what Ned said. It was a start. Ned had talked the old man out of his apparitions before. But say this apparition had become too real? It was likely enough one day, or night. Ned, though, did not have much time to think it out. Nick was almost on top of him with a swinging axe again. He couldn't argue with an axe. However real the apparition he, Ned, was real enough to have a real head cut from his shoulders.

He dodged once more. Jesus, he thought, is a man to get no bloody rest tonight?

His retreat began. It was not really a chase, except in patches. He would talk, reasonably, then Nick would charge. In this way they progressed around the whare once, twice, then across the paddock and around the cowshed. Somewhere along the way Ned extinguished the lantern, which made him too easy a target, and cast it away. But it was not altogether a help. The thin moonlight, those wild cries from the dark, and sometimes the crack of an axe connecting with something, tended to be unnerving. Nick seemed to become only the more ferocious, the more reason he was offered.

So in the end Ned gave it away. Let the old bugger do for himself, he thought wearily, but not me. He set about placing a considerable distance between himself and Nick, and then crossed the creek for good measure.

After a time, behind him, there was a cry of triumph. Nick, by the sound of it, was having a victory march somewhere near the cowshed, staggering around with the axe over his shoulder. For he began to sing:

> Onward Christian soldiers
> Marching as to war
> With the cross of Jesus
> Going on before

A pretty weird sound, altogether, up there. Like some beast giving birth, with echoes. Ned found a flat rock, about as comfortable as he could expect, on which to rest. And he left Nick to sort himself out.

He must have slept. Quite suddenly, it seemed, the sky was a rage of light. He looked across the creek and saw Nick on the front step of the whare. Fallen asleep, the axe beside him, as if on sentry duty. Birds fluted in the bush. The night might never have been. Ned rose stiff from his rock.

Thank Christ, he thought. Thank Christ it's only once a year. It was time to milk the cows again.

Six:

IN THE DRY FOREST, IN THE VALLEYS UNDER THE MOUNTAINS, IT seemed summer might never end. They made their picnic, more often than not, in a pleasantly ferny clearing beside a creek. They might have been the first to discover the spot, to speak human language there; there was no way of telling. Sun and shadow had intricate arrangements in the clearing, and tiny leftovers of light were scattered upon the swift water of the creek. Whether bird or creek or wind high in the trees, all sounds were mellifluous. Their words, though, could fall suddenly, and disconcertingly, not really native.

'Things are easy for you,' said Peggy Campbell. 'You know what you want.'

'I don't know about that,' he answered clumsily. 'What I mean is, I wouldn't say things was easy. But I know what I have to do.'

'And what is that?'

'To stand on my own two feet, and fight back. And not let anyone beat me down.'

'I see. And who pays the price?'

'Price?'

He did not understand.

'It doesn't matter,' she said finally. 'It is just that I do not think we can buy anything cheap. Not our own honour. Or dignity. Or faith. Someone else pays, even if we don't, sooner or later. Even if we never see it ourselves.'

He was still not sure he altogether understood her. She often puzzled him.

'I am willing to pay my own price, if you mean getting hurt. I have paid it often enough. It has to be paid if things are to be done.' He tossed a small stone into the air, and it plopped down

79

into the creek. 'But then,' he added, 'I don't know much about women. Perhaps they see things different.'

Or things otherwise invisible. He did not know. Either way it was disturbing.

'My father, for example,' she said. 'He seems to himself to have done the right thing. About my brother, I mean. His honour is not impaired. He has his dignity. All that has happened is that he has put my brother out of our lives, perhaps forever, and my mother has taken to her bed. It is like somebody has died. But he is all right, with his pride. Three other people are paying the price for it.'

Bill Freeman began to see her direction, with some relief. For it was not towards him after all.

'And your brother?' he said. 'What was the trouble?' It was necessary, after all, to know.

'My brother? That is very simple, though some would make it more. He has never been like other men. There are some like that. And so he got into trouble. You might as well know the truth.'

'Thank you,' he replied. 'There are some would never tell.'

'I am not ashamed to tell. Though it is difficult. I don't understand my brother, it is true, but I am not ashamed. He has his own life. If love came to him in a different way from most, isn't that hard enough for him? Must he be punished also, and forgotten? He might as well be dead, for all we know. For all I know.'

'You were close to your brother, then?'

'As children. Yes. We were close. I was younger, and he was gentle.'

'You would go to him now?'

'If I could help. And if I could find him. But there is my mother.'

'Yes. Your mother. I forgot her.'

'She is not so easy for me to forget, in her bed all day. And also my father. He might be wrong, but what can I do? He has been made poor in his own way. Though perhaps you might not see it. You have been a help to him, and the Party. He has new interest.'

She had accounted, anyway, for the puzzle of the school-teacher's house. But she could not account for the surprise she was, often, to Bill Freeman. Nor could he account for it himself. He had to make what he could of his soft shocks of wonder, and take things as they came.

'You don't speak much about your own people,' she observed quietly.

'There is nothing much to speak of. My mother died, when I was young. My father lived longer, he was big on making a new go of things in this country, with no smoky factories, and people not tipping their hats to the boss. But he got the quartz dust in his lungs in the gold mines at Waihi. I had two brothers, but they didn't take their lives much to heart. They fought a lot, and drank. And they both died, I am told, the same day at Gallipoli.'

'You hate too much,' she said.

'There is plenty to hate, the way things are.'

'But still things to love.'

'Of course. For them that have the time.'

'There is always time.'

'Then I have never had much of it.'

It wasn't altogether true; he had, after all, had this summer. But to say so would have been as good as outright confession. That was beyond him. But he did concede, 'You might be right. There are times it seems I don't know much at all. And it would be easy for a man to lose his grip.'

As he could, too easily, now. He lay back, against a warm boulder, and looked up a trunk of a tall tree rising above the fern.

'Lose your grip?' she said. 'I don't understand.'

'I mean you are not too good for me,' he said.

'Oh?' She did not appear dismayed.

'From one point of view, that is. From another point of view you have done me a lot of good. It just depends, mainly, on the point of view.'

He paused. Perhaps he was confusing her.

'And which is yours?' she asked.

'Myself, I don't know. I don't think I have much of a point of view just now. Not when I'm with you. I mean you make some things not so important. It's hard to say what I mean. I'm not too good at it.'

'I see.'

'What I'm trying to say is I like it, anyway. Being with you, I mean.'

It was the nearest to a declaration he could make.

81

'Thank you,' she said, 'from my point of view.' She was teasing him only slightly. 'I should like to say the same. Perhaps I can now. But not at first. At first you worried me. Because I couldn't see the point.'

'The point?'

'Of us being together. Except that you seemed to need company sometimes, different from what you have.'

'You think we might make a thing of it, then?'

'A thing of it?'

'You know. Something regular. You and me.'

The creek was noisy. There was faint wind up in the trees.

'I don't know,' she said at length. 'I don't know what you mean, exactly.'

Well,' he said. 'Get married, like. If I have to say it.'

'You don't have to say it.'

'But I do,' he insisted.

'We are different,' she observed.

'Yes. But not too much. In some ways we might find we are alike. We are only both human beings.'

'Is that enough, then?' she asked.

'It might be more than enough,' he suggested.

'Please tell me. Because the subject isn't an easy one for me, you see. Please tell me if it is enough that two people are human.'

'All right. It might not be much, but it is something for a start. The thing is whether we would be better off together than not. I think I would be better off. So it's up to you.'

'I will have to think,' she insisted. 'Because I have not thought of it. We have not been like that.'

'Like what?'

'Like two people intending marriage.'

'No,' he agreed. He had to agree. 'But then I don't know what other people are like.'

'We have just walked and talked a lot,' she went on, 'like two people anywhere who happened to meet.'

What did she expect? 'Well, that is the fact of the thing,' he observed. 'We are just two people who happened to meet. I never been much good at the romantic stuff. And I told you before I don't know much about women. I mean I've been around, I've been with a woman or two. But it was nothing special.'

'I see. Well, I don't know much about men. So we would

both have something to learn.' This thought caught her between a nervous smile and a frown; and the frown prevailed. 'I will have to think about it. It is all so different.'

'Different to what?'

'Different from what I expected. So it's difficult for me, you see.'

He began to feel irritation. What did she expect? And she must have seen it was difficult for him too. Difficult, say, to talk about love, if that was what she wanted. It was true he hadn't mentioned it. He just hadn't organized himself that far, not yet.

'You won't hurt me too much if you say no,' he told her. He did not really care to determine whether this was true. 'It's just I'd like to know your mind before too long. On account of it doesn't look like I'll be here much longer. On the Coast, I mean.'

'You're going away?'

'Looks like it. The Party has asked would I make a shift to the north, to Wellington first, as an organizer. Because they got too many intellectuals up there, not enough workers. And it seems it's me that is best to go from here. Comrades like Charlie Higgins are too tied up with the union, or married. I'm more free.'

'You're not very free if you go where the Party tells you.'

'But I need the Party, just like the Party needs me. And unless a man does what he needs to do, he's a slave.' He paused. 'I could write out my resignation and become a slave tomorrow.'

'Do you really have to go?'

'There is only one thing I can't do,' he said, 'and that is waste my life.'

'I see.'

'It has to have a point. It has to amount to something.'

'For some, yes. I can see that.'

'Then that,' he said, 'is a fair sort of beginning.' He paused. 'I'd of taken my time about talking to you. But it's just things are happening this way.'

'Yes.' She turned quiet.

'It doesn't rain in Wellington so bad, they say,' he went on presently. 'But there is pretty wild wind.'

'Yes. The wind.'

She was plainly untangling thoughts, somewhere beyond her

83

remote expression. And he did not think she was considering the Wellington winds, exactly.

'We could talk about it again,' he suggested.

'Yes. That would be better. The time is getting on.'

They rose, and began to walk home. A bird sang somewhere in the dying day. The creek raced beside them, quite bright and wild, towards the anonymous sea. He respected her silence, and her thoughts. He could not do otherwise. Gloom grew in the forest as the last sunlight withdrew from the valley. Yet the warmth hovered. Their feet made dry, cracking sounds as they walked.

'We will be all right,' he said, at length. 'You and me.'

He did not explain how he knew. For he could not. He took her arm tentatively.

'Yes,' she agreed presently. 'Perhaps.'

And they kept walking.

The trouble started in Australia, as good a place as any, with a miners' strike in New South Wales. The Party was strong in the union there, but weak elsewhere. So the loss of coal supply in New South Wales was made good from other parts of Australia. At that time a Party man from the New South Wales union travelled across the Tasman, looking for support. For the mines on the Coast were also supplying New South Wales. This Australian talked with the Party executive, which was now in the north, and Bill Freeman received a message from the executive. So he met with Charlie Higgins, down in the port, to pass on the message.

'It's quite clear,' he said to Charlie. 'The executive has met with this Australian comrade and passed this resolution. Not a ton of coal for Australia. That is Party policy.'

'And they know what they can do with it,' Charlie Higgins said.

'I don't get you.'

'They can stuff their bloody policies. Who are they, to tell us what to do? Let them have their fucking fun, and pass all the resolutions they like. So long as they don't interfere with us. Tell them that, if you like.'

'You're not serious, Charlie. This is an instruction to all Party Members.'

'It sounds like an instruction to a lot of bloody sheep.'

'It's not like that at all, Charlie,' Bill said patiently. 'These men in New South Wales are out. They need our support.'

'You think I don't know that? Do you think I don't know what it's like to be out? And we are supporting them. We're raising money and sending it over. What more can we do?'

'Stop the coal.'

'It wouldn't make no difference; it wouldn't help them. There's other Australian mines still supplying. That's their problem, not ours.'

'Ours too. The working class is international, Charlie. An injury to one is an injury to all.'

'That sounds like we have to cut our own throats because they do. That it? We can help them with money if they want to stay out. That's all we can do. You want us to call all the mines on the Coast out to stop coal going to Australia?'

'If necessary. Yes.'

'Then tell them to go to hell. I thought I helped make a Party for the workers. Not a bloody army.'

'The Party has an overall plan.'

'And I got some overall common sense, thank Christ. And that's what I work by, not instructions. For me the workers come first.'

'The Party means the workers, Charlie. Read your Lenin again. The advance guard of the proletariat.'

'Listen, Bill. I said the workers come first for me, and that means the union comes first. Follow? If the workers didn't have a union for protection, they wouldn't have nothing. We been building up a strong union. You think I'm going to try wrecking it all on account of someone has the bright idea we should stop coal going to Australia? When it won't do them, or us, any good?'

'It would be a gesture of working class solidarity,' said Bill Freeman, who believed it.

'Then I'm too long in the tooth, Bill, to believe in gestures much. I just believe in doing what's best. Gestures might be all right for the young. But you're talking about men out of work, families going hungry, maybe even scabs coming in to take jobs while the union is wrecked. And all for what? Not for this working class solidarity. But because some bone-heads in New South Wales don't know the right time to call quits with the boss. We're making our gesture. We're sending money so their kids

85

don't go hungry. If we go out, we won't even help them that way. We'll have enough trouble feeding our own kids.'

'I see. So that's the way it is.'

'That's the way it is,' Charlie agreed.

But they might have been talking different languages.

'And you won't accept a Party directive,' Bill said.

'No,' Charlie answered. He had never had a God to wrestle with anyway. 'See, Bill,' he began slowly and patiently. 'I've always depended on my own judgement. I can't go against it. I been too long in the game. Take that away, and I might as well be nothing.'

'So you won't accept it,' said Bill. He was not listening. He was making himself believe it.

'Not much use our talking, is it Bill? You got your way and I got mine. We got to make the best of what we have.'

They had been talking, for almost an hour solid, down in a pub at the port. They had talked in a lot of pubs, a lot of places, in the past few years. Bill Freeman knew suddenly that this would be the last; he had never seen feet of clay disposed so carelessly before. And Charlie's dark suit, in which he did union business, was a little shiny here and there, probably where the bosses had begun to rub off. They no longer knew each other.

'You'd turn your back on history,' he accused finally.

'History, Bill? I don't know much about it. I never known much about it. That don't mean I haven't read Marx or Lenin. They might be right about history. The Party might be right. All I know is I got to do the right thing, regardless, and too bloody bad about history.'

'And you'll betray the workers in the end.'

'You and me both, Bill. In that case. I don't want to argue. Can we shake?' He offered his hand.

Bill Freeman turned away. He couldn't give his hand in anger. It would have been, more likely, a fist. He walked fast out of the pub, not looking back at Charlie, and found himself trembling, bumping blind through passers-by in the sunlight outside. Not in years, not since Charlie found him walking an Auckland street, had he felt so lost in the human forest. The undergrowth was too thick, too high, seldom a real tree to be seen. It was not a matter of just hacking his own way out, if he could. For it would all of course have to be cleared one day, perhaps real trees along with the rubbish, wherever there was shadow, for a fresh start. So that the light could pour in, and truth.

86

But he was, after all, just walking one of the drabber streets of the port, with old women hunting bargains along the cracked pavement, and delivery trucks banging over potholes. He might discard Charlie, but there were other pieces of his life he had to consider, before he fitted it together again. There was, for example, Peggy Campbell. It seemed he might be able to do very little about her. He had delayed his move north long enough. And her mother, in that permanent sickbed, had taken a turn for the worse. Peggy couldn't leave.

The fact was he had work to do. He would make a move at the end of the week. He walked steadily, with some decision.

Before the end of that week, though, there was another change. He had a new, personal directive. He was to stay on the Coast, in the mines, so long as the New South Wales miners were on strike. He was to fight against coal being shipped from the Coast to New South Wales.

He might have replied that such a fight was hopeless now. But he didn't, because if he wasn't to fight there was no point. He stayed. He stayed long enough to see Charlie Higgins, and most of the miners he knew on the Coast, walk out of the Party. The social democrats, of course, took most of them. There were few comrades left when that fight was finished. Some said the day of the Party on the Coast was over. He also stayed long enough to attend Mrs Campbell's funeral, and to marry Peggy Campbell.

Mrs Campbell, it turned out, had suffered cancer as well as grief. Her son, Peggy's brother, was apparently not informed of her death, because he did not get across to the Coast for the funeral. But no one was altogether sure. Afterwards it was said that he had been seen watching from the edge of the cemetery, some distance from the crowd at the graveside.

Bill Freeman and Peggy Campbell married a month or two later. They did not, however, leave directly for Wellington. They honeymooned first, since this was expected. They took a cottage for a week on a lonely beach just along the coast. The bush rose high on the hills, and the hills dropped abruptly to a vast plain of sand, darkish and vaster still when the tide was out.

A noisy bus left them there with the hills, the bush, the cottage among tall treefern, and themselves. They were shy, for they still did not know each other well. They had not even kissed much. There had not been the time.

There was not the time now, either. There was a fire to be lit,

87

for the cottage was damp from weather and lack of occupants. It had rained for the best part of a month and even the sun, when it showed itself, appeared limp and watery in the sky. Because of the season they rented the cottage cheap. There was that much to be said for the place, if not much else. It was isolated, the nearest neighbour five miles away, and once the home of a hermit gold prospector. Since his death the honeymooners had come year after year. Within the thick wooden walls of the cottage passion must have been kindled, but it was not evident. They were aware most of the cold and damp, and advance of darkness. There was just enough wood to get a fire going. Bill went out to fetch more.

The night came down swiftly from the hills as he gathered driftwood on the beach. The surf heaved and pounded raggedly up the sand and the wind flicked back fine spray, like smoke, from the crests of the shattering waves. His ears accepted the rhythm, the regular roar and crack of the sea, as he carried armloads of whitened wood back towards the lit windows of the cottage. He liked the knowledge that Peggy was beyond those windows.

And, within, she was brisk enough, busy with food. She seemed happy. He could never be sure.

After a time he could no longer hear the surf outside, though it still crashed as loudly. It became a kind of deafness in this place, a deafness into which the other sounds of the world only fitfully entered. He thought he could speak to Peggy now.

'It isn't so bad,' he said at length. 'For the price, that is. It could be worse.'

'We have it to ourselves, at least,' she replied. She seemed, as she hurried, more determined to make the food her answer.

'Too bad if we didn't have it to ourselves,' he joked heavily.

'I mean,' she said, with difficulty, 'it is hard to believe that I don't have to think of anyone but you, now. Now we are really alone together at last.'

He could have kissed her for that, and perhaps should have. But things were still strange. Instead he squatted before the fire, lighting one of the thin cigarettes he needed to roll himself on occasion. She rustled about the room while he tried to steady his unease.

'Yes,' he agreed. The word was inadequate, too small, a tiny island. Beyond were vast waters in which he had yet to involve himself.

'Properly alone,' she explained. 'Not being tugged apart, this way and that. By people. That is what I mean. I know you have got nothing much against people, except that they seem to disappoint you often, but there are times when I could do without all of them.'

She could express herself passionately at times, no doubt of it.

'Yes.' He seemed trapped on that island; he could not launch himself.

The food steamed from the two plates set down on the chipped wooden table. They sat at the table and began to eat, since this presented no problem. They spoke very little, though, and his appetite might have been larger. The fire crackled and flames leapt. After the meal they sat for a short time before the fire. Then Peggy moved away, into the shadows, to make up their bed. She appeared to take the task for granted; she was really quite noiseless. Presently she returned to the fire. She did not sit, however. She stood.

He became aware of the sea again, that rhythmic deafness.

'Perhaps you will write a poem here,' he suggested. 'It is a good place for poems. Wild, I mean. And strange.'

There seemed nothing but themselves and the sea.

'Yes,' she said. 'I might. Anything is possible.'

For they had to begin, all else was evasion. She continued to stand.

'We have a week,' he observed, 'to get used to it.' He could not say what he meant.

'And to get used to ourselves,' she insisted, saying it for him. 'It is really not much time.'

'No.'

There was a silence. Then, perhaps it was the sea, he could not be sure who had spoken last. He had been certain of most things in his life. A man could lose his grip too easy, the way things were.

'We will be all right,' he said.

For the moment had arrived, it seemed, when he was obliged to prove it, or prove something, with his angular body. He rose awkward beside her. His flesh had never seemed so hard, so ugly, and he flinched at his own clumsiness. Yet after all she did not fracture at his first touch. He took her to the bed.

Upon the bed they discarded, eventually, all obstacle to union. Though his mouth was dry, and his throat thick, he was surprised at the tender compositions his body began to design.

She held his face lightly between her hands, gentle enough to take his breath away. Yet he grew aware that he was giving, rather than taking; her breathing was eloquent. An erratic traveller upon her flesh, but still not altogether lost, he began soon to see end to the journey. The world outside grew enormous in his ears, the sprung waves toppling, and all rhythms one. The tumult in the body beneath told him he was giving and giving. Then he had given, with a shudder, and was empty and still. After that it was incredible that she should still move so fervently beneath him, as if he had more to give. She did not seem to understand he had nothing left. Nothing, except perhaps one thing.

'I love you,' he said at last, in despair.

Seven:

WHEN THE HERD DRIED OFF THAT WINTER, NED LIVINGSTONE
began to make weekend visits to the Crimmins place. He left Nick
to look after the farm and milk the couple of cows still supplying.

On the third visit, he collected a pig. For he and Jack
Crimmins were successful with their shooting on the flanks of
Pirongia at last. After the fourth visit, he collected a question
from Nick.

'You and that girl Nance will be getting married soon,'
Nick said. 'Is that right?'

Ned, who had barely got out of the steaming Ford, was
troubled by the question. Of course Nick was more or less right,
the way things were shaping. He had gone up to the Crimmins
farm for more than the shooting, and certainly for more than
Jack Crimmins' yarns. But his visits hadn't got much further
than that, perhaps because he hadn't wanted to look too much
further. He was still uncertain, and it was hard to think why.

So he didn't answer Nick. He laughed it off.

Not long after, though, he arrived at last at the serious business
of knocking up a house. It had been a plan years enough, long
grass was growing around the timber he had ordered, and
the whare was decrepit. By the time spring came half a house
had risen. He didn't waste that winter.

Calves tottered on thin legs, and there were surprising flowers
in the bush. The days lengthened and the land grew ever
warmer, under the sheltering hills. He no longer got up to the
Crimmins place; there was the milking morning and evening,
with more cows coming in all the time.

'She's going to be a dry summer,' Nick announced. 'That is
what the Maoris say.'

For Nick, after the last shambles at Mother Murphy's, now

took up with Maoris on his visits to town. The Maoris seemed to like old Nick, with his yarns. And he could, with his colour of skin, arrange to order a bit of booze for them from up north, cheaper than through a sly-grogger. The Maoris also appeared impressed with his talk of Lord Jesus Christ. He took religion almost as serious as they did themselves, now Tane and Tangaroa were taken by the missionaries, and their old lands had shrunken almost to nothing under their newly shod feet. They had reason to make the best of Lord Jesus and a bit of booze.

'A dry summer, they reckon,' Nick continued, 'on account of the big flower in the cabbage tree.'

'Superstition,' said Ned, who had no use for omens, or anything of which he could not take hold. 'Just bloody native superstition.'

He could not explain his irritation. It was not entirely with Nick.

'They been here a long time,' Nick observed. 'They know things we don't.'

'And a hell of a lot of good it's done them,' Ned answered. On the whole, he considered, a man had more than enough strife with the things he knew.

'Well,' said Nick. 'We'll see.'

It was not yet time for their shift to the half-complete house. But Ned had begun to fidget with furnishing it while they continued sleeping in the whare. The completed part of the house looked solid, the rest a skeleton through which imagination could wander. Ned planted pines for a windbreak.

'What are you planning,' Nick persisted, 'about this girl Nance?'

As if it concerned him.

'Nance is all right,' Ned replied. 'Or would be, if you laid off the subject.'

It was one of the few rebukes Nick had suffered from Ned. 'This house,' he continued, risking the implication, 'is coming on. Another winter should see it up.'

But Ned was busy with a scythe. The long grass swayed, shivered and fell as he attacked it for a future garden; the stalks bled under his trampling boots. It was an easier job than most. The grass, after all, was his ally. He had brought it, sown it, in this place which before had known only tall trees, involved scrub, birds, and perhaps Maori hunters. But even allies, sometimes, had to be ruthlessly shown their place.

Still he should have preferred, at this moment, to be working with a slasher, chopping at tenacious old manuka or fresh yellow gorse, enemies native and new, both too ready to take over this land. Also they resisted, and gave him more satisfaction as they fell to his abrupt blow. A man knew where he stood, and that was alone on the land he had earned, and flavoured, with his own sweat. Alone, or almost alone.

Nevertheless, it seemed time for trimming allies back.

'I am paying you now, Nick,' he observed at length. 'Paying you good money. But not to talk. There is plenty of work about this place.'

And Ned, having finished with the scythe, hacked angrily and possessively at the earth under him, with sweat springing out on his face.

Nick stood aside bewildered. He had never heard of a sheila who wasn't good for a laugh, and he couldn't see this Nance as different. But he had only begun to see the change in Ned. He was growing harder. And he sometimes wounded Nick, if not fatally.

Love. Was that it, then? Nick struck sputtering matches of thought in a labyrinth, illuminating only the start of passages which he would never now traverse. For Nick had never gone much on love, so far as the sheilas were concerned, but he knew that it sometimes announced itself in anger, as if there had been a defeat.

So Nick, that day, shifted himself to a hillside well removed from Ned, who could work things out of his system. The sun, slow across the cloudless sky, warmed them impartially.

I am old, thought Nick, and will die pretty soon. For death stands to reason. I have shagged about, and not been much use. What have I been here for, and who will remember?

Lord Jesus have mercy, he prayed. I am not such a bad old bugger, and might of been worse. He could have fallen on his knees to plead and might have, if Ned had not been near enough to see.

He could almost understand Ned then.

And he stood there on the hillside, trembling, with spittle bubbling on his lips, an old man in scarecrow clothes who might otherwise have been naked and bleeding.

When the mist had risen from his eyes, he looked toward

93

Ned, who still ignored him. Ned was stripped to his black singlet and the wintry white of his flesh was sharp against the green of the young grass.

Would Ned know this pain too? He was young yet, of course. And he wasn't to be blamed, perhaps, for thinking he could give it a miss by filling his life with a woman. Perhaps he would. Or perhaps he would just postpone it. Anyway he could almost forgive the boy now.

Days passed in this way, the sun still warmer, with Nick tormented and Ned taciturn. There came a day when they recognised the season as summer. Then the trees at the edge of the bush offered cool grottoes of shade. There were new sounds across the land now. Early morning and late afternoon a clattering and a chugging echoed against the hills, and back over the tight-fenced paddocks. Ned had his milking machine at last. He had his machine, his Ford, and almost his house; what more could a man ask?

A man could have asked for some bloody rain. Under Ned's feet the earth grew dusty, the grass crackled; the shiny skies offered nothing at all.

Just when a man was getting started. He sometimes felt he would use up his life getting started. For what, in that case? He would study the sky.

When the sky darkened, it was only with smoke from a blaze or two which had got out of hand down the Waiatarua valley. Up Waikato way, they said, things was bad with the drought.

At night Ned listened to his restless cows, in search of feed, and in the morning fed them with the last of the past winter's hay, and then with the hay he had put aside for the next. The sky was indifferent.

It was time he wondered how things were up the Crimmins place, and with Nance. It was the first letter he had written to a woman.

Dear Nance, he wrote. Then he considered. While Nick watched furtively, he waited for his blunt pencil to continue.

Looks like things is bad everywhere but hope theyre not too bad with yous up there. I hope your okay Nance

This seemed sufficiently personal, so he went on:

and Jack is holding on all right. Tell Jack I would like another go at them pigs on Pirongia sometime.

And he appeared to have said just about all he could say. He moistened the edge of his lips, trying to concentrate, but the blankness of the rest of the page became dazzling. So he concentrated for a while on rolling and lighting up a smoke. Then he took hold of the pencil and attacked the paper again. *I reckon things will probably come out all right. The important thing is*

Puzzled, he sat looking down a vast crevasse. Words he might use as slender bridge just swayed there, and fell. Outside, dry wind scratched through the dry valley. The moon silvered the window of the whare. The pencil circled in his fidgeting fingers. He could get no strength behind it. And it wasn't his implement anyway. Nevertheless, he resented this weakness, which he seemed committed to explore. Once more he looked at the words. *The important thing is*

Nick could tell him, doubtless. Sweat began to form on his forehead as he fronted up to the paper. Yes, Nick could tell him and that might be right for Nick, who was old. Was there nothing better, or more?

For the sentence clamoured to be finished.

The important thing is

Then he thought he had it. Anyway the pencil began travelling clumsily across the page.

to hang on, I reckon.

He gave up, then, and went to bed. Actually it was some time, nearly a week, before he commanded strength enough to finish the letter, with a fresh spurt of words directly for Nance, and lick down the envelope with relief. It was not the things he had said which troubled him so greatly; it was the things he hadn't. And it was still another two days before he took it down to Te Ika to mail. But once in Te Ika, possibly the heat confusing him, he drove first not to the post office, but to a back street off to the side of town, where he parked the car and knocked on a familiar door.

A woman answered. He had never really taken a good gander at Mother Murphy before. She was bulky and grey-haired, and wasn't mean with the mascara.

'Yes?'

His tongue wandered up to the roof of his mouth.

Then, evidently, she recalled his face. 'If you're looking for your mate Nick, he's not here, thank Christ. I haven't seen the bloody old ning-nong in months.'

'No,' he said. 'I'm not looking for him.'

'Some beer, then?' He had never been a particular customer. He shook his head.

'Then what?' She had company inside, plainly, and was impatient.

'There was,' he uttered at length, 'a woman here called Mabel.' His throat was quite dry; he could have stood a beer after all.

She laughed. 'You mean you're looking for our Mabel?'

He nodded. 'That's right.'

'Well, you're a bit on the late side, matey. Our Mabel's shot through. She's took off up the line with a boy friend on the ran tan. Some fellow on the railway, a big brute too. She didn't say when she'd be back. Or if she would. Christ knows.'

'I see.' He had, it seemed, pretty well changed his mind anyhow. 'Well, it doesn't matter.'

She gave him a speculative stare. 'There's no one else,' she asked, 'I could find to suit?'

'No,' he insisted.

'Well, then, good luck to you, matey, and good day.'

He turned from the shut door, walked back to the car, drove to the post office, and mailed his letter to Nance. It was, he knew, what he should have done in the first place. For it was clearly his fate to mail the letter. But it seemed he had always to give fate a fair run for its money. And make sure, possibly, that fate wasn't confusing him with someone else. Afterwards, though, he might wonder, sweating, what would have happened if Mabel had been there, and what other fates he could have found. He might never know.

Nance replied quickly. Her answer came inside a parcel with a thick woollen pullover she had knitted for Ned. She was posting it, she said, on account of Ned not getting up to see them lately. She said she hoped it fitted and things wasn't so bad up there, it could be worse Dad said, but some were losing stock. She hoped Ned was looking after himself and would write again soon.

So it began again, this agony of words. Possibly it had been a mistake to write the first time. Once begun, there was evidently no end to the business. Still, the last line of his new letter turned out rather surprising. The pencil seemed to travel of its own accord over the page, while he watched. *Nance I would like to marry you if thats okay* And sat, his heart thumping. He looked across at Nick, calm on his bunk, who apparently felt

96

no reverberation. He considered the sentence again, signed his name hastily, and sealed the envelope. For some things could never be unwritten; it was done now, forever.

He spent most of that night wondering if sleep, like the bloody rain, had gone to another country. Only Nick's snores, rumbling and crashing, told him otherwise.

But he was up earlier than usual with his cows the next morning. He did not wake Nick; he was happier by himself. And when late-sleeping Nick emerged at last from the whare he found Ned, nails between his teeth, hammering up a house for his love.

Jack Crimmins and Nance arrived the following weekend. They sent a telegram naming the time of their train, and Ned drove down to Te Ika station to meet them.

'We have knocked off for the weekend,' Jack said. 'The cows have half gone dry anyhow. We left the kids to milk the rest.'

Nance, behind Jack on the platform, had nothing to say. She was having trouble where to look.

'Anyhow congratulations,' Jack went on, 'we are all damn glad for Nance.'

Nance decided to look beyond the railway yards to the hills above Te Ika.

'Nance,' said Jack, 'you ought to say some bloody thing. And not leave all this effort to your old man.'

He grabbed her shoulder and propelled her towards Ned, whose arms hung bewildered until he saw he must catch hold of Nance, if only to keep her from pitching forward upon the gritty platform. She clutched a small purse, a bright beady affair, and was awkward in her thin cotton frock, patterned with red roses.

Her flesh shivered as he caught her.

'I am looking the other way,' Jack announced, half turning his back.

There was some perfume Ned could not remember having smelled before. And Nance had distinctly reddened her lips.

She was trying to smile. His hands were so hesitant, upon the thin cotton, that the roses might have been real, with thorns. He looked at this insubstantial girl who was evidently to be his wife. Then he saw he must kiss her. That, it appeared, was the way to end all this confusion.

He placed his dry lips upon that part of her forehead nearest

97

his mouth. There really wasn't much to Nance at all; it surprised him how thin.

'Hullo Nance,' he said. He was obliged, surely, to say something. His voice was thick.

She appeared to awaken then. Her eyes grew bright with something like tears. 'Hullo Ned,' she said. 'I am glad.'

'I am glad too,' he replied.

No one would suggest otherwise. Jack was all over them again. 'When you reckon on getting it fixed up, Ned?' he asked.

Ned and Nance were apart now, and lost. 'Fixed up, Jack?' Ned inquired.

'With my little girl here,' Jack said. He placed a hand firmly on Nance's shoulder, as if about to make some bargain.

'We better talk about that,' Ned answered.

'Nance is not keen on waiting.'

'I'm not one for waiting round much myself,' Ned agreed.

So it seemed pretty well settled, but for a date. He drove Nance and Jack up the Waiatarua valley. They passed through the gorge and entered the stripped land beyond.

'Them cows of yours,' Jack observed, 'are looking damn skinny.' He had no eyes, evidently, for anything but the beasts.

'Nothing wrong with them,' Ned said defensively, 'that a bit of rain won't fix.' He paused. 'I have jacked up a place for Nance and you to sleep in the house. Two of the rooms are near enough ready for sleeping in. Nick and me are still in the whare. But the house is coming on.'

Nance climbed out of the Ford and looked across Ned's land, as if testing herself against it. First her eyes measured the hills and the durable trees which still greened the high ground between limestone outcrops. Then the slopes where black stumps burst out of patchy pasture. Lastly she considered the thirsty lowland, filigreed with fences. But it will all be mud in winter, she thought, and not much better than our place. Still, the house will be something when it is finished, because it will be my own.

Besides, she remembered, there is Ned.

She lost all thought of the other things, the land, the house, and felt weak. This man Ned, this stranger, to be her husband? Her imagination wilted. Her flesh panicked. Did no one see?

But Jack and Ned were just talking, pretty casual, not looking at her at all.

She could manage, of course. She could cook, keep house, and do a man's work outside. But more was expected, surely.

98

More? She cringed. She expected she probably loved Ned, all right, the way she said. Would love, though, be a help? No one had told her.

'Does it look all right to you, Nance?' said Jack Crimmins, who was now seeing beyond the beasts.

But he did not expect an answer. He started on about shooting prospects to Ned. And Nance, silent, was left to wander among her strange thoughts.

Now Nick shambled over to the Ford from the whare. 'A good day for it,' he said conversationally.

'Too many more good days,' growled Jack, 'and we might as well cut our throats.'

Nance looked away, dreaming. In the city it was different. In the city they would be enjoying the sun. They sea-bathed and walked in bright parks, among flowers, where bands played. She knew because she had seen them once. And she could not really detest the sun herself, ever. And not on a day like this, even with its fears.

'Rain,' Jack went on. 'That's all us poor bloody cockies are interested in. Rain and good grass. Isn't that right, Ned?'

Ned agreed while Nick mumbled.

Anyhow, Nance thought, it will be quiet enough here, strange and quiet, and Ned and me will have a chance to get used to each other.

She tried to persuade herself to the idea. Ned, though, was difficult to get around; he was too solid to shift. There seemed, when she thought about it, some curious menace beyond his shyness. What was it, though?

Her mind scrabbled for an answer, but she had only the sun warm on her face and arms, like ridicule.

And he will expect me to have his kids, Nance remembered, palpitating.

They stood there, Nick and Jack, Ned and Nance, confused by the ambiguous sun.

Nancy Crimmins and Ned Livingstone were married soon after, on a dry day of a warm month. The parson, an elderly man with mince in his walk and squeak in his voice, scattered old words liberally over their heads, then appeared to mutter to himself. When it was over, anyway, they concluded they were married. They were dazzled by the sun which slanted through a stained glass window where Christ was crucified prettily, and it was a relief to step down from the altar.

Mrs Crimmins, a huge sagging woman, stepped forward, 'Here Ned,' she said. 'You kiss the bride. Or have you forgot?'

But Ned had never been told. He did what he could, against Nance's face, with shaky lips.

They had a breakfast, or boozeroo, at the Crimmins place before Ned took Nance home. There were neighbours, kids, and gallons of grog. And tin cans rattled from behind the Ford as it started back to Te Ika. After a mile or two Ned stopped the vehicle and stripped off the paraphernalia. Nance, sitting prim inside, watched in silence.

'That's that, then,' Ned announced. He flung the cans into a ditch. 'We might of been better off without all this nonsense.'

'Nonsense?' Nance said.

'The church,' Ned told her, 'and all the rest.' He paused. 'I don't go much on none of it. That parson, he give me the creeps.'

'It is a sacred moment for a woman,' Nance said, for she had been told this.

'Well,' Ned replied, 'He got five quid for it. That's sacred enough, if you ask me. A fiver's a fiver. I could work me guts out all week to make a fiver.'

'Or ride a horse,' she said, 'at a rodeo.'

She blushed at her own precocity.

'By Christ,' he said, amused, 'you're right there.'

He climbed back into the Ford in better mood.

'Mrs Livingstone,' he said, and tickled her under the chin, 'I think you might know all the answers.'

She coloured again.

'I don't know much,' she said. 'I wish I knew more.'

They arrived soon at Te Ika. He grew expansive. 'Here it is,' he said. 'The town the railway built. What do you think of it, eh? Look all right to you?'

'It looks like a town,' she said. She would like to compare, but could not. Towns were towns. And she had seen only the one city, once.

'It's all right, I expect,' he said, answering his own question. 'A foggy and frosty bloody hole in winter. And the shopkeepers are all crooks.' On such evidence he could not, of course, justify the town. All that could be said was that people lived there, for some purpose, and died. He was glad he did not have to

100

reconcile himself to the necessity of such a place; he was really not obliged to think about it much at all. It was true, though, that he still sometimes puzzled over the point of things, the purpose, until the threads of his thought tangled. At such times he would peer into his scratched, scabby hands as if they might disclose something. Since they did not, he would soon enough fasten his hands upon something, the shaft of an axe or the handle of a spade, to fill the emptiness he saw.

'A man can't amount to much in a place like this,' he explained to Nance. 'There's nothing for a man to get his teeth into. He can't get very far, or grow very big.'

So they carried on through the town of strangers. Past small, perplexing lives.

Ned sometimes thought that if he believed in God he could put things together easy. But he had no faith in the bastard.

'There is the school,' he said, 'where our kids might go.'

'Yes,' said Nance. 'It is a nice looking school.'

'And there is the pa,' Ned said, 'where the Maoris get up to their tricks.'

The meeting house, the carved posts, the ugly faces, the old gods, rocked past.

He could believe, he decided at last, in Nance and himself. He could believe he was taking her home. He could believe in their kids. He could believe in this gravelled road, this slow valley, this dark river, this gorge, this land.

'Here we are,' he said. 'We are home.'

There were the acres of brown grass, the tight fences, the patchy bush, the taut hills, the sun in an orange sky. Nick stood outside the whare, waving.

'Here is your house, Mrs Livingstone,' announced Ned, as he clambered from the Ford and helped Nance down. 'All yours. I thought I would have it finished. But there is still the verandah to put on. The verandah will face the sun.'

'It will be nice,' she agreed, 'facing the sun.' Then, excited, she added in a breathless rush, 'And I would like to have one of the rooms as a front room. A proper front room, I mean. Where we can keep nice things, little knick-knacks, and china, and entertain visitors now and then. I have always wanted a front room.'

'Then we must see about that,' Ned promised.

The cicadas drummed from the bush, and the birds played woodwind.

'I will like it here,' Nance said. 'I know.'

101

Nick came running, staggering, from the whare.

'Having milked the cows,' he insisted, 'I am surely entitled to kiss the blushing bride.'

Nance looked in appeal to Ned, who nodded. Old Nick left a drip of saliva bright on Nance's cheek.

That night the iron roof contracted after the heat of the day. It sounded like haphazard gunshot. Nick had gone off to sleep in the whare. Ned sat fidgety in the kitchen while Nance disappeared into the bedroom. He listened to the sounds of clothing and linen. He heard bare feet upon the floor, then a creak from the wire of the double bed as it took a body's weight. At last everything in the house was quiet. A morepork cried faintly from the bush. Cows chafed and chomped in a nearby paddock. The sounds of thinning water floated musically across the evening. Ned washed himself, with a cloth, at the kitchen sink. Then he stripped his clothes, his wedding suit, and went to the room where his wife waited.

Her slight body offered possibilities to him, possibilities more than flesh. So he searched, in hope of finding them. It appeared, at times, that he might succeed; that lust might have some richer harvest. He could not doubt that there was more to be won. That night was the first of many in which he tried to twist and trap some dimly conceived finality from the flesh of the woman. So that even she, in the end, might have suspected desire had some more intricate choreography. For she must have sensed his disappointment, when his body had done its best, and was gentle enough, and patient. They could only do what they could, after all. But she could not tell him this; it was not a subject for speech. He became blunter, more taciturn. He wished to give himself to lightning, perhaps, yet he remained tangible, too solid altogether, listening to the dwindling thud of thunder as it moved away, his body limply joined to hers.

Still in the night, it seemed, the girl who had become wife reached across for her husband, but found herself the only occupant of the bed. Light trembled upon his crushed and vacant pillow. Panic took her. She climbed from the bed, with its smell of their first night, and swiftly hung clothes upon her skinny body. Then she raced out into the gaudy morning. 'Ned!' she cried, for fear was beginning to throttle her.

But Ned was there. He was real, and safe. He stood there, on his two legs, among the faintly steaming pats of manure, slapping cows into the milking shed. With old Nick, his mate, beside

102

him, coughing and spitting. There, on his two legs, with a torn shirt on his back, and she could almost have died for love.

'Ned!' she cried again, happily.

As he turned to look at her, he was grinning. Her speeding feet seemed slow through dewy weeds and grass.

Still he grinned. 'Them clouds,' he called to her. 'Look at them, Nance. Look. They're building. I reckon it will piss down today.'

She stopped, as if hit. But she really did not know, it appeared, what else she might have expected, or what she might have said to him anyway, And she certainly had not seen the clouds. They were there, all right, grey and darkening above the hills, climbing towards the sun.

The world seemed to be shrinking, visibly.

'You're all right?' he inquired, when she arrived beside him at length.

'Yes, Ned,' she agreed. 'I'm all right.'

'That's good, then,' he observed.

There was a silence. They were both, in their ways, having difficulty.

'My first morning here,' she said finally. It was not all she meant.

'Yes.'

'And I am just about to get the breakfasts ready,' she said, 'and the house tidy. It is too much to believe. Almost.'

The milking machine began to make a racket.

'So,' she finished, 'I better get ahead with believing it.' For she was, on the whole, a practical girl.

She went back to the house and got ahead with things. The air inside grew heavier, and there was rising wind outside. Soon, when she looked, the rubbery clouds, bouncing and stretching, had erased the sun. Trees with gossiping foliage bent to the wind; the bush up on the hills seemed in uproar.

Not long after they sat to breakfast, the first rain cracked upon the iron roof. With clatter of chairs, the meal was abandoned. They raced out to the back door for the spectacle. The drought at last was over. The wind was angry now, snapping and slashing, while rain roared.

Soon Ned was worried. With an oilskin over his shoulders he hurried across paddocks to shut gates and make things fast. The rain hurtled down from the hills in huge grey gusts. Pools formed and fattened. She ran after him, across the paddocks, perhaps to help, perhaps just to keep him in sight.

The valley seemed to be rocking. She could not remember a storm like it. There was thunder now, and lightning playing on the limestone cliffs.

The rain was sharp on her face; she could feel it spidery beneath her dress. Then she caught up with him, and her feet slowed while her heart leapt like a hooked trout.

'What you think you're doing?' he demanded. 'Out in this?'

'I might help,' she said, stricken.

'There is nothing much,' he said. 'Nothing much to do.'

His words seemed to rattle in the wind. The rain swished between them.

'I didn't know,' she began, and stopped.

'Didn't know what?'

'That rain could be lovely. To feel, I mean.'

She was just standing there, happily, while the rain fell.

'It is clean,' she said inadequately, 'and beautiful on my face.'

'You ought to be back at the house.' He was baffled now. 'Keeping dry.'

Leaves flew past them. 'But I feel good,' she insisted. 'I feel mad.'

'Mad enough to catch a death,' he said. 'What you think you're doing?' He came closer, as if to see. The rain streamed from his bristly face. His eyes were strange. He could not recognise this girl he had taken. 'Come on back, Nance,' he pleaded.

'Ned,' she said. She rushed at him, all damp dress and dripping hair, a thing of storm. 'Ned I love you, Ned.'

There could have been nothing more dismaying.

'I would like to dance,' she said. 'To sing.'

He tried to steer her back, but she floated away through the rain. He plodded in pursuit.

'We could do everything, Ned. You and me. We could do everything. Whatever we like. Because we are us.'

He could not recognise his handiwork, any more than he could comprehend it. The land squelched beneath his feet, while her words veered around him. They were among trees by the creek now. The air was filled with falling leaves. Lightning splashed through the branches.

'We are us, Ned,' she announced again. 'We can do everything.'

And this eventually she tried to prove, beneath a tree. She dragged him down, and they fell there among sodden leaves and broken sticks, holding tight to each other and breathing hard. It seemed their chilled bodies needed to make no effort at all; it was over soon. 'You see,' she told him, 'we are mad, Ned, both mad.' For there was possibly no other explanation. Then she added, 'Perhaps we have made a kid now. You think we might?'

Their regained clothes were wet and unpleasant, and the violence in the storm was abating. They peered out from under the trickling trees. 'We better get back,' he declared. 'Old Nick will be wondering.'

'Nick,' she sniffed. 'He's got nothing to wonder about.'

But Ned turned out right about something else. Nance almost did catch herself a death. She spent four days, afterwards, sneezing and coughing in bed. And she never lost the cough altogether when she rose from bed. She went down with cold after cold that winter.

So Nance never did trap Ned out in the rain again. But she could tease.

'I think I am having that kid now, Ned,' she would say.

Just to watch his face. It was a good face, not much damaged yet by age and experience. She could take great pleasure in it when she teased, glimpsing things otherwise hidden within his skin.

She would have teased him for hours, but she hadn't the heart.

'You think so?' he would say. He could be almost breathless.

'I am late this month,' she explained. 'You never know.'

She had him really on edge. She had never felt power before; she could make the eyes of this man tremble.

'You better take things easy for a bit,' he said. 'Just in case.'

At once she was ashamed of her teasing. 'We will wait, Ned, and see.'

They did not have very long to wait. The months sped, her belly fattened, and the child was born. Ned drove her down to the Te Ika hospital in the morning, and when he drove back there after milking in the evening he discovered himself a father. Nance was asleep, and he was shown his child by a terrifyingly crisp nurse who seemed indifferent to the fact that his tongue was paralysed. 'Here we are, Mr Livingstone,' she announced, wheeling in the basinette. 'Seven pounds and eight ounces. A lovely boy.'

Ned, leaning over, saw a small blotchy red face with clenched eyes. The lips parted slightly and a tiny bubble formed.

'This one?' he said, attempting to believe it.

He thrust a finger forward, not quite touching the child's face.

'That's the one, Mr Livingstone. That's your boy, all right.'

'My boy,' he said. But it was absurd.

The nurse had, of course, seen men stunned by fatherhood before.

'He's all right?' he remembered to ask at length. 'Nothing wrong?'

'Nothing wrong. He's as he should be, a perfect little human being. All his fingers, all his toes. Now, Mr Livingstone. Don't touch. We don't want your boy to get an infection, do we?'

He withdrew his wandering finger. It had brushed only the slightest particle of the child's flesh; he felt cheated.

'He'll be all right?' he repeated.

'Perfectly. He should be a healthy, strong young boy. You ought to be proud of yourself, Mr Livingstone.'

Pride? Pride had not revealed itself to him. But power had. Perhaps Nance was right, they could do anything. He felt giddy with his strength. And he couldn't shift his eyes from the child; he wished most to sample that vivid, quite incredible flesh with his blunt and shaky finger again. The nurse tapped her toe impatiently.

'Time for baby to sleep,' she said, and swiftly wheeled the basinette away.

Ned Livingstone had lost his son for the first time.

Then he was taken into the room where Nance had awoken. 'I'm sore,' she said. 'I'm terrible sore, Ned. Sit here.' She patted part of the bed. He sat. 'Well,' she said, 'we got a boy, Ned. A big boy. Isn't that good?' She waited for answer, but there was none. 'Ned, you're all right, aren't you?'

'I'm all right,' he agreed presently. 'I'm just thinking.'

'Thinking? What about, Ned?'

'About things. You and me. And living and dying. Everything.' He paused and confessed, 'Sometimes I get scared.'

She frowned. All this seemed to her irrelevant. At this time, especially. Ned should have been joking and laughing, full of

106

beans, like the other boozy and happy new fathers she had seen. She did not like to see her husband set himself apart.

'Scared? What are you talking about, Ned?'

'Scared of things,' he explained ponderously. 'It is like – ' But he could not say. So he tried again. 'It is like seeing God, in a way. Only I don't see him, I never see the bugger.'

'This is no time to be morbid, Ned,' Nance said firmly. 'Or for blasphemy. We have a son, a fine boy. You ought to be happy.'

'But I am,' he replied. 'That's the trouble.'

At times he maddened her, he was so difficult to understand. He sat there in his tough skin and old clothes, as if determined to irritate.

'I have been thinking,' she said, 'about the name. I should of made up my mind before.'

'The name?' he said, blinking.

'I think Timothy is as good as any. I can't think past it.'

'Timothy,' he repeated.

'You remember?' she said. 'After my brother. The one I told you about. My dead brother Timothy.'

This boy, Ned remembered hearing, had been a strange child, a little light in the head; he had gathered flowers, woven garlands, and wandered through the bush talking to birds and singing to himself. He died of some slight illness when Nance was a child. Possibly he had never been strong enough for life. Nance had loved her brother Timothy because he loved her, when she was small, and told her stories.

'Timothy?' he said. 'Yes, that could be a good name. We could call him Tim.' But he couldn't imagine this, not yet. He was speaking to humour Nance. He was also recalling a yellow snapshot Nance still carried, almost all that remained of the original Timothy. He remembered most the large strange eyes, quite melancholy. He did not care for the thought of his own son, still blinking in the light of the world, being burdened by association with such eyes. Ned, however, continued to humour Nance.

Until it was time to leave the hospital. It was a large square concrete building with humming sounds, white light, and quick feet. As he left it, and looked back, trying to guess which lighted window his son lay beyond, he thought that perhaps Nance was right. It was not really a place for a man to brood on things.

107

This mechanical building, with its metallic noises, dealt only with flesh, sometimes cruelly.

He walked among large trees and flower beds. The night air was pleasant, scented thinly with growth and decay. He stood by his car for a time, as if trying to make measure of himself, and finally lit a smoke. I have got a bloody son, he repeated in his mind, I have got a bloody son at last.

He could not believe the world indifferent, or unshaken. And the boy, after all, might turn out to be a bloody marvel. He could not wait to know his son.

Whatever he told himself, however much he repeated it, it was all inadequate. He would, doubtless, have years in which to believe it. Meanwhile, though, there seemed nothing he could do with his wonder; there was nowhere to take it.

His stomach growled, a low rolling sound. Jesus, he thought, the old guts are in real uproar.

In the end he drove back, fast, to the only place where he could take himself, and where his mate Nick would be waiting for the news. Nick had put a couple of bottles aside, in a rare act of self denial, to wet the baby's head when it came. That would have to do. At least his gut might have a chance to settle.

Eight:

THEY DID NOT LAST LONG IN WELLINGTON. THEY DID NOT LAST
anywhere. The woman dreamed of permanence, some place
of rest. She flung lines of longing to towns and landscapes, as
they drifted by, but never made herself fast. The man disengaged
without effort, and they moved on. She attempted to have a
child, which miscarried. There was no promise of another.

He had jobs. He worked cargo on the waterfront. He used a
knife in slaughterhouses. He stacked butterboxes nine high in
freezing chambers. He dug coal again. He did most of the jobs
that were to be done, and his own.

He knew the dream, knew how to scatter the seed. Sometimes
with whisper or iron joke, sometimes with speeches and limp
leaflets. His fist became a hammer as it pounded the texts.

He discovered that he could share his anger. He could bring
bitter light to grey, perplexed faces. He could make a crowd
rustle as if in high wind.

He found the time his ally now; the time was on the side of
his dream. And the dream itself, as he spoke, began to solidify
in his palpitating mind; he could distinguish the turrets and
spires, the fountains and parks, of the just city. He seemed
already to be walking those precise squares, those straight streets,
where never a brick, nor blade of grass, was unaligned. His
imagination faltered only when he tried to populate the city
with recognisable human forms; his footsteps were still lonely
there, and left no echo. He was only faintly troubled. For he
was always back soon enough in the forest, in the undergrowth
of ignorance and superstition, with treacherous nettles everywhere, his words slashing and hacking.

He talked of twopence an hour, strike action, eviction laws,
economy measures, relief works, protests, and the Russian Five-

Year Plan. It seemed the old forest had grown brittle. Just the right spark, possibly, and a blaze might devour.

The land quietened. Men walked out of dead factories, into the streets, and sought him out. They froze into crowds and then, given warmth by his words, melted back along the asphalt streets. Farms died too, less swiftly, under yellow weeds, as men walked into the hopeless city, sometimes to ask why. His voice grew hoarse with explanation. Marches began. First dozens, then hundreds. His stomach, often otherwise empty, could rattle with exhilaration.

'It's coming,' he told Peggy. 'How can anyone not see it?'

They were in Auckland now, a futile city, grown for profit on mud and swamp, and now, with splitting asphalt, sinking down to swamp again. Yet people still bought and sold, as if it mattered. And worked in jobs, if they had them still. He had a job himself, for that matter. But his pay as Party organizer wasn't more than token. Peggy had a part-time factory job which helped, three afternoons a week at Betta Shoes.

'Coming?' Peggy said. She was tired. Her back ached, and her feet. He had met her at the factory gate, where he sometimes attempted to sell the Party paper. But her fellow workers, a disorganized lot, mostly middle-aged women employed as cheap labour, were pretty tight fisted. They hurried past when he tried to sell.

'What is coming?' Peggy said. 'And when?'

'An end to this,' he announced. 'Before long. An end to the way things are.'

Many things moved her, mostly with dismay. Peeling fences, children with dirty faces, old men cadging outside pubs, women with bleak eyes, shabby churches with pleading posters. There was a woman next door, for example, who must have sobbed a week, because her husband had gone elsewhere to find work, if he could, and instead had found a woman to keep him. But she was also moved by skies fantastic with sunset, above the distant blue hills which edged the city. Under such skies the old wooden houses, in the gully where they lived, took on a cruel and dreadful glamour. She almost expected people to flee. But they did not, of course. They tugged down blinds against the night, and lit fires if they could get the wood and coal. An end? She supposed she saw an end too, a different end. One which would herald no beginning, for man was an incurable illness of the earth.

110

'Yes, Bill,' she agreed.

He always walked a little too fast for her. And his eyes flitted from side to side, as if auditing the city.

'There will be five thousand more on relief by the end of the month,' he announced, almost as if he had arranged it.

'Then where is the end?' she asked.

But they were home, and she was fidgeting among coins in her handbag for the key to their door. The door squeaked on its hinges, allowing them entry to a dark passage which smelled of gas and cabbage. Something rustled underfoot and she picked up a letter, heavily postmarked, which seemed to have been re-addressed a half dozen times.

'Look,' she said. 'Look at this.'

'At what?' He had gone heavily into the room they rented for eating and sleeping.

'This letter for me. It has followed us around everywhere. All over the country.'

'Who from?' he grunted.

But she was already gorging upon it.

'Who from?' he repeated. His stomach grumbled.

'From my brother,' she said. 'He has written at last. And he is here, Bill. He is up in this part of the country. Not far outside the city, he says. In a little place.'

When she had finished reading, she placed the letter near him, where he might pick it up if he wished. But he did not look, or touch it. Those thin pages, with spidery writing, might have had contagion.

He watched her flutter, all alight, as she began to prepare food.

'Well?' he said. 'What is the point?'

'What point, where?'

'The point of his writing. What did he write to you?'

'To tell me about himself. Why else do people write?'

He did not know. He grew hostile now.

'What's he want, then?'

'Nothing. He doesn't want anything, Bill.'

'No? Then why'd he write?'

'Because,' she explained hopelessly, 'because he'd been thinking about me, wondering. He'd heard I was married.'

'So he was just thinking, wondering, and he wrote?' He made it seem unlikely. But he still declined to touch the letter. 'And he wants to see you again?'

'He didn't say that. But I expect he would.' She paused, briefly defiant. 'Just as I would like to see him again. He is my brother.'

He could not deny it. He began counting loose change from his pocket, and then checked the total against his unsold copies of The Red Worker. 'So he just wrote,' he summed up presently. 'He didn't want nothing.'

'No,' she insisted. 'Why must you always think that people want something?'

'Because they do,' he said.

'Then what do you want, really, Bill?' She mercilessly stripped potatoes of their skins.

'You know what I want.'

'But I want you to tell me, quietly.'

'Something better,' he began.

'I don't mean politics,' she interrupted.

'Oh?'

'I just mean what you want most, in your own heart.'

'Then I don't see the difference.'

'There must be something special you want. Something good.'

'All right,' he said. 'There is. Men like brothers.'

She placed the potatoes, presently, on a steady gas. 'But, Bill, men are brothers, for what that is worth. Already. Sometimes for better, sometimes for worse.'

'I mean we should behave like we are brothers. Decently.'

'I think what you really mean is that people should be made to behave like that.'

'Up to a point.'

'And what point is that?'

'Up to the point where we're finished with the old greed. Finished with profit, wage slaves, and the capitalist system. Then men will be free. And that is the way things are going now.'

He was orating again after all. This did not always dismay her, though it did now. At other times she wondered at his strength. And sometimes, perplexed, she wished to save herself by squeezing into his skin. But that was something for which she was ill-fitted by nature.

'I don't know what is happening now, Bill,' she said mildly. 'I wish I did. I only know what you tell me, and it is mostly people's misery.'

This seemed to pacify him.

112

'So what about your brother?' he asked, after a time. 'What has he done with himself?'

'He has been to Europe. All over, with a swag on his back, looking around. He hasn't been back here long.'

'What did he want to go over there for?'

She was grilling some cheap mutton chops; the room began to smell of melting fat. 'He didn't say. To forget his trouble, perhaps, and get away from things he knew. Or perhaps just to see new things. A number of reasons, I expect. He's interested in everything. He's an artistic sort of person.'

'I bet,' he grunted, since he had struck artistic sort of persons before. And had to defend himself, once. It confirmed the worst about this brother. And about artistic sort of persons. The more he heard of this mythic brother, the less he liked the sound of him.

She was silent, and remained silent. They seldom, anyway, invaded each other's minds.

'He'd meet that kind over there, all right,' he went on. 'Does he reckon he liked it?'

'He seems to have liked it.'

'Then why didn't he stay over there?'

She shrugged. 'I am obviously not my brother's keeper. I cannot be expected to account for him.'

'I hope not,' her husband said, seeing humour.

She placed food upon the table.

'My brother is all right,' she insisted. 'It is people who are wrong. You should understand that, of all people. Because you know what intolerance means.'

There seemed, then, some slight change in his involved face.

'All right, then go and see him,' he told her. 'It's all the same to me.'

But it wasn't, altogether. It seemed that, to have Peggy, he was obliged to own this brother-in-law too. He disliked situations where he had no choice.

'I think I will,' she answered carefully, as if negotiating a narrow path. 'You must understand that I cannot desert my brother. He is a good man. No matter what people say.'

'I am saying nothing,' he announced.

'No,' she said quietly, 'but you are thinking.'

'All right. So I am thinking.' He placed food within his mouth, and began to work his teeth. 'I am entitled to think.'

They reflected on this. She was glad of the silence. And it was

113

pleasure to be off her painful feet. All afternoon the banging machines seemed to have been moving in upon her. So that once she almost screamed aloud, for escape. Survival, each time, was still a matter for wonder. In her gentle childhood, beside the forest under the mountains, she had never thought much about factories. Bill might overturn the country and half the world with his talk, but there would still be factories. It didn't seem important to her who owned them. They would still be there, with people captive.

'How was the meeting?' she asked at length. For she remembered his meeting that afternoon. She was vague about all his committees and meetings, but tried to take an interest.

'It was all right,' he answered. 'Though there's some there I'd trust about as far as I could kick.'

'What's wrong with them?'

'You should ask what's right with them. Smart alecs, social democrats, opportunists who can see a good thing. Their eye on the main chance. We got this anti-eviction movement under way, and they climb on the bandwagon.'

'You ought to be glad,' she observed. 'With more people, there's surely a better chance of stopping the evictions. Isn't that so?'

The argument did not appear to move him much. 'I don't trust them,' he insisted. 'That's all.'

'Then how can you get anywhere if you don't make the best of people?'

'If you expect the worst, and hope for the best, you can't go too far wrong. Trust no bugger, and you're not too hurt in the end.'

'I see.'

'I trusted one man, once,' he went on. 'I'd of stuck with him till hell froze over. And I got taught a lesson I haven't forgot. Because he was like all the rest in the end. Ready to sell out when the going got tough.'

She let him go on about Charlie Higgins, and retreated into the cool of her mind. She wasn't sure what selling out meant, exactly. Perhaps it just meant changing and compromising. But it was inconceivable, of course, that her husband should be different. To wish him different would be to wish him death. He would win on his own terms, or not at all. She was suddenly quite afraid.

'Look at them now,' he was saying. 'Look at them all. The

114

ones in jail in the war. The ones I knew down on the Coast. All scrambling over each other as fast as they can go, to get their bums comfortable in Parliament. Social reform, they talk about now. For a regular salary, of course. And so they can cheat the people again. You reckon I should trust the likes of them?'

She had nothing to say for a while. Perhaps what he said was true. If so, she didn't go too much on truth any more.

'I don't know,' she confessed. 'I only know it is better to trust than to hate. I don't even know how I know that. I just know it. I am entitled to think too, Bill.'

'All right,' he said. 'So we're quits.'

It was a rare concession.

She still felt gratified, next day, as she travelled by pale ferryboat, past anchored ocean liners, across a brilliant harbour. Their peace, or truce, left her serene enough. Perhaps she would not have made this trip otherwise. Lean gulls drifted across the bright sky; a widening band of sea excluded her from the city, and she began to feel excitement.

The boat bumped against piles, a gangway rattled down. She went ashore and caught a bus which carried her through patchy maritime suburbs. There were still small farms, and orchards. She glimpsed beaches, where huge old pohutukawa reared, lined with pleasant wooden bungalows. The bus travelled further. Houses became fewer. She was dropped, finally, in a scrubby seaside place; the bus went no further. The signs spoke confusingly, but she decided she had a mile to walk. The road of clay and stones was brutal to her feet. Her body soon became slippery with sweat beneath its garments. A shiny car, with two grinning blonde girls, kicked dust in her face. She passed paddocks and grazing cows, beginning to limp. Eventually she stopped at an isolated house for a glass of water and to inquire about her direction. She was sure she had missed a turning somewhere, as she explained to the lanky woman, with hair in curlers, who fetched her a glass of water from the rainwater tank.

'No,' said the woman. 'You're right, dearie, you're dead right for the bay. Only a couple of hundred yards and you're there. Whose place you wanting?'

'Name of Campbell,' she said.

'Youngish fellow? Thought so. You should find him there, all right. Not been here long, that right? In a little bach. Yair. No, there's not many down in the bay. You can't miss it. My

115

hubby knows him, to pass the time of day, but I can't say I've had the pleasure. Know him, do you?'

'My brother,' Peggy said.

'Well,' said the woman. 'Fancy. Sure you wouldn't like a cuppa, dearie? I could put the kettle on.'

'No thanks,' Peggy said. 'But it's kind of you.' She sipped the water, and the glass was suddenly empty.

'Well, any time you're round here again, just pop in for a yarn. Bring your brother too. Rose is the name. Rose Sullivan. It's a lonely sort of place, and I don't see many new faces. Not since we shifted out here, Christ knows why. But we had a little money, you see, on account of my hubby having some luck at last with the horses. So before the dumb bugger pissed it away on the booze I told him he better buy a place. And this was going cheap. He wanted to live near the sea, on account of he was a seaman. You can see the ships from here, most days. But I mean it's not much good to me. A woman wants a back fence to yarn over, doesn't she? I mean ships isn't much consolation.'

Peggy began to look for escape. She could feel herself being drawn down; she was too reassured by unsurprising lives.

Rose Sullivan's curlers clicked in her jostling hair as she guided Peggy back to the gate. 'Remember,' she said. 'Any time, dearie. I'm always here.'

Peggy fled down the road, and presently came to what she took to be her brother's place, near the sea. It was more or less as he described it, a small weatherboard cottage in a scraggy little gully. A creek ran beside the property, trickling toward the sea, with a few thin young willows. A large pohutukawa held a bank at the back of the place together. Much of the property was still thick with native scrub and alien weeds, but in a clearing, a patch of sanity in the confused vegetation, there was a considerable garden, with cabbages and onions and potatoes and less identifiable plants growing in sandy soil. A thin path took her past this garden, up to the rickety porch. She knocked upon a door, heard papers rustle within, then feet. Ben came to the door with sandalled feet and shorts, on thin brown legs. He was paralysed with sight of Peggy; they both were. 'My God,' he said at length, still incredulous. 'And what are you doing here?'

His face was vaguely puffy with sunburn, perhaps, or sleepless nights; his eyes, though, were shrewd and bright. He was no longer young.

'I got your letter,' she announced. 'So I came.'

'From where?'

'From here, Ben. We're living up here now. Bill and me. Bill,' she remembered to add, breathless, 'is my husband. We've been here the best part of a year.'

'My God,' he said. 'All this time. Come in, come in.' He stood aside, waving her into the house. His hair, she saw with dismay, was thinning on top. And his face had several days' growth of blackish beard, as though he didn't care too much about himself now. In a sunny room, jammed with books and papers and bachelor paraphernalia, pots and pans and vegetables, she took a wobbly chair. Ben took another seat, but couldn't shift his wondering eyes from her face.

'Well, Peg,' he said. 'It's been a long time. Sometimes I thought I might never see you again. Particularly since I sent that letter, and had no reply. I was lucky enough to meet someone who told me you were a Mrs Freeman now, and gave me an address.'

'It took a while,' she explained. 'Following us round. We are never anywhere long.'

She was sitting beside his desk, on which she could now distinguish separate things. Notebooks, volumes opened at marked pages. A typewriter, rather antique, with a sheet of paper fastened in it. And ranks of neat words. Her eyes lifted.

'I got it yesterday,' she added. 'I came today.' She wasn't sure whether she was declaring affection, or loneliness. Or both.

'I'm glad,' he said, and then explained, 'sometimes I have the feeling I possess no past at all. That I don't belong here, or anywhere. I haven't been very settled since I came back from Europe. Probably that's one reason I fired off that letter to you. A selfish reason. I wanted to make contact again – with you, but also with what past I do have. Can you see what I mean?'

'Yes,' she said, but didn't altogether.

'I'm still trying to make sense of things. Of myself too. Hopeless, of course, but one tries. Can I make you a cup of coffee?'

'Don't go to any trouble,' she pleaded. 'I can see you're busy. I won't stay long.'

'But you've only just come,' he said, astonished. 'After more years than I care to think.'

'I just wanted to see that you're here. That you're all right. Now I can see you're all right.' She moved uneasily in her chair;

117

she thought she would never be comfortable here, or with Ben again.

'I'm lucky to have this place, that's true. The owner cleared off to England about the time the bust came. So he let it go for almost nothing. I was lucky to have a few quid in my pocket for once. It's quiet. People don't bother me here. I have a small dinghy down on the beach, so I can fish for my supper. Or there's shellfish, failing a bite. I've all the time in the world to make sense of things. Too much, sometimes.' With a rueful, rather urchin grin, almost the only thing still familiar about this man, he set about making coffee. Beyond the window, between clumps of cabbage trees, she glimpsed sand and rock and dazzling water. Distant islands seemed suspended on the haze of the horizon. Out there, she thought, there might be places where we could know each other again. Surely. Here the room, the debris of his curious life, impeded. Everything was alien, even her flesh and blood.

The room began to smell of coffee. He was still trying to relax her with his conversation, and she could not help him much. 'So you thought you'd try making a go of things up here?' he asked at length.

'That's what we thought,' she agreed. 'It's bigger. Bill is always losing jobs. Once the bosses get to know him. We thought it might be better here. But there are no jobs to speak of now.'

'Tell me about Bill.'

She tried, but found it hard to tell. It was not for lack of attention from her listener. Ben appeared fascinated, and kept chipping in with questions. It was just that all these details did not add up to Bill; they did not explain him, if there were an explanation, or make him seem real. To Ben, and perhaps to herself. She needed Bill Freeman's large presence. He was altogether plausible then. And made explanation trivial. She felt, as she talked of him, what might have been a shiver in her soul. It seemed she was afraid again.

'He sounds a real fighter,' Ben observed. 'A determined man. Hard.'

'Hard? I expect he sounds like that.'

'And not like the kind of person I should have expected you to marry.'

She did not reply. She could not imagine another husband.

'He sounds,' Ben summed up, 'very much like someone who knows where he is going.'

118

And where, Ben, is that? she wanted suddenly desperately, to ask.

But Ben was busy, his back to her, pouring the coffee into mugs. She found herself, with her mind slowly emptying of urgency, reading along the ranks of words trapped in his typewriter.

While one must travel into the centre first, the nature of a civilization is sometimes best comprehended at its extremities. Habit and inhabitant alike take on, or revert to, something archetypal in character. Inessentials of character, of behaviour, are often stripped away and, picked clean, the bones of being become almost luminous. Those who come from a frontier society go very naked in the world. This is one view. But

It might have been another language, something foreign. And it seemed unlikely that such words were the property of the only Ben Campbell she knew, who had run laughing with her on beaches, and made mysteries of the bush, before he went off to university and murkily out of her life. She knew nothing of this man near middle age, an impostor grotesquely posing as her brother. She could accept the coffee from his soft hands, but very little else.

So she sat, and felt her spirit dwindle within its lumpy shell. She sat, and sipped her coffee.

There was a painting above the mantelpiece. It must have been what people called abstract. Nothing recognisable, something yellow lit with red flashes. It soon, this strange thing, began to hypnotize her, for she had nowhere else to concentrate her gaze safely; the red flashes began to move apart, or flow together.

This Ben Campbell's voice was strange too. Soft, almost silky. For a moment she yearned to engage her fingers in its texture. So that she lost the sense of what he was earnestly saying.

The panic passed.

'Anyway,' he finished, 'if you and Bill get desperate, remember there's always a refuge for you over here. I'd like to meet this husband of yours sometime. He sounds interesting. And I like meeting new people anyway. I only have one friend here regularly; he comes to stay on weekends.'

She didn't ask who. She was relieved, retrospectively, to have found him alone. This meeting with her brother was unmanageable enough, without his friend. Where, then, would she have begun?

For she had to begin. 'You haven't any job?' she asked.

'No. And I'm not greatly grieved yet. I manage, as you see, to survive. Also one gets time to think. That's been the trouble with this country. People have been too busy settling it to think much about what they're doing. Or what it's all about. And I'm writing, as you might observe.'

'Yes.' Her gaze blinked back to the typewriter, and flinched away again. 'I see.'

She did not know how to comment, or what to ask.

'It's about all I have to show for myself since I saw you last. A handful of poems, a few essays. I'm not prolific. The more I learn, the less I write.' He shrugged, rose, and began to rummage for something on his desk. 'I meant to send this to you. Here.'

He pushed a thin booklet into her hands. *This Island Harvest,* the title read. And underneath, *Poems by Ben Campbell.*

'You may not,' he added, 'find it especially interesting. But there's something dedicated to you in there.'

'To me?' The room was altogether too bright now; her eyes began to smart. 'But why, Ben?'

'Why not?' he said. 'I wrote it, in point of fact, while I was away. I was looking back on things, especially childhood here. It all became very real again. I believe the experience is not uncommon among exiles, temporary or otherwise. Though it's said nostalgia is an inferior starting point for a poem.'

He had lost her again. She had a chance to gain control of her eyes. But her fingers seemed frozen around the booklet. She did not dare consider it.

'I was unloading, if you like,' Ben went on. 'Unloading a lot of mental baggage. To make my journey back lighter. And so I wouldn't expect too much.'

The room settled, dust motes turned in the sunlight; she felt strong enough to chance herself against the occasion. She rose. 'I think I had better go, now,' she announced.

'Don't feel you have to,' he insisted.

'It's just Bill,' she explained. 'Bill will be expecting me.' Bill Freeman was now entirely familiar, and precious, not at all strange. 'And thank you,' she added, 'for this.' She clutched the book of poems tight now, a souvenir of the day in which she might believe soon. As she moved in flight towards the door, Ben caught her wrist, and held. So that she had to face him.

'Peg,' he pleaded, 'you will come back, won't you?'

For now his misery encountered hers. Her flesh grew white where he gripped.

'You won't just forget?' he asked.

She was appalled. And had to answer, evidently.

'I will try,' she promised. 'I'll try to come back again soon.'

'And bring your Bill. Bring him too.'

'I'll try.' She could not promise more.

'We all have to hold on, Peg. In our different ways. And sometimes there's not much to hold on to.'

Yet he appeared to find her wrist substantial enough. His fingers unwrapped it reluctantly; he appeared to marvel, for a moment, at his own ferocity. She had wanted to say: Tell me, Ben, tell me what is good and true, what is right, if you can.

But such words declined to turn on her tongue. Released, she went through the door. Ben still pursued.

'I'm here most days,' he said. 'Any time.'

And what could he tell her, after all, a man so afraid? She could think of Bill again with gratitude.

'My garden,' he said, guiding her along his path. 'It is not coming along too badly. The white butterflies are a problem. And it's thirsty. It could do with some rain.'

So they paused, in the end, to contemplate Ben Campbell's garden, under a hot and ransacked sky.

'I have found,' she said, 'the derris dust best for the white butterfly. And a touch of lime and sulphur elsewhere wouldn't hurt.'

'Really?' He seemed delighted. 'I must remember that. This gardening bug has only just taken me. It's being back on one's own soil, I expect. One's instinct is to grow what one can, no matter how obstinate and unpromising the ground. Our first instinct, perhaps; the dream of the garden. And perhaps that is what this country is really about, after all.'

It seemed to her a long way from derris dust, and lime and sulphur. She would, if she tried, only grow breathless trying to catch up. They walked on towards the bus which would take her back to the city, and Bill Freeman.

That night, beside her husband, she said, 'Sometimes I am scared, Bill. Sometimes I am terribly afraid.'

'What about?' he asked sleepily.

121

'If I knew, perhaps I wouldn't be so afraid. The things which frighten me are the things I don't know. Please hold me, Bill. Hold me very tight.'

He was willing to do this, for quite a time.

'It's probably seeing that brother of yours again,' he observed afterwards. 'It doesn't seem to have done you any good. Probably best if you didn't see him again too soon.'

Her reply was indistinct, but peaceful enough.

Betta Shoes closed between one day and the next. When Peggy arrived, for her afternoon shift, there wasn't even anyone in the office to inform her officially of the closure. There was just a note on the door, and the machines were quiet within; the place was a dark shell. Cats and children prowled the gritty street, and the wind tossed scraps of paper. The day was bleak, with random showers. She hurried back the way she had come. When she reached their room, she shut herself in, and experimented with ways to stop a draught, while she waited for her husband.

Bill Freeman was at an unemployed meeting that afternoon, and organizing a protest. The protest concerned the slave camps. The government was trucking single men off to these camps in thousands, working them for sixpence or a shilling a day, with tucker. It was a way of building roads, or planting forests, on the cheap.

'World capitalism,' he announced, 'doesn't even pretend any more. It's been stripped of its last rags. And stands there naked. Because it's only interested in surviving now.'

He was mild; he knew his men, that afternoon. Most were from the executive of the unemployed movement. Some were delegates from outlying districts. He had met most before, and sized them up. Some were almost friends, like Alex O'Leary, the Liverpool Irishman with broken teeth, flat nose, and wild eyes; or Harry Jones, a short, shrewd and tough ex-miner. Both were good Party comrades.

It was expected, and arranged, that Harry and Alex would rise in support when he said, 'It's time for us to show our hand now. We're ready to call thousands out into the streets. Make no mistake about it. We've never been nearer the hour of challenge. Never. So let's think about that, remember it, when we make our next move.'

'The question is, when?' said Alex.

'And where would the chairman propose?' asked Harry.

They knew the answers, of course. But he had to give the others time to brood. A few clearly panicked at the idea, and had to be won over. And the movement was gathering more than its share of cranks and compromisers. After a time, the usual social democrat rose to say, 'We don't want to prejudice our organization by reckless behaviour, mister chairman.'

He knew that sound, too well.

'If we are not here to take chances,' Bill Freeman replied, 'then we are here to do nothing. Anyone not ready to take a risk can leave the meeting now.'

He waited. No one moved, though the social democrat once looked towards the door. Evidently he wanted someone else to leave first. The silence became reassuring.

So Bill Freeman began to steer the meeting his way. It was soon settled. Trade unions were calling a demonstration to protest against a wage cut for public servants; it was to be a respectable affair, finishing inside the town hall, with resolutions to the government. But the unemployed, who had no wages to cut at all, would now be invited into the streets too, in thousands, with their own demand. After the meeting Alex and Harry shook his hand in congratulation.

'You swung them all the way,' Alex said.

'Good lad,' Harry Jones said. 'You could of had them eating out of your hand there, at the end.'

They began to speak, in lowered voices, of a Party cell meeting to consider urgent problems. Until they were joined by a stranger, a delegate from some outlying place, and fell silent. Bill looked at this face. It was at once familiar and unfamiliar. Yet he was certain that he had never seen this man before. He was looking at Bill and holding out a hand to be shaken. A police spy, perhaps. This was their casual approach.

'The name is Campbell,' this strange face said. 'I imagine you know the name.'

For a moment he didn't. He couldn't connect.

'Ben Campbell,' the stranger persisted. 'Peg's brother.'

There was something for Bill Freeman to consider then.

'I've been involved in the movement for the last month or two,' Ben explained. 'I've been hoping I might see something of you. After hearing about you from Peg. I did suggest to her, that once she came to see me, that you might both come over and visit sometime. But I can see you've been busy.'

It was Peggy in this man's face, Peggy who was familiar. A masculine caricature, a mockery. And this soft hand to be shaken. It was absurd. Yet he discovered he was shaking the hand. Or had already shaken it. Words climbed clumsily from his throat.

'Yes,' he said. 'I heard about you. A lot about you.' It might have signified everything, or nothing; he did not know himself. 'I'm glad,' he added, conventionally, 'to see you at this meeting today.'

'I must say,' Ben Campbell offered, 'that I'm an admirer of yours.'

'You reckon?' Bill Freeman might have been seen embarrassed.

'I'm impressed by your ability to pull men together. Really quite remarkable.'

Bill Freeman wasn't in business for compliments. 'People have to be pulled together,' he said, 'if we're going to move anything. Or move anywhere.'

'Quite,' Ben said. 'It's just that you seem to have the gift of doing it.'

'It's half the battle,' Bill conceded.

'And what's the other half?'

'Holding them,' Bill Freeman argued, 'when you've got them. When the fight begins.'

'You seem to be talking from bitter experience.'

Bill was not really in the mood for memory. 'I been around', he agreed at length. 'And I'm going to do my best to stay around.'

'I don't doubt that. I suppose you realize you're fast becoming a bogey-man? No; silly question. Of course you must. What I mean, perhaps, is that you seem to unnerve some on the left as well as the right.'

'There are always some would sell out.'

'And you're a marked man. You must know that too.'

'How would you know?' Bill asked, suspicious. His first impression might not have been altogether wrong. The police could make use of some pretty queer fish, even stray brothers-in-law. It could be a warning.

'Because it's logical,' Ben said. 'Entirely logical. They can only let you go so far; and no further.'

He felt relief, mainly for Peggy's sake, that this brother of hers was just giving him a lecture. 'Then,' he said, 'I better see how far that is first. And we can have a yarn about it when we're across the other side. There's no stopping now. Just look at history.'

'I have,' Ben replied. 'That's the trouble.'

'Then we read the books different.'

'Perhaps. Or different books.'

They exchanged other words, like thin coins, as if attempting to purchase something, and possibly not entirely failing. Because they parted with promises, and some goodwill.

'My brother-in-law,' he explained to Alex and Harry. 'First time I ever met him. And I expect I could of met him in worse places. A funny thing, though. I'd never of expected to see him at a meeting like this, from all I heard.'

But of course it did not concern them. He had to puzzle over it alone. When he arrived home, he reported to Peggy, 'I met your brother. Ben. He was at the meeting.'

She was at the stove. Her face lately seemed shrunken; her stomach was never strong in the mornings. She would insist, if he asked, that there was nothing wrong. And he had to accept this. To have done otherwise would have been too distracting. Anyway they hadn't been talking much. Sometimes, at night, they lay separate.

'At the meeting,' he repeated. 'And we had a yarn.'

He couldn't determine if he was getting across to her at all. He couldn't see her face. She remained quiet.

'There are,' he added, 'all kinds of intellectuals coming into the movement now. Useless, most of them. But you never know.' He was trying to be fair.

Yet he still had not made much of an impression on Peggy, at the stove. And she had gone on so often about this brother.

'He reckoned we ought to go over and see him,' he went on. 'And stay with him, even, if things get rough.'

'What did you say?' She had a reaction at last.

'I said I'd think about it.'

'Well, you'd better think about it, Bill. Really think hard about it. Because my job's gone. The factory's shut. We can't afford the rent here now. And,' she added, after a moment, 'we're going to have a child, Bill. I didn't want to say until I was sure.'

'I'd thought we was pretty careful,' he observed. They had decided to postpone a child until things were better. Yet he was not as dismayed as he might have been.

125

'There was one night,' she said. 'One night when I wasn't up to much. When I was scared of things. And we weren't careful; I didn't think to be.'

He strained to recall, but found it difficult. There were, after all, so many nights when she confessed fear.

'All right,' he said. 'So we're going to have a kid.'

'Is that all you have to say?'

'Only that there's nothing we can do about it. We're probably due for a kid, either now or later on. And later on might never come.'

'So you're not angry?'

'There are more important things to be angry about.'

'Then,' she said, 'I wish, in a way, you were angry. Because a child is important. Our child, any child.'

'Christ,' he said abruptly, 'I can't win. Give me a chance.'

'For what?'

'To be glad, for instance. I have to get used to the idea first. You know I'm not much good at pretending.'

'No,' she agreed. Then, 'I'm sorry.' For she was.

'And we're damn well going to make the best of it,' he insisted, 'and give the kid a fair chance.'

'Yes.' She was almost meek now.

'I'll go and see your brother about moving over there next week sometime, when things have quietened down a bit.'

'When what's quietened down?'

'The city. Right now I got a lot of things to do. We're organizing a big demonstration.'

'Another one?' she said.

'But this one's different.'

'I expect it is,' she said, since they all were.

'I think things might be on the move at last. The thing is to keep the pot boiling, but not let it boil over. Not yet. People are getting angrier every day. And hungrier. But they still have to be steered the right way.'

'You talk yourself hoarse with some people, Bill.'

'So I'll talk myself hoarse, then,' he said. 'And if my voice goes, I'll use a blackboard. Do you think I'm going to give up because some people only hear what they want to hear?'

'No,' she admitted. When he grew so large, she knew the worst of her fear, for there was a limit. There would be too many willing to make him small again.

'This kid,' he said presently. 'You sure about it?'

126

She felt relief; he was more her size again. 'As sure as I can be,' she said. 'Otherwise I wouldn't tell you.'

'I'd better look after you decent this time,' he said. 'Last time I was pretty ignorant.'

'It wouldn't have made any difference last time, Bill. It was just nature. Something wasn't right, that's all.'

'All the same. I could of done better.'

'It would have made no difference,' she insisted.

'And I'm sorry,' he said, 'if I let you think this kid wasn't important to me.'

She felt mean, now, because she had diminished him.

'A man's got to have some stake in life,' he went on, 'otherwise he doesn't amount to much. It gives me even more to fight for.'

She would, perhaps, have to think about that. Nevertheless, words unsaid, all grateful, fluttered like a flock of wild things in her mouth; she could not speak at all.

'And about this factory job,' he said. 'Don't worry about it. You're better off without it now. Things will come right.'

'Will they Bill? Will they come right?' she said at last. She would have liked him to prove it.

'You got to have some faith,' he observed.

'Faith? That does not sound much like you, Bill.'

'Not faith in God. In man.'

'But you have said you don't trust people.'

'Faith is different from trust.'

'It is hard for me to see the difference.'

'Faith is what keeps you going. When you haven't got much trust left. Or hope. That is what I mean.'

'Then what is faith, when there is no trust or hope?'

'It is what keeps you going,' he repeated. 'To keep going you got to have faith. And to have faith you got to keep going.'

'I see,' she said, though in despair again of ever seeing. 'Perhaps I need some of that kind of faith too, Bill, if you have some to spare.'

That night, near sleep, Bill Freeman was jerked awake again by a sudden and vivid memory of the conversation with his brother-in-law, as if there were something there he had not understood, some piece of grit still irritating his vision. It was no new thing, really, to be told he was a marked man. Marked for what? Ben Campbell had not said. But marked for defeat, of course. That was the point. And it wasn't much of a point.

127

Because it didn't mean he was too crippled to confront his defeat, wherever it might be found, preferably on some ground he had chosen, and settle the issue once and for all. For it was no longer an entirely personal problem, to see how far he could go. There was also Peggy to consider, and the child now. And after all, defeat was really no stranger, more an old companion. At least he knew where he stood with defeat. He mightn't have much patience with the other anyway.

Peggy stirred beside him. 'You're restless tonight,' she observed. 'Is it the child?'

'Yes,' he agreed. 'And other things.'

'Other things?'

'This demonstration next week. It looks like we're going to bring it off, all right. I reckon it will be a huge success.'

Alex O'Leary approached him, in subdued fashion, a day or two ahead. 'Look, Bill,' he began. 'We better have a talk. About this demonstration.'

'I thought we'd pretty well used up all our talk.'

Alex coughed; he was clearly about to undertake some task he disliked. 'The Party feels – well, Bill, the truth is that the Party feels that perhaps you better not speak at the demonstration.'

'Why not?'

'Because, if anything goes wrong, you'll be looking down the barrel of a gun. Things are looking pretty tense already.'

'Are you saying the Party needs to look after me? That I can't bloody well look after myself? That it?'

'In a way.'

'What way, then?'

'Well, the fact is, Bill, and you got to admit it, is lately the Party is starting to look too much like Bill Freeman, and Bill Freeman too much like the Party. So far as most people are concerned. That's about the guts of it, if you must know.'

'And I been getting too big for my boots. Is that right?'

'We're not saying that,' Alex answered cautiously.

'Then I'm buggered if I know what you are saying. Except that you want to put me down in mothballs.'

'This time, Bill. This time.'

'And it's a directive?'

'Yes. To march; not speak.'

'So we let the social democrats make the running. That it?'

There were times when disgust seemed to paralyse him; the contempt he tasted in his mouth would not find shape in words.

'The feeling is you might misjudge the situation and get carried away. We can't afford it; the Party can't. Things are too dicey. We're still too weak to have you putting us in the gun. Party policy is to let these moderates put up their respectable front, while we give them a short sharp push in the arse. So either they expose themselves or go our way. Too much risk otherwise. For the Party; for you.'

'Thanks for nothing,' Bill Freeman said.

For he had been cheated. He had been cheated, after all, of the only ground he might have chosen; he should perhaps have reckoned on defeat contriving this ambush before he even arrived. And from behind a friendly face. Charlie Higgins once; Alex O'Leary now. There was no end, evidently, to the disguises it wore. And it didn't want a straight fight to a finish, that was clear. It just wanted to needle and nag, until he could think of nothing else.

Feet. There were feet everywhere, drumming and scraping, as thousands gathered at the assembly point. Some drifted in, others marched. Contingent after contingent arrived from the slave camps. Banners rose jerkily, as if thrown up by internal tremors of the thickening mass. The last light had gone from the sky, and faces and banners alike took thin colour from the feeble street-lights. Blue smoke rose and swayed, in the still air above the shaggy heads of the young, the bald crowns of the old. Bill Freeman, pushing among bony bodies, had never seen anything like it before. He tossed out pamphlets and talked as he moved; faith grew abrasive in his throat. When his hands were empty at last, his voice still functioned; it made a slow, twisting track through the crowd. There were the smells and voices of city pub and slum, country clay and swamp. Unemployed fresh from road-gangs still had mud splashed on their trousers. And more came riding in, unkempt and bearded, on the back of covered trucks. They had their banners and cardboard slogans too, END SLAVERY and IF BLOOD BE THE PRICE OF YOUR CURSED WEALTH, GOOD GOD WE HAVE PAID IN FULL. He saw few men he knew, though he made it his business to remember faces. But many seemed to know him. Perhaps too many; his shoulders began to ache from

129

friendly pounding. And his progress was made slow by insistent handshakes. It seemed his jubilance would have no end. Once, walking this same street of the city, he had thought himself lonely in his anger, the impossible only too solid around him, all brick and stone and men beyond salvage. Now he had multiplied, and saw himself in every face. He could measure triumph in fists and feet. He could almost believe the city was theirs.

He came to the edge of the crowd. Noise and smell began to break off like a tattering froth. For the silence was solid beyond. Each side of the street, as it rose wide into the city, revealed the glint of police buttons. Here and there mounted men stood stationary, in silhouette, among clustering onlookers. A tram or two echoed away up the route the march would take. Otherwise the city could not have been quieter.

It was time. He took his place near the head of the procession, between Harry Jones and Alex O'Leary. He did not speak to either of them; there was nothing much to say. Behind them the ranks formed. And soon the feet began to move, first in uncertain shuffle, then in quickened and steady beat as the asphalt route unrolled. The banners jutted, rising and falling with the motion of the march, like debris upon a river of men. Rags of old song fluttered back in the ranks, but not for long. Onlookers tossed out applause and abuse, but the sound was small. For the feet overwhelmed. Even the mounted police did not care to interpose; their horses shied now and then as the feet played a slow drum upon the city. Bill Freeman walked tall enough that night. At those times when he looked back, it seemed the march was coming on forever. IF BLOOD BE, and the faces came flowing on.

It hardly seemed necessary for anything to happen in his life again.

They arrived, too soon, at the end. It was a square of sorts. An open space allowed, between the city's bulkier buildings, by the confluence of streets at the town hall. High wires gleamed; the town clock shone like a spotty moon above. Everywhere uniforms swarmed, silver buttons bristled, horses pranced. The doors to the town hall were open for the wage protest meeting. But the police appeared intent now on blocking the place off altogether. They made a cordon before the doors. Some marchers darted free of the ranks to find gaps or scuffles in the police line before the doors could be closed; few got into the building. Then the doors were bolted.

Bill Freeman, stopped short of the police line, felt the pressure behind him now. It mounted impossibly as rank after rank of marchers jammed up behind him, as thousands filled the square. Trouble was a matter of time; the only question was where it would begin. Where? But it had begun. He swung his gaze and saw a baton bounce brutally off an old man's head, then the flash of fists. A police helmet spun high.

'Steady,' he called. 'Steady.'

No use. A woman's cry this time. He could not see what was happening. But the crowd howled and surged; it was like boulders kicking together in flood. He just managed to stay on his feet, but was carried away from Harry and Alex. Again the cry forked, thin and wailing. Feet scratched over the asphalt, wearing at the flesh of the city.

The crowd had became aimless explosions of flesh. He used his strength to find Harry and Alex again.

'What do the bastards think they're doing?' Harry asked. 'They got us penned like pigs here. They don't just want to keep us out of the meeting. It looks like they want things to get out of hand.'

'Then,' Bill Freeman said, 'you'd best call on your moderate friends to pull the fat from the fire.'

'They're all inside. In the meeting. On the platform.'

'And in their best suits, no doubt.'

He could enjoy this moment, for there was little else to enjoy.

'We got to hold the crowd together,' Alex said. 'Otherwise we're lost.'

'I think we're pretty damn near lost now,' Bill Freeman said bitterly.

There was a police charge somewhere in front. People tumbled back, grabbing each other as if trying to impart messages, and falling underfoot.

'You could do it, Bill,' Alex conceded at last. 'You could pull them together.'

He had, of course, been waiting for this. Fear chafed in his chest, nevertheless.

'I expect I could try,' he agreed. 'I expect I could give it a go.'

Then he was hoisted. His legs dangled, and his buttocks sat on bony shoulders. They carried him, through the churning crowd, to the front of the town hall. To a small railed-off area, a prominence with a patch of lawn, where people parted.

'Tell them, Bill. Tell them.' Alex was actually pleading.

But he'd had enough of that satisfaction now. It was time to measure himself against the din. And give it some shape, some point or purpose; he might have been a sculptor about to inflict himself on stone.

And it might have seemed, for a minute, he would never begin. For he looked graven there himself.

'Comrades,' he cried. 'Comrades.' But he could have been shouting into storm. Sweat sprouted on his face with the effort; he had to bunch his being behind the word. 'Comrades. Comrades.'

Then he knew he could do it. It was not something he could afford to doubt.

'Comrades, listen to me. We got to stick together.'

Incredibly, they were listening now. Or some were. There was a spreading quiet, a stillness, as faces turned upward; he had become a distraction from the police. So he scattered his words over them. And, like pebbles skipped on water, they struck off the crowd with swift splashes of response. He could hear his name called, several times, out there in that mass. And cheers. It began to have form.

He allowed himself to take breath. It might all be downhill now. Even his loins were looser.

'So here we are again,' he announced. 'It could be a bloody sight worse.'

He paused. Some seemed to see humour. He played it gently.

'And it might be,' he went on, 'if we aren't careful.' He didn't need the hammer yet; a nick at the theme was sufficient. 'It seems to me, comrades, that the police have something pretty precious to protect in that meeting. Our politician friends, for example. The kind who get paid in Parliament to be friends of the workers. They're all in there, while these coppers keep us great unwashed at bay. So give these boys in blue a round of applause for doing their job. After all, it's good to see somebody actually in a job, for a change. Come on, now. Give them a hand. Sorry. I don't think I heard that. Try again. That's better. But you can do better still. Of course you can. Now, that's more like it. And remember now, that copper nearest you may not have a father, but it might be kinder not to say so. He's a worker too. So give him a break, will you? If he pulls his baton, just press close around so he won't be silly enough to use it, and get himself hurt.'

There was laughter where his bait had been; he thought he

had them hooked. People at the back of the square were pressing close, straining to hear. The scuffles with the police had ebbed at the edges. Things had some sort of shape now. He was undecided what to do with it, exactly, unless that was to be discovered in what he was saying.

'There's some would like trouble tonight,' he insisted. 'There's people in high places gunning for trouble so they get an excuse to smash our movement. So don't let yourself be provoked. Because that's what they want. What we want is different. What we want is a fair return for the sweat we put into this country. What we want is justice. And we're going to get it.'

If this was defeat, it still hadn't introduced itself. The sound crashed up from the darkened square. And he was lost within it. The solid city seemed to sway. He had to wait before his voice was useful again. In the meantime, perhaps, he could enjoy the pained question on Alex O'Leary's face. For there seemed nothing he could not do, give or take an Alex O'Leary. Or a Charlie Higgins. He could even step down, if he liked, and bequeath defeat this creation, this roar, as a parting souvenir. But it was, after all, even more tempting to resume his speech, when the crowd had quietened; to assault that silence and see what lay beyond.

'And one day soon, comrades, we might be able to call this country our own. And make something good of it as last. And we'll do that, all right, if we stick together. So don't let yourself be provoked. Don't – '

He saw what lay beyond; he saw the raised baton. It seemed to move very slowly, yet there was not the time to duck beneath it. He was quite paralysed; there was no one more lonely in that square. The baton caught him across the side of his face once. Then split his head. There was a sighing, a soaring. Alex and Harry were picking him up, propping him. The policeman had been torn away, perhaps to be torn apart. They were inhabiting a world of batons and fists and murderous feet. It seemed Bill Freeman was being told something. They were asking him to speak again, these urgent men around him. They appeared to think they had the right to ask. They appeared to think him their own property. He understood then, in this bruising confusion, as men pawed and held him, that he could never be more than others chose; and had never been. The rest was a desert of deception: he wasn't even his own creation.

133

For he was thrust up again, by many hands, above the lurching crowd.

And was given sight of the disaster. The roar was endless now. It wasn't just angry; it was hungry too. The fractured crowd was a thing of hurtling, spinning, swarming bits and pieces. It had a dozen directions, and none at all. The police were swamped, their batons still flailing, wherever they stood. Then his own blood blinded him.

'Hold on, comrades. Hold on.'

Perhaps he said that. He was no longer sure which voice was his own.

'Listen to me.'

That was certainly his own, however thin and strange. And a joke. For it was given to him to listen now. That roar seemed to fill his thudding brain; he thought he would never forget it.

He cleared his eyes. Men, having stripped palings from a church fence, were launching themselves insanely upon the police. Or stabbing and swinging with the shafts of broken banners. Some lay prone. There was blood enough already. Freed of flesh, it leapt and spun in sticky patterns over clothing and hair. Plate-glass windows began to smash open around the square.

It was all over, or just begun. They lowered him to the ground again. 'No use,' he confessed to Alex. 'No bloody use at all. I've lost them now.'

'They just went mad when you got hit,' Alex said. 'It was all they needed.'

'Then who needs me?' Bill Freeman asked.

Alex was puzzled. 'You sure you're all right, Bill?'

'I'm all right. Only this blood.'

They tried to pass through the fighting. An eager young constable, surprised to find himself in a gap with a target so clear, seemed to think he might finish off Bill Freeman. Alex tripped him as he came, and Bill swung a rabbit-killer; the constable fell at their feet. Bill held him there, by the throat, while Alex took away the baton. That pale flesh was soft under his throttling thumbs; it would have been easy to strip it entirely of life. But he couldn't. There was no satisfaction in a frightened kid with acne. Disgusted, he laboured on through the brawl with Alex. The police seemed in total retreat. And as the fighting subsided, the crowd found its direction at last. Hundreds, then thousands, were moving back down the main

134

street, the way the march had come, and plate-glass windows were falling fast.

The worst, in fact, had only just revealed itself. It had become total riot.

'We could,' he told Alex, 'try and head them off.'

'Don't be a bloody fool, Bill. You done your dash. Christ, man; where do you think you're going?'

For he had begun to run, jerkily, trying to catch the foremost of the rioters, and Alex was soon lost somewhere behind. But he might have entered a race with some blind, battering flood. There was no sense to be seen. Here and there police lay shredded. The street was silvered with glass. And some men stood perplexed by what they had done. There was hardly a window left intact, so far as he could see, as the roar moved down toward the wharves. Other men looted casually, standing inside the shattered windows. They flung out clothing, food, jewellery. A man, who evidently did not recognise him, thrust a watch into his hand. 'Be in, mate,' he said. 'Get your chop.' An old woman danced and sang in a bulky fur coat. Bottles of looted whisky smashed.

'Comrades,' he pleaded, 'you're only hurting yourselves.' Then, 'This isn't revolution. This is just anarchy.' Then, 'You're playing into the hands of capitalism. Can't you see? Call it off before it's too late.'

But it was late enough for him to be punched and kicked aside when he tried to restrain some. And they trampled away, these people he thought he led, to the sound of breaking glass. He lifted himself off the pavement slowly, the despair in his mouth flavoured with blood.

'Let them go,' said a deep, caressing voice. 'On and on. For there shall be an end.'

He recognized the man. A blond Swedish giant, with huge golden moustache. Seen only once, but hardly forgotten.

'Out of chaos,' he said, 'will come our kingdom.'

Blood from some scalp wound had reddened his immaculate hair.

'The chaos,' he went on, 'where the spirit will triumph. Where man's new cities will flower. So let us make haste. Let us destroy.'

He flung a bottle through a still unbroken window, in emphasis.

'And let us hate,' he finished, trembling, 'so that we can love.'

135

'Christ,' said Bill Freeman. 'Get out of my way.' For the man impeded. 'Bugger off before I hammer you. You hear?'

The giant did not seem to hear. His eyes grew wilder.

'For we will love one day,' he declared desperately. 'All of us will love.' He was clinging to Bill Freeman's sleeve now. 'I heard you up there. I heard you speaking. But words, words, all words. There are no words in the blood. Only deeds. Deeds.'

So Bill Freeman was obliged in the end to prove the point, and strike the man, again and again, until he fell aside.

Further down the street there was nothing much to see. Unless it was women trying on shoes, and prancing about the pavement. Or men lighting a dozen cigarettes at a time, and loading themselves with liquor. The scavengers seemed to be moving in now. They followed the fighters, the despairing wreckers. And jigged jubilant under the street lights with their loot.

There was no news in this. He had always known men might shit upon themselves, given the chance.

He said that, or something like it, to Ben Campbell, who rose abruptly and vaguely before him. 'It's finished,' he said. 'All we had tonight. Finished.'

'I've been looking everywhere for you,' Ben told him. 'Where've you been?'

'To hell,' Bill Freeman said, and meant it.

'This will wake up the government, if anything will.'

'Wake the government up? We want to finish the bastards off, not wake them up. Can't you bloody see either?' He felt clumsy then, out of his own control, and dizzy.

Ben steadied him, and stopped his fall. 'My God,' he announced, 'you're a mess. What am I going to do with you?' Then, with alarm and dismay, 'You're not crying?'

'No, you fucking fool,' Bill Freeman answered savagely. 'It's this blood. Can't you see? This blood in my eyes. Can't you help me get rid of it? Jesus.'

It seemed his wound was open again. Ben did his best to clean him up. In the nature of things that couldn't be much.

Panic spread up the street. Someone ran past and cried, 'The navy's coming.' There were boos and ironic cheers somewhere distant.

'Look,' Ben was saying, 'it's risky for you in the street. Anywhere in the city. After tonight. You'll be safe at my place. Peg too. We'll pick her up on the way. You should be very safe there.'

'Safe?' Bill Freeman said. He could not seem to extract

meaning from the word. He had never been able to make much sense of it.

'From any more trouble,' Ben said. He added, 'They're right. The navy's coming.'

There was a measured clashing of feet. And the fixed bayonets were tipped with light. The pale ranks snapped past. The feet again. Feet.

Bill Freeman allowed himself, at length, to be led gently away. Ben now and then sheltered him in shop doorways, when any danger was evident. And almost the last thing he saw, in that slow retreat, was his old adversary, the Swedish anarchist, being gripped between two constables and led away, still raving quietly to himself.

'Bugger me,' he said. 'I am nothing either.'

He could not see anything to contradict him. Even Ben Campbell could not.

The sun was warm, and small waves flickered on the bright sea beyond Ben Campbell's garden. It made some things difficult to believe. Yet he had a bandaged head which hurt, and a cut hand in plaster. He became fidgety as the day went on. And Peggy was quiet, with the waiting.

Ben took him aside.

'The chances are the police are looking for anyone connected with the affair last night,' he said. 'And especially you. They'll never find you here. You should be all right until things cool off.'

'Then what?' Bill Freeman asked.

'I don't understand.'

'Do I just sit quiet and hide forever? Is that it?'

'If you like, I expect you could go off down country later, and find somewhere you aren't known. But you can stay here as long as you like. You know that.'

'Then I might as well be in prison after all.'

'But there's Peggy,' Ben observed. 'And this child.'

'And a knock on the door one day.'

'Perhaps,' Ben had to agree.

'I think I'd sooner choose my day. And place.'

Ben was silent. 'Yes,' he said presently. 'I expect you would.' He paused. 'Silly of me; I should have known that.'

'It's all right,' Bill said. 'You mean well.'

He had, in fact, begun not to object to this brother of Peggy's.

He was not so bad, considering. His heart was in the right place if not other things.

'You don't need to worry about Peg,' Ben insisted. 'I'll look after her. And do all I can.'

'Then perhaps,' Bill Freeman suggested, 'you can make a start by explaining to her why I have to go back to the city now. I'm not too good at explaining these things.'

Ben was surprised. 'Of course. But all the same, I don't see that you have to charge off yet. I can't see that you can do anything over there. Not now.'

'You mean I'm beat?'

'I didn't say that. I'm just saying I can't see that you can accomplish anything.'

'Same thing.'

'Possibly. But I didn't mean it, all the same. And I expect you know your own business best; it's rather impertinent of me to suggest otherwise.'

He was a gentle apology for a man, really. Bill Freeman could not find it in himself to be irritated.

'I do know my own business,' he agreed, 'even if I seem to know bugger all else. You might be right. There might be nothing for me to do any more. I probably am beat. But I still have to know, don't I?'

'I expect you do,' Ben said.

They found themselves shaking hands.

A hat disguised his bandaged head. Most windows in Queen Street were boarded up, the broken glass swept away. Patrols of special constables, enrolled that day, roamed with armbands and batons. Mounted infantry volunteers, farmers up from the Waikato, cantered in clusters, with rifles slung on their backs. Iron hooves struck sparks from the electric streets.

Darkness was further disguise as he took side streets and progressed deeper into the city. He tried to make contact with the movement again. But doors were shut, with no lights showing, and sometimes the police stood guard. He did not know where to begin, but it was not as if the feeling were unfamiliar.

He got news, eventually, from an old plug in the movement whom he met by chance in the uptown shopping district. It was a Friday night, with shops open for those who could buy. But the crowd was huge, and most were not there to buy.

138

They were simply standing, watching and waiting. Most announced themselves, in dress, as working men, unemployed or otherwise. But their sullen vigil would have been sufficient announcement. The horsemen clattered back and forward. The special police shoved through the crowd, trying to move people along. But they remained stationary, and largely silent.

This old plug approached him with surprise. 'What the hell you think you're doing here?' he demanded. 'There's a warrant out for you. They're out to bloody get you. They got some of the boys already. Alex O'Leary, he's in the nick. They arrested him this morning. And Harry Jones. Jesus, boy, what you think you're doing?'

'Standing here,' Bill Freeman said. 'That's what I think I'm doing.'

'Half the bloody coppers in Auckland know your face, boy,' said the old plug, whose name he recalled as Henry Something. 'And you mean to say you're just going to wait for one to spot you?'

'I told you,' he replied. 'I am just standing here. On my two feet. I have a right. To stand on them, where I choose.'

It was, after all, what most people in the street were doing. It seemed unlikely that he could have chosen better. Some nervous shopkeepers had begun to fasten their doors. Horsemen, impatient for trouble, whooped along the street, calling insults. Their language suffered, perhaps, an excess of colour. For it seemed the useless parasite pricks on the pavements were both bloody yellow and fucking red. All bleeding the country white.

It appeared the farmers had arrived to save the country.

There was only an old lady to dispute their possession of the open street. She dared to cross it with a pound of sausages for the weekend meal. Or perhaps she was quite oblivious. She clutched her package tight and hurried head down.

'Get off home, granny,' shouted a horseman who seemed to think she might be good for a laugh. He tried to wheel around her, and rather miscalculated. His mount reared and skidded, bumping the old girl, who went down with her legs in the air and sausages spilling.

'Bastards,' Henry called. He flung a bottle which he had just emptied. It caught the horseman in the face and sent him over. So that he hung, one foot in a stirrup, his head bumping on the street, as his panicky horse careered.

The horsemen were galloping in from all directions now,

and the specials on foot were running and swinging as they came. Some women and children, not moving fast enough, went down under a charge; others were flung against, and through, shop windows. The crowd divided swiftly between those who would save themselves with fists and those who would save themselves with fleeing feet. The fighting was confused, once it began. The enemy was not especially clear, once dragged from a horse or stripped of an armband. This Bill Freeman discovered when he took a baton from a felled special. He had to be careful not to use it on his own kind; farmer and worker looked too much alike. So he used it with discretion, if effectively enough, chopping into heads and arms wherever they appeared to threaten. But it was all, in the end, retreat; it could not be other. The fighting progressed along the pavement, to the sound of breaking windows, and around a corner. It appeared the specials, and their horses, were trying to box the worst of it in. And slowly succeeding, though someone had used the uproar as an occasion to set fire to a church. Flame crackled up the wooden steeple and the cross at the tip stood emphatic in the trembling red light.

It was, of course, only a matter of time. Most things were.

'That big bastard there, Ned,' someone said. 'That's the one. Watch him, though. He's grabbed a baton.'

Which Bill Freeman was using even more efficiently. For there was no problem identifying friend or enemy now. The enemy was all around him. Old Henry had gone down bleeding. The horsemen were tightening their box, and the specials were at him.

'Watch him, Ned,' said the voice. 'Get the bastard from the back.'

The baton collided with monotonous skulls, and his arms ached with the jarring. He began to take blows across the face and shoulders. Everything was dancing red. Everything was time. Flame flicked up the cross now.

'That's it, Ned. Oh, no. Oh, Christ.'

He managed to get his back against a wall. But they had him now, or near enough, for there was a limit to this too. They were coming again and again. They would never stop coming. They would hammer him into nothing. If this was the worst defeat could do, then he had been cheated again.

'Ned, you beaut. You bloody beaut.'

One came in low, surprisingly, and even the baton was

useless against his head; they fell together, locked, under indiscriminate batons and trampling feet, rolling over and over as they wrestled.

He was saved, perhaps, from too much damage because he held the other so tight. True, they were both booted around. But some farmer called a stop.

'Careful, you lot. That's me mate Ned down there. It's not him we want, it's the big bastard. That's it. You all right, Ned? Christ, what a bloody awful mess.'

They put hammerlocks on the big bastard, just in case, and twisted experimentally to see how far his bones would give. That was where Bill Freeman was reported as taken, after some strife beside a burning church. Later he was identified positively by regular police who had grievances of their own, but who were more particular about where they left bruises.

Before he was sentenced for sedition, policemen queued to enter the witness box and assert that they had heard him encourage and instruct crowds to riot and wreck the city.

Alex O'Leary and Harry Jones were given lesser sentences.

Inside the stone prison where they took him afterwards, the warders made him strip clean, and examined his mouth and arse to make sure he had nothing hidden, and also to make clear he no longer counted for much. For they left the tall man naked for quite a time, just skin and bone and a clump of pubic hair, blue and shivering with the chill of the place. Until there could be no doubt this Bill Freeman was nothing much at all.

Ben took Peggy home after the trial. They had already said most of what there was to say.

'There's a neighbour to see you,' Ben announced next morning.

'A neighbour?'

The woman Rose Sullivan stood on the step of the cottage in the shiny winter day. 'This hubby of yours,' she said, 'has had a rotten bit of luck. I come to see if there's anything I can do to help.'

'Thank you,' Peggy said, 'but – '

'Because I hear you're having a kid too,' Rose Sullivan insisted on saying.

'Yes, but – '

'Nothing like a kid, I always say, to keep a woman's mind off

141

herself. Or, come to that, off a hubby who's been put away a year or two.'

Peggy Freeman wept then.

'Come on, dear,' Rose said, nursing Peggy into the cottage, and down in a chair, while Ben stood by. 'Do you think he'd like to have you fretting on the other side? And it's no use weeping about the way the men carry on with each other. The poor bugger only did what he thought was best, when all said and done.'

'I think, perhaps – ' Ben began, helpless.

'And I think perhaps you better keep out of it,' Rose told him. 'There's time when a woman needs a woman. Men can have their fling and make their noise, I always say, but the women have to get on with it.'

'Get on with what?' Ben asked, in confused retreat.

'Life,' Rose Sullivan said. 'Children.' She bent to Peggy again. 'The rest,' she added, 'all comes out in the wash, I always say. And I'd say by the look of you, dear, you was a good six months gone.'

Nine:

'YES,' OLD NICK SAID, LEANING AGAINST A VERANDAH POST. 'I think I will shoot through. It is no life for me here. And I'm not much use to no one any more.'

'You don't need to,' Ned said. He had often considered the possibility of Nick dying. He had never thought of him walking out. Just like this.

The cows were milked, and the sky darkening. Inside the house the kid was crying. He still cried a hell of a lot. But at least he could walk now, and say something like words. Ned would listen to these confused sounds with patience; it was about his only distraction from the many things which troubled him. There was, however, little consolation or satisfaction there. For the things would still be waiting after. Nick was the latest. The old man had been sulky for some time, and now talked about shooting through.

'Things is different on this place now,' Nick explained. 'I am not complaining. It is just that things is different.'

It was undeniable. There was Nance around, for one thing. And the kid.

'I didn't want to walk out on you when things was crook,' Nick went on. 'But the way I see it, things aren't going to get no better.'

'You reckon?' Ned said. Wool-prices had gone, then butterfat. Men had walked off the land.

'I reckon,' Nick said. 'I reckon nobody can get us out of this lot. All the great men are dead. The men who made this country. All dead.'

'I don't know nothing about that,' Ned replied. 'I never heard of them.'

'And I'll tell you another thing. Before things is finished you'll

143

wish you never seen this place. You can wipe your sweat with the slack of your gut, but it won't make no difference. Because the place probably won't be yours anyway. There won't be a good man left on the land. The vultures will feast. The Jews, the banks, the stock and station agencies. Men will cry to let the day perish.'

'Nobody is taking this place,' Ned said. 'It is only worth what I am. Also I have a shotgun in reasonable shape.'

'Then there are none so blind,' Nick said. 'You and all the rest, Ned. I won't be here to see. I'm sorry, Ned, but it is time for me to shoot through. The good days have gone. And I have done my dash. I got nothing much to show, not even kids. Too late to be sorry now. I just got to make my peace with this bloody shambles, and give God half a chance to make his peace with me. I need a good long rest, and I know I got it coming. That's the one good thing I know.'

Ned, who had been thinking bitterly of rats and sinking ships, now felt a perplexing pity for the old man. It was easier to feel pity. His mind, these days, brimmed with sour things anyway. He could often taste this sourness leaking into his mouth, and spitting did no good. It even invaded his food as he ate it, and played hell with his digestion.

He placed a friendly hand on Nick. They had, after all, been mates ten years or more, and Ned might never find another. 'But where will you go?' he asked Nick gently. It was true Nick wasn't good for much any more, unless for that grave to which he now looked forward.

'Don't worry,' Nick said. 'I got friends.'

Friends? Ned tried to imagine them, but failed. They lived in some wild strange part of the country, perhaps. Some part Nick had known when he was young and strong. There were parts of the country which were still wild and strange, though it seemed unlikely here, upon these acres tamed and fenced.

They went inside to eat, while Nance and the kid kicked up noise around them. The kid was tired, and didn't want to eat. Ned didn't handle him much, it was easier to leave to Nance. On the few occasions Ned had been left with the child, he was terrified by his own impotence. It was difficult to believe that this screaming arrangement of flesh had anything to do with him.

'Tim,' he would say, 'Tim.'

While the child raged on. And Ned would grow brittle with

144

his own foolish expectations. He thought he would never get to know this son. He would never walk with him, and tell him yarns. Or do any of the other things he planned. The child often screamed just at the sight of his father.

Nance could quieten him. She had her ways. She would sing, or bounce the child. Or interest him in some toy. She even sat him at the table, with pencil and scraps of paper, where the child scribbled happily. Something Ned would never have thought of.

So he had this disappointment, among many.

Kids were for women. He should have known.

Nick finished his meal and went off to the whare. Nance put the child off to bed and came back to the kitchen, where Ned was brooding over his tea and rolling thin cigarettes.

'Nick is clearing off,' he announced. 'He wants to finish up.'

Interestingly, Nance showed no surprise or dismay. Had Nick talked to her first?

'It will make things simpler,' she said presently. 'One less mouth to feed. He is not much help any more. And he is beginning to smell, Ned. An old man's smell. He brings it into the kitchen with his mud. He is always trampling mud everywhere. No matter how often I tell him to leave his boots at the door. He doesn't look after himself proper. That is why he smells. Him and his mud and his smells. He doesn't belong in a civilized place.'

'He kept out of that front room,' Ned observed, 'after you told him.' Ned had cause to see the front room, which Nance had arranged with her knick-knacks and china, as a civilized place. He didn't often feel at home there himself.

'Just as well,' Nance said firmly, 'or I would of had a fair bit more to say.'

'He is old,' Ned suggested. 'He needs looking after.'

'We been looking after him,' she replied. 'Long enough.'

A suspicion nagged in some dim part of his mind, but he wanted to ignore it. 'He has been my mate,' he went on. 'He worked for me when I had nothing, Nance. Bloody nothing. Just for his tucker, that's all, and a place to sleep. I never been able to pay him much anyway, even when I could afford to.'

She sniffed, and went to the stove. She was evidently determined to say nothing, for some reason of her own. So he could no longer ignore his suspicion.

'Is it the mud, Nance? Did you tell him to go on account of

145

the mud? And the smell?' The thought that this might be so appalled him. His mouth hung loose after he had uttered the words.

'I told him I'd had enough,' she agreed finally. 'I told him he better learn we was civilized people.'

He still could not believe it. 'You said that, Nance? You said that to him?'

'Why not? I got rights, haven't I? I got rights to say things.'

'And you came right out and told the poor bugger to go?'

'I didn't tell him direct, Ned. Not direct.'

Nevertheless, he rose wearily from the table and struck her. He had never done anything like this before. Yet he bunched his fist solidly enough, and swung it with some effort. The shock of the blow jarred his shoulder. She fell into a chair and covered her face. She made, after a time, small moaning sounds. And blood dripped between her fingers. He stood there for a while, on the spot where he had delivered the blow, and watched with curiosity. He was astounded, not least by the fact that she made so little noise. Jack Crimmins, no doubt, had given her bashings worse. She might have thought Ned wasn't up to it. If so, he had given her something to think about. And remember. He moved, at length, to mend the damage he had done to her face.

The next morning, though, he did not tell Nick he could stay. Perhaps things were for the best. Perhaps Nance had done the right thing for the wrong reason. It wasn't just that the old man wasn't up to much; he had begun to cause strife in the home. And Ned had no answer to that, or to anything much. He just wished he could feel sure about things, or know more. The sourness was in his mouth again, and he spat as he milked. Nick came over to the cowshed to help with the separating, and had nothing to say. Afterwards he went back to the whare to pack.

And Ned, after breakfast, sat in the house he had built and looked at the rain which travelled in gusts down the valley. He sipped tea, and wished it stronger. He found it difficult to believe there had ever been a time when he was happy with himself upon this land.

After a time the child scrambled on to a stool beside his father. Ned was surprised; it had never happened before. Not that the child gave him any attention worth noting. After a brief look at his father he took greater interest in the pencil and

146

paper Nance had placed ready for him on the table. He took
the pencil inside his small fist and began to mark the paper
in various ways. Back and forward, up and down.

'What good is this going to do him?' Ned asked.

'Good?' Nance said. 'It is not a question of good. It is a
question of keeping him quiet.'

'I never notice he is terrible bloody quiet.'

'He is an active child. Active children hurt themselves often.
He walked sooner than most children, so he hurt himself more.
Now he is talking.'

'Talking? I never hear nothing that makes sense.'

'Because you don't know how to listen. Everything cannot
come at once in this life. Look at him now. Perfectly happy,
scribbling his shapes. As quiet as my brother Timothy with his
flowers and birds.'

'Your brother Timothy was crackers,' Ned observed. 'I just
hope to Christ it's not in the family.' He looked swiftly at his
son, as if alert for first signs. 'Anyway,' he went on, 'I'll give
him jobs soon enough. That will keep the little bugger quiet.'

Nance returned to the pained silence which distinguished that
morning. She had a large blue bruise under her right eye.

'There'll be a few small jobs around now,' Ned finished.
'Now we have got rid of old Nick. Which reminds me, it's
about time I ran the poor bloody old sod to where he wants to
go.'

'He isn't staying?' Nance said in surprise.

'Why should he be staying?' Ned's voice was sharp, perhaps
in defence. 'He isn't welcome here no more, and he knows it.
So he is buggering off, which is fair enough.'

'I thought you might of spoke to him this morning,' she said
softly.

'I might of done a lot of bloody things, but he's shooting
through, and that's the finish.'

'Then I am sorry, Ned. You are right and I am wrong. I
mean I wish I hadn't spoke to him in the way I did. He is your
mate, I mean.'

'Then you can afford to be sorry now, can't you? You can
afford to be wrong. Since you have got your way and he is
going anyhow.'

'That,' she insisted, 'is not what I meant.'

'It doesn't matter. I am not very bloody interested what you
mean. He has friends elsewhere. It is no use grieving now.'

'Friends?'

'How should I know what friends? He says he has. That's all I know. If he says he has friends I got to believe him, don't I?'

His voice had risen.

He looked at his thin wife and his mind trembled with the knowledge that he might have enjoyed striking her. He could have struck her again, to prove it one way or the other, but instead he went to the door and pulled an oilskin over his shoulders, laced hobnail boots on his feet, and left the house to Nance. The rain fingered his face coldly as he walked.

The whare was empty, Nick gone.

Ned travelled a mile in his Ford on a puddled, muddy road and found Nick walking in the rain, swag on his shoulder and trousers tied with string again, through the gorge. After some hesitation Nick climbed into the vehicle.

'I am not one for goodbyes,' he explained. 'And I walked into this place. I might as well walk out.'

'It wasn't pissing with rain the day you walked in,' Ned observed.

'You're right there. I remember now, you was burning off. You was burning off, and I could see smoke up the valley. The end of the road. By Christ, it felt like it too. The end of the road's always a bloody sight further than you think. It was that day. It is today. You was burning off at the top of the valley and I sat down to rest me feet. Me feet was giving me hell. They're not the best today neither. And me boots are full of water.'

They rode in silence. The windscreen wiper scraped. Beyond the gorge the rain was lighter.

'I'll take you down to town,' Ned said. 'It's the best I can do.'

'That'll do me, all right.'

'These friends, Nick, where are they?'

'I'll find them, all right. They'll be waiting.'

The town drifted out of the rain. The houses, hedges, trees, and shops.

'The railway station?' asked Ned. 'That do?'

'Anywhere,' Nick said. 'But there's shelter there, and I can get meself a cup of tea.'

There were few people walking or standing under the corrugated iron verandahs in the main street of the town. It had become a desolate place, worse with the rain.

'You will write to me, Nick?' he said finally. 'You will tell us how you are?'

'I am not too good on the writing,' Nick replied. 'And I never wrote too many letters anyway.'

Ned appeared to wrestle with some internal pain after he stopped the vehicle beside the railway station.

'You could tell me where you are going,' he suggested. 'At least.'

'I am going,' Nick said, 'to keep on going.'

He hoisted his swag on his shoulder, standing in the rain beside the Ford. Ned leaned out and pushed a blue piece of paper into the old man's hand.

'Then there is a fiver to help you get there. Wherever it is. I know I owe you more, but it can't be helped.'

'God bless you, son. I am not a great one for goodbyes, but God bless you.'

The old man shuffled out of Ned's life, through the rain, into the shelter of the railway station. He didn't look back, or wave.

And Ned, after a time, said to himself : My name is Ned Livingstone. Once I was sweet bugger all. And now I am not. So why should I grieve?

But he did, all the same.

He bought a newspaper but did not look at it beyond reassuring himself that the date was a day in April, 1932; the year was all that mattered. He drove out of Te Ika, past the men with nothing faces aimless beneath shop verandahs, past the relief gang chipping weeds on the roadside, past the peeling churches. The rain was lifting; thin sunlight coloured the soaked paddocks of the Waiatarua valley. The roadside trees, most shedding, shone gold. The river ran fast and muddy. He bumped over bridges, then entered the gorge. More than once in his life, as this craggy limestone closed around him, he felt he was leaving the world's ill behind. Now that illusion lay shrivelled. Perhaps the infection had taken grip here, on his land, when the first cut of his swinging axe bled a tree. He did not know, and might never; he was only a man.

He dismounted from the Ford, and opened his front gate. There was the blast of a horn behind him; the sound ricocheted from the hills. Something, someone, had followed him home.

Tom Jackson in his boneshaker Chev. Tom Jackson who had once ridden up with the war. He rolled up to the gate on which Ned was now leaning. Ned made himself a smoke and Tom shut off his engine.

'You seen the news?' Tom said. 'Or heard it?'

'I seen nothing,' Ned said. 'Nor heard nothing. I got me own problems without every other bastard's too. But I bought a paper, and was planning to have a read of it sometime.'

'You ought to keep up,' Tom insisted. 'Things is bad.'

'If it's another bloody war,' Ned said, 'they can go fuck themselves. They're not roping me in again.'

'It's these bastards in the city again, Ned. They're raising hell.'

'So let them raise it.'

'They've fucking near torn Auckland apart. The bloody Reds. They're at the back of it. They're after us. It's only a matter of time. They'll take your land away as quick as look at it.'

'They're welcome,' Ned said, 'the way it is. It only earns me a pain in the gut.'

For he couldn't believe it. Or believe Tom.

'We got to stick together, son. Now or never. Let them get away with this, and they'll get away with anything. And everything.'

'We stuck together in the war, Tom, and a lot of good it done us. I reckon it's every man for himself now.'

'So you'd let your land go without a fight?'

'I wasn't saying that.'

'Then what are you saying? That you're scared?'

'I'm just saying that right now I'm just too bloody tired to care.'

'You'll care, all right, when you lose all you got.'

'I just told you, Tom, I haven't got a hell of a lot to lose. Not the way things are.'

It was perverse, considering. It was just the way Tom Jackson affected him.

'All right, so you don't care about your land, your wife and kid. I'll let the others know.'

'What others?'

'The other boys. We're all off to town, Ned. We're going to teach these bastards to pull their heads in. The way my old man did back in the 1913 strike. Nothing like a few bashed heads to show them who's boss in this country.'

'And who is that, Tom?' Ned had never taken much to any boss.

'The man on the land, of course. And the governments we vote in to keep order. It's war again, Ned, and you better choose your side. If you're with us, you better say so now. It's

150

time to make a stand, and they need volunteers up there. We're going up today, in Frank Robson's truck, a whole gang. All of us that was in the war together. We thought you might like to come along too.'

There was a long silence. Finally Ned flicked away his cigarette.

'There was a time,' he said, 'when I thought I'd done my fighting.'

He returned to his farmhouse to collect some gear and to tell Nance she would be milking the cows he hadn't dried off.

There was booze pretty well all the way to Auckland, in the back of Frank Robson's covered truck; they stopped at pubs for fresh supplies. There were songs too, songs that Ned hadn't heard since the war. He sat quiet in a corner of the truck. He didn't drink much. He tried to listen to his own thoughts when he had a chance, which wasn't often. As they got near Auckland the others became noisier. They swung like kids from the back of the moving truck and called to women. Empties rolled off the tail of the truck and smashed.

Just south of Auckland they met up with another truckload of farmers, from round Pirongia. Ned's father-in-law, Jack Crimmins, was among them.

'You in for your chop too, I see,' Jack said, wiping his mouth with the back of his fist and passing Ned his bottle. 'There'll be bloody murder before the night's out, I reckon. Bloody murder.'

There was much laughter and slapping of backs when the two truckloads combined.

'How's my girl, Ned?' Jack asked. 'You treating her right?'

They stood pissing together on the roadside.

'As well as I can,' Ned said. 'The kid is growing now. He keeps Nance busy.'

Jack retrieved his bottle.

'Well,' he said, 'we'll certainly give those buggers in the city a lesson. Good to see you, boy. We might meet up again before the day's out. Go for their balls, Ned. Don't forget.'

The trucks started off again, with whooping and shouting. It might all have been a picnic, Ned thought, a bloody great picnic. He had still to find out what it all had to do with him. Braced against the jolting of the truck, he rolled himself cigarettes with care and watched the countryside give way to suburb.

'Auckland, here we come,' yelled Tom Jackson. And, 'Up you, darling, with bells on,' to a passing woman.

It was about mid-afternoon. An hour or two later they were all enrolled as special constables. Near dark they began to patrol the city. Most of the city's broken windows were boarded up now. The Friday night shopping crowd was quiet and indifferent.

He could soon begin, all right, to be irritated with smug faces; he could even, before long, feel tempted to fracture them.

Yet he would sooner have been back in the mud, tramping through rain to the cowshed, than walking asphalt with his baton, waiting for a chance to teach someone a lesson.

'I think we're wasting our time,' he told Jack Crimmins, who walked beside him.

'Wait and see,' Jack said. 'Just walk. Keep walking. Put the fear of hell into them. Show them we're here.' Jack gave his baton a casual swing; he seemed to enjoy the feel of it. 'And if there's trouble, Ned, remember their balls.'

Large buildings blocked out most of the night sky. But there were stars up there, if he looked. It was a mild enough evening for autumn, for April. Probably cooler inland, though, back on the farm. This time of an evening he was usually shut in the kitchen, Nance having packed the kid off to bed, and rolling smokes beside the stove.

'Why don't you hicks get the straw out of yours ears?' a voice hissed behind.

Jack swung round, his baton erect, but the owner of the voice was not to be distinguished. People laughed.

'You'll laugh, all right,' Jack promised. 'By the time we're finished with you buggers.'

They walked on.

'They don't love us, boy,' Jack observed. 'That's a fact. Ungrateful bastards.'

Ned listened to his feet. Finally he spat.

'These mugs,' Jack went on, 'loaf on the dole, while us poor sods sweat it out on the land. What hope have we got with them riding on our backs?'

Ned spat again.

'So where do we start?' he said. 'Who do we bash first?'

But meaning, why am I here? He could taste an accumulation of bitternesses in his mouth now. He could still taste too the beer he had not particularly enjoyed. He would like it all over and done.

'Patience,' Jack said. 'Just have some patience.'

They passed others on patrol who were also being patient. They exchanged greetings in doorways and sampled from hip-flasks. They began to make their way uptown where the crowds were big and the shops still intact. Mounted volunteers paraded. The crowds were soon blocking the pavements.

'Trouble coming,' Jack predicted. 'This place stinks of it.'

They waited. Violence seemed to flash from several places at once. Bottles were flung, horses charged and reared, windows smashed.

'Here's a go,' Jack cried, jubilant.

Their batons grew huge in their hands as they rushed toward trouble. But the actual fighting was elusive. Hostility would melt back into the crowds, to spring out in another place. Behind them, perhaps.

A flung bottle caught Ned behind his right ear, and he dropped to his knees.

'Shit,' Jack was saying. 'Shit.' His baton dangled useless as he helped Ned back on his feet. 'Where did that bugger go?'

There was no telling. The crowd churned, absorbed. There was no one to strike, unless there was everyone.

Up ahead there were more windows smashing, and a fire siren. A church had started to burn, and the red light leapt over upturned faces.

For Ned, though, it was all on a queer tilt, as if sliding away endlessly. He needed to grab something for support, but there was only the baton on which his two hands were fastened. He pushed it out ahead of him as he ran forward with Jack into the new brawl. And then swung it, perhaps at the right man. Anyway the man went down.

'The big bastard,' Jack said. 'Get that big bastard. That's the one. Get him. Watch him, though. He's grabbed a baton.'

There was no mistaking this one. He was large against a wall beside the burning church, and smaller figures fell away from him as he swung. Some had lost their batons and grappled vainly with their fingers. But the man was difficult to hold. When Ned rushed in, he was knocked back with a blow on his shoulder. He went low the second time, just as Jack told him, and the baton cracked on the side of his head. But they both went down, their heads colliding, their teeth uncovered with the pain, rolling

153

over and over, battering and twisting. In fitful flashes Ned thought he saw the face of the other. It could have been anyone; it could have been himself, Nick Bell, Nance, some German he thought forgotten, anyone. He also saw nothing, unless madness was more, as he strained to strangle. Then a boot struck at his head and after a while he was being bandaged, propped against a door, and there were faces looking down at him. They were safe enough faces. Tom Jackson, Frank Robson, Jack Crimmins.

'You all right, Ned?' Jack asked. 'You got him, all right. The big one. They just took him away.'

'They think he's one the police are looking for,' Tom said. 'A ringleader. Christ, there'll be tales to tell when we get home, boy.'

'Easy now,' Jack said. 'Don't get excited. We're going to whip you into hospital for a check. Just to make sure your thick skull's not broken.'

'Bloody wonderful tales to tell,' Tom said. 'Have a drink, Ned. It'll settle your guts.'

Ned forced himself up, fighting away hands, his bandage unfinished and trailing. 'Fuck off,' he said. 'The lot of you. I done my bit. I done what I was supposed to do. Now leave me alone. I'm shooting through.'

'Concussed,' Jack explained. 'That's his trouble, boys. Easy now, Ned, easy. Just take it quiet.'

He had to push them clear as he walked away. He arrived home just after milking the next morning, Christ knew how.

Nance looked at him with fright and concern. 'What happened up there?' she asked.

'Nothing.'

'But you been hurt. Who did it?'

'Some poor bloody fool like me.'

'I don't understand,' she said.

'There is sweet bugger all to understand,' he replied. 'Unless why men are mad.'

'But you said you was all going up there to put the country to rights again.'

'Then I come back, haven't I? I come back to put myself to rights.'

After a while he went outside to take a look around his land again.

If there were tales told, he never heard them, up there on his

154

farm beyond the gorge. They said he'd always been a cranky sod at the best of times, Ned Livingstone. Some reckoned he hadn't come right after those cracks on the head.

The kid grew. Nance often got sickly in the winters. In general, things became worse before they got better. Not that Ned Livingstone was heard to complain. He was seldom heard on any subject. Some said his lack of interest wasn't decent. To take an example, it was by chance only that he came to vote in the election. It happened because of a Maori who arrived unexpectedly on the farm. This was an early summer day in 1935, three years after the riots. The Maori turned up about noon, riding a horse.

'That old fullar,' this Maori said, 'he pretty crook now. Not last much longer, they reckon. He say he want to see you.'

Ned was baffled.

'Old fellow?' he said. 'Who you mean? I don't know any old fellow.'

'You know this one, all right. Old fullar used to work here, for you.'

The hills, rocks, creek – everything seemed to shift slightly but perceptibly.

'Nick?' he said. 'You mean old Nick?'

He hadn't heard a thing of Nick in three years or more. He sometimes imagined Nick swallowed up in those wild, strange places from which he claimed to come.

'That's the fullar, all right. Old Nick.'

So the hills settled, and the rocks. And the creek ran bright, between willows.

'Well, I'm shagged,' Ned said, and shifted back his hat. 'You mean you know where he is?'

'On our place,' the Maori said, 'a couple of mile outside Te Ika.'

Ned felt cheated. He could not say why.

'He's been there all the time?'

The Maori nodded.

'And he's crook, you say?'

At that moment Tim came trotting from the house. To study the Maori and the horse, but from a distance. The boy was shy.

'Come here, son,' Ned called.

The boy approached with short, cautious steps. Without shifting his eyes from the Maori and the horse, he pushed up one hand, almost experimentally, towards his father.

155

Ned, surprised, took the hand.

'This is my boy,' he explained to the Maori, unnecessarily. But he would have said it louder, if there were more to hear. 'My son.'

The hand was tiny in his.

'Not a very big kid,' Ned added apologetically. 'But he's toughening up. He's just turned five. Off to school soon. He don't remember Nick, of course.' He knelt to the child. 'What do you say, boy?' he asked. 'Would you like to go for a ride in the car with your Dad?'

The boy thought. After a while he nodded.

'There,' Ned went on, as if he had proved something. He rose and looked at the Maori. 'We'll follow you home. A couple of miles outside Te Ika, you said?'

'Old brown place on South Road,' the Maori said, swinging back up into his saddle. 'A cowshed and a couple of cabbage trees outside. Just past the old quarry. You can't miss it.'

He rode off. Ned led the boy back towards the house.

'We are going for a ride together, Nance,' he called.

He lifted the boy into the Ford, which was showing age; torn canvas flapped, and the paintwork was chipped and scratched. But the engine had a healthy enough kick, when he cranked.

Nance appeared on the back porch, still in dressing gown. She had become a late riser, when off colour, and often Ned cooked breakfast for himself and the boy. 'You won't be late?' she asked.

'We could be back any time,' Ned announced. 'We are going to see Nick. The old bugger has been living with Maoris all this time. And he is dying, they say.'

'Dying? With Maoris? Is this a suitable place to take your son?'

'It will just be a ride for him. A ride in the car, there and back. And I will get him an ice cream on the way.'

Ned pulled shut the door of the throbbing car and travelled off with his son beside him. This warmish November day was clear and bright, with the willows newly green. They bumped across bridges and potholes. The hills were vivid against the sky. Now and then Ned looked sidelong at his son, to make sure the boy was happy. The boy was peering out the window.

'I see a bird,' he announced presently.

'A bird, son?' Ned asked, uncertain.

'A bird,' said the boy, 'in the sky.'

156

Anxious to oblige, Ned slowed and then stopped the car. 'Where?' he asked.

'There. The bird is falling in the sky.'

'Flying, son. Not falling.'

'Falling,' the boy said.

They started off again. They rumbled towards Te Ika. After puzzling for some time, Ned explained, 'You would fall from the sky, but birds fly.'

'Why?' the boy said.

'It is just the fact of the matter,' Ned answered, which was unsatisfactory. So he added, 'It is in the nature of things. We fall, but birds fly.'

The boy was silent. Ned manouevred across a shaky bridge. He tried to recover some thought he had about Nick, but Nick was elusive.

'There is another bird,' the boy said. 'Falling.'

'Flying,' said his father.

'If they are flying,' the boy said, 'then why can't I?'

'All right,' Ned sighed, 'so they are bloody falling then.'

Te Ika lifted out of the sunny landscape, a brimming basket of houses with hills tawny beyond. They passed the railway yards where engines shunted and wagons crashed. There was an unusual amount of activity in the town for a Saturday. Outside the council chambers were a number of vehicles and a large number of people.

'We will stop here,' Ned said. 'And get your ice cream. And perhaps learn what all this fuss is about.'

He led his son through the crowd. Many people, he saw now, were wearing ribbons and rosettes, red or blue. And Tom Jackson was sitting behind a table on the pavement.

'Good old Ned,' he said, 'I'm glad to see you here to vote the farmers' man.'

They hadn't often conversed, the two of them, in recent years. Tom handed Ned a card.

'There,' he said, 'is the name of your man.'

'My man?'

'Our man, Ned. The farmers' man. He needs you today.'

'And you reckon I need him?' He could humour Tom.

'If you want to stop this country going soft, Ned. Yes. It's our man or theirs. And you know what they'd do to the country.'

'No,' said Ned, to give Tom his fling.

157

'Then you should of been paying some attention, Ned. Look at this Higgins character, for example. He was a raging Red up to a few years ago, made no bones about it. And he's probably still one, for my money. Now he's up for the other crowd, all democratic, an official candidate. Could you trust the country to the likes of him? Could you, Ned?'

Tom was earnest, and seemed to be suffering.

'Anyway, Ned,' he added, 'you got the right name on that card. The name of your man.'

'Then,' Ned said, 'that is news to me too.'

Someone else pushed up to Tom's table, so Ned moved on with the flow into the council building, where the polling progressed, and was given a ballot paper. There was a hush there, with pencils at work behind screens.

'Why are we here?' asked Tim, too loud in that place.

'To vote,' Ned told his son. 'It looks like we are here to vote, God knows why.'

'What is vote?'

'It is,' he explained, 'something men do to keep themselves happy. So they can think they have done something real.'

They went behind a screen. The boy pulled at his trousers.

'Can I vote too?' he asked.

'In a minute,' his father said.

He looked at the names printed on the ballot paper. Tom Jackson's man was at the top. Without thinking, Ned struck out the name. That left one. That name was unfamiliar, but probably no better. So he struck that out too. Then he sealed the paper, with some relief, and pushed it into the ballot box.

'But I didn't vote,' whined the child.

'I forgot,' Ned apologized. 'Never mind. I will get you an ice cream. And that will be real.'

On their way out of the council building they passed Tom Jackson again. Tom winked. 'I think we can trust you, Ned,' he said, 'to vote the right man.'

'You can trust me, all right,' Ned agreed. And surprised himself by laughing. It was not at Tom exactly, nor at his blue rosette and absurd anxiety. Perhaps it was at the farce of men sweating over tiny bits of paper in so vast and inexplicable a world. He could afford to laugh, if he could see.

'You can trust me, Tom, because I only trust trouble. It is all the same to me.'

And Tom, perplexed, looked down at the wooden surface of

158

his table, as if seeking reassurance there. 'All the same?' he muttered. 'I don't know what you mean. Ned.'

'I mean we went to war and bayoneted Germans. We went to the city and broke heads. And I can't see things is any better. Or we're any wiser. The world is still going round. And we are older. So what difference does one fat arse more or less in Parliament make?'

Also, he wanted to add, my old mate Nick is dead, or bloody near, and he is the only man I could ever call my own.

But he could not seem to make this fact fit.

'Please yourself, Ned,' Tom said, angry now, and finally turning to another customer.

Ned, even angrier, and not sure why, walked his boy swiftly to the ice cream shop.

He sat tight in his ageing skin as he drove out of Te Ika on to the South Road. The boy beside him licked elaborately at his ice cream. They were driving into swampy country, and gorse flicked at the car along the narrow road. Soon they passed the scoured-out hill which had been a quarry.

'Never let any bugger use you, son,' he said.

Perhaps the boy looked up while his father drove.

'And be your own man,' Ned said. 'I hope to Christ you learn.'

Ned could get no great satisfaction from the words. But they seemed to be all he had. Perhaps the boy would remember, though.

Ned turned up the drive toward the brown house with cowshed and cabbage trees.

'There is a man here,' Ned went on, 'a man who is pretty crook. I want you to be good while I see him.'

Maoris appeared on the verandah of the house when he stopped the car. Chickens clucked away in fright, and children came skidding around. They watched, quiet, while Ned lifted his son from the car.

'Stay here,' Ned instructed. 'Be good. Play with these kids, if you like.'

The boy stood as though paralysed.

'I will be back soon,' Ned said carefully, and then walked into the house with the Maoris. He could not think how else he could manage the situation, and leave the boy.

For behind him the boy began to weep. Thus he had to nerve himself doubly as he was led down a long gloomy passage

159

and into some side room. It was difficult to see at first. A mattress flung on the floor, a heap of blankets. Shadows became
people. Old Maori women, two or three of them, sat each
side of mattress. Then he discerned Nick's shrunken head,
almost a skull already, among the blankets. His eyes were open
and staring.

'You old bugger,' Ned said. 'Why didn't you tell me you
was here? Why didn't you tell me you was crook?'

Nick had nothing to say, evidently. He continued staring.
What did he see?

'It is me,' Ned said slowly. 'Me, Ned. Your old mate.' He
paused, his tongue dry. As though to convince himself, he added,
'Your old mate, remember?'

A Maori hand dropped on Ned's shoulder. 'He been like this
the last hour or two', a voice explained. 'Not saying nothing.'

'Then I'll wait,' Ned announced, and began to roll a smoke.
Nick's eyes were still open. What, for God's sake, did he see?
Ned was afraid to think.

'Doctor wanted to take him to the hospital,' the Maori
voice said. 'But he said no, he'd die among friends.'

So Nick had made up his mind. Certainly he appeared to be
doing his best to die. His body was now the only obstacle, and
there wasn't much of it left. From time to time it gave a small
shudder, as if under attack.

'He did say he wanted to see me?' Ned asked.

'That's what he said, all right. He said you was his only
other friend.'

'Than I'll wait,' Ned said again, and rolled another cigarette.

He rolled a great many smokes, waiting for Nick to die; the
extinct butts gathered on the floor beside him. The afternoon
passed, the shadowy Maoris shuffled. There wasn't much in
the way of conversation. Now and then he took a walk outside
the shabby house, to ease his bladder and see Tim was all right.
The boy was quite happy now, it seemed, careering around a
paddock with a gang of Maori kids, chasing a football. Often,
since he was smaller than the others, he would fall behind or
trip over. But he would always find mates to help him up. And
sometimes the ball was set up especially for him to kick while
the other children stood aside. When thus favoured, the boy
crowed in triumph before he kicked the muddy ball. He shone
pale among the other children, though his clothes had become
grubby enough.

160

Lonely little bugger, Ned thought, and too much Nance's boy. But there was still time to put that right.

There would be hell to pay, of course, if the boy picked up some Maori sores. In that case he would just have to tell Nance that you couldn't go out in the world without picking up something. For some reason he looked down at his hands which were good for some things, if not voting.

Shadows were growing long on the grass. Ned went back into the house to sit beside the dying man. His body heaved less often now, perhaps beginning to surrender. And his eyes had closed. There was no sense to be got out of him. He would take Nick's hand, which seemed quite lifeless, and try to talk.

'It's Ned,' he would insist. 'Your old mate, remember?'

It was no good. The old women clucked in sympathy.

And the wild, strange places had shrunken to this. To a musty room in a Maori house, a mattress on the floor, and old women fussing. Had these people liked Nick, perhaps loved him? Ned Livingstone looked into their faces and could not tell. He was sure, though, that they hadn't cared too much about his muddy boots and old man's smell.

Ned thought he could stand most things, except Nick forgiving him.

It appeared he was weeping, or damn near, and trying not to make it plain. Soon one of the women was offering him tea again. And outside young Tim was calling for his father. The afternoon was almost shot, his tobacco tin empty, and there was the milking.

'I want my Dad,' Tim was calling. 'Where's my Dad?'

Ned thought he might cope with this demand, at least. He journeyed clumsily through the house to his son. The boy was tired and tearful and jumped up into his father's arms. Ned had never held him tighter.

'Come on, son,' he said presently. 'We'll get home to the cows.'

To the Maoris he said, 'I'll be back later, when I got the milking done.'

He hoisted Tim up on his shoulders and carried him out to the car. He sat the boy gently in the front seat and placed a blanket over his dirty knees. Nance always worried about the boy taking a chill in the car. But it was only Nance who collected the chills.

'Where is the crook man?' Tim asked. 'I didn't see him.'

161

'Because he was too crook,' Ned answered. 'Too crook for a boy to see.'

'Why is he crook?'

'Because he is old. And tired. And because – '

Ned and his son hurtled homeward through Te Ika in the late afternoon.

'And because,' Ned said, 'because too many people let him down. Nothing worse you can do to a man than let him down. Something else to remember, if you can.'

The boy wanted another ice cream. Ned bought it at the nearest shop and they resumed their journey home. Outside the council chamber there were still thin arrangements of people. Tom Jackson was doubtless off home for the milking.

'Sometimes you wonder what it's all for,' Ned said. 'And then you know it just comes down to that one thing. Not letting people down.'

Ribbed hills shone in the afternoon light. They shifted, congealed, and grew tall before the travelling car.

'I won't let nobody down, then,' the boy decided, his face involved in his ice cream.

'If only you could understand,' Ned offered. 'I wish to Christ you could, or someone.' He took one hand off the steering wheel and placed it on the boy's head as he drove. He felt he might almost have got across to the boy today. They might get along yet.

'You enjoy your outing with your Dad?' he asked.

'I enjoyed it, all right,' the boy answered. 'I liked the ice creams.'

'And those kids. You liked playing with them?'

'They were big. They kicked a ball.'

'I think you liked it,' Ned said, as though to convince him.

'A lady gave me some cake. They were big. Other kids are big.'

'You'll be big enough yourself soon,' Ned promised. 'You see.'

The point was lost; the boy began to bounce in his seat. 'There are the birds again,' he said. 'Falling, everywhere.'

'Everything is falling everywhere,' Ned generalized as he drove into the gorge. For to be particular was to see in his mind the old man he had just left dying in a Maori bed. And himself, quite powerless.

When they were home, Nance had some sharp things to say

162

about Tim's muddy condition, but there was no time for Ned to listen. He got stuck into the milking, and had the herd finished before dark. Impatience was large in his throat by the time he got back to the house.

'And where are you going now?' Nance said, after he bolted his food and pulled on a jacket. She had not asked him about Nick since his return. Nick might have been dead for all she knew, and evidently cared. But she was on edge.

'Back to where I been most of the day,' he replied. 'Watching an old bugger die, and trying to say something to him before he goes.'

He watched her face. But there was nothing to see. There had never been much to her as a woman, and there had become less over the years. It seemed she was only good for the one kid.

'What is it you want to say to him?' she asked, and shifted a pot on the stove.

'That is the point. I got nothing to say, except I am sorry. But you wouldn't understand that neither. I got nothing much to say to anyone any more.'

'Not to me you haven't,' she agreed. 'You don't have to tell me.'

'Not to anyone,' he said with sudden anger, and stalked from the house. Behind him the door slammed. He crashed into the seat of his car and fled his tame land and tidy wife.

He had been gone three hours from Nick's side, because of the cows, and he hoped it hadn't been too long. The car creaked and thundered with speed along the country road, and the cool night air rushed over his hot face. Stars speckled the sky; a fine night after a fine day. The streets of Te Ika were scantily lit, and there were few walkers about. Too early for the picture show, but the windows of the council building were bright. The election was over, and they would be counting the votes. He supposed Tom Jackson might be present for that, in the interests of the farmers' man, whoever that had been. His brakes squealed, to avoid a collision with a truck, as he escaped Te Ika and sped out on the other side towards the Maori place by the old quarry. He drove stiff and upright, a hat aslant on his balding head, a dead cigarette gummed on his lower lip. His hands were big and brutal on the wheel of the car as it jerked and bounced out of potholes. He appeared ready to rend the wheel, or the car, or the world. Anything to clear a space for himself as he moved.

163

At the house he left the vehicle with cooler face and cast the neglected cigarette away. He was met at the door by one of the younger Maori men, who shook his head and did not speak. Ned followed him inside. The house was without electricity, still remote from progress, and kerosene lamps sent huge shadows jumping up and down the walls. Then Ned heard the weeping, the first wails, and knew. He didn't need to go further than the door of the room. Nick's body was no longer a hindrance. His face had gone slack, the life emptying out of it, the struggle won. The old women crouched close. Ned felt sick.

The bloody cows, he told himself.

For the young Maori was saying, 'He talked just before. He was talking good-oh. Then he stopped, and his eyes went queer. Just now.'

Ned found his throat difficult. 'Did he ask for anyone?' he asked finally.

'He didn't ask for no one. He just talked.'

'I see.'

'It wasn't that kind of talk,' the Maori explained. 'It was wild things.'

'Wild things?' Ned hesitated. 'He didn't,' he added, 'say there was anyone after him?'

'Anyone after him?'

'A big dago devil, wanting to take him away.'

'No.' The Maori was baffled. 'Nothing like that.'

'Thank Christ, then,' Ned said. 'Thank Christ for that, at least.'

'He was talking about God, mostly. He talked a lot about God.'

'That would be right,' Ned agreed. 'He would.'

'Right at the finish there, just before you came, he was still going on about God.'

'He wouldn't need to ask for no one else, then, would he?'

The Maori looked surprised. 'I don't get you,' he said.

'It don't matter. When you got nothing else, or no one, you talk about God. When there is nothing else, but has to be.'

It was the same with the wild strange places, perhaps. Anyway Nick had seen the strangest now.

It was too much for the other. His face was troubled.

'About this funeral,' Ned went on. 'If you let me know, I could help with some money. I owed him some. He would of liked to be buried decent.'

164

But saying this was little relief. He walked back down the passage and out into the evening. The boards of the verandah moaned faintly under his step, and the stars were as bright. He clamped himself into the car rather than sat in it. After a while he lowered his head to the cold corrugation of the steering wheel. It remained there some time. Then he straightened and started the car, lurching, off the Maori land.

Just short of Te Ika he punctured. He took his time about changing the wheel. He thought about it first, and rolled a smoke. Then he strolled diffidently about the car, examined the flat tyre, and relieved himself on the roadside. For a while he stood just looking into the dark : the countryside was quiet and black, and the only lights distant. He spat, as if to assert himself, but the sound was small. All things were indifferent under the coldly glimmering sky. For comfort he could listen to his own tight breathing, if he liked, or the rustle of his clothing as he moved back to the car and began to change the wheel. For confidence he had only his own hands, in the end. They untightened the nuts and dragged off the wheel. Then he slammed the spare into place and spannered it tight. He wiped his greasy hands on his trousers, the job finished. Silence again, apart from his thickened breathing, and even those distant lights looked fewer; the hills might have moved in while he worked. Stones rattled under his feet as he walked around the car to give it a crank.

So Nick has gone, he thought. It is all the same, and must be.

The engine became clamorous on the second crank. He sat behind the steering wheel, flicked a switch, and the road ahead was lit. A man got most things off his back, given time. Or all things. All things in the end.

In Te Ika the lights were off in the council building, the votes all counted, for what that mattered. And men thus satisfied or dismayed. It was, after all, a day no more than any other, a year no more than any other. He and Nance were that much older. Only the kid changed, and grew.

As he drove home that night, he felt the farm long before he reached it. It seemed to have become some dull ache which hardened about his body, and suffocated, and through which only anger could spurt, so he could breathe. As he drove through the gorge, at a speed higher than usual, the limestone walls might have been collapsing behind him, blocking any way back, trapping him with this land ahead. His land, he once dreamed of owning. His muddy paddocks, his fences, his cows, his shelter belts of trees pale under the headlights. His anger seemed to rise with the speed of the car.

Then it was offered substance. The bull rose abrupt and dark into the headlights, eyes shining, straddling the road. In his haste to leave earlier that night, to see the old man before he died, he must have left a gate open, for the bull to escape. It entirely filled the road. It did not shift, nor would. He had no time to brake, even if he wanted to, at the speed he travelled. And no space at all. He sat his hand on the horn, for all the good that did, as they rushed together. Yet with the violence close he felt a certain anguished relief, near exaltation, rather than fear or dismay. The bull took the impact of the vehicle sideways. Its bulk flew up momentarily into the headlights as Ned felt his body jar brutally and the metal of the car crumple; he could hear glass as his right headlamp smashed, as the broken fender snapped up into the windscreen, and as he pitched forward. He must have braced just enough to save himself. Then everything was still. Outside the damaged car he could hear the moaning of the beast. He eased his shaken limbs into the night and found himself intact. The car had not come off so badly, considering, but the bull was altogether beyond repair. Its legs were shattered, and probably its back and neck. Flanks heaved and dying muscles twitched. One eye bulged from its socket in the light of his torch. He reached back into the car for a spanner and struck the beast once, powerfully, between the eyes and once at the base of the skull. All resistance went. There was a sound of expiring breath, a last twitch or two, and it was still. There were murmurings and shufflings as the evening rearranged itself: a final fragment of glass tinkled down from the fractured headlamp. He tried to feel something: regret, perhaps. But he felt nothing. He was numb, quite disentangled from the flesh in which he went disguised as Ned Livingstone. And he floated giddily, rather than walked, towards the lights of the house. Nance, who must have heard the noise, was standing on the lit porch as he approached.

'Ned,' she said, panicky. 'What happened?'

'Nick is dead,' he answered. 'The poor old sod went off before I got back. They said he was too busy getting himself on side with God to talk any sense. What you might expect. Nothing I could do.'

'But the noise. The car.'

'I had a smack. A little argument with the bull. Finished up having to kill the old bastard.'

He really surprised himself. Nance stood aside, wondering, to let him go into the house, and then placed a tentative hand on his arm, to help him along. For it seemed he had begun to limp badly. In the kitchen he lay heavy in a chair. Nance fussed, then decided he needed a cup of tea.

He was tired, even of anger, quite spent. And he sank back into his flesh with some relief, despite the pain, when Nance brought him the tea and bandaged the long graze on his arm. She no longer irritated. She was simply there.

'Poor Nick,' she uttered. 'I am sorry, Ned.'

He no longer cared. He had a sense of some door closing, of things impossibly past.

'There's an end to everything,' he said at length. 'I will have to think about the bloody car tomorrow.' He closed his eyes briefly. 'And the bull. That was the biggest bloody write-off you ever seen.'

'I was sitting up by myself, waiting,' she offered. 'Listening to the radio to pass the time. But there didn't seem nothing on but election results.'

'No,' he said. 'I don't expect there would be tonight.'

'Just before I heard the crash,' she explained, 'and came running out, I heard the latest news. There is a new government, Ned.'

'New? There is never nothing new about government. There is just government. They make their different speeches, blue-arsed or red-arsed, but their shit is always the same colour.'

'Well, it's this new lot, this other crowd. These Labour socialists or whatever they are. They have got in, they say, almost everywhere. Or seemed to. They are promising a fair deal for all. There is great excitement.'

'That'll give Tom Jackson a bad night, then.'

'What do you think? Will things be better or worse?'

'I don't think nothing. I am just bloody tired.'

'Come on, then. I had better clean you up and put you to bed. Just like little Tim. You certainly had a big day.'

'Nance, girl.'

'Yes?'

He pulled her head awkwardly against his shoulder, and she slid to her knees beside him. He could not remember how long it had been.

Ten:

OUTSIDE THE NEWSPAPER OFFICE THE CROWDS WERE THICK, banked up across the city's main street. Cheers grew as results flashed on to a lighted screen. The government was changing. The tall man worked back and forward through the crowds, copies of the *Workers' Weekly* over his arm, selling the odd paper, talking, arguing.

'The truth, comrades,' he offered. 'The truth.'

But the cheers deafened, at times. And the faces were almost all upturned. He was perhaps the only one in the street who did not look at the results. He did not need to look. The cheers were enough.

After a time he met an old militant he had known on the waterfront after the war. 'It's a great day,' this man said. 'The workers are taking over this country now.'

Bill Freeman grunted, 'Not yet,' he said, 'not by a long shot.'

'No?'

'No. Don't fool yourself. These social democrats, these respectable reformists, you ought to know them by now. They'll always knife the workers in the end. Every time. They won't change nothing. They'll just make capitalism more efficient. But I expect they got to have their day, so the workers will see them in their true colour.'

Though he had, that day, abstained from voting without effort. They wouldn't have any sort of day with his help.

'Look. There's Charlie Higgins' name. Old Charlie. He's five thousand votes ahead.'

'He's the kind I mean,' Bill Freeman said. 'In Parliament he'll sell you out as quick as look at you. Like Ramsay MacDonald in the old country, like every so-called Labour man there's ever been. Out for himself, number one every time.'

'I don't know,' said this aquaintance, shaking his head. 'At least things should be better for the ordinary man.'

'If they can get a new charge out of capitalism,' Bill Freeman conceded, 'you might get a few crumbs.'

He made a sale and pushed on through the crowds. Three years before he might have had these people with him, all the way, to some savage end. Instead they had broken windows and then retreated in panic to live on hand-outs. They were happy now to mark their ballot papers the right way, cheer the result, and go home to wait for the promised land to blossom around them. Nothing was ever so cheap and easy. Yet if he rose now to say that, he would doubtless be hooted down. All his effort might never have been, unless to put a Charlie Higgins in Parliament. He couldn't have been more alone again, among so many.

Charlie Higgins in Parliament now. He could imagine.

Still the names and figures flashed upon the screen, and voices rose in excitement. Even if they cheered the wrong men, perhaps it was for the right reason. If you could call hope a reason. There was consolation there, if he tried. But it still stuck in his throat. It didn't help him either to see good Party men losing their heads and cheering loudly in the crowd with all the rest. Men who should have known better. Everyone was wild with victory, as if some new day were really dawning. But Bill Freeman, walking home with his bundle of unsold papers, hadn't lost his head, though he felt he had lost much else; he took defeat very personally.

His time in prison had left him still leaner. Though he was several months out, he was still looking for a way to make use of the world, and of himself. And he had a son. This child, so quickly grown, unnerved him almost as much as he appeared to unnerve the child, when he returned to look for his life again. The kid, it seemed, had grown used to Ben, and didn't need another man, no matter how often persuaded. He could begin to doubt whether anyone needed him. For Ben and Peggy seemed to have managed well enough in his absence. Ben with radio talks and articles, Peggy with cleaning jobs in large homes. They scraped along and kept the child well fed and clothed, if not themselves. They were mistaken quite often, and they seemed to think this a joke, as man and wife. Bill failed to see any humour, but perhaps prison hadn't left him much. He stayed on with Ben, though, since there was nowhere else. And never felt more than a guest with his wife and son. He talked to Peggy about pulling out from the city, looking for work in the south, and otherwise making himself necessary again. But Peggy wasn't keen to shift; she pleaded the child. Also Ben began to irritate. There were many things he did not like, including the looks Ben and Peggy exchanged when he had something to say. He seemed to be married to both of them; they appeared to think they shared a problem called Bill Freeman. He made the mistake, once, of expressing this thought to Peggy.

'When I took you on,' he told her, 'I didn't take on your brother too.'

She was shocked, of course. 'I hate to think,' she replied, 'where we would have been without him.'

'Fair enough,' he observed, 'but there has to be an end to it.'

'And you should know,' she went on, 'that he hasn't done everything just because I'm his sister. It's also because he, well, admires you so much. Because he thinks you're a marvellous man.'

'Then that,' Bill Freeman insisted, 'is his problem.'

Things came to a head, anyway, on election night when he arrived back at the cottage to find Ben jubilant about the result, and pouring Peggy a small glass of sherry. When Bill came into the room, Ben turned down the radio.

'So it's done,' Ben said. 'We kicked them out. Peg and I are just having a quiet celebration.'

'Celebrate away,' Bill replied. 'I'm off to bed.' It seemed he was to feel a stranger everywhere.

'You won't have a drink first?'

'I'd choke on it.'

'Come on, now. Let's at least greet our social democratic revolution with goodwill. There's still room for yours later.'

'I told you I'd choke on it. I seen enough happy idiots tonight.'

'Be reasonable,' Ben said. 'You can't fight the whole country, can you? Not now. There's a new mood. People have got to be given what they want. Jobs, homes, an easier life.'

'And that's justice?'

'Of a kind.'

'I'd say it was more like a bribe. To keep things the way they are.'

'Look, Bill, you don't know yet. There could be some real

change with this new crowd in. They aren't all crooks and fools. They'll try. So give them half a chance. Anyway it's no use shouting them down at this stage, unless you like making yourself hoarse. They haven't had time to do anything.'

'And they won't. You can be sure of that.'

'Hasn't the world got any surprises for you, Bill?'

'I don't believe in fairytales. If that's what you mean.'

'But it's not all grey. What do you believe in Bill?'

'Struggle. All there is. All there's ever been. Men struggling for justice. Nobody ever got anything without struggle. Nobody ever will.'

'But dreams, Bill? You must have dreamed, once.'

There was a silence.

'Everyone dreams,' Bill Freeman agreed. 'But dreams never made nothing by themselves.'

'Did blind struggle ever do anything by itself either?'

'How would you know?' he said, losing patience. 'How would you bloody know?' He got his breath again. 'You intellectuals, you flirt around the movement so long as it suits you. From choice. It never strikes you that some of us have never had the choice, if we was going to call ourselves men. It's been war, all the way, for us. I seen the inside of prison more than once and I expect I'll see more of it. How would you ever bloody know?'

'We mightn't know in that sense,' Ben conceded, 'but we can feel, and imagine.'

'Great,' Bill said bitterly. 'You go right ahead, then, with your feeling and imagining.'

There was a pause.

'Nevertheless,' Ben replied quietly, 'I don't need imagination to see that you can't take on the whole country. Because that's what you seem to be telling me.'

Bill looked at Peggy. 'I'm off to bed,' he announced again. 'You coming?'

'All right,' she agreed. 'I'll be with you in a minute. There are some dishes.' She paused. 'And Ian. He was awake earlier. I'll just make sure he's settled for the night.'

The child: of course. It was not easy to take into account yet. In prison he had often been obliged to remind himself that he had a son. He still had to. So he went off to bed that night as much dismayed with himself as with the world.

In penance, next morning, he took the child for a walk down to the shore. The boy was beginning to talk sense, and to under-

171

stand. And he was probably not a bad kid, as kids went. Bill Freeman did not know much about them, and had been given no time to learn. This one played with the sand on the beach, heaping it over his feet, while his restless father rolled cigarettes and looked out on a hazy sea.

'You must be three soon,' said the father, uncertain of dates.

'I have just been three already,' the boy said, indignant. 'I had a birthday cake, and candles.'

'Four, then.' He had forgotten.

'I will be four soon,' the boy agreed, 'and then I will be five. And then I will go to school every day.'

'I think we will go away soon,' his father said.

'Away?' the child said solemnly. 'Where is away?'

'Away from here. Somewhere.'

He paused. He was at loss to explain.

'Will Ben come too?'

'No. He can't come. Because your father has things to do.'

They seemed to cross that obstacle easily enough. For the boy was curious.

'What things?' he asked.

Bill Freeman searched for words to suit. 'Difficult things,' he offered finally.

'What are difficult things?'

'Things hard to do.'

'Do you like them?'

Bill Freeman thought. 'No.'

'Then why do you want to go away and do them?'

'Because someone must.'

This appeared to be an adequate answer after all. The boy lost interest. He continued heaping up the sand.

'I am making mountains,' he informed his father. 'I would like to see mountains. Mountains with snow.'

'I might show you some soon.' Bill paused. 'And other things.'

'Promise?' the boy said.

'Promise.'

A few days later they left Ben's cottage, the three of them, and travelled by train down into the country. It happened that they left the day after Charlie Higgins and his friends were sworn in as Cabinet Ministers. A photograph appeared in that day's newspaper showing them smart and smiling in their dark suits. Bill Freeman was prompted to shred the newspaper and toss it

172

out the carriage window as the train hammered south. He sat in silence, avoiding Peggy's eye, for some time afterwards.

He had gone to the Party, of course, just before he left, and told them what he was doing. 'It looks to me like we got to start all over again, from the ground up,' he said. 'So we might as well begin.'

'Well, take it easy, Bill,' Harry Jones suggested.

Harry had just made a trip to Russia. He spoke with new authority.

'Take it easy? What does that mean?' He could almost smell something.

'It's just that we don't know how things stand yet,' Harry expanded. 'With this new crowd in, I mean. We might have to take a different atttitude.'

'What is different, that we got to be different?' Bill challenged.

'Things are changing fast,' Harry announced, always bulky on the line. 'All over the world. There could be a war. If this Hitler has a go at Russia, or anyone else. We got to consider the interests of the world's only workers' state. You see that, don't you?'

'We got our own interests.'

'Sometimes one thing has got to be balanced against the other, Bill. It might mean, for example, we got to work with these social democrats, with pretty near anyone, against fascism. So we don't want to get ourselves too much offside.'

'You mean we might have to drop our principles?'

'It's not a question of principles, Bill.'

'Then what else is it a bloody question of?'

'Tactics, Bill. Good sense.'

'At the price of principles.'

'Now steady on, comrade.'

'Don't comrade me if you can't talk principles.'

'Listen, Bill – '

'All I know is we got enough problems without taking on the Russian ones too. We got our problems, they got theirs. And it seems to me they have more people to cope.'

'All the same, comrade – ' Harry had begun to sweat.

'What it means is,' Bill suggested, 'we got to help this new crowd of crooks in Parliament sell out the workers, because the Russians have got problems.'

'Now just hold on a moment. This new crowd might do some

173

good things. Things we have to support.'

'Extra money on the old age pension?'

'Well, yes,' Harry said.

'So long as I know,' Bill said finally. 'I never thought I'd see the day.'

'Now just a moment, comrade –' Harry began.

But Bill Freeman had risen and gone his own way. He never really came back.

On the train south, though, he was still sure of himself even if others were not. His conversation with Harry might have left him uneasy, his parting with the Party might have left him groping, but he had his wife and son beside him and a suitcase filled with literature in the luggage rack above his head. Now and then he looked at his hands. They were ready for work. It was some time before he could account for his good feeling about things ahead. Then he understood. He was independent again, of Ben Campbell on the one hand, and of the likes of Harry Jones on the other. He was his own man, even if he had the country against him. He took a deep breath of satisfaction and watched green landscapes race past. He was reminded briefly of another train journey, the one after his first time in prison, sixteen or seventeen years before. Had it really been that long ago? Things now seemed much the same. Apart from Peggy and the kid, of course. He looked at them and was surprisingly reassured by their presence. Anyway he saw them as he had never quite seen them before, and might never again. Because they seemed, things considered, to be all he had done with his life. He reached out slowly and placed his hand on Peggy's. Her response was quick. She smiled at him, perplexed, and then her eyes grew tender. He was glad of one certainty. He lifted his sleeping son from his wife's knee and nursed the boy for the next hour or two of their journey.

Finding work was one thing, holding it another. He had three jobs in a half dozen months. But there were more shifts than three. His reputation always caught up with him, and sometimes preceded. A job would sometimes vanish the moment he arrived near an office. But there were more jobs about now, and Charlie Higgins and his crew were promising still more. He saw the inside of a timber mill, a fertilizer plant, and a public works camp. After each job they started again. No job was altogether a loss; he made contacts here and there, and

174

left literature behind. Then he and Peggy and the boy boarded train or bus for another place. They went much further south than he intended. They came out of the country, at one stage, and saw the sea again. It was winter, with grey cloud low. The sea was dark, the heavy waves crashed. In that town he looked for a job in the freezing works, but there was nothing casual available, the killing season over and carcasses shipped away. Finally he found something just outside the town, cutting scrub for a farmer on an hourly rate. He saw no one on the job but the farmer himself, who was usually about to see he got good value for his money. Peggy and Ian stayed in a cheap boarding house in the town, while he slept in a scrub-cutter's shack, and he walked five miles to see them on weekends. That way, they lasted most of the winter. His hands grew hard on the slasher, chopping yard by yard into the tough scrub. But it had to come to an end. There was only so much scrub. And there was nothing on the other side of it, nothing at all. A chill from the saturated earth seemed to gather in his body, an indifference. A man might as well be an animal, he thought, as live this life. He would last the days to each weekend, which sometimes restored him, and then walk back to the farm to start over again. He had neither time nor energy, the way things were, to do any-thing about making contacts or passing on literature in the town. The newspapers he sometimes saw told him about things at a distance. There was fighting in Spain. But the rest of the country seemed about as remote. He could not do much, except survive, and keep his wife and son fed. He put his head down and attacked the scrub. On Saturday nights he and Peggy groped for comfort on the metal bed in the boarding house.

'You could write away,' she said. 'You could write away to see what jobs are going now in other places. There must be some don't know you, or have forgotten if they did.'

Otherwise there was only one way out, it seemed, the way back.

'You must find something steady, Bill,' she pleaded. 'Soon Ian will be going to school. Then where will we be? At least our son should have some chance in life.'

'All right,' he agreed finally. 'If we can find something steady, in some place, I will play it quiet.'

He lay awake for a long time that night, his body twisting into tight shapes, listening to the rain chip at the iron roof of the boarding house while his wife and son slept. He might have been hollowed out, left quite gutted, for all he could feel. And his mind raged in this echoing shell. Certainly his dialogue, that night, was more with echoes of himself than substance. He had almost said it to Peggy, he had as good as said it. He might just as well have admitted outright that he had done his dash.

In Spain, though, he could have done something with a rifle still. He might have been born for a place like Spain, for all he knew. Not born to play it quiet, though he might learn. What else was he doing anyway? No one could be more quiet, or dead.

He was oppressed, suddenly, by the truth, that he had only the one life.

Thirst flared in his throat and he rose from the bed in search of water. Peggy stirred. 'You aren't sleeping, Bill,' she said.

'No,' he agreed.

'Something is worrying you.'

'Why should I have anything to worry me?'

'But you were so tired tonight.'

'Then I am too tired to sleep.'

He felt his way back to the bed, and found her arms waiting. 'You are not saying what you want to say,' she observed.

'No,' he agreed again.

'So what is it?'

'There is too much to say.'

She drew him down beside her, and then into her body. They drank each other's tongues. It was all as gentle and easy as the sleep which came later.

'I will write those letters,' she offered. 'Don't worry about them now. Everyone says the country is on the move again, there is more work about. I will start writing them tomorrow.'

A reply came eventually, when he was cutting through the last of the scrub, and they set out again.

He didn't sleep that night either. Gashing the mist on the carriage window, he watched the grey of morning grow above steep yellow cuttings of clay and damp dark bush. Shreds of steam from the engine ahead hurtled past the window.

A guard trundled through the swaying carriage, pushing his way among outflung limbs of sleeping people in desperate shapes, and called the name of the next station, a one-minute stop. After so long a wait, it came as a relief. And there was a future in the name. He wished he knew how much. He made

176

one last gash in the mist of the window, but was offered nothing but a swift, gloomy blur of thick bush tangling close to the track.

So then he woke his wife.

'There?' Peggy said vaguely. 'Already?'

'It's morning,' he said. 'Look out the window.'

But she was looking at him as if she had not seen him before. He looked back at her, in silence, for a moment. Weak spots of light travelled over their faces. Their hands reached out and touched briefly. Then she looked guiltily at the child.

'Ian,' she said. 'Ian, wake up.'

The train, moving along a flat stretch of track now, had begun to slow. While she whispered placatingly, Peggy fastened shoes on the child; her husband removed luggage from the rack above their heads. There was a hoarse whistle. The train shuddered, with a prolonged clash of couplings, and was still.

The three left the stuffy warmth of the carriage for the chill of the sunless and misty morning. They were the only passengers to leave the train. His thick black coat flapping about his legs, the man carried two suitcases alongside the stationary, hissing carriages. The woman followed, carrying a smaller case with one hand, guiding the slow child with the other. Their feet crunched on gravel.

They came to the waiting room, a dull red box empty of all but feeble yellow light. The buildings of the settlement around were dark and obscure in the mist. 'Early yet,' he observed, as he set down the suitcases. 'We can wait here.'

The room smelled of soot and urine. They sat on hard wooden seats, the child's feet dangling. Peggy covered the boy with a blanket and pulled the lapels of her coat over her pale throat. Her husband hunched forward, his large veiny hands falling fidgety between his knees : he looked at his hands presently, turning them over for inspection, as if seeking some answer there.

'It'll be all right this time,' he said at last. 'I know it will.'

Peggy was quiet.

'I got a good feeling about it,' he said.

Or he would like to have. He became annoyed with looking at his hands and pushed them deep into the pockets of his coat. The engine whistled and a long line of carriage windows streamed past the waiting room. He found a tin of tobacco in one pocket and began to make a thin cigarette. He wished he did not feel so tired. A scrap of newspaper scuffed under his feet. He looked down: a photograph of Charlie Higgins, smeared with grease, looked back at him. MINISTER DENIES said the torn headline above.

And he thought he had forgotten, as if he could.

A solitary railway employee, walking homeward, looked into the room. He was puffy-eyed; and under his railway uniform a pyjama-top showed. 'Anything I can do for you people?' he asked.

Bill Freeman looked up, hostile. 'We're just waiting here,' he said. 'No law against waiting, is there? That's what this place is here for, isn't it?'

The railwayman blinked. 'Don't get me wrong, mate. Just wondering if I could help, that's all.'

'You can't. Fuck off.'

'Strike me dead,' the railwayman said. 'No need to bite me head off, mate.' He retreated, still astonished. His feet crackled away into the dull morning.

'He was only trying to be helpful,' Peggy suggested. 'You could have been nicer to him.'

'Helpful?' He laughed. 'Nicer?' He stopped laughing. 'I pick his sort a mile. Bloody snoopers everywhere.'

Peggy shrank. The boy, who was half asleep against her, stirred and muttered.

'Sorry,' her husband said. He seemed dismayed. 'You're right. I don't know.' He shook his head. 'There wasn't no need for me to go crook like that. I'm just a bit jumpy about everything. I didn't sleep. I suppose he might of been all right.' He drew hard on his cigarette, but it refused to function. He threw it away, and took a soiled paper bag from a pocket, tearing it open to reveal three stale sandwiches. He offered them to Peggy. She shook her head. 'You eat,' she said.

'I'm not hungry neither.'

Suddenly the woman looked sick with exhaustion or something like it. She touched his arm lightly. 'Where are we?' she asked. 'Do we have to go far?'

'This place here's a timber-milling outfit,' he said. 'This settlement. The mine's a couple of mile or so from here. There's a road down to the mine, and a railway track. Don't know how the loco runs from here down to the mine. That's what we got to find out.'

'You could have asked that man then,' she observed cautiously. 'He could have told you how the loco runs.'

178

Bill sighed. 'I could have,' he agreed. 'I just wasn't thinking. When I seen him come along I was thinking of other things.'

She seemed althogether satisfied by his reply, by his admission that he had been wrong. It was, after all, an event of a rare kind, and she could afford satisfaction. He sat forward, looking out the door, thinking of his other things again. While Charlie Higgins denied and proclaimed, while Harry Jones counselled caution and compromise, he sat his bum in a waiting room in the middle of nowhere. Everything he had done, in the end, had been to put Charlie where he was, to give Harry something to compromise about, and to leave him here waiting for his life to begin again.

He sat there for a long time, fitting his thoughts together, until there were fewer sharp edges.

Soon the light outside was bright. Mist fled up the sunlit flanks of hills, revealing the settlement. The boy slept against Peggy, and Peggy against himself; he was still very much awake. He reached for a sandwich and fed it carefully into his mouth. The movement awoke Peggy, then the boy.

She took the boy to a tap outside the waiting room and washed his face with a moistened handkerchief. Then she gave him the last of some cream-flecked milk in a bottle, and a sandwich. There was one sandwich left. She looked at Bill, then at the boy; and her hand darted out, as if on its own volition, and carried the sandwich to her lips. She ate it almost furtively.

Her husband stood. 'I'll find out what time the loco runs down to the mine,' he announced. He went out of the room, across the tracks, and into the settlement, walking with an abrupt, jerky stride. Presently he returned.

'There's a loco comes up about ten,' he said. 'It don't go back again till about one. That's five hours yet.'

'We can wait,' Peggy said patiently. She fingered back her lank hair.

'Wait?' he said. 'I've got a gutsful of waiting. It drives me up the wall. I want to get started. Before I change my mind. We can walk to the mine. It's not far.'

'Walk?' Peggy said faintly.

'All right?' he said briskly, but gave her no time for answer. He took up the two large suitcases. 'Let's go.'

They walked over the tracks and through the settlement. Along a thin stony road, puddled with recent rain, there was a

179

store and post office combined in an ungainly wooden building which looked near collapse. One or two early morning loungers watched the strangers pass. Further along was a string of old houses, knotting at the end into a ramshackle cluster of single men's huts. The timber mill, which stood at the end of the settlement, was already alive with grinding, tearing sounds.

They walked in silence. His pace, even with the two suitcases weighting him, was too fast for Peggy and the boy. Soon he was several yards ahead.

'Wait,' she called, her voice mild with old despair.

He sat on his cases and waited. She expected irritation in his face, but found only concern. 'Sorry,' he said. 'I keep forgetting him.' He nodded toward the boy. 'Let's take a rest.'

The boy was still sleepy, and bewildered; his mother sat him on her case. 'Where we going?' he asked.

'I told you before, sonny,' Peggy said, sighing. 'We're going to a new place.' She was tired of the question.

'Why?'

'Shush, Ian,' she said, annoyed. Then, repenting, she straightened the boy's small cream beret.

'Why?' the boy repeated.

'Because,' she said, raising her eyes in appeal to Bill, 'because Daddy's taking us.'

'Why is Daddy taking us?'

She didn't answer; she didn't look at Bill. He knelt beside the boy, and the boy looked back at him gravely. 'We're going to a new place because it should be a better place,' he said. 'That's all.'

'Have you got hard things to do there too?'

'Just work. Hard work.'

'Will I see mountains? The mountains with snow?'

Bill was perplexed, then amused. 'That's funny,' he said to Peggy. 'I'd forgotten. I promised him that months ago. He's got a memory, our kid.'

They started out again. The sun, climbing the pale sky, lit a lacerated landscape. On the upper slopes of the hills, where limestone outcropped against the sky, were long-dead trees, fallen in whitened tangle, and giant ulcers of erosion scabbed with weeping crusts of clay and papa. On lower ground slack wire fences straggled about small, pine-sheltered farmhouses. The pasture was a dead green colour, and loose bellied cows grazed, with their spindly calves. There was a steady silvery

180

dripping of moisture from the telegraph wires above the road. The day grew warmer. And the road unwound slowly, a narrow strip of clay and bluish stone edged with manuka and gorse.

'I thought you said it wasn't far,' Peggy protested.

Bill didn't argue. 'A bit further than I thought, that's all.'

'We should have waited. We should have waited for that loco.'

He seemed to agree. 'I just wanted to get there. I just don't like hanging around. Not this time. I want to make a start.' He paused. 'I didn't think it would of been so far.' He paused again. 'I'm sorry.'

She was appeased; she nodded. 'I don't like hanging around either,' she said. 'But we should have waited.'

They came to a rise. Bill, walking ahead again, was first to the top. He stopped and set down his suitcases. 'There she is,' he announced, pointing, as his wife and son arrived beside him.

The mining settlement discoloured the end of a verdant valley; the hills around seemed black with bruising. Two groups of buildings made the settlement, one group large and dark and tightly gathered, the other small and white and more scattered. The large dark buildings belonged to the mine itself; the small ones were the miners' homes. Above and beyond the valley were hills tall and blue and remote.

'What's that?' the boy asked.

'Where we're going,' his father answered. He spoke with some satisfaction; he sat on a suitcase and rolled a cigarette. 'Might as well have a rest now,' he announced. 'It doesn't look so bad, down there.'

Peggy sat beside him and looked down the valley with a pensive expression. He touched her playfully under the chin, tilting up her face. 'What do you think, mother?' he said. 'Look good to you?'

'Any place,' she said. 'Any place looks good now.'

'I think you'll like it. I just got a feeling.'

'I'd like it anywhere. Just as long as it's somewhere. For a while.' She continued to look pensively down the valley.

'I don't want to go,' the child said. 'I want to go back.'

'We can't go back,' Peggy said. 'Not ever.' She didn't look away from the distant settlement.

'Why?'

She didn't seem to hear. She might have been unravelling something.

'Why?'

181

'Shut up,' she hissed suddenly, jerking her eyes to the boy.

Astonished, he began to whimper. She softened. 'Shush, Ian,' she whispered. 'We're going to a new place. A nice new place.' She pointed. 'See?'

But the boy couldn't or wouldn't see. 'There aren't any mountains with snow,' he said. 'My feet are hurty.'

Bill picked up the suitcases. 'Let's go,' he said. He set off with a jaunty stride, humming a tune.

The sun grew hot in the empty sky. A few hundred yards down the road they came to a rough wooden bridge which spanned a clear, glittering stream. Upstream they could see a sandy place, a miniature beach, strung around with toe toe and flax, and shady with willows. They made a halt on the bridge. 'Pretty place,' Peggy murmured.

'Nice in summer,' he offered, as if he already owned the spot. 'We could have picnics here. And swim. And eat our lunch under the willows.'

'Yes,' she responded. She had heard this before, or something like it. But there had never been picnics.

Their stops along the last circling stretch of road became more frequent. The boy complained of his feet and Peggy became tired and ill-tempered. And Bill seemed to increase his pace as they neared the settlement.

It was late in the morning when they came to the place. The pale miners' homes, attractive enough from a distance, were crude boxes dumped almost at random where the bush had been cleared at the valley's end. But they doubtless sheltered life of a kind. Each had a black strip of garden and a green patch of lawn.

Bill nodded towards one. No curtains showed in the window, no smoke came from the chimney. The lawn was unkempt. 'That's empty,' he said. 'That could be the one we get.'

Peggy considered the place. There wasn't much to consider. 'Like it?' he asked.

'There'll be a lot of work to do,' she said, though she hardly dared hope. 'The inside's probably a mess. And the garden's full of weeds. But it couldn't be better, the way I feel now.'

He did not need to ask how she felt. 'I had a feeling,' he said, 'you was going to like it.' He spat on his parched palms and took new grip on his suitcases.

Beyond the store and post office they found the squat grey

182

building which advertised itself as an office. 'Wait here,' Bill directed. 'I don't think I'll be long.'

Peggy found a place to sit with the boy outside. She removed his small shoes and was gentle with the tender feet she found. 'We'll be all right soon,' she said.

'Why?'

'I just know,' she answered.

The reception office was a small, gloomy room. Beyond a chipped counter were two desks. At one a grey-haired woman sat typing. At the other was a clerk, a slight mousy man of about fifty. He had a shiny bald head with a slender periphery of silver hair, and steel-rimmed glasses on a bony nose; the face itself seemed dehydrated. He worked in a limp black smoking jacket. Just beyond him was a door displaying the sign, *Mine Manager*.

The clerk looked up from his papers, evidently to ascertain that the visitor was of not much account, then bent to them again.

Take it easy, Bill Freeman told himself. Take it quiet. He looked at the clerk's shiny head with conviction.

The typewriter ticked and stopped. The clerk's pen scratched briefly, and he rose without haste, flicked some spot of dust from his papers, and minced slowly to the counter.

'Yes?' he said. 'Anything I can do for you?'

'I'm here about a job. I wrote a letter –'

'The name?'

'Freeman's the name. William Freeman.'

The clerk screwed on the top of his fountain pen; he began to twirl the pen slowly in his fingers. 'Ah yes, Mr Freeman,' he said. 'I remember.' His expression was pained; the pen twirled.

'It's all right, isn't it?' Bill Freeman said. 'You said in your letter –'

'There were two letters actually, Mr Freeman.'

Easy, he thought. Quiet.

'Two letters? I only got one. You said there was a job for me here.'

'It's apparent you couldn't have received our second letter then. We only posted it two days or so ago. We hardly expected you would turn up here so soon. You see, there was some mistake.' The clerk smiled with nervous goodwill.

183

'Mistake?' His voice trembled. 'What do you mean, a mistake?'

'About the job. An error in the office here. Really most unfortunate. What it amounts to is that there isn't really a job here for you at all.'

'But you said – '

'As I've explained, Mr Freeman, there was a mistake. We tried to tell you that in our second letter. Unfortunate that you set off before that second letter arrived, but we can hardly take the blame for your enthusiasm.' The pen still twirled between thin fingers. 'The whole thing is really most unfortunate.' He shook his head. 'I'm sorry.'

Something heaved under his ribs and he saw his fist slam surprisingly on the counter. 'Don't lie to me.'

'Please, Mr Freeman. Please.' The clerk retreated from the counter; he gave a small, despairing shrug.

'I don't want none of your bloody lies.'

The grey-haired woman, startled, looked up from her typewriter. The clerk appeared to wither. 'Please, Mr Freeman. Please. There's a lady present.'

'Tell me the truth. The bloody truth.'

'I'm afraid I don't understand,' said the clerk weakly. 'I've explained all there is to explain.'

'Let me see the manager.' Bill Freeman pointed to the door beyond the clerk's desk. 'Maybe he doesn't feel the truth's so bloody precious that he can't give me any.' He went around the end of the counter, but the clerk blocked his way.

'He's a busy man. He wouldn't want to be disturbed. He really – '

Shoved aside, the clerk collapsed back upon the woman at her desk. She gave a small cry, and just managed to save her typewriter as it teetered.

Without knocking, Bill Freeman pushed open the door of the manager's office. This room was bright after the gloom of the other; too bright. He could not see at first. Sunlight fed through a long window in the opposite wall, silhouetting the desk and its occupant. The walls were cream-coloured, and there was now green carpet underfoot, and light-varnished filing cabinets around.

'The name's Freeman,' he announced.

He could see the occupant of the desk now, as he rose slowly, removing thick tortoise-shell glasses. A short stocky man, amiably

184

moon-faced, in a pepper-and-salt suit; a gold watch-chain was looped across his waistcoat. He looked mildly puzzled.

'I beg your pardon?' he said.

'The name's Freeman. I want to know why I can't have a job here. After you people said I could have one. And I don't want none of your bloody lies.'

'A job?' the manager said. He resumed his seat and began cleaning his glasses with a white handkerchief.

'The job you people promised. Now your bum boy out in the office says I can't have it. I want to know why.'

'Why?' the manager repeated. He seemed amused. 'You want to know why?' He gave a significant cough, and added, 'There was a mistake. No doubt you've been told that.'

'I told you I don't want no lies. I'm sick of lies.' And sick of much else too, his inward enemy told him, but it was not the time to qualify.

The manager replaced his glasses and studied the man before him. The glasses seemed to increase his assurance.

'Well, Freeman,' he began casually, 'if you must know, as of course you do know – '

The clerk put his head cautiously around the door. 'I tried to stop him coming in,' he started to apologize.

'Fuck off,' Bill Freeman said.

The manager appeared to agree; he also irritably dismissed the clerk. The door closed softly.

The manager straightened the file on his desk and closed it. 'Now,' he said slowly, fingering his lower lip. 'Your name, if I have it right, is William Freeman.'

'That's right. And I'm proud of it. I wouldn't be anyone else. Not now at least.'

'I daresay, Freeman. I daresay.' He slipped the file into a wire basket. Then he sought another file in a cabinet beside his desk. The item he wanted was evidently near the top of this file. 'You're the Freeman who was jailed for sedition four years ago, aren't you? You seem to get around quite a lot. And everywhere there seems to be trouble. Odd.'

'I'm not ashamed of it. I've found trouble, all right. The kind you people make when you don't give men a fair go. All I do is fight back. Why should a man behave different?'

He seemed, more or less, to be asking the question of himself too.

The manager took this thoughtfully. Or with the appearance

185

of thought. 'That, of course, is no concern of mine, Freeman. My concern is that we don't have trouble, or trouble-makers, here. Up till now we've been remarkably free of trouble. The management's on excellent terms with the men. We wouldn't like any change. We want to keep things pleasant here.'

'Keep the men down, you mean. I know your kind. I expect you run the union too.'

'I don't want to hear speeches. Speech-making might be part of your business. Listening to them is not part of mine.' He paused before a less delicate thrust. 'Anyway,' he added, 'my impression is that your audience has shrunk lately. Is that why you feel the need to practise on me?'

'You can't get away with this. You can't victimize –'

'No one, to my knowledge, is being victimized. No one is being discharged from employment here. There was just a mistake, as I told you. In any case, I'm sure if I discussed this thing with the men they would certainly prefer to be without your company.'

'Or else,' Bill Freeman said heavily. 'I know your stunts.'

'They would,' the manager repeated, 'certainly prefer to be without your company.' With a pleasant expression of innocence, he held up his hands. 'The clerical error which led us to advise you that we had a job available is, of course, most regrettable. Also any small inconvenience caused.' He placed his hands flat on the desk, to signify that he was finished with the subject.

'Bloody liars.'

'If you persist in seeing things in that light, Freeman, then of course there is simply nothing I can do about it. I could, perhaps, see my way clear to offering you some small sum by way of compensation for the inconvenience.'

'You mean a bribe to go quietly.'

'Compensation. How would, say, ten pounds sound to you?'

'Thirty is the usual figure for blood money. And in silver, not pounds.'

The manager did not appear to understand for a moment. 'Fifteen, then. How does that sound?'

'Your hide would sound better. Go to hell.'

'The sentiment, Freeman, is reciprocated.'

'If everything's so sweet here, what are you so scared of? You know as well as I do. This place is known up and down the country as rotten.'

'If it's as bad as you say,' replied the manager calmly, 'why

186

did you come here, Freeman? Why don't you,' he added, 'go to Russia?'

'You really want to know? Because I don't like your kind. Because you're not Russian. And I'm not.'

'Just as well for you,' observed the manager. 'Over there they'd shoot you.'

He did not trouble to deny it. 'And you,' he said. 'So it would be worth it anyway.'

'I've a considerable amount of work to get through today,' the manager said abruptly. 'I'm sure we could have a most interesting discussion some other time.'

'Like hell. Scared, aren't you? All your kind.'

'If you'll excuse me, Freeman.' The manager opened a new file. 'I have work to do.'

'Take a good look around you sometime.' Bill Freeman pointed out the window. The colliery workings, the mine shaft, blackened sheds, rakes of coal trucks shunting, were all visible against scarred hillside. 'One day that's not going to belong to you. Or any of your kind. One day this country's going to belong to the people who sweat into it.'

'Get out,' the manager said. 'Get out before I call the police.'

Bill Freeman strode out of the mine office, past the bent clerk and the typing woman, into the street; a door crashed behind him. He went past Peggy and the boy as if he hadn't seen them. Peggy ran after him and caught at his sleeve.

'Where are you going?' she said. 'It's all right, isn't it?'

He stopped to look at her, but his face was remote. He hesitated, turned, and walked silently back to the suitcases. He lifted the sitting child aside.

'It's all right, isn't it?' she said, still plucking at his sleeve. He shook her away, picked up the large suitcases, and began to walk. She took her own case, and the child's hand, and hurried after him. 'Where are we going?' she pleaded. 'It's all right, isn't it? There's nothing wrong? You got the job, didn't you?'

He stopped, and let the suitcases fall heavily. 'No,' he said. 'They knew. Or found out.'

Her eyes trembled. 'But the letter,' she said.

'They must of found out after they sent the letter.' He was not looking at his wife now. 'They said it was a mistake. All a mistake. Bloody liars.'

Her shoulders quivered; the boy began to whimper. Bill Freeman took his wife by the arm. 'Stop it,' he said. 'Not here.'

187

He looked up and down the quiet street, but there seemed, at that moment, no onlookers. 'Not here,' he repeated.

'Bill, there's something I must tell you – '

'Not now.'

'It's important.'

'Another day.'

'Where are we going?' she whispered. 'Now?'

He avoided the question. 'We'll wait,' he said. 'Until the men come up from the pit. The day needn't be wasted.'

'Bill, you really ought to know that – '

'Later,' he insisted. He paused. 'You see, don't you? I got no chance of being anything but what I am. They wouldn't let me anyway.'

Peggy gave her attention to the boy. 'Shush, Ian,' she said. 'He's hungry,' she appealed to her husband.

He wasn't listening. He had taken the letter from his jacket pocket and was shredding it. 'Liars,' he said, more quietly now. A breeze fluttered the torn paper from his hands. 'Well?' he said at last. 'What are you waiting for? You can get something to eat from the store, can't you?'

In the late afternoon a low siren moaned : echoes circled the valley. Wire rope strained upon turning winches as the cage from the pit screeched and rattled upward. Presently men emerged, dusty and blackened, in scarves and helmets, with eyes negro-white, through the colliery gate. They carried lamps and lunch-boxes and blinked against the bitter sunlight.

On one side of the gate they saw the short woman, drab and pale, with a child and some suitcases; on the other, the tall gaunt man in evangelical black. They were giving out leaflets with huge, exclamatory headings. The woman gave out hers almost apologetically. The man appeared confident, entirely with out apology, and called friendly slogans to the miners as they passed. 'The truth,' he said. 'Get the truth, comrades.'

Puzzled, most of the miners accepted the strange, rustling sheets of paper with urgent words : though some, as if fearing infection with a malady which they could not themselves properly define, side-stepped the outstretched hand, the humourless slogans, and hurried away. Some accepted only to repent, crumpling and discarding the leaflets as they walked with quick-ened step towards their safe homes. One or two stopped briefly to talk to the gaunt man in black; one pressed money into his hand. And then they were gone, all of them, into their ugly box homes with strips of garden and patches of lawn. The streets were empty again.

The man, moving slowly, gathered up the remaining leaflets and crushed them into a suitcase. 'All this stuff,' he said, 'it's no good anyway. It's all near a couple of years old, propaganda from before the election. Everything's different now. I ought to of thrown it out.'

'How are we going to get back to the station?' the woman asked, as though waking from a dream. 'Can we get the loco?'

'Walk,' he said. 'The way we came. There's no loco back now. Too late in the day.'

'Walk?' she said faintly.

They walked. The sinking sun coppered the land; the valley was quiet and still, dry and dead. The road had whitened, and their feet stirred up pools of dust.

'Where we going?' the child said.

'Shush,' said the woman. 'Daddy's taking us.'

The sun sank; the valley was shadowed. In the east the clouds were pale and curdled, in the west they were gold and pink.

'Why?' said the child.

Dusk smoked fine and blue from the land. When they reached the rise in the road from which they had first seen into the valley, they paused and looked back. Bill Freeman set down his cases. 'I'll get rid of that stuff,' he said, 'those leaflets. And lighten the load. They're no use to anyone now.' In the distance the mining settlement was an island of weak lights under the evening stars. The child was tripping and crying.

'Why Daddy taking us?'

'Shush,' said the woman patiently.

Bill Freeman picked up his son. 'He's tired,' he said. 'Poor kid.'

'Why?' asked the child stubbornly.

Their wait for a train to take them further was a cold one. He and Peggy sat close together for warmth, and the boy slept on his knee. He told himself he had better face it : Peggy was looking grim. Worse than he had ever seen her before. It was plainly more than the walk, more than tiredness, more than disappointment. More than their lives. Her face, under the feeble bulb of the waiting room, was pale and stark and quite bloodless. Almost the complexion of corpses he had seen. He felt his first, furtive terror.

189

'On the train,' he promised, 'it will be warm. We'll have time to think.'

She tried to smile, with colourless lips.

'Things will get better,' he went on, 'we'll find somewhere. We'll sleep on the train and tomorrow we'll be back in the city.'

This time she made no response. She might have been afraid of falling apart.

Soon the train, whistling escape, roared out of the misty hills. He nursed his wife and son aboard, and their luggage. The warmth of the train was relief. He felt better, hearing wheels turn beneath them again.

'Thank God we're out of that lot,' he said. 'That hole. We probably wouldn't of liked it there anyhow.' He paused. The train roared on. Restless, half-sleeping passengers muttered around them. Peggy sat up straight beside him. 'You'd best get some sleep,' he added 'Don't worry about anything.'

But she was incapable of rest, or still afraid. He had his arm around her in comfort. He could not acknowledge his own fear yet.

'Bill,' she said presently. 'It's no use. You've got to get me off.'

'Off?'

'Off this train. The next stop. It's no use, I've got to. You've got to get me off to see a doctor.'

'A doctor?'

'I tried to tell you today. I would have, but all those other things happened. I was frightened.'

'Peg,' he said, 'what's the matter, girl?'

'I don't know yet. But you must get me off. The doctor will know. He'll tell you.'

He had never felt more threatened. The entire dark land seemed to move, to loom and shift in upon them now, and even the train made them no less vulnerable. This time, for the first time, it was nothing he could stop and fight.

'Peg,' he said, 'Peg.'

But she was going clean away without a sound. Soon the train was racing out of hills and noisy tunnels into the lights of a town. The panic lurched up into his mouth with numbing taste. For his stomach was empty of all but terror now.

'Peg,' he was saying, 'Peg girl. For God's sake.'

He must have been shouting. There were awoken passengers about his seat, and the guard. His son was weeping.

190

The train slowed. 'We got to get her off,' he said, blindly bumping people away, lifting his wife. 'Got to.'

There was a platform. Lights, station attendants, a policeman. And people about, helping, obstructing. 'Easy now,' someone said close to his ear. 'We got an ambulance coming. She wants hospital, not just a doctor. No point wasting time.' Their luggage was taken from the carriage and dumped on the platform. The train hurtled away with gusts of steam toward the city. Shortly afterwards a tinny ambulance squealed into the parking bay beside the platform. He helped carry his wife into the back of the ambulance, then remembered his son. The boy had to be rescued, still kicking, from the policeman.

'My mother,' he screamed. 'Where's my mother gone?'

There was a nurse with Peggy in the back of the ambulance who resisted their attempt at intrusion. So he crammed the boy on his knee in the front seat of the vehicle. The ambulance turned with speed into the wide main street of the town, quiet and empty with hardly a light showing in any window and the town clock stopped. The boy weakened, collapsing in his arms.

'Where are we?' he asked the driver. 'What's the name of this place?'

'Some call it a bloody dump,' said the driver tersely as he accelerated toward the hospital, 'others call it Te Ika. It's the kind of place, once you're in it, it's hard to get out of.'

He chewed on a dead cigarette. He was not a happy man.

'But I got the wife to think about,' the driver added. 'She wouldn't shift, once she got her roots down. So here we are. What's the trouble with yours anyway?'

Bill Freeman didn't answer. He let his head fall against his limp son.

His life began to seem a composition of waiting rooms. This one smelled antiseptic and leathery. The cushioned seats creaked under his restless body. There were shiny magazines he could not touch, and the bright steady light burned his eyes. At some stage his fretfully sleeping son had been taken from him. The polished hospital squeaked and whispered around him. Doors sprang open and closed noiselessly, and nurses moved pale beyond frosted glass. Flowers glowed in a vase but offered no scent. His large, twisting hands were grainy with dirt, scratched in a few places. Erect and sweaty in his narrow body and

191

sagging clothes, he waited on the doctor. It seemed the bugger would never come.

There was only a black-haired woman, an orderly, shaking him awake. With a cup of tea to offer. It was still night. She found a flattened packet of cigarettes somewhere in her white uniform and offered him one. 'There,' she said in a cheery Irish voice, 'just hold on, and everything will be all right. You see.'

He started to shake his head, then nodded.

'I heard your name was Freeman,' she went on. 'You wouldn't be Bill Freeman. I mean the Bill Freeman we used to hear about.'

He hesitated. For the first time in his life he was tempted to be irrelevant; he had a faint sick feeling, and the cigarette smoke was rough on his throat.

'I suppose I must be,' he agreed.

'God bless you then,' she said. 'There's some people still remember, even if others don't. The way you fought. I heard you speak once, before they put you away. So I know why they was frightened.'

She seemed just to vanish. For a moment he wondered if he had dreamed her. But there was the cigarette burning between his fingers, the cup of tea in front of him. Then the young doctor at the door.

'Mr Freeman?'

'Yes.'

'You're a lucky man. Your wife's going to be all right. And with any luck we've averted a miscarriage.'

'A miscarriage?' Bill Freeman had to think about the word. It might have been something foreign.

'That's right. I don't think your wife will lose the child. But it was a near thing.'

'Jesus,' Bill Freeman said. 'Jesus Christ.' He felt for his head, and appeared to find it solid.

The rest of what the doctor said made no sense, much. He had enough to understand, or make himself believe.

'And she's going to be all right?' It was still the most important thing to believe.

'With some rest,' the doctor agreed. 'We can't let her out of here too soon. She's at pretty low ebb; she needs as much rest as she can get.'

'Can I see her now?'

192

'She's asleep,' the doctor said. 'She'll be out for quite a while. Perhaps late in the morning. But what about yourself? You look as if – '

'I'm all right.'

'But – '

'I tell you I'm all right.'

'Please yourself then.' The young doctor shrugged. 'I'm just trying to say you look all in yourself. But that's your business.'

'It is,' Bill Freeman agreed.

'So if you'll excuse me – '

Bill Freeman sat on in the waiting room, believing what there was to believe, and regretting what he could. He became, at length, irritated with his irritations. The cigarette had left him dizzy, the tea had gone cold, and there was pale morning beyond the windows; his body was a collection of diverse pains. In this waiting room, with walls vaguely receding every time his head nodded, he could identify nothing familiar other than himself, and even that disguise was difficult to penetrate. He had a son asleep somewhere near; that was evidently important to remember too. Where were they, where had they arrived? He might have asked what there was to this place other than a railway station, a main street, a hospital. It seemed he would have to get up, get out, and manage a new grip on the world before it flowed out and away from him altogether. He rose heavily, and his legs all but refused his weight. Then the woman appeared, the black-haired orderly, to recover her cup and saucer. He had almost forgotten her, though she had sugared his tea too sweet.

'Your wife,' she said gently. 'She's going to be all right?'

'So they say.'

He was still shaky on his feet, and she put a hand on his shoulder.

'Everything's fine then, like I knew it would be,' she said with conviction. 'So you just take it easy.'

'What is there here?' he said. 'In this place?' He had to manoeuvre each word from his mouth with effort. 'In this town?'

'There is a couple of thousand people,' she said, 'and not much else to speak of.'

'There might be work?'

'There might be,' she agreed, 'now things is better. Depends what you want. There's a quarry just outside town, and a limeworks. Then there's the railways, maybe. But you're not looking for work yet. Surely.'

'I got to, you see,' he explained. 'On account of her having to stay here. I got to find something to keep us going.'

'You got to find some sleep, it looks to me. My house is just near. I think you could make good use of the spare bed.'

'When I got my hands on a job,' he said, 'I'll have all the time in the world to sleep. And that might be about the truth of the thing.'

He started to move past her, out the door. Then he remembered. 'There's the boy,' he said. 'My son. He's somewhere here.'

'You go and find yourself that work you're so keen on,' she said, 'and I'll look after him. And ask near the end of this road for Mary Leary. The white cottage with the silver birches. You'll find your boy there, and a bed.'

'You're kind. You don't even know me.'

'But I do know you, Bill Freeman,' she said.

Bill Freeman walked into the town. There was not much to it, as towns went. A drab sort of place, the buildings dulled with drifting soot from the railway yards. A main street, tidy enough, and little else. The streets behind, beside the river, were ramshackle. At one end of the main street was a carved Maori meeting house, at the other a school. It was a Friday, a sale day at the stockyards, and later in the morning there were muddy vehicles in from farms, and dusty men in crumpled hats. There were clusters of dark-dressed Maoris, perhaps mourners at a tangi. He might have known, perhaps, he would finish up in some such place; he might have been freshly trimmed to inhabit it. And the place, besides, had the anonymous colour of his deepest and bleakest expectations. So he walked, and kept walking, until his feet began to grip.

Eleven:

ON A GREEN DAY, BETWEEN MORNING AND EVENING, NED LIVING-stone lost his wife. Not entirely, and not quite all at once, but enough to put a damper on his life.

It was the year things began looking up too. In the town, where men gathered to yarn on street corners, some said it was the new government. Whatever the reason, even farmers like Tom Jackson, around the saleyards, were not heard much to complain. There was a better price on the cream anyway, and the butter factory was busier than it had been for years when the cows came into milk that spring. Abandoned land around Te Ika was refinanced and reoccupied. There were more people in town on sale days, and storekeepers were happier with credit. If Ned Livingstone noticed the change, it was because he did not go into town much, no more than he could help, and each time some improvement was visible, even if only long-neglected potholes in the main street patched with fresh asphalt. And after the battering rains of winter, it seemed the land had never been as green as it was that sunny spring.

When Ned took on a hand to help, it was because it seemed necessary again; he planned to run more cows. He hung on to his new heifers, bought in some higher-producing stock at a decent price, and culled his neglected herd. All this appeared worth doing at last. Even mending and rewiring fences had some point. Aspirant second growth had risen on slopes he had once cleared, but never really claimed; he found himself chopping and burning again, and attacking weed. There was much satis-faction in the work. But he needed help and a new hand, he hoped, might mean company. He'd had none since Nick departed and, slaving solitary from before sunrise to after sunset, he grew conscious of the lack. Then there was Nance. She was

195

even less help around the farm itself. She tired easy, and the kid was not longer so obviously to blame. For Tim was off to school five days out of seven now, and not anywhere near as demanding. But Nance would take crook more often than ever, with coughs and sniffles. 'It seems to get colder every year,' she would say, 'colder and damper. This is just a bog, this valley.'

She would forget the drains he had dug. Sometimes she grew shrill on the subject. He hadn't much to say.

'This is a dreary place for dreary people,' she would needle. 'I want something better for my son.'

He would roll a smoke, perhaps, or lift the newspaper. He thought he knew the trouble. Her father, Jack Crimmins, had dropped dead on his land the year before. Her family was scattered, remote. Sometimes she got letters from a sister in the city. Something had gone, at the centre, but the problem was one he could not name. Like her resentments. He had his own, after all.

'I would like to see Timothy a scientist,' she went on, 'in some clean laboratory. In a white coat, looking at test tubes.'

He could wonder at the idea.

'He will get out of this mud,' she promised. 'Are you listening?'

'The boy is just bloody five,' he said. 'Give him a chance.'

'Six,' she said. 'Nearly seven. He has ideas. He is independent.'

'All right,' he said. 'Six or seven. He has still got plenty of time to grow and decide.'

'It is just as well he has someone who cares,' she announced. 'You sit there in your old clothes and never think. You smell of cows.'

He could find no sequence in her thought. He had given up trying. Sometimes indignation blushed on her milky cheeks.

'I might as well be dead,' she accused, 'for all you listen.'

'You was talking about the boy.'

'And other things.'

'And other things,' he agreed. 'I was listening.'

'Is that all you got to say?'

'I thought enough was being said.'

He made up his mind that Nance was no longer herself. He did not know why, and at times it was difficult to remember what else, or who else, she had been. And if she was not herself now, then who was she? That was a puzzle too. He could see

196

no connection, and would sit lonely in his surprise. Now and then he would, against his will, find his way back to the day he struck her in the face on account of Nick. Had that been the beginning? He could not remember. The only thing sure was that he felt more and more on the outer in his own place, in this wooden dwelling he had nailed together, on this land he had chopped and razed to farm. True, there was the boy. But young Tim was not often around, with school, and when at home mostly close to his mother. Ned had begun talking to himself again lately, as he traipsed about his land or sat in the cowshed. This solitary dialogue was no great comfort. If anything it took him back to the time, just after the war, before Nick came tramping up the gorge. The time when he was alone, beyond dispute, and not alone with a couple of troubling strangers, one of whom was evidently his son. He might have been happy in that earlier loneliness, with only the land to impose himself on, but he could not exactly recall. It was tempting to think so. For then he had needed only to be certain of himself, and there had been no problem in that. Or was memory trying to trick him about that too?

Still, so far as Nance was concerned, he had hope that things would come right again, if he hung on. He had no clear cause for such hope. It was just there. And he tried not to provoke, since his existence seemed provocation enough, and at night she often lay stiff and apart in their bed. The boy was something else again. He would have to wait and see. And the boy, after all, would one day own this land his father had earned.

When Ned made his need for a hand known in the town, response was slow. A year earlier he would have had no difficulty in finding a man; he might have had to fight off contenders for the job. But those of the unemployed not become unemployable had begun to shift from the town on to construction jobs the new government was starting. And in the town itself there was suddenly work to spare. Ned waited, though, and in time there came to the Livingstone farm a lanky streak of a boy, puffing at his first cigarettes, in his father's car. His father's name was Archie Daniels. Arch was a bookmaker, and in a small way a sly-grogger, in the town. Ned had heard of the man, but never met him until that day he arrived at the farm and introduced his son. He had a smile filled with gold teeth.

'Young Alan here is just out of school,' Arch explained. 'I thought he might give farming a bash. I got to find some way of keeping the young bugger out of trouble. A bit of a hard yacker never hurt anyone his age.'

Ned looked at the boy he was offered. There wasn't much of a lily to gild.

'I'd like you to give him a try,' Arch went on. 'See if you can make something of him.'

'I'm not running a school here,' Ned observed. 'We better get that straight. I'm offering pay, and keep.'

'You'll get the work out of him,' Arch promised. 'And naturally, him being new to it, you don't need to pay him so much.'

Ned was slow deciding. It was true the boy wasn't what he expected, but it was also true there wasn't much risk involved, or money. He could always give the boy his marching orders at the end of a week. And his need for help had grown more urgent. In his thin way Alan looked healthy and perhaps wiry enough. He had begun to shave, and his acne problem appeared to be fading. 'All right,' Ned agreed finally. 'I'll give him a try.'

'Any problem,' said Arch Daniels, 'just give me a buzz. And I'll put a flea in his ear.' He looked at his son. 'I don't want to see you coming home for a year. Right? Make a go of farming, and I might just set you up on your own place later on.' To Ned he added, 'I just got married again, you see. And the kid always seems to be damn well underfoot.'

Arch Daniels climbed back into his shiny vehicle and drove from the farm. Ned set young Alan up in the old whare by the creek. He would, of course, come across to the farmhouse for his meals. As soon as he was settled in, it was clear he had some promise as a worker, though his arse could get heavy after a couple of hours on the slasher or shovel. Still, he wasn't afraid of working up a sweat, and Ned gave the boy credit. And his real problem soon became obvious. It was girls, or the lack of them. He papered the walls of the whare with glossy portraits sliced from magazines. Girls with high breasts and plump buttocks, half-draped or undraped entirely, in high heels or barefoot, reclining on couches and rugs and floors. Corridors of limbs, an army of flesh. Ned had never seen anything like it before, but what the boy did with the whare was his own business. Nick was exorcised from the place altogether, and Ned no longer felt easy there. He would feel dead in his heavy skin. Those walls, with their abundance, seemed merely to tell him of

198

lives he could have led, worlds he could have known, and would never. His irritations on this account were in exact proportion to his disbelief; there was no other life he could have led, no other world he could have known. And he doubted if the rest was more than dream anyway, a fevered dream from which the flesh was sure in time to awaken desolate. So he called into the whare only when he had to, and was always glad to escape the door, and find himself surrounded by evidence of the solution he had imposed upon the land. That near fence, or that far stump; the trees he had chosen to leave rooted, like God, and the pines he had planted himself; these long-legged calves he grazed, because he had decided they would live; that house he had built and painted, and those acres sloping up to the hills he made green. He had no cause for doubt. But then he always felt better outside. Even mud could comfort after listening to Nance, or looking in on Alan.

Alan was not much company. That had to be conceded. But perhaps Ned couldn't have everything.

'I don't think I will take up farming,' he confided. 'Your life is not your own.'

He was not a bad-looking kid, once you got used to him, and not deliberately disagreeable.

'Then what is it?' Ned asked.

'I don't know. I just know it is not your own.'

It was doubtless something he had heard somewhere. And he had come to the end of the received wisdom.

'I can't see it myself,' Ned offered pacifically. 'Your life is more your own here than it is under some boss.'

It was years since he'd tried to shape this in his mind. The words were rusty, those he retrieved, and the rest evidently mislaid down the years since he last used them.

'I don't know,' Alan said. 'A boss is human. He can be looking the other way.'

'If you're lucky,' Ned allowed. 'But that's not saying much.'

'I mean, here everything is boss,' Alan said. 'Like the cows, the weather. Nothing ever looks the other way.'

They had been carrying buckets of curd to the pig-pen. When they filled the trough, they leaned on the rails and smoked. It was a pleasant day, easy enough, and Ned could not feel especially bossed.

'If it comes to that,' he observed, 'everything is your boss, whatever you do. But here you got a chance of sorting yourself

199

out. Other places you haven't. You always know where you stand here, anyway, because you can only depend on yourself. And you always know it's just a question of getting your back into it.'

He felt optimism again in his body, warmth almost forgotten, as he lectured young sceptical Alan.

'Work's not everything,' Alan said.

Probably something else he had heard. But he appeared less certain. 'I mean, is it?' he added.

Ned had to feel his way slowly about that one, like a sudden rock in the dark. 'A man ought to care about what he does,' he said finally. 'See something for it, I mean. Like I can. I can see something for what I done. And my kid might see it too, one day.' He thought it time, though, to shift the subject slightly. 'I suppose you'll be getting tied up with some girl yourself one day soon. Then you'll see. Your life won't be too much your own then.'

'That's different,' Alan said, quick.

He did not like this shift, apparently. He took his cigarette from his mouth and his tongue felt the edge of his lip.

'Anyway I'm still young,' he added, but without confidence.

'We all have our fun,' Ned agreed, though he found it hard to recall his own. 'But you got to see what everything comes down to, in the end.'

'I don't know too much yet,' Alan acknowledged with unease. He pushed himself back from the rail, and stamped out his cigarette. 'I suppose I'll learn, like you say.'

It seemed he wanted to escape the conversation entirely.

'It's just I hate to think of some people never learning,' Ned Livingstone said.

A month or two after Alan came, the day after they finished planting turnips for next year's winter feed, Ned Livingstone set off alone for town on a Friday. Less than a mile from the farm his left front wheel developed a wobble, about half way through the gorge, and he finished up in a ditch, the entire vehicle tilted and slewed in a patch of mud. He hadn't a hope of shifting the thing alone. So after a smoke and some thought he started home on foot to get Alan's help. He didn't mind the walk. He almost enjoyed it. The sun was warm, not too hot, and birds sang from the high crags and native trees clinging each side of the gorge. The musical river, where the

200

creeks joined, had a cold shine. Kowhai trees here and there were in mustardy bloom, shedding beaky flowers which lay like yellow snow; and roadside broom echoed the colour. Here almost nothing had changed since he had bumped up a rutted track on a dray, the horse tugging ahead, and his cases and tools clattering behind. Or since the winter evening, freed from the army, he had walked up here with his kit-bag on his shoulder. The track had become a decent enough road; that was about all the difference. For the crags were as tall, and he could feel as small here as at the beginning. The gorge had been witness to his arrivals and departures in all weathers, in all seasons, in bad times and good; he had never much thought about its obstinate permanence before. There was nothing to be got from it except stone, the timber was mostly stunted, and it was too sharply lifting for even one useful grazing slope. He felt its presence, when he crashed through it in the car, but he hadn't really seen the place since the beginning, when he was new. Now it gleamed with spring, and the birds chuckled and chimed. Ned Livingstone, despite himself, and despite his afflicted car, began to feel as amiable as the day. To his own surprise he picked up a pebble and tossed it far up, far over to the other side of the river. And then trudged with a tuneless whistle.

He came out of the gorge, and in sight of the sweep of fenced green where everything was changed. He expected to see young Alan somewhere handy on the farm, fencing in one of the nearer paddocks, but there was no sign of the boy. Then his eye picked up movement at a distance. Nance going down and into the whare by the creek. He hadn't known she tidied up for Alan during the day. It surprised him, all things considered, an unexpected point in her favour. She had become less conscientious a housekeeper as the years drifted. He walked, still taking his time. Now and then he stooped to pull out roadside weeds, mostly yellow ragwort. It was wicked how the stuff persisted, for all his effort to stamp it out, and crept back up from the gorge, from the world outside, like some creeping sickness carried by wheel or hoof. He kept his eye open for Alan, but still couldn't pick him up. He might have been in the tool-shed, of course, on some small repair, for the boy was occasionally useful with hammer or spanner there. But there was no sound, no echo, across the land. The farm was perfectly quiet, with cows shuffling across the far paddocks, and the grass soaking up the sun. As he neared home Ned struck off towards the

creek, and the whare. Nance might know where Alan was working, if she had half an interest in what happened around the
farm. He just hoped he didn't find the boy slacking because his
boss was out of sight. The whare stood, its door ajar, among the
long grass and wild potatoes of Ned's first garden, willows tall
with fresh leaf behind. The noisy creek buried his sounds as he
brushed through the grass, up to the step, and pushed the door
open wider.

'Nance,' he listened to himself say, too late. On the bed
Alan's body was pathetically thin and almost anguished between
Nance's upthrust knees. Her hands had left red marks on his
bony back. And all beneath those regiments of receptive thighs,
those corridors of glossy limbs through which Ned would never
wander. But the pair on the bed gave the lie, if he looked. It was
so grotesque, all hair and feet and clutching hands and angly
flesh. Only the sheets and blankets crushed and kicked to the
floor looked soft. Nance's thighs were wide and the boy's
shoulders quivering.

'Nance,' he said again, quieter. For he had to ensure he was
not sunk in some dream with leaden feet. He took a step closer to
them, though he would rather have not. 'Nance, you better get
up off there.'

It seemed reasonable.

But there was, of course, panic then.

'It wasn't me,' the boy had to say, quick on his skinny white
legs. His hands shot down to cover his difficulty. 'I only – '

Ned struck the boy just the once, sideways, between the jaw
and the neck. When he fell away, there was only Nance to be
seen, still sprawled, but more than enough to occupy the mind
wholly. She appeared to be making some effort to cover herself
with an inadequate towel. But her hands were unsure, her body
uncoordinated, and her eyes huge. Thus disposed, she looked for a
moment wildly like those pasted women above and around her,
also imperfectly covered, with whom she had evidently tried to
compete. Though she obviously could not. Compassion fluttered
in his throat like a dying bird.

'Christ, Nance,' he said. 'Christ, girl.'

His hands, however, were more articulate. He watched them
reach out to grab, wrench, or shake sense into her. Perhaps even
to strike, for all he knew. She cringed away. There was high
strange colour in her cheeks.

'Don't touch me,' she said. 'Don't touch me or I'll – '

But she did not appear to know what she would do. And when he started tugging her off the bed with his big hands, and she became heaving flesh and struggling limbs, what she actually did was begin to cough. Not alarmingly at first. He just let her drop to the floor, by way of experimental contempt. He still seemed to lack the conviction for anger. It was all just happening, regardless. And his naked wife was crumpled at his feet. He was not sure how he was supposed to handle things from this point on, he knew of no precedent. For a moment he was quite numb with indecision. Finally he spoke.

'Get up,' he uttered. To no effect, and he did not try to help her. Behind him the boy Alan was dressing furtively and fumblingly. The distraction was a relief.

'Get out,' he instructed Alan. 'Get all your things and get out. Wait for me outside.'

'It wasn't me. I only – '

'I don't want to hear.'

'She wanted – '

'Say any more and I'll have your guts for garters. Get your gear and get out.'

In terror the boy scratched about the room, recovering one thing and another from near and around Ned's feet. He didn't take long, his possessions seemed to be few. Then he was out. Nance was still collapsed and uncovered on the floor. Her coughing was more violent now, almost explosive. Ned stooped clumsily.

'Come on,' he said. 'Get dressed. We better see about all this. We better get it straight.'

He pushed her garments tentatively in her direction. She did not appear interested. She was totally absorbed by the behaviour of her erratic body, clinging frantically as it bucked.

'I can get away now,' she muttered, between coughs. 'That's what I want. That's all I want. You won't stop me now, will you?'

'Get dressed,' he said. He was groping on the floor, in some dream, with a naked woman. 'Get dressed and we'll get it all straight.'

'You couldn't stop me,' she said. 'Not even with the kid.'

There was hair all over her face.

203

'We'll see about that,' he promised. But he did not mean it as an offer. 'Get decent first.'

This plea seemed to have no appeal, not now she had begun, among tears and phlegm. 'You couldn't even prove the kid was yours,' she coughed bitterly. 'Not now.'

'You don't know what you're saying.' He knew then that he could get no lower than this uneven wooden floor. He could only scrabble, here, with this woman who had been Nance.

'I know what I'm saying, all right. You poor goat. How could you be sure of anything now? What about your old friend Nick? He could of had some kick left in him, for all you knew.'

It seemed she was determined to leave him nothing at all. But a convulsion overtook her before she could do more damage. If he had been going to strike her, the moment was gone. But he did start pulling her up roughly, and her head fell back, the tight muscles in her neck showing. That was when he saw the flecks of blood among the stuff which made her mouth shiny. He got her on to the bed again, but it seemed the coughing would never bloody stop. He covered her with a sheet, since he could think of nothing else. It was then he remembered his trapped vehicle. He went to the door. The boy stood a few yards away, waiting exactly as instructed, still shaken. Once again he tried to speak.

'I told you I'm not interested,' Ned insisted. 'It looks like we got to get this woman to a doctor. Or the hospital. You better come and help get the car moving.'

It was a year before they got to the car in the middle of the gorge, heaved it out of the ditch, and changed the wheel. Another year before they got back to the woman, dressed her decent and packed her into the car, on the way to the doctor.

Ned Livingstone did not get back to the farm with his son until late afternoon. He had collected Tim from school after delivering Nance and Alan to their separate futures. He didn't have much to say to the boy on the drive home, and made no explanations, since he had none himself.

'Where's my mother?' the kid asked, when they walked into the empty house.

'Away,' Ned told him. 'It looks like she will be away a while. It's hard to say.'

'She didn't say she was going,' said the kid in dismay.

'Well, she has gone. We don't know when she'll be back.'

Her lungs, or so the doctor seemed to think, would make the decision. At least one looked shot. The doctor couldn't understand why they had left it so late. It was no use Ned saying he'd never bloody known. Or that he'd never gone much on doctors anyway. It was really no use him saying anything. He could only watch while they rolled Nance along on a trolley from one part of the hospital to another, doctor and nurses hovering, until they told him there was not much point in his staying. Since his wife was, beyond argument.

'Where is Alan, then?' the boy asked, after a time.

'He is gone too. But he won't be back at all. He wasn't much use around this place.' Ned took a deep breath. 'So,' he added, 'there is just you and me now. Just you and me to look after each other.'

The boy didn't weep long for his mother, his curiosity soon died. He could accept what was, when it was sufficient, and he ate the thick jam sandwich his father made, and drank a glass of milk. When his stomach was satisfied, his eyes were distinctly less inquiring. He unhooked himself from his stool and ran after some interest of his own outside, while Ned went to chase up the herd for evening milking. He would need the kid soon, he thought, the way things were. Now Nance was no longer there to make objection, there was not much problem. He would have to get around to the kid soon anyway, there was leeway to make up.

It was a heavy evening after a heavy day, but Ned had no time to contemplate the burden. When he slapped the last cow out of the shed, and finished the separating, he walked back to the house through the dusk, and found the kid asleep on the couch in the dark of the cold kitchen. He would, he thought, have to organize things better than this. While the boy slept, Ned started a fire and fried bacon and eggs in a pan. He wasn't as proficient at the business as he might have been, and burned his hand with spitting fat. Then he woke his son. There was more warmth in the house, at least. Their plates were set on the table with a glass of fresh milk for the boy.

'Get it into you,' Ned said. 'You got some growing to do.'

The boy rubbed his eyes over the greasy meal. Then he looked up at his father.

'Go on, boy. Eat up, for Christ's sake.'

205

He did not mean to sound brutal, but he was tired. The day had become a numb thing in his gut. It seemed he dare not remember yet.

The boy began weeping again, and would not stop.

'Jesus,' Ned said, while he groped to console, and his own food grew cold. It seemed the day would never bloody end. He nursed his son on his muddy knee, and coaxed. 'Just the one egg, then,' he compromised, 'and a little bit of bacon.' He had never felt so helpless. 'Come on. I can't eat it for you too. You got to give your old man some help, don't you?'

At last he persuaded the boy to chew on something while the tears dried on his face. But Ned's triumph was small. By the time he got back to his own food it was quite congealed into cold fat. He ate, and the boy finicked, and the night was black on the windows.

'We can't have this every night,' he observed. 'We got to start out right by ourselves, don't we?'

His son was evidently not up to an answer.

'Never mind,' he added, without great conviction. 'We'll learn, you and me. Go and wash your face, then. And get your pyjamas.'

He knew that much about the business, at least. He would have to get hold of the rest. They probably both had a lot to learn.

'And your teeth,' he remembered, as the boy left the room. 'I think you got to clean your teeth too.'

He rose to stuff more wood in the fire. The dishes at least could be left. And as he sat before the stove on his haunches, warming his hands, he had a strange sense of storm passing over. He found himself listening in the quiet night, as if for stray winds left behind. But there was just the small voice saying, 'Dad.'

The boy offered himself in pyjamas, his face clean.

'All right,' he said, when he had his son ready for the night, 'now off to sleep quick. We'll get things straight tomorrow.'

With his son no longer about to occupy him, Ned was restless. He arranged himself in his usual evening position, feet up beside the stove, a newspaper in his hands, but changed his mind. He looked at his worn slippers to see how much longer they would last. He put more wood in the fire. He opened the back door and looked out into the night, as though to see if the house

206

had shifted, and shut it again. He hung up an oilskin which had fallen from a hook behind the door. He carried dishes absently from the table to the sink, and for the second time decided not to wash them. He tried to see out the black window but the night still seemed no different. He rolled a smoke and put the kettle on for a cup of tea. Finally he recognized what he wanted to do. He went into the boy's room, knelt down by the small shape in the narrow bed, and struck a match.

The sleepless boy's eyes fluttered open and shone. 'What's the matter?' he asked.

'Nothing,' his father said awkwardly. 'Nothing is the matter. I just come in to have a look at your face.'

'Is something the matter with my face? I washed it, like you said.'

'No, boy. There's nothing the matter with it. I just come to have a look at it, to see you was asleep.' This explanation did not sound quite right, but he left it there.

'It's hard to sleep,' the boy confessed.

Ned struck another match, still staring, and reached a hand around the back of the boy's head. His hair was soft. 'Then you must try harder,' he said. He struck a third match. The fact was he could see nothing but a child's face. Nothing, and certainly no one else.

'Why are you looking at me like that?' his son asked at last.

'Just to see you are all right.'

'I'm all right,' said the boy with surprising confidence.

'Yes,' said Ned Livingstone, though hestitantly, before he tucked the blankets down and left the room on quiet feet.

An hour later, when he thought the boy sure to be asleep, he laced on his boots with sudden decision, lit a lamp, and went outside. Shadows jumped huge in the sway of yellow light about his feet as he walked across the grass, around the garden, past the cackling fowls he had forgotten to feed, and through the pines. From a shed he removed a can of petrol. He continued until he came to the old whare by the creek. He scattered petrol through the place, along the floor and over the walls inside and outside, until he had no more. Then he set his lamp clear, on a stump, and put a match to a puddle of petrol at the door. The fire took quickly, around the door frame, spurting, snapping, and up into the roof. Soon the rest of the whare raced to join. There were volleys of sparks, then spinning explosions as the roof crumpled noisily. He remembered that he had

207

nearly broken a leg in a painful fall from the roof, while nailing down the corrugated iron, the year he went to war.

He looked to make sure there was no chance of the flame spreading, and then he walked back to the house. On his way he snuffed out the lamp. He had no need of it. The blaze, even as it diminished, lit the entire farm strangely, even the hills beyond. He saw his way back to the house in the pale red light.

Part Two

Fathers and Sons

Twelve:

THERE WERE NO MOUNTAINS WITH SNOW, UNLESS IN THE SOUTH, where he had never been. There were hills though, hills heavy and green, and veined with dark bush. He thought he might never grow tall enough to see over those hills.

Te Ika school lay in a bend of the river. The school could be found by way of the town's main street just before it struck across the railway track and became the highway north to the city. Or it could be found by way of swingbridges, and a long dawdle along the riverbank. There were oak trees along the riverbank, maple, sycamore, chestnut, and willows trailing in the water. In this lower part of the river there were tyres and tins and giant eels. Some kids said they had seen them twelve feet long and thicker than your leg. The school was half hidden behind tall poplars. The buildings were high-gabled, wooden and austere, surrounded by asphalt and lawn, and beyond trimmed hedges was a rugby field. There was also a paddock where country children left their horses, if they did not travel by school bus. The classrooms, with their high windows, were dim and chilly in winter, with blackboards all around, on which *I must not* might be printed twenty, fifty or a hundred times over. It depended. Swearing was a hundred times over, fighting fifty, and spitting twenty. And there was always the cane, if improvement was slow, on backside or legs.

After school was best. After school he did not have to hurry home. He did not go by swingbridge and riverbank, but along the main street and then through the back of the town. Some of the older shops still had creaky boardwalks in front, though the streets were paved now. There were two blacksmiths noisy with hammer and anvil and fire and bellows, where horses were shod. There were garages, petrol pumps, and mechanics in oily overalls. And scrap yards, bottle merchants, and the printing press which rumbled out the *Te Ika Gazette* twice a week. Some houses, in the back streets, were not really homes at all. They had signs saying 'Guests Taken' or 'Private Hotel', and tired-looking men peering out between the lace on the windows. There were some buildings empty and open for exploring, though you had to be quick if someone saw.

No school, of course, was best of all. There was the riverbank then, and the swimming holes, and the hills above the town.

Home changed. Once it had been a tiny place at the lime-works end of town, a long walk from school. It was near the railway track and shook with trains passing. There were pad-docks around, and cows. And loud booms when explosive went off at the limeworks quarry. Men going home from the lime-works in the evening were dusty white. They walked or bicycled home soon after the siren sounded, and then everything was quiet, except for the trains. The house water came from an out-side tap on a tank which caught water from the iron roof, and sometimes froze over in winter. There was enough water for drinking and cooking, but not enough for washing clothes. Clothes had to be washed down at the river, and his mother went down there two or three times a week. Maori women washed down there too, and strung the clothes over the scrub to dry.

Once a man came from off the road. He had come from somewhere south with a bag tied to his back. He wanted a drink of water and he wondered if the shed in the next paddock was used. He was a swaggie. He said things was tough on the road. He took a gift of tomatoes and eggs and made a fire for himself by the shed where he planned to sleep. He cooked him-self food and made tea in a billy and when it was dark sat look-ing into the fire. In the morning his fire was cold ashes and he was gone off somewhere into a different part of the country. The boy wondered where.

His mother said you didn't see many like that around now, not now there was work.

His father had work. Work was something you had when you were big. His father worked in the limeworks and then on the railways. After work he was tired, and not to be pestered. He would sit by the stove and pull off his boots and read the newspaper. Sometimes he sighed and said it was getting hard to make bloody sense of the world. Then he would just look into the fire and put more wood into it until dinner was ready. But he was still not to be pestered. And his mother would be putting the baby to bed.

After a while they moved to another house. It was right in town and better and warmer in winter, and they did not have to go outside for water, or take washing to the river. It was nearer school too, and he did not have to walk so far. The house was up a bit, on the side of a hill, and you could look over tall ferny trees, some of the river and part of the town. Grape vines clung to the wall of the house, heavy with fruit in late summer, and a lemon tree grew in the garden, a shady place in the heat. In front of the house was a lawn where his sister learned to walk, and soon she was talking too.

He was getting bigger, though it seemed too slow. He knew when he was happy or hungry, but otherwise thought he did not understand much. People came from the city, passing through, to talk to his father. These people had different names and different faces, but mostly they would say the same things. They would talk about war coming, Russia, the working class. Sometimes they would argue loudly with his father. After they had gone his father was often bad-tempered for a while.

Another person who came from the city was his uncle. Uncle Ben would stay longer than the others, and talk to the boy and buy ice-creams. If it was summer he would take the boy swimming in the river. His mother would say he must be nice to Ben, because Ben had a difficult life. Uncle Ben was a gentle man, with sad eyes. He would talk about things with his father too. And sometimes then his eyes grew sadder, and even trembled, if his father spoke too loud. The boy would feel sorry for Ben if his father got angry. Because Ben would look almost hurt enough to cry, though he didn't. Once he heard his uncle say to his mother, 'Well, I suppose you people know what you are doing, living here.'

'We do,' his mother said.

'I can see it's a pleasant enough place for the children to grow up. But as for the rest – '

'The rest is peace and quiet,' his mother said. 'More than I ever expected.'

There wasn't much to understand. Ben was soon gone again. Sometimes his father said, 'Let's go for a walk.'

Those times were good. He would walk with his father in the

213

early evening. His father had leaflets in his hand. When they came to a new street, he would peel off some for the boy.

'You put those in letter boxes that side of the street,' he said. 'I'll put mine in this side.'

At the end of the street, when they had finished, he would say, 'You're a good kid.'

They might keep walking, then, and see Mary Leary. Mary Leary wasn't really his aunt, but she had looked after him once, when his mother was sick, and liked to be called auntie. She lived alone. She had orange drinks and a biscuit barrel, and she would give the boy a book to read or a toy to play with, while she talked to his father. She also had a plum tree which he climbed. She would give his father blackberry wine. Sometimes he heard what they were saying.

'She's never been the same, Mary,' his father might say. 'Not since that second kid.'

'You must be patient, Bill.'

'Patience is one thing. But it goes on.'

'Time is a healer in these things. In most things. You see.'

'I can't see much healing done in different beds. Because that's how it is.'

'Then I'm sorry, Bill. I can't say more.'

'She always had a strange streak. But then there's no accounting for women.'

'Or men, sometimes.'

'True. But what I mean is, she got things more or less her own way, in the end. Anyway she seems to think this town suits. So why this? Why don't things come right?'

'Perhaps they will,' Mary Leary said gently.

They might have noticed, then, that the boy was listening. For the subject changed. There wasn't much to understand. And he was soon walking home with his father in the dark night. His father would take his hand. His father was cheerful after blackberry wine at Mary Leary's house. He would joke, sometimes. And point out stars in the sky.

'And that,' he would say, 'is the Southern Cross up there. Those four stars. They used to use it, once, to find this country when they was sailing out here. So you better remember it. If you ever stop seeing the Cross you know you're lost, too far from home.'

Or, 'They reckon men might travel up among the stars one

214

day. Even live on other worlds. You might see it. Not me, thank Christ. This world's enough of a problem for me.'

And they walked home with a sense of the problem vast and obstinate around them. His mother would be quiet when they came in, and not ask where they had been, though she might have things to say about the boy being kept out so late.

Soon there was war, and not just in Spain. He knew not only because his father shook his head over the newspaper more in the evenings, but also because at school the games were different. They were war games, with Germans. Before long there were men in khaki in the town.

If anyone came from the city now, the arguments in the front room with his father were louder. 'I'll make up my own bloody mind about it,' he heard his father say. 'I made up my own mind about the last one, and I'll make up my own mind about this one. One day these Nazis are monsters, killing workers everywhere, the next day you tell us not to fight them on account of their signing some piece of paper with Russia.'

'It's a question of tactics,' one of these visitors said.

'I've heard that shit before too. And always before some sell out.'

'Capitalism would kill workers here too, given the chance.'

'You're telling the wrong man.'

'We know you've had things rough, Bill. But the fact is you been too long out of touch. You're a bloody anarchist. We don't want to expel you. People remember your name.'

'Then tell them Bill Freeman expelled himself.'

'Why, Bill? On account of you not having the stamina to see the thing through?'

'No. On account of me not being Russian.'

'Same thing, near enough.'

'Then too bloody bad. Just say I had to be myself.'

After that, all he understood for certain was that when he walked with his father in the evenings they no longer delivered leaflets. Parcels stopped arriving from the city. People stopped coming too, though that didn't altogether end his father's bad temper. In the evenings, even if tired, his father would now settle down before the fire with some book instead of with the newspaper. 'History's got its consolations,' he would say to Ian's mother, who perhaps was busy with her own.

If he walked in the dusk with his father, they went more or

215

less straight to Mary Leary's, her orange drinks and blackberry wine.

'It's been a long road,' his father said to Mary, 'and I seem to have got bugger all to show at the end of it. And it seems, the way they tell it, I am just another turncoat after all.'

'You have a wife,' Mary observed, 'and two fine children. Count your blessings, Bill.'

'Sometimes even that's not easy.'

'She's a good woman, Bill. And don't forget it. And your children couldn't have a finer mother.'

'I can see,' his father said, 'I need you around, Mary. You keep a man sane.'

At school things changed. Men teachers went away for a while, and returned disguised as soldiers to say goodbye. The favourite game was still killing Germans along the riverbank though it wasn't fun if no one wanted to be German. But there was still another game. Children learned from their fathers about his father, or overheard something. They circled him with confused messages, chanting, 'Your father's a German,' they would say, but he denied it. 'Your father's a spy,' they said, but he denied it. 'Your father's a traitor,' they said, but he was soon out of breath. 'German, spy, traitor,' he heard. 'He's a colmunist. A fifth colmunist. We know.' 'And they stuck him in prison once. My Dad says. They stuck him in prison once, and they'll stick him in again. About time too, my Dad says, all these colmunists ought to be locked up.'

Sooner or later he had to fight, first one and then another. That was the idea.

It was not a regular game, more one of desperation, when Germans were reluctant to volunteer. And it was always possible, each time it happened, that it might be the last. He could hope. His knuckles, as he grew better at the game, were often as bruised and scratched as his face. At home he pleaded accidents. Sometimes his shirt was torn. That was more difficult to explain.

'He is growing into a roughneck,' he overheard his mother complain. 'He needs more control. I think he is getting hurt in fights, though he tells me different when he comes home.'

'Then he will have to learn to fight better,' was all his father said. 'If he doesn't learn now, he will only have to learn later.'

'What sort of advice would that be from a father?'

'It is not advice. It is fact.'

'Is that the sort of world you want, then?'

'It is the sort of world there is. It has nothing to do with what I want.' He paused. 'Nothing has anything to do with what I want. Christ knows you ought to know that by now.'

His father's voice was strange. He did not know why. It was the first winter of the war. The lawn was spiky with frost in the mornings, and the newspaper had photographs of soldiers in small boats coming from a place called Dunkirk. In winter he wore his boots to school, crackling through icy puddles.

It was the lunch hour. He was between the river and the horse paddock, well out of sight of the school buildings, within the chanting circle again. Sometimes he thought it might all be a dream. For his feet did have a nightmare heaviness, and his arms. Feet scuffed through soggy heaps of rotting winter leaves. Now he fought only because it seemed he must. Around and among the high bare trees, through snapping sticks, banging, battering. He thought his head might burst, or his lungs. His small hope, that it would end, grew smaller still. As despair scratched in his throat, he discovered the advantage of seeking vulnerable places, eyes or neck, and kicking up between the legs, learning that much anyway, and more effective than he had been. He heard the chant, 'Dirty, he's fighting dirty,' and it seemed now he was fighting two or three at once. His head struck back against a trunk and his eyes, already blank and bright with pain, were pounded. His bones felt chipped by violent kicks. They were all about, all at once, excited by the excuse they had now. His teeth cracked together, then again with his tongue between, and there was a taste of blood.

Suddenly everything began falling apart. He was curiously free. He thought perhaps the bell had rung for the end of the lunch hour, and he had not heard.

But the others were flung and falling.

He did not know the boy who had newly appeared. He was bigger, older. Lean and fair, with an angry face. But he had seen him before. He was, this boy, two or three classes ahead. Now he cuffed the last of the smaller boys away.

'What's going on here?' he demanded. 'I seen you at him before.'

'His father's a dirty traitor,' someone breathless pleaded.

'Does that mean you got to kill him?'

'He's dirty like his father. He fights dirty.'

'With you all on to him, I suppose he's got to fight some way.

217

Now get out before I belt you myself.' He paused. 'You hear what I said?'

The others were unwilling. And still unashamed. They shone with the heat of virtue.

'What's wrong with your father anyway?' the new boy asked. He knelt beside Ian, whose tongue was thick and painful.

'Nothing. Nothing's wrong with him.'

'His father's a jailbird. A rotten colmunist. My Dad says.'

'I told you to get out before I belt you. You want me to start now? I bet there's none of you would fight for your father. Not unless you were in a crowd. Now get moving.'

They began to shift away, but with reluctance, on their just feet. They looked back with silent complaint.

The new boy helped Ian up from the roots of the tree where he had fallen. 'You hurt much?'

'Not much.' But his eyes throbbed, and his shins. He felt queer.

'They were really knocking you about, weren't they?'

Ian nodded, tasting his tongue.

'Think you'll be all right?'

'I'm all right now,' Ian insisted.

'What about trying to get up?'

He tried. His legs were wobbly. 'I could have fought them one at a time,' he said. 'But it wasn't fair.'

'No,' said the bigger boy. 'I saw that.'

'It isn't true about my father anyway.'

'I don't expect it is.'

'He's just different, that's all. My mother says he always stands up for his rights. He argues.'

'Probably like my father. He argues too.'

'My mother says they only put him in jail because he didn't shut up when he was supposed to shut up. That's all.'

'Well, they never put my old man in jail. But I expect that's because he mainly argues with himself, most of the time. We're on a farm and there's no one to listen much. Except me.'

'I don't really know much about it. Except I know he's not like what they say.'

'You don't want to listen to what they say.'

'I have to, if they're all around.' He paused. 'Then I fight.'

'Good on you. But there's too many. If it happens again, you better come and find me.'

'I don't know your name, even.'

218

'Tim Livingstone. I'm usually easy to find. Except after school. Then I have to catch a bus straight home.'

'Mine's Ian Freeman.'

But the taller boy did not appear to think this relevant. 'So you feel all right now,' he said.

'I feel better,' Ian agreed. And he watched the other move away among the bare trees and thick humus of the riverbank.

That night two or three boys, who evidently felt cheated of their game, tripped him into a patch of mud on his way home. He decided, before he faced his parents, to go to Mary Leary's place to clean up. With Mary he could be more free than with his parents. She had fewer distractions, or consolations, and listened to what he said. So that her white cottage, with the canaries whistling beyond the silver birches, was like another home. That afternoon, while she cleaned him up and disinfected and dressed his scratches, he told her everything, more or less.

'And you stood up to them?' she asked. 'On account of your father?'

'I fought them,' he said. 'Until today, this boy came along to help.'

He couldn't understand why she was tearful. She might have taken the blows, the hurt.

'Dear God,' she said. 'Haven't you told anyone about this before?'

He shook his head.

'But the teachers,' she said.

'That would be telling tales.'

'Then your mother and father.'

'That's no good either. Anyway they always seem worried by enough things.'

'Dear God,' she said again, strangely. She had become clumsy and groping. 'Suffer little children.'

'I think I better go,' he said, panicky.

'Then I'll tell them,' she said.

'No.' He was firm. 'You mustn't.'

'Why not? They ought to know.'

But he could not explain his fear. Perhaps it was of an even greater commitment. And of an inadequacy. This was something his own, he did not know why.

'You must promise not to,' he said. And added, 'Or I'll never tell you anything again.'

She appeared unmoved by the threat, but perplexed. 'Tell me,' she said, 'what do you know about your father, really? Anything?'

'Not much,' he confessed.

'Don't you think you'd better know, if you're going to fight his battles?'

He shook his head. It wasn't clear. Very little was clear.

'I'll get you an orange drink and a biscuit,' she said, 'and then you're going to listen to me.' She paused, and rearranged her face with the help of a handkerchief. 'It wasn't as if I ever knew him in the old days, you see. But my hubby was alive then, and Gus and I used to hear your father speak in the unemployed days. You're growing up in a time where ordinary people are looked after, for a change. Where there's jobs and houses, and money around for everyone, and hospitals for the sick. It's all different. And you know why? Because of men like your father, who weren't afraid to shout and fight. So you sit there, son, and listen to me.'

It seemed he had no choice. He settled for an orange drink and Mary's biscuit barrel. Less than for learning something, though he might have. And it all appeared part of a bargain, if his secret was to be kept. Later he got her promise.

'I still think you ought to say something yourself,' she said, when they parted.

He considered this again on his way home through the back streets of the town. But at home his mother was cooking, and complaining about his late arrival and the condition of his clothes. His father, just home from work, was involved with the newspaper. And his sister wanted him to read a story. 'I see,' said his father, before using the newspaper to light a fire, 'they're talking about Charlie Higgins being heaved out of the War Cabinet. On account of him still insisting on conscription of wealth along with conscription of manpower. I thought the old sod would know when he was safe.'

His mother had nothing to say.

And his own moment had gone. He would never tell them now. He went to find a story to read to his sister.

It was almost the end of it anyway. For some time afterwards, when she wasn't on duty at the hospital, Mary Leary met him at the gates of the school when he was leaving. The lunch hours, perhaps because of the threat of the Livingstone boy, became safer too; Ian had no need to call on him again. In any case the war soon changed, with the Russians also fighting the Germans, and it seemed colmunists or communists were no longer so dirty, or such traitors. His father told Uncle Ben, down on a visit from the city, that he had been right all along, not that he cared much now, one way or the bloody other. And it was true that his father seemed happier, these days, reading his books instead of talking to people.

There was, though, one night different. It was a Friday night, and Ian walked with his father through the shopping crowds along a main street of brightly lit display windows. Then his father stopped, and he stopped too. Across the street, on the lawn beneath the town clock, was a noisy crowd. Someone was up high on a ladder, talking. They crossed the street together, his father taking his hand. 'We better see what's going on,' he said. 'Probably just some Bible basher.'

The man on the stepladder had a Bible, all right, but he wasn't bashing it. He just held it close to his chest, or heart, as if afraid of someone taking that talisman. He spoke so softly that it was hard to hear what he said above the jeers. At the foot of the stepladder stood a solemn young man, perhaps his son, in a dark suit. He looked pale and frightened. After a while Ian heard something of what the man on the stepladder said. He was talking about love and peace.

The noise around them grew ugly then. 'Throw him in the bloody river,' someone said. 'He's insulting our boys in uniform.'

'Get the police,' said someone else. 'They ought to shoot the bugger.'

There was a lurch forward, with people bumping each other, and the man on the stepladder toppling. There were fists high.

'You get out,' his father instructed. 'Get well away. Quickly.' He shoved his son.

He stayed close enough to see his tall father break through the crowd, pulling and pushing to the centre. He heard the sound of the stepladder breaking up and splintering as it was kicked about. And there were torn pages of Bible fluttering pale under the street lights. He wondered about his father, and thought about the men in the centre, and felt sick. The young one had looked so frightened. Perhaps he would see pieces of the men thrown too. He wanted to look away, but couldn't.

Then the crowd swung, shifting enough for him to see his father again, arguing, standing in front of the two men, his arms spread to protect them. The young man had been hit,

221

and held a white handkerchief, quickly staining, to his bloody nose. The older man's shirt collar was torn, and his tie twisted. The crowd grew quieter, though Ian could not hear what his father was arguing about with the people around.

His father then seemed to make up his mind suddenly and started dragging the two men with him through the bystanders. One or two people shouted, but most might have been too startled to protest.

'Now look,' he at last heard his father saying, 'get out of here fast. Back to your farm or wherever you come from.'

'We have our message,' the older man objected. 'We – '

'You're lucky you weren't lynched,' his father said.

'But our message. We – '

'You're among the deaf. Don't talk to me about bloody messages.'

'You don't understand.' The older man became stiff.

'I do. That's my bloody trouble. And what you better understand is that you might easy have gone into the river tonight. And still might, if you don't pull your finger out. You got a car or something?'

'We have a vehicle,' the man conceded.

'Then get into it and put your foot down.'

People were now beginning to follow and press behind, bickering. Ian felt his father's hand on his shoulder. 'I told you to go away, son,' he said. Otherwise the boy had no rebuke.

They stood beside the two men while they climbed into their small pickup truck and backed out into the street. The younger one was still bleeding. The last Ian saw of them was the pale handkerchief in the gloom of the cab. Around them the crowd argued and parted. And a constable arrived, too late.

They crossed to the other side of the street again, to finish their Friday night walk through the town, and buy ice cream. His father evidently had nothing to say about it all.

'Why did you help those two men?' the boy asked at length.

'Why?' his father said. 'Why?' He laughed. 'Because they was such poor fools, I expect. Because they was such poor fools like the rest of us.'

This was not very satisfactory. But he had learned not to persist in asking his father why, however often tempted.

'There is,' his father went on, 'some sense to be got from human beings sometimes. But I can't say I ever found much of it myself. I hope you have better luck, boy.'

Later that evening, tight in his bed, he felt unfairly young and small. For he couldn't even fit together, now, the things Mary Leary told him. He wished he knew his father. Or had, instead, one he could understand. It wouldn't have been so bad getting in fights for one he could understand.

He saw the mountains with snow, in the end, without his father. It happened that when he was about ten years old his grandfather Campbell down on the Coast became ill, and his mother travelled down the country to nurse him. She took along the boy and his sister. They travelled through the night by train, then another night by boat, and endlessly by train again. The boy made believe he was in other countries. He saw towns and seaside cities peaceful in pale sunlight, and wild coast where surf boomed. And wide tangled rivers, gentle lakes, bleached plains and finally the mountains. Under these mountains, in a town tucked away in bush, was an old man dying. It was too late to know him now. So he had to make the best of what the mountains told him, marching away into the distance, perhaps all the way to the frozen south pole, though books told him different.

He could climb hills and high trees to consider the mountains. For they did not always answer back. Then his mother would call, or his sister pester.

Uncle Ben arrived too. The boy was about his grandfather's house that day. His mother was tearful when Ben arrived. Ben looked tired and pale. He went straight to his father's bedside and sat there, his head in his hands, all that night and the next day too. Until grandfather Campbell had nothing more to say, and was dead.

So there was a funeral. Ben and five other men carried the coffin through the showery afternoon. The green hills beyond the cemetery were streaked with sunlight, and the mountains, those he could see, could not have been more white. There was a huge crowd. A red flag flapped on his coffin. A man who spoke at the graveside said his grandfather had been a great teacher and grand fighter. His mother wept. Ben took a shovel and dumped dirt down into the grave. Then other men followed and did the same. It was, his mother explained, the custom of the Coast.

Then they journeyed home again. The mountains diminished behind. Soon there were just his own hills; his father was waiting

on the platform of the railway station. After the greetings, the
kisses, the tears, the boy's father bent to him. 'Well, son,' he
said, 'you been a long way. Did you see much?'

'Not much,' he said. 'Only the mountains.'

But he could not make them appear relevant. At least not so
his father would notice.

At home, unpacking, his mother observed, 'The place is
looking neat, Bill.'

And his father said, 'I can't take all the credit. Mary was
around, now and then, to keep the place tidy.'

'Mary?'

'And to cook me the odd meal. She's got a big heart, Mary.
What I mean is, she's always there when you need her.'

'Evidently,' his mother said.

'Come on, Peg. No tears again. You're tired.'

'Did you have to?'

'Did I have to what?'

'Have someone here, while I was gone.'

'Christ almighty,' his father said. 'Things are what they are.
I didn't organize life.'

After a time the boy walked outside. He looked across river
and town. And at his own hills again; he could not believe that
anything ever really happened here, or would. Yet they inched
taller again around him while he watched. Nothing was explained, but everything was plausible.

He hardly spoke to the boy called Tim Livingstone again. The
other, though, sometimes took notice. 'Hello, young Freeman,'
he usually said. Sometime he just smiled. That was all. Before
long he was out of sight altogether, moved on to high school.

It was not important. He had friends now who would share
his fights if he had them. And if he had them, they were for
his own reasons, they were his own fights. Not that there were
many, unless on the football field. He played in the school
rugby team with his friends. Sam Kahu, a chunky Maori boy
from a poor and swampy farm just outside town, was one.
Cedric Black, whose father ran a hardware store, another. And
Fred Saunders, from a tribe of brothers and sisters on a father-
less farm, a third. They were not much alike, other than in
their football jerseys, out on the field; they did not play to lose.

In time they also moved on to high school. By then the war
was ended with howling sirens, ringing bells, and detonators ex-

ploding under a railway engine. At school they were lined up to sing and pray, then given the freedom of the main street to watch the town brass band march up and down until its drunken members began at last to fall. At home his father was quiet.

The end of the war was soon less important than being alone again in the corridors of the new school. It was something he hadn't expected. But his friends, Sam Kahu, Cedric Black and Fred Saunders, moved together into the agricultural course at the school, into a different classroom from his own. While they studied the advantages in clover pasture, he pursued French verbs without enthusiasm, and made do with the football they still shared.

Now and then he saw Tim Livingstone and was again acknowledged. It was now more than five years since the one occasion when they had really spoken, and it did not seem likely that they would have anything to say to each other again. The Livingstone boy, it seemed, lived with his widower father on a farm some miles out of town. He was bright at school and teachers had their expectations. He was also a prefect, and a powerful forward in the school's first fifteen. A large athletics cup on which his name was engraved stood in a school corridor. His distinction wasn't so much that he was different. It was that he was ordinary, only more so. Younger boys might aspire.

So Ian was allowed to feel a glow, now, if Tim Livingstone selected him for a smile or a word among others his own age. After his first game of the new rugby season he found Tim Livingstone, clad for a senior game, waiting for him as he left the field. 'Good,' he told Ian crisply. 'Very nice teamwork.'

It was Sam Kahu who had scored the tries, Ian who had made the breaks to send Sam over.

'And I see you do your brawling on the football field now,' the other added. 'You were lucky the referee didn't see that punch-up.'

'I was held.'

'You might have been. But you looked pretty fierce to me. As if you just had to belt someone, sooner or later. But I suppose if you have to swing punches, it's better out there than on a riverbank.'

His voice was dry; he moved on.

It was the only reference the other boy ever made to the past. Ian preferred not to remember anyway. He had learned to become inconspicuously part of a team, uneasily at one with

225

others. He might have been fervent about his football, but it was less religion than refuge. He would sooner make breaks for Sam Kahu than go on his own for the line. If his triumphs were known best to himself, then so were his failures. He didn't want to be caught outside again, outside and alone, or inside some other and equally vicious chanting circle. He had no wish to risk it either, for he knew that in the long run he would have no chance of winning; he was not the kind. To stand out was to be vulnerable, in the classroom or on the rugby field, and to merge almost painless. His magpie interest in his father's books and magazines gave him, in general knowledge, an advantage which he seldom used in the classroom, though he could at times be provoked. It depended on the subject at issue, or the teacher, but afterwards he had regrets. He could not burn outwardly with relevance; that was a fire he lit within. He didn't need to prove anything.

Tim Livingstone, meanwhile, became someone to pity. Towards the end of Ian's first year at the school there was an accident. And Tim did not return to school until the following year. He had, it seemed, finished his term as school hero. The doctors had stitched his skin and set his bones but he walked with a limp. He could not play rugby again, or earn the engraving of his name on silver cups. He no longer had even a spectator's interest in these things; he used sport time in, of all places, the art room, where the teacher was interested in him. And in that room, after a time, a wall was hung with some pale, pleasant water-colours bearing the name Livingstone. The art teacher used them as examples, clearly proud. Tim Livingstone continued to limp his way around the school. He may have been deprived, but his expression did not concede it; his expression did not really concede anything at all. He could smile when the occasion demanded. He was, after all, still a fair, good-looking boy with a polite manner. And still really quite ordinary, apart from his uneven gait, and a pale blue scar, travelling up from his throat and across part of his jaw, which also told of the accident. Ian, though still acknowledged, kept a distance, intimidated by the pressure of sympathy; he could not imagine Tim Livingstone wanting sympathy.

Then pity became mystery. The Livingstone boy vanished from school between one day and the next. The sequence of things was never clear because, among other things, he was on the point of becoming a school hero again, in a more minor way, for having won some art competition for schools the length of the country. At first it was said his father had made him leave school. Then it was reported that he had even cleared out from his father's farm. And gone to the city to take his prize money. He never came back. Nothing was announced officially within the school. The headmaster evidently felt the affair brought the school no credit after all. And it was made more embarrassing by publicity in newspapers. At school Tim Livingstone ceased to exist, apart from some soon forgotten stories, his name on the cup for athletics, and one or two paintings in the art room. They were still there, though no longer so prominent, when Ian was in his last year at the school.

By that time most of his older friends had dropped out. Sam Kahu was occupied trying to improve his parents' run-down farm, the farm all the other Kahu boys deserted sooner or later. Cedric Black, who had always been slow at school anyway, now served behind the counter of his father's hardware store. Fred Saunders helped his older brother milk the Saunders herd. In the rugby season they still saw each other often enough, at training nights, and Saturday club games. He could be jealous of their freedom. He had few friends among those of his classmates measuring themselves as schoolteachers, accountants, doctors and lawyers.

His mother took it as certain that he would be moving on to university. 'You can stay with Ben in the city,' she said. 'That way, your living expenses won't be so high. We can't give you as much financial help as we would like. But with Ben's help, and some holiday work, you should be able to manage. I know Ben is keen to have you up there.'

Ian had less certainty. Ben, though his only distant relative of account, had become a fitful presence at the margin of his life. He had become more strange and bleakly solitary, with the years, in his untidy bachelor cottage. These days Ben worked as a landscape gardener around the city, laying crazy pavement and digging flower beds. In grubby boots and old clothes, pushing a wheelbarrow or forking compost, he looked relaxed enough. Ian could not really associate this dour labourer with the poet his mother saw and never really allowed him to forget. 'Ben's different,' his mother insisted. There was, of course, no doubt about that. The problem was that Ian did not want to be different, even by association; his anonymity had been won too painfully and well. He really could not imagine himself, with his strange uncle, in that vine-hung cottage. He couldn't even begin to see it.

'I know your company will do Ben good,' his mother added, and her secret was more or less out.

'Yes,' he replied at length, 'all right. We'll see.'

'What do you mean?' she said. 'It's the only practical way, if you want to go on to university.'

'That's it, you see. I don't know that I want to go. I haven't made up my mind.'

'But you can't stay in this town. There's nothing here for you, when you've finished school.'

'I don't know yet. I might find something.'

'Here?' She seemed appalled. 'What is there here?'

'Life. At least most people seem to think so.'

'Your father and I made our home here because we had to, because there wasn't anywhere else. It wasn't an easy thing for your father to lose himself among other men. But he had to. You don't have to.'

'I get along all right here,' he argued. 'I have friends.'

'You can't waste yourself, not now. You have a responsibility to yourself. And to your father, to do something decent with your life. Otherwise what has all his effort, and all these years, been for?'

'It's my own life,' he insisted. 'In the end it has to be.'

She was wordless.

He still visited Mary Leary in her cottage near the hospital on occasion, though no longer with his father. She was a gentle fixture in their lives. Sometimes she came to visit, and brought gossip and pickles and jam. If his father still went alone to see Mary, it was not obvious. But then nothing had ever been obvious, or altogether understandable. Ian usually found sympathy with Mary. The next time he saw her, she sighed and said, 'I hear you're being difficult again.'

He was inclined not to dispute it. But as a matter of form he answered, 'Not really.'

'You have your parents worried. This obstinacy of yours. It seems you refuse to see what's good for you.'

'It's just that I don't like having my mind made up for me,' he said, 'and my life planned.'

'There's people,' she said, 'who'd have given their right arms to better their minds at university. For a man like your father, it was impossible, some dream. Think how he would have used the chance. And now you – ' She appeared at loss. 'I can't believe it.'

'You'll have to.' He felt more stubborn than ever, though he had really come to no decision. 'Mary,' he pleaded, 'don't you go on at me too. I've been getting enough at home lately.'

'Too soft,' she said. 'That's the trouble. You don't know what hardship is any more, or striving. When I think of what your father went through to put you where you are now, the world at your feet, and you turn your back.'

'Mary,' he said. 'Please.'

But her disgust was large. She turned away trembling. It seemed he would find no comfort anywhere, if he persisted in trying to be heard. So he did not persist. He learned the use of silence. His parents argued themselves into despair. He was surprised, and often unnerved, by how hard he could become. Nor did he try Mary Leary for consolation again. Her first concern was to make his father's life tolerable. His mother was no different. The two women, in their different ways, worked at the same thing. They worked at making whatever it was his father had done have some meaning. And Ian, in wanting to make his own life tolerable, had become a threat. He could trust neither of them. He could trust very little other than his own instinct to survive, which so far appeared seldom to have been astray. Survival meant choice, his own. Otherwise he was nothing. Or someone else, someone who existed merely to give point to another's life. The idea was at first a rough vast shape in his mind; he had to whittle at it to find what lay inside. And he still couldn't express it entirely, though he tried when he talked to Sam Kahu. Ian now often stayed on Sam's farm, and hunted with him in the hills beyond Te Ika. Sam had become a good six feet tall, with powerful arms and an attractive smile. His intelligence was really as sharp off the rugby field as on, but it seemed, sometimes irritatingly, that he preferred not to make this obvious. He was certainly not much help in conversation. When Ian confided in him, he spoke slowly.

'Your parents probably know best,' he said.

'Do yours?' Ian challenged.

Sam shrugged. 'Usually. Your old man, he's been around. He knows a lot.'

'That's not the point.'

'I don't know. If you didn't think so too, what would you be worried about now?'

'Who said I was?'

Sam just smiled.

To make it worse, Ian heard himself saying, 'They're just determined to make me feel guilty, that's all.'

Sam continued to smile. He was really no help at all. 'Would university kill you?' he asked finally.

'It's not that. You know perfectly well.'

'Then you tell me.'

'It's making up my own mind.' But he had grown tired of the sound of those words, and knew no others.

Sam laughed. 'Well, then, I'll tell you what I'll do. I'll help you with a job. You can cut my scrub and mend my fences if you can't find anything in the town.'

'Don't worry. I'll find something.'

He did. Towards the end of that last school year he arrived home with the news that he had a job as junior reporter on the *Te Ika Gazette*.

'For the holidays?' his mother asked hesitantly. 'Until you go up to the city?'

'For the next year,' he replied. 'And probably a year or two more.'

The silence in the house was long.

'I won't be wasting my time,' he explained. 'I'll be learning something.'

'Learning what?' his father said.

'A job,' he said. 'Just a job.'

'As the Romans said, when they nailed Christ to the cross.'

'That's a pretty big idea of the local rag. It doesn't count for much.'

'And nor will you.'

'That's my business,' he told his father. 'You don't understand.'

His mother, in considerable disarray, had left the room. In the past she had been present to soften the confrontations between father and son. Or, at least, the rehearsals.

'I think I understand, all right. I think I understand that you'd sooner sell yourself for sweet bugger all rather than risk your neck in the world. And peddle someone else's cheap little lies rather than hurt yourself sorting out the truth. I think I understand that you're gutless.'

230

'I'm sorry, but I don't feel obliged to count for anything.'

'That's what I mean. Gutless is the best way to say it.'

'It's no use talking to you.'

'You can try. Tell me more.'

'I'll be learning to use words, at least.'

'I never noticed you having difficulty.'

'It might be something to keep me afloat later.'

'Or sink you now.'

'You see,' he said. 'How can I talk to you?'

'I'm still listening.'

'Even if I go to university, I still have to find something to do with my life, don't I?'

'If that's the best you can tell me, you might as well cut your throat now.' His father shook his head. 'Find something to do with your life? Jesus Christ. A man worth the name knows. He knows. You hear? He knows. The rest is just picking your way through the garbage to get what you want.'

'That's what you did?'

'More or less. Yes.'

'And what did you get?'

'You, by the look of it. So much the worse for me.'

There was really nothing more to be found in that direction. But they still faced each other as if some victory were possible, and not just more damage done.

'It's impossible,' Ian said. 'You say you're listening but you're not. Perhaps you're really arguing with someone else. Someone back in the past. Where you belong, probably.' This attempt at cruelty surprised him, but he seemed short on defences now.

His father, however, didn't take long to consider that.

'And I suppose you live in the future?'

'No, I wouldn't say that altogether.'

'Then what in God's name would you say?'

'Well, for one thing I'm not sure there's a future to live in, the way things are going. You ought to know; you talk as if you're eavesdropping on the end of the world every time you pick up a newspaper.'

'So nothing's worthwhile any more. Is that it? You don't really need to make an effort? Or have any principles, believe in anything? It must be all very convenient for you.'

'I won't find it very convenient if your old friends in the government put me in uniform for this next holy war. They seem pretty determined to arrange something.'

'It seems you haven't been reading the newspapers either. The only old friend I have in this government – and I haven't seen him for twenty years or more – has just been thrown out on his scraggy old neck. For standing up for what he used to believe in. He must have looked at himself in the mirror one morning.'

'This is Charlie Higgins?'

'Yes. He's done his dash.'

'You used to call him a rat.'

'Well, he turned out an honest rat then. Maybe he just saw in the end that socialism amounts to more than buying a man off with a job, a full stomach and a roof over his head. While others exploit him. It isn't even justice.'

'You always seem to take it so personally.'

'Why not?' His father seemed, at last, touched in a tender place. 'Unless a man takes what he believes bloody personally, there's no point. Either in the belief, or the man.'

'Still, making people happier seems fair enough to me. Whatever you like to call it.'

'It's still not enough.'

'What is enough, then?'

'I'm still making up my mind.'

'So you're in a marvellous position to give advice, aren't you? You've had a lifetime to make it up, so far as I can see. And now you want to make up mine for me – instead.'

'That's different.'

'I can't see it. You're happy to judge this old friend of yours without saying what you'd have done in his place. And you're quite ready to condemn me without actually saying what you'd do in my place.'

'That's not the truth, and you know it. I'm telling you to take the chance to make the most of yourself. And walk decent in the world. It seems I spent the last dozen years of my life giving you that chance. Now you throw it back in my face. What's got into you, boy? What is it?'

Ian found he could not say anything. Unless he said everything. And that was impossible. He shook his head.

'All right, then,' his father said finally, 'it seems I got an idiot for my pains. An idiot son who can't see further than a hick town and the end of a rugby ball. If you can find another word to suit, I'd be happy to hear it. Please yourself.'

'I have to,' Ian insisted. 'I have to please myself.'

And it seemed there was nothing more to say, though they made an effort.

The next weekend he arranged a shooting trip with Sam Kahu, after the Saturday game, to keep out of the house. Cedric Black, who often made quiet company on these trips too, trailing his hero Sam with dogged devotion, was ill with bronchitis. Ian was glad to have Sam to himself this time. He needed someone to hear him out.

'You might be right,' Sam said, as they sat in front of their camp fire.

'It's not a question of might be,' Ian answered. 'It's a question of having to be, now.' He took a deep breath. 'I just have to be right.'

'So why worry?' Sam asked cheerfully. 'You don't have to make a religion out of it.'

'That's it, I suppose. If I'd known staying ordinary was going to be such a hell of a business, I'd have quit long ago.'

Sam's laughter rang against the firelit trees.

In the end comfort was in being free of home, and away with Sam in wild country, walking with his rifle through the quiet bush in the early morning as the first sunlight yellowed the tall bronze trees.

At home he found a peace of sorts with his sister. Diane had grown quietly, just behind him, into a shy and long-legged fourteen year old. Smaller, she had made demands on him; now she doted from a distance. She followed him to football, for example, but never came near him when a game was over. She seemed content to press no claim as sister. She seemed content in most ways. And her company became a refuge; her gentle life offered relief from his own. They began walking together, for the first time since they were young, along the riverbank or up tracks into the hills behind the town. It gave her a chance to show off her knowledge of plants and rocks. Her bent might have been towards science, but there was poetry in her fervour. It delighted him. And he was delighted too when the nervous momentum of her speech carried her far beyond anything she meant to say. She seemed to stun herself, at times.

'You're never very happy,' she once concluded out of nowhere. They were walking; she put a hand to her mouth in dismay.

233

He wasn't disposed to dispute it. 'I'm all right,' he suggested, 'when I'm doing something I'm sure about.'

'Like your football?'

'Yes,' he agreed. 'Like that, I expect. And that's about all. Because it doesn't connect with anything else much. And it can't last.'

He was always oppressed by impermanence at the end of a rugby season.

'You do what you want to do, in that case,' she insisted. 'Don't go away. Stay here if it's going to make you happier. I hate seeing you upset.'

She spoke with passion. But happiness seemed more likely, then, in watching the wind wild in her hair. For that could not last either. They were climbing a hill, the town below them, and the gleaming river. At the top he placed a hand on her shoulder, she steadied his life.

'In ten years,' she said earnestly, 'I wonder where we'll be, and what we will have done with ourselves.'

'Don't go strange on me again.'

'No. It's just interesting to think about.'

And unnerving, though he did not say so. 'All right,' he said, 'so you'll be married with four kids at least.'

'And you – ' she said and stopped, puzzled.

'Go on.'

'I can't.'

'You could try.'

'I can't, you see, because I don't really think you'll be much different.

They began to feel the wind, and made their way down the hill together.

He began on the *Gazette* the day after election night, and his first job was to collect figures from the district's polling booths. The government had changed, and the *Gazette* post-election editorial was fervent: 'After fourteen years of pampering the nation with ill-conceived welfare schemes, after fourteen years in which the country has gone soft and simpering, after fourteen years of socialistic mismanagement and strangling bureaucracy, it seems that all is not lost after all. The question is really whether the country can still be saved from creeping corruption. Discipline can save us yet. Let the early return of capital punishment, with a taste of the rope for our now coddled murderers, serve as a symbol. There is much, apart from pseudo-

humanitarian snivelling, of which this country can be well rid
– to make it worthy again of its pioneer founders.'

Ian would have preferred not to read it. The editor of the
Gazette was a severe, dusty little man with a frowning squint.
He had once been editor of a newspaper much larger. His
wife had left him, and he was said to drink. His thunderously
phrased editorials came from a boxy and untidy office where he
was supposed to have a secret bottle. He was occasionally quite
amicable, and had a quick eye for split infinitives.

He encouraged Ian in his first weeks. 'You've got the idea,'
he insisted. 'We shouldn't have any problem making a newspaper man out of you.'

Doubtless meant as a compliment.

Still, he was free to inhabit the illusion of freedom, and otherwise apparently just where he wished to be. At least he was
learning to use a rackety typewriter.

It was a long summer. Heat lay thick on the land, and the
office stifled. Home was never more than tolerable at best,
despite Diane. So he had cause to be grateful for autumn, cooling rain and yellowing leaves, and the first games of the rugby
season. His young body came to life, then, with the crisp slap of
leather from hand to hand, the bite of sprigs into the shiny
new turf. And he could take much pleasure in what he could do
with it. He knew who he was, in a football jersey and with
the crowd roaring, cutting swiftly inside his man and passing
precisely to Sam Kahu outside him. For eighty minutes of his
week, tackling, running, kicking, swerving and diving, it was a
relief to care about winning; an almost illicit pleasure as he
burned through tackles, racing free to draw the opposing full
back once again and then send Sam flying towards the line.
For Sam, though, it was never more than a game, a pleasant
break from the farm. But they said, the wise heads on the sideline, that he and Sam were going to go a long way, with their
kind of understanding. A long way? Possibly they meant an
international team. Snap; Sam had taken Ian's pass again and
was roaring clear of the full back towards the corner flag. The
truth was, together they would be lucky to see another couple
of seasons out. Sam didn't take it seriously enough, and he took
it too seriously. Something had to give. Crash; Ian was
grounded and winded by a heavy late tackle after he had kicked
neatly out to Cedric Black's wing. Cedric fumbled, slithered,
lost the ball altogether. A knock on; the referee's whistle blew.

Ian, tense, groaned and fumed at the waste of his work; Sam winked and smiled reassuringly at nervy Cedric. The ball shot cleanly out of the scrum and suddenly Fred Saunders was running on the blind. He gained lost ground before a tackle jolted him over the sideline. Ian could relax again and remind himself that they were, after all, ten points up. A long way? He and Sam would never travel further together than the end of a game well won. And even then Sam seemed amiably indifferent.

In the office he began to supply special items to a city newspaper. A senior reporter resigned and passed to Ian the job of local correspondent. 'I can see you've got the knack,' he said. 'You shouldn't have any trouble.'

Very soon, it seemed, he had been on the *Gazette* nearly a year. He had more money in his pockets than he thought he had a right to expect. He bought an old car. He failed to see change in himself, though Diane was growing swiftly beside him. His interest in other girls had fitful fervour. Sometimes, at football dances, he found himself with Fred Saunders' sister. Margaret. A cool and competent country girl, she helped manage her family and farm now that her parents were dead. With Margaret he learned the pains and pleasures of riverbank petting. She had a hard, vigorous body and a quick tongue.

'You and Sam and Cedric,' she said, 'and brother Fred too. You've got to grow up sometime.'

'What's that supposed to mean?'

'Just that you can't be boys forever.'

'That's no news.'

'I wonder.'

'What do you wonder?' They were together, more or less intimately, on a bench beside the river. Beyond a certain point, she tended to needle, for relief or protection.

'Well, I wonder, for example, why you should still be wasting your time in a town like this. So far as I'm concerned, there's only one good reason for this place existing. That's as something to get out of. No one ever got anywhere here.'

'Probably not,' Ian agreed.

'And you don't have to stay.'

'True.'

'So I think my thoughts, you see. And wonder what game you're playing. Other than rugby, of course.'

'Nothing else. There's no mystery.'

236

'You're not tied down to land. Or a family business. So why hang on?'

He shrugged. He might have said, Because my father's name happens to be Bill Freeman, and I happen to be his son. But that might not have begun to explain, at least not to Margaret.

'Does something out there frighten you?' she persisted. 'What is it?'

'It's just that I seem to be all right here.'

'You're not answering the question.'

She had begun to unnerve him, for some reason.

'Possibly not,' he answered coolly.

'You know something? I still don't think you're quite as innocent as you look. Or quite such a fool as you sound.'

'Thanks.'

'I even imagine, sometimes, that you might know what you're doing. Or think you know.'

'I try,' he conceded.

'Anyway,' she went on, 'I'll be out of here soon, with any luck.'

She surprised him. Suddenly he saw himself cheated of one of life's possibilities. But he could only think to say, 'So who is going to cook and housekeep for the Saunders family?'

'I think it's time for someone else to take a turn, now we're almost all grown up. Their problem. I'll have my own, making out in the city. I'll leave Te Ika to you. I'd be happy to bet you'll be editor of the *Gazette* inside ten years.'

'Decent of you,' he replied, more bitterly than he intended. All pressure had gone from his flesh now. Possibly what she wanted. It was always the same with Margaret, advance and retreat, and she appeared to take perverse delight in it. A game she played less with him than with herself.

'Another three weeks and the football season will be over. What will you do with yourself then?'

'I usually manage.'

'Why don't you come out and see me on the farm soon? While you can.'

'I might.'

'It's an easy place to find. You know,' she added bitchily, 'on the way to Sam Kahu's place.'

'I think I've had about enough of this,' he announced and rose from the bench.

'I do believe you're angry. I can't think why. If you prefer other company, why pretend?'

'No comment,' he said.

'Quite the professional. The man has nothing to say. And everything to hide. Well, don't let me stop you getting back to the boys.'

'Look,' he began, 'you might think this is funny –'

'But it is,' she insisted in a queer, strained voice. 'Desperately.'

She was, it appeared, on the edge of tears. Now and then he glimpsed something perplexing in her nature, some inner havoc he preferred to avoid.

Anyway it disarmed him now. The few times he had seen her on the Saunders farm, usually when he dropped in to see her brother Fred, Margaret had invariably been in old shirt, trousers and gumboots, trudging back and forward from house to cowshed. The absence of parents had bent and burdened her life, though she made her effort seem small. Her father had been a well-read and articulate spokesman on agricultural affairs, running a model farm, until his early death in an accident with his wife. Margaret and her older brother Clem were obliged to give up everything not farm or family. She left school early, despite lively intelligence, to look after younger brothers and sisters. Lumpy and arrogant Clem, on the other hand, gave up little more than football to rule his family self-righteously and pull the farm together again. Perhaps Clem was the reason why Margaret was leaving for the city, though family loyalty wouldn't let her say so.

'All right,' he promised. 'I'll come out and see you soon. Perhaps some Saturday when the season's finished. How's that?'

'Thanks,' she said quietly. There seemed to have been some inner collapse; anyway her aggression was punctured. 'I'd like that, if you could. But don't leave it too long. I mightn't be playing mother and milkmaid much longer.'

It was a relief the next day to walk with Diane. She at least was undemanding. Their Sunday mornings together had become ritual.

'I'm thinking about the city again,' he confided, as they walked.

It was true enough. But it was also true that he had only just begun. Perhaps end of season; perhaps other things.

'You've changed your mind, then?'

238

'Not really. I mean it's still my own mind. And I'll make it up for myself. Not change it.'

He heard himself with some dismay. Was that the best he could offer?'

They walked in silence for a time. The hills were bright with dew that sunny spring morning. It seemed possible, already, to place them at a distance.

'But you'll go to university after all,' Diane observed presently.

'I might,' he agreed. 'But in my own way. I can support myself now.'

She grabbed impulsively at his arm. 'You planned this,' she insisted.

'It would be nice to think so,' he said.

'I mean you planned it all along. That's why there was all the trouble last year. You're too proud. You had to do things your own way.'

Her benevolence was hard to resist. Anyway he did not feel inclined to argue. Truth, it seemed, was never tidy. And mostly inexplicable.

Thirteen:

HIS MOTHER WENT AWAY AND DID NOT COME BACK. AFTER A while he stopped asking about her. Because he was told nothing. But he went to see her once, in the hospital where she had to live. She did not say anything much. She held on to his hand tight. He became frightened. His father came back soon and took him home to the farm. On the way he remembered he hadn't told her about the new spotty heifer, or anything. His mouth had been too dry. And she had been too thin and watery in the eyes. He began to weep and soon fell asleep in the back of the bumpy car, under the woolly rug.

When he was a bit older he once had to stay on another farm, the other side of the gorge, with Mr and Mrs Fletcher. His father said Jock Fletcher was not a bad sort of cove. He had a game leg from the war and limped about puffing a big black pipe. Mrs Fletcher was a long stringy woman with brown hands and she always wore a floppy sun hat around their farm. She had been a teacher once, before she married Jock, and taught girls needlework and art. They had come late to this farm up the Waiatarua valley, and didn't have any kids. He had to stay with the Fletchers because his father had gone away for a bit. Jock Fletcher went up to the Livingstone land every day to look after things. It was easy for Jock to leave his own place, and keep another farm going, because he had sheep instead of cows, and a few days lost was neither here nor there. Mrs Fletcher looked after Tim. One day she walked with him along the bank of a creek which ran through the Fletcher property. It was a pretty creek, shady with autumn-coloured willows. Under her arm Mrs Fletcher carried a wooden box and a thin contraption which she did not explain to Tim. They stopped

240

first at a long bend in the creek, shingly about the edge, where gorse flowered bright under the willows.

'Ugh,' she said. 'It smells.'

For a dead lamb rotted at the edge of the water. So they moved further along the creek.

'This is an easel,' explained Mrs Fletcher. 'And this box has colours and brushes. I am going to paint a picture, if you like to watch. But you can play, if you like.'

He watched. She fastened a sheet of stiff paper on to her easel and began to paint. Trees, creek and hills appeared in faint colours.

'You are a very quiet little boy,' she observed. 'You are really very good. I hardly know you are there.'

She offered a sweet as reward. He took it absently.

'Is something the matter?' she asked. 'You could go behind the trees, over there.'

He was too shy to say.

'Is that it?' she persisted. 'Do you want to go somewhere? Do you need to do something?'

He shook his head.

'Then what is it?'

'I would like – ' he said, and was dumb again.

'Yes?'

'I would like a turn,' he got out at last. Then his breath raced. 'At that. I would like a turn at that. I would like to paint a – ' Then his breath failed, as though he dared too much. 'One of them, like that,' he finished. 'A picture.' He paused. 'With colours.'

'Of course,' she said. 'Why not? I was going to suggest you might. Just as soon as I have finished.'

He could hardly wait, and shifted from one foot to the other, excitement fluttery around his insides, so that in the end he did have to go somewhere, behind the trees. He fumbled to release the bright stream upon the grass, wetting his pants, and ran back to Mrs Fletcher. She had nearly finished. Everything was neat in her picture, and tiny. There were even sheep grazing, under dim and distant hills. Everything shrunken, far away. And there was a road winding towards the hills where there was not a road. A windy white road with a person walking.

'I cannot see the road,' he observed, 'or that person.'

'That,' she said, 'is imagination.'

241

He was silent a moment. 'I don't know that place,' he confessed.

She laughed. 'Imagination is not a place, dear Tim.'

A road, then. He knew of no road either, like that, called Imagy Nation. It was not near Te Ika anyway. She placed her hand on his head.

'Imagination is something in yourself,' she explained with care. 'It is something you should bring to whatever you do. There is no road here, no person – but there is, you see, in my head. In my mind. That is why it is painted here. That is imagination. I have brought it to what I am doing.'

He was more confused than before, and his first idea was hard to shift. Imagy Nation was a road, with a person walking. He could understand that, all right, if only she would not pester. As she did with other, even more confusing words.

'Imagination is a different world,' she was saying, among other things. 'A different world altogether.'

But it obviously was not. That road, that person, could be anywhere. What was so different? What was so different, if he believed her, was that the road and the person lived in Mrs Fletcher's unlikely old head. He looked at her and considered this. He wished he could be sure about whatever it was or where-ever.

'Do I have to paint a road too?' he asked at length. 'And a person walking?'

She laughed again, delighted. His earnest innocence made the morning seem quite wildly wonderful about her. 'Of course not, Tim,' she said, ruffling his hair. 'You must paint whatever you see. And bring to it whatever is in your own head – and in your heart too, of course. That is all your affair.'

He nodded as if he understood. Often it was best to pretend.

She adjusted the easel to his height. She would always regret having no child of her own. Jock had come along too late.

'These are the brushes,' she said, 'and these the colours. You can choose your own colours. Or make them, if you must, by mixing. I cannot help you there. I can just show you how to hold the brush. The rest is your individuality – the rest is Tim Livingstone, not me. We each have our own private language, Tim, and you must learn your own.'

The colour of the fresh paper she fixed to the easel was white and terrifying, perhaps to infinity. It seemed he must make some mark to begin. So he did, rather muddily: a brown, nervous streak. And now it was there, he had to do something with it. It couldn't be left. He plunged again, and was surprised. Now he saw the brown could be hills, or broken earth along the creek, or anything. He tried other colours, blue like sky, yellow like the trees, rusty like the scrub.

'You will learn to be neat,' she suggested. 'In time.'

Now the colours were coming so fast he could not cope. They ran and dribbled; he tried to slash them back into place, or into something, with the brush. Or they would overflow, and he would drown in rainbows. He had no time to think about Imagy Nation, or anything Mrs Fletcher had said; he had to fight back before he was lost.

'You seem,' she said patiently, 'to need some control. Restraint. That is the essence of art.'

For the trees, if they were, rioted. The creek, if it was, ran dark. The sky was smudgily ambiguous at the point where it might have joined the hills. At the centre was some unburied white; he could not think why he had left it. But he began to work upon it because it interested him. It took time to find what it was, but then he did.

'It is all very interesting,' said Mrs Fletcher. 'All very interesting indeed. But what is happening there, in the middle?'

'It is something,' he said, distracted.

'Obviously. But won't you tell me?'

He worked tenaciously at his secret.

'It is,' he announced presently, 'a dead lamb in the water.'

'I see,' she said, faintly worried. 'You mean the one we saw?'

'No. This one is in my head.'

'But like the one we saw?'

'Yes. Only I see it better in my head.'

'Then that, Tim,' she said, though disconcerted, 'is imagination.'

He thought about that, and reached a conclusion. 'Yes,' he answered. 'Like you said.'

'It is not a very pleasant subject,' she observed after a time. 'And what is what you are painting around it now?'

'The smell,' he said. 'The way it smells.'

Appalled on her two feet, she bent close to him. 'Dear me, Tim,' she said quietly, 'you really mustn't take what I say so much to heart. Imagination is all very well. But there are limits.'

It wasn't what she meant to say. She wasn't sure what she meant to say.

'It is just the smell I am painting around it,' he went on, 'and then I will be nearly finished.' He hesitated. 'The smell is dark, like that.'

She couldn't quite bring herself to object. She supposed she was, after all, at fault for not having made herself more clear at the beginning. 'All right,' she conceded in disarray. 'I suppose it is. You have,' she added, 'made a very brave try, Tim. The neatness will come in time, I have no doubt.'

Though she prayed quietly, and wished she knew this lonely child better. His mother was dying in a sanatorium, and his father had gone to the poor woman. How much did the child guess, how much was his small mind clouded by what he knew? Was this some morbid, autumnal vision? But his eyes, when they lifted at last from the picture he had made, were bright and healthy enough. So she was more perplexed than ever.

'We will go home now,' she announced, 'and get Jock's lunch ready.'

'Can we do this again?' the boy asked cheerfully.

'I imagine we can,' she answered, for it would have been more difficult to say otherwise.

His mother died. His father did not think to say so until some time after his long trip away. And then it was only because the boy had just asked the question he had almost forgotten to ask. 'When will my mother be back again?' he said.

For he could still remember the time she left. He had woken weeping in a night of strange sounds and red dreams.

'She won't be back again,' said Ned Livingstone, who groped around for his tobacco tin, mislaid somewhere in the kitchen while he cooked up some tucker for the evening meal. 'She is not here any more. She has gone. Gone right away.'

He was trying to remember how he should explain. People had suggested how.

'Where?' Tim said. 'Where has she gone away?'

That was an interesting question, if considered. Sometimes he was frightened he saw her in the boy's eyes.

'She has gone to sleep,' Ned said, remembering one possibility. And then added, 'The way people go to sleep when they get all worn out. And when people go to sleep, that way, they go right away from us.'

'You mean she is dead,' said the boy.

244

'Yes,' the father agreed with relief. 'I suppose that is what I mean.'

He felt lighter as he sweated over the stove, and free. The boy did not weep. He went out to feed the fowls. He was useful about the place now.

They were not always alone on the farm. Sometimes men came to work, to help his father, but they never seemed to stay long. There was a thin man who came walking up the road one day. His name was Mr Smith. He slept in the spare room off the back porch. When he was not working he shut himself in there with his ragged heap of books. The books had ugly covers, with men and guns, and women with ripped clothes. Mr Smith had funny eyes and did not like to talk much. His books and his sour smell were still in his room when he left, quite suddenly, with all the spare cash he could find to take in the house. The police came, not long after, and said the man's name was not Mr Smith and they had been looking for him. Later on the man's real name was in the newspaper, when he went to prison.

'There's no one you can rely on, in the end,' his father said. 'Only yourself.'

It was just near Christmas, anyway, and better to be alone. When the boy woke that morning, the light outside still grey and the birds starting to sing, he found a model train set arranged beside his bed. He began to play with it. Then he looked up and saw the bare bony feet, and pale hairy legs, which had arrived quietly beside him. His father stood there smiling, with sleepy eyes and hair untidy, in his night shirt. 'That,' he announced, 'is for being a good kid. And for not being a bother to your old man.' He knelt down beside the boy to show him how to fix the rails. They played so long with the train together they almost forgot the cows had to be milked. Later that morning, when the cows were finished, his father took a dusty bottle of beer from a high cupboard. He gave the boy a taste of the beer, in an egg cup. Beer had a cheerful smell. His father drank it slowly, shaking his head now and then. 'You're a good little mate,' he said. 'The only one I got, and the only one I want. You tasted your beer yet? Drink up, now. And learn to be moderate. Cheers.' He lifted his glass, and the boy lifted his egg cup. They drank. Beer had a sour taste. The smell was better. Then his father whistled about the kitchen while a fowl was in the oven. The boy could not remember having heard his father whistle for a long time. The fowl was burned a bit, by the time they sat down to eat, but his father picked out the parts that were all right. And they had the Christmas pudding Mrs Fletcher had cooked. In the hot afternoon, their stomachs full, they went outside to chop out some gorse, for his father said they couldn't afford idleness, not even on Christmas day. So that night he was too tired to play with his model train, and in the end his father must have carried him off to bed, because suddenly day was shining through his bedroom window.

Through the school holidays he saw Mrs Fletcher now and then, but mostly with his father. He didn't need to see her often now, for she had given him a small box of paints of his own.

'What is the idea, boy?' his father asked.

'To paint pictures,' he said, though it seemed obvious.

'That's all very well,' his father observed, 'for those who have the time. Life is not pretty pictures.'

His father seemed to know. He might have been, then, looking at sad pictures of his own which the boy could not see.

So he did not use the paints much if he saw his father irritable. And he kept the pictures he painted in his room. If he took them out, it was usually only to show Mrs Fletcher, when she asked to see.

'You have an unusual sense of colour, Tim,' she would say. 'Unusual, if not downright perverse. Do you really look at your subject? Tell me, what is it that makes you choose one colour against another?'

'It is the colours,' he said.

'I know. But one against another?'

'It is the colours,' he repeated impatiently. 'The colours that make me.'

'I see,' she said, but perplexed. 'Then you must learn order, harmony and restraint. Otherwise you shall be lost.'

He tried to understand, but words were in his way.

'This red, for example,' she went on. 'In this painting it seems to be everywhere, for no good reason.' She paused. 'Even the hills – aren't they hills? – this extraordinary hue.'

'It is dreams,' he explained, 'and things dying.'

'Then you have a great deal to learn indeed,' she said. 'You must learn not to let your imagination run away with you. Try this one again.'

For she spoke less of imagination, now, than of discipline.

246

And gave him exercises to encourage. 'You could almost do without the colours for a time,' she said. 'Unless you feel absolutely obliged.'

To Ned Livingstone she observed, 'Your son has a talent. But what for, I am not sure. I hope, anyway, that this keeps him out of trouble.'

'The boy is no trouble,' Ned grunted.

'In that case – ' she began, and then wondered at her point. 'In that case, perhaps it will keep him out of trouble in the future. To have an interest, I mean. One never knows, really, with the young.'

'Or the old,' he said, shrewd. He had never known quite what to make of this gangly woman, though he got along with Jock Fletcher all right. Yet he had no real complaint about her interest in his son. She had been good to the boy when he went away to help Nance with her dying. It was just that his son had not been the same after. It was always the way with other people; he found it harder to get a grip on the boy again.

'True,' she agreed. 'But still. The important thing, of course, is for young Tim to sort things out for himself. I imagine he will. He is a bright enough boy.'

'If you say so,' he answered, for he did not see where this could get.

Afterwards she wondered if her suggestion might have been less gentle, the point less implied. She was never easy with this slow and taciturn man, and she could feel resentment when they discussed the boy; it was not her intention to come between boy and man, but she could hardly say that in reassurance. Without, that was, the very suspicion attaching. But when she wondered what they might be like together, this father and son, her heart shifted in her thin chest and there was a perceptible thickness in her throat.

His father didn't always know quite what to do with himself in the evenings. Most nights, if he couldn't find something to keep himself busy, he would fall back into the most comfortable chair, put up his stockinged feet on another chair, and tenderly balance steel-rimmed reading glasses on the end of his nose. There was always a large heap of newspapers for him to read. Always too many, for all the time new ones arrived at the farm. Now and then he threw out all those unread and began again with the latest issue. The heap grew again. Because some

247

nights he did no more than sit tired and look up at the spotty ceiling through eyes half closed. He might have been considering something there, perhaps a fresh coat of paint; anything was possible. If the boy spoke, asking a question while he read or puzzled over homework, his father answered with effort.

After the boy had been sent to bed, the kitchen light would burn until late. From his warm blankets he saw its reflection under his bedroom door. Sometimes, awake longer than usual, he slid out of bed, opened the door quietly, and went lightly over the cold floor down the passage to the kitchen. Often he found his father still in his favourite chair, sprawled asleep, the glasses teetering off his nose while he made loud snoring noises in his mouth. Tim moved closer, then, and touched his father gently on the shoulder. And he always woke with a jerk, with wild red eyes, amazed, as if the boy were a stranger. As if he had expected to awaken somewhere other than under the cold glare of electric light in the kitchen, the fire burned out, with Tim standing before him frightened and barefoot in outgrown pyjamas. Then he removed his glasses like an irritation.

'You ought to be in bed,' he said slowly. 'Asleep.'

The voice made Tim run fast back to bed. After a time he heard the jangle of easing chair springs as his father stood up. There were kitchen noises, and presently the kettle hissing for a cup of tea. And suddenly Tim's door swung open, and the light behind showed his father large. He would bend and give Tim a glass of milk and a big slice of fruit cake.

'And after this you better go to sleep,' he said. 'Early to bed and early to rise makes a man healthy, wealthy and wise. Goodnight, boy.'

'Goodnight,' the boy said through his mouthful of cake.

The door shut again. Soon he heard the rattle of cup and saucer as his father finished his tea, the splashing of water as he washed himself, the lights clicking out, and his bare feet moving up the passage to his own bedroom. Finally there was the grating sound as his father wound the shrill alarm clock, and the wire of the big double bed straining as his father lay his weight on it. Sometimes, not often, he would even hear his father begin to snore again.

Out of a noisy shower, one gusty night when the wind sent loose leaves spinning, a young Maori came to the door. His name was Tui, and he said he'd heard there might be a job.

He came from the south and he liked the look of the country around Te Ika. It was just on meal time, so he was invited to sit down to eat.

That was when the boy learned his father could still talk after all. The more he talked, the more carelessly he ate. Stew splashed off his plate and stained the table cloth he had specially laid; bits of food clung to the corners of his mouth. His father's table manners were never good when he talked too much. The boy could remember his mother complaining. So he shifted in his chair, trying to catch his father's eye, and signalled by rubbing at the corners of his own mouth. When his father at last took notice, he looked stern.

'What's the matter, boy? Eh? You got St Vitus dance?'

He seemed ashamed for an idiot son, and the bits of food still clung. And he went on talking.

Tui stayed the night, and got the job. The house was different. His father had someone to talk to now, in the evenings. The boy had someone too. He liked being with Tui. Sometimes, when work was slow, they walked across the farm up to the bush, and Tui told him names of trees and birds, and Maori stories. He showed the boy how to catch eels in a trap. The boy often left his homework until late so he could work longer with Tui after school, in the cowshed or forking out hay from the barn.

'Your Dad's a great man, eh?' Tui said.

'Yes,' Tim would say, pleased.

'I can tell you're pretty proud of your old man,' Tui said. And added, 'Yes, he's a great man on the work. He never stops. All day and half the night. He's a great man on the work all right.'

'He works pretty hard,' Tim agreed.

'Too much work's no good. What do you think, eh?'

He had to consider this. Finally he suggested, 'It makes you pretty tired, sometimes.'

'Too right. Too right it makes you pretty tired. All work, no play, eh?'

'Yes,' the boy answered, though he wasn't sure.

'You got to have fun sometime, eh? You're a long time the corpse.'

Stopped in his work, leaning on his fork, Tui looked down at Tim as if he expected an answer.

He didn't see Mrs Fletcher much at all now. And sometimes forgot his paints for a week or two at a time.

Tui liked to sing when he milked cows. He reckoned the cows liked a little song. And they gave up their milk easier too, he said. The cowshed was never the same with Tui around.

Or the farm itself, and the places beyond. His father didn't seem to mind him being with Tui so much. His father said he was pretty pleased with Tui. Because Tui was a pretty fair sort of Maori. He worked hard, never complained, and was a big help around the place. Educated too, and sensible. Not like the Maoris who gallivanted around spending their money and having a good time. Tui worked and saved his money. He supposed Tui was doing it with the idea of getting married and settled on some place of his own. Anyhow, whatever it was, his father hoped Tui wouldn't pull out too soon. Even a couple of years would be too soon.

The boy listened. He also wondered. 'When are you going to get married, Tui?' he asked. They were lying on the bank of the creek one bright winter day, waiting for their eel trap to fill.

Tui laughed. 'You get some funny ideas,' he said.

'When are you going to? Not ever?' The boy was hopeful.

'Sometime I might. No big hurry, eh?'

'My dad thought you was going to.'

Tui's smile was big. 'Why, eh?'

'Because he says you probably want a place of your own. Because you save your money.' He thought for a while. 'Why do you save it?'

'So I can keep it. So I can do things.'

'What things?'

Tui didn't seem too keen to tell.

'Please,' the boy said.

It seemed in the end that Tui planned on some shooting later, and needed a good new rifle, among other things. He planned on a good long spell of hunting and fishing. And he needed money to keep him going, for clothes and food. 'I'm spoilt now, I reckon,' he said. 'I can't go living off the bush for everything. And you can get pretty sick of the taste of wild pig anyway.'

'Then you won't be stopping at our place?' the boy said with dismay.

'No,' Tui agreed. 'I reckon I'll have to be moving on for that. What do you think your old man would say about me taking it easy and having a good time?'

Tim had to think; he was silenced. They filled their sack with eels and started the walk home. They climbed a ridge and saw the farmhouse and trees in the distance, tiny in the tidy valley which the bush overhung. His father was hammering at something; the hard, rhythmic sound rose up to them.

'He's a great man all right,' Tui said. 'A great man on the work.'

It was spring soon, then hot summer again. Tui came into the kitchen one evening, while his father was bent to the stove, and said he wanted to leave. The windows were lit with a cool orange sunset.

'Well,' his father said, shocked and sad. 'I'm sorry to hear that Tui. I am sorry. I'd of thought you'd be with us a bit longer.'

Tui went to bed earlier than usual that night, soon after the meal, leaving his father with his newspapers again. They had begun to heap high in the last few months, since Tui arrived. The boy sat up with his father, offering his company, and reading a book. He lifted his head when his father spoke at last, but it seemed he was just talking to himself after all.

'He must be going to get married. It's the only thing. That's why he's been saving so careful. Been putting away every penny. He must count on getting himself a solid bit of land one day.'

After a time there was a rustle, and the boy looked up again to see a newspaper slide from his father's dangling hand. He slept with his mouth fallen open, and the deep lines on his brow gone. But he looked older than ever, and new grey hair patched the side of his head. The boy rose, gently removed the precarious glasses from his father's nose, and placed them on a table. Then he began to prepare his father a cup of tea. For he was becoming useful in the kitchen now. And he was too busy feeling sad for his father to feel much for himself. He looked out a window, his arms resting on the sill, while the kettle boiled. The stars were bright. And he could hear, somewhere in the dark hills around, a morepork calling lonely in the night.

It was a Saturday when Tui left; the boy was home from school. The sun had yet to smother the clean smell of morning; it was still climbing clear of the hills. Tui sang as he packed in his room, and his father tinkered noisily with the old Ford out in the back yard. It seemed the engine wasn't up to taking Tui down to town.

The boy sat on the porch, between.

His father was still swearing at the Ford when Tui came out of his room, his swag dangling. So then his father walked back to the house.

'Sorry, Tui. It's no go with the car.'

'It's all right,' Tui said. 'Don't worry.'

'You better wait for the cream truck.'

'He's usually late,' Tui said, impatient. 'I think I'll walk down the valley. I might pick up a lift on the way. I want to get started.'

The two men faced each other across Tim, and then rolled smokes.

'She a nice girl?' his father said.

'Girl?' Tui was puzzled.

'Don't you think we can guess?'

'There's no girl,' Tui said quietly.

His father got stiff. 'But the money you been saving up. Aren't you going to get married? I thought you might of been thinking about settling down on your own bit of land.'

'No fear,' Tui said. 'Not me.'

'But what about the money?'

'That's for me. To keep me going through the summer. I got some relatives over Taupo way. I might look them up this year. Then I might take a look round the east coast. I got some relatives there too. Then there's some things I want on the way along, like a rifle and stuff.'

'And that's all you worked for?'

'Sure thing,' Tui said with a grin. He pulled his swag on to his shoulder. 'Well, I guess I better be starting off.'

But Tui and his father just stood for a moment looking at each other, and the silence was thick. Too thick for the boy to penetrate, even if he had found words to say. All he could see was that the two men did not understand each other, and could never. They frightened him.

Then Tui remembered something. Presents, he said. He went back to his room and returned with a fishing rod for Tim, and a new adjustable spanner for his father.

'You shouldn't of,' his father said, not seeming to know what else to say.

For then the boy could see that they were all lost now.

They followed Tui down to the front gate, under the shady trees which lined the drive. His father leaned on the gate and the boy sat, his legs dangling, on the top rail. Tui grew smaller, walking away down the white road. Now and then he turned to

252

wave. After a while they heard his voice, a faint song in the morning. The day was shiny and the hills stood up clear with their black stumps and banks of yellow clay where slopes had slumped in winter rain. Then he was gone, his song too. His father thumbed back his hat and rolled another smoke. Together they walked back to the house under the cool trees. A wheeling fantail flickered in and out of the shade. On the back porch the boy fingered his fishing rod while his father smoked and puzzled.

After a time he got jerkily to his feet. He tossed Tui's spanner away. It fell with a dull sound on the hard earth.

'There's no one you can ever really rely on,' he said. 'Only yourself.'

He started off towards the broken down car again, stopped, looked back. 'Remember that, boy,' he added. 'And remember most people don't amount to nothing.'

The boy understood, at least, that his father was still having trouble finding things to say. For he was saying the only things he knew.

He picked up the spanner, examined it, then changed his mind once more, and threw it away for a second time. It vanished into long grass.

That night, over their meal, his father observed, 'Anyway we're together again, boy. Aren't we?'

It was difficult to doubt.

Yet sometimes, after, he dreamed he was running, swooping, down a white road. Now and then he seemed to catch up with Tui's song, which still floated around, but never Tui himself : he was always much further than his song, and couldn't be caught up. When he woke in the morning the dream still seemed real, even if it wasn't, even if it was all just in his head. That wasn't so surprising, after all. Imagination was a windy white road, with a person walking. Hadn't Mrs Fletcher told him that in the first place, though afterwards she tried to confuse? A windy white road, with a person walking. She really needn't have told him at all; he had found out for himself.

All the same, he showed Mrs Fletcher the new picture. 'I must say I usually expect something more original from you, Tim,' she observed. She examined it with some care. 'Still,' she added, 'it is done very well. I can't deny that. I'd be quite pleased with it myself, to tell the truth.'

He made, however, the mistake of leaving the picture lying

about the house, where his father found it. 'And what is this?' he asked.

He had thought the boy past this business now. His suspicion leaked through his intended unconcern. After all there had been another Timothy, who finished talking to birds, quite loony.

'Just something I done,' said the boy. 'In my room.' But he did not mean it to sound so furtive.

'I see,' said his father, but puzzled. 'And what is it all about?'

'There,' said the boy, 'is a road. And there,' he went on in another breath, 'is a person walking along the road. And those are hills there, behind.'

'So what does it amount to?' his father asked. 'Did you have something in mind?'

'It came out of my head,' the boy explained. 'Just the other day, when I was in my room.'

'All right,' said his father, impatient. 'But what is the point, what is that person doing?'

'It is,' said the boy, 'just a person going away.'

It was really quite simple, and he didn't understand why his father should look so queer.

'That's all,' he finished. 'Just a person going away.'

For you could paint just a person. Not songs, or smells. He had learned that, in time. There were limits.

He might even have explained, if he could, but his father seemed to have lost interest. He tossed the picture back.

'All right,' he said. 'But we mustn't forget there is work to be done around this place.'

And he went outside again, to prove it. The boy followed. A day or two later he put his paints away. And when he found them again, perhaps a year later, he threw them out altogether.

He wouldn't have minded school, if it hadn't seemed test for his impatience. The idea, perhaps, was that he shouldn't grow up too soon. The kids, and their muddly games and silly shouting. The teachers, and their blackboards and repetition. He learned, though, to answer sums efficiently, and to spell words. He learned also to kick a muddy ball, and to tackle kids so hard that they took fright when he came near. He could do most that was expected, and sometimes more. But some days, because he had been up since early with his father, he fell

254

asleep on his desk in the afternoons, and had to be woken by the teacher for the bus home.

'Perhaps you can manage some homework tonight,' the teacher might say. 'For what you have just missed.'

Other teachers were not so gentle. He woke with the cane stinging his legs.

So he would sooner the farm. And his father. Mornings were best. His father would wake him and they would go into the bathroom and splash their faces with water. Then they would go out to the cowshed. Sometimes the grass was dusted with frost, crackling underfoot while their breathing steamed in the quiet air under the solid hills. In winter it might be misty, rainy, and still dark; the house lights would be yellow behind them, and their feet heavy in the mud. In summer the paddocks glittered with dew under the cool early sun. In autumn the grass was freckled with mushrooms.

'So we are back at war again,' his father said one night, and threw the newspaper down.

'What will happen?' the boy asked.

'Nothing much,' his father said. 'There will just be more poor bloody silly buggers killing each other.'

'What for?'

'That,' his father answered, angry, 'is what they bloody forgot to tell me in the last one.'

'What did you do?' the boy thought to ask.

But his father, it seemed, did not care to say.

'Never mind, boy,' he said at length. 'We're all right here, aren't we? They can all go to hell out there. We're all right here, you and me. We're safe.'

The boy would have found it hard, then, to believe otherwise.

Outside, his father often said, 'Now take a good look around you, boy.'

He would do as he was told. He would consider all the land up to the hills. Then the hills.

'Right,' his father said. 'Now, have you got it all locked in your head?'

'Yes.'

'Everything?'

'Everything.' Perhaps he was not meant to include the hills; he was never sure.

'Good. Then don't forget it. Because it's all we got to show for

255

ourselves in the end, you and me. It's all we got between us and that lot out there. So it's all we are.' He paused. 'Now close your eyes.'

The boy would.

'What do you see now?'

'I still see pretty near everything.'

'Tell me, then.'

The boy, with eyes shut, made lists of what he saw. He excluded the hills, for safety. Thus they became more intimate.

'Good. You got the idea. Because it's as good as yours. You know that, don't you? So what is it you see?'

This answer was easy; he knew it by heart. 'Our land,' he said, 'which will be mine one day.'

He could open his eyes then.

'Right,' his father said. 'So that ought to make you feel safe. Now let's get on with our work.'

And there was, in truth, only one place on this farm under the hills where he ever felt strange and uneasy. That was the front room of the house. His mother had filled it with fancy things, frilly chairs, and painted china behind glass. And pictures on the walls. His father never went in there. It had a strange smell now, always cold, and things were dusty. Sometimes, when he was small, he hid in that room to think things, and make believe. He could make believe, for example, that his mother still lived there in secret, and might appear to surprise them one day. But she was never there, quite, when he opened the door. Or when he sat on a couch, imagining she might appear, trying to terrify himself. There were only some murky photographs which refused to live. And a doll, a gypsy doll with a silly look on its face, sitting on the mantelpiece. Later he became like his father, and never opened the door of that room at all.

Another night, near the end of the war, his father announced, 'I have a note here from your headmaster. It seems this geezer thinks you are pretty bright. And he hopes there is no question of you leaving school before you should.'

Tim took a quick breath, but did not speak. He had felt this coming.

'Speaking for myself,' his father went on, 'I reckon it's none of this bastard's business. What do you think?'

'I don't know,' Tim said.

256

'You don't know? And yet he says you are bright.'

'It is just his opinion. He is entitled to an opinion.'

'He is not bloody entitled to tell other people how to live their lives. Or am I mistaken? Does this bugger think he is God, or a headmaster?'

'It is part of his job, I suppose,' Tim said. 'To worry about kids.'

'It isn't part of his job to interfere. Why should he interfere now, or anyone?'

'It must have been a talk we had,' Tim said quietly. 'He asked me my plans. I said I expected I would leave soon, to help on the farm.'

'And whose idea was that?'

'Ours,' Tim said. Because it was true.

'That was between us,' said his father. 'At least I thought it was. Not for nosy creeps in the pay of the government.'

'I had to tell him something,' Tim insisted.

'By rights I ought to push his face in. I would, if it was worth pushing in. So what does he want you to be, then, this bastard? Some creep like himself? Or someone in a laboratory with a white coat?' He had never been able to loose that fear from his mind : it could be Nance's last triumph. Still could.

'Nothing like that. He just said it would be a pity if I left early.'

'Next time, if there's a next time, you just tell him to mind his own bloody business. You hear?'

'All right.'

'And just tell him you're my son. And not to forget it. You understand?'

'Yes.' He understood, all right, even if he did not understand why his father should begin shouting so bitterly. Or his face twitch, as if he were ill. He muttered to himself a long time after, behind Tim's back, and read his newspaper restlessly that night. Tim finished his homework early and went to bed. He woke late in the night with a torch shining in his face. His father was behind the torch in night shirt and bare feet.

'It's all right,' he reassured Tim. 'Just seeing you are all right. Are you?'

'Yes. I'm all right.' It was puzzling.

'Good.'

He was slow, though, to shift the blinding beam of the torch and go off to his own bed. Tim, quite dazzled, was unable to see the expression on his father's face, if there was anything to see. And nothing was explained. When his father left, he could be heard heaving sleepless on the wirewove of the creaky double bed for some time. Then, just before Tim went to sleep again himself, he heard his father pad out to the kitchen to make another cup of tea. It must have been after midnight.

Later the torch seemed to flash across his sleepy face again. This time, though, he thought he might just have dreamed it. For his night became quite wild with dreams which left him sweating.

He still saw Mrs Fletcher, though not as often as he had when younger. Their meetings were mostly accidental, and seldom comfortable; he always seemed to disappoint her in some way. 'I hear good things about you from the school,' she told him. 'One or two teachers speak very highly. The art teacher, for example.'

This was her first disappointment, that the boy had lost interest.

'He's easy to please,' Tim said. 'They all are.'

'Easy for you to please, perhaps. But I wouldn't despise his or anyone's judgement on that account. Or have you contempt, now for your own gifts?'

'No,' he replied. 'I just mean that he's easy to please. If I just do something the way he wants it, he's perfectly happy, like all the others.'

'I see. And what about the way you want it?'

'That's not important.'

'A gift for anything requires some commensurate strength of character, don't you think? Otherwise you die as a person, as an individual. And I find it hard to believe you don't have that requisite strength of character, Tim.'

'I just mean that nothing is very important. Nothing at school. I expect I'll be leaving soon.'

'But that's absurd.' Mrs Fletcher was clearly distressed. 'You must keep on.'

Tim shrugged.

'I'll speak to your father.'

He was quick to reply. 'I don't think that would do any good. Really.'

'After all, you've only another year or two before you finish school anyway. That much education never did anyone any harm. I think your father may be a little old fashioned in his notions about schooling.'

'I'd still rather you didn't say anything.'

'We'll see,' she said. 'I won't make a point of it, unless the opportunity arises.'

He knew she would make the opportunity, and felt depressed as much on his father's account as his own. He wished he had said nothing. After all, his life was no great problem, when left alone. It was true that he had begun to have surprising dreams, and yearnings. But he was not without places to invest these. Not at school, of course, or with other kids. He didn't have much use for other kids, though he could act the same, for convenience. When he got the chance, he would flee across the farm, the grass streaming green under his quick feet, and his heart thudding in his chest. And collapsed only when he had punished his body sufficiently. He would usually fall under some willow trees by the creek, where light flashed off the fast water. He swam there in summer, in the frosty water, behind a dam of his own devising. And fished in winter. Sometimes he would just walk, and climb, until the sky grew around him, and the farm became remote, like most things, though the forested hills could not have been more substantial wherever he looked. Up there, a place where only skinny scrub grew, there was a limestone summit with which he became familiar, and where he could experiment with the clumsy feelings in his body when it became impossible not to. And when his flesh was coherent again, if not longer articulate, he would begin the descent to the farm.

'That Fletcher woman had a yarn with me today,' his father told him. 'She seemed to think I got something against you getting an education. She as good as said I'm not treating you right.'

He had nothing more to say, evidently. And Tim had nothing to say at all. They ate their meal in silence.

'I told her it's no odds to me when you leave,' his father continued after a while. 'This year or next year or the year after. I said you had to please yourself.'

Tim still had nothing to say. It seemed they were never to be left alone.

'I suppose so,' he tried to agree.

'Isn't that right?' his father demanded. 'Suppose so? What do you mean, suppose so? Either you

259

please yourself or you bloody don't. Whose son are you, anyway?'

It was always the same, now, if something like this came up. The same question, in a shout. And afterwards the heaving on the wirewove in the other bedroom late at night, and the torch-lit wandering in the house.

'Are they taking out your tongue at school?' his father asked. 'Is that it?'

Now he really dared not speak. Whatever he said might enrage.

'Well,' his father finished, 'the way I see it, if they haven't stuffed you now, another couple of years isn't going to make no difference. And if they have stuffed you already, then they got another couple years to make good the damage they done. I'm not going to have it said I don't treat you right. Or give you a fair go.'

'But,' Tim was moved to protest, 'I thought you said I had to please myself.'

'Say what you mean, boy.'

'Then I'd sooner get all this over. Leave school now.'

'Good. That's more like it.'

'So I can?'

'I didn't say that. No.'

'Why?' The boy was baffled.

'Because that would be too easy.'

'But it's not pleasing myself.'

'No one ever ought to be able to please themselves too easy. I didn't; I earned this place hard. It looks like you got to earn it too.'

'You said – '

'We'll get around to that later,' his father promised. 'I just wanted to see, in the meantime, that they hadn't got you stuffed.'

His father seemed quite pleased, on the whole. And the house, after all, was quiet that night.

So he continued also to please at school, sometimes with honours. There was no real effort to be made, unless in contest with his impatience. It was just a question of using his brain when obliged in class. And his strength as efficiently on the football field. When free of school, he worked steadily and often silently beside his father. He began to see his appearances, in one role or another, as disguises merely. How the idea began he did not know, but once in his head it did not shift. The

260

more disguises he wore, the safer. And the more he seemed to belong elsewhere, the more he belonged to himself. The vacuum behind his smile became his natural territory, much like that lonely place among skinny scrub. He could laugh, and feel absolutely nothing; he could stand off and watch himself behave with other people; and he was, perhaps best, his own cool retreat in crisis.

'You're all right?' his father would ask.

'Yes.'

'I suppose if you weren't, I'd never bloody know.'

He could not really disagree.

He did not become familiar with the stump at the edge of the south paddock until his seventeenth year. Yet it had been there from the beginning, a giant lump of hardwood durably rooted, which Ned and Nick had tried to blast out with gelignite after the rest of the bush had been felled and fired. They had, on the surface of things, been successful. For the stump was levelled, if not erased. If this last limb of the old forest had an existence still, it was not evident upon the evenly sloping land. Until a lurch in the land, one winter's erosion, gave it slight prominence again. It lay near the edge of the jagged slip, or crevasse, the heavy rains had made, and through which a flash torrent had torn. The land dried out again that spring, and the damage to the south paddock did not appear so great after all; the erosion seemed eccentric in that corner of the farm, which took the sun longest. Certainly not to be taken seriously, as it might be elsewhere on other, steeper cleared slopes. His father saw no reason why, in fact, they shouldn't break in the south paddock and plant a crop of turnips for winter feed. So Tim, upon a tractor, dragged discs across the land, ripping open the earth for the crop to come. The old tractor throbbed and rattled beneath him; he looked back, as he worked the paddock, to see the discs churning the green pasture to even dark corduroy. He could see no cause not to work as close as he could to the edge of the slip, since the ground was dry and settled again. Looking frequently over his shoulder, he did not notice the freshly exposed stump until he was quite upon it, and be began to wrench at the steering wheel at the same time as the tractor was moved to protest by tilting sideways with stump's impact. Also at that point, perhaps, some ground gave way, enough to turn the jolt into a slide, the slip became large on his left, and everything was moving, the sky too. The land seemed to be slowly sucking him down into its ugly wound. Amazed and helpless, and then with late terror, he watched himself become altogether involved with the tractor and discs as the slide into the slip gathered pace. There was, of course, no escape; nowhere to jump. But on the other hand there was surprisingly little pain as he was flung and crushed by machinery and sharp edges within the crash at the bottom of the slip. There was just a quick hell of razored flesh and splintering bone, and then he was unconscious.

They said, in the hospital where he woke, that he was a very fortunate young man. They did their best to make him intact again, to patch and mend, and arrange his bones in order; his plastered legs were hoisted on pulleys above the level of his head, and where he wasn't cased in plaster, he was mostly bandaged. Blood dripped into his wrist through a tube. He was given injections to deaden pain. So that even his daily discomfort became a hazy thing.

There were visitors, of course. His father first. His father seemed seldom to leave the bedside, except to see the herd was milked, that first week or so in hospital.

'Jesus, boy,' was about all he could say at the beginning. And he would try to touch Tim somewhere unbandaged, usually on the face, to reassure himself his son was solid. At the end of the week he began to say, 'Thank God.' It was only at that point, anyway, that Tim could begin to pay much attention. His father often just sat at the bedside with his face buried in his hands. He might have been trying to shut out some memory of the sight he had seen at the bottom of the slip after the accident; it was impossible to say. The nurses in the hospital were gentle with his father. They did not try to turn him out after visiting hours were ended. And they sometimes fed this dismayed, distracted man while he sat with his son.

After a time he also began to say, 'They tell me you'll be all right again, more or less, by the time they finished with you. All I can say is thank God. I thought you was gone there, at one stage.'

He even talked about the farm again. Earlier, he appeared to find the subject distasteful. The tractor, it seemed, had been a write-off. But otherwise things were fair. He was managing all right.

262

Time passed, and much of the pain. He should have expected Mrs Fletcher at his bedside.

'You're a very brave boy, Tim,' she announced. 'I can't say how glad I am to see you making such a good recovery.'

She looked distraught, though. And once she had to turn away to do something with her tears.

'I imagine,' she said, recovering, 'that you are beginning to be bored. I hear you will be here for a while yet. So I brought these. Some books which may interest you. All light and pleasant enough. Nothing melancholy. These verses, for example, I found quite entertaining. Also I brought this box of paints, and this drawing book. Also some charcoal. If nothing else, they may help you find a way of passing the time easily, while you are confined. Illness and incapacitation often mean a time of falling back on one's inner resources. Otherwise boredom sets in.'

It was possibly true that he was bored. Certainly he felt empty, like some vacant receptacle into which sensation, or the world, could slowly enter. He could watch the sunlight endlessly, as it played across the hospital window, and lit in turn each object in his room; and contemplate the nature of darkness when the sun had gone. He was most at peace when left alone. Yet he could sometimes enjoy the nurses as they fussed and flirted in and out of his room, where he was kept separate from less serious, or less damaged, patients. They appeared, especially the younger nurses, determined to make him happy. They would tell him that, with such a good looking face, he would go far with the girls; they would invent romance for him while he lay there. And rearrange his pillows, and giggle.

His white skin toughened and his scars healed where the bandages had been. His bones, however, were a persistent problem. He was taken to the operating theatre, more than once, so that they could be freshly broken and set again. It seemed he would never escape plaster solid around his limbs. And one morning there was a doctor at his bedside.

'They tell me,' this doctor began, 'that you've been quite a fine young rugby player. Quite the pride of your school. And not only that, a promising young farmer too. As well as being a bright enough boy in general.'

He saw, to his relief, that he was not expected to agree. He was just being told, for some reason.

'Well,' the doctor went on, 'I don't find it pleasant having to discuss this; I'd much sooner not. But it might be easier if I

263

told you now, so you can get used to the idea. The point, I'm afraid, is that your rugby days are over. Or anything athletic, with acute physical demand. Oh yes, you'll walk again, of course. Perhaps not as easily as other people. But reasonably. You won't be greatly handicapped or anything like totally crippled; and you may not suffer more than twinges to remind you of this unhappy time in your life. As for the farm, I imagine your father will still find you useful there. In fact, if you take things easy, you'll live as normal a life as most.'

After the doctor had gone, he tried to consider what he had been told. He was doubtless supposed to feel something, and he tried to free himself from the impassive disguise he had devised for the doctor. It was then he discovered that the disguise was, for once, the truth. So he felt relief, if anything.

He turned after a time to the books Mrs Fletcher had deposited on his bedside table. And read them from duty, more or less. It was certainly true that they were light and pleasant, as she suggested, but they were not equal to entertaining or interesting him. They could not, for example, tell him anything of his sick terror when the land turned over; there was no black pain in the pit to escape, or even acknowledge. They might have been designed, in fact, to fuel his impatience. For he turned at length to the paints and charcoal she also left, and the blank pages in the drawing book. He doodled, listing the discoveries his awakening eyes made, as the days grew longer and his body repaired so far as it would.

There was a nurse, then, with whom he imagined himself in love. She wasn't the prettiest of the nurses. She was just a small birdy girl, sometimes rather shy when alone with him, who bathed his body gently, lifted him into wheelchairs, and pushed him out into the sunlight on good days. She didn't pester, or giggle too much. Yet she was quietly bright enough, most of the time, and seemed to enjoy inhabiting her trim brown body. Her name was Nurse Pratt; he was never more familiar, though their hands often touched by chance. She talked of some place by the sea where she swam in wild surf on her holidays, and walked across miles of lonely dunes. Though she did not actually say she was alone; it could be presumed that she had not. She said Tim would have liked it too. She was a good swimmer, once a school champion. She was careful not to ask if there were some activity at which he might have excelled. But he could almost wish himself upon a rugby field again, hammering through a ruck or taking a pass, with Nurse Pratt applauding from the touch line. Instead he began to make her pictures which might please.

Also for Mrs Fletcher, who appeared even more gratified. The pictures were still life, mainly. And, at first sight, as light and pleasant and airy as the books she brought him. Fruit on the table. A chair by a bright window, with sunlit sky beyond. A vase of flowers Nurse Pratt had arranged by his bed. And that was, after all, quite reasonable. His life could not have been more stationary. He could not believe himself growing older. Or in the world elsewhere. Not even, for example, if he closed his eyes tight, as a trial; he saw not what he should have seen, then, but something which he preferred not to see again. So he did not try. He painted still life.

'I do believe, Tim,' Mrs Fletcher said, delighted, 'you are coming back to life again. And in more ways than one. Some of these are quite superb. The attention to detail in this one, for example. Such patient observation. And yet your treatment is really quite imaginative.'

'I have nothing much else to do,' he offered.

'Better still,' she went on, 'there's this splendid sense of design you have. I know you had it, doubtless instinctively, when younger. But it is, I suspect, more conscious now. You are older and able to make more sense of things. And that, after all, is what design is all about. Making sense of things. To discover order where there seems none. Isn't that so?'

She might have been expecting an answer. It was hard to say.

'Never mind,' she said, 'the main thing is that you're making a very good best of yourself in here. I hope you don't mind, by the way, if I convey some of this work to your art teacher at school. So that he can know it's possible for you to try harder after all. When you want to, that is. And,' she added, 'I must say too that it's a pleasure to see such cheerful, charming work from you, Tim. It would have been perfectly forgivable if you hadn't chosen to look on the bright side.'

Nurse Pratt might have been the explanation, if not altogether. Her pleasure in the pictures he painted was quieter. She said she had tacked some up on the wall of her room in the nurses' home, for other girls to envy. She confessed also that she was sometimes teased, but didn't mind. She walked him on the hospital terrace, persuading him to use his legs, and then through the hospital grounds, which smelled fresh after rain.

His father, who did not know about the painting at all, was simply pleased that his boy, after so long, was coming right.

So he was pleasing everyone again, it seemed, except himself. He wouldn't know where to begin. He was, to everyone, that brave and likeable Livingstone boy; his disguises had become single, and he was almost inextricable.

There came a day when he was allowed to leave the hospital, hobbling on a stick. His father arrived in the car to collect him. He tried to make his departure as quick as he could, for he had already said goodbye. He had said goodbye, in truth, at twelve the night before, which was the time Nurse Pratt went off duty. She arrived at his bedside, bearing a cup of tea. She was pale in the dark, and her starched uniform had a crisp sound. He had not been asleep, though the lights had been off for hours; he had grown numb with waiting. And she was shy. They did not know what to say to each other. They could not seem to make themselves say anything. She began, professionally, to make him comfortable in his bed for the last night. Then her hand encountered his, this time deliberately, not by chance. 'Perhaps,' she said, without much conviction, 'we will meet each other again. And have things to say then.' At length she leaned over him, her uniform rustling in the dark, and kissed him lightly on the lips. He could feel, through the starch, her small breasts pressing softly against him. He wanted, then, to know more of that undamaged body she occupied with such satisfaction. But she withdrew, and squeezed his hand again. 'Never mind,' she said. 'You're still young. It's just a pity I'm not younger. Or you're not older. It seems one of our lives isn't arranged right.'

Then her swift feet sounded away down the polished hospital corridor, and altogether out of his badly arranged life.

Back on the farm things were much the same after all. He could not imagine why he should have expected change. His father fussed, for a time. That was about the only difference. Apart from the place looking slightly shrunken under the hills, after his months away.

'You got to take it easy for a while,' his father said. 'That's what they tell me.'

'I can manage some things around the place,' Tim insisted. 'I'm not a cripple.'

266

'You leave the hard yacker to me. Don't worry about it. About anything. I wouldn't say you was a box of birds yet, by any means.' He paused. 'Anyhow you still got school to think of.'

They had not discussed this. Tim had taken it for granted that he would not be returning.

'School?'

'That's right. You might as well see the thing out. You can't be much use on the farm anyway. It'll keep your mind off the place.'

'I don't see the point.'

'Look, boy, I don't want you brooding around here. The way I see it, I been pushing you too hard. I got a lot to forgive myself. And I'm lucky I still got you.'

Tim felt discomfort. He usually did, when people showed feeling. 'I don't see the point,' he repeated, 'if I'm just going back to kill time. And leave at the end of the year.'

'If you take something on, boy, you see it through. I can't stand quitters. Never could. Besides I don't want you, or anyone, saying I never gave you a chance. So go back to school and finish off there. The farm will still be here when you finish. You know that.'

So he found himself a schoolboy again. Despite the stump, the gap in the land, and Nurse Pratt.

The teachers all made allowances upon his return. And were gentle with their demands. All, that was, except the art teacher, Mr Grey, who tended to be rather excitable anyway.

'You've certainly been hiding your light under a bushel, Livingstone,' he said. 'I always thought you were up to more than you showed me in class. Though that was good enough. But this work Mrs Fletcher has been showing me is really quite fine. So I think we should spend longer together, if you don't mind. And, after all, your other activities are limited now.'

This was impossible to dispute. So he was trapped, more or less, with Mr Grey in a room of the school while battle sounds rose from the rugby field outside.

'Patience,' Mr Grey insisted. 'Patience. That is what you need, above all else. And it seems you had some in hospital. This work, by contrast, is rather sloppy. Good, but sloppy. It seems you have difficulty concentrating again.'

This also was undeniable. His disguise here had become thin. Irritation had begun to corrode it beneath.

'Precision,' Mr Grey said. 'That is what we must work

267

towards together. It might help if we return to some basic things, which you rather tend to take for granted. I should like to think we are not embarked together on some rather futile exercise. But instead on something which might allow you to lead a fuller life – something rather richer, say, than cows and rugby.'

For Tim tended, sometimes, to look through the window to see what was going on outside. Still life was no longer sufficient.

'Well,' Mr Grey said, 'we have made some progress, of a kind. I should like to think we had made more. But still. Your work, let's say, is worthy enough. It's just that there is something missing.' He shook his head, perplexed : he could hardly know about Nurse Pratt. 'Conviction, perhaps. Certainly not talent. If only we had more time to sharpen it, perhaps conviction would come. This late start, under these circumstances, is most depressing. I've been hoping for someone like you to arrive on my hands, and now you're here I can't quite see what to do with you. Except wait. And there isn't time.'

His precision, however, began to announce itself colourfully on the walls of the art room, where his pictures were hung.

Towards the middle of that last year Mr Grey approached him with some excitement. 'There is this national art competition for schools,' he said, 'which might interest you. Each school selects its own entries, and there are money prizes put up by the brewer who is sponsoring it all. You might prepare something for the senior section. I think we can take it for granted that yours will be our entry.'

So Tim obliged again, with nothing to prove, or lose. But this time there was in the end no satisfaction in pleasing, if there had ever been. There was just more irritation, until his disguise was altogether split and obligation became repudiation, though he wasn't sure of what, as he laboured upon the painting he was supposed to produce. The problem was simple, a matter of some chosen landscape. And that chose itself. The rest was detail, even if he was impatient with detail, and Nurse Pratt no longer in his life. He was left, it seemed, with this scarred body, and with limbs which still haphazardly functioned. So he painted. He surprised himself. He had never cared less, or more. A bitter wind might have grieved through the dead trees and charred stumps; there might have been black frost in the shadow of the crude hills. And he felt, if not free, at least elated.

'There,' he said at length to his teacher.

Who considered. He took a long time to consider.

'Livingstone,' he said, 'I have just one question. You haven't copied this from somewhere?'

'Should I have?' he asked. 'Was that the idea?'

'It is just,' Mr Grey said, 'that it doesn't seem to be yours. It is unlike – well, so unlike your work.' He shook his head. 'Unlike anything. I don't know. I just don't know. What happened?'

Tim really could not say.

'You must have had some idea of what you were doing,' Mr Grey protested. 'Or of what you meant to do. Just a hint would help. A little hint.'

'I just painted,' he explained finally. 'Perhaps I wasn't in the mood.'

'I see. And am I supposed to take from this that you've lost interest?'

'I don't know,' Tim confessed. For he didn't. He had still to consider the cause of his satisfaction.

'I know you're finishing up this year, not taking anything further. All the same, though, I didn't expect a swan-song quite so explicit. You're sure this is all you have to submit, quite sure?'

'Quite sure.'

'My God,' said Mr Grey, despairing, 'I don't know how I'm going to sort this lot out. Can't you be any more help to me?'

'It doesn't seem like it.'

'All right. Well, there we are. Or here I am, rather. With this. You realize, I suppose, that I've virtually committed my-self? I didn't press for competition among senior pupils because I know they have other demands at this time of year. And because I was so certain yours would be the only real entry anyway. You might have told me you were losing interest.'

'You didn't ask.'

'True.'

'And I mightn't have said that anyway.'

'So I can't win. You've made it admirably clear. Now you'd better go and give someone else a headache.'

But his entry was forwarded, after all, for he won the competition. Mr Grey, at first stunned, was soon proud. 'There you are,' he said. 'I knew you'd make it.' And was graceful enough to add, 'I really shouldn't have had any doubts at all. What will you do with the money?'

'Money?' Tim said. He had forgotten.

'It's a substantial enough sum, for a young man. And for this kind of competition, in this country. I don't doubt that you will find some use for it. You could invest it, perhaps, or use it to further your education. You know which I would prefer. By the way, we're both expected to attend the ceremony, both teacher and winning pupil. I take it that there's no problem about this for you. Our fares will be paid.'

'Where to?'

'The city. Next week. Until then it's officially a secret. We'll have to make arrangements.'

So he had to tell his father, finally.

'Whose idea was it?' he asked.

'It was just a competition,' Tim repeated. 'I was asked to submit something.'

'Who asked you?'

'I just told you. My teacher.'

'Why did he ask you?'

'I suppose because he thought I might have a chance.'

'He might of asked me what I thought. I'm supposed to be your bloody father, after all.'

'It was a school thing.'

'So that means it's got nothing to do with me, does it? Who keeps you at school? And whose idea is it that I sent you to school to paint pictures?'

'I do other things. This was something special.'

'Too right it's something special. So special I'm not even told about it.'

'You've got it all wrong.'

'I'd just like to know what they think you're up to.'

'They're not up to anything. You don't understand.'

'I got them sized up, all right. Don't worry about that.' His father brooded for a time. 'Well,' he conceded, 'that money will be handy, anyhow.'

'Yes,' Tim said. 'That's what I'm trying to tell you about. I've got to get it. Collect it.'

'You just said you bloody won the money. What do you mean?'

'Well, I'm supposed to get it at some prize-giving in the city. I'm supposed to go up there with my teacher.'

'I might of known,' his father said. 'I might of known all along there was some other bloody stunt. Who said you was going up to the city?'

'No one said. I just said I was supposed to.' He added quickly, 'The fares are paid.'

'They would be,' his father said. 'Of course they would be. They wouldn't leave a little thing like that to chance. They plan everything neat.'

'I don't see what you mean.'

'You wouldn't. Of course you wouldn't. You're only the one they're after, the innocent. You'd be the last one to know. But I been around. If these people, whoever they are, are so keen on throwing their money about on pictures, why don't they come down and give it to you, eh? Answer me that.'

Tim couldn't.

'I'll tell you why,' his father went on. 'Because they want you up there. For some reason of their own. Your teacher's probably in it too, and that headmaster for all we know. It's as plain as a dirty window. They want you in the city, and they made up their minds to get you there. Well, just let them try.' Ned Livingstone rubbed his hands together. 'Just let the bastards try.'

'All they want to do is give the money to me.'

'And you think they'll rest content with that? Do you? You think that fare to the city is to be spent for nothing?'

Tim was quiet. He could see a cranky logic in what his father said, but where logic ended and crankiness began he could not tell.

'You have to admit it, boy,' his father insisted. 'This whole thing has a smell. No one in his right mind would want to throw all that money about on just a kid's picture.'

Now he couldn't see where the crankiness ended. With a sick feeling, quite helpless, he realized there might be no stop. It was as if a falling pebble had dislodged stones, and stones boulders. And his father rumbled on.

'But the money,' Tim said finally.

'Don't worry,' his father announced. 'We'll get it, all right. We'll keep them to that. Even if we have to bloody sue them. So you go right back and tell that to your smarmy bloody teacher.'

At school, though, all he said to Mr Grey was, 'My father's being a bit difficult about this trip.'

'Perhaps someone ought to have a talk to him.'

271

'No,' Tim said quickly. 'I don't think that's a good idea.'

'It's rather important, you see, this award ceremony. The first time, and all that. I still have to go, even if you can't. But it's much better, from all points of view, that you collect the prize in person. I'll speak to the headmaster. There must be someone who can talk to your father.'

'But I've tried to talk to him. It's no good.'

'We'll see, then.'

Tim made a last effort, before everything slid away again, quite out of his control; this time he saw the stump coming, and a crack in his life opening as large as the last. 'I think I'd sooner not go anyway,' he said, and he might have been wrenching the wheel again. But too late.

'Most commendable loyalty,' Mr Grey observed, with the faintest of smiles.

'This teacher of yours,' his father said over the evening meal, 'I hope you spoke to him straight today, and told him just what we thought.'

'I talked to him,' Tim agreed.

'And I bet we took the wind out of his sails too. The last thing he'd expect.'

'Well – '

'A bit of a pansy, is he?'

'I wouldn't say that.'

'Married?'

'Yes.'

'Some of them are,' his father said. 'Just for show. You never know where you are with these tricky bastards.'

'But you haven't met him.'

'I pick his kind a mile. Didn't he come to you on the quiet about doing this picture?'

'In a way. But – '

'There you are then. Next time he tries that, tell him to go and stuff himself. Make this one the last. This picture.'

'It's just his job. I mean, part of his job. He takes English too.'

'Well, let him stick to that. Next time tell him you're not at school to mess about. You mightn't be so lucky, the way you're lucky this time. I ought to make a complaint, pull you out of school. You sure you can't give me something more solid to go

272

on? That's what I ought to do. Make a complaint and pull you out.'

'All right,' Tim said. 'So it's all finished.'

But it wasn't. Mrs Fletcher arrived at the door, skinny and awkward, in a straggly dress and floppy hat. She brought a freshly baked cake as excuse.

'By the way,' she said, 'I must offer my congratulations. I really can't say just how delighted I am by the news.'

It was true her bony face shone. Tim didn't dare look at his father.

'I think,' she went on, 'I can fairly claim – well, some small contribution towards Tim's success. I'm so pleased and proud. You must be proud of your son too, Ned.'

There was a silence; they all seemed tied to weights.

'All right,' Ned Livingstone said at length. 'So the boy has painted a picture.'

'There's really a little more to it than that,' Mrs Fletcher said amiably. 'Don't be so modest, Ned.'

'I got no plan to stand up and cheer,' he replied. 'If that's what you mean.'

'But all the same – '

'The sooner there's an end to it, the better. I didn't know this was going on, behind my back. I thought the boy had grown up out of it.'

'But it's part of education, part of making the whole person. You sent him to school, Ned, and kept him there.'

'Because I thought a bit of education wouldn't hurt him in life. I mightn't know much myself, but there's one thing I'm sure of. Life isn't bloody pictures. I'm sorry now I didn't pull him out of school when I should. But there was others thought I wasn't doing right by the boy.'

He didn't accuse, since there was no need. He just left it there.

'He's brought credit to his school, Ned,' Mrs Fletcher pleaded. 'Credit to the district, credit to us all. You've a very talented son. Can't you see?'

'I'm thinking about the boy,' Ned Livingstone said. 'I am thinking about him. Not credit for anyone. I have never gone much on any kind of credit anyway. Generally I pay cash, or take it. The boy can get his hands on that cash, and there's an end to it. I suppose he earned it fair. I wouldn't know.'

'Then you will let him attend the ceremony?' Mrs Fletcher said in surprise.

'I didn't say that. What do you know about it anyway?'

'I just heard.' Mrs Fletcher realized the blunder.

'Now that's very interesting,' he said, shrewd. 'I reckon I hardly had time to hear anything myself. I didn't know news spread this quick, even round Te Ika.'

Mrs Fletcher, quite trapped, said nothing.

'I can see,' said Ned Livingstone, 'that there's been a hell of a lot going on behind my back. More things, more scheming than I thought. And you're in it too. Who rung you up today and told you to try and talk me round into letting the boy go?'

'I just heard, Ned. Quite by chance. Quite accidentally.'

'A quick accident, then. Convenient too. Who is it wants the boy so much, and why do they want him? It seems they're after him terrible hard. The more I see and hear, the more it smells. By God, it does. How long have you been in on this? Was that why you came to me before and talked me into keeping the boy on at school? Who was it rung you up then?'

'No one. I just – '

'You been in it all along. You and how many others? I thought once there was neighbours I could trust, after all. Now I can see there's no one a man can trust. Not that I ever really knew different.'

Mrs Fletcher took a lean stand at last. 'You mustn't let suspicion run away with you.'

'Don't you think I got any common sense to use? And I got eyes, I got ears. Whoever it was rung you up today, you can ring right back again. And say the boy's not going to this damn ceremony. Not even going back to school again. After today, he's finished. We made up our minds, Tim and me. Just tell them that. And tell them to send whatever cash is due, or I'll see my lawyer.'

'Ned, please – '

'And you can take this home again,' he said, pushing the cake back into her unwilling arms. 'I think I'd choke on it. Tell Jock I'm sorry, but I don't want to see him up here again neither. Tim and me will have more than enough to keep us busy without wasting ourselves on useless conversation. More than enough. Won't we, boy?'

Both his father and Mrs Fletcher waited on him to speak, Mrs Fletcher in dazed appeal. He tried to nod in agreement, but it seemed nothing showed; perhaps his head hadn't moved at all. Mrs Fletcher's tongue then fluttered absurdly in her open mouth.

'Ned – '

'Get out,' his father said. 'Get out before I'm bloody angry. Get out before I throw you out.' He paused. 'And don't come near the boy again, any of you.'

She went, all legs and quivering skin, and sudden tears. She did not look back at Tim. She vanished around the house and they heard the car leave, coughing away down to the gorge.

He tried to find the shape of words in his thick throat. The expression on his father's face seemed to have made up its mind at last. It was one of satisfaction, after all.

'You needn't have,' was what he said to his father finally. 'You needn't have done that. She was only – ' But he could not finish. Only what?

'The bitch,' his father said. 'The two-timing old bitch. Coming here like that, to tell me what to do.' It appeared his father had not heard Tim at all. 'But we showed her, didn't we?'

'She was only trying to do what she thought best,' Tim finished. 'She meant well.'

This time his father did hear. Though he could not seem to believe what he heard. 'What are you talking about, boy?'

'You needn't have done that,' Tim persisted. 'It wasn't fair. She's been good to me. And don't keep saying we. When it really means you. Because we didn't make up our minds about anything at all, the way you told her. You made up your mind. Not me.'

His father's expression seemed to shift with a creak. 'What is this?' he asked, and groped for a word. 'Are you defying me?'

'No,' Tim said quietly. 'Not defying.'

'Then what? Have they turned you against me? Have they got you by the bloody balls after all?'

'I'm just telling you,' Tim said.

He lay awake that night considering what he would do with the money. Then he knew. He would use it to paint another picture, like the one which had won the prize. Only larger, and better. It would have to be both, perhaps, if he were to find out not so much where he went wrong as where he went right. For he wasn't sure, no more than baffled Mr Grey. He would like it so large that he could almost step into it, look around, and breathe; he would like it so real that people might be bruised and scratched, if they entered. And so no one could doubt, in the end, not even his father. Also, he might find out this time what it was that made him feel so good and strange the first time he tried. The memory of that pleasure could still reverberate in his flesh, not unlike another memory, the gentle pressure of Nurse Pratt in the dark. And that was gone. Half asleep, his imagination working, it seemed he had already made this picture. But when he woke in the morning he had not even begun; he did not even have the money to buy what he needed to begin. And he had to. He was terrified he mightn't.

'I think I'd better go up to the city,' he announced, 'and get this money. I want to make sure I get it.'

'What this?' his father said. He could not seem to understand what he heard; he was still rather distracted.

'I said I'm going to collect this money. To make sure I get it.'

'We'll get it, all right. Don't worry about that.'

'But I must make sure. So I'm going up there to collect it.'

'What are you talking about, boy? You just sit tight. It'll come. We'll make sure of it.'

'I want the money quickly. I don't want to wait.'

'Why? What the hell's so desperate? We're not short, if you want a bit of pocket money. In fact I'll put you on a regular wage now you've finished with school. So forget that other. What the hell use would all that be to you just now anyway?'

He was obliged, it seemed, to tell his father. And he did, in the end.

Again, though, his father was unwilling to understand, or believe. 'What's that?' he said.

'I said I want to paint another picture. Like the one I did. Only different. Bigger. Just to see if I can. To make sure it wasn't a mistake. I've got the time. I'm still not much use around the place; you've said so yourself.'

'Jesus Christ,' his father said. 'You've never took this serious before.'

'Other people have.' This was not convincing, but it was all he could find to say.

'Does that mean you got to be an idiot too?'

'No. It just means I want to have another try.'

'Then it seems I better give you another try at some more of the farm work.'

'And I want to get that money.'

'We'll see about the money, all right.'

'I want to make sure of it myself.'

'We'll see about it,' his father repeated. 'Are you arguing with me?'

'Not arguing with you,' Tim said. 'Just telling you again.'

'Telling me?' His father tasted the words.

'Yes. Telling you.'

'By God,' his father said.

He moved in upon his son heavily. Tim lurched sideways, trying to duck, and his worst leg sang with sudden pain. His father's blow went wild. Ned Livingstone fell defeated against a chair. 'It's for your own good,' he breathed. 'I never wanted nothing that wasn't for your good.'

But his son, standing beside him, listened only in a technical sense.

'So they got you, the bastards,' his father went on. 'I might of known. I woke up too slow. Too late. I ought to of lumbered you before, for discipline. Now that's too late too.'

Standing above the chair, in vivid shock, Tim saw somewhere safe. A place of cruel colour and cool form where nothing could touch him and hurt. He had begun to set foot there before he knew it. And before he knew himself free. So it was possible, then, to bend his father after all.

'I'm sorry,' he could say with ease. And add ruthlessly, 'we've just got to accept, you and me, that we see things differently.'

It was only truth which had to be said. Otherwise he was forever disguised, forever prisoner.

'Dad,' he said, 'are you listening to me? I'm not your little boy.'

'You never were,' his father replied, lifting himself at last. 'Never bloody were, but I never wanted to wake up to it. Not even when your mother, the bitch, wanted to tell me.'

'What are you talking about?'

'You got nothing to do with me. Nothing at all. Even your name.'

'No,' said Tim, who could never doubt.

'Never were. Nothing to do with me.'

'You're off your head,' Tim said, unable to stop. 'I mean – '

But it was meant. They entered silence.

He attempted repair. He went to Mrs Fletcher to apologize,

but she wouldn't hear him out. 'I know you feel obliged to stand by your father,' she insisted, 'and that is a very praiseworthy thing. Indeed, a most natural thing.' So he was unable, really, to confess the truth. Or say he was, in fact, going to the city. He also looked in on Mr Grey, when he picked up his possessions at school. 'About this trip to the city,' he said. 'I think it will be all right now. I'll be able to make use of the money right away.'

He didn't say what for.

'So long as you're sure,' Mr Grey said.

'I'm sure. I'll meet you at the train.'

'Then that's fixed. Great relief all round. It's just a pity you felt obliged to leave school beforehand, but that doesn't affect your win, of course.'

'I hope not,' he said. For it seemed to be all he had.

'I don't mind telling you, Livingstone, I'd sooner not have heard of this award. The way things have turned out. You might be able to put a brave face on it. But it seems I've lost my brightest pupil. I can't believe that your precipitate departure from school is unconnected. Or that you've left of your own accord.'

Tim chose not to say.

'All right, so I'll meet you at the train,' Mr Grey said, vaguely despairing.

Finally, of course, he had to tell his father again too, in case he hadn't been believed the first time. 'I'm going to the city tomorrow,' he said, 'to pick up this money I have coming to me. This way, I make sure.'

He wasn't inclined to expand. It should have been clear.

It was warm in the kitchen, a cool sunset light on the windows and frost in the air outside. They had just come in to eat, having used all the daylight. The first calves had arrived, and the herd was coming into milk again.

His father might have been expecting something of the kind that night. Anyway his reply was quick.

'All right,' he said, 'so it's your way. Their way. I won't expect you back.'

'But I am,' he insisted. 'Coming back, I mean.'

'I said I won't expect you.'

'But I –'

'Jesus, boy, haven't you got any wit? I'm saying if you go, you go. And don't come back.'

That was clear too, even more so.

278

'There is,' said his father, 'no use in us buggering about any longer. We got to know where we stand, you and me. Either you belong here or you don't. Either you're my son or you're not.'

Tim hesitated. 'I see,' he said at length. 'All right, then. At least I know, don't I?'

What he saw, though, was some last test, contrived for truth or satisfaction. Was he supposed to live his life as proof, and would it satisfy anyway? Certainly such a life could offer no truth, of any kind.

'Do you? I'm interested, boy, in what you really do know. But I'll let tomorrow tell me.'

'Then you needn't wait. I'm going anyway. Because now it seems I have to.'

The next day his father did not offer to take him by car to the train, and he did not expect it. He started the long walk down to Te Ika, carrying a light bag, and taking things slowly on his uneven legs. If there was no goodbye, it was because neither believed it. His father was at a distance, across the paddocks, under hazy hills and dull sky. The road was rough on his feet, and his pauses frequent. He could still imagine himself back in a month or two, when he had done what he wanted. So he was actually within the gorge, surrounded by high crags, before he really troubled to look back, too late.

At the railway station, waiting for Mr Grey and the train north, he thought of something he might do before he left. He went on his stiffening legs to a telephone box and made a call. He was not sure what he was going to say, but he hoped to find out.

The voice he finally heard, however, was brisk and strange. 'Nurse Pratt,' the voice said, 'is no longer with us. She has had a transfer.'

'Thank you,' he said politely, and placed the receiver down.

279

Fourteen:

SAM KAHU WAS KILLED ON THE LAST SATURDAY OF THE SEASON
when he tried to hurdle a tackle on the opposition goal-line; he
grounded the ball for a try in almost the same instant as his neck
was broken. They had, he and Ian, travelled the full distance
after all. For Ian had tried to warn Sam off his dangerous
delight in hurdling tackles, and been amiably ignored. The
game was won, and lost.

Yet there were still ten minutes to play after Sam was taken
off in the ambulance. Ian took command of the bruised and
diminished team, which had to hold off crushing forward charges
upon their line. It seemed this anti-climax would never end.
He kicked and kicked, trying to clear the ball; he tackled
endlessly. His hard fit body might have been made for such
contingencies, but he found no comfort in it now; his mouth
was dry with terror, and not from the savage rucks into which he
found himself flung, or the boots which crashed into his face.
He journeyed to the last of his strength, and then into the
delirium beyond. And the referee's whistle sounded at a great
distance. The game, incredibly, was over. And the season,
though he might have been slower to see it. For he and Cedric
Black changed urgently and followed the ambulance up to the
hospital. Sam took six hours to finish dying. His body lay three
days in the Maori meeting house before the tangi concluded and
he was buried. The *Gazette* carried a short obituary : there was,
it seemed, nothing much that Ian could really say about Samuel
Kahu. The obituary said that he had been a promising rugby
player, and a credit to his race; the last phrase was actually
the editor's. 'You've got to say something about him,' he said, as
he added the line to Ian's copy. 'I know he was a friend of

yours, but you've got to learn to be objective. That's what you're here for.'

'Then why not just say he was a credit to himself?'

'He was a Maori, wasn't he? Or have you got your facts wrong again?' The editor looked at Ian with something like pity. 'Credit to our brown brothers when credit is due. And they buy our paper, after all.'

'But you don't really give a damn, do you?'

'That's what I mean,' said the editor, 'about being objective. I never liked the smell of shark and muttonbirds anyway. Why we didn't finish them all off, when we had a chance, I'll never know. They'll probably breed us out of this country again one day. Still, that's one less.'

'Lucky, then, aren't we?' Ian said.

'How?'

'That no one will ever expect us to be a credit to our race,' he said, as he started to leave the editor's room.

'You're smart, young man, but not smart enough,' the editor called after him. 'Not yet. But you'll learn. Your kind always do.'

There was a strange scene at the graveside. A young and pretty Maori girl flung herself at Sam's descending coffin; there was a flurry as she was pulled back and carried away. Ian saw hopeless love. The girl, whose name he seemed to remember as Weri, had been one of Sam's neighbours. And rather irrelevant. He had noticed her shy gaze on Sam, at times, but Sam seemed immune. And he would no more have thought of mentioning the girl to Sam than the other would have thought of mentioning, say, Margaret Saunders.

Who was waiting for him, afterwards, at the cemetery gate. Exhausts were jetting, cars rolling back to the town.

They exchanged words with effort as the crowd dwindled around them. The spring sunshine began to soften the cemetery again. Then he heard Margaret say, 'It was more than you knew. You didn't really know anything. You see, Weri's pregnant. Yes, Sam. And before Saturday they had an arrangement to get married. Quite soon, naturally. But it wasn't just a sudden thing. It was going on for a while, only you never saw it because Sam didn't – '

She twisted her face away. Embarrassment was unlikely in Margaret.

'Because he – because I don't think he cared for you and Cedric to know about it, not right away. He wanted to stay one of the boys as long as he could. Until the end of the season anyway.'

He didn't go back to work that afternoon. Partly because he didn't feel up to it; partly because of Cedric Black. For Cedric still appeared quite numb and bewildered. No one, other than the girl Weri perhaps, was left quite so lost. Certainly no one had depended on Sam more. Without Sam always laughing and coaxing, gentle Cedric's pleasure in life wouldn't have amounted to much; he wouldn't even have made the grade for a decent football team. And with Sam's colour gone, he was left with his father's hardware store and a functional future in Te Ika. Ian could see that too clearly. What he could not see was how properly to console. But he drove Cedric out of town, towards the coast, and home again, trying to talk. Until there was nothing left to say. And Sam Kahu still quite dead.

Sitting in his car, he listened to Cedric's feet scrape hopelessly away down a dimly lit street. And he encountered himself again, unwillingly. At least someone he could once perhaps have presumed to have been himself; the sensation was strange. He could have been looking at himself across a divide. Or from Margaret Saunders' viewpoint at the cemetery gate. His character, then, seemed more her possession than his own. It wasn't that she appeared to see through him, exactly; it was that she saw around him. And that might be sufficient. For he needed reassurance of his substance. He drove, not homeward, but towards the Saunders farm.

He arrived there not long after the evening meal. Clem Saunders was smoking his pipe before an open fire, his feet propped up against the mantelpiece, though the night was mild enough; he appeared to enjoy the commanding position of this fireside role. Around him the rest of the family flowed: he was, with his austere face, the still centre. Margaret and her young sister Judy were busy in the kitchen. Peter was fretting over homework, and Fred was contemplating an agricultural journal without enthusiasm.

'We don't see you out here often,' Clem observed.

'An unusual day,' Ian answered.

'No argument about that,' Clem agreed. The entire family had been at the funeral, and Fred one of the pallbearers along with Ian. 'Something the matter?'

'Nothing in particular.'

'I thought it might just have been something to do with that girl. Sam's girl. Sad business.'

'Yes. I don't know whether there's anything the rest of us can do.'

'The Maoris usually look after their own,' Clem suggested. 'A pretty moody lot. Best to leave them to it.'

'Probably.' Ian was not inclined to debate with Clem.

'If it's Margaret you're looking for, she's in the kitchen.'

'I can see that.'

Clem returned to his newspaper with a responsible frown. Ian passed a few words with Fred and Peter before he went into the kitchen. But his delay doubtless didn't deceive anyone.

Margaret looked up from cleaning the stove, a faint smoky smear on one cheek. Judy muttered some shy excuse and left them together.

'Surprise, surprise,' Margaret said.

'Hardly. I promised to come out at the end of the season.'

'True. But I didn't expect such speed.' She lifted an eyebrow. 'Or is the word haste?'

He shrugged. 'Please yourself.'

'How's Cedric?'

'Alive, at least. I just saw him home.'

'Poor Cedric. At the funeral I wasn't sure who was going to break first. Weri or Cedric.'

She almost spelled it out: the lovers. His own claim to Sam Kahu began to seem a flimsy thing. Sam was a safe childhood, gone. And the world beyond was spiky.

'I'd sooner not talk about it. I came to see you.'

'I hardly ever see you out here, and you turn up tonight. Of all nights. Why? To keep some dusty promise? I don't believe it.'

'You did say you might be going away soon.'

'Agreed,' she said. 'But still.'

'And are you?'

'As a matter of fact, yes. I'll be gone within the month. It's definite.'

'I see.'

'I didn't think the news would leave you prostrate. And I see it hasn't.'

'It might be because I'm leaving myself. Or coming around to the idea. The way things are, I could be gone in a month or two.'

283

'That's that, then. So we might have that much in common after all.'

They seemed tense enough about it. So he tried again.

'It's a pleasant night,' he said. 'I could suggest a drive.'

'About time too.' The tension vanished with her sly smile. She swept past him into the living room.

'Ian and I are just going out for a bit,' she announced to the family. Fred and Peter looked up with interest; Judy too. Clem, though, remained fastened to his newspaper before the fire and made no sign he heard. 'I imagine you can do without me for an hour or two,' she added. 'You'll have to get used to it.'

She tugged a windbreaker over her shirt and they let themselves out the back door. 'Thank God you came,' she said. 'I was starting to stifle in there. They've only just begun to believe I'm going. And things have gone sour. Clem says I've got no loyalty, I'm breaking up the family, I'm selfish. All possibly true. But I still have to go.'

'Yes.' He thought he understood.

'Do you think our lives are important?' she asked. 'Yours and mine, say.'

'Probably not.'

'But we still have to find out, don't we? We still have to find out what they amount to. Even if we find out they don't amount to anything. At least we know.'

'I think I'd prefer not to find out. But it seems I have to do something anyway.'

The stars were bright, and the rising moon. He could smell the dry pines sheltering the farmhouse; the warmth of the spring day lingered over the needled path. A season he could dread, this one more than most. Tonight, though, his feelings were mixed. Margaret took his arm as they walked to the car.

She suggested a gorge further along South Road, the town's one rather limp attempt at a scenic reserve, and not much used other than by children and lovers. Though they didn't strictly qualify for either category. They were past childhood and not yet lovers. It had begun to seem they might never be. They bumped along South Road in silence for a few minutes, past the Kahu farm and the scrubby Maori land around, gorse and clay banks sharp in the headlights.

'A penny for them,' Margaret said.

'Not worth it,' he insisted.

'Next football season?'

284

'Hardly.'

'Don't tell me you've finished up.'

'Since you ask, yes.'

'Good God, So what, dear melancholy one, will you have instead?'

'I expect I'll find something.'

'You don't have to commit yourself, you know. I'd be the last one to keep you to it. You know that.'

She might have been trying to tell him something.

He swung off the road in a slight skid, down the narrow and winding track into the gorge. There was only a foot or two to spare between a limestone bank on one side, and a sheer drop to the river on the other. Foliage clattered across the windscreen, snapped at the windows. The night seemed to thicken, though moonlight silvered the tops of the tallest trees. The road dipped, swung, and levelled out beside the river. He stopped the car and switched off the headlights; the dark rushed in to isolate them with the cooling tick of the engine. 'We seem,' he observed, 'to have the place to ourselves tonight.' She said nothing; she rested her head on his shoulder, as if her devils were at peace for once. The river was loud. And the air was chillier here. The moonlight travelled deeper into the gorge. He had an arm around her. But when he tried to involve himself more with her body, she resisted, and presently grew restive again.

'I'm getting cramp,' she insisted. 'Let's walk.'

They left the car and walked beside the river. He skipped flat stones to the other bank: tiny explosions of spray flew up shining. They seemed back to where they began, or had never begun.

'All right,' she said finally. 'Perhaps we haven't got anything to say to each other after all.'

'I wouldn't say that.'

'No? Then what would you say? What are you ever likely to say?'

'Perhaps it's not my night.'

'And obviously not mine either.' She faced him, shadow and moonlight mingling to make her face indistinct. 'Those times you were off with Sam Kahu, in the bush. I imagine you had something to say to him then.'

'What's that got to do with it?'

285

'I'm away in the bush with you now. Or as good as. So I can't help wondering, can I?'

'If you say so.'

There was a silence. He skipped another stone.

'What I really want to know, I think, is whether you slept with Sam Kahu.'

The night seemed to freeze about him. He let the new stone in his hand drop.

'You're joking.'

'I wish I was.'

'We could drive home now,' he suggested. 'There's nothing to stop us.'

'How do you think Cedric would react to the same question? Any differently?'

'Cedric?' Again the cold seemed cruel against his skin. 'Cedric – ' He stopped. He could not, he knew, speak for Cedric. It had grown difficult enough, now, to speak for himself. For the truth was, in a sense, irrelevant.

Her hand appeared on his arm, quite gentle.

'You just don't make any sense otherwise,' she insisted. 'And never have. Hiding away in this town and pretending to have half your intelligence. Acting the tough bruiser on the football field. How else can I add you up?'

So that was all. He could have laughed with relief or erupted with anger. Instead he stood divided. Perhaps truth would always unravel as soon as he touched it. For it no longer seemed true simply to say his friendship with Sam was innocent. Or to say the town was safe. It was no longer even the whole truth to explain that he was Bill Freeman's son, if he could. Because he was more than that, and less. How much more, though, and how much less? The world appeared to be conspiring to exact a precise statement of account. And he had outrun his credit, and credibility.

With Margaret, say. She was still talking.

'Anyway,' she went on, 'I'm just trying to say you're not the only one with problems.'

'So go on. Now you've invented mine, tell me yours.'

'I not asking for polite interest. Thanks all the same.'

'Then what the hell are you asking for?' he said.

There appeared only one possible answer; he had some use for his hard body after all. Anyway he had her brutally on the ground, evidently to some purpose. Her limbs were wild, not so

286

much in resistance as in demented welcome. She bit and scratched, and her breath was sibilant between her teeth. At times they might have been heaving towards the same end; at times they might have been contriving to fly apart. Tangling garments gave way to the clash of clean flesh. Yet she still seemed in two minds, or two people. Her knee jabbed bruisingly into his groin : in the next instant it locked around him. Only when he was within her, tight, was a direction clear. It was not that violence ceased : they were still battering each other down through roots of grass and brittle sticks, deeper into the dark alluvial earth on which they lay; her teeth made a final desperate attempt on his shoulder. His largeness, or her tightness, surprised him; he could hardly feel more secure. He tried to bury her mouth beneath his, but it escaped with strange sounds, then dazed words in his ear.

There was Clem's name, among other things. He was slow to understand. Then he knew, and more than he bargained for. He should have seen.

Her bitter cry carried him suddenly along too, into the blank and blinding current their flesh arranged. Then they fell apart, limp with relief, and lay still.

'Thank Christ,' she breathed. 'Thank Christ for that.'

For they had survived. And the night grew cool again.

He sold his car to a wrecker. People were another problem.

'The city?' his mother said.

'Yes.'

'Then I'd better write to Ben.'

'Thanks all the same. But I'd sooner make out for myself.'

'But university. Your future.'

'I'll keep it in mind.'

'What does that mean?' his father demanded.

'It means I have a job on a large newspaper.'

'Where you can learn to tell larger lies, no doubt.'

Perhaps it was just a question of how much wreckage he left behind. Other farewells were simpler.

'Write to me,' Diane insisted.

'God bless you,' Mary Leary said.

There was one he did not have to make. Margaret had already been gone a month. In the end it was only a matter of watching the town recede, early one morning, until green misty hills shut it from sight as the train gathered pace. Until he became prisoner of the journey.

Margaret could be postponed; the city could not. He had, it seemed, to give his mind to the place. He found a room to inhabit, a noisy tram to catch to his office, streets to walk. It did not after a time seem so great a problem. But he still did not get in touch with Margaret, though he had made a promise. It was easier not to have an identity yet. It was easier to measure himself anonymously against gritty pavement and stubborn stone. Or against palm-shaded parks and sleepy waterfront on weekends. In the office he was almost as anonymous as elsewhere. He sat at a desk among other desks and worked among clacking teleprinters, ringing telephones and deadline commotions. He was sometimes sought, but mostly ignored. His work appeared satisfactory: at least no one informed him otherwise. His conversation with colleagues at neighbouring desks seldom passed beyond the perfunctory; they were lean, tight-lipped and diversely self-important men in shirt sleeves, trying to trap history in their cryptic typewriters. So it was a surprise when a fat and friendly face appeared at length beside his desk. Ian had observed this journalist before, at a distance. Perhaps because he looked, and appeared to enjoy, the part more than most. His tie was always loosened, a small hat often tilted back on his head, and his face could shine with sweat. He was clearly, with his brisk efficient manner, the colourful office professional. And a reliable workhorse, frequently in earnest conference with chief reporter or assistant editor.

'How's the new boy?' he asked. 'On top of it all? That's the important thing. Once you're on top, ride it.'

Ian hardly nedeed to offer an opinion.

'The name's Stan Coates,' he added, and put out his hand. 'I know yours. I made a point of noticing it in the assignment book. I like to know who's round here and who isn't. It gives me a sense of security. No one creeping up behind my back. Where you from?'

'The country,' Ian confessed.

'We were most of us country boys once,' Stan said pleasantly. 'They murdering your copy?'

'I never notice much change.'

'You've made it, then. Not that anyone's going to tell you

around this place. You might ask for more money. Tell me, is this your life's ambition?'

'I suppose I'm still making up my mind.'

'That's it. Don't give the bastards an inch.' He considered Ian. 'You educated?'

'Up to a point. I haven't tried university yet. I might later.'

'Pity. It won't do you any good in this place. An uneducated bugger like me suits them better. You might turn out too clever.'

'I see.'

'That's the boy. You might have the makings.'

They met again while leaving the office for lunch. This gave Stan Coates a chance to talk about himself. Though only two or three years older, he had already written his way through a dozen newspapers. None had been quite tailored to his talent. Anyway it began when he left school at fifteen to work in a newspaper printery. There he wrote a story on an accident he witnessed. The editor, impressed, moved Stan from the printery to the office. And Stan had been moving on ever since.

'I suppose I should still be in that printery,' he said. 'I wasn't even an apprentice. Just an odd job boy. Someone to run messages, mainly. And sweep floors. If I get depressed, it seems nothing much has changed after all. I'm still running other people's messages. And sweeping away unsightly things into corners.'

Perhaps Ian was meant to be impressed. But it also began to appear surprisingly possible that Stan was just lonely, for some reason, and liked to talk. He was, after all, the least anonymous person in the office, gritty and sweaty among the bland white shirt sleeves.'

They were sitting in a wooden cubicle at the rear of a chromed coffee bar. It was some distance from the office, but Stan explained their walk by saying the place sold the only real coffee in town. He seemed to know a number of the young customers who straggled in off the main street to occupy other cubicles. They were rather uniformly distinct in appearance, often untidily bearded, and girls lank-haired, unextravagantly garbed in jeans and corduroys, windbreakers or shawls. They all appeared to know each other. There was a great deal of talk and smoke. It was more like a club than a coffee bar.

'This might strike a country boy as some den of iniquity,' Stan suggested. 'The truth is it's just a rather pathetic haven for what passes for the arty-crafties of this town. And other strays who have nowhere else to feel at home. I must confess I have a soft spot for the place. Apart from the fact that I occasionally pick up an off-beat story here. After the office, I almost feel human again.'

'It's past our hour,' Ian said. 'Perhaps we should get back.'

But Stan was calling amiably to an occupant of another cubicle, 'Where's the party Saturday night?'

'Livingstone's, I hear.'

'Well,' Stan said to Ian, 'that's Saturday night shot down in flames. Another quiet night at home.'

'What's wrong?'

'The host and I don't hit it off. Or rather we do – we hit it off at a party a couple of weeks ago. I got a blood nose, but you should have seen him.'

'I knew someone by the name of Livingstone once,' Ian said quietly.

'A Tim Livingstone?'

'Yes.' Something had gone very still inside him.

'You ever have a run-in with him, a brawl of any kind?'

'Not exactly.'

'Then it may not be the same one. You never know.'

'Tell me about him.'

'He's supposed to be an artist of sorts,' Stan said. 'He possibly is, some of the time. And a positive bloody lunatic the rest of the time. How does that sound?'

'Interesting anyway.'

'He's also young. Fair. And walks with a limp.'

'Then it is the same one.' He shouldn't have doubted.

'My sympathy,' Stan said. 'But that doesn't help my problem. I can't afford two blood noses in a fortnight.'

They walked back to the office.

'You've turned very quiet,' Stan observed.

'Yes,' Ian agreed.

Fifteen:

THERE WERE SPEECHES. IT SEEMED HE MIGHT NEVER GET THE money. People talked, instead of talent and values. But then a flash-bulb snapped dazzling in his face as he was passed the cheque by a large sweaty man. His hand was shaken, and Mr Grey's. The large sweaty man said he couldn't have been more pleased that a farmer's son, a country boy, had taken the prize. 'The wealth of our country is on the land,' he said. 'And not all in a cow's udder or on a sheep's back, as our young friend shows.'

There was polite laughter, and clapping. A flash-bulb dazzled again as he was pushed forward to stand in front of his own painting. His eyes hurt, and it seemed the thing would never end.

Nevertheless, the large sweaty man finished, he felt constrained to point out that his company, as sponsor of the prize, had rather unfairly not been given a say in the judging of the competition. A more attractive prize-winning painting, designed to show the country at its best, and worthy of reproduction on his company's annual calendar, would have been in order. Not that he wished to tell the judges their job, but he thought the feelings of his company might have been considered. Perhaps this was not the proper occasion, but all the same –

Tim understood only that whatever was happening now was not concerned with him. It was over, so far as he was concerned. For he had the money. And there was no point standing still. He folded the cheque and placed it safely in his pocket, looked around the cryptic faces once, and left. He noticed, peripherally, a silence in his wake.

'Livingstone.' Mr Grey was calling from behind, clattering down the stairs after him. 'Livingstone.'

Tim waited for him to catch up.

'You really shouldn't have done that,' said Mr Grey,

breathless. 'You might have ruined everything, for God's sake. I know that fellow was a bit much to take, but we've got to be patient. It's possible they won't put up the money again.'

'That's got nothing to do with me.'

'Don't you understand? You just can't walk out on something like that. It's not only rude, it's – a disaster. It might even get in the newspapers.'

'I've got the money. It seems to me I had enough trouble getting it. All the rest is none of my business.'

'You mean you didn't walk out because of what he said?'

'I don't know what he was going on about. I had my mind on other things.'

'Other things?'

'My own things.'

'Are they so very vital, at the moment?'

'Yes.'

The word might have been a blank wall to Mr Grey; he looked baffled. 'I'd better go back and see if the damage can be repaired. I suppose I can always invent something about a weak bladder, or your being overwrought by the occasion. God help us. Where are you going now?'

'To have a look around the city. To get on with it.'

'I'll see you at the train later, then.'

'No. I'm staying.'

'But your father – '

'He doesn't want me back now. So I have to, don't I?'

Now Mr Grey was in a sweat: crisis upon crisis. 'You sure about this? Oh, sweet Jesus.'

'I'm sure about it,' Tim said. 'So I'd better get on with it, thanks all the same.'

In the end Mr Grey fled back up the stairs to the other crisis, for preference. And quite vanished from his life.

The rooms had already gone at the first place where he called: it was over the hill from Queen Street, among old houses in a gully. 'But there's a shed out the back,' the landlady said. 'We used it for coal until we switched to electricity. I could let you have it for – let's see, now – thirty bob a week?'

They went to look at the shed. It barely stood, but it had a roof. Long grass grew at the door.

'Perhaps twenty five bob,' she said. 'It's not much. I'll put a bed in, and a chair and table. You'll have to come inside the house to cook, with the others. I'll tell you what,' she added, when he still hesitated, 'I'll make it twenty bob a week. You're just a young fellow. How's that?'

He nodded, having added up at last. And having learned the value of diffidence.

'Yes,' he said. 'All right.' He ran an idle finger over the inside wall of the shed. It came away black.

'And I'll clean it up,' she promised.

Here the earth grew only tall weeds under high wooden walls streaked with damp. Yet he thought he could make a home here, for as long as he needed. He did not think beyond, for anything beyond need was difficult to conceive. He was a fact, and the shed, and his money. At noon, he discovered, the winter sun appeared above the wooden houses, and lit the tiny window of the shed for a quick hour or two. He worked best and fast then, with paint or charcoal, upon the paper he tacked to the table. Sometimes he would sit all morning before blank paper until the sun appeared. Then, with the window stained faint yellow, and a feeble criss-cross of shadow over the table, he would begin. Not upon his big picture. Or not yet. He had to get used to himself again, if he could. Otherwise he might make nothing to bruise and scratch, only tickle. Also he was unwilling to shut his eyes for too long, lest the hills grow too large. Because they would, until he was dizzy. To get used to himself again, then, he drew messages to convince himself of what he saw around him. That was a problem too. For there seemed nowhere to stop. And he was still not convinced.

On rainy days the shed leaked, and grew damp. He could buy food for himself, and cook. That was not enough of a problem to be diverting.

He also bought books which appeared useful. And which seemed likely to tell him, if not how to start, at least where to stop. He found the art gallery, a high cold place, gloomy and quiet, with ushers who watched him suspiciously if he paused too long. He was never comfortable, and his feet echoed. And it appeared, after all, that the place had very little to show. When his first excitement was gone, he was left with some heroic Maoris and dim dusty watercolours. He might have met Mrs Fletcher peering around some corner, and almost expected to. Nevertheless he waited before the paintings as if something might reveal itself, with patience and mental persuasion; but the colours, like the subjects, were obstinate in their absence of secret. So he would step out into the bright city again.

He simply walked, when he had the patience. The streets were noisy with purpose, and people. With truck and tram, and scraping feet. There was nowhere to be alone, and everywhere to be lonely. From his shed at night he heard banging, shuffling, coughing, clinking bottles and sometimes shouting in the houses around. He shared a kitchen with a collection of solitary and battered men, often old and eager to talk.

At the end of two months he wondered what he had to show, and to whom. He certainly had no big picture. It was more remote than ever. He had, instead, apologies for not beginning. But he had money left, at least. He had been careful.

If he felt unease, and fidgeted his time away, it was possibly because he did not know enough, and might never. He had not thought of this before. He could, of course, call the whole thing off. He began a letter to his father, but found himself unable to finish it, or confess defeat. It was never an effort, though, to convince himself that his father existed, and the land on which he stood. Perhaps his father had a man to help now. He could wonder about that. And wonder too if the willows were in leaf along the creek.

Sometimes he had to conspire against himself. The sun came longer through the window now.

On the waterfront one day, trying to convince himself of precise ships on an immaculate tide, someone near his side spoke to him. He expected the usual old man. But it was a young man with gentle voice, stubby black beard, and curved pipe. He wore corduroys and a thick tartan shirt, and his old boots were suede.

'Would you mind, I wonder, if I could see what you've done?' he asked.

Tim was too surprised to speak. No one had ever asked before.

'I've been watching with some interest,' the stranger explained. He took his pipe from his mouth and his sleepy-looking eyes opened wider. 'But of course if you don't – '

'No,' said Tim quickly. 'I don't mind.' And showed.

'Well,' said the stranger at length, 'your approach seemed rather confident. That was what interested me. I can see this has got the makings, all right.'

'It's just a drawing.'

'Of course. Up at the art school, are you? This some exercise they've set?'

'No. I'm not at any school.'

'No? Well, then ...' The stranger considered the drawing again. His scrutiny seemed more careful this time. 'So what is it you do for a living, then?'

'Nothing. Unless this.'

'You don't look idle rich.'

'It's too complicated to explain.' For it was.

'I'm in no hurry, if you're not.'

If he could not explain, he could at least talk. He had not forgotten how. There were gulls drifting high above the ships. And there were potato peelings in the water.

The stranger laughed, after a while, and slapped his knee in delight. 'So you're the one,' he said. 'My God.'

'What do you mean?'

'I mean the one in the newspapers.'

Tim stared, and shook his head.

'Don't tell me you didn't read about yourself. How did these headlines go? School art controversy. Prizewinner's walkout.'

Tim shook his head again.

'So you're the one. The kid who walked out on those bastards. With the cheque – that was the part I liked best. You kept your hands on their cheque, all right.'

'That was what I went there for,' Tim explained, in case this point had been missed.

'Of course. But it's just that – ' The stranger paused, seemingly in difficulty. 'Just that – well, someone else might have been goat enough to throw the cheque back in their faces. Out of wounded feelings.'

'Why?'

'Well, exactly. There you've got me. So that's how they spoiled an honest country boy. Now you're at a loose end in the city. Living off their money. It's almost too good to be true. No wonder they've decided not to put the money up for the prize again.'

Tim tried to be interested.

'It was in the papers again last week. Great puffing and blowing. Everyone seems to have had their say. The sponsors said, if I remember right, that they weren't prepared to subsidise an insidious and unhealthy cult of modern ugliness in the schools.'

295

'Then I'm glad I don't read the papers.'

'That makes it even richer. A culture-hero entirely unaware. Oh, dear God. It's too much.'

'All I did was paint a picture.'

'All you did – ' At this point the affable stranger appeared to have difficulty with his throat. 'Do you realize that even the Minister of Education, whatever his name is, has been called on to declare himself? Jesus, boy, you all but caused a Cabinet crisis. And all you did was paint a picture.'

'I don't think I want to hear any more. Thanks all the same.'

'I suppose one might have guessed you were a pretty cool customer,' the stranger observed. 'Tell me one thing, though. What will you do when the money gives out?'

'I haven't had time to think about that. I suppose I can always go back to the farm, if – '

'If what?'

'If my father will have me back. It's all a bit difficult. And it might be even more difficult now.'

He couldn't make up his mind about that. His father had doubtless read the newspapers. What he might prove with them was impossible to say, exactly. Probably that he had been right all along.

'I suppose it might be. I don't imagine he ever expected to breed a cultural outlaw.'

'It's not that.' It wasn't that, because he wasn't sure what this person was talking about.

'No? Then what happens if you don't go back?'

'I'll live, I expect.' He saw no reason to doubt this, unless he doubted everything. And that was always possible.

'Is there something I can do to help? I know one or two people. For a start, you might show me some more of what you've been doing lately. The name's Ted Connolly, by the way. I meant to chase a job on the wharf this morning. Then I found the sun too tempting.' He stretched lethargically.

'The rest of my work's at home.'

'Good. So do we walk, or take a tram?'

'We can walk, if you like. But you don't have to bother.'

'Bother?'

'To be polite.'

'I don't know how,' Ted Connolly said.

They walked. The other noticed his limp.

'Had an accident?' he said. 'Sprained an ankle?'

'Something like that,' Tim agreed.

Ted Connolly, it turned out, was a migrant bird, moving with the seasons. In winter he might go into the forest to shoot deer for a living, or work on hydro construction jobs on remote rivers. In summer he liked to work nearer the sea. For an Irish misfit, he said, it was a reasonable sort of country. Because nothing fitted. He couldn't complain.

'Here,' Tim said, and turned in at the gate.

They followed a path around the bulky wooden ruin of the house, with its sagging verandahs, and then beyond. Rusty tins crunched underfoot.

'Here?' Ted said. They faced the shed.

'Yes. It used to hold coal.'

'The underworld of the artist. Magnificent. You've got it made.'

'It's cheap,' Tim apologized as they ducked through the door, 'but it's not always as dark as it looks.' He switched on the light, a swinging bulb on a long flex.

Ted Connolly went straight to the books beside the bed, and flicked over a few pages. 'You're dead keen,' he observed. 'I can see that, all right. Perhaps you don't need anyone to help.'

'I didn't say I did.'

'True.' Ted Connolly gave him a sudden shrewd look.

Tim arranged a few things on the table. 'These are just a few drawings I have done,' he offered, 'since I have been here. Mostly people. I have never been very good on people. But they are all around, here.' He paused for breath. 'This,' he went on, 'is a woman I saw singing with a band, in the street.'

'God save the Salvation Army. You got her, all right. And who is this here?'

'A man I saw sitting outside a pub. After he'd been thrown out at closing time.'

'Well, he doesn't look too unhappy about it, after all. Look at me, the great big fat boozy king of the world. And who owns this mournful face?'

'My landlady. And this is an old man I saw delivering coal up the road.'

'Where does the coal end and the man begin?'

'He was pretty dirty.'

'It wasn't that I meant. Well, never mind. You got him too. Anything else?'

There was much else.

297

'It is not all I want to do,' Tim explained. 'There are things I haven't even begun.'

Ted Connolly did not ask what things. He was going through the rest of the work swiftly. With a frown of concentration, and sometimes a smile of pleasure.

'Yes,' he said at length. 'Well –' He hesitated. 'I suppose I should tell you that I like this, for what the opinion's worth. And that's nothing. Instead, I'll ask what you want.'

'What I want?' He could not think how he would begin to tell. It was too large to explain.

'Because if you care too much you'd best get home to your father. In every way to be preferred, unless –'

Tim found his mouth dry. 'Yes?' he said.

'Unless you're prepared to go along for the ride. And enjoy it, while it lasts. Or you last. Because it doesn't matter, you see, if you don't care. If you care, it becomes another thing. A fatal illness. Even a little talent can be a deadly thing. Caring too much can kill.'

Tim shook his head, unsure.

'I almost cared too much,' Ted Connolly explained. 'I almost tried to do another James Joyce on Dublin. Until I found out that he'd already done it. So I had to cure myself, one way or another. And of Dublin too. And have, more or less, as an antipodean bum. I don't have to care much now. This is a good country for not caring too much. You see.'

Tim tried to. It was difficult. He only wanted to paint pictures. Or a picture. He couldn't see what that had to do with countries. Or with someone called Joyce.

'So you might be safe here,' Ted suggested. 'I hope so. If not, it wouldn't be the end, you know, if you went back to the farm.'

'If I went back now, I'd just look a fool.'

'Better to look a fool than be one.'

'You mean,' Tim said, 'only fools don't quit.'

'Well,' Ted Connolly agreed, 'yes. Holy fools, some of them. Poor fools, the rest. But all fools, nonetheless.' He appeared to be trying to convince himself with his vehemence; and groped, with curious clumsiness, for his pipe and tobacco pouch. 'I'd sooner swallow pride than wisdom. Easier on the digestion.' He shook his head. 'Never mind. I'm just trying you out. If I can't persuade you to go along for the ride, then perhaps life will. You're obviously not up to quitting yet.'

'No.' He only had to think of his father. Or, if necessary, of hills beyond.

'All right,' Ted said, and sat on the bed with a creak, 'so it's not the end of the world. We'll just have to see if we can make the patient more comfortable.'

Ted Connolly wasn't long in the city, that trip. His stay was cut short by news of a job in the southern fiords, chopping out tourist tracks for the summer. But before he went he steered Tim through his accumulation of acquaintances, and perhaps friends, in the city. 'You might find some of them interesting,' Ted explained. 'Most will be a dead loss. But it's up to you to pick and choose. I can't help you there. Take Ken over there.' They were at a noisy party in an old house, and Ken was a bespectacled and crew-cut poet, a student and editor of the university literary magazine, at that moment rocking clumsily about the room with a fat Samoan girl. 'Ken McAdam might be just a drunken fool, and he might not. That's for you to decide. Or Sandy West.' Sandy had a long rather skeletal face, with a drooping ginger moustache in the style of a Mexican bandit. He was plucking half-heartedly at a guitar, with smoke drifting into glazed eyes from a limp cigarette in the corner of his mouth. 'Sandy might be dead serious about his communism, or it might just be a clown's act. I wouldn't like to say. The same way as Charlie Bates might even be serious about architecture.' Charlie Bates, with wild hair and gaunt face, was asleep on a torn mattress near their feet; a stub of candle flickered behind his head, and he left the impression of a laid out corpse. 'He might really be brilliant. On the other hand he didn't have to get himself thrown out of architectural school by designing a fucking seat for a certain professor, and then trying to call a strike. Unless he wanted to fail in his own way. Which he has. You might argue that he's a successful failure. But it's all the same. Take words like success and failure away and there are just people trying to make sense of themselves. Here are a few to get along with, if you can.'

'All right,' Tim promised. 'I'll try.'

'Then,' Ted Connolly observed, 'it looks as if you have company. So you'd better just go ahead and enjoy the party while it lasts. This is where I exit. I have to be out on the road south early in the morning. But about my room – you'll definitely be taking it over tomorrow?'

'Yes. It'll be better than the shed.'

'Those books I'm leaving behind. I know you'll look after them, but that's not the point. The point is that you read them.'

'I'll try.'

'And when your money runs out, you can always find work.'

'Yes. You told me.'

'Then I've told you everything. Except good luck. I imagine I'll be seeing you again before too long. I'm always back.'

They shook hands, with the party still heaving around them, and Ted Connolly went to the door. His gentle departure went unnoticed : there was no one else to say goodbye. Tim watched Ted stride off. The house backed on to an old cemetery and, in the fitful moonlight, pioneer headstones rose pale. Ted followed an obscure track among them, flickering ghostly through shadow. But he might already have been out on the road, on his way, striding steadily down through the heart of the country. He was soon out of sight.

And Tim remembered that he hadn't said thanks. It was too late to call.

He returned to the party. A tipsy girl, with an awkwardly held cigarette and a slopping glass of beer, blocked his way. She was having trouble with her long hair; she tried to toss it back, and then peered at him through the remaining strands.

'You're new,' she announced. 'What's your name?'

It was easy enough to confess. She didn't look in the least like Nurse Pratt, but that had already begun not to matter.

When he moved into Ted Connolly's room, he found an envelope propped prominent on a shelf. It contained a short note and a sum of money. 'This is so you don't run out too soon,' the note explained. 'This place is going to cost you more. If you insist, take it as a loan. Otherwise as a down payment on a painting of my choice sometime. And don't forget the books. Don't drink too much and remember penicillin does marvels with the syph.'

He had an unfamiliar head and gritty eyes. The room was not large, but the furniture offered drab comfort, and the place was almost intimidatingly bright. It overlooked a sunny backyard with trimmed lawn and a large lemon tree, and there was a glimpse of sea beyond concrete buildings and waterfront cranes.

There was the smell of pipe-smoke and liniment in the stuffy warmth of the room. Ted's books, those he had chosen to leave, were in a solid and impressive line beside the bed. The bed was

300

unmade, as Ted had left it, blankets and sheets churned after a restless sleep. A dented alarm clock ticking. A junk-shop radio. Tim switched it on experimentally and, when music came, switched it off again. He became aware of a slight sweaty smell from the bed. Already strange, he had the suffocating sensation of being someone outside himself, perilously resident in another's life. In sudden terror he went quickly to the window and heaved it open with a creak and a bang. The clock on the sill crashed on to the radio, then the floor, its glass splintering. Yet the sound was as much a relief as the new cool air invading the room.

The clock was beyond recall, the ticking stopped; the radio cabinet was chipped. There remained the books upon which he might also impose himself, given time. It seemed he had begun to make his own space to grow. He looked out on city and sea.

'I understand,' said Hans Wiemken, 'that you have some interesting work to show.'

They had just been introduced in the coffee bar to which Tim had been taken by Charlie Bates. Hans was lean and continental with pleasant accent. He was perhaps forty, balding, and with remarkably slender hands.

'Of course he has,' Charlie Bates urged. 'Haven't you, Tim?'

'Well –' Tim hesitated, though Charlie nudged.

'Evasion is no use,' Hans said. 'I know you are this young man who caused so much trouble in the schools.'

'Trouble?'

'I do not have to be told. You see, I was judge. One of the judges on that occasion. I remember your painting quite well. It might not have been original, but it was alive, which was more than could be said for the others. So sad. All those young people dead before they could begin. I wept after I judged. Wept. For it was all too much. I could never do it again. Never. So why, please tell me, should yours have seemed alive and the others not?'

Tim shook his head.

'I think,' said Hans, 'perhaps because there is something in you harder to kill. I cannot think otherwise. It must be. Or else it must be that there is nothing to kill at all. And I will not believe that.'

He smiled. And his long fingers cupped his chin as he looked at Tim.

'And now,' he went on, 'you have something new to show. True? My friend Charlie here says so.'

'One or two things,' Tim conceded.

'A bloody roomful,' Charlie said. 'He works like a bat out of hell.'

'I am hanging a small exhibition. Various people. Charlie here seems to think I should consider you. So I have said to Charlie, very well. Bring this young man to me and let me consider him. Thus, I consider.'

He smiled again. His thin bright eyes never shifted.

'Do you think you might have something to please me? I am not so difficult to please. I make allowances. One must.'

It was not dislike Tim found. It was his neutral face again, like an old friend.

'It's all the same to me,' he replied, 'whether it pleases you or not.'

'Hans is just offering to help,' Charlie pointed out amiably.

'I didn't ask for help.'

'Ah,' said Hans. 'Spirit.'

'You could be more gracious,' Charlie said. 'You mightn't ask for help, but you're certainly going to need it.'

'No, no,' Hans said. 'Give the boy his head, Charlie. Hear what he has to say.'

'I haven't got any more to say,' Tim announced. 'Except that I didn't know why I was brought here tonight. I mightn't have come if – '

'Now, now,' Hans interrupted. 'Such spirit is beautiful to see, within reason. You must understand that Charlie and I are friends. And that it was natural for Charlie to mention you, since he is recently a friend of yours too, I gather. Please do not see conspiracy where there is none.'

'It's not that.'

'No? In that case, then, we shall speak no further of your work, if this offends you.'

'I just don't like anything behind my back.'

'Sorry, then,' Charlie Bates offered. 'All quite innocent, really.' To Hans he added, 'I warned you he was touchy.'

'True,' Hans said. 'So let us forget the subject for now. Perhaps you and Charlie might join me for a drink one Saturday night when I am having friends around. And then perhaps we can – '

'There's no need to go through all that business either. You can see my work. That's if you really want to. I didn't say you couldn't. All I said was it was all the same to me whether it pleases you or not.'

Charlie appeared nervous now. 'It's good, Hans.' He hesitated, then corrected himself. 'Some of it. I mean, it has possibilitities. You really ought to see it.'

'Then I will, Charlie, of course.' Hans seemed amused. 'Since our young friend here has made it plain he doesn't mind. And a little temperament has never deterred me. Surely you wouldn't think that.'

Charlie looked relieved. 'Well, that's settled, then.'

'When I'm ready,' Tim said.

'Pardon?' Hans appeared briefly off balance.

'You can see it – my work – when I'm ready.'

That was a month away.

Hans Wiemken was something new. Since Charlie was always willing to talk, he learned that Hans Wiemken was a German refugee from before the war, an art teacher when he felt like it and an itinerant the rest of the time. He hadn't gone back after the war, Charlie explained, because he was on a Pacific thing. He had travelled the length of the country, and gone up to the tropics, in search of primitive themes he might use. 'He knows his stuff,' Charlie insisted. 'Don't let the European manner fool you. You were lucky, that night, you didn't get his back up altogether.'

'Lucky?'

'He could very easily have decided you're just another arrogant young prick, not worth the time and trouble.' Charlie hesitated, apparently in search of reaction, but there was none. 'That's if you don't mind me saying so,' he added by way of apology.

'He saw my work first,' was all Tim felt committed to saying. 'That painting in the competition.'

'True. I was forgetting. But all the same.'

All the same? Charlie evidently preferred not to specify. The blind could not be cheerfully invited to see.

They were travelling across town in Charlie's antique Ford. The back seat, which Charlie frequently used as bed, when the vehicle served him as home, was now burdened with several paintings. They were on their way to Hans Wiemken's flat, Charlie uneasy and rather pained about his involvement now.

He had often enough been victim of crossfire in petty feud, a clownish martyr. His hurts were never mentioned when the stories were told.

'You hear from Ted?' Who, when it came right down, was really to blame for this situation, Charlie's haphazard involvement. Not that Charlie would bear grudge.

'Just a note to say he's still south, and not much else.'

'No one ever hears much more than that. Then one day he's back again. A happy-go-lucky sort of life.'

The thought of it did not make Charlie more cheerful, as his clacking wiper scraped rain from his windscreen, fitfully revealing the sterile streets which funnelled him towards Hans Wiemken's. Tim was quiet beside him. Charlie was never sure how he should manage indifference, or if he should.

'Here we are,' Charlie said at length.

They conveyed the paintings awkwardly and quickly through the rain to Hans Wiemken's door, and pressed a button which rang a bell remotely. After a time slippers tapped down a staircase within. The door opened and Hans peered out; music jingled somewhere behind him.

If he was pleased to see them, damply disposed on his step, he did not show it. His face preserved an obscure melancholy as he invited them inside, and went ahead up the stairs.

'So,' said Hans, when they were arranged in his living room, 'I have the pleasure – or should it be honour – at last.'

There was a fourth person in the room. A limp young man who appeared as uneasy as the two newcomers. He rose from a couch, without introduction, and set down an empty glass. His lips had no colour, and his dress was precise in its contrasts. 'I think I must be on my way, Hans,' he observed. With this acknowledged, he made his way past the damp paintings and out of the flat without further word. The music, which seemed faintly scented, continued at high volume from the record player.

'My anticipation has been aroused, all this time,' Hans said, though his voice made it seem unlikely. 'Come, now. Let me see.'

Tim Livingstone stood leaden in that strange room. He certainly made no effort to thrust that part of himself which was in the paintings forward; he simply clung.

'Make yourself at home, please,' Hans offered, with gestures.

He continued to stand. He was in a room of paintings, for

304

one thing. And convulsions of artefacts crowded shelves and surfaces. He needed time to disentangle.

Hans, with slight impatience, was contriving now to accept the surrender of his paintings.

'Let me arrange them,' he insisted, 'so that I can see as I wish.'

It appeared he and Charlie were permitted to remain, to sit and smoke, so long as they were quiet.

'This is earlier,' he once objected, 'and that later. You should have them the other – '

'I prefer,' said Hans, 'my own discovery, if you please.' His thin smile might have conveyed condescension, but it was not obvious.

'Come on, Tim,' Charlie said. 'Sit down. Give Hans a fair go.' He pulled Tim down to the couch, beside him.

Hans switched off the music, to help his concentration. His breathing could be heard, quite distinct, as he went from painting to painting. He seemed faintly tubercular, or asthmatic. Now and then he coughed over his cigarette, but soon lit another one. There appeared to be no system in the way he studied the paintings. He chose at random, sometimes travelling out with a backward shuffle of feet, sometimes closing with a painting as if in struggle. His fluttering fingers, at times, certainly seemed tempted to grip.

'This country,' he was once heard clearly to mutter. 'This damn country is a disease.'

He offered nothing more, apart from occasional headshakes. And long pauses of perfect stillness. He returned to some paintings more than others, but there was no clear link between those to which he gave most attention. Then he quit, quite suddenly. He sat, nursed his head gently with one hand, and gazed at the floor.

'Charlie,' he said quietly, without looking up. 'I am grateful to you for bringing your friend. But there are things which might be said more easily without you. Without the embarrassment of another, if your friend is sensitive.'

'It's all right, Hans.' Charlie was quick on his feet, in apparent relief. 'I have to shoot through anyway.' He stood for a moment in the doorway, pushing back his floppy hair. 'See you,' he said to Tim. 'Good luck.'

He received soundless acknowledgement. The kid sat tight, with no expression.

Outside, the car howled through its gears, down the road. Hans Wiemken still gazed at the floor.

'So,' he said, a stone tossed in a pool, to ripple.

He lifted his head at length. His expression was hardly generous.

'So what am I supposed to say to you?' he asked. But obviously expected no reply.

He shrugged. 'I could say, yes, very good, try harder. That is what I am sometimes paid to say.'

'I didn't,' said Tim Livingstone at last, 'come to be told anything. It was something to do with an exhibition.'

'But you will listen, all the same. Even if you move to the door, and attempt to gather up your paintings, in protest. I will still have time to speak.' Hans seemed accurate in his anticipation. The other, after a slight move, was still again. Hans lit a cigarette. 'I wish, first, for you to see my problem, if you will listen a moment.'

The other was quiet.

'You see, it is this. Fundamentally you are still primitive. If you had teaching, it has not counted enough to tell. Primitive, with all the vigour – more – and health which that implies, but sadly often does not. This work is honest, which is something to be said. But honesty is not art, any more than all good artists are honest men. So if I say it is honest, alone, that is all I can say by way of consolation. No, sit. I have yet to finish, by far. My problem is not how to tamper, but whether to. You see.'

The other plainly did not, but after all continued to sit. There was, anyway, the problem of moving the paintings, without the Bates vehicle as carrier. The situation might have been contrived as trap, he should have seen. Charlie might by now be joking about it, with some of his embattled coffee bar friends.

'This exhibition,' he repeated firmly, since Hans appeared determined to forget. 'That is what I'm here for.'

'Of course,' said Hans, undismayed. 'The exhibition. But even to include your paintings – one or two – with those of these other young men is to begin to tamper. It is to set off the judgement of others, and eventually your own, whether you care or not, in a different context. A context which you have hardly begun to contemplate, and perhaps should not. That is really the crux.' He sighed, but peripherally. 'I would sooner not have the problem. To tell the truth. I would sooner you went, with your paintings, out the door.'

It was test and challenge. They waited. There was the sound of rain on the window.

'All right,' Hans continued. 'Then it will not vanish, after all, so simply. And at least I appear to have your attention. So listen. The real question is if you could be anything more, or anything else, and if it is worthwhile trying. And the answer is probably no. So many with talent, so few with light. And you have everything against you, anyway, before you even begin. An entire country. A way of seeing, or never seeing. A land where giants should walk, and instead midgets burrow. All this energy to make a place to sleep. On the other hand, you have the advantage that no one here, yet, has quite ruined you with teaching, or crippled your vision. You still have a certain childish wonder, and imagination.'

It was just the accent, of course, which seemed to break the final word down into two parts, much as he had first heard it from Mrs Fletcher. Imagy Nation, an echo upon echoes, grass and tree and creek, and the smell of death. He appeared, after all, to understand about as much as he was told now as he did of what he was told then. It was faint progression. Yet he could listen, perhaps, to take what was needed. Or as much as he needed. He had always taken that much, without particular greed.

'All right,' said Hans, suddenly restless and gesturing on his feet, 'so where does that leave us? You are here, in this quaint and curious dead end of Western man. You have friends, or at least acquaintances, already – people who would sway, even if they do not wish. One such, our friend Charlie, has brought you here. You have not been left alone and will not be, it seems. The fact that I talk to you also becomes part of the damage, of the total. Will you flee before it is too late? I think not. An artist's worst enemy is himself. After that, his friends. No other enemy is worthy enough to be considered. Society? Just fertilizer. This country is very poor quality fertilizer. Too new. Like all new fertilizer it burns, rather than nourishes, the roots. Fast growth, then death. Or nothing at all.'

'Then why should you stay here?' Tim said, provoked enough to ask at last.

'Do I sense real puzzlement,' said Hans, 'or is it but again the sturdy voice of the patriot?'

'I don't know what it is. I just want to know.'

'Because I make meaning of my own, in spite,' Hans answered. 'Perverse, perhaps. But of my own. And perhaps because I choose to be – or have been chosen for – victim. I prefer the role of victim here to the other, the role of victim I escaped, being half Jew and unashamed, in Germany. And now this second role is habit to me, as well. So, does that answer?'

It might have. He would need time to consider.

'Never mind,' Hans continued, 'it is your problem, not mine, we have on hand. This farm I understand you to come from – is it too late, too far? Are you going back?'

'I still have to decide.'

'Is that why you are here, then? So that something can be decided for you, in absence of your own decision?'

'In a way,' he agreed finally.

'What way?'

He was reluctant to be precise. 'Only that I haven't much time left, or money. And I still haven't done what I thought I could do. I could let those things decide for me. Or I could let my paintings decide, since I have nothing else to show.'

'In an exhibition?'

'Yes.'

'And that is all you care about?'

'Yes.'

'Then perhaps I should send you back to that farm.'

'Say I'm not going back, then.' He might have arrived somewhere, it was hard to tell. The words seemed far too easy. They left no abrasion in his throat, which might have been his expectation, and left the visible world unchanged.

'Then I shall be willing to say that, if you are. It brings us to a possibly hopeless problem. The makings of an artist, from the scattered bits and pieces you are. You have not even begun, and may not. But there is strength in your honesty, and your mind may be single enough. Or would your prefer not to listen?'

It appeared this had been decided too. Anyway he sat.

'If this pathetic exhibition, which I have contracted to choose, is still most on your mind, then let me set it at rest so that we can forget the damn thing. I am willing to select some of this – your juvenile rubbish. I offer this only as bribe, so that you will listen without distraction. So don't stand up yet. The exhibition is still conditional on you listening.'

Hans briefly resumed his chair again, and gave silent attention to the ceiling, placing the tips of his fingers together, sure now of his audience. Then, with theatrical jerk, he was on his feet and striding, in perplexity or irritation. 'This,' he pronounced finally, over the propped paintings, 'is just pull, all pull. You are all pull. As with the brush strokes, so with the whole.' His hands seemed given imagined wings by the word. 'Pull, pull, pull. Which means grab, grab, grab. Like a man drowning. Pull at anything, grab at anything. A man drowning. But in a sea of ignorance – or innocence, which is the prettier word. Grabbing, pulling, less at the real than at some phantom of the real, for that is what it becomes in the act. A shallow phantom, without truth or life. Life is in opposites. Love and hate. War and peace. Birth and death. Male and female. In your work there is no clash of opposites. How can it grow? If it is all this grab, grab – or pull, pull? You want everything, and you want it quickly. You cheat your subject. Worse, you cheat yourself. So what, to begin, is the opposite of pull? Why, push; that is all. Push. As simple a word. To pull, merely, is to be a creature of reality. To push, merely, is to resist reality. From their clash is one man's truth – to answer pull with push, push with pull. As with the brush strokes, so with the whole. First you take your subject – pull. Then you separate yourself from it again – push. Subjective, objective; new opposites between which to find your own point of balance. And each painting should have its own fine point. One which can drive cleanly to the spine of the onlooker. So I say you have not even begun. Begin to answer pull with push and you will find yourself no longer reality's captive. You may even discover something of your own.'

The lecture was over, evidently. Hans Wiemken stood by the window. Tim Livingstone got to his feet.

'You probably will not understand much,' Hans suggested finally. 'But you will, if you must.'

'The exhibition is all right, then,' Tim said. 'You will take my work.' His flat voice conceded nothing.

Hans Wiemken for a moment looked incredulous. 'You,' he began, but after all did not continue. It might have been the start of a bitter laugh, or cigarette smoke, which choked him off. His hands mimicked drowning. 'My God,' he finished. 'I wonder if you really heard a word.'

The other still waited, on his feet, apparently for sure confirmation.

'Yes,' said Hans at last, despairing. 'It is all right, the exhibition, all right.' His fingers, intending to snap dismissal of the subject, clumsily misfired; and bit back into a limp hand at the end of a slender arm which drifted home to his side. 'I should have known I could not compete with yet another young fool in a hurry.'

'Which paintings, then?' asked Tim Livingstone.

'That and that,' Hans Wiemken said, stabbing blindly and obscurely. 'Or that and that. Anything. To save problem I would just as soon say everything, if you like, but there would not be the room. Is that sufficient nourishment for your ego?'

His harassment may have been implausible, but his coolness was not. They stood.

'I will have to get Charlie to come for the others.'

Hans Wiemken, an addict, returned to his record player. 'By all means. By all means get Charlie. And remove them from my sight.'

The music was loud. Gypsies might have danced to it once, with rhythms to squander.

'Then,' Tim Livingstone said, 'I would like to begin.'

'What is that?' Hans said. For the music deafened.

'I said I would like to begin. Or try to.' It was not a decision, because there was no longer a choice.

The music was silenced as Hans turned a switch. 'You would?'

'Yes.'

'Then God help you,' Hans said.

Ted Connolly did not reclaim his room, but found another. 'Keep it,' he said. 'It seems to suit you.'

'I've done a lot of work here.'

'I can see that too.' Ted's beard was untidy, his hair more so. His boots were still muddy. He held a bottle of wine in one hand, a glass in the other, and sat on the bed. His gaze shifted critically over the contents of the room. 'It can't be much more than a year,' he said. 'You've certainly moved. Almost painted yourself in.' He seemed to be picking over words to suit, in the first awkwardness.

'It is a bit of a clutter.'

'Started to unload yet?'

'One or two. Here and there. I've had a little luck.'

'Jobs?'

'Enough. I've usually found something easy.'

'Been home?'

Tim hesitated, as if the question needed thought. Perhaps it should have.

'No. I thought not.' Ted looked into his emptied glass and filled it again. 'Silly question. I feel I'm to blame.'

'Why?'

'Perhaps because I should have left you where I found you. Among those seagulls. You'd have gone back, in time.'

'Why should you worry?'

'Because I do. Reflexive guilt of an ex-Catholic.'

'It's not your business,' Tim insisted. 'It's mine.'

'If you say so.'

'I do. It's my own life. It has to be.'

Ted seemed taken aback by the sharpness. 'Yes,' he answered carefully, setting his bottle down on the floor, and tightening his feet around it, for security. His moves were all very deliberate. He might have been avoiding prickles which, conceivably, still clung to his dusty trousers. 'All right. So we have a deal.' His eyes shifted to the paintings around. 'It's certainly changed,' he observed, at length, 'your work.'

'It had to,' the other was prepared to offer, more agreeably. 'Didn't it?'

'Perhaps. But it's still a surprise.'

'Good or bad?'

'I'd have to think about that. And know a bit more. About how well you know Hans Wiemken, for example.'

'Who told you I knew Hans Wiemken?'

'No one told me. I've only been back a few hours.' There was a pause; the bottle clinked against the glass. 'First thing I always do, back in town again, is fill myself up with the worst Dalmatian plonk I can find. It helps cushion the shock. Tomorrow I'll only have a headache to worry about.'

'What is it you're hinting? That you see Hans Wiemken in my work?'

'I thought it was more than a hint. But still.'

'I don't like the way you raised it.'

'Sorry about that, then. No offence intended.'

'Hans has just made me interested in trying new things.'

'No doubt.'

'And he's given me a lot of his time.'

'I imagine he would.'

'What's wrong? Don't you like his work?'

'No one,' Ted said, 'would suggest that he doesn't know what he's doing. And sometimes it even seems that it's worth doing.'

'That's not an answer.'

'I don't expect it is,' Ted agreed.

'Anyway there's nothing wrong with trying new things.'

'No. So long as they're your own.'

'Who said they weren't?'

'I suppose I'm saying it,' Ted acknowledged. 'Look, this is a hell of a start. I'm sorry. Since you're not prepared to share this stuff with me, perhaps we could get out of here and try a walk somewhere.'

There wasn't much left in the bottle anyway.

But the walk offered them only sodden city parkland, a misty harbour and dull sky. They progressed into the centre of the city. And there rain sent them, predictably, into the coffee bar for shelter. At least they had relief from each other. For Charlie Bates moved into their cubicle soon after they arrived, and then Ken McAdam and a girl friend. Ken flourished proofs of a new magazine he was editing. The crowd became steadily more oppressive and irrelevant. Ted was not surprised when finally Tim eased himself out of the cubicle and said a cool goodbye.

'What do you think of the kid now?' Charlie asked.

'The kid?' Ted was for a moment confused, heavy in a private gloom.

'The wonder boy,' Ken said. 'Wiemken's wonder boy.'

'Hans' new darling,' his girl friend said. 'Didn't you know?'

'He might be doing himself justice,' Ted said. 'But I wouldn't know.'

'I suspect he's one of these quietly arrogant buggers who think they've got the world sewn up,' Ken said.

'I wouldn't say that, altogether,' Charlie Bates said in characteristically mild intervention, also characteristically neglecting to add what he would say, altogether. 'It's just that no one sees much of him.'

'Except dear Hans,' the girl said.

'Except Hans,' Charlie admitted.

'How long has this been going on?' Ted asked.

'I introduced them,' Charlie said. 'Not long after you left. I could see Hans was interested right away.'

The girl, rather shrill with drink, laughed.

'And Hans,' Ken went on, 'seems determined to protect him

312

from the local boys – other artists. He appears afraid his wonder boy will be tainted. Our exotic flower has drawn a bee at last.'

'Hardly the first,' Charlie protested.

'The first that's any good, at least,' Ken insisted. 'Though that probably won't be true for long. The other sweet boys haven't mattered a damn. Besides, this one's not sweet.'

'He always looks sour to me,' the girl agreed.

'Or shy,' Ted suggested.

'Well, you know him,' Charlie said. 'The rest of us never got that far. We tried to give him a helping hand. Only Hans whisked him off.'

'How far off?'

'Well, he doesn't live with Hans. The others have. Perhaps you can make some sense of it, now you're back again. You are, aren't you?'

'It begins to seem like it,' Ted sighed. 'So where's the next party?'

Sandy West pushed into the cubicle, crowding them still further.

'On second thought,' Ted went on, 'where's the revolution?'

'Monday,' Sandy said. 'In the town hall if it rains.'

Their greeting was ritual. Ted might resist the city a day or two longer, but it seemed he was home again, among his own kind, and his time away a pretence. He might wish himself different, and hope for the chance, but without much illusion: he supposed he might be preparing for retreat. A life without answers was all too possible; he had even, lately, begun to forget the questions.

'Your trouble, Ted,' Ken McAdam was saying, 'is that you hate to come back and find anything changed. You want us all frozen, exactly as we were. That kid, for example. You weren't really so involved with him. What you really resent is that he's different. It wouldn't matter which way different. You'd still resent it.'

Ted could understand, at least, that Ken was attempting consolation. 'You might be right,' he agreed amiably. 'Nothing stands still. We only have to ask Sandy here.'

'The law of life,' Sandy said. 'Quantitative to the qualitative. Something has to give, sooner or later.'

'So what do we do about it?'

'Go with it,' Sandy said. 'Ally yourself with history. Organize.'

'It's cut price day,' Ken McAdam said, 'for a trip to the Finland station. All aboard.'

His girl friend giggled.

The city was still coloured with rain, the buildings, pavements and people. Everything. Any other colour seemed to drain away down the raging gutters. Still shaken by Ted's return, he walked quickly away from the coffee bar. Until, quite at random, the city offered him another face.

Nurse Pratt, it seemed, her face bright with rain.

'Why, Tim,' she said. 'Of all people. What are you doing here?'

He might once have dreamt of this. Once even sought it.

He tried to explain. But he did not altogether convince himself.

'I read about you, of course,' she said. 'It must be a year or two now. And I must say I wondered.'

She was a very ordinary looking girl, with an ordinary voice. He could not really understand this.

'So you're here,' she said. 'I've been here all this time too. And enjoying myself, I must say. A pity we didn't meet up sooner. Or perhaps just as well.'

For she had a diamond ring upon her left hand. She was engaged, and to some doctor.

'And now you're a real live artist,' she said. 'Fancy. I should have known.'

'Not exactly,' he insisted. For one thing, he did not feel very real, or live. And Ted Connolly put the rest in doubt.

But she was determined to be entranced. She wanted to find somewhere dry where they could sit and talk, though he did not see the point. It was her day off.

And a day off, in all senses. For it finished in his room. She insisted on calling it a studio. The paintings perplexed her, but she announced she had never seen such colour. 'I am sure you know what you are doing,' she said.

She certainly did. Her birdy body shone in the dark, upon his bed. Even softer than he expected, and extremely functional; she wrapped her cool legs around him and moaned with exquisite surprise as she encouraged him, with swift hands, to make use of her. Until she, it appeared, was making even more efficient and urgent use of him.

314

Then she was engaged to her doctor again, dressed, and pulling on gloves. Quite brisk.

'It is all romance, Tim,' she said. 'And there is no future in romance. One must get on with life. There are practical things.'

He could not believe he had craved her legs so much. And would not enjoy her body again. Yet she was making it clear. He began, for the first time, to see life as a bleak enemy. The problem was to make himself safe from attack. Some risks could not be run.

'I daresay I'm one among many,' she suggested, 'so I can't imagine this will hurt you too much.'

She could not imagine at all.

'We might even be better,' she added, 'for having got it out of our system.'

He had got one thing out of his system. Her name was no longer Nurse Pratt. It was Liz. Liz Pratt. There might not be another Nurse Pratt, but there were doubtless many girls with names like Liz, or something near.

He walked Liz Pratt home, then, to her room near the hospital. 'Amazing what use I've made of my day,' she laughed, as they parted. 'Who would have dreamt it?'

There had never been need to suffer illusion about Hans, strutting and self-caressing. His father would have expected Hans; Hans, or someone like him, had actually been invented in anticipation. Perhaps not actually all the way down to those fluttering fingers, but near enough.

'There is no rush,' Hans observed. 'You must learn to live with time. Make it ally, not adversary. Only at my age does it become such. You have long to go, before then. There will be time enough for that fight.'

Hans liked to leave the impression he was still just riding punches, by way of preliminary. Tim, having heard it before, sat silent. He sat increasingly silent through most of Hans' repetitions, which had now begun to irritate. Perhaps because they had stopped moving. He had offered his impatience to Hans, like so much else in the past year, only to have it rejected again.

'In the long run,' Hans finished, 'it is not the distance one's work has travelled which counts. It is the depth to which it has gone, how far the roots grip. You are just beginning. You follow me?'

Tim stirred in a comfortable chair, something stale in his mouth, which Hans' vermouth would not rinse away. He might have stayed on the farm to send down roots. He had not, surely, exchanged one standstill for another. Yet Hans could offer plausibility, if not much else now, and logic so transparent that he was tempted to fling words, like stones, to see if there was something to shatter.

'All right,' he said at length, when he had collected sufficient words. 'But who is to judge?'

'Pardon? I do not follow.'

'Who is best to judge the point, the place to send down roots?' He found himself even more restless in his chair. 'Only the person himself. If he gives that up, what has he got left?'

It was so obvious, at last, it left him slightly breathless.

'Nothing,' he answered before Hans could. 'He's got nothing left in the finish. He's not his own man any more.'

Now he was angry with himself, as much as with anyone other. Easier to have seen sooner.

'I do not deny you the right to judge,' Hans said. 'Nor have I. I hope simply to have given you the information on which you may base judgement. I never remember you needing the confidence.'

'It has all,' Tim went on without pause, now wholly involved in his theme, 'been a kind of blackmail all along. Unless I do this. Unless I do that. I see it all now. And in the end I'm nothing. Nothing, anyway, that doesn't belong to you.'

'But Tim,' Hans appealed, 'no, not – ' He might have been obstructed by some inner pain. 'Never have I denied myself more,' was all he could say finally. And inadequately. So his feet took him to a place beside the younger man's chair, and his hand involved itself with Tim's shoulder.

'Never mind,' Tim said, and swallowed the rest of his drink in haste. 'Forget it.' He made an effort to rise from his chair.

'No,' said Hans, restraining. 'Listen to me. Perhaps we have seen too much of each other. But that is all. Irritations can quickly breed from nothing.'

Tim tried to shake his shoulder free of the obstinate hand. When he did rise, it was to find two hands claiming him.

'It is a trifle, Tim,' Hans said. 'All this. It has begun from nothing, and will end nowhere.'

'Leave me,' Tim was obliged to say, since the two hands

remained firm on his shoulders. Hans' face was slack and crumpling : a child deprived. 'For Christ's sake.'

It had been easier to escape his father's sudden despairing lunge, and wild fist. That too seemed to have begun from nothing. But it had ended somewhere.

He was aware most of Hans' thin dry lips, near his face. But disgust seemed to weaken him. He had flung stones, experimentally, and set another boulder rolling. He had not to hold it, but to escape its path. Those grappling hands, those near lips; he felt panic rise, perhaps just in time.

All the same, he did what he must with regret. Though the shock of knowledge was less vivid this time, the place he walked was as cool and cruel. Those shaky lips, and pleading eyes, invited the ruthless. So he struck Hans, for release. Though the blow had only tentative impact, the other reeled away, doubling up. The theatrical had become real; he was his own parody.

'That's it,' he gasped, leaning across a chair. 'So I have made you feel at last. Hurt me. But don't leave me, not now. Hit me again, if you must. If you want.'

It was incredible, absurd.

'Again,' he repeated, a shrilling plea. 'Again.'

And Tim Livingstone seemed to understand the word obscene at last. Impossible to believe that this man once welcomed him with indifference to a music-filled room and talked of truth, and push and pull. There he was, then, victim of no more than his own teaching; the push had come.

'Tim.' The supplicant fingers fluttered. The eyes were watery now. 'Tim, please.'

The blow had been light, and anyway unwilling. Yet he could not contrive innocence, altogether. There had been satisfaction, along with relief. He could not risk staying; he could not risk further gratification.

He tried to step around Hans as he might something with sharp edges. But not quite carefully enough. For Hans, sliding to floor level, grabbed at an ankle.

There was no room for regret now. He kicked blindly, yet in full knowledge. And kicked again, in terror.

Hans collapsed altogether, clutching his damaged face. 'Tim,' he gurgled, mucus and blood slippery between his fingers. 'Stay, Tim. Please.'

He could almost have kicked again in simple emphasis. But

317

he didn't: he was at the door, breathing hard, opening it, and finally looking behind him. His paralysing disbelief fixed it all: the music, the drapes, the paintings, the rugs and bric-a-brac, and the man crawling brokenly across the floor in insect motion.

'Don't run away from yourself,' Hans said, more lucid though still gasping. 'In this, too, you find merely what you are. You see your need for me?'

He looked up with the eyes of some creature waiting for axe or last bullet.

Tim felt not so much need as something which rose thick and trembling in his throat, quite ambiguous in its command; he shut the door at last, and ran towards his twentieth birthday.

For that was what it was, the next morning, when he woke from patchy sleep. All night he had been flailing at phantoms, sometimes at half-dreamt hands upon his body. And they did not seem to be those of Liz Pratt.

He washed himself with particular care, but this hardly seemed sufficient to mark the day. He began to see how he might. The idea took hold until it became as vivid as water seen distant in desert.

It was evening when he left the train and walked through Te Ika. He had a light pack on his shoulders. The night was fine and cold, with stars. He took the road up the Waiatarua valley slowly, though the land was elastic enough. Farmhouses showed lights beyond pine trees. An occasional car passed, headlights flashing over fences, leaving the taste of familiar dust in his mouth. The hills began to rise, as he walked. At first separate, dark lumps in the night, and soon dimly massing. Then he was in the gorge with the sound of water. And fern brushing his face as he descended carefully to the river to drink. He bent among boulders, the river loud around him, and bathed his face and hands in the chilling water. He drank finally, in quick thirsty gulps, for the taste could not have been cleaner. Or the cold more satisfying. Even the hills seemed lighter.

He left the gorge and there was light in the farmhouse ahead. His legs pushed the last mile behind him.

He was knocking at the door, to his own surprise: the act of a stranger and stood waiting, still a stranger. There was noise, a rattle and then a shuffle, inside the lit kitchen. It was just such an unexpected time of night, he remembered, when the knock of a young Maori stranger had been answered. His own knock seemed an echo.

There was damp in the night, perhaps frost. The floorboards of the porch had the same creak under his feet.

The door opened. His lumpy father, in torn shirt, stood there, squinting. He seemed so much smaller.

There was no other difficulty about recognition on his side. And none on the other, evidently. They faced each other and there was after all not much to say.

'I suppose it had to be you,' Ned Livingstone observed, 'this time of night.' He backed from the door, a sole flapping from one of his aged slippers, and stood aside. 'So you had to come back. Come in, then. If you're coming.'

A burnt-out cigarette was stuck to his bottom lip, and wobbled as he spoke. His hair was thinner.

Tim Livingstone entered his father's house and stood unsure.

'Travelling light,' his father said. 'You walk it?'

'From the town.'

'Well, I didn't think from the bloody city. Take that thing off and sit down. If you're going to.'

He seemed determined, from the start, to make everything a challenge; and everything his own small triumph. Perhaps until he had sufficient in accumulation. He shut the door while his son unshouldered his pack.

'I suppose you could go a cup of tea,' he said, and went to the kettle without waiting for answer.

Tim was aware most of the smell. He sat uneasy on a couch, against a cushion of cracked leather, while his father moved through the preliminaries of what might have been welcome, if he forced interpretation. The smell was thick, and probably made of many things. Perhaps dust gathered in crevices and high surfaces; perhaps mould and slow decay; perhaps heaps of sourly sweaty clothes. Anyway it was unmistakable. He was home: he could not have been elsewhere.

'Like something to eat?' his father said.

'It's all right. I'm not hungry.'

'What's the matter? Isn't my tucker good enough for you now?'

'It's not that. It's just that I had something on the way.'

Then his father appeared to relent.

'I got a drop of beer, up to the cupboard,' he said. 'That's if you got a taste for the stuff now.'

319

'Tea should be all right for the moment.'

'You don't look too much knocked about, boy. I mean they haven't changed you much.'

Tim shrugged. He would have liked to have found something to say.

'So you had to come back, eh?'

'For a day or two,' Tim said quickly.

'A day or two? I thought – '

Ned Livingstone, shaking his head for a moment, was saved by the kettle, arrived conveniently at the boil. He turned to it on his slow feet.

'I thought,' he finished, 'that it might of been longer.'

He seemed to be speaking, more or less, to the kettle rather than his son. Anyway he looked at the kettle, as the boiling subsided, as if expecting answer. His heavy body seemed to need a sudden effort to bear.

'You see,' he persisted, 'I been expecting you back, sooner or later.'

Tim, who could have held off challenge, felt vulnerable now. He had really nothing to give, except himself, wholly. And that was out of the question, however much it might have been possible once. What was in the question, then? Perhaps nothing much. Only the need to inhabit his own skin. Only the need to find what he could do, or couldn't.

'It was just,' he began, and hesitated, 'just it was my birthday. So I thought a trip home wouldn't hurt.'

To say more would be to offer hope where there was none. And to confess flight, or failure. He had no intention of this. He had to go back, if only to begin again. Futile, and cruel, to pretend otherwise.

'Funny thing,' his father said. 'I had a feeling there was something special about today. Since I went out to the cows this morning. Maybe that's why I wasn't too surprised to find you at the door. Not that I remember birthdays, you know that.'

Even if he could remember the day of his son's birth, and prodding lightly at that incredible flesh with a blunt finger. Ned Livingstone seemed suddenly blind, quite uncoordinated, as he grappled with tea and teapot and boiled water. Tea leaves shook from the spoon in thin stream; water splashed his trousers. Yet he imposed himself, in the end. The tea was made, and he found cups.

320

'Never had a head for dates,' he explained. 'Your mother used to say I even forgot our first wedding anniversary.'

And the calendar on the wall, Tim saw, was anyway two years old. It had not been changed since the time he left, like much else. He supposed that the floor had been swept on occasion, though the evidence suggested otherwise.

'What was she like?' Tim asked. 'My mother? I never really asked you before.'

Perhaps because he had never seen the house as womanless before.

'Your mother? There isn't much to say about her.' Ned Livingstone placed two slopping cups of tea on the table. 'She was a girl, once. And she was a woman.'

He made it sound hard to forgive.

'But where did she come from?'

'Another farm. A few miles up the line.'

'What happened to her family, then? My grandparents? It doesn't seem like I ever had any.'

'I lost track, boy. Jack Crimmins – he would of been your grandfather – dropped dead when you was small. The others could be anywhere, or all dead too, for all I know. Your mother never really liked it here. Though I didn't know it till the end. Too lonely, I expect, she being used to a big family. And flat country. Once she said the hills made her feel like an insect caught in a slippery basin, never able to get out. And the climate didn't suit. Too much rain, and mud in winter. Of course I didn't really see that till the end, neither. I thought it was just something to complain about – the hills, the rain. I couldn't take it serious till I had to.'

The use of memory appeared to exhaust his father. He sat very quiet, rolling a cigarette and looking into his tea.

'We should of had that beer,' he said at length. 'I could of done with a booster, if this is what you want to talk about.'

'It isn't, exactly,' his son said. 'It was just something that crossed my mind. But I'm glad to know.'

'You're welcome to know. Your mother was a sad bitch. I don't think I ever got the strength of her. Not at the end, or any time. I find I don't even remember her too well. I remember other things better.'

Like fire flashing off the hot hillsides, and arriving back at the whare to find Nick Bell with his tied trouser-legs and swag. He often woke from such memories to find youth and strength

321

emptied from his sagging flesh. They had bled away into the land, into a dead marriage, and a lost child. He should have known, but he had no chance to start over, and do better. No chance at all. Life was ruthless with mistakes, the slightest stumble. It just rolled on like a dream, or nightmare, out of control. He looked up slowly at the son his dream had damaged. He was, after all, glad to have the boy again, or as much of him as still existed, for it seemed he had bugger all else.

'I said some hard things to you, boy,' he went on, weary now, and letting his eyes fall again. 'When you left. Hard things.'

'Never mind.'

'I'm not saying I'm sorry I said them. Or all of them. But you gone your own way now.'

'It's all right, then.'

'You're making a go of it? What you want to do?'

'I don't know.'

'You ought to know by now. You've had the time.'

'Not enough. A year or two isn't enough.'

'Then you'll never know, at this rate.'

'You might be right,' the boy conceded.

'Anyway,' his father said clumsily, 'you can always come back. This place is still here. This land. I want you to know that. It's all yours when you want it. You can forget anything I might of said to you.'

But Tim Livingstone, quite unprepared, everything shifting under his feet, might really have preferred the old things said again. He might have preferred anger to concern so naked and durable. Anything rather than the temptation to place an arm about his father's solid shoulders. Anger would have been less brutal.

'I've forgotten anything you might have said,' he lied, since it was necessary. 'Otherwise I wouldn't be back, would I?'

'I suppose not, boy,' Ned Livingstone said. 'I don't know.' He faltered, having some difficulty with speech. 'I just know it's good to see you. To see they haven't been knocking you around too much. I been having a lot of time to wonder about you.'

Tim, with a faint sick feeling, could imagine.

'Sorry,' he said. 'I'm tired. It's been a long day.'

After a longer night. He could feel Hans Wiemken clutching at his ankle again. He twisted abruptly in his chair, then rose.

His father rose too, brushing crumbs from the pitted table.

'Then I better find some clean sheets for your bed,' he said, 'if you'll just hang on.'

'I can make the bed,' Tim insisted. 'I'm not that helpless.'

'The least I can do. My boy home.' Ned Livingstone left the room to fossick in cupboards, then carried musty sheets to the bedroom. Tim followed. 'I expect you'll be up early with me for the cows,' he said.

'Of course.'

'And then I expect you'll be wanting to take a look around the place.'

'I expect I will.'

'You won't find much change.' His father grunted as he laboured over making his son's bed, refusing all help. 'I culled down the herd a bit last year. Easier to manage now. And I let a couple of top paddocks go. Not so much ground to cover. There, that should be right, three blankets and a quilt. Now you go to bed and sleep easy. We got all tomorrow to talk.'

He seemed ready to undress his son for sleep, as he had once. But he just placed a hand briefly on Tim's shoulder, then left the bedroom with apparently no more to say.

In bed, stripped to his underwear between chilly sheets, the boy lay awake, though his body craved sleep. He could identify each sound and movement his father made in the other part of the house; each seemed to echo in the perspective of the silence beyond. For he was aware now of the silence. He closed his eyes. The sounds continued; and the silence.

Then his father was standing by the bed. He might have come bearing a glass of milk and a slab of cake. Instead it was just another cup of tea.

'I was making myself a fresh one anyway,' he said. 'Goodnight, boy.'

He left the tea beside the bed, then retreated as far as the door, where he paused. 'You're comfortable?' He seemed obliged to say something, even if he could not say all; the rest might have been in his face, if Tim could have seen it.

'Fine.' He hesitated. 'Thanks, Dad.'

It seemed he had found the word the other was waiting for; it was as simple as that, after all.

'Goodnight, boy.' The door was shut.

Still there were sounds. The cup of tea, the faint slurping, the snip of a tobacco tin; then a long silence merging with silence. His own tea was left untouched. It was a long time before he heard the feet through to the bathroom, the splashing of water, the light switches clicking off one by one; and the grating as the alarm clock was wound.

And then wirewove crackling as it took the weight of his father's body. The sound of the old double bed; that was unlikely ever to change.

He waited for the sound of sleep. There was none. Perhaps his father was waiting too.

He woke once in the night, though. His father was crying out in his sleep. It was the cry of a man strangling.

It subsided to a reverberant groan, then a whimper. Finally there was nothing but the sound of a restless sleeper upon an old bed.

The boy tried to find sleep again. He dozed uneasily, in fits and starts, jerking awake as if in anticipation of another cry. He was well awake long before dawn. The entire house, even with his father asleep, appeared indifferent to any change in him. And the night appeared to insist that nothing had changed, nor would. For he had no answer to such a cry. He had been less helpless with Hans.

His first protest was to escape his childhood bed, and dress; his second was to find his pack in the dark, and slip a strap over his shoulder. Then it was only a matter of closing the back door quietly as he went.

At the end of the front drive, swinging the gate shut, he heard the alarm clock in the distance, calling his father awake for milking. It might be five minutes before his father rose; another ten or fifteen before he found his son's bed vacant again, and perhaps sat upon it, fingering the emptied sheets, in bleak wonder.

It was a picture hard to support, or justify. Some physical assault would have been less cruel, and at least comprehensible.

So he would have to justify it. He would have to begin.

The day was close now. The eastern hills were taut in a widening band of light. His father was right; nothing much had changed. The hills had not shifted, though they might have shrunk. The cows shuffled close to the milking shed, over their winter pasture, the cropped grass. The pines stood dark, the poplars bare and ghostly. The bush had an edge ragged with second growth now, where his father had surrendered ground;

once the margin had been precise. And there were clumps of gorse flourishing unchallenged along the roadside.

The road widened as it received him. Soon the light was pearling the dew wherever it trembled and fell. He walked without haste. There was no sound behind him of starting motor, something he might have expected, though the birds were noisy now. He looked back several times, carefully perhaps even hungrily. Then he left the rising sun, his father's land, for the gorge, still shadowed, and the river. He drank from it, as he had the night before, and then let his hands rest in a pool, until they were entirely numb.

This time he could not doubt goodbye. He tried, with some ferocity, to persuade himself that he had lost only what he had to lose. But he could not believe it, altogether. At length he withdrew his blue hands from the pool, dried them beneath his armpits, and walked on down to Te Ika. He would likely never try to taste a birthday again, certainly not in this fashion, though it had been one way of killing off his first twenty years, and rather more. He might have drawn into his flesh more than the chill of a dark river on a late winter morning.

His first ride towards the city was in a cream truck. Impatience, and perhaps hunger, scratched in his stomach. For he could believe in beginning. It seemed absurd that he had been gone only a day. And if he was impatient, it was because he still had to find out how he felt, and would.

Sixteen:

So he merged and suffered no loss. Perhaps only with Stan Coates, and then just in flashes, did he shed his chameleon colours. He still did not altogether trust Stan, and his urgency. And his unlikely friends. There were other people, though, for whom his concern should have been immediate. Margaret Saunders, somewhere in the city. Ben Campbell, his uncle. If he still saw neither, it was because they might take him back to where he began. He allowed the weeks to drift. Until a telephone rang, as he might have known.

'An old friend sends her regards,' the voice said. 'If you have the time to receive them.'

'Margaret,' he said. 'Sorry.'

'You're always sorry for something,' she observed. 'And guilty for same. When will you learn that life's too short?' She paused. 'Well, go on. Ask me how I am.'

'How are you, then?'

'Miserable.'

'Missing home?'

'Technically. No; that's not it. Try another question.'

He preferred not. 'I was going to get in touch. I'm still settling down.'

'That saves my question, then. How you are.'

'Making out.'

'You disappoint me.'

'Give me a chance.'

'Go on. Excite me. Interest me. Tell me about life in the big city.'

His problem with Margaret was not whether he could cope, but whether he wished to try.

'I'm on a story right now. Perhaps we could meet.'

He named the only place he knew. And arrived there that night ten minutes early, and to give no further ground for grievance. He took coffee to the only vacant cubicle. There were few of Stan Coates' acquaintances about, and not Stan himself, a relief. Most of the listless customers appeared ordinary enough.

In the next cubicle four students were occupied in desultory dialogue. Probably from art school, if their flashy dress and talk were indication. He eavesdropped on a few shiny fragments of ego, a splinter or two of malice. Nothing coherent. Until he heard, or thought he heard, the name Tim Livingstone mentioned, in some connection. The name seemed just to surface, then to sink again among clinking cups and mumbles. He wished himself less troubled by the name. Like irritant grit in the eye.

He was glad to be waiting for someone, even if she was late. A quarter of an hour late, at least, when she made her way to him, smiling, without apology. A big-boned country girl, emphatic in this place, though she was out of gumboots and dressed smartly enough; perhaps it was the confident stride, and lack of inclination to lower her voice.

'You look as if you've survived,' she announced. 'Though you look a bit thin on it.'

'You don't look bad either,' he said.

It was true; she didn't. Her voice on the phone had been one thing; her presence was something else altogether. He could wonder now why he had been so slow. He seemed to be coming to life again; at least he was aware of his body.

'I'll get coffee,' he added.

'No,' she insisted, her hand on his. 'I didn't come to drink coffee politely. I came to see you.'

They left the place. It was a pleasant night for walking, early summer and warm, with the damp of a quick shower shining on the streets. Not that they walked far. His room was less than a mile.

'Very neat,' she observed, shedding her jacket and unknotting a scarf. 'You're a good housekeeper. Are you going to make me supper later?' She tossed jacket and scarf across the chair, and kicked off her shoes. 'I mean, when we've got the greetings over?'

'I'll think about it,' he promised.

'And the drinks and music?'

'I haven't arranged those yet.'

'Then we can do without. I don't mind. I mean I'm not a hard girl to please. As you ought to know.'

He did. Perhaps that was why they were undressing without particular haste, however much the urgency. It was all so casual. Even fitting together on the single bed.

'Let's take it more slowly,' she said. 'More slowly than we have before, I mean. We might find more.' Her tongue and teeth worked around his neck.

They did, in the end, find a great deal more. Only the tightness, when he was inside her, was entirely familiar.

The end, though, was much the same. They clung to each other, almost in panic, as their strong bodies buffeted. And then they fell apart.

'Now that's cleared the air,' she said presently, 'we might find time to talk. You want me around, or don't you? I prefer trying for the truth afterwards.'

'Well . . .'

'Yes or no. Not if or but – or well.'

'Yes, then. We seem to get along.'

'No need to let caution overwhelm you. It's not marriage we're talking about.'

'I realize that. Tonight hasn't been much of a problem after all.'

'I like the after all bit,' she laughed. 'I really do.' She moved her bare legs lazily. 'Never mind. When do you suggest I move in?'

He was slow to answer, because he hadn't understood, entirely. 'Move in?'

'I'm not hitting it off terribly well with my aunt anyway.'

'I see.'

'There'll be another complaint tomorrow about the curious hours I keep at business college.'

'And you want to move here just because of that?'

'Not just because of that. Obviously.'

'It's not much of a place here. I mean, it does me for a while, but that's about all. Cheap – that's about the best I can say for it.'

'And the landlady's no problem? Can you say that for it too?'

'I suppose so. Yes.'

'So where's the problem?'

'I'm not saying there is one. It's just a bit sudden.'

'You want time to think it over, then?'

'Look; give me a chance. I've just got used to coping with myself. And now this. It's sudden.'

It sounded lame. But he felt possessive about this shabby room now, even about the makeshift bookshelves of brick and board, and the creaky bed he had bought cheaply. He had been so grateful for the surprising pleasure of privacy he hadn't felt need to clothe or colour the room particularly: a few magazine pictures of appeal, odd sticks of furniture, his books. His tidiness might not have been obsessive, but the place was neat, well scrubbed and swept.

He rose from the bed, pulled on a dressing gown, and began to make supper. Margaret rummaged through his wardrobe and found a sweater to pull over her slip. Amply covered, she apparently felt able to face him again.

'All right,' she said bleakly. 'So what's the verdict? Sudden is meaningless.'

So perhaps was peace. He hesitated, though, before reply. Then all fire seemed to leave her entirely.

'Never mind,' she went on, 'I've had it anyway. What does it matter if I tell you the truth? I'm fed up already. You probably guess I've been on a spree. From the moment I hit town, in fact. And now the party's over.'

There was a silence. 'You're pregnant?' he asked.

Her laugh was dry. 'Who said anything about pregnant?'

'What is it, then?'

'Just that I've had it, I'm sick of it already – scratching around for company. I even found a suitable married man in the office. A little Dane with a beard. He lasted two weeks, nearly. Then his wife came home from hospital. The others? You wouldn't want to know about them.'

He was surprised at his own calm. 'Probably not,' he agreed.

'If I have to sleep with someone, why can't I sleep with someone I like? And someone who might need it – it, or me.'

'And the point is I qualify?'

'Almost; near enough. I like you, up to a point. And you do need it. Or need someone.'

'All right. So I'm overwhelmed.' Perhaps he was. But he wished feelings more precise as he toasted cheese on bread to go with the coffee.

'What's wrong, then?'

'It seems I'm supposed to need you, but you're not supposed

to need me particularly. It doesn't sound a very happy arrangement. Does it?'

'Jesus wept,' she said. 'Do you want everything? Do I have to prove it again? What is it I have to do, how far do I have to go?'

'If you'd made it clear, then –'

'Made it clear?'

Tears were almost the last thing he expected from her; and they were, in a way, the last thing. And the cheese was burning, the coffee bubbling over. When he reached out for her, she pushed him away. At least the cheese and coffee were manageable, he found; and when he turned back to Margaret she didn't resist him altogether. He started to help her towards a chair, and then the bed, it seemed. He wasn't sure of any direction in his clumsiness, and hers. Yet she wasn't sobbing; her tears were silent. The agitation became his. And the direction, it turned out, was hers. She caught him, held him, just short of the bed, and slipped down his body; until she was half-knelt on the floor, her arms locking his thighs to her face, and her impatient mouth. He fell back the rest of the way to the bed, since there was nothing else to be done and certainly nothing to resist.

'There,' she said, when her mouth was free. 'Am I proving it? There. There. There. Enough? You don't need it?' She went to work again, his body now quite trapped beneath her, and her hair a tent from which he might never escape as shock after shock wilted his will. 'There,' she said. 'There. Come on, now; come. That's better. You can't act the cold fish now. I want the truth with it this time, not after.'

She lifted her head. Apparently to ascertain that he was satisfyingly helpless.

'You could say stop,' she observed. 'So why don't you? If you don't, it can only be because you need this, and me. Wouldn't you say? And if I go on, it's because I need something too. Right?'

Her logic appeared incontestable. But he was hardly looking for argument anyway. 'You must,' he agreed.

'It's yes or no again.'

'Then yes.'

'And I go on?'

'Yes.'

'That's better.' Her hair flowed back over his thighs again. She was gentler. 'There,' she said quietly. 'Come on, now; come.'

330

At the end, he seemed to have given her all the need he had. Margaret stayed the night and had never been more affectionate. 'A long time ago,' she said, sleepy beside him, 'we were country kids. And I had a brother called Clem. Remember?'

'Yes,' he said. 'I seem to.'

'It was rape, of course, with Clem, the first time.'

'I supposed it might be.'

'But not the other times.'

'No.' Only half awake, he was not sure what he should say. Or what she was trying to tell him anyway.

'So sooner or later I had to do something I hadn't done with Clem. Didn't I? Until tonight, even tonight, I wasn't sure. But it wasn't so difficult after all. I found I meant it. I didn't mean it when I started, and then I did. And that was all the problem. I couldn't, until I meant it. And now I feel quite free. You see?'

He hoped he did. It was true he had never known her more relaxed beside him. Soon they slept as easily as country kids.

'You're bloody quiet today,' said Stan Coates in the office. 'Sickening for something?'

'Perhaps. I seem to be tired.'

'Not sleeping well?'

'There's that too.'

'Frustration,' said Stan. 'Night starvation. Bad dreams. Cold sweats. I know it all, a sorry business. Time you snapped out of yourself. A party or two wouldn't do you any harm. Go on a good bender, or get a good woman. You're too damn earnest. Anyone would think your life depended on this pathetic job. Look as if you don't care and you might strike a raise.'

A telephone rang. 'Excuse me,' Ian said.

'Well,' Stan said, as he left, 'the professional advice is free.'

It was Margaret on the line. 'No,' Ian said presently. 'I'm fine. Really. And I shouldn't be late tonight.'

The cottage was difficult to find. New houses and tidy suburban gardens had grown around it. Asphalt streets, power poles, telephone boxes, a shop or two. At length he found a narrow right of way and followed it until he came to a thick wall of bamboo. An opening had been hacked through it, and on the other side was the cottage, the vines, the tropical trees. Just as

331

he remembered, nothing changed, a faintly yellowed photograph in the afternoon sun. His uncle lay in a hammock, evidently asleep, a book on the greying hairs of his chest. His head had balded down the centre, leaving his remaining healthy hair to fluff out above his ears. He wore only a ragged pair of shorts and soiled tennis shoes, an improbable Adam at rest in an embattled Eden. Somewhere beyond the bamboo there was a roaring motor-cycle.

But his eyes opened as Ian approached. He sat up, swinging his feet out of the hammock. 'I heard from your mother you were likely to turn up at some stage,' he observed, with a quizzical and perhaps kindly stare. 'Seems you've been something of a rogue elephant in your family. That right?'

He pulled on a shirt, and walked Ian through dappled shade to the cottage.

'It depends which side you see,' Ian said, 'or whose side you're on.'

'I don't take sides,' Ben said. 'Not any more, and never so far as families are concerned. Apart from the fact that your father was the original rogue elephant. Come on in.' They bent to enter the low door of the cottage. It was dim inside, and musty. The windows looked out on to dense foliage rather than sky, and were not particularly clean. Untidiness emerged from the gloom. Green peppers and tomatoes ripened or rotted on sills. The remains of perhaps two meals lay on the table : plates, cups, a half sliced loaf of bread, lettuce leaves, crumbs. Everywhere there were books : bursting off shelves, in tumbling corner stacks, open on the arm of a chair or on the floor, half read and evidently abandoned.

'Find yourself a place to sit down,' Ben said. 'You going to stay for a meal, or just coffee?'

'I'm committed to a meal back in town.'

'Well, that's all right too. I didn't really expect to see you. You didn't sound to me – from your mother's letter – as if you'd be driven over here out of some sense of family duty. You used to be a pleasant enough infant, as I recall. But you became just another bored kid to me. And I was just a boring uncle.'

Ian didn't attempt to deny it.

'So there we are,' Ben went on, 'you don't know what to make of me, and I've no idea what to make of you.' He fidgeted with a packet of coffee, then tore it open. 'We're in roughly the same boat. So if you want to get it over quickly, so you can tell your mother you've been, that's all right by me. You don't have to sit there ill at ease, wondering what you're supposed to say. I have the same trouble myself. And a little honesty might make it easier for both of us. Fair enough?'

'Fair enough,' Ian agreed. He felt able to smile.

'We'll just take it that we're two strangers, thrown together for an hour or two. And make the best of it.' Ben banged the coffee percolator down on the stove, for emphasis. 'So how are you liking the city?'

'A relief. To get off on my own.'

'You have this newspaper job. And I hear you're going to start university soon. What's it likely to add up to?'

Ian shrugged. 'Does it have to add up?'

'Not political, like your father?'

'No.'

'From a distance, or middle distance, he could overwhelm, at times. Believe me. Middle distance was mostly my vantage point.'

'I suppose he must have been remarkable, if so many people say so. I seem to have been hearing it half my life.'

'Well, possibly he's started to shrink. He could only grow so far.'

'So far?'

'So far as his time would allow him. Or his place. But then that might apply to a great many people, one way or another.'

Ian had no opinion.

'What about the other side of the family, your mother's and mine? No literary ambitions?'

'Faint.'

'So you haven't inherited much either side.'

'As little as I can manage, I suppose.'

'Well, don't make a point of rubbing the slate too clean. Or you might find yourself writing the same things again.' Ben paused. 'And how do I strike you? Don't be polite.'

'I don't know; I need more time.'

'You must have some impression. Anything like your father?'

'Possibly. Though quite unlike, most ways.'

'A bit shrunken too. That it?'

'I don't know if I mean that.'

'But it fits, fairly. Wouldn't you say?'

'Well – ' Ben was insisting on likeness.

'We're both history's left-overs, after all. No one had much

333

use for either of us, in the end. For my verse or his speeches. You take your coffee black?'

'Thanks.' The visit was turning out far different from anything he expected. Ben should have been weary and perhaps bitter. Instead there was this sunburned man with eyes alert in a leathery face, and a lively smile. He sat comfortably, his bare legs crossed, in a chair opposite Ian.

'Still living alone?'

'Not any more.'

'Some colleague?'

'A girl friend.' It seemed, after all, that nothing needed to be hidden from Ben. 'Quite an old friend. She moved in a week or two ago.'

'No plans?'

'None. We just happen to get along for the time being.'

'Then good for you. And her.'

'It may not be so good for her. She seems to expect something of life. Of the city anyway.'

'And you don't?'

'Not that I've noticed.'

'She's from Te Ika too, I take it. Home town girl.'

'Yes.'

'Then I imagine you both have a great deal of growing to do yet. Just remember, if you do break up, that there's not an original line in the script. It will all have been said – or screamed – before.'

'I'll try to remember.'

'If one ever does. Mention of Te Ika reminds me. You never knew a family by name of Livingstone?'

'Here we go again,' Ian said.

'You did?'

'I knew someone – a boy – called Tim Livingstone. That's the name you want, isn't it?'

Ben nodded. 'You knew him well, then?'

'Hardly at all. Except once. But I've heard his name two or three times since I arrived here. I assumed it was the same person. It had to be.'

'A remarkable young man.'

'So I hear. Though it hasn't been complimentary.'

'I don't see why. He's aggressive enough, of course. But possibly only as much as he needs to be. I've only met him once. An acquaintance of mine, a German named Wiemken, coached him for a time. Though now he's out on his own, in every sense. I've never seen a young painter who could borrow so much and owe so little. Incredible.'

'And he's good. Is that what you're saying?'

'It's unnecessary to say it. He's interesting, which is rather more to the point. I find it takes a great deal to interest me these days.'

'I'd like to see his work. Even if I don't happen to meet him again.'

'Then you'll possibly do both. It's not such a big city, after all.'

It wasn't.

'Let's do something,' Margaret said as she lay beside him one lazy Saturday. 'Take me out.'

They had, for the moment, exhausted the possibilities of their own company. There was rain on the windows.

'Something in mind?' he asked.

'Nothing. And don't suggest another movie.'

She fidgeted. He hadn't learned how to manage her restlessness, beyond a certain point. Usually he just tried to see it out. For they were comfortable enough, on the whole.

'Haven't you any imagination at all?' she said. 'And if you haven't any imagination, haven't you got some friends?'

'Friends?' This was something new.

'Friends we could visit. People. You know, on two legs.'

'Well, let's see. There's you.'

'I already have some pretty sad company.'

'There's Uncle Ben.'

'He doesn't sound up to much.'

'And there's Stan Coates. I work with him. That's about it.'

'It looks like it has to be this Stan Coates, then. Is he nice?'

'Friendly anyway. I might have his phone number somewhere.'

'Try it, then.'

At length he was persuaded off the bed. Talking to Stan Coates seemed, for the moment, preferable to bickering the rest of the afternoon away with Margaret; it was one or the other. He groped bleary into his clothes and went down the hall to phone Stan. His finger, though, hesitated on the point of dialling the last digit of Stan's number. He could, after all, tell Margaret there had been no reply. But she would still be on

his hands, with an abundance of unsatisfied energy. So he spun
the last digit like a gambler.

An indistinct voice answered; there was a great deal of noise
at the other end of the line.

'Stan?'

'Stan's off down to the boozer to get some more grog. Can I
do anything for you? Take a message? Pour you a drink?'

'I just wanted to get in touch with Stan. I work with him.'

'Urgent? Life or death?'

'Nothing like that. I wondered what he was doing.'

'I'm wondering too. He's been gone an hour. If you want to
see him, come around.'

'Thanks, but – '

'Open invitation. If Stan doesn't want to see you after all,
blame it on me. His flat's rather a shambles. So we can take a
bit more blame. Just tell him Livingstone told you to come
around. That's if he's heaved us out by the time you get here.'

'You're Livingstone?'

'More or less. Today it's less. I don't even know why I'm in
Coates' flat at all. It's just that I woke up here this morning.
What time is it?'

'About four.'

'Four in the afternoon?'

'Yes.'

'God almighty. Who's talking, by the way?'

'Ian Freeman.' He paused, then added, 'We met once.'

'Freeman? Wait a moment – a name but no face. Where was
it? Whose place?'

'No one's place. School. Te Ika.'

'Christ, that's all I need now. Four in the afternoon and someone says Te Ika.' The voice shifted from the phone in mid-
sentence; Ian thought the other was about to hang up. 'Hey,
shut off that racket, will you? Can't you see I'm having a
conversation?' Then the voice returned more clearly. 'Te Ika,
you said. You did say it? Then who are you?'

'We hardly knew each other.'

'Freeman, Freeman, Freeman. Hold it – not the kid who got
bashed on the riverbank?'

'If you like.'

'The kid on the riverbank. What do you know about that?'
A pause, and the voice distant again. 'For Christ's sake, didn't
you hear me telling you to lay off and shut up?' Another pause,

and the voice was clear again. 'Did you say you were coming round?'

'Well – '

'Come on round. I'll pour you a drink. This is bloody hopeless.'

'If I can find the place.'

'A hundred yards down Ponsonby Road. Behind a second-hand shop. You'll hear the noise. See you.' The phone went dead abruptly.

Ian went slowly back to his room. Margaret, still on the bed, flashed a look of inquiry. 'Well,' he said, 'it seems we've got some kind of party on our hands.'

'Marvellous,' she said. 'How did you manage it?'

'Sunny personality. No problem at all.'

'Whose party?' she asked, as she slid from the bed and looked out clothes.

'I would know. But it's in Stan Coates' flat. And we were invited by someone called Livingstone. I suppose you wouldn't know the name.'

'Should I?'

'Well – ' The connection with Te Ika might not appeal to her. Perhaps it wasn't relevant anyway. 'He's an artist. Also supposed to be rather a lunatic.'

'Then I'd hardly know, would I?'

They had less than a mile to walk. They found a subdued din as predicted, behind a second-hand shop; and rang a bell. Stan Coates emerged from somewhere in the shabby wooden building. He looked at Ian sadly, then at Margaret speculatively.

'I rang up and got invited to a party,' Ian explained.

'More than I was,' Stan said.

'Stan Coates. Margaret Saunders. Margaret's an old friend.' He thought he should make something clear, if not everything.

'Sorry I'm not at my best. This, apparently, is just a peacemaking effort by Livingstone. As is the international custom these days, he makes peace through total war. Come on, now. I need allies.' He shepherded them down a short hall, then into a room murky with tobacco smoke and dense with shifting people. There was the smell of spilt beer. And a clash of music; there seemed to be a guitarist playing in opposition to a radiogram. It was hard to see. Blinds had been drawn against the day.

'I'll fetch some bottles,' Stan said. 'I bought some on condition they leave. They're sampling it first.'

'Doesn't anyone breathe here?' asked Margaret vaguely. 'Or am I a victim of country air?'

They were bumped apart by a bearded drunk, who lurched to a standstill and then regarded them both for a moment without apology. They were too obviously newcomers, and sober. 'Some more buggers without grog,' he observed briefly, and then crashed out the door in the direction of a permanent cascade of water.

'Here we are,' said Stan, returning with a pair of frothing bottles. 'And good luck to you.'

'Where's this Livingstone?' Ian asked. He was still trying to see.

'Underfoot, I hope,' Stan said bitterly. 'Trampled to death by his so-called friends. That's what the bastard deserves.' Stan then, with an offhand gesture, pulled someone by the shoulder out of the crowd. 'Listen, Tim,' he said. 'Enough's enough. What about packing it in soon and moving on?'

Tim Livingstone, it turned out, was still ordinary enough. And, beardless, distinct among his friends. He was as tall and lean as Ian remembered, and as fair. With the kind of craggy face which might have been anonymous above a mounted horse, upon a football field, or behind the wheel of a tractor. He wore jeans and unbuttoned shirt and appeared unsteady on his feet.

'People are only just arriving,' he said, looking Ian and Margaret up and down.

'Friends of mine,' Stan said. 'On a social visit. That's all. I'm trying to get rid of yours, remember?'

'Telephone,' Tim Livingstone said. 'Invited some friends of yours on the telephone. Just to make up the number.' He steadied, then looked at Ian. 'You the one, then?'

'We spoke,' Ian agreed.

'The kid on the riverbank,' Tim Livingstone said. 'You him? You look too smooth by far.'

'What the hell's this?' Stan asked.

'We knew each other once,' Ian explained. 'I told you.'

'Te Ika?' asked Margaret, perplexed.

'And who are you?' Tim Livingstone said. 'Don't remember you. You think I ought to?' He draped an arm over Margaret's shoulder.

'If this is a reunion,' Stan said, 'Then I'm better out of it. Christ, I was expecting allies.'

338

'The kid on the riverbank,' Tim Livingstone said. 'Can you still fight? I seem to remember you taking on half the damn school. And coming up for more.'

It wasn't difficult to disbelieve in the Tim Livingstone he was offered. Nothing was quite true, and everything faintly inflated. The drunkenness. The arm about Margaret. Even the unbuttoned shirt, possibly, and certainly the bottle he tilted into his mouth. The substance might have been there; the edges were unreal.

'Ian fighting half the school?' Margaret laughed. 'Never.'

'Fact. Fought like a tiger. Can't remember why, now.'

But he gave Ian a sober flick of the eye : of course he remembered, however much the memory was unlikely here.

'I've never seen him hit anyone,' Margaret insisted. 'Off a football field, that is.'

'Let me tell you, then, that day I had to step in and save a dozen kids from slaughter.'

Again the slight, unmistakable flick of the eye. A private game, almost.

'You actually fought Ian yourself?'

'Hell no. Not my job to tame him. I just suggested he keep his fighting to the football field. Which he did thereafter, evidently.'

And he smiled as he delivered up the myth. So pleasantly, and fluently, that Ian could almost prefer to believe it.

'Livingstone,' Margaret said. 'I've only just clicked. Of course. I remember you. Ahead of us at school. And wasn't there some trouble? Some accident? You came from some farm up the Waiatarua gorge.'

'It sounds convincing,' he said.

'My father knew Tom Jackson. Who knew your father.'

'Who hated Tom Jackson's guts. And probably your father's too, if the truth were known. Where was your farm?'

'On the flat, on the old road south.'

'I know. Clem Saunders – big burly brute.'

'My brother.'

Another ghost loosed in the room. Stan Coates, understandably, had vanished in despair, and given Tim the victory. Margaret turned on Ian.

'When you said Livingstone,' she went on, 'you didn't say anything about Te Ika. You asked me did I know the name and didn't say anything about Te Ika at all. You just said something about him being an artist. An artist?'

'Well, that's supposed to be true too,' Ian said, and looked to Tim in appeal. 'Isn't that right?'

'An artist from Te Ika,' Margaret said with scorn. 'Who do you think you're fooling?'

'That,' said Tim, 'is a difficult question.'

'Which end of a cow do you paint?'

'Your guess.'

'I don't believe it, that's all. An artist from Te Ika. That place.' She made it sound some final infamy.

'Look, Marg,' Ian said reasonably, 'you haven't even seen his work. So –'

'I can see him, can't I?'

'Yes, but –'

'And I know where he comes from, don't I?'

'All right,' said Ian, 'but I don't see –'

'Aren't I entitled to an opinion, then? Is that what you're telling me?' He went to look for Stan.

'I don't know that I'm trying to tell you anything,' Ian sighed. 'Never mind.'

He was sitting maudlin and lonely on a stool in his kitchen, among empty bottles and crushed cartons; the floor was awash. 'So how did you find Livingstone?'

'Reasonable, in his way.'

'A fascinating qualification. You'll go far in journalism, let me predict. Never mind. It's his friends, possibly. That's what I'd like to believe anyway. The thing is how to tell him apart, and whether it's worthwhile trying. Which somehow reminds me never to tell by appearances again – you're a dark horse. That filly you fetched along. You really surprise me. Seeing you in the office and elsewhere, I was convinced you were either celibate or sexless.'

'Old friend,' Ian insisted.

'How wrong could I be?' said Stan gloomily. 'All this time I've been feeling sorry for you, wanting to bring you out, and you've been having that spectacular harvest. I can't trust myself to make an educated judgement again. Never. Did you open that bottle? Pass it over. Mine seems to have evaporated. What do I do with this crew? Any suggestions short of massacre?'

'Not really,' Ian said.

'Then let the day dissolve,' said Stan wearily.

But in the end the day collapsed inward. When beer grew short, Stan produced a venomous bottle of red wine, which they drank by the tumbler; everything seemed to swell outward, then shrivel. Faces at a distance swarmed close again; the kitchen filled, emptied, filled. Bearded faces, girls' faces. A fight bounced into the kitchen; he found a girl weeping in his arms. The day died and the power fused, then there were faces grotesque by candlelight, surging away and crashing back again. Margaret danced giddily in a circle of clapping hands. There was shouting, night air, taxis, cartons of beer. He was vomiting into long grass with strange buildings around and Stan surprisingly still beside him. A glassy house somewhere with high beams, flagstoned floor, more red wine, more people. Margaret dancing again. His limbs were leaden, his head threatening to slide from his shoulders More night air, more taxis; slamming doors. He had to endure, for some reason. Stan's voice, still cheerful. Shouts, fading.

He opened his eyes to find his own room, and morning sunlight. His eyes hurt; his mouth was bitter. He could hear children playing in the street outside.

His room did not appear much damaged. It was just that Margaret did not occupy the pillow beside him.

Perhaps indifference had been his undoing. Anyway he was undone; and she was elsewhere. He had been expecting something like this. What he hadn't expected was that it would arrive so painlessly. He was as numb with relief as regret, waking lonely again, pushing bedcovers aside and placing his feet on the cold floor. He couldn't remember where he'd lost her, where he'd last seen her. She had still been dancing, doubtless, among admirers. But who had put him to bed?

The answer seemed Stan, collapsed and asleep on the floor, an overturned bottle staining a mat.

He carried his hammering head through to the bathroom and, on return, decided against waking Stan with questions. Instead he prepared coffee and tried to enjoy silence and sunlight. Stan soon stirred. He seemed to claim his limbs one by one, then his head almost as an afterthought; he sat up with heavy eyes. And looked at Ian in grieving silence.

'You look too bloody good to be true,' he announced at length. 'You've no right to be sitting up there on that stool

341

passing judgement on lesser men. You should have seen yourself last night. Give me some coffee, quick.' He rose dishevelled from the floor, gently fingering a split lip. 'I think we can fairly blame Livingstone. You can't say I didn't warn you.'

'No,' Ian agreed. 'I can't say that.'

But they were silent together over coffee.

'Well, aren't you going to say anything at all?' Stan demanded.

'What about?' Ian asked.

'For God's sake, man. Your girl.'

'She can look after herself. Margaret's never had any problem in that connection, so far as I remember.'

Stan looked stunned. 'You're kidding,' he said.

'We just happen to have been living together,' Ian said. 'An arrangement of sorts. It's been convenient.'

'That's all?' Stan was still incredulous. 'With her?'

'Roughly,' Ian said. 'Very roughly.' He could smooth it all out in time, perhaps even polish it, so there would be no roughness left at all; no unexpected edge to hurt. He was supposed to be hurt : no doubt about that.

'You're either a cold fish,' Stan said, 'or you're nuts. Or I'm a sex maniac who can't see straight; that's a third possibility. There is a fourth, that you – you and me both – are still in a state of shock. I don't suppose you'd remember who I fought with last night?' His fingers approached his lip again.

'Sorry.'

'Most unsatisfying. I lost track after my landlady called the police in.'

'I lost track before then. But I gather you managed to put me to bed before you fell on the floor yourself.'

'Me?' Stan said. 'That was one thing I didn't do, put you to bed. Not my line at all, old son.'

'But you were the only one – ' Then Ian remembered that he'd been stripped down when he woke between the sheets; his clothes had been folded neatly. Too plainly Margaret. His guard was instantly down; something did hurt after all. 'Never mind,' he finished.

'The party moved in here and moved out on the way to somewhere else, as I recall. We were the casualties left in its wake.'

'Never mind,' Ian repeated. 'I'd sooner forget it.'

'With my head,' Stan said, 'not bloody likely. And today

342

I've got to think about finding a new flat. Bloody Livingstone. I hope he was the one I belted. Incidentally, you came out with some interesting truths last night.'

'Me?'

'Well, I didn't intend to mention it right away. About your being Bill Freeman's son, I mean. He was a depression hero of my father's. Your father, that is.'

'My father?'

'Yes. Look; are you with me this morning?'

'Within limits. It's just that sometimes I can do without people talking to me about my father.'

'Understandable,' Stan observed. 'I can also understand your not advertising your ancestry.'

'One of the times I can do without hearing about my father is with a hangover. I've just discovered that. So do you mind, Stan?'

'All right. I'll lay off. But it's a funny thing.'

'What is?'

'The way I seemed to smell you out from the beginning.'

'Oh?'

'I suppose it's time to tell a little truth of my own.'

'Can I cope with it before breakfast? Or can it wait?'

A certain concern for Margaret had begun to nag, and distract him from what Stan was saying; he hoped she was all right, though he could not hope for much else. So he found relief in frying bacon and eggs. Behind him, though, Stan persisted.

There was, evidently, to be no escape.

'Look,' Stan was saying, 'How do I strike you in the office?'

'Very efficient, I suppose. And you seem to know your way around.'

'You wouldn't guess, then.'

'Guess what?'

'My double life.'

'You mean these friends – or enemies – of yours last night? Well . . .'

'No. They don't count. I'm more genuinely schizophrenic. I'm talking about the stuff I write for the Party weekly. In the time I'm employed by the capitalist press.'

'I see.' But he didn't really, though he felt a faint tremor, perhaps a warning, through his general numbness.

'No reason not to tell Bill Freeman's son. So far as I can see.

343

Writing for them, my secret life, makes the office almost tolerable. Not quite, but almost.'

'I don't see why you should tell me, particularly. My father broke with it all years ago.'

'But his heart was in the right place.'

'Perhaps. I wouldn't know. But I seem to remember him called a traitor.'

'You don't think I take all that nonsense seriously?'

'Then aren't you with them?'

'Up to a point. I carry a card, if that's what you mean. Like a rosary – to finger when in doubt. But that doesn't mean I have to take all the nonsense seriously.'

'I've only just realized you took anything seriously.'

'I take myself seriously. Otherwise I'd be off my head. If I carry a card, I can pretend to call my soul my own. I have to have something. What have you got?'

'Bacon and eggs,' Ian said. 'Don't let your food go cold.'

'Seriously, though. What have you got?'

'This room. My job. University soon. And bacon and eggs right now. Eat up, Stan. Waste appals me. And I can't be too intense on Sunday morning, besides.'

'Never mind,' Stan said. 'You're young, of course. I'm forgetting. Sex is sufficient unto the day. So just quietly forget it.'

'Forget what?'

'Anything I've said to you. If it doesn't interest you, then you've never heard it. I talk too much with a hangover. And if I have confused you with your father, my apologies. Fortunately, I never get confused with mine. He's an alcoholic ex-pugilist, as talkative as hell.' Stan filled his mouth reluctantly and winked.

Margaret stepped in the door, with a faintly worried and abstracted air, as if she'd lost something. 'Oh,' she said with apparent surprise, 'you're all right. I came back to see.'

'Nice of you,' Ian observed. 'But we're really making out quite well.'

She showed amazingly little trace of the long night. She still glowed, in a subdued way.

'Pity to walk out on the party on our account,' Stan said. 'Does it still survive, somewhere?'

She ignored Stan. Ian felt her eyes on his face; she seemed to be studying him with some concern or concentration. He kept his own eyes on the food, so far as he could.

Margaret still had nothing to say. She went across the room, fell into a chair, kicked off her shoes, and looked at the ceiling.

'Breakfast?' Ian offered.

She shook her head.

'Coffee, then?'

Since she made no response this time, he fetched a mug of coffee and balanced it on the arm of her chair. She looked up at him with what might have been appeal. But he didn't linger to determine the expression or return her gaze; he turned his back and went again to the breakfast table. And Stan. Earlier, he could have done without Stan; now he was glad of him.

All the same the silence, for a time, was difficult.

'Thank Christ for that food,' Stan said finally. 'My stomach isn't half so introspective.' He wiped egg from his mouth. 'Tell me, Freeman, you got any plans for today?'

'No,' Ian said. He could not have been more precise.

'If you feel like it later, give me a ring. We might be able to salvage something sane from the weekend. Even if it only amounts to resuming our conversation where we left off. Meantime, I'd better shuffle off home to face the music. I imagine my landlady, despite having ordered me out by the end of the month, will still be singing an interesting tune.' He finished his coffee and rose. 'Good luck.'

Ian saw him to the door. Margaret didn't shift her eyes from the ceiling. So far she hadn't acknowledged her coffee either. With Stan gone, Ian returned to his silence; and hers. They could, he supposed, sit like that all day, each wondering about the other.

'Sorry,' she said at last. And sipped her coffee.

He was not sure he understood.

'Walking out on you,' she explained.

'No reason to be sorry,' he said shortly. 'That's your business.'

'But I want to be sorry for once. It's my turn, surely.'

'Then be my guest.'

'I'm interested in whether you're angry.'

'Well, thanks for putting me to bed. Is there anything else to say?'

'You don't care, then,' she said flatly. She did sound tired, at last. And began to look it. She closed her eyes. 'But I don't really need to be told.'

'Look, Marg –'

'It's perfectly all right. It really is. I knew long before last night. You're a cripple. You can't feel. Except once – one night when you really happened to need me. Since then, since we came here, I've had to make you need me. And there's an end to that too. Right?'

He didn't answer.

'So there's no point in my being sorry, or anything else, about last night,' she went on. 'Is there? As it happens, I didn't go to bed with anyone else. I was almost enjoying myself, for once. I haven't been. I can't share that shell with you. So that's it.'

'I suppose I needed more time,' he said. 'Time to straighten myself – '

'Time to hang yourself.'

'Possibly,' he allowed.

'So thank God for last night. If this had gone on much longer, I might really have forgotten I was still alive. And to think I was ever idiot enough to think you could be different. That's the biggest joke. On me.'

She was swift to her feet, her face without expression, and swept out of the room. A minute later there was sound of the shower. Ian made gestures toward disposing of the breakfast dishes. A sunlit Sunday morning seemed as good a time as any for things to come to a head. He didn't believe her, of course. He preferred to believe she had slept with someone last night. And that courage had failed her in confession.

The shower stopped. His unease was distinct now, in his knees, and his throat. And somewhere in his belly too, it seemed.

Then Margaret appeared, holding a thin blue dressing gown tight about herself. Her feet and legs were bare, her skin flushed, and her hair damp. 'I won't bother you any more,' she announced. 'I'm off to bed. I expect I'll sleep the day out.'

He knew whom she had been with, of course. He didn't even have that question to consider as he stacked away the dishes. Behind him, Margaret made the bed and slid between the sheets.

The day was surprisingly warm already. And the room had grown airless.

'Coming?' she said quietly.

There was a prickling in his dry body which he might have acknowledged.

'Only if you like,' she added. 'It only means as much as you want it to. And it doesn't have to mean anything at all; I shouldn't have to tell you that, though, should I?'

The test had only just come after all; everything else had

346

been by way of preliminary. He knew what he would have preferred to say. He also knew what he had to say.

Her hair drifted across the pillow. She was smiling, and with some evident confidence. 'Come on,' she said. 'We've never stood on ceremony.'

'Sorry,' he said finally.

He didn't look to see if her smile changed, or faded. He went to the bathroom to shave. He wondered whom he might visit. Stan, in the debris of the night, had no appeal. Besides he needed a less sluggish mind, now, to keep Stan at a distance. Ben, then. It could be said for Ben, at least, that he wasn't young, and no longer cared much. What kind of refuge was Ben to be, then? From Margaret, or from life? The two had become indistinguishable.

His actual departure from the flat was quiet, an anti-climax: Margaret was asleep, or appeared to be.

And so later, much later that day, was his arrival home to a dark flat; perhaps nothing in his life would be dignified by genuine climax. He could smell difference in the place before he switched on the light; it was also perceptibly cooler. Hardly a trace of Margaret remained. Perhaps a hairpin, if he looked. And, surprisingly, she had restored the place to its original austerity. Stockings no longer hung to dry in random places; undergarments were no longer scattered about the room. And the bed was doubtless made with fresh sheets. The wardrobe door did not bulge open with the pressure of her clothes and his; it was shut tight. She might have neglected to empty an ashtray. But that was about all. Otherwise she had emptied his life almost too efficiently.

He sat down slowly, and wondered what else he might have expected. Ben, after all, was wrong. There could be original lines in the script. Margaret would always write one or two of her own. She hadn't even left a goodbye note.

Seventeen:

He followed the creek, beyond spring willows, into the bush. The path along the creek gave out; rocks split and eroded grew on each side. He had to wade in the cold water now and, in deep places, scramble from rock to rock. At times the pressure of the noisy water kicked spray into his face. Trees branched overhead, and the creepers hung thickly. There were gloomy limestone hollows along the creek where water circled, and beards of slime tangled. And perhaps muddy eels twisted. Pale green tree ferns dipped toward the water and brushed lightly over his face. Then he came to the waterfall, a sudden curving flare of white in the gloom, and a welcome roaring in his ears. For he knew where he was at last, and why he had come. There was no surprise in the discovery at all; it was something as natural as drawing breath, for all the wonder. And the real wonder was that he hadn't seen it before. It wasn't such a big waterfall. The creek dipped down three or four ledges, and then hurtled perhaps twenty feet, through flashes of sunlight where rising spray sparkled and mistily drifted. He made his way, rock by rock, towards it.

His shoulder was knocked, and he spun dizzily off balance. 'Livingstone,' someone was saying, 'are you going to sleep all day again?'

He was among blankets, not water, but he floundered nevertheless. Strength seemed sucked from his flesh. In fright, his body was vulnerable, still prone to laceration.

It was Ken McAdam by the bed. Ken McAdam smart in a suit. Ken was in advertising now.

'A small job for you,' Ken said. 'That's if you're interested in money this week. Are you with me?'

His eyes were still difficult.

'I'm on my way to the office,' Ken went on. 'I'll leave this stuff by the bed. You can sort it out yourself. If there's any problem, ring me. All right?'

Ken had gone by the time he was ready to speak. So he closed his eyes again. But the dream, the waterfall, was gone. Impossible to rediscover. And the lightness of his limbs was gone too; his flesh felt bruised and heavy and awkwardly knit. He might have been drowning among hot blankets for a month, waiting for a sign.

Ken with a job. His wooden room tight around him. The sounds of the city beyond. He rose, relieved and washed himself, and made toast, since his kitchen contained some stale bread. And some tea, which helped his throat. His eyes improved.

Outside the city raced. Monday morning. Money. He moved himself to Ken McAdam's proposition at last, concerning something called Ship Biscuits. 'Suggest you try Cook's *Endeavour* as a theme,' Ken scribbled. 'For local appeal. Perhaps the immortal Captain Cook himself with a spyglass. If you use as much imagination as you did on the last job, then you're home and dry.'

Dry, at least; he made more tea. And considered. *Endeavour* had been a small ship upon a large ocean. Too large for comfort. So perhaps he could try the ocean first, to see what it suggested. He found pencil and paper and tried to arrange himself plausibly beside the window, since he could not believe in himself yet, and that difficulty was not at all unfamiliar, even if he were only doing something for Ken McAdam. It could be still worse at other times. Worst, now, if he were trying to.

After an hour or two, however, he had something credible, though he was not sure whether the *Endeavour*, tiny and tossing in mountainous water, had two masts or three, or perhaps even four. It was clearly time for some research. He shaved, in hope of feeling better, and walked down to the city library.

'Cook,' he said to the girl behind the desk.

'Fiction?'

'The man who discovered this country. Captain James.'

'Upstairs. Reference.'

He found his way about, in the end, and sat at a table where another girl heaped volumes. He did not expect to be any time at all, and should not have been, since he found illustrations of *Endeavour* in plenty. But he swam around these illustrations,

349

through cascades of words. There was crack of canvas, surge of sea, gulls circling the masthead. The words became, in time, tributaries to the one tide, and he went on the tide, until a huge horizon began to fill with land. Headlands grew around him, crags, bays, hills lumpy and hills sharp, mountains beyond; and everywhere the leap of light.

Hans Wiemken might have leered at him behind some rock.

Yet he might have gone further into the vision, and pierced that thick foliage, or been pierced, for leaves gleamed like glass; and somewhere beyond, and within, have found his father, to shake his hand, as if they had found themselves together at a funeral. For it could not be other.

Then he imagined himself where Cook had never seen. And watching from within, upon a high hill, he saw *Endeavour* pull up anchor and set sail. The silent sails tugged the ship away on the evening wind. Everywhere the birds swarmed, in the darkening trees; everywhere the sound of water. He would have gone back to his village then, to his tattooed brothers, and attempted an explanation, or a legend. And for truth he told, perhaps have his brains dashed out. Or be set aside, ignored, as a madman.

The library was closing. 'You're a funny sort of student,' the library girl said. 'All these books, and I haven't seen you make a note all day. Or didn't you find what you were looking for?'

Endeavour had three masts. He was back in the world of Ken McAdam and Ship Biscuits. He was also hungry and excited. He could do something about the hunger, if not the excitement, for he had money in his pocket. Sufficient, say, for a toasted sandwich and coffee. Beyond that the week ahead held only promise.

Ken was not in the coffee bar; nor Charlie, Sandy, anyone predictable. Just the girl, and she was alone. He recovered her name without effort; she had been almost the only thing to shine in the manufactured murk of his weekend.

'Cheer up,' he said. 'This time of night is usually worst.'

She still shone, in her way, even if she did not smile. 'Thanks,' she said.

'Trouble?'

'Not really trouble; not any more. It's just Ian and I have given up.'

'Ian?'

'Your old friend, remember? Te Ika.'

350

'Sorry,' he said. 'I'm a bit dislocated tonight.'

'It was probably time we gave up,' she said. 'But still.'

'And you feel like going home to Te Ika now?'

'I didn't say that.'

'Then I misheard. How do you come to be here tonight, anyway?'

'Because Ian arranged to meet me here once. And tonight, when I was walking by myself, I dropped in to rest my feet. It seemed as good as anywhere.'

'I see.' His excitement appeared to have an edge to work on now. 'So you really are alone. You've got somewhere to stay?'

'For the time being. A scruffy little private hotel. No hot water after nine, no visitors after ten. It'll do. I knew Ian and I wouldn't stay the distance, from the beginning, but it was worth trying.'

'Why?'

'Just in case I was wrong. I thought in the city we might be ourselves. And that's the trouble. We are. Only more so. So perhaps the city's to blame after all.'

'Or Te Ika.'

'Perhaps.'

'Or even yourselves.'

'You're not much help. Why do people take you seriously? They seem to. I can't think why.'

'I'm not to blame for other people.'

'That's your story. You stick to it.'

It seemed, before long, that he liked the girl. There was none of the nonsense. He had grown used to earnest little girls lifting their eyes from volumes of poetry and wanting to know what he thought of Eliot and Pound. And then wanting, quite logically, and even more earnestly, to improve him. He had often found his way blind to bed through fogs of elegant advice. He might also have been waiting for this capricious messenger from nowhere. Well, almost nowhere. Te Ika could hardly be nearer.

Later that week he asked, 'You're not really thinking of going back, are you?'

'Would it matter to you?' she said briskly.

He took time to answer. There was, after all, a limit. 'Yes,' he said finally. 'It would.'

'All right,' she said. 'Let's say I'm not, then.'

She slid so naturally into his life he was still surprised. Certainly he was better able to avoid pubs and people, and tangled talk. Other things helped too, of course. Ken McAdam and Ship Biscuits, for example. He finished the job at amazing speed, complete with Cook, and three-masted *Endeavour*, so he could settle to see.

'I think I can afford a bigger room,' he announced.

'Why?'

'For one thing, too many people know this place. For another, it's growing too small.'

'Because of me?'

'I need more room to move around now. If ever I'm going to get down to work again. It would be easier, of course, just to talk about it. But this time I am.'

'Why the sudden panic, though?'

'Because I have to get on with it.'

He was grateful that she allowed him to make it a practical thing. They found a place they could share in a quiet dead-end street. It was large enough; and there was a view of mud-flats and mangroves from their small kitchen, just a glimpse between houses. They could also see a calm tide glimmering there, at times.

Best of all, no one came; no one knew he was there. He could always ring Ken McAdam, for work.

'You've really dropped out,' Ken said. 'No one seems to have seen you in weeks. What's the story? I hear rumour of some woman. I can't find you in the pub. Or the coffee bar. And I find you've cleared out from your old place. The rent paid too. That's a change. Ted Connolly was in town the other day, looking for you. No one could help him. He looked a bit down in the mouth. I hear he's taken off again.'

'Sorry about Ted. But still.'

'Well, what is the story?'

'Just that I'm all right.'

'Then you're working. I seem to recognize the tone.'

'I don't admit anything. But I would be glad of any money I can make, on the side.'

'I'll see what I can push your way. It's just that jobs are a bit tight at the moment. Keep in touch, though. And you really are working?'

'You don't miss a trick.'

352

'I like to keep my ear to the ground. You know that. And it's true about this woman?'

'Everything they say,' Tim agreed, 'whatever it is. She's French, with sixteen grandchildren, and keeps poodles.'

'And keeps you out of trouble, evidently.' Ken sighed. 'I wonder how long.'

How long? Margaret took him on trust, more or less, and that was sufficient. She would watch him prepare board or canvas and begin to paint.

'I suppose,' she said, 'you know what you are doing.'

He continued. One day he would paint a picture all in black, and its shades.

'Or someone does,' she added. 'I wouldn't know.'

For the bush was growing darkly on the hills, and he was trying to contain winter in the rocks, and more. Each day he would try more, but carefully, as if the rocks might split, or the painting, with the weight. And the weight of black. He still had to measure it with caution. An intricate act of balance. It could kill so quickly, leaving nothing but itself. His own problem entirely, but one he had to contrive, to see how far he could go. Otherwise there was nothing, no challenge, nothing at all to give the act point, and certainly nothing to satisfy. Not that he did find satisfaction, but there was always the possibility, if he could shorten the distance between what he wanted and what he got. And that, after all, was reason to try again.

'I suppose,' Margaret said, sceptical, 'you are thinking of some place you know. Some place around Te Ika perhaps.'

She was not altogether blind. And her presence, while he worked, was something upon which he could test himself. It might have been less real, but it was also relief. She could be rich in relief.

'But I'm sure I wouldn't know,' she added pleasantly.

Sometimes they could not have been more serene.

'Actually,' he tried to explain, 'the thing is not to find what you know, but what you don't.

For it was almost ready; he could feel the balance in himself as much as in the colours, which had taken about as much black as they could stand, or he could risk. It was not the time, not yet, to gamble everything. He had to be sure, first, what he was gambling for, and why. Anyway the painting stood almost intact, if still quivering. There were hard shiny edges here and there, slow to dry. He took a new brush, quite clean,

353

and tried the white. Because only the white could tell him, finally, what the gamble had been. Just the one stroke, at first thin, then slowly spreading; the one slow pull, no push. He dared not look at the rest, to see what was happening, to see if it were pulling together. It was quite enough to imagine. Even Margaret knew, by now, not to speak, if she were present. All pull; risk enough to take. But if he were to be captive he could be so, at least, with his eyes open; the point of rules, really, was to comprehend their breaking. Then the white was finished, utterly. He still dared not look. But he wiped his hands at least, and walked away.

'Well,' said Margaret, by way of punctuation, 'so I was right. I thought it was going to be another waterfall. Just another waterfall, after all. After all that. Never mind. Better luck next time.'

So he had to look. There was bitter truth in the black, but elusive. Remote, and still receding. But he was used to dismay. It would return as discontent. He would be more worried without.

'I could,' he said, 'take a cup of coffee. Or some of that wine, if you haven't guzzled it all. I feel entitled to flop.'

'And all on account of a tiny waterfall,' she mocked.

He crashed into an old chair regardless.

'Would you,' she asked, as she fetched coffee, 'like me to take you seriously?'

'Not just now,' he replied. 'Thanks all the same.'

'Any time. Just let me know.' She placed the coffee beside his chair and then sat on a rug near his feet. 'But it's easier for me not to. And perhaps easier for you too.'

'Yes,' he agreed. 'So don't go queer on me. And start talking about painterly textures and symbolic values.'

'You're safe,' she promised. 'Relax.'

'It's just that I've had four years, or more, of people trying to put me right. And make me like themselves, one way and another.'

The coffee was hot enough to blister. But he began to drink it down.

'They probably meant well,' she observed.

'It's just that I want them to mean well somewhere else, now. Not around me.'

'It's all right,' she insisted. 'I'm not complaining. It's just I thought you might be avoiding people because of me.'

354

'Because of you?'

'Well,' she explained, 'you know how hard it is for me, with some of these people. I'm just a country girl.'

'I've heard that once too often.'

'Someone else felt the same way.'

'Your friend Ian? I do notice you make a point of not talking about him.'

'Do I?' I haven't noticed at all.'

'Come, now.'

'I saw him in the street the other day,' she confessed. 'With some of his slick new city friends. Journalists, perhaps. It was hard to tell him apart anyway.'

'How is he?'

'We didn't actually find anything to say. Sad to relate. But never mind. I saw him. He looks as if he's still alive, and possibly he is. I'm no judge.' She paused. 'Of anything much, it seems.' She nodded towards the painting. 'When do you think you'll be finished with this one?'

'When it finishes with me, probably.'

'I see,' she said, puzzled. She appeared to be considering the new painting with interest, despite herself. 'But you seem to be doing the same thing over and over again.'

'Not quite. Each time, I like to think, I'm getting a little closer. And I might be.'

'Closer to what, though?'

'To the edge of nowhere,' he suggested.

He looked to see if her expression changed. But it was still puzzled.

'Or closer to what I want,' he added. 'And don't ask me, now, what I want, because I won't know for sure until I've got it. That's the way it is. Sorry.'

Looking again, he was able to see what he didn't want anyway. He didn't want the falling white water to serve simply as seam, the place where the hills were stitched together, and the bush, and rocks; that was only half the truth. And he didn't want it just as limb of light to hold the painting steady; that was no truth at all, though it might be sufficient for some. And he didn't want the white simply to describe the black; that was to miss the point entirely. Yet in all these things, and out of them, should be what he wanted, if he could see. He felt the first twinge of fresh impatience. Though he was able to subdue it, and finish the coffee, which had grown cool and slightly bitter.

'And was I right?' Margaret asked. 'About it being some place around Te Ika? Some place you know?'

'Some place I am trying to know anyway,' he agreed.

'It's not any place I recognize specially. That's if it is around Te Ika. You ever feel like going back?'

'I've been back,' he said crisply. 'Once.'

'Because,' she went on, 'I'm thinking of going back. No, not for good; at least not at the moment. To see my family. I have a promise to keep, that I'd go back to see them soon. I imagine you don't make promises like that to your father, or have one to keep.'

'True.'

'I was thinking of some weekend. Perhaps we could both go.'

'What so good about your family?'

'That's not the point.'

'Return of the black sheep.'

'Perhaps. But I'm going back, just the same.' She paused and then added, 'Well, what about it? Will you come?'

'Ask again in a couple of weeks. Where's that wine?'

'I'll get it. So you won't answer me?'

'Can't you see,' he said, edgy, 'I'm doing my best?'

She looked astonished for a moment. 'You actually mean to say that I'm tempting you?'

So they did go, after a couple of weeks.

The weather was warm, and skies clear. Margaret pleaded illness to escape two days early from her job. They left on a Thursday and had to be back before Monday.

They hitch-hiked. They left too late for a clear run through, and besides lingered to browse here and there, between rides, where the countryside appealed. They met evening short of Te Ika. They left the highway, crossing barbed-wire fences, moving between gloomy trees, pushing between blackberry bushes which plucked at their clothes, and came at length to the sloping bank of the river they sought. Grass grew tall there, above the water, sheltering and cushioning. They lit a fire on a shingle bank and made tea in a billy. The highway was just a fitful flash of headlights in the distance. They ate cold pastry, chocolate and fruit. But the tea was warming, after they had bathed in the river; the water was still innocent of summer, and left them breathless.

'I'm glad we didn't get all the way,' Margaret announced.

'Think of what we might have missed.' For the stars were thick, above, as she leaned back to look and sip her mug of tea. The dry grass crackled as he sat beside her. She sounded oddly nervous; the fire was flickering low. 'If I talk too much,' she went on, 'you only have to say.'

'It's all right,' he insisted. 'Talk away.'

But evidently she found it difficult. They had sense of the hills, if not the sight. With walls stripped away, for the first time since they met, their voices were different; most things were. The night was large, and the river loud. The last glow of their fire bled away in rippling reflections. There was distinct cool in the air now, and the night would be moonless.

They had not touched.

'You might,' she said presently, 'roll me a smoke too. I wonder whose farm this is. I can't remember. It's near enough to home. I should know. Yet I feel quite lost.'

He finished making her cigarette, and passed it over. Then at least they touched, or anyway their cold fingertips. 'Do you feel lost too?' she asked. 'Is that it?'

He struck a match to light her cigarette, and for a moment or two they could see each other clearly. But there was not much to see.

'Different,' he allowed. 'In a strange country.'

'Strange?' she laughed.

'Or enemy territory.'

'I see.' This time she didn't laugh. 'Too dramatic for me, I'm afraid. It's just home, or near enough. It can't hurt me now. At least not much.'

'It doesn't matter.'

'But I'm sure it does.'

Conversation lapsed again; their words seemed to leave no useful residue. He still sat stiffly. There was a morepork sounding off methodically among the riverside trees.

'I shouldn't have come,' he said suddenly.

'Ah,' she said. 'So that's it.'

'A mad idea in the first place. But I don't blame you. I blame myself. I should have known.'

The night could not have been cooler, after the day. And there was dew.

'You could,' she observed, 'go back in the morning. The road's over there. It's just a question of going north instead of south with me. I'll find my own way back on Sunday.'

357

'It's all right. I can wait.'

'I'm saying you don't have to.'

'Then I'll decide in the morning.'

'I can see it's going to be a long time coming. Morning, I mean. Tonight seems to have gone on years already. What's the trouble?'

'Nothing.' His tone was sharp.

The night flowed on; the dark was endless, and the sound of the river. She shivered, and tried to make herself comfortable in the grass.

'Come here,' she said finally. 'Closer. I'm cold.'

He appeared to relent. His arms were cool, and his face.

'There's that blanket in my pack,' she went on. 'And a coat.'

They contrived a nest in the grass into which they could fit warmly. And within which, before long, their bodies could manufacture still more warmth, without any real effort at all. They slept to the sound of the river.

He was first to wake in the morning. The sun was already touching the hilltops above, and there was thin mist across the river, out of which dark trees bulked. There were gleams of faint light upon the river itself, subdued flashes of silver where the current crumpled against black lumps of rock. Then, slowly, a flare of lemon light swept along the ragged ridges above.

Margaret still slept. Her face against the grass was cold and pale.

He had forgotten summer mornings so cold. And he had not seen her before.

He examined the morning again, to see what the light had to say; the day, after all, was quite eloquent. Everywhere hills rose, near and distant; small hills scattering up to large hills, all exact in the still morning, and pointed peaks just visible beyond. The greens of the native bush were dark beyond the pale grassy slopes, where man had trampled the old vegetation down, and where cattle stirred dimly in the vanishing mist. Yet the old order of things could reassert itself, in random rhythms, which began to merge. Until he saw beginnings, if he tried, and endings, all equally indifferent. Until there was only indifference left to see. Untidily captive, scratched and scraped to the bone, the land still marched, after all, to its own chilly logic. It wasn't that it had to be seen; it had to be unseen. Or peeled off layer by layer for the colour of the truth beneath to

358

seep through. And it seemed he had begun. He shivered, perhaps with the cold; he had not perceived the finality of the thing before. It was as if he had not seen death before.

So he saw, or tried not to see, and Margaret slept. Her pale face ebbed back into his sight. She made reassuring measure. He would have preferred to share her sleep, if he could. He could understand that ephemeral flesh was all they had.

He began to free himself gently from their blanket. She stirred, muttered, and finally opened her eyes. 'Where are we?' she asked. 'Oh, bloody hell. I remember. So this is where we finished up.'

'I'm about to boil some tea. I think we have some chocolate left.'

The hills had already begun to shrink to decent size. He fastened his trousers, tucked in his shirt, and went barefoot down to the river. He began to make a fire.

'I recognize this place now,' she said at length.

'You do?' He was not sure he wished precision.

'Have you made up your mind what you're going to do?'

He fed some dry wood into the fire.

'You've come this far with me,' she went on. 'You might as well come the rest of the way now.'

'Well,' he began, and was silent. The fire was flourishing.

'What's the problem?'

'Just that I'm not sure I can afford to stay.'

'Three days?'

'It might be three days too many.'

'You weren't especially broke when we left.'

'I don't mean that.'

'I see. Well, I'm not going to ask what you do mean. I gave that up weeks back. And I'm not going to say that sometimes I don't understand you. Because it's pretty well all the time. Is the tea ready?'

'By the time you've dressed. Here comes the sun.'

Warmth began to fill the riverbed. Margaret, zipping up a jacket, descended leisurely to join him beside the fire. A lean, tall girl with handsome and rather troubled face. The long grass, bent with heavy dew, was spangled with light. A pair of birds in obscure panic took wing behind her, scrambling into the sky.

He hoped he might hold that intact too. And the silences beyond. He had to go back. He must.

'And here I was hoping,' she went on, 'that we might find that waterfall of yours.'

'Or lose it.'

'What do you mean?'

'We mightn't find it. That's all.'

Margaret took a mug of tea. 'Well,' she said, 'anyway we found this place. Perhaps that's enough. Why are you so frightened of your father?'

An hour later they parted.

Margaret returned to the flat on the Sunday night, as expected, but remained restless weeks after. At least things were never quite the same.

'You shouldn't have left me there,' she once said, by way of oblique explanation. 'I needed you. And I couldn't cope.'

She was no longer so quiet and patient. And she smoked too much. She gave up her job, and found another, and also forgot about business college.

'I'm not important to you,' she insisted. 'I expect I've been useful to you, but not important. What I mean is, someone else might have done as well, or better.'

He might have spent energy recklessly in an attempt to disagree. But she plainly wished more than disagreement. He tried, though, to locate the direction of her discontent.

'Have you seen Ian lately?' he asked, by way of experiment.

'Not really.'

'So what does that mean?'

'Just the once or twice, in the street. Accident; that's all. We've talked, yes. But you can't make any more out of it. Because there is no more. He's starting university. And he seems all right. Beyond that, there isn't much said. Not much at all.'

'You don't tell him about yourself, then.'

'And what would be the point of that? Possibly he already knows more than enough anyway. I shouldn't be surprised.'

She seemed sullen.

'All right,' he said. 'So there's nothing more to it. If you say so.'

'I don't really care whether you believe me or not. Why should I?'

Again he was powerless. If he had to take a stand anywhere, it was by saying nothing. She had begun to irritate.

360

'I suppose I'm interested,' he said, 'because it was through him we met.' Since he had started, he might as well go on, to the finish. 'And whatever it is you want, perhaps it was from him you wanted it. Not me. I haven't been important to you either, though I might have been useful. What would you say to that?'

She said nothing to that. But she did pull on a jacket, a few moments later, and leave the place. 'If you're interested in knowing,' she explained, 'I'm just going out for a while.'

'But it's raining outside.'

'What's that got to do with it?' she replied, and banged the door.

What indeed? It was almost certainly a rehearsal, if he cared to think about it. He didn't, however, for too long. He simply sat, and after a time began wondering if he shouldn't get in touch with Ken McAdam again, or someone. The rain was thick on the windows.

She didn't return until late; she dripped her way silently back into the flat. He could wonder. He wished he could return to the dream, or wherever it began. But it seemed the waterfalls were over now. There were just the hills, daily more precise. They could terrify him with their precision; he could wonder where he was going, or if. At times he felt a cartoon character, fled solid ground, over the edge of a precipice, with legs still pumping in empty space, nothing at all beneath.

He would give anything to see a soft edge in his work. But the ridges were always razory.

That night Margaret was rigid in bed beside him, as if challenging him to fall asleep first. Perhaps he did. He certainly didn't know what he was supposed to say.

One day there was the threat; the next she was gone. It was all pleasant enough, perhaps, up to the last moments. Her bags stood ready at the door, for the taxi to the train.

'It's just that I have to go back to Te Ika,' she said. 'I know where I am, back there. I'm not cut out for this kind of life. People like you, and Ian too, don't really know where you're going.'

'And you do?'

'Yes,' she said. 'I certainly do. I'm going back home.'

'And what do you think you'll find back there?'

'I've a pretty good idea what I'll find. Which is more than you have. Or Ian.'

'Why do you have to keep mentioning us in the same breath? I hardly know him.'

'I have my reasons.'

'Obviously.'

He didn't really want to pursue the subject anyway. He was already empty of regrets, and much else.

'People like you,' she announced, 'deserve each other. And all you'll probably find. People like me are only an inconvenience.'

He shook his head, still mystified. 'Have it your own way, then.'

'I am. That's exactly what I'm doing. Having it my own way. And good luck to you. I think that's my taxi.'

He helped carry her bags outside. It was a mild evening, still short of sunset. He handed the bags to the taxi driver, then opened the door of the car for her.

'Is there something you haven't told me?' he asked finally.

She appeared to hesitate, then make up her mind. 'No,' she said. 'Nothing you need to know.'

'You must tell me if there is. Write, at least.'

'No point,' she said crisply. She turned to the driver. 'The railway station, please.'

She closed the door of the taxi against him, but he could still speak through the open window.

'There are things I should have said,' he began.

'Quick,' Margaret said to the driver. 'The railway station.'

The taxi escaped his grip. It sped away up the street, a direction light winking. He thought he saw her, for an instant, bent over in distress. But she could, of course, have been hunting money or tickets in her handbag. And he might just have imagined it anyway.

The direction light continued to wink, in his mind, for some time after. More indelible, really, than anything said.

His own direction turned out, for a time, to be along that littered loop of coast the city allowed him. Rusty cans crunched underfoot, broken glass rattled. Sunset reddened the full tide, and the mangroves. There was a dead seagull, stained dark with oil; one version of beginnings. He turned for home, in the thickening night, with ooze dragging at his feet. His flat, on his return, appeared to have been redecorated, in colder colours. He fell asleep in a chair and woke with an intricate pattern of aches and cramps in his flesh; the flat was stunningly quiet.

That day he tried, several times, to begin work again.

Part Three

Sons

Eighteen:

Documents

Avarua P.O.
Rarotonga
Cook Islands
August 4, 1966

Dear Mr Kennedy,
Your letter received late. Mail services to this lonely part of
the Pacific are erratic – by stray ship or odd air force plane.
By this time you are doubtless wondering if I intend reply;
and it could be some time before you receive this. Your project
sounds interesting, and I wish I could be more help.

To be specific, then, I was not a childhood friend of Tim
Livingstone's. I can easily see, however, why you might have got
that impression. We did grow up in the same country district,
but he was some three years my senior. And he lived on a farm;
I lived in a township of sorts. We did go to the same school,
and I was aware of him once or twice during my schooldays.
And that was about it. I met him briefly in Auckland in
1950, soon after my arrival in that city, but not again until
some distance into the following year. Chance threw us together
at that time. Yes, we did share accommodation in Auckland,
perhaps for a couple of years, in the early 1950s.

As you know, he left for Europe in 1956. I went to Europe
myself a year or two later. In 1959, in Paris, I met with fairly
recent news of him. And I did try to seek him out in that city,
without success. I have had no real news of him since. But I
gather it is no part of your intention to establish his continued
existence in the world. You are interested in the work –
'historically as much as artistically', you say. Fair enough. But

367

it surprises me that anyone should be interested in the age of op and pop. Or is it something new now? News travels rather slowly to us here.

Naturally I agree that near-success, or half-failure, is sometimes critically more interesting than success. But is that entirely the point? Yes, I am very familiar with what you call his 'waterfall' paintings. But there isn't a great deal I can tell you about their origin; and I certainly can't date them exactly. But you are right in assuming that the black paintings, and the others which interest you, do come later.

Nor can I help much in locating such of these paintings as still exist. You have obviously seen those I possess, in storage with my uncle, since you mention his name.

Sorry I can't be more help. Good luck with your project.

Yours sincerely,
Ian Freeman

Commentaries

The rain was heavier. Stan didn't seem troubled. He pushed a hat low on his head, buttoned his raincoat to the top, and strode off into it, leaving me with the empty flat. It was late, after eleven, by the time Stan made up his mind to leave and risk the rain. He wanted to talk a number of subjects into the ground, his weariness with the newspaper, his problems with the Party, a strike on the waterfront, and apparently I was his most useful listener. I watched him vanish beyond the rain and shut the door.

All the same, I had an odd sense of an evening unfinished. I should have been thinking about my year ahead at university, and beginning to read towards it. Instead, Stan.

So I wasn't entirely surprised by the knock on my door. At first I thought Stan was back again, having forgotten something; but the knock was light. And when I opened the door, Margaret stood there. Soaked and pale. But recognizably Margaret.

It was like finding again a symptom of an illness from which I thought myself recovered. For a second we just stood there. The rain gleamed on her face.

'I'm sorry,' she said. 'At this hour.'

'I'm supposed to be the one who always says sorry,' I observed. 'Remember? Don't stand there. Come in.'

She moved into the flat, looking about gently, as if the place were totally strange to her.

'Well, I am sorry,' she went on. 'I didn't mean it to be this hour. It's just I saw you had company earlier.'

'It was only Stan Coates,' I said. 'And he'd move if he wasn't wanted. Here. Let me get your coat off.' Puddles gathered around her as she moved. She still had a bewildered air; I still had the impression she couldn't altogether understand finding herself here again.

'But you might have wanted Stan to stay,' Margaret suggested. 'I had to get you alone.'

'All right,' I said, hanging up her heavy coat. 'So here I am. Or here we are.'

'It's hard,' she said, still looking around, 'to believe it's only two or three months. Yet everything's still the same. Another bookshelf; that's all.'

'University texts,' I explained. Then, 'For a while I wondered if you were still in the city. If you hadn't gone home.'

There was another pause, more awkward this time.

'And you heard different,' she said finally.

'Something like that,' I agreed. 'Then I saw you, out of a bus window. You and Tim Livingstone walking somewhere together. That's about all. Just a flash, the once. And when I saw you later, alone in the street, you seemed to be looking happier. At least.'

'All right,' she said. 'So we've got that over.'

'Actually what made me think you might have gone home was the fact that you never came back to say goodbye. I half-expected it.'

'Better late than never, then.'

'You mean – '

'I mean I'm here. And saying goodbye. I suppose that's what it amounts to.'

She didn't seem too sure. She fell in a chair.

'And I'm curious,' she added. 'It amounts to that too. Curious about you. About how you are managing.'

'I seem to be busy enough.'

'Fine,' she said.

That word seemed to dispose of conversation for a while. She looked quite exhausted. I made coffee, and gave her a cup. Her face was pale enough to make me wonder if she had been ill, but I found it too difficult to ask the question. The silence was so solid. The rain hit at the windows. In the end I had to say something.

'Why tonight?' I asked. 'After leaving it so long? Why pick tonight to say goodbye?'

I felt obtuse, as if there were something I should have understood.

'I'm sorry,' she said, in a small, oddly vague voice, 'if it's inconvenient.'

'I didn't mean that. And don't say sorry again. It's not answering the question.' It was the first time I'd ever had the advantage of Margaret in a conversation.

'Then the answer is that I'm going home,' she confessed at last. 'Back to the farm. I am quitting, after all.'

'I see.'

'Never mind. I came here to see you. To see how you were. Before I left. That's all.'

'That's all? Really all?'

'Really all.'

In one way I was relieved. In another, disappointed. I seemed back again to where I began, three months before. As if she had never left my life. I could never be sure of myself with Margaret, however much I tried. I could be reasonably sure, though, that this uncertainty was something I had to escape.

'You might have given me some warning, then,' I said, 'that I was due for inspection tonight. Can I ask why you're going home? Or is that question out of bounds?'

'I think it's out of bounds,' she said. 'Yes.'

'Well, that's that. There isn't much to talk about, is there?'

'If you say so.'

'I'm just left to imagine that the other thing didn't work out.'

'I don't know that it was supposed to work out,' she observed. 'I'm not even sure what you mean.'

'Well,' I said, 'it seems, for example, that we didn't work out.' I disliked having to put that into words too. 'I mean more or less the same thing.'

'This was different.'

'I'm sure. Clem too, I expect.'

I could hardly forgive myself for that; but the arrow was shot, and quivering. There was a longish silence then.

'I'm sorry,' I offered at last. 'I didn't mean to say that.'

'Of course not,' she said. 'But you did.'

She was too vulnerable entirely. I didn't have to make any

effort to hold my own. But nor was there any point in any advantage, unless I wished to hurt again, now that I had discovered I could. And my desire to hurt, once I acknowledged it, left me feeling faintly sick. For it was there, all right. It seemed Margaret still hadn't finished teaching me about myself.

'You're all right?' I asked. 'There's nothing really wrong?'

'No. Nothing really wrong. Just me, I expect. Just me in general. And the easiest way to fix that is to go home, you see.'

Silence again. 'Is there something you haven't mentioned?' I asked. 'Something you wanted to talk about?' I had the distinct impression there was something; she was still sitting there tense; she hadn't looked relaxed for a moment since she entered the flat. I tried to imagine the decision which had carried her across the city to me, through a rainy night. For there must have been some decision, with some impetus. More than the need for a belated goodbye. I was surely an indifferent retreat from a lovers' row.

'No,' she said at first. 'Nothing.' Then, 'Yes. There is one thing. One thing I'd like to ask you, if I could. If it's not too late.'

'Go on, then. Ask away.'

'Do you think we might have finished differently? If things had been different?'

'What can it matter? Say I said, yes I could have been different. What difference would it make? None at all. It's too late.'

She didn't seem inclined to disagree.

'Too late altogether,' I emphasized, a twist of knife.

She sat very still. Her expression told me nothing. But I couldn't look at her face for long. I wondered what my own expression said, or if there was one. And hoped my inner trembling wasn't visible. I suppose I should have felt pity, mainly. Instead I knew disgust, disgust with myself, for feeling so weak; I needed very little, it seemed, to tilt in her direction again. And never grow up.

'I know that,' she said, very quietly, at last. 'I know it's too late. Perfectly well. I suppose I just had to make sure.'

She rose, suddenly brisk. Her eyes made summary of the room, as if she were still expecting to find something. It was a thick night, grown more humid with the rain.

'My coat,' she said. 'Where did you hang it?'

'You haven't finished your coffee.'

'But we've finished all we had to say. Surely.'

('I almost told you then,' said Margaret eighteen years later. 'I almost came right out with everything, there and then. But I didn't. What if I had?'

'I don't know,' I confessed. 'I really don't know.'

'It would have made no difference at all,' she said. 'You'd have run a mile.'

'Possibly. Probably.'

'I wasn't equipped to cope either,' she said. 'But at least I knew it.'

'You don't seem to realize,' I said, 'how easily everything could have started again. I really wanted nothing more than to go to bed with you. But I grew up.'

'Is that what you call it?'

'It's what it is. Learning not to have what you want. As good a definition as any.'

'Then I must have grown up too,' she said. 'That night among others.'

'Among others?'

'There were others. Perhaps growing up was more painful for me.'

Something I couldn't dispute.

The smile was light at first. Then she laughed. 'Life. That might have been our trouble. You were scared of it. And I'd just learned it was real.'

'And perhaps words,' I said. 'Speaking for myself, that is. I didn't have enough then. And I have too damn many now.')

'Well,' I said lamely, 'obviously you know best. And I'm not allowed to ask why.' I helped the coat over her shoulders. 'Good luck anyway.'

'And good luck to you too,' she said, swinging around suddenly, so that it was inevitable that we kissed, if clumsily; my mouth found her cheek; it was largely a collision of faces. It might just marginally have been more. Then we drew apart. Or perhaps the motion was hers. Her eyes were cool.

'It's raining outside,' I observed.

'So I've been told,' she said. 'Earlier in the evening, by someone else. Or do you mean something more?'

372

'Just,' I had to define shakily, and with no certainty, 'that I could call you a taxi. If you like.'

She finished buttoning her coat and opened the door. The rain was quite loud.

'I think,' she said, 'I prefer the rain to waiting around. Thanks all the same. And goodbye.'

Once out in the rain, she began to run. So she was to be seen for only a few moments; then she was gone altogether, and the rain streamed under the streetlights and overflowed the gutters, and I shut the door and had my evening again.

('Well,' Margaret said, finishing her coffee eighteen years later, and looking at her watch, 'that's about it. We're due at the studio in fifteen minutes. Have you thought about those questions I'm proposing to ask you? Never mind; we'll manage. I remember how soaked I got, going home, that night. The rain was terrible. I walked all the way and got home half-drowned. I think Tim was asleep, or pretending to be. He never asked where I'd been, and I never told him. Did he figure at all in our conversation that night?'

'Not that I recall, especially.'

'I left him two or three days later.'

'So you've already told me.'

'But it was over well before then. We'd made a trip together down to Te Ika, something he'd promised me for quite a while, but he walked out on me. I felt it was always going to be like that, and worse. And then there was the other thing; I had to face that too, and make up my mind.'

'I'm sorry I was so little help.'

'You were a great help, in fact. If that last meeting with you hadn't been quite so awful, I might still have have been tempted to stay. Instead, I went home. And that was the best thing I ever did, as it turns out. The only thing I can be sure of – the one good thing.'

'I can understand that,' I said. For I could.

'Tell me,' she said quietly, 'if you can. There's one opinion of yours I'm interested in. Do you think he was a good artist?'

'Good?'

'Reasonable, then. Worthwhile.'

'I used to think so.'

'You're still not good at answering questions. Come on, you're not in the studio yet. And you don't have to commit yourself forever. Besides, it's the one question I won't be asking you tonight. Who cares, now?'

'We do. Evidently.'

'So, go on. Tell me. Not what you used to think, but what you do think.'

'If I try hard, then, I possibly still think the same. He must have had something to agitate people. And make them feel committed to him.'

'Like who, for instance – '

'Like me, for instance.'

'Oh,' she said, 'I see. Well, of course, that was something I wouldn't know about. I only see my tiny side of it.'

'Perhaps it wasn't too tiny.'

'What do you mean?'

'Things you've been telling me. Without, perhaps, you knowing they were particularly important. Perhaps they'll all add up, in time.'

'You make it sound a dark mystery.'

'Well, it is. It is, in a way. A mystery anyway. The darkness is optional. I don't know that I can explain that too.'

She looked at her watch again. 'Ten minutes,' she said briskly. 'Five minutes' walk to the studio from here. That leaves you five to explain yourself.'

'There's too much ground to cover. Perhaps we should walk slowly.'

'It's only a couple of hundred yards to the studio. Nervous?'

'Mildly. I hear the interviewer can be rather acid.'

'A dirty rumour. All you have to do is account for yourself. Not to me specially; to the great antipodean public. The expatriate returned. Why you did, and why you didn't. You ought to be used to it already. All I can do is trip you, when I can. And stop you, if you rave on. And that, by the sound of it, isn't likely.'

'It's the tripping that worries me.'

'All over in a flash. At best it's like the guillotine. And people won't remember a damn thing you say. Just your nice honest face, or otherwise. So cheer up and finish what you were saying. If you were really saying something, that is, and not just making conversation.'

'I've forgotten where we were.'

'Mystery.'

'I've lost the thread of that too.'

'You must be nervous.'

'I was interested in what you were saying earlier on, about those waterfalls. His waterfall paintings; remember?'

'I can hardly forget. I seemed to be drowning under them, sometimes. One after another.'

'There's been some interest in the time they were painted. While I was up in the islands there was a fellow writing to me. I should have put him on to you. He had plans for a piece on Tim, as part of something larger; I think he planned to call the chapter "The Spoiled Primitive as Culture-Hero".'

'That sounds pretty pretentious.'

'So this fellow evidently decided, in the end, too. He had a hobby horse to ride, and he hoped Tim's work was going to help him into the saddle. But it didn't work out that way, I gather.'

'Oh, well,' Margaret said. 'Let the dead bury the dead.'

'If he is.'

'Is what?'

'Dead. We don't really know.'

'Odd you should say that. I thought I saw him a year or two ago.'

'Where?' I felt suddenly breathless.

'Here. In the city. The other side of the street. Looking very different, of course – after all these years. I couldn't be sure. I had to wait for the pedestrian light to get across the street, to make sure and by the time I crossed he was gone. If it was Tim. I hurried in the direction he was taking, but I never caught up with him. He was gone with the crowd.'

'I thought I was close a couple of times. Once in Paris, as I told you. And elsewhere. Never mind. I wonder if you did see him.'

'Come on, now. I'd forgotten it by the day after. And I've never had cause to mention it to anyone till now.'

'It just could have been him, you see. He might just be back in the country.'

'Well,' Margaret said, 'at least we know for sure that you're back in the country. And you're due to account for yourself in just – my God, look at the time – three minutes. Come on, let's run.')

'You look down,' Stan Coates said. 'Way down. What's the trouble?'

It was nothing I could tell him but Stan insisted on dragging me from my desk and up the street for lunch. On the way he had news to offer.

'This strike's going to be a big thing,' he announced. 'The biggest thing to hit this country in years. The government's out for a showdown with the unions. And they're going to have it. I hear the army's being primed to scab. And emergency regulations become law on Monday. Three months' jail for anyone who has a good word for the strikers.'

It sounded a little unreal. I was only half-listening anyway. It was a week or two since Margaret's visit in the middle of the night. But that wasn't it, entirely. I could smell the end of summer: perhaps an early and empty winter.

We turned into the coffee shop. We hadn't been there long when Stan was approached by an earnest little individual I'd never seen before. He had a creamy baby face, rather solemn, decked with emphatically black-rimmed spectacles; a long and spectacular scarf was wound wild about his neck, and he wore a black beret askew on his curly hair.

'You haven't,' he said to Stan, very confidentially, 'seen Livingstone around?'

'No, thank God,' Stan replied. 'Not for months. Should I have?'

'He's around,' the other replied cryptically.

'Again?'

'Yes.'

'Thanks for the warning. I need a better lock for my door if Livingstone's on the loose again.'

'His last woman's gone, you see.'

'Oh,' Stan said. 'I see.' Stan was very careful not to catch my eye. 'So that explains it, does it?'

'Yes. Mind if I sit down here?'

'Go ahead. This is Paul Wiseman, by the way. Paul Wiseman, Ian Freeman. We're moving off in a minute. Unlike some, we have work to do. Such as keeping capitalism in business. Please don't give Livingstone my regards if you happen to see the bastard.'

'I'll make a point of that,' said Paul Wiseman gravely. 'Anything else?'

'Nothing else.'

'Then,' said Paul Wiseman, 'I wonder could you give me the price of a coffee.'

Stan sighed and produced money. 'Here. And buy yourself a

sandwich too. I suppose, as usual, you haven't eaten for a couple of days.'

'For four days, actually.' He had a very precise, crisp voice. There was a certain shyness in the way he took the money. And he seemed always to be looking over his shoulder, as if pursued. He went to the counter.

'Behold,' Stan said, 'how I subsidize the hangers-on of Livingstone. I should have my head examined. But I can't resist those little doggy eyes; Paul is rather lost, and sweet. I'd say he was one of Livingstone's more pleasant acquaintances, on the whole. Paul, I predict, will finish up with his throat cut – and perhaps more – in some obscure corner of the city. See if I'm wrong. He can never quite find a fit. Though he tries to tailor himself to most situations, socially and sexually. He writes sensationally erotic verse about the death of sex and art.'

Paul returned to wolf his sandwich and gulp his coffee in our cubicle. After a time Stan and I walked back to the office.

'You think I'm right about this strike?' Stan asked. I didn't see why he looked to me for reasssurance. 'You could be,' I offered vaguely.

('Take a seat,' said the fussy, precise managing director of Paul Wiseman Arts Ltd, London, W.1. fourteen years later. 'So you're going back to the little country.'

'Bit by bit. Yes.'

'And I expect you've come to ask again if I've seen or heard of Livingstone.'

'Yes again.'

'The answer's no, of course. And I can't imagine that I'm likely to see or hear of him again. Can you imagine it?'

'I thought there might just be the chance.'

'I imagined I put you on his trail – well, it must be six years ago. 1959? And I haven't seen him since. Have you?'

'Not really.'

'I might as well be frank and say I don't particularly want to see or hear of him again either.'

'Fair enough.'

'All that's in the past now. So much in the past it seems quite unreal to me. All those years out there. When I think how near I came to wasting my life.' He produced a mock shiver. 'But no – I can't think about it. I daren't.'

'Understandable.'

377

'What do you mean?' He was still too sensitive, by far.

'I mean I only have to look around this place.'

'And what do you hope to achieve by going back? I seem to recall some mild success you've had here. They forget quickly here, you know. Very quickly. Now consider my position.'

I considered his position at some length. But I found, after escaping his gallery, that I preferred on the whole to consider the mini-skirts of springtime London.)

('Take a seat,' said the plump and amiable head of Coates Public Relations Ltd, eighteen years later. 'So you're back with us again. I saw you on the telly the other night. You looked a bit tired. Nervy. Perhaps it was the interviewer; she's rather tenacious.' Stan offered a sly smile.

'Quite possibly.'

'You know, it took me some time, after I first saw her on the box, to accept it was the same Margaret Saunders. Even the name didn't click at first. But my wife still remembers the wild cry I uttered when the penny dropped at last. By Christ, I told her, she's Ian Freeman's old girl. You're a familiar enough name in our household, you see. Though you don't know my wife, of course.'

'No.'

'You must meet her. Come around. Make a date to suit yourself. Anyway she's quite different. Margaret, I mean. Very smooth indeed. To think you upturned that field when it was virgin.'

'Well – '

'Come, now. Credit where it's due. Well, now, what can I do for you? Not looking for a job?'

'Not at the moment. No.'

The question seemed to explain, and ease, a certain business-like tension in Stan. 'That's that, then,' he said. 'Not that I possibly couldn't find a place for a fellow refugee from the past. Quite a few have passed through this office. If you are looking for a job, any time, try me. You might find me full of helpful advice. At the moment I'm trimming my sails a bit. Politics again. I've been offered a reasonably safe seat in Parliament.'

He must have seen some query in my face.

'To the left,' he added. 'Naturally. I haven't changed that much. I didn't have a God that failed; it's just that the Pope died. And we all make our peace where we can.'

378

In Berlin, say, beside a wall: the cement still fresh between the bricks. But the memory was difficult to sustain in Stan's comfortable office, in a chair which sank into executive carpet, beside a picture window with an attractive view of serene harbour and shadowy islands. The sounds of the city were muffled; most things were.

'Well,' I said, rising suddenly, 'I thought I'd just drop in, Stan, to say hello. I won't keep you.'

'And it's marvellous to see you. Really great. We really must get together soon, to talk over old times. You got a telephone number?'

'Not yet. But I'll let you know when I have.'

'Great.' Stan paused. 'Talking about old times,' he said, 'whatever happened to Livingstone?')

Stan was right. The strike grew, the length of the country, with surprising speed. And the government deployed troops on the waterfront, and elsewhere.

I left the office early, most afternoons, to attend my first university lectures. I didn't see so much of Stan; he seemed particularly busy, and quietly agitated. I managed, though, to get over to see my uncle one Sunday. His place was still an oasis in the city; I could relax there, and Ben made no large demands. 'So you're settling down,' he said.

'Reasonably.'

'I've been meaning to ask – how's that home-town girl friend of yours?'

'She finished, some time ago.'

'Well, university then.'

'All right so far.'

'You don't give much away, do you?' Ben laughed. 'So what about the job? It still suits you?'

He tipped more wine into my tumbler. We were sitting out in his garden, in the shade of banana fronds. There was a thick drumming of cicadas.

'Up to a point. The atmosphere's not particularly pleasant at the moment.'

'Yes, I'd forgotten; the strike. I was over in the city the other day. Troops and police everywhere. Like the 1930s all over again And I suppose it is, in a way.'

'How do you mean?'

'The same words, the same faces. A last stand.'

'I still don't quite follow.'

'Take Alex O'Leary and Harry Jones; both strikers' leaders. And both old friends of your father. Even old Charlie Higgins grumbling away in the background – he was once a friend of your father's too. That is, before he ratted, in your father's considered opinion. They all fought the battle for some grand new order, and finished up with sufficient of an old compromise to put society off to sleep. As elsewhere. So they haven't a chance now. Not because they've everything against them; because they've so little with them. The trouble isn't that working class leaders have been bought out; it's the working class itself that's been bought. Perhaps for good.'

If it was politics I wanted, I might as well have spent the afternoon with Stan Coates. But it wasn't; I might have spent the afternoon with Chaucer more profitably. Nevertheless, I accepted more of Ben's faintly acid wine. At least his wine, like his pleasant garden, could make the world recede. Yet I could resent his complacency too. I didn't, however, feel need to express this resentment. I didn't feel need to express myself at all. That was where people who expected something of me, or appeared to, made their first mistake; I wasn't my father's son. That was Stan's touching faith, despite the evidence, and Ben's too. I suffered no illusions. Not only wasn't I my father's son; I didn't expect anything of myself either.

'What do you think?' Ben asked presently.

He would have to wait a long time for answer to that. 'It's quite possible,' I replied, at length, 'that you're right.'

('Let's face it,' Ben said, reclining in the same garden, in possibly the same aged chair, eighteen years later. 'You were a pretty shy kid in those days. When you first came to the city. You hardly had a thing to say for yourself.'

'I didn't imagine you noticed. You had so much to say.'

'That was just me trying to draw you out of hiding,' Ben said. 'Or didn't you see that?'

'Not really,' I confessed.

'Then who did draw you out, in the end?' he asked. 'Tim Livingstone?')

When I went into the office that morning, Stan was already at his desk, at his typewriter, hitting out sheets of copy. He didn't see me; I didn't make a point of greeting him. Shortly afterwards he approached a sub-editor. Before long there were two or three sub-editors examining his copy. Stan, all the time, was talking earnestly and quickly. I could see argument developing. One sub-editor went to the telephone; another went to a teleprinter, apparently with a stand-by message or query. The next time I looked up from my own work, Stan was being ushered towards the editor's office with his copy. His face was flushed; he was obviously irritated.

I tried to concentrate on my work. It became more difficult.

Then there were raised voices above the sound of teleprinters and typewriters. Stan was leaving the editor's office. He wasn't just irritated now; he was livid. And shouting. He was still clutching his copy. He tossed it high in the air as he passed the sub-editors; the separate pages floated down.

'You ought to,' he informed them loudly, 'give a better imitation of working for a newspaper.'

One made indistinct reply, to the effect that Stan shouldn't lose his head.

'At least I've got my balls,' Stan replied. 'Which is more than you eunuchs can say.'

He went to his desk and emptied it of his possessions. The job didn't take long. Then he approached my desk.

'There's no one else worth saying goodbye to,' he announced.

He didn't take long to explain. It appeared he had been approached, the night before, by some naval ratings concerned about the plight of three or four of their fellows; they wanted Stan, as a newspaperman, to do something. Their friends had refused to blackleg on the waterfront, or anywhere else, and had by way of intimidation been locked a week in a latrine block, without bedding, without food, with no other sustenance than the water they could drink from lavatory cisterns. At least one of the men already required medical assistance, which had been refused by his commanding officer. So Stan had written the story. First, as he expected, it had been officially denied by the navy. Then a government censor had instructed the newspaper to kill the story. And the editor complied with the instruction, without hesitation.

'That's it,' Stan said. 'So I quit. And I must say I feel a whole lot better for it.'

'But what are you going to do now?' I asked.

'At least I imagine those navy boys are unlocked now,' he said.

'Which was the point of the enterprise. The story probably scared shit out of the navy brass. But there are other things going on as bad, or worse. So I've plenty to occupy me at the moment.'

How? I wanted to ask. But I decided it safer not to ask. If Stan really wanted me to know, he would doubtless tell me anyway.

'Well, I'll see you,' he finished. 'It was nice working with you, while it lasted. I'll see you around, or you'll see me. Good luck.'

He had nothing to say to anyone else in the office. He left without looking back through the door, without smile or wave.

Yet I couldn't pretend not to feel some relief. Stan had kept me something of an outsider in the office. I still didn't belong; I still hadn't found my own feet; I was still uneasy among other journalists. And, afterwards, I listened to them dissecting Stan, without any protest on my part; without any interjection at all. Stan was a fool, it seemed, a hothead: he didn't know which side his bread was buttered and, above all, he wasn't wise in the ways of the world. It was to be assumed his critics were. But I kept silent, kept my peace. If I was betraying Stan, in a small way, it was so as not to betray myself. For to speak up would have meant identifying myself wholly with him. With Stan, that is, or my father: the two, in this context, had become confused. So I sheltered in silence.

And I was easier in the office, making my own way. True, Stan had lent a certain drama; I sometimes missed that. I received a small promotion, became junior crime roundsman. My enclosures became tidier by the day. The other enclosure, university, was peaceful enough too, though a few students, spiritually kin to Stan, distributed leaflets in lecture rooms in support of the strikers, urging students not to scab.

I occupied myself almost totally with belonging. And even my visits to Ben became fewer.

In the office I was sometimes asked, 'What do you think, Freeman?'

Now an idiot question, in the circumstances.

Nineteen:

Documents

Avarua P.O.
Rarotonga
Cook Islands
September 15, 1966

Dear Mr Kennedy,

The delay in reply to your new letter is again not of my making. You say you feel at a dead end in your search for information about Tim Livingstone. Well, you have my sympathy, since I felt the same way in Paris in 1959. That was when I abandoned my unprofitable quest. Perhaps by the time you receive this you will have abandoned yours. I'm sorry I wasn't more forthcoming in my first letter. It seems I misunderstood your request: I took it that you wished to establish that I had been a childhood friend of Livingstone's. And I simply clarified that. I find it very difficult to believe that I am the only person about who knew him 'reasonably'. Among other names I might suggest are Ken McAdam, now an executive with commercial television in London; Sandy West, when last heard of a correspondent for an American news agency in Asia (perhaps Vietnam now?); Ted Connolly, an anthropologist – I heard that he had been doing field work in New Guinea, but whether he is there or back in the United States, where he had a post at Stanford, I wouldn't know; Stan Coates, who I understand is head of an advertising and public relations business in Auckland – perhaps the only one left in the immediate vicinity. (You will understand that, having been outside the

country for the last eight years, I'm very much out of touch.)
There is one other person who could conceivably be useful to
you – Paul Wiseman, who also knew him in Auckland, and is
the only person I know to have seen something of him after his
arrival in Europe (in fact they travelled together); Paul isn't
difficult to locate as he now cuts an impressive figure on the
business side of the international art world, incredible as this
still seems to me. The question is whether you might persuade
him to give a little of his time to correspondence ... Until
your letter came, I didn't know Hans Wiemken was dead;
otherwise I should certainly have suggested him too. Though he
really belonged to an earlier period, before my arrival in the
city and encounter with Livingstone, about which I knew little.
You say you get the feeling there has been some kind of epidemic
or blight, with virtually everyone gone or dead except Livingstone's work. That seems to be putting it rather dramatically;
but it is possibly true enough that his milieu doesn't exist or
persist. Why should it, after all? I can only give a rousing amen.
Incidentally, you still haven't made it very clear to me why you
think the work remarkable, or worth particular attention at this
late stage. Agreed that it meant something then, to a few of us.
But now? Anyway I'd be grateful for anything you have to say,
by way of clarification.

No, I don't mind recounting the circumstances under which
I met him in 1951, though I'm afraid you'll find them largely
irrelevant. That year, as you may not be old enough to recall,
the government of the time set out to provoke and then break
the old militant trade unions. And the best way to do this was to
make the country a tight police state. Propaganda for the
strikers had to be produced illegally, in elaborately conspiratorial
conditions. Stan Coates, earlier mentioned, was in charge of some
of this. And I became involved peripherally – likewise Livingstone, as a result of some police violence. The risks were real
enough, with likely arrest as threats to public order. Perhaps I
should stress that his involvement was primarily a human
reaction; he was never really a political artist. Does that cover
the ground sufficiently for you?

Yes, you are welcome to borrow those paintings from my
uncle.

Best wishes again.

Yours sincerely,

Ian Freeman

Dear Ben,

I gather you know someone called Max Kennedy who is pestering me to death with questions about Tim Livingstone. He threw off your name in his first letter, saying you had been one of those who interested him in Livingstone's work. True? I assume you must also have given him my address. If so, why? Is he serious? I find it hard to believe. My two replies so far have given him, I imagine, a certain amount of help, if a minimium of encouragement.

I've just fossicked out your last note, and see with shock that it is four months or more since I wrote to you. All's well here. I've just arrived back from a four-week journey by tiny copra boat through northern atolls, up near the equator. Quite a journey, 1800 miles never moving faster than six knots. We were caught in storm at one stage, and spent much time surfing on 30–40 foot waves, blown in the direction of Tahiti. The atolls themselves? Sad, beautiful places; coral husks in immense loneliness, in this incredibly bare ocean, swiftly emptying of the last of their people. (Soon there will be only the very old left, and they will die off.) Remarkable, when you really think about it, how all these minute lumps of rock and sand, hundreds of miles apart, were found and settled by man in the first place; it just couldn't have been chance, but only the most determined and desperate voyaging; and possibly too as good a gamble as anything in the history of our species. Anyway, all that heroic past and now no future at all. Just ruined temples among the palms. Quite haunting, the people too. Tough, lean, a different Polynesian entirely, even if vanishing. And amphibious. Must tell you some day about my fishing experiences with them; fish stories to end all. Went down with pearl-shell divers among sharks. They explained to me that it was perfectly safe. (We prayed before we dived.) They explained to me that it was only men of little or no faith who had anything to fear from the man-eating *papera* – the black shark. But I was most reluctant to put my faith, whatever it is, to the test when I saw a *papera* moving elegantly in on me. I could see myself lending rather messy substance to the local belief. I now have an island motto graven on my heart : Watch for the black shark.

After all that, it was good to see the serene green peaks of Rarotonga, with their spiky tips, rise out of the Pacific again. You ask what I'm doing here. No, it's not that I'm afraid to come home; at least not entirely. (I see you still have the knack of putting me unfairly on the spot.) Have I really been here the best part of a year? Well, I can't argue with the calendar, though I'm tempted. I only have cause to look at it when writing a letter like this, evidence of a kind. When I jumped ship here, only three days short of home, it was because I wasn't feeling ready. But perhaps that's not sufficient answer. Let me try again. What am I doing here? Well, I'm not writing a book called *The Death of Polynesia*. (Titles are all that occur to me these days.) But that's not really a joke. The place does concentrate the mind wonderfully. Rarotonga is Polynesia's last stand. In ten years its people, those who remain, will be hewers of wood and drawers of water for the world's wealthy; the windows of luxury hotels will glitter along the shore; bulldozers will be ploughing palms under for chalets and marinas; supersonic jets will be crashing in and out daily. For the time being, though, there's still a touching innocence, the sound of sea on the reef, bush-beer and the *tamure*.

Hope all is well. Tell me this Kennedy fellow is not some hoax.

Very best for now,
Ian

Commentaries

I'd just come back from a profitless hour in the magistrate's court, and was checking my scanty notes, when Derek Martin, the chief reporter, called me to his desk. 'I hear,' he said, 'the strikers are marching this morning. Or trying to march. I've sent a couple of men along, in case anything happens. You'd better go too. You might see something the others miss. Up the road as fast as you can.'

Then he seemed really to see me and remember something, perhaps my association with Stan, and reconsider his request. He looked around the office: I was the only reporter obviously free; he would have to make do with me, after all.

'Get going,' he added. 'You might be too late as it is.'

He appeared reasonably certain, then, that something was due to happen. I wondered what, exactly, as I left the office in haste. But I didn't doubt the direction from which the information had arrived; Derek Martin prided himself on his rapport with the police. And only a day or two earlier the newspaper had editorialized: 'In this time of national anarchy, let the government announce that The Police Will Be Armed. And let it be known, in the event of challenge to authority, The Police Will Shoot.'

Derek himself was supposed to have tried his hand at editorial-writing that day. It seemed likely enough; he expressed himself even less mildly in the office. He had even proposed concentration camps for dissidents, though that proposition had still to find its way into editorials. He seemed about to spit on those occasions when Stan Coates was mentioned in the office; Stan was now rumoured to be preparing underground propaganda for the strikers. 'In a war,' Derek said, 'treacherous bastards like that would be stood against a wall.'

He was a thin dapper little man, rather nervous, and otherwise kindly to his staff, particularly to me for some reason. Perhaps that was why I felt rather paralysed when I heard him speak. It was all unreal: I felt sure things were going to blow over; they were bound to, it stood to reason.

The demonstration was quiet. Perhaps a thousand strikers straggled along, with crude and hastily painted banners, in twos and threes up the rising street. *Hear Our Side Of The Story*, one of the banners read. Women, strikers' wives, were mingled with the union leaders at the head of the procession. There was some ragged singing; the atmosphere was good-humoured. It was all quite harmless and a little pathetic. What had Derek Martin been expecting?

I found one of my colleagues in the roadside crowd, along with a photographer. 'Very quiet,' I observed.

'Wait and see,' he said. 'They're not going to get away with this.'

Then I saw they weren't.

Further up the street police cars were pulling into a shiny, solid line; the street was being sealed off. And ranks of dark blue uniforms were gathering.

'Look,' said my colleague, 'you'd be a help if you kept your eye on some of the leaders.'

'For example?'

'Harry Jones; the little fellow with the curly hair up front.

And Alex O'Leary, the one with the broken nose and the old hat. Those two for a start. I assume you're familiar with their names.'

'Reasonably,' I agreed, as coolly as I could. And I looked at the two men with whom my father had once marched. They seemed, in their way, as ordinary as my father. Except that they were still marching.

The roadside spectators were largely indifferent. There was little applause for the strikers, but not much hostility either. After two or three months of strike, the marchers looked pale and threadbare in the wintry sunshine; it was as if the procession had been dusted with a fine grey powder. Yet there was still a steady, rather powerful beat of feet.

'And that grey-haired fellow in the dark suit,' my colleague said. 'The well-dressed one. That's Charlie Higgins, the old Labour cabinet minister, until his own party kicked him out. I don't know what he's doing here. Unless he imagines he's lending moral support. The old buffoon.'

But Charlie Higgins walked with his head high enough. He, and probably most of the forward marchers, could see the police up ahead. The police ranks were still thickening. For a man my father styled a renegade, he looked oddly unashamed, and unafraid; he appeared to be joking with marchers beside him. His face had a shiny and distinguished air, if rather corroded by age and perhaps disappointment.

'Come on,' continued my colleague. 'Don't stand there gaping. We've got a job to do. Let's get up ahead and see the action.'

We pushed up the street, through the crowd, and took a vantage point beside a small park and near the police. The distance between the head of the procession and the police shortened slowly, fifty yards, twenty yards, finally ten. 'Hold it,' called a police inspector. 'Hold it right there.'

The leaders stopped. The rest of the marchers began to bank up behind.

'I'll give you five minutes,' the inspector shouted. 'Five minutes to disperse and go your ways. You've had your fun. Now get out; go home. Is that clear?'

Perhaps it was. Alex O'Leary and Harry Jones, among others, turned their back on the police to speak to their followers; they appeared to be urging retreat. Some of the marchers broke ranks and began walking away, according to instruction. Others stood indecisive. Possibly a minute had gone. Charlie Higgins was

388

one of those still standing their ground. The police were more or less ignored. Most of the marchers were soon turning their backs, and the movement away became general. I looked at my watch : still less than two minutes since the police warning. Everything seemed safe; there would be no trouble after all.

Then, incredibly, I heard the inspector call to his men, 'All right, boys. Break it up. Move in there and break it up.'

The lines of blue, with gleaming buttons, crashed across the few yards to the strikers; line after line with batons drawn and swinging. Like a machine, with the trigger tripped. The strikers began to spin around, but too late; most took the first baton blows on the back of their heads. As they fell, they were kicked aside. Women were screaming; I saw one being beaten across the face as she clawed at a constable's arm. Two or three others were knocked aside in the park, sent rolling down a slope. As for the men, the police seemed beserk with their boots and batons; they looked determined to hammer the strikers, and their protest, not just into the ground but under the ground. Here and there, when the blue ranks parted, I saw police feet working efficiently on the fallen. Blood was beginning to colour hair, faces, clothing.

An elderly man was trying to crawl away; his head was split, and one arm seemed crippled, possibly broken, by a baton. His freckled hands were shakily searching the asphalt, as if for understanding. I moved towards him; my colleague grabbed my arm and pulled me back.

'Don't be a mug,' he said. 'A good journalist never gets involved. Besides, you're liable to get clobbered too.'

I was saved from decision by two detectives. They gathered the old man up roughly and arrested him.

Some of the strikers were trying to fight back, to hold the police off with their fists. But the black batons ripped endlessly in the sunlight; a bristling tide. And before long it was over. A few stunned and moaning men were left, being pushed into a Black Maria; there was amazingly little blood left anywhere; a few broken placards and a buckled police helmet lay in a gutter. Traffic began to move up and down the street. The city was credible again.

I waited for my colleague to finish a conversation with the inspector. He returned and said, 'Well, that's it. He said he gave them the full five minutes. Then they attacked his boys. No option, he says; they had it coming.'

'But – '

'They were spoiling for a fight. You saw it yourself.'

I had seen Alex O'Leary and Harry Jones turning their backs. And Charlie Higgins standing his ground with some dignity. Perhaps he'd known, or guessed, all along. What had happened to him? I hadn't seen.

'They were leaving,' I objected. 'They were starting to leave. And it was only two minutes.'

'Then,' said my colleague, 'you go tell that to the editor.' He paused. 'Come on back to the office. We've got work to do.'

'You might have,' I said. 'It seems I've gone blind.'

'Look,' he said, after a moment, 'If that's the way you feel, why don't you go up to the hospital? And check the number of injured? Ring me at the office when you've got a figure. That way, you'll keep out of trouble.'

'Kind of you. But I think – '

'Listen,' he went on, 'there's no point in you risking your future on account of a bunch of troublemakers. Is there now? Go on up to the hospital; keep out of the office. See reason.' He grabbed my elbow as if to steer me. 'Go on, now. You're not a bad kid. I'd hate to see you go the same way as Stan Coates.'

But he was, as it turned out, literally pushing me in the same direction as Stan. Stan was at the casualty department of the hospital when I arrived there. So were half a hundred strikers, many of them injured, and several dozen police. The police seemed to have taken over the hospital. I hadn't seen Stan in the demonstration, but it was evident he must have been; he looked shaken, if unhurt.

'Well, well, bright-eyes,' he said. 'So you're on the big story. You saw it all, then?' He was trying to put up a cheerful front; but inwardly, it was clear, he still fumed.

'I didn't see anything. Or so I'm told. I've just been sent up here to count casualties.'

'There's no deaths yet. Or won't that satisfy them?'

'I'm sorry, Stan. I've just got a job to do. You know that.'

'I could suggest a useful way to be sorry.'

I imagined I might need time to think about that; then I discovered I didn't. 'Tell me then,' I said.

An hour later I scrambled into a telephone box and rang the office. I asked for Derek Martin instead of my colleague on the story. 'What the hell has happened to you?' he asked.

'I'm at the hospital.'

'And you should have rung an hour ago. We've had to call the hospital ourselves for casualty figures.'

'It's just that the story's a little bigger,' I said. 'A little bigger than casualty figures.'

'Another brawl up there?' he said quickly.

'Not exactly. But you might be interested in this. All the casualties so far are suffering from severe head wounds, mainly to the back of the head. And concussion, some severe.'

'Facts,' said Derek. 'Facts. Not opinion.'

'And the men are being stitched up without anaesthetic. And being bundled out of the place by the police without dressings, without any chance to clean up. Still bleeding. And stitched up like sacks. Two of the concussion cases collapsed before they'd gone fifty yards from the hospital.'

'Facts,' said Derek Martin. 'Facts. If you've got something printable, for Christ's sake tell me.'

'One of the men who collapsed was carried back to the hospital again by his mates. It appears he may have a fractured skull. The other one fainted from loss of blood.'

'Jesus Christ,' said Derek Martin. 'Don't waste my time with this garbage. Have you got anything useful to tell me? Otherwise come back to the office.'

'I just thought you might be interested to know that the police have followed the suggestion of the mayor of this city – to let the strikers go around bruised and bleeding for a bit. I should have thought it was highly relevant.'

He hung up.

Stan was waiting for me outside the box. 'I'm wondering,' I said, 'whether I've still got a job.'

'Come on,' he said, 'I'll buy you a beer. I think we have one or two things to talk about.'

(Stan crossed his thick-carpeted living room and switched on his hi-fi. He set a record to play and singing strings, of some brand name or another, swamped the room. Then he topped up my drink and settled down to his own. He appeared rather fidgety, with something on his mind; I was content to wait. And in point of fact rather relaxed, having sampled Stan's swimming pool and liquor cabinet.

'Of course,' he said at length, 'we were rather naive in the old days. Imagining a couple of blasts on our trumpet would bring the walls of Jericho tumbling down.'

It wasn't difficult to agree.

'The world's not built that way,' he added. 'Or the walls of Jericho.'

He seemed to be drinking himself into pleasant melancholy, though his own walls also appeared substantial enough.

'All the same,' he finished, and looked at me with regret and appeal, 'our hearts were in the right place, weren't they?')

The house was old, in a back street where half the buildings were likely condemned. A rather shy woman met us at the door and took us through the house, down stairs, and into a basement. There a sweaty man cranked a cyclostyling machine; another man fed it. Bulk paper sat around in stacks. There were a couple of typewriters on flimsy card tables.

'Well,' Stan said. 'This is it for tonight. We never spend more than three nights in the one place.' He introduced me to his two friends. One was a seaman, the other a waterfront worker. 'And this,' Stan explained to them, 'is a friend of mine from the capitalist press. Probably better that you don't know his name. He saw everything today, and he's going to write it the way he saw it.'

While he talked, Stan was stripping off jacket and tie, and rolling up shirtsleeves. 'All right?' he said to me. 'Choose your machine.' He indicated the two typewriters. 'You tell it straight, and I'll editorialize. You can be your own sub-editor too, if you keep it down to six hundred words. Otherwise we'll have to cut it. You've got a good hour to write the story, if we're to have it in tomorrow morning's strike bulletin. Fair enough?'

I took off my jacket, but left my tie. 'Fair enough,' I agreed.

'Sorry we can't give you ordinary office comforts. But Mrs Harris, upstairs, obliges with tea whenever you feel like it. She's a striker's wife, incidentally. Her husband's in jail for hitting a scab. Thus the police, we hope, won't be watching this place, with her husband away.'

With hardly a breath for preliminary, Stan began typing. I sat longer, in the unfamiliar atmosphere, trying to sum up scenes; and choose words, if I could find sufficient to choose between. I wasn't helped by the other two men in the room watching me with gentle interest, possibly with suspicion: a stranger, after all. I was risking words; they were chancing prison.

I looked over Stan's shoulder, in hope of guide. He was well into his editorial. 'Capitalism,' I glimpsed, 'has again shown its mailed fist. This black and bloody day. . . .'

And saw I couldn't compete.

Stan stopped typing. 'All right?' he asked.

'Just getting up to the start mark.'

He looked at his watch. 'Fifty minutes,' he said. 'Think you'll make it?' Without waiting for answer, he resumed typing.

Then I saw what I could do that Stan could not. The larger things might escape me, but there was still truth in an old man crawling away from a baton. Or in a broken banner. And if everything was information, then information was everything. The sunlight, the winter trees; the quiet street, the shiny cars in line; the flash of police buttons, the blood.

I was aware, from time to time, of people coming and going from the basement; of messages delivered, instructions passed; of a cup of tea set gently beside me. Within my fifty minutes, I delivered my words to Stan. He looked through them quickly.

'They'll do,' he said. 'Good stuff. Just a little cautious, but good stuff.'

Mrs Harris called down the stairs. 'Lights off,' she said urgently. 'There's a car just parked outside.'

The watersider went for the light switch; the seaman opened the window, for quick escape.

'Just sit quiet,' Stan said in the sudden gloom. 'We have these false alarms. A half dozen a night, usually.'

We heard a knock on the door upstairs; and after a time Mrs Harris answering it. There was indistinct conversation. We continued to wait in the dark.

'It must be all right,' Stan announced. 'She planned to knock over a stand in the hall if it was the police.'

Presently there was a rap on the door at the head of the stairs. The light went on. Stan went up to unlock the door and returned with Alex O'Leary. It was interesting to see him close: his eyes were red and tired in a wrinkled face.

'I've brought you fellows along another story for tomorrow,' he explained. 'This one's on the hoof.' He called up the stairs: 'Come on down, boys.'

Two men came down the stairs in damaged condition. Their clothes were torn, their shirts bloody; both had crude bandages on their heads. One of the two was Tim Livingstone.

He looked at me, then at Stan: we both looked back with disbelief. Nothing was said.

393

'I want their story in tomorrow's bulletin,' Alex O'Leary was explaining. 'It's as bad as anything that happened in the open, out in the street, today. Worse. We've got to spread word about what is happening. About just what terror tactics the government is using. One of these men' – he pointed to Tim Livingstone – 'had nothing to do with strike at all. He's a student. That right?'

'An artist,' Tim said mildly, by way of correction. He still looked at us with some interest, without a smile.

'Artist?' Alex O'Leary considered this doubtfully. 'Just for the record,' he said, 'student might sound better.'

'Artist,' Tim said.

'All right, then. Artist. And this other man is Monty Nolan. Monty is a member of the Seamen's Union.'

I really hadn't looked at the other man. He was stocky, with quite a powerful build, and rugged face. One eye was considerably bruised. Otherwise he might have been good-looking, in his way.

'These two men,' Alex O'Leary went on, 'took themselves up to the police station tonight, as ordinary citizens of the city. They were trying to find out whether a friend of Monty's arrested today could be bailed out. What happened was that they were pushed out of the police station and into a back alley, where they had hell hammered out of them. These two can fill in the details. Afterwards, someone can take Monty up to hospital. It looks like he has a couple of broken ribs.' He looked at Tim Livingstone. 'What about you?'

'I'm all right,' Tim said. 'I could do with a chair, though.'

Chairs were found for the two men. And the seaman cyclostyler produced a hip-flask. Alex O'Leary began to depart, with the explanation: 'I shook the police on the way here. But I don't like the car left too long outside. Can you make it a good bulletin tomorrow?'

'Promise,' Stan said.

'Who's this man?' Alex O'Leary paused at the foot of the stairs, evidently noticing me for the first time. There was a certain challenge in his stare, as he tried to sum me up.

'He's all right, Alex,' Stan said. 'I'll vouch for him. Besides, his name's Freeman. That ought to be familiar to you. Enough for you.'

'You don't mean – '

'I mean Bill Freeman's son.'

'Jesus Christ,' Alex said.

His handshake was solid. Then he gripped my shoulders and looked at me. His stare was intense.

'Young Ian, isn't it?'

'Yes.'

'I remember bouncing you on my knee,' he said. 'Now I look at you, I see you got your father's nose.'

I felt embarrassed, with the others looking on. Stan was smiling.

'And maybe more of him than that, eh?' Alex added. 'How is he?'

'Alive,' I answered. 'And reasonably well.'

'He became a very bitter man.' Alex shook his head. 'Very bitter.' He paused. 'What does he think about you being here?'

'I haven't asked him.'

'I see.' This time he shook his head as if to indicate that he didn't understand altogether, and didn't want to intrude. And it was true that it was, after all, my business. 'Well,' he said. 'I'm glad to have you with us, boy. Good luck.' With a last smile, he went up the stairs, leaving us with our fresh story; and Tim Livingstone.

He sat smoking, his feet up on a table, rather abstracted.

'It seems I'm not safe from you anywhere,' Stan said.

Tim just smiled vaguely. Perhaps he was concussed.

'All right,' Stan went on. 'Who is going to tell the story straight? Perhaps you'd better. Tell us how you got involved; and what happened.'

'I just happened to be drinking with Monty tonight,' Tim said finally. 'Among others. That's what happened.'

'Come on, now,' Stan said. He looked at me. 'You'd better take notes, Ian.' Then he switched back to Tim. 'You were drinking with Monty. So?'

'So he mentioned that he was worried about whether his mate had been bailed. And said he wanted to go up and see. But he didn't want to go alone.'

'And you volunteered?'

'Monty asked me.'

At this stage Monty intervened. He had obviously been hurt more than Tim; he spoke slowly. 'I said to Tim,' he explained with a feeble grin, 'I wanted a respectable friend to go up to the police station with me.'

'Don't tell me,' Stan said, 'that Livingstone's the best you can do by way of a respectable friend?'

'He was around,' Monty said. 'And he wasn't in the strike. So I asked him. And Tim said okay, he'd come along with me.'

But the effort of explanation was too much for Monty. He started to slide sideways in his chair. I grabbed him before he fell to the floor.

'I think that's it,' Stan said. 'So far as Monty is concerned. You'd better get him up to hospital, Ian. I'll get the rest of the story from Tim.'

Stan was still, really, the cool professional. All I could think was that Monty might be dying; the bandage on his head had slipped, and I could see thick fresh blood oozing through his hair. Mrs Harris called a taxi, and I half carried Monty through the house and out to the car.

On the way to the hospital, perhaps with the fresh winter air, he seemed to revive a little as he lay against me. At first he was incoherent, cursing the police. Then he said: 'He's a good boy, Tim. You know him?'

'A little,' I admitted.

'A good mate. He could of buggered off when the johns went for me tonight. They didn't touch him at first. They went for me; they knew me. But he didn't bugger off.'

'It's all right,' I said. 'Take it easy.'

'I hope he's not hurt too bad.'

'He's all right.'

'You know him?' he repeated. 'You know him, then?' His brain was starting to travel in circles.

'Yes,' I said again, ' a little.'

'I wouldn't of thought he was much of a fighter. Tim. Not with that crook leg. You tell him from me I'm going to fix one or two of them bastards with a bicycle chain across the face. One dark night. You tell him from me.'

He lurched against me with the motion of the taxi; I had blood on my jacket. Less than eighteen hours before I had been setting off to fit myself into a quiet, uncomplicated day at the office. The taxi turned into the hospital gates.

'We worked together on the same job, once,' he went on. 'When I was ashore. He was just a kid, new to town.'

It didn't take the hospital long to admit Monty. He had broken ribs, a cracked wrist, severe head lacerations, and concussion. I said goodbye to him as he was wheeled away on a stretcher. He was even more vague; he found it difficult to focus his eyes; he was confusing me with Tim Livingstone now. If I had to be confused with other people, that at least was a change.

'You're a good mate,' he said, gripping my arm with his good hand.

(The Victorian fortress rose grey in the day; its dirty, rain-streaked turrets stood stark. The place hadn't changed much in my years away : it had just sunk more darkly into the city, a region of rot, among tall new buildings and motorway fly-overs. I cut the engine, the windscreen wipers ceased to scrape at drizzle, and I took a deep breath; and then locked and left the car and went up to the front gate. I pressed a button and a bell rang somewhere inside; presently a face peered through a barred slot. I presented my visiting permit and the gate was unlocked for me.

'You sign the visitors' book first,' the warder said. 'Nolan's down in the maximum security block. I suppose you know. Turn sharp left and down the steps.'

I arrived at an evidently new section of the prison; but it looked even grimmer and tighter than the main building. Inside was a wilderness of concrete and steel bars; there were remote bangings and rumblings. Some electronic equipment clicked and hummed in a control room after I presented my permit for inspection again; gates clashed open and shut; the duty officer appeared. 'You might find Nolan difficult at first,' he advised me. 'He hasn't had a visitor in years. They drop away; they always do.'

I signed another visitors' book. With formalities finished I was taken into a visiting booth. Painted concrete blocks; the smell of damp; bitter cold. The other side of the visiting booth, beyond two sheets of bulletproof glass, with bars between, sat Monty Nolan. He had balded, his face was sunken and sunless : I wouldn't have known him. But his eyes were still shrewd and lively.

There was a voice-box between us, through which we were expected to communicate. His voice came booming out, 'You have to shout.'

'Shout?'

'Through this apparatus. There's a microphone in there, by

the way. We're bugged and taped. A little game to keep the screws occupied.'

'I see.' A clanging gate somewhere near drowned me out; the visit was going to be even more difficult than I thought. And I couldn't find a conversational opening appropriate : to ask how he was would be absurd. He was clearly waiting on me to speak.

I tried to smile. 'It's a long time, Monty.'

As inept as anything else I could find to say. How long was life?

'What's that?' He strained to hear.

'I said – it's a long time. Since we saw each other.'

He nodded. 'A long time, all right.' He paused, squinting under the feeble light. Then he again tried to launch himself through glass, bars and concrete. Or at least his voice. 'I read you was back in the country,' he said, 'and I wondered how I could get in touch with you. One of the screws reckoned he'd seen you on television. So I sent you that note care of the television station.'

'You were lucky, then. A girl friend at the station forwarded it to me.'

'Girl friend?' He still heard me only fitfully.

'An old one. She works in television. She passed your note on to me.'

'I hope you didn't mind,' he said. 'I mean, I hope you didn't mind me getting in touch.'

'Mind? Why should I mind, Monty?'

'I just thought you might of. I mean, you're respectable now. I mean, I thought you mightn't of wanted to be reminded. You know how it is, sometimes.'

'Then I hope I never know how it is,' I strained to reply.

He smiled for the first time. I seemed to have put him more at ease.

It was true, though, that there were things I should have preferred not to remember. Not in connection with Monty especially, though he might have been part of it; and not that I could or would tell Monty, or anyone. Such as : a shattering window, a falling body, Tim's cry; Paris, 1959, September. Such as –

'Well, you look respectable,' he was saying. 'Damn smart, in fact. You not only done well for yourself. You actually look like you have.'

Such as the fact that we were both serving life sentences. But I'd turned that to profit. Hadn't I? And we'd both tried escape, after all : with roughly equal lack of success.

We looked at each other through the glass and bars.

I realized I'd never know Monty well. And that sooner or later he was going to say why he really wanted to see me; he was going to ask the question to which I could give no truthful answer. Or no answer at all.

'Ten years you must of been away,' he said.

'At least,' I agreed.

'A hellish long time.'

'Yes.'

'Ten years ago can seem like yesterday here.'

'I can imagine.' Could I, really? Yes; in my way. 'Is there anything I can do to help, Monty? I hear you don't have visitors. I'll come again, if you like.'

'Only if you want to.'

'I'd like to.'

'I can always do with books.'

'What about fruit and chocolate?'

'Not allowed here. There might be marijuana in the fruit, or LSD in the chocolate. Or a revolver in a pineapple. They can't be too careful. Not with us bad boys. No, books do me. I don't need too many vitamins to read anyway.'

It sounded more like the Monty I remembered. He winked through the glass. Then, while the guard observing us turned his back, he flashed a note in large block letters : I PROBABLY WONT TRY ESCAPE AGAIN BUT THEY DONT KNOW THAT. KEEP THEM GUESSING. KEEP YOURSELF GUESSING. THE ONLY WAY TO STAY ALIVE. RIGHT?

'Right,' I said. 'I'll remember the books next time. Let me know if there's anything you want specially. What else do you do – apart from reading?'

'Slop out in the morning. Shower Tuesdays and Fridays. Eat the garbage they feed us. Brood in the workshop, type braille for the blind. Paddle around in the exercise yard when it gets some sun. That's about it. The time goes. That's the funny thing. It really does.'

'What about the art, Monty? I remember you used to paint, now and then. Do you still try that in here?'

399

I was trying to make it easier for him to ask the question he wanted me to answer. We should be close, now.

'For a start,' he said. 'For a start, I did. Then I lost interest, or ran out of gear. I forget which. It was years ago.'

'If I brought you in some gear, do you think you'd start again?'

'Well,' he said, 'I could always give it a try.' He paused. 'That's if they let me have the gear. Very suspicious bastards they are here. They might think I'm trying to paint a hole through my cell. Or pole-vault over the wall with paint-brushes. Christ knows.'

It seemed I had to try another tack, then.

'What about your case, Monty? You ever have any luck in reopening it?'

He shook his head. 'Never. I realized I was stuffed very early on. After that time I went over the wall, I didn't have a fucking hope this side of hell. That fixed it for good. I'll be lucky to get out of here alive.'

Yet there was only a flicker of bitterness. He said it smiling.

'Still,' he conceded, 'that's what they say about the whole bit. Life; the world; whatever. You never get out of it alive. That right?'

'So they say, Monty.'

'You ought to know. You been around. People listen to what you say; they read what you write. You tell me now, what's the point?'

'The point?'

'The point of the whole bit. Being alive. There must be something. I got time to brood. I could do myself in, easy enough, before the screws got to me. It'd be all over quick. Why don't I? I got nothing to look forward to, except more of the same.'

'Then you're more likely to have the answer than I have – so it seems to me. And perhaps you have.'

'What do you mean?'

'Keep guessing; that might just be it. As good as anything I know.'

There were renewed clicks and hums from the control room: then clashing of gates again, and boots on concrete. I realized the guards were coming to unlock Monty from his side of the booth, and take him away. Our half-hour was up. He took a deep breath, and looked at me with a certain intensity: now or never.

400

'All that time you was gone,' he said, 'did you ever come across our old mate? Did you ever come across Tim Livingstone?')

When I got back from the hospital, after about an hour away, I half expected to find Stan still in conference with Tim. But he was at his typewriter, apparently preparing the story. And Tim was at a bench in a corner of the basement, his back turned, obscurely occupied; my arrival didn't distract him. Stan looked up, though.

'You might be interested to know,' he said, 'that I've just recruited another staff man. Livingstone, no less. He's just undertaken to produce some drawings for tomorrow's bulletin. And for one or two propaganda pamphlets. I wish the police had hit him on the head sooner.'

'How's Monty?' Tim called, his back still turned.

'Surviving. They're mending his ribs and keeping him there. What about you? You sure you shouldn't go up to the hospital too?'

'I'm all right,' he said. He didn't pause in what he was doing; he was extremely concentrated. 'Monty was the one the police went for. I was just too slow to move.'

'So I heard. That, and a little more.'

He made no response. There was no point in persisting.

Stan said, 'Look, Ian, now you've got your story out of the way, I wonder could you help with one or two other things? That's if you have nothing better to do.'

It was difficult to think of anything.

'There's some more copy to get out of the way. I'm running late. And Sandy West is due here shortly after midnight to take delivery of the first batch of bulletins. He drops them around town, in various places.'

'Sandy?' Tim looked up from his corner at last. 'He in this too?'

'And a few other no-hopers you could name. The thing is, you see, we're useful just because of that. Most of the prominent strikers are being watched. We're not, if we're lucky. So far we have been.'

'But why are you doing it?' Tim said, with a trace of amazement.

'Because someone has to,' Stan said.

'What about you?' Tim looked at me.

401

'Because I twisted his arm,' Stan said. 'And why are you here?'

'Because of Monty.'

'Obviously. But what's he to you anyway?'

'He's bought me meals and drinks when I've been broke.'

'You still didn't have to go up to the police station with him.'

'Then say I was drunk. Or looking after a meal ticket.'

He went on with his work. We went on with ours. I began to enjoy it; I felt relaxed as I stitched up sentences for Stan. Even the seaman and the watersider seemed to have accepted me wholly, since Alex O'Leary had. They accepted that I belonged, after all. Perhaps I did.

Tim produced his drawings. Most were simple, effectively along the lines Stan had prescribed: a police helmet with swastika emblem; a baton gripped in a fist; a heavy police boot trampling a placard; a fallen striker.

'Good crisp stuff,' Stan said. 'How's your head?'

'Still there,' Tim said, 'so far as I know.' He touched it tenderly and then, with decision, tugged off the bandage. The blood had coloured most of his hair, but the wound wasn't deep.

'Go upstairs and let Mrs Harris clean you up,' Stan said. 'You can't walk around like that.'

When he'd gone, Stan said, 'Surprise; the boy's good. He knew what I wanted, and he delivered. He can oblige when he feels like it. Or when he's hurt enough.'

When Tim returned, he traced his drawings carefully on to the skins for the cyclostyling machine. Stan and I typed in the last of the text. Soon the seaman and watersider were in full production. Towards midnight more people arrived to staple up the bulletins. And not long after midnight Sandy West arrived. He was a jaunty, lanky individual with vivid eyes, narrow face, and straggling red moustache. 'I thought,' he announced, 'there might be machine guns and road blocks up tonight. The way things are going. So I brought along a couple of friends to ride shotgun.'

Two companions followed him into the basement; both looked equally unlike strikers. One was bearded blackly and untidily; shaggy hair fell down to his shoulders; he wore a soiled windbreaker, shapeless khaki trousers, and heavy boots. His eyes were friendly. He was introduced as Ted Connolly. The other was less easy of definition: short, pale and bony, and perhaps

402

nervous; in a black polo-neck sweater. His name was given as Charlie Bates.

'So this,' he said, looking at Tim, 'is where the party is tonight. Livingstone's had his first fight already.'

Tim had nothing to say. He and Ted Connolly were looking at each other.

'What are you doing here?' Ted Connolly asked.

'I could ask you the same.'

'Then say I've always been a sucker for lost causes. And I happen to be back in town.'

Sandy said, 'If you haven't got my first two thousand bulletins ready, have you got anything to drink?'

'Mrs Harris,' Stan said, 'is always happy to oblige with tea. You only have to ask.'

Stan continued stapling. The cyclostyling machine was noisy.

'You're all right?' Ted Connolly was saying to Tim; he spoke with a gentle concern.

'Fairly.'

'I missed you, last time I was in the city. No one seemed to know where you were. Except that you were shut off, somewhere, with some girl. That was one story I heard. Otherwise I drew blanks. You still haven't told me what you're doing here.'

'I got hit on the head.'

'Spoil a good peasant,' Ted Connolly said. 'Sandy seemed to suggest that he was taking me into the inner council of the revolution. And who do I find?'

'Well,' Tim said, 'Ian Freeman here, for one.' He seemed aware of me for the first time that night. 'Ian's an old school friend of mine. He didn't get hit on the head. He hasn't the same excuse.'

'I'll work with Stalinist bastards when it's necessary,' Ted announced, 'but I'll never forgive what they did to Trotzky.'

'It's not the point,' Stan said irritably.

'No?'

'The point is there's a strike on, the country's shut up tight, and we're the only people who can tell the story. And there's a certain amount of propaganda to be produced and delivered tonight.'

'I wouldn't be here if I wasn't willing,' Ted said. 'What really worries me is whether I'd be here if it wasn't hopeless.'

'Hopeless?' Stan snapped. He was tired and quick to anger. 'What do you mean hopeless?'

'I mean the strike's beaten,' Ted answered. 'It's been beaten from the start. The battle can't be fought the old way. It's over; dead.'

'Then,' Stan said, still furious, 'there are still a lot of dead men being beaten up.'

'The third act,' Ted explained. 'All good drama has a convincing third act. We just happen to be waiting for the curtain line. Or pretending we haven't heard it.'

'You're a cynical shit,' Stan said with disgust.

I really wanted to side with Stan, but found it easier to believe Ted.

The first bulletins were ready. Sandy West, Charlie Bates and then Ted carried them out of the house, after someone had checked that the street outside was free of police cars. Sandy's old truck ground off into the central city. All this time, no one noticed Tim much. When I went downstairs again, after seeing the truck leave, I found Stan bending over him. He'd quietly collapsed.

'See if Mrs Harris has some brandy,' Stan said.

Mrs Harris hadn't.

'Then I'll take him home with me,' I said. 'If he's not all right in the morning, I'll see he goes into hospital.'

Stan was bathing Tim's face with cold water. His eyes were open again, if weakly. 'Tired,' he managed to say. 'Bloody tired.'

'It's all right. Ian's taking you home.'

Tim looked at me puzzled. 'You?' he said faintly.

'He'll see you're all right,' Stan said. 'Thanks for everything tonight.'

Another taxi was called, and ten minutes later Tim Livingstone was at home on my bed. I pulled off his shoes and unbuttoned his shirt. He was reasonably conscious again, and I offered him coffee.

'Not a bad place you've got here,' he observed finally. 'Big enough. Margaret lived here too?'

'Yes,' I agreed. 'She did.'

'Do we need to talk about Margaret?' he asked.

'Not specially. No; I don't think so.'

'That's all right, then. It's just that I thought there might be things to be said. I'll talk about her if you want to. She's gone, you know.'

'Yes. I know.'

'I wasn't what she wanted, exactly.'

'I said I'd sooner not talk about it.'

'Fair enough. Is this going to be all right? Where will you sleep?'

'On the couch. I have a sleeping bag.' My eyes were heavy and I had a job to face in the morning, if it still existed.

'I can easily bugger off. I'm feeling much better.'

'You're under observation, in case you don't know it. You may have to go to hospital.'

'Not me. But thanks, all the same. I mean thanks for looking after me.'

'No problem. Come to think of it, you looked after me once.'

He looked at me queerly. 'You mean that?'

'Yes. Or I'd like to think so.'

A couple of minutes later I switched off the light. It took me, however, some time to find sleep; it wasn't just the discomfort of the sleeping bag on the couch. It was incredible that the day had begun not so unlike any other since my arrival in the city.

The street; the sunlight; the blood. Then Alex O'Leary gripping my shoulders.

But of course there was more. I heard rain on the roof, then a faint rumble of distant city traffic. Tim was noisy in his sleep. Company had comfort.

Twenty:

Documents

Avarua P.O.
Rarotonga
Cook Islands
October 7, 1966

Dear Ben,

Thanks for your reply, rather swift as these things go here. We must have caught the ships right. And, for me, dismayingly swift.

I wish I could say your reassurance about this Max Kennedy was gratifying. That is, I wish I didn't have to take him seriously. But it seems I have to: I have still another letter from him. Is Tim's work now worth all his time and trouble? Once, of course, I wouldn't have had doubt of the answer. Now it seems all so remote. Yes, I'll do my best to help him – so far as I can, which may not be far.

Three weeks' rain. Everything damp and mildewed. The *tamure* is a dance, not a fish. Captain Cook called it the 'timor-dee' when he first saw it in Tahiti. Very indecent, he said. Women use their hips, men their knees. It took me a couple of months to find the right joints; they're well seasoned now.

Very best for now,

Ian

Avarua P.O.
Rarotonga
Cook Islands
October 7, 1966

Dear Mr Kennedy,

Thank you for clarifying your interest at such length, and

with such patience. I'll come clean and say I haven't been able to take you very seriously until now. Perhaps that is why you say you find my letters of tantalizing interest. It's true that you have rather a mystery story on your hands. But are you sure your interest isn't in the mystery – more than anything else? Rather than in the art, say? I may not be able to do much in this letter, which is being written to catch a plane here for a brief stopover.

First, yes, the young artist who does figure in some of my early fiction was, more or less, modelled on Tim Livingstone.

Second, girl friends. I don't think you'll find much joy here. There was, however, one girl with whom he lived for a period – perhaps three months – and therefore knew him more intimately than most. A home town girl. Her name, in those days, was Margaret Saunders. She is almost certainly married, probably to some dour farmer, and buried in the countryside.

Third, childhood background. Only child, brought up by widower father on a farm not far from Te Ika. Terminated school before end of his final year, after winning some national schools' art prize, and moved to city; also after a partially incapacitating accident on his father's land. Possibly fortunate (or unfortunate, depending how the light falls) in his early friends in the city. The art certainly became serious. Exhibited young anyway. Much of this you probably know. At the time of my arrival in the city he seemed to have established a reputation of sorts; I encountered the reputation before I encountered him. Yes, you could say he was 'taken up early', I suppose. On the other hand you might also argue that if he didn't exist, he would have had to be invented. He seemed necessary not only to his time and place, but also to people.

Fourth, my relations with him. I mentioned our meeting during the strike; we came to share a flat in consequence. Did I explain his involvement? He had a friend, a seaman named Monty Nolan, who since has had some notoriety; I imagine you could locate him without problems, if you wished, still serving life sentence for murder (though there was dispute about his total guilt) and violent escape. I doubt, though, whether Monty could really be much help in your research. Tim left the country shortly before, or at the beginning of Monty's trial. There was a suggestion he could have been a witness, though my memory is hazy on this point.

But this is doubtless digression. Closer friends around him

over the period I have named already; we were all made closer, to some extent, by the strike. Stan Coates, if anyone, was initially the dominant figure. Afterwards, in the general demoralization, it was Tim Livingstone. To explain the thing fully, which I won't, I would have to account for the deadly conformity of the time and country. (That should be your business anyway.) It was a question of who could offer challenge, if anyone could. Does that help? Possibly not; human beings aren't accounted for so easily.

Fifth, I haven't time – the mail clearance for the plane is close – to go into anything I know, or rather learned incidentally, of the European period. Not that there is a great deal I can tell anyway. I thought I made clear that I didn't find him there – in Paris, I mean. Or anywhere else.

Best wishes

Sincerely

Ian Freeman

PS: Apropos of mystery. Thoreau: 'It is remarkable how long men will believe in the bottomlessness of a pond without taking the trouble to sound it.' The greatest depth of Walden pond, he says, was no more than one hundred and two feet, 'yet not an inch of it can be spared by the imagination.' Wouldn't you prefer that I left it all to you?

Good luck anyway.

Commentaries

Another basement. Not that of Mrs Harris; there had been a half dozen since then, and the police still hadn't caught up with us.

But this one was uncannily still. The cycostyling machine had thumped to a stop; Alex O'Leary had just left the place after saying his sad piece. For a while there was silence. Tim was the first among us to make any definite move. He picked up two or three cartoons he had just completed and very carefully delivered them to the wastebasket. He didn't say anything.

Communication of any kind seemed unnecessary. Even Ted Connolly, pessimistic enough from the beginning, looked dismayed; he sat slumped on an old couch beside Charlie Bates, who appeared busy looking at his feet. Monty Nolan, with his healed and scarred scalp, leaned on the cyclostyling machine, at which he had been employed; he rolled a cigarette.

At our centre sat Stan, head in hands, bleakly gazing at some inflammatory copy no longer needed.

'Well, I'm stuffed,' Monty Nolan said at length.

'A pity,' Sandy West said. 'I thought for a while there it had the makings of something.'

'I was just beginning to enjoy it,' Charlie agreed.

'Not with a bang,' Ted Connolly said. 'As we might have known.'

'All over,' Stan said at length. He got clumsily to his feet; he still looked stunned. He looked around at us, face after face. 'Well, thanks for everything. All of you.'

'We could always try again,' Sandy said. 'There has to be a 1905 before a 1917.'

That did not seem to cheer Stan. For the first time I saw him as totally exhausted; and a different person from the cocky, self-assured journalist I'd first met. He'd burnt himself out, or near enough.

Tim still hadn't spoken. He was tugging on a windbreaker. It was almost midnight, and the strike was over; or would be in the morning, after nearly six months, with final and total defeat, and not a strong union left alive in the country. There was nothing left for us to do. And little more to be said. It was Stan who moved me most: perhaps he would never live so intensely again. He seemed to be shrivelling up before my eyes.

Tim looked at me. 'I could do with some sleep,' he said. 'I don't know about you.'

Sleep had seemed unnecessary for weeks. We had often gone through until four in the morning. And my efficiency in the office, where Derek Martin saw that my assignments had no potential political hazard, was fairly minimal. My university work had been forgotten altogether.

'Sleep sounds reasonable,' I agreed. But I was still watching Stan.

Perhaps I should have been watching Monty Nolan. Monty was far too quiet.

Tim and I were first to leave. It wasn't a long walk to my flat. We'd been sharing it now for three or four weeks, ever since he had been forced, through non-payment of rent, to vacate the place he had evidently shared with Margaret. We didn't talk much about that. Which, of course, suited me; we might, in our new friendship, have sprung freshly from that first meeting, nearly a dozen years before, on the muddy river-bank. With nothing at all between.

Our feet clicked on asphalt pavement. 'Well,' he said presently, 'I expect I'd better call Ken McAdam in the morning, to see if he has any work he can steer in my direction. Money, I mean.'

'There's no hurry,' I observed. It had seemed the least of our problems, so long as we had police to evade. While I held a job, I could pay rent and buy food. It was natural enough to share.

'I'd sooner get it out of the way,' he said. 'The money problem.'

'But,' I protested, as I unlocked our door, 'why not get back to painting first? Settle yourself. Think about money later.'

'While you support me? No thanks all the same. And I'd better think about moving out.'

'The place is big enough. I don't use it all anyway.'

I switched on our light. He fell in a chair.

'Well,' he conceded, 'perhaps I could stay a day or two longer. Just to get my breath. Now it's all over.'

All over? For Tim it had largely been adventure – and perhaps distraction – in which he had not been slow to join. Something of chance which became challenge, and outlet for anger. For Stan Coates it wasn't all over. He'd already talked beyond the strike, about some book he planned to write. For me? There were certain things I couldn't banish, or put into storage. A grip on my shoulder, for instance; and an undeniable relief, as if in some way I had found myself home. I should miss the basements, the work in the night.

'Look,' I said to Tim, 'I'd like you to stay. I'm trying to put it on the line now.'

Evenings, in any case, might barely be bearable alone.

'The room's bright enough,' he said crisply. 'And I've had worse.'

'Well, then, make some use of it. I'm out all day, most days. If you can work here, go ahead. And so far as evenings are concerned, I need quiet too – if I'm going to catch up on university work.'

Though that did seem, everything considered, unlikely now; and irrelevant too,

'All right,' he said finally. 'I'll stay, if you like. It's just that – '

'Just that what?'

'Just that, well, I thought you might still be sensitive about

410

Margaret. And might have taken me in here as a kind of sacrifice to the cause.'

'The cause?' I couldn't quite see the point.

'I didn't mind helping out, and you've helped me out. Fair enough. But if you want to call quits now, go ahead. I don't need charity. I can move out tomorrow morning.'

I was suddenly afraid he might. He had made slight attempt to occupy the place. His belongings were still tidily arranged in an inconspicuous corner of the room: mostly stacked books and neatly folded clothing. And his paintings were still in tight, tied parcels. It wouldn't take him more than ten minutes to shift again; he appeared more camper than long-term guest.

'It hasn't been like that at all,' I objected. 'And so far as Margaret is concerned, I thought we'd finished with that subject.'

'If you say so.' He had my face under intense observation.

I turned my back and began to prepare late food. 'We could say,' I suggested, 'that we're just a pair of home town boys washed up on the same beach. We do have that in common.'

'Well, Christ,' he said, 'I can't imagine why you want to remember the place. I seem to remember kids beating you up on account of your father.'

'There was more to it than that.'

'You've got a good story there. You stick to it.'

'Don't you ever go back?' I asked.

That seemed to silence him. I finished making the supper.

Since I appeared to have advantage, I persisted. 'Your father, for example,' I said. 'Don't you ever go back to see him?'

'You mind your business,' he said abruptly, 'and I'll mind mine.' But he couldn't resist adding, 'And how often do you go back anyway? And see your father?'

'I'm overdue for a visit,' I admitted.

'You mean you haven't been back at all?'

'Not yet. No.'

He laughed: quite surprisingly.

'All right, I'll stay. We'll see how we make out.'

While we settled, while Stan Coates fretted and while Sandy and Charlie drank Ted Connolly's bad red wine, Monty Nolan finished off the strike in his own way. According to the very precise courtroom version, he found an iron bar and used it upon three policeman congregated at a street corner. Two were taken

411

to hospital; the third managed to subdue and arrest him, with some belated assistance. The magistrate remanded Monty for sentence. Monty had no lawyer and wasn't interested in defending himself. Even his own unionists seemed unwilling to help, in the circumstances; he was on his own.

Through minor misjudgement on the part of Derek Martin, I was covering court the day Monty appeared for sentence. His face was still dark with bruises. Since he hadn't denied any of the charges brought against him, there was possibly no point in his being defended anyway. Though the judge did ask Monty if he expressed any regret.

'Only that I didn't flatten all three of the buggers,' he said.

That appeared to settle it; he could expect five years' prison. But before the judge could pass sentence a detective, who had earlier offered evidence about Monty's arrest, rose from the body of the court; he produced a revolver and pointed it at Monty. Or in Monty's general direction; it could also, the way the object trembled, have been pointed at the judge. There was sufficient of a pause, before he came to decision about pulling the trigger, for the detective to be overpowered by fellow officers; he was taken raving from the court.

Perhaps the judge was too shaken to offer Monty more than four years. He gazed with a certain indifference in my direction, and I attempted a friendly smile in return. Tim and one or two of the others were sitting at the back of the court; perhaps they signalled sympathy too, with equal lack of response. Monty seemed to have accepted the bargain as fair, the price as worth paying; he looked a man secure in his satisfactions.

Back in the office, I tried on my typewriter to make accurate account of the scene in court; and presented the result to Derek Martin, as he requested. He made certain predictable alterations to my story. There was no point in protest. It wasn't a question of belonging now : rather of half-belonging, as with most things.

'For example,' Derek said, with critical brow, 'I don't see the need to specify this man with the gun as a detective. It can be assumed that he's just a member of the public, reflecting public feeling against the vicious troublemakers who have tried and failed to destroy everything decent and disciplined in our society.'

Derek was beginning to talk like one of his own editorials. It worried me more, though, that Stan Coates was too. Stan always seemed to have had a certain cynicism in reserve when talking things political; now he had no reserve at all.

'All right, so there's a battle lost,' he told me. 'That doesn't mean there's still not a war to be won.'

The Party, with the end of the strike, had given him a job on its weekly newspaper; he wrote for the paper with a great deal of ideological zest, and hoped I might contribute too. He was also preparing his short history of the strike.

'There are certain Marxist lessons to be learned,' he explained, 'if the working class movement is ever to be a coherent and commanding force again.'

Stan was beginning to lose me somewhere; but I was reluctant to lose him, for reasons I didn't begin to determine. There was always the possibility, now, of relaxing with others.

Tim, on the whole, was surprisingly quiet and even company. He insisted on paying his way, some of his share of the rent and food, with odd jobs picked up from Ken McAdam. This commercial work was almost all I saw of his activity when I got home from the office in the evenings. I assumed he engaged in what he called his real work when I was elsewhere. And that, for me, largely remained mystery. The paintings he had brought with him were still stacked and tied tightly.

Saturdays, though, were more restless. We might hunt down Paul Wiseman in the coffee shop, since Paul had a sensitive ear for information about social activity in the city; no one was more knowledgeable about parties in or around the university's corduroy fringe, or in the homosexual belt. Paul was so inconspicuous; people possibly didn't notice him at all when passing quiet invitations. Impossible to estimate how many crashed and wrecked parties for which he was, one way and another, responsible. Failing Paul we could always search out Ken McAdam, Sandy West or Charlie Bates in the pub; and Ted Connolly, if he were in town. Often enough, however, we found they were similarly searching for us. Out of such stalemates we could contrive parties ourselves, though these were seldom satisfying. There was, for example, the problem of arranging sufficient girls. These were most easily acquired at parties to which we had not been invited. The same girls, confronted with the suggestion that they might enjoy a small evening in Ken McAdam's flat or mine, seemed to be considering the hazards of gang-rape; they excused themselves. So we found ourselves, perhaps, still totally masculine in company at three in

413

the morning, in bleak rooms growing bleaker, among puddles of beer and wine and sodden cigarette butts, in some grey haze and daze and silences which grew ever longer. If we were waiting for something real again, it was slow to arrive. There was one thing for which I wasn't waiting. I hadn't caught up with university work; it coasted towards collapse.

'You could at least try,' Stan Coates advised me.

'Well,' Ben said, shrugging, 'it's your own funeral.'

'I wouldn't worry,' Tim said.

'What is it you really want?' Ted Connolly asked. 'That's the question you have to face, sooner or later. If you don't face it, you're wasting your time. And you have less and less time.'

Of all Tim's friends I preferred Ted. He had a certain calm of character; he seemed often to be examining us all in a detached way. I noticed too that he left Tim uneasy. Not that anything was ever said, at least in my hearing; perhaps it wasn't necessary for anything to be said. For when Ted addressed me, it often seemed his words were also directed elsewhere.

There was one thing I clearly couldn't leave to time; one thing I had to face. That was a visit back to my parents.

A day or two before my trip, Stan Coates appeared at my flat. 'There's someone I'd like you to meet,' he said, 'if you can spare the time. An old friend of your father's. Charlie Higgins. I'm going around to his place this evening, to interview him for my book. What about coming along?'

I hesitated.

'What's the trouble?' he demanded. 'You don't have to think about it, do you?'

Tim was lying flat on his stomach, on the couch, leafing through a magazine. He didn't appear much interested in our conversation.

'I suppose I could come along,' I conceded finally. 'Though I don't see how I'll be of any use to you.'

'It wasn't use to me I was thinking about. I was inviting you for your interest. Or the good of your soul.'

'I see. Well, if that's the case, I'll come along.'

Charlie Higgins had a modest suburban home among other modest homes: there was nothing to mark it out. The same shaven lawn, the same characterless shrubs, the same flower-beds. And after we had knocked on his door, Charlie Higgins himself appeared to present the same surprising lack of distinction. In slippers, cardigan and open-neck shirt, a pipe gently smoking in his hand, he could have been a retired businessman, shop-keeper or clerk. The stiff-backed demonstrator I had seen, the distinguished retired politician, was quite gone; there was just a quiet old bachelor showing us into his living room, and offering us a drink.

'So you,' he said to me presently, 'are Bill's boy.'

For a moment it seemed to be Alex O'Leary all over again. Yet it wasn't, exactly. He didn't take a grip on my shoulders. He seemed entirely without passion.

'Yes,' I agreed. 'It seems I have to live with that.'

'I haven't seen your father, of course, in more than twenty years. We went our different ways.'

'So I gather,' I understated.

'And had our different failures,' he added. 'No grief to anyone now. Least of all ourselves. We're both out of it now.' He passed our drinks. 'It could have been different, perhaps, in small degree. He could have been where I've been, and I could have been where he has. But the ending would have been much the same. Wouldn't you agree? It doesn't matter. We tried. It's not much of an epitaph, but the best we can manage. People have full stomachs, at least. If they can be happy with that, so might we. Full stomachs don't encourage a passion for justice or reason. One day they might be empty again.'

Stan was visibly impatient with the old man.

'Where would you say,' he asked, 'the failure of the militant working class movement has been?' His notebook was open, and his pencil hovered.

Charlie Higgins didn't appear to hear a word. 'I'd like to see your father again,' he went on, 'if he'd like to see me.'

'Would you ascribe it,' Stan persisted, 'to ideological lack? To a generally blind syndicalist or anarchist spirit?'

'At times,' Charlie Higgins said, 'I've felt him very near, and wondered how he is. Now it's all over.'

'Could you tell me how you feel?' Stan pleaded, plainly afraid the old man would wander further. 'Just how you feel about the whole thing? Now you can look back on forty years of class struggle?'

'Tired,' Charlie Higgins said.

Stan parted from me, that night, in bad humour. 'The old bastard,' he said, 'didn't tell me a thing. What a waste of time.'

I had nothing to say. I could remember the old man's eyes.

'You're not really going to take him down to see your father?' Stan said.

'I could do worse,' I argued.

I drove Charlie Higgins down to Te Ika in a rental car on a Saturday morning. It was a pleasant drive; he dozed most of the way. When we reached town, I dropped him at the private hotel where he'd booked, and then drove on to my home and parents. It was a cool spring day, with the hills sharp against a clear sky. The willows beside the river were showing new green; there were scatters of spring flowers through the streets of the town.

I arrived home in relaxed mood. My mother's welcome was warm and tearful, and my father gripped my hand tight.

'We thought you'd given us up,' he said.

I hadn't really seen them as old before. Nor had I seen them with such relief. My mother's hair was distinctly grey, and my father carried his age leanly. There no longer seemed much distance between us. Behind them Diane hovered, with a delighted smile, waiting to greet me in her own way.

'You could have written more often,' my mother said. 'But Ben's been giving us news.'

I didn't ask what kind. That could wait.

'And you're making out?' my father said. 'That's the main thing. You look fit, anyway.'

He put his hand on my shoulder and steered me into the house. There was more laughter in my presence than I could remember. Diane kissed me on the cheek, and took my hands. It seemed I had a lovely enough sister.

Out of the confusion I found myself, at length, walking in the garden with my father. The town appeared asleep around us, in the Saturday sun; most sounds were faint and distant. I was aware of Diane watching from the house as we walked together.

'I gather,' my father said, 'you've become a bit of a fighter. According to the letters Ben writes your mother.'

'I wouldn't say that,' I protested. It was hard to think of a more unlikely description.

'Anyway I hear you've been pretty well involved,' he went on, 'and with one or two old friends of mine.'

'True,' I agreed. 'Up to a point, for a while.'

416

I hadn't expected him to sound quite so pleased. And I couldn't disappoint him entirely.

'Well,' he said, 'I was wrong about you. You haven't sold out. I don't mind admitting I was wrong. You got your own life to live, the way you see best, and that's all right by me.'

I began to see he was really making his peace with his own version of me; and there was nothing to be done but let him make it.

'It worries your mother, of course,' he added. 'She'd like to see you getting ahead with university, and improving yourself. But I say you've got to have your head. She might see that in time too. But do your best to keep her happy meantime.'

We were on difficult ground. But I had a distraction in hand. 'Talking about your old friends,' I said, 'I brought one along with me.'

That stopped him. He stood blinking.

'A friend of your youth,' I explained. 'Charlie Higgins. He's put up down in the town for the night, hoping to see you. I'm driving him back to the city tomorrow.'

He couldn't accept it.

'Charlie Higgins?' he said. 'This is not some joke?'

'He's no joke. Not now. And he wants to see you, very much. I wouldn't know why. But I daresay he has some reason of his own. He's old, for one thing.'

He still looked at me with total lack of comprehension.

'But why should that respectable old phoney – ' he began, and shook his head. 'And why should you – '

He was quite incapable of completing a sentence.

'Never mind,' he said at length. 'All right, I'll see him. I'll see the old bugger. But Christ knows what we'll have to say.'

Yet he seemed to be accepting the idea, even warming to it.

'In town?' he added. 'Well, why don't you go and fetch him?' He showed sudden impatience with me. 'You didn't need to leave him sitting there.'

'It was just that I thought you mightn't want to see him. And he thought the same.'

'And yet he came all this way, in case?'

'Yes.'

'Well, go and get him. Quick.'

It didn't take me long to drive back into town and find Charlie Higgins sitting bleakly in the parlour of his private hotel, between pots of maidenhair fern, a magazine long out

417

of date in his hands. There was relief in his eyes as I approached him and spoke; his gratitude was pathetic.

'And he really does want to see me?'

'Yes. I just said so.'

He evidently found some things difficult to believe too. He rose heavily, with a slight sigh, and I escorted him out to the car, and drove him to my father. At least to the front gate; my father was advancing slowly down the path. Charlie Higgins opened his door, slid out of the car slowly, and then rose erect to face him. They both hesitated for a moment, gazing at each other as if without recognition, and then closed with each other swiftly; and shook hands. I preferred, in a way, not to hear what was said; I occupied myself parking the car safely. Anyway I had become unnecessary now.

They were talking, smiling: I could see that much. And see enough.

They were turning, walking back up to the house, between beds of bright flowers. My father had even dropped an arm over Charlie Higgins' shoulder. It was almost too ordinary a scene to imagine: two elderly men walking in a sunny day. There were trees around, and the grass was shiny with spring. And the birdsong was agreeably dense. Two elderly men walking. I tried to imagine them once outcast, once in prison together; it was ludicrous. I tried to imagine them as two names which once made a country tremble; even more ludicrous. The hills, the houses, were so indifferent around; the land was so quiet. And the two old men seemed to grow small.

I followed them up the path as they made their peace together. I appeared, in my fashion, to be making my own. I might have been following them down a suddenly quiet street where broken banners and a buckled policeman's helmet lay.

I had the afternoon with Diane; that was a pleasant prospect. 'I expect you want to go to the football,' she said amiably.

I thought about that. I would almost certainly see one or two of the Saunders boys there, perhaps Margaret too.

'I don't know,' I said finally. 'Perhaps I can do without football now.'

Her surprise was plain. 'You have changed,' she said.

'It's too good an afternoon to waste sitting still,' I observed. 'Perhaps we can take a drive somewhere. Since I have a car.'

She was altogether delighted, restless from the moment I

made the suggestion. She raced about the house preparing a basket of food and drink to take in the car. My mother, meanwhile, appeared occupied with her guest: Charlie Higgins sat on the verandah with my father in the mild noon sun. Diane and I were hardly noticed as we left the house and drove away.

'Where to?' she asked gaily.

'Let's just drive and find where.'

We slipped across the river, through the town. Most traffic was headed towards the football ground; we left it behind, and soon were in open country. Diane continued to offer bright words beside me.

'I didn't think you were ever going to come back,' she said suddenly. 'Ever.'

'Would that have been so terrible?'

'Yes,' she announced. 'For me.'

'Why?'

'Because you're my brother.' She paused. 'And,' she added, with terrifying ease, 'because I love you.'

I was ill-equipped to cope. The countryside divided before the windscreen. Farmhouses, farms, hedges, grazing cattle and sheep. Hills on each side growing taller. There was still a splendid sparkle in the day.

'Listen,' I said slowly, 'it would be a good idea if you didn't depend on me. Not too much. You understand?'

'No,' she answered resolutely. 'I don't.'

It was no use. She didn't want to hear a thing. She simply smiled as if deaf, and blind.

'You'll do wonderful things,' she insisted. 'I know.'

That was even more terrifying, in its way. She spoke with such absurd assurance for her sixteen years. I would have preferred my father's expectation, anyone's.

'Leave me alone,' I said sharply. More sharply than I meant.

She sat quiet, perhaps wounded, for a mile or two. The countryside was changing. The land was growing steeper, with bony ridges, on each side of the road. I should soon have to decide where we were going.

'I suppose you've had girl friends in the city?' she said.

'Yes,' I conceded. 'One or two.'

'And you've gone to bed with them, I expect. That kind of thing.'

'That kind of thing,' I agreed. 'Look, does it matter – '

'What's it like, then?'

419

'Do you have to know?'

'Yes.' She paused and took a deep breath. 'Because you're my brother. And I want to know you.'

'Then it would be better if you didn't. If you didn't know me. Let's forget it.'

It wasn't meant to be cruel; but it must have been. She was silenced again.

We had arrived somewhere, anyway. We had arrived near the end of the Waiatarua valley. I should have acknowledged the direction earlier. And might have without Diane distracting. For there couldn't have been any doubt of the direction from the beginning. Ahead was wild country; and a single narrow road through a limestone gorge. On the other side of that gorge was the Livingstone farm; I had never seen it, but I had found my way towards it easily enough. And it wasn't too late to turn back.

I drove into the gorge, nevertheless, and parked the car by the side of the river. Diane revived instantly. 'Lovely,' she laughed. 'I've never been here before.' She escaped the car, kicked off her shoes, and ran barefoot to the water's edge. I followed slowly. She was paddling ankle-deep in the swift river. The trees around were vivid with spring, and the unfurling ferns; the gorge was filled with sunlight and the sound of the river.

It was all so unexpected and improbable; the rest of the world was lost. And my sister, a child again, was calling me to explore.

('You do remember that afternoon, don't you?' Diane said eighteen years later.

'What afternoon?'

'The afternoon you were home. And we went exploring. Up through that gorge, and over the other side. I think of it, sometimes, as the nicest day I ever had, as a child. I don't even remember just where the place was, or how we got there. It was something all by itself. Surely you – '

'Of course I remember.'

'I hoped so.'

Her twins, a plump boy and plumper girl, came squealing into the kitchen, announcing hunger and thirst. Diane disposed of them without effort. Soon they were outside again, their sound subdued.

420

Diane, however, continued to stand in the centre of the kitchen; there was a baffled look on her face. 'What was it we were talking about?' she asked.)

We left the river's steep edge and began to climb. The dense vegetation made the journey slow; we paused often to rest. Diane refused to be detached from her basket. After perhaps an hour we left thicker bush behind, and emerged in a high place, a limestone plateau, deeply weathered and broken, where only tough-rooted scrub grew. It was quite warm up there; the day was windless. In one direction we could see all the way back to Te Ika, across farmland. In another, hills and bush blocked any distant view. In the third, we could see an isolated farm, in the valley beyond the gorge, its pale pastures chipped into the dark bush; there was a farmhouse among trees. It was possibly mid-afternoon, and the valley was still sunlit, though some of the hills were taking shadow; there was a sparkle of water at one boundary of the farm, and giant willow trees. Another boundary approached the plateau where we rested, but the margin was scruffy with scrub; it was hard to tell where the farm ended and the bush began. I glimpsed, in one shrunken clearing, a fallen fence.

There was a slender road into the farm: it ended among trees at the farmhouse. The lower ground, near the creek, was spotted with grazing cattle. There was no other movement; no other evident life.

As if the place could tell me anything, anyway. But my eyes continued to search.

Diane, having got her breath, and sampled all the views available, was emptying her basket; and uncapping a thermos flask of tea.

I felt immensely lazy in the warm sun. And peaceful.

'Here's luxury,' Diane said. 'Sandwiches from my own fair hands.' She paused. 'Have you been very lonely in the city?'

'Did I say I had?'

'No. But I expected you might be.'

'I've one or two friends. More than one or two now.'

I would, though, have found it difficult explaining them to Diane; it was difficult enough, sometimes, explaining them to myself.

'At least I won't be lonely, when I get to the city,' she observed. 'Because you'll be there.'

'You mustn't count on me. I told you that.'

'Oh, but I do. I will. That way I'll make sure, you see.'

She offered a shy smile. She couldn't lose, in her way. I'd doubtless be there, if she wanted me. And so, in all likelihood, would a great many others.

My eyes wandered over the solitary farm again, the hills and bush looped tight around. True, there was a road out. But that didn't do more than announce its own nature. I tried at last to imagine Tim Livingstone down there, but the effort was too great. I gave up; and gave in to the day, to Diane.

'I'm happy here,' she said. 'Aren't you?'

'I expect I am,' I conceded.

'Then say you love me,' she went on.

'I love you.' It was easy enough to say.

She sighed. 'That's all right, then. That's all I want to hear.' She paused and added, 'You can go off to sleep now, if you like.'

I'd certainly grown drowsy, bedded on the warm limestone. My eyes fell shut. Then there was a slight, unmistakable kiss on my cheek; and the sound of fleeing feet. Before I could say anything, Diane was gone. I didn't doubt she would be back again. I slept.

When I woke, most of the afternoon had slipped away. The sun was low, nearing the hills; and Diane was standing above me with some wild clematis freshly gathered from the bush. 'I walked miles to find this,' she said. 'All around the edge of the farm down there. And I found it, in the end. Shall we go home now?'

'I seem to be ready,' I said. But I rose with reluctance.

'A funny little farm,' she said, 'with a funny little man.'

'You saw someone, then?'

'I just told you. A funny little old man. Like a shrivelled-up gnome. He came across the paddocks to me. I was a bit frightened, he looked so queer. He seemed to own the place. He had a rifle. Perhaps he was just shooting rabbits, but I thought he might shoot me. For just a minute. But he was all right, really.'

'What did he say?'

'Not very much. Just that I was trespassing, but that he couldn't take offence at a pretty girl who trespassed. I thought he was sweet, in the end. When I told him I was just looking for flowers, he told me where to go. He said his wife and boy used to pick them there once. But I didn't see any wife or boy

422

around. I didn't see anyone. I think he's all alone. He stood there watching me until I left the place. And he waved goodbye.'

'Just think,' I said, 'you probably made his day.'

Though I preferred not to think. At least not for long. It was the nearest I came to Tim Livingstone's father.

We left the plateau and descended through the bush, back into the gorge. Diane's pale dress flashed ahead of me, rippling beyond the thick foliage; she was always yards ahead. And soon there was the sound of the river again. The sun had withdrawn from the gorge. We met the first chill of evening.

In the morning my mother had me to herself for a few minutes. Charlie Higgins had been altogether successful as a distraction; she'd hardly had a chance to talk to me at all. She revealed, in passing, that she and my father were thinking of leaving Te Ika, with his retirement near; she mentioned a seaside place nearer the city.

'But you've been here so long,' I began to protest.

'We never meant to come,' she explained, 'and we never meant to stay. But we did, mainly because of you and Diane. And because there seemed nowhere else for us then. Now you've gone, and Diane will be going soon. And it will be better for her if we're closer. A girl doesn't make her way in the city as easily as a boy. You haven't told us much about yourself yet. About university.'

'There's not much to say.' I stood up; we had, until then, been reasonably relaxed at the kitchen table. 'I really should go around to see Mary Leary before I leave.'

'Well, you won't see her this morning. She's ill, in hospital. And at the moment she probably wouldn't know you if you came. She's under drugs. Your father and I visit.'

'You should have said.'

'You were so busy with Diane yesterday.'

'She's dying, then?'

'Yes. I expect she is.' She spoke with extreme control.

'Poor Mary.' I couldn't believe it.

'I'll give her your love. Sometimes she understands what we're saying. And I'll say you wanted to visit, and didn't have a chance.'

'I wish you'd said earlier.'

'Mary has always been a great strength to us. To your father particularly.'

'I know.' It had taken me years to understand.

'Without her, we might never have managed here. She had patience with your father when I hadn't. When I had you on my mind, and Diane. It hurt me, of course, when I saw how close they had grown. It hurt me a great deal. But I learned to live with it – the hurt, I mean. And it was all right in the end. There might have been much worse than Mary; and no one ever had a larger heart.'

'I could at least have tried to see her yesterday.'

'Diane needed you more. You can't do anything for Mary now, but you can do a lot for Diane. She misses you. You could write to her, and us, more often.'

'I will,' I promised.

'You've made your father happy this weekend. That's the other good thing you've done. I expected you might be charging off, the moment you got here, to see old friends. Instead you've been with your family all the time.'

'There was no one I particularly wanted to see, except Mary. And it seems I can't see her. With her dying, and you leaving, I probably won't want to see this place again, or anyone here.'

'Well,' she said, 'there's the Saunders family. I expected you might go out to visit them, at least. Margaret's back, by the way. I don't suppose you saw anything of her in the city?'

'Why?'

'Just that I remember you went out with her once or twice. Anyway she didn't last long in the city. And she sounds quite a brave girl.'

'How?'

'The way she's kept her child, despite the town.'

'She's what?'

'She's kept her child. She came home, you see, to have a baby.'

I hardly looked at Te Ika as I drove out of it; I didn't have the heart for a silent farewell. The houses flowed behind, the river and the riverbank, the shops and churches; and Charlie Higgins was quiet beside me. Soon there was just the open highway, aimed straight at the city, and mild and mellow countryside. The heartland hills, which had framed my childhood, shrank quickly behind.

Charlie Higgins began gently to snore beside me. I tried to consider the city ahead, and other things.

I would have to tell Tim, of course. I didn't doubt that I

424

should. And how would he react? Indeed how would I react, myself, if told I had a child, back there, in Te Ika? I could only assume that conscience, or something like it, would sooner or later twist my life out of its present shape. Shape? Out of its present shapelessness, then. And perhaps give shape, where there had been none.

I remembered Margaret out of the rain. There was no doubt, now, what she had wanted to tell me. But what more might she have wanted?

Then it struck me that I wouldn't be bringing news at all. If she had known, then, he must also have known why she had gone home to Te Ika. That was plainly why he didn't like mention of Margaret. I had assumed the sensitivity was mine alone. Now I saw his conscience at work. It explained his indifference at times, his apparent apathy.

The best thing would be to use my knowledge gently. Just tell him I knew, no more. And watch carefully for reaction, if there was any. I would tell him as soon as I got back, as soon as I saw him, in the first minutes.

The highway seemed to be sucking us, faster and faster, into the city. The day darkened as I drove; rain flecked the windscreen. Soon there were the city lights, from a distance. I could feel something near affection for the place after all.

Charlie Higgins revived, and began to talk in a rambling way about my father when he was young. 'When I first met him after the war, he didn't seem to know where he was going,' he said. 'That was after his first time in prison. Never knew where he was going. I suppose I was the one who put him right. Or wrong. God knows. I don't know myself now. All I know is that man's wasted himself, or been wasted. All those years in that town. What's it add up to?'

'It adds up to raising a family,' I suggested. 'For one thing.'

'I suppose it does,' he agreed. 'But all the same – that town, all those years. A leader of men. Can't you see what I mean?'

'Up to a point,' I said.

'He walked out on me,' he went on. 'In the old days. Or I walked out on him. I've never been sure which. We both thought we were doing the right thing. But it turns out we never knew any bloody thing.'

'I wouldn't say that.' But, if it came to a point, I wasn't at all sure what I would say.

'Things seemed possible, in this country, when we were

young.' He paused. 'But of course you wouldn't understand that.'

'No,' I agreed. 'Possibly not.'

I began to feel tired. The weight of the weekend, perhaps.

'People were starting again,' he explained. 'At this end of the world. That was why things seemed possible. Of course it was a dream. All just a bloody dream. I woke up too late. All those years in politics. I learned nothing. I only had time to think about playing my cards right. I never had time to think about what I was playing my cards for. And now I got nothing. No wife, no kids. And no answers. I don't know what it was all for.'

'I thought it was for people.'

'Then I don't really give a damn about people any more,' he said. 'Perhaps that's it. I think I might even hate them. Ungrateful bastards. When I think of what we went through to make their lives decent. Who cares, now? No one.'

He soon subsided, however.

'All the same,' he finished, as I drove through the city, 'I'm glad to have met your father again. Something seems to make sense after all. Even if it's just that young men grow old. Never mind. Thanks for taking me to see him. And,' he added, when I dropped him at his door, 'I'm glad to have met you. A young, fresh fellow like you seems to make some of it worthwhile. Your father's been lucky.'

The responsibility was too great; I felt more suffocated than ever. I watched him walk away up his path in the suburbs, an old man, and alone, and wondered if I could really have said anything to cheer him. Then, with a certain sense of liberation, I turned the car in the direction of my flat; or mine and Tim's.

Actually I had reason to doubt my possession of the place at all when I arrived.

The change was incredible; the change was everywhere. It was difficult to believe that I was only two days gone. It could have been two years. There was little enough sign of the place I knew. It wasn't just the reorganization of the flat, the displacement of furniture, the transposition of bookshelves and beds; I could, perhaps, have accepted most of that with small shock, and adjusted quickly enough. It was the paintings most of all, the paintings I had never seen before, the paintings broken out of their parcels and spreading everywhere; the place, after

426

all, seemed to hold little else worth attention. Some were hung, jammed tight against each other, and others were casually propped against furniture. I was completely checked at the door; I had, for a start, to be careful where I put my feet. Tim stood at the centre of the room. He had moved the table there; and buried it beneath sheets of stained newspaper, boards, bottles, brushes and tubes of paint. An amazing clutter, really; I had never seen its like.

I said, 'What's happened?' Or something equally idiotic.

'I got going again, while you were away,' he explained. His cheerfulness was quite disarming; his hands were black with paint; it was also vivid, patchily, in his fair hair, and spotty on his clothes and bare arms. I had seldom seen his arms bared before; they were badly scarred, presumably like the rest of his body. 'I just got going again. That's all.'

'I can see that.'

But I wasn't sure what I was seeing; not yet. The paintings resisted immediate impression. The room certainly hadn't filled with colour, but little else was obvious. The first effect, if anything, was gloom. But a considerable gloom, hard, very precise. Everything was edges. And some of the edges seemed sharp enough to cut. At first these looming shapes had little more than themselves to tell me. Their real surprise was in their context. In that place; and on that evening.

I found my way, by degrees, to an uncluttered chair. Possibly I felt dismay; possibly I had been expecting an easier homecoming, one much less demanding, in a place grown familiar. But it was still hard to tell just what I felt. I might have been too tired to feel much at all.

Tim made a gesture towards cleaning his hands, with a dirty rag. Then he lit a cigarette. 'I'll clear the lot away, if you like,' he said pleasantly. 'I mean, if it's a bit much to take. I really intended to do something about the mess, at least, before you arrived back. It seems I got carried away. But as for the paintings – if you can't take them, you only have to say so.'

'No,' I said, without great conviction. 'It's all right.'

'It's just I needed a look at them again, to see where I was. I haven't been sure.'

'Fair enough.' This was probably inadequate too.

'You're to blame, in a way,' he observed.

'Oh?' I tried to imagine how. It was difficult.

'You going back down there. I expect that had something to

do with triggering me off, one way or another. And Monty. Monty Nolan.'

'What's Monty got to do with it?'

'I was visiting him in prison, remember?'

I'd forgotten. Tim had been getting dressed to visit the prison at the same time as I was leaving for Te Ika; we'd both been in a rush and had hardly spoken.

'How was he?'

'All right. Cheerful. Or pretending to be. He seemed glad to see me anyway. I must take you along to see him too.'

'What's Monty got to do with all this, though?'

'Well, just that I suggested he might like to take up painting in prison, as a way of passing the time. When I got home I rustled out some paints and brushes and other gear to drop into the prison for him.'

'So?' It still didn't make sense, quite.

'So I sat here with this gear, and must have started brooding. About how I could start Monty off. And after seeing Monty I felt like company. The place was so bloody quiet with you gone. Then I started thinking about where you had gone. It hadn't really registered. I thought about how you might feel, back there. That was about it. The next thing I knew, I had paintings everywhere. And they looked better than I remembered, but still not good enough. So then there was nothing else for it. I got started again. With the gear I dug up for Monty.'

'I see.' Perhaps I was starting to.

'I suppose the idea was to produce something good enough. But I need more time. I can't do it in a weekend.'

'You mean you've been going all weekend? What happened to Saturday night?'

'There were some knocks on the door, late. I heard Ken's voice, and Sandy's. But I didn't answer.'

'I suppose I'm another interruption.'

'You're all right,' he said graciously. 'I'm used to you around. Besides, this place is yours, after all. And I've pretty well done my dash. Perhaps I'll have another try tomorrow. You look done in. Can I make you a cup of tea?'

'That would go well.' I began to see the real change wasn't so much in the place itself, but in Tim. Since I'd met him in the strike, and since he had come to share the flat, his apathy had been something I could easily share myself. But now he seemed entirely alert, his eyes brighter. And there was a certain

428

fresh and jaunty arrogance too. He was himself again, or near enough. Perhaps that was it.

'If you want me to toss the paintings out,' he said, as he made the tea, 'you only have to say. It's your place.'

He appeared determined to remind me of this. Perhaps he'd selected a frontal attack as most likely of success, in getting his own way. And naturally he would. He couldn't have caught me weaker.

Anyway I was starting to look at the paintings, for the first time. They had begun to separate sufficiently for me to see them as individual things, though I still couldn't resist total impression. It had taken me some time to realize that the paintings were not, after all, abstractions. They were landscapes, more or less. But landscapes of dream as much as of the world. Here a chipped hill, quite stark. There mountains like muscles. A glimpse of wandering river. A flow of bleak bush. An angrily eroded valley. Then the waterfalls; it took me time to see the waterfalls, still longer to feel them. They recurred in painting after painting. Just slight ribbons, sometimes slender to vanishing point, or tangling trembles of pale paint. Then I became aware of light. Feeble here, luminous there, and most often just gentle incandescence. But I did begin to see that one had to accept the dark first, to find the light, and feel its presence.

Finally I was looking not at the paintings, but at Tim. And looking at him as if I didn't know him at all. He was standing before me with a cup of tea, and a thickly cut sandwich.

'Get this into you,' he said. 'You'll feel better.'

He was being very gentle with me, everything considered. Possibly that was a tactic too. But I was prepared not to care. I might have been as much tired as receptive.

'You're not obliged to like this stuff, you know,' he added. 'Or pretend you do. Or any damn thing at all. It's all the same to me. Whether you like it, whether you don't. Whether you want to throw it all out, whether you don't. It's all the same.'

I knew then that it wasn't. Did he protest too much? Anyway it seemed I was on test. It wasn't just a question of him using my flat, my life, or anything else. He had to have me care too, after all. Why me? Perhaps I just happened to be around.

'Give me time,' I said. 'I might get used to it.'

There didn't seem much else I could say.

'I'll tell you something,' he went on. 'You're the first person

429

to have seen any of this. It's all new. Different from anything I've done before. I don't know whether it's any good either, but this time it's my own.'

'Yes,' I said. 'I suppose I can see that.'

Or at least it was beginning to seem impossible that the work should belong to anyone else. But it was, all the same, difficult to connect with those gentle rural watercolours which perhaps still looked down on crude and sweaty schoolboys.

'So,' he was saying, 'it doesn't matter whether you like it. It's a question of whether you can put up with it around you.'

'Or put up with you.'

'Or put up with me,' he agreed.

'I think I can put up with you,' I observed. 'I have so far. It hasn't been too difficult. And if I can put up with you, I don't see why I can't put up with your work. So long as I have some space for myself.'

'I was about to start cleaning up the mess. Sorry. It's just that the weekend ran away with me.'

'All right, then. I don't see that we need to talk about it any more. Though I would like to talk to you about your work, sometime, when I'm less tired.'

'That shouldn't be a big problem,' he said, as he went to the table and began clearing it, 'since there's not too much I can say. Just that I paint this way and not another way. That's about all.'

'Fair enough.'

'Don't drain your brain on my account. It's my problem, not yours. You've got your own.'

'Meaning?'

'Meaning you don't seem to know where the hell you are. Or who. It's your problem. Not mine. If you want my advice, you probably won't get it. Advice ends too many friendships.'

It was interesting to hear him at last define our relationship, and perhaps its limits, since neither of us had before, or found it necessary: we still seemed, chance met, together for mutual convenience. Otherwise he had no news.

I looked at his painting again; and saw more in one way, less in another. Whatever it was, good or bad or indifferent, obscure or lucid or both, it continued to insist on attention. And respect, on that account.

In any case there was no evading it now.

Before I went to bed I asked if he was planning to exhibit the work soon.

'I'm still thinking about it,' he explained. 'Trying to make up my mind whether it's worthwhile. If I do, you see, it might only be to prove to some people that I haven't quit. And I can't think of a worse reason. What I really have to do is invent a better reason. If there is one.' His tone was acid. 'You can always fool other people. So long as you don't fool yourself.'

'Why should you want to fool other people?' I asked, faintly puzzled.

'Because other people bring out the worst in me, I expect.'

'Then who brings out the best in you? Like all this, for example. Your work. Who brings that out?'

The question seemed to take him off guard. He appeared, as he looked around the room at his own handiwork, to be trying to make up his mind about something, testing adequate answers. After a time he just shrugged.

'Other people too, I expect.'

I supposed it some kind of concession: I didn't at the time see it, and couldn't have seen it, as particularly potent truth.

'Well, time for sleep,' I said.

Much later that night, too late, while Tim slept and I lay sleepless, I remembered that I hadn't mentioned Margaret. I wondered if I ever would.

431

Twenty-one

Documents

... With that preliminary over, let it be said that the exhibition of new paintings by Tim Livingstone at present hung in this murky mid-city gallery represents his best work yet. It is not to be expected that more than a handful of citizens will see his work; and buyers so far have been conspicuous by their absence. Doubtless, of those who genuinely come to see, as many will be repelled as attracted by this talented young artist's view of his native land. But of those who come to jeer, many may yet stay to cheer. Livingstone offers us not the saccharine views of the tourist-poster painters, in fact nothing sweet or cosy or comforting at all. He offers challenge. He offers us a land of heroic proportion, if we care to see. But do we care to see? Will we ever see? Let's beat it back to the suburbs, and sleep easy.

     – Signed review by Ken McAdam, university newspaper

....Sometimes, the less than casual visitor may feel landscape has never really been painted here or anywhere before. Whatever their possible peripheral failings, the paintings offer something new. Whether many will see that is open to question. Most will be puzzled at first. But those who are patient with this young artist could find considerable reward.

     – Unsigned newspaper review, written by Ian Freeman

... Ugliness. And more ugliness. Truth is beauty, said Keats, and beauty truth. There is no truth and no beauty in this grubby show. One wonders about the motives of this young painter, still more about the motives of those who encourage him. This is diseased art, a calculated insult to this country.

     – Unsigned newspaper review, author unknown

... How can your reviewer style this an exhibition? This obscure and witless shambles? There is no respect for paint, or for craft, in the work of Mr T. Livingstone. There is nothing at all for the genuine art-lovers of this country. Give a lunatic a paint-brush. ...

       – From prolonged newspaper correspondence

CONTROVERSIAL PAINTINGS DAMAGED: POLICE INQUIRIES

         – Newspaper headline

       Avarua P.O.
       Rarotonga
       Cook Islands
       December 2, 1966

Dear Max Kennedy,

You seem to be encountering the difficulties I anticipated with your project. It's not to be expected that people would have clear memories after this length of time. I really didn't suppose you were likely to get any help from Paul Wiseman, for example; but I did think that Ken McAdam might reply. Appalling to hear about Sandy West being blown up in a Viet Cong ambush. I seldom see newspapers here, of course. I'm glad that Stan Coates was at least amiable in being unhelpful. Possibly he was suspicious, and didn't quite see what you were after; Stan, after all, has a past to outlive and he may not have cared for reminders of wild youth (which actually was staid enough, from this perspective). There is one other person I neglected to mention – Charlie Bates, a mad young architect once fired out of university for something of obscene design, as I remember. He may still be about, possibly still unqualified. I haven't heard anything of Charlie in years. Track him down, assuming he is still about, and you might find he has something to say.

Yes, that exhibition was something of a cause célèbre – it seemed considerable to us at the time, however tiny a tempest it seems from this distance. We did our best, one way and an-other, to stand by Livingstone. And our best possibly didn't amount to much. Possibly the trouble was that we didn't alto-gether know what to make of Livingstone ourselves. But some-one had to defend him, since no one else would. People con-ventionally avante-garde in their taste, for example, had in the past resisted philistine attack on exhibitions derivative of outside fashion. Confronted with something reasonably native-grown, they allowed the philistines a field day and even joined in the hunt themselves. The apparent crudeness of his paintings resisted easy labels, and quick defence. Perhaps the point is that his work offered itself up to be put down. Does that make sense?

The damage to his paintings was a final touch. The police never laid a charge.

How did all this affect him? Terrible to admit, since I perhaps came closer to him than most, but I never knew. I never knew how much.

Perhaps his life – or apparent absence of life – is the only reply you're likely to get.

But I wouldn't draw quick conclusion from that either.

I must say I admire your persistence. You must have been tempted to let the whole thing go.

Best wishes.
Yours sincerely,
Ian Freeman

Avarua P.O.
Rarotonga
Cook Islands
January 15, 1967

Dear Ben,

Yes, it looks as if I might have done my dash here. The sweetness is melting away. And the world seems to be moving closer. No escape after all. The big new preoccupation here is the French nuclear testing, and how much radiation the islands can safely absorb. Even the exciting prospect of a big new airport, of size for jumbo jets, tourist laden, becomes secondary.

Alas the last dream, one way or the other.

Ina – I think I mentioned her earlier – was unusually soulful last night. I asked the trouble. 'You're becoming damn *papaa* (European) again,' she announced. 'You've gone away.'

Note: gone away. Not going, or about to go. Gone away already. Another damn *papaa* after all. They never come back, though they promise to.

Incidentally the origin of the word *papaa* is intriguing. Literally it means 'four layers': don't ask me, though, why such a word was originally necessary. And the word was used to describe the early European voyagers here – the locals were astonished to find Europeans capable of burying themselves within four layers of clothing. A wild kind of magic, or lunacy.

Anyway : four layers. The name still stands even for such belated voyagers as myself. And Ina I suppose has had reason to think me freed. So actually, for too short a time, have I. Perhaps I did shed two or three layers, but never four.

Did I tell you the place to learn the *tamure* was not on a dance floor, or within some firelit circle of beating drums and clapping hands, but in bed? In bed or, better still, in some quiet place by a lagoon? Never mind : another irrelevance.

Our friend Max Kennedy still hasn't given up. I find it an increasingly immense effort to reply to his letters. I usually put them aside in hope that they will go away. They never do. Perhaps that is where the blight has begun.

So this is to tell you I've started to think about a ship out. Any month now. I'd better confess to Ina soon. But I don't think she'll be in the least surprised.

Come to think, I doubt if you will be either.

Very best,

Ian

Commentaries

I never mentioned Margaret or her child. The occasion never came. Besides, I didn't doubt he knew. And there was no point in twisting knife in the wound, if there was one. Or actually wounding, if there wasn't. He had his own life. And I had mine, though I sometimes wondered.

The paintings multiplied. And our flat could only hold so many.

'Perhaps I will have to exhibit soon,' he announced. 'Even if it's just to make more space here. On the other hand, if I don't sell anything, where will we be? Perhaps we can have a bloody great bonfire.'

'Don't be ridiculous.'

'Well, what can I do? Send them back to the farm?'

'You could do worse. They'd be safe.'

'You're joking, of course.'

'As much as you're joking about the bonfire. And I don't think you are.'

The physical problem was very real : to the point of being absurd. He lent out work to people whose lives, and rooms,

435

could contain it. To less itinerant people like Ken McAdam, say. But such relief was only temporary; the new space in the flat would soon begin to diminish, with fresh work. His pace was sometimes frantic.

Some months we hardly talked at all. Other months we found ourselves still talking at three or four in the morning. Sometimes the talk concerned his work, but as often it concerned our separate childhoods in and around Te Ika. Sooner or later everything was said about most things. At least we had hills in common, and rivers.

His other friendships seemed soon to become backdrop to our own. Like mine, perhaps, with Stan Coates. Though Stan would not easily abandon me as a lost cause. He made it clear he thought my friendship with Tim a profound mistake, and implied it was something I would get over, in time. Now the strike was receding into the past he again found little use for Tim. 'Ratty, and no sense of responsibility,' was how he put Tim down. 'He'll have you running in the same shrinking circles. You're bright enough to see that, surely. And bright enough to see he's making use of you.'

'Perhaps I don't mind being made use of,' I suggested.

'God help us all. It's one thing to be an innocent, another to know you are.'

'Besides,' I added, picking words carefully, 'I'm beginning to think he's worthwhile. His work, at least.'

'Then you're under the spell too,' he said. 'Another one. I've seen them come and go. Ted Connolly was first, by all accounts. Now it's your turn, it seems.'

'You forget we knew each other as kids.'

'That hasn't seemed very important to you before. And, as I recall it, he celebrated your first encounter in the city by stealing your girl.'

'I was asking for that, or something like it. Or she was. Anyway it doesn't matter now.'

I could, in fact, feel only a very slight twinge. If anything at all.

'What happened to her, anyway?' Stan said.

'She drifted off,' I replied vaguely. 'Probably back home again. I don't really know.'

'Pity,' Stan said. 'I might have done myself some good there. Shocking waste.'

436

'Look, Stan,' I said patiently, 'would you like me to see if I can put you in touch with her? How would that be?'

'No,' he answered quickly. 'I've got too much on my plate at the moment. Thanks all the same.'

His reaction was reasonably predictable; I'd called his bluff. And now felt sorry for it. Stan could be too naked. Our eyes no longer met, though mine were ready.

'So what's new?' I asked.

That helped him. 'The class struggle is never new,' he replied, 'however much people like you choose to ignore it. There's a regrouping of forces going on at the moment, a revision of policy.'

He talked cheerfully for half an hour. And, at the end, resumed his central theme. 'Just remember what I say. Livingstone's doing you no good. And he won't do you any good. Are you with me? I wish you'd damn well listen.'

It was difficult not to smile. He made it appear that Tim and I spent our time together plotting orgies, each bigger and better than the last. It would have sounded almost as absurd if I attempted to explain how tame most of our evenings were. That is, when Tim was working, which then seemed most of the time.

His father I soon began to imagine, to the point where he sometimes became as vivid as my own.

'You've seen our farm?' he once asked.

I admitted I had. But didn't say when.

'What do you think of it?'

'Lonely.'

'Lonely, all right. And damn near buried under those hills. Though the sun usually managed to climb over them. Sometimes enough to clean all the shadow away. But it's the late light I remember best now, when the shadows thickened. And sharpened. You just got the glow on the ridges between. They seemed to become something else altogether, the ridges.'

He appeared to be considering just what they became. I saw slender slips of light. And then other things, if I tried. Perhaps that was the point. I had to try. He didn't.

'Anyway,' he added, 'interesting. The forms, I mean.'

'I thought we were talking about the farm itself.'

'We are,' he said. 'More or less. I'm just trying to give you some eyes to see with. That's all. You don't have to be blind. It's your own choice.'

437

Which might have been Stan Coates talking. But I had the feeling that he wasn't so much giving me eyes as exercising his own. I was useful provocation.

I began to see, all right, if not altogether in the way he meant.

'So,' I said, 'the farm. You obviously can't forget it.'

'I only have to shut my eyes,' he insisted. 'And sometimes not even that.'

I could believe it.

'And I'll own it one day,' he added. 'I don't forget that either.'

The idea was new to me; and difficult to take.

'I suppose you'll sell it up.'

'I suppose I will,' he agreed. 'Though it's hard to imagine. And anyway, who knows? I might need somewhere to hide. For Christ's sake, let's forget it. I don't even know how we got started.'

I had a fair idea. But if he wanted a hurt to finger, that was his own business. Sometimes, when we talked, I was more than usually aware of the ragged blue scar up his throat. I wished I'd actually met his father. He seemed, in my imagination, as crude and craggy as his own land. Not at all the shrivelled gnome of Diane's report.

He continued to paint. Our lives were without large event. Often, on Saturdays, we visited Monty Nolan in prison. Monty was brighter, and more interested in himself, since he'd begun drawing and painting under Tim's instruction. His first work was rough, but he had a certain gift. He composed colourful fancies of the outside world, with flowers, trees, birds and cottages. And showed the result with pride.

'All very sweet,' Tim said curtly. 'But where've you gone, Monty?'

'I'm here. Four years, that bastard said. I'm gone four years, remember? What's it like out there anyway? Does the sun still shine? Do people still play football? You tell me your news and I'll tell you mine. Mine isn't much. Just that last night I saw the biggest fucking rat I ever seen in my cell. A man-eater. Jesus Christ, I was still shaking with fright an hour after I killed it. The bastard could of done for me. I'm not joking.'

We had no reason to disbelieve him. The flowers and trees, and bright birds, appeared even more wistful.

'How did you kill it?' Tim asked coolly.

'With the only thing I had handy. My bucket. I brained

the bastard. He didn't come back for more. But you could say I sent the shit flying. The cell still stinks.'

'Well, that's where you are, then. That's what I want you to paint.'

'What? A fucking great rat? You're having me on, boy.'

'These paintings' – Tim indicated the work Monty had produced – 'aren't telling us anything about where you are. You're not there at all.'

I would have disputed that myself, but still: Tim knew, or was supposed to know. I kept quiet, though the colours in Monty's work seemed all the richer; there was no smell of excrement in those sparkling scenes.

'You better tell me what you're talking about,' Monty said, plainly puzzled. 'This is no place for painting, in here. You don't seem to see.'

'I'm trying to see,' Tim said patiently. 'Tell me about inside. Tell me about your cell.'

'What do you want to know? I got four walls. Solid brick. A door; it's mostly locked. A table. A chair. A bed. A window.'

'Tell me about the window.'

'It's got bars. Two ways. Up and down. And across.'

'But it lets the light in?'

'That's the idea. But I can tell you it would let a lot more fucking light in if I filed the bars away. Not that I'd still be around to appreciate it. You got any ideas about a file? Right now I'd sooner have a file than a paint-brush, I don't mind telling you.'

Monty didn't appear concerned, much, about the warder watching us. The man remained with a blank face. Doubtless, if he had heard, he had heard it before. And would hear it again.

'Look, Monty, I want you to think about those bars.'

'Jesus Christ, I give them enough thinking already. I spent a lot of time studying those bastard things. By now I even got their weak places figured out. I reckon I could even manage with a knife, if it had a decent edge. With a clear run, I could do it in a day.'

'I mean I'd like you to draw them. At different times of the day. I'd like you to draw them for me. Really to look at them, then draw them.'

Monty looked stunned. 'Next thing' – he nodded towards the

439

watching warder – 'you'll be asking me to draw that bastard of a screw there, with his bunch of keys.'

'Well,' Tim conceded, 'you could do worse.'

'Fuck me,' Monty said. 'Now I heard everything. You know what we call that fat cunt? Rosy. He gets his shine from the kids in here. A virgin a month. That's old Rosy's reputation.'

Rosy, if he heard, remained impassive.

'Like your picture painted, Rosy?' Monty called. 'A real fancy job?'

The man allowed a feeble smile. But otherwise was not provoked. Tim was starting to look irritated with Monty but his control was surprising, his voice still cool.

'I'm serious, Monty, if you want to get anywhere with this. You've got to paint what you know, all you know. Not some dream of what things might be. That's what it amounts to, at the moment. You're not in this work at all.'

'You don't like it, then. You don't think I'm up to much. Is that what you're bloody saying?'

'That's what I'm bloody saying,' Tim agreed.

'Well, that's all right. I'm not sold on being Rembrandt anyway.' But he grew more serious, more attentive. 'You think, like, I should have a decent gander at these bars.'

'Yes,' Tim said. 'And see what they say to you.'

'I could write a book about what they say to me. No trouble at all.'

'Just some drawings. And perhaps some paintings, later on. I want you to use your eyes, Monty, as well as your imagination. Could you try?'

'All right, then. I'll give it a go.'

'And when you've finished with the bars, I want you to try the walls. Those brick walls. And the locked door. And the pot by your bed. Your chair. Your table.'

Monty blinked.

'You've got a world in there,' Tim went on. 'A world, if only you see. I want you to tell me about it, show me what you see. But you've got to start trying to see. You've got to.'

I had never seen Tim speak with such vehemence. He certainly impressed Monty.

'You might even,' Tim finished, 'find it starting to make some sense, after all.'

I found it starting to make sense in more ways than one, and wondered if Monty could. When Tim lit a cigarette, after his

440

harangue, his fingers trembled. He left it to me to carry on conversation with Monty for the remainder of the visit. He seemed to grow distant from both of us. I should really have liked to pursue the prospect of a file with Monty; instead I talked about a couple of books I'd brought him to read. Perhaps the next best thing. Soon Monty was led away to his cell, his world.

Afterwards, walking aimless through the city on a quiet Saturday afternoon, with surprisingly little to say to each other, Tim and I stopped for coffee and ran into Paul Wiseman and his world.

'You interested in a party tonight?' Paul was quick to say. 'I've got two lined up. One sounds quite bizarre. Really fantastic. the other – '

'No thanks,' Tim said shortly. 'Not tonight.'

Paul looked stunned.

His eyes were large with surprise and then interest behind his black-rimmed glasses. 'You mean you've got something better?' he said. 'Where?'

'Nowhere,' Tim said. 'It's just not my day. Or night.' He turned to me. 'You go along with Paul, if you want.'

He might have been putting me on test. On the other hand he might also have been indifferent to what I did. In any case Paul's bizarre parties weren't really my style.

'I think I'll just coast along,' I told Paul. 'It's possibly not my night either. We've just been to the prison, you see.'

Though that really didn't sound adequate explanation.

'Well,' said Paul. 'Please yourself. You don't know what you're missing.'

He went his way cheerfully, doubtless to scatter more invitations.

'You don't have to stick with me, you know,' Tim said after Paul had gone.

'It's all right.'

'I'm not asking you.'

'I know that.'

'You own yourself. At least I hope so.'

'Look,' I said, 'if you want to be alone, you only have to say. Or if you're irritated with my company. Just say.'

'You're making an issue of it. There's no issue. I'm going back to the flat because I feel like going back there. That's all.

What you want to do is your own affair.'

'Well,' I said with care, 'there are one or two things I may do. Such as dropping in on Stan, if he's home. Or – '

'For Christ's sake,' he replied, 'you don't have to account for yourself. Not to me, now or ever. Get that straight.'

He walked out on me, and left me in the coffee shop alone. The explanation was probably that he had a girl somewhere, and had to shake me off: usually, though, he was more explicit.

Finally I sought Ken McAdam in a bar where he was likely to be drinking.

Tim's friends had become more or less mine too; and Ken, whatever his connection with Tim, didn't take himself or anyone too seriously. Or didn't appear to, though rumour said he was engaged on a novel of spectacular proportion. Anyway it was possible to take his company lightly. 'The only way to survive,' he once advised me, 'is to convince yourself it's a joke. A bad joke perhaps, but a joke. That's the trouble with Livingstone. No real sense of humour at all. And his strength, I suppose, when I think about it. Or if I think about it, which I can't afford to do too much. Like a kick in the stomach. He almost convinces me the whole thing is beyond a joke.'

Ken had a vaguely cosmopolitan air. His parents were English wanderers. He had spent some time as a professional hunter before settling down to university and advertising. He published short, cryptic sketches of tough men in bush country in university magazines; also oddly dreamy poems about sunrises and sunsets beyond tall mountains. He could disguise himself as another loud-mouthed student, rather too boozy, or the dapperly dressed, crew-cut advertising man of weekdays. He revealed himself sometimes, such as in his uncharacteristic outburst about Tim, or when he explained how best to stalk deer through rugged country.

When I found him, that afternoon, he was in company largely and intimidatingly literary. There were a number of students gathered about him at the bar. Their conversation concerned the future of some magazine. It was clear, despite the general incoherence, that Ken had a large say in the contents of the magazine; it was also clear that he had been ambushed by a number of potential contributors. Most had a sad and fragile air, though they were articulate enough, and variously bitter. Ken finally saw me eavesdropping; he pushed his way through to me.

442

'Alone?' he said. 'Where's your mate?'

I shrugged. I still felt faintly dispirited, and the question didn't help. 'We've been up to prison to visit Monty Nolan,' I explained. 'Then he took off somewhere.'

'A woman,' Ken suggested.

'That did cross my mind.'

'Never mind; drink up. And talk to me about something real.'

'I thought we were talking about something real.'

'Livingstone? He's real, all right, but I can't think of any subject I exhaust faster. What I really want you to do is excavate me from my present company.'

It might have been affectation; I wasn't sure that he didn't enjoy being surrounded. On the other hand he did seem interested enough in what I had to tell him about the prison and Monty Nolan and Tim's attempts at art instruction. 'Marvellous,' he said. 'So now he's going to paint his rat?'

'Or something like it,' I agreed.

'Tremendous.' Ken was all enthusiasm. 'We'll have to do something about a show for Nolan, if he comes up to scratch. Win him some sympathy and perhaps get him an early release.'

By the time I'd finished my stories of the prison visit, the students were pressing close around Ken again, implicitly demanding his attention.

I felt more cheerful.

It might have been the beer, or just the relief of relaxed conversation. I had little sense of restraint with Ken, as I often had with Tim. Perhaps I took on too much of Tim's colouring. Anyway Ken's candour could be infectious.

'This is Ian Freeman,' Ken said, introducing me around, 'our man in the fourth estate.'

The others did not appear greatly impressed.

'Come to think of it,' Ken went on, 'why don't you write something for us?'

'Why not?' I said cheerfully. If it was a joke, I could take it.

'We've enough bloodless bloody poetry. We need something hard and real and down to earth.'

He was serious, after all; he had me trapped. The students continued to elbow around, impatient with Ken.

'All those courtroom dramas you witness,' Ken went on.

'Christ, man, you've a ton of material there. So long as you don't use too many adjectives.'

'I'll think about it,' I promised.

'Don't think about it. Do it. And you know you can.'

He seemed determined to make it a challenge. But it wasn't so much challenge I felt as the temptation to make myself, perhaps, in some way distinct. From what, though, or whom? Anyway the need was there, suddenly seen, suddenly real; it expanded to fill my empty afternoon. And then, almost as suddenly, the balloon pricked by reality, I was back again at the bar, with Ken, among the noisy students, the city bleak beyond. It was all, of course, absurd.

'We'll see,' I answered finally. 'It must be my turn to buy the beer.'

(I had arranged to meet Ken in a bar off the side of Soho. It was my favourite hour of the day in London, late afternoon, smoky-blue autumn light; the braziers of chestnut sellers glowed along the Charing Cross Road. The bookshops were still open, brightening patches of yellow light, as I paced past them, already late. I turned into Soho and found the bar: a small, comfortable place, a warm retreat in a reassuringly solid city; I was, possibly for the first time, grateful for London's cosiness. Even for such a bar as this, with its melancholy drinkers; they probably hadn't changed in five years, and likely wouldn't in another five. They were like actors left behind with the drama over, the curtain fallen. It seemed I was in love with London, if only because it was unlikely to be sliced by a wall. And it seemed to have become as much mine as anywhere, a second-hand suit, comfortably fitting.

Ken was distinct among the drinkers; he hadn't entirely blended. A neat Italian suit, an American shirt, pointed suede shoes: as much with it as always, but not too conspicuously; the young man forever on the rise. He finished off a large whisky as I approached.

'Two more,' he said to the barmaid. 'Doubles again. No, make it triples.' He shook my hand. 'It's nice to see you again, all in one piece. I've sometimes wondered.'

'Wondered what?'

'Whether you'd make it in one piece. I've never seen greater potential for schizophrenia. Never mind. Try this for size.' He handed me my drink. 'I'm paying,' he added reassuringly. 'All on expenses. Entertainment of prospective something or other. Can you sing? Light entertainment's my baby at the moment. Not literature, or foreign affairs, any of the heavy stuff. Yes, I think I'll put you down as a prospective singer. That should do nicely. Well, where were we? You're looking well anyway. I can't think why.'

'Nor can I.'

'How has the continent been? I've tried to keep up with you, in my way. At least I've been trying to read your stuff, when it appears. You were in Berlin, I noticed, when the wall went up.'

'Yes,' I agreed. 'I was there.'

'All very exciting. Such times we live in. You know your trouble, Freeman? You make me feel I'm missing out on something.'

'You're not missing much. Believe me.' I tried to be as casual as I could: it was still difficult.

'You don't have to go out of your way to convince me. Sandy West was in town a couple of months back. He'd just done an agency stint in Washington, and was off to Cairo. He seemed in touch with history too. At one stage, he said, he was following Eisenhower around a golf links, waiting for pearls to be dropped. He may actually have picked up one of the great golfer's lost balls; I don't really remember. He was off to Cairo seeking to prove something or other about Nasser. I wished him luck. Now there's someone who's changed. There's not much room to the right of Sandy. Not these days.'

'So I gather.'

'The scourge of the left. That's how he likes to think of himself. And the mailed fist of the right. He regards you as a dangerously corrupt and sentimental liberal. When I pointed out that you seemed fairly anti-communist, he wasn't at all impressed. He said it wasn't enough.'

'Probably not. I sometimes have that feeling too.'

'Poor Sandy. It all has something to do with his being up in the Sierra Maestra with Castro, before Castro made it in Cuba. In the days when he was a fine clean cause. I think, actually, he was in love with Castro. And he feels Castro betrayed him, personally, by turning out a communist after all. Anyway he can't forgive himself, for some reason. And compensates. Do you think he might have slept with Castro? Does that sound possible?'

I shrugged and finished my whisky. And hoped we might be finished with Sandy too.

'Thank God it's not my problem anyway,' Ken observed. 'I don't have to see further than next week's light entertainment on the idiot box. Castro and Berlin crises come and go, but bread and circuses go on forever. At least I know where I am. Do you?'

'No,' I confessed. I saw no reason not to be honest.

'You ever think about going home?'

'Now and then,' I conceded.

'I'd have thought so. Yes. You need a nest. Come on. Drink up. You don't really have to sing.'

The whisky was going very quickly to my head. No obstruction at all.

'Last time I saw you,' Ken went on, 'four or five years ago, you were on your way to Paris. Hoping to catch up with Livingstone, as I recall. Did you, ever?'

'Not really. No.'

'Did you ever get anywhere near?'

'As near as I could.'

'But no go?'

'No go,' I agreed.

'So what's your conclusion?' Ken asked. 'Does the bugger still exist?'

'It's hard to say. Your guess is probably better than mine.'

'That's rather enigmatic.'

'Well, that's the truth. I don't even pretend to know.'

'So,' Ken said, and raised his fresh whisky, 'here's to absent friends, wherever they are.'

I began to relax. The whisky, the warmth; and someone I knew. I could foresee a tolerable evening with Ken.

'The critics,' he said presently, 'were reasonably pleasant about your last book. Very civil indeed, I thought. All things considered.'

'What things?'

'Well, to be honest, I thought it was pretty rough. Well short of your best, if you really want to know.'

'Perhaps I was pretty rough. At the time I wrote it.'

'I wouldn't know about that. Don't get me wrong. All I'm saying – '

'I know what you're saying. It's all right. I can take it as said.'

446

'Look,' Ken said quickly. 'What's happened? You never were that sensitive.'

'Perhaps I'm a slow developer, then.'

'At the beginning, I admit, there was a certain amount of envy. The usual brew. That was when we were still competing. I might have got some satisfaction out of seeing you fall flat on your face then. If you don't mind me saying so, you seemed so bloody unlikely anyway. Livingstone I could see, yes; and one or two others. Including myself, of course. But not you. Not you at all. So it seemed all wrong. And only a matter of time before you got your just deserts. How wrong could I be? Never mind; it's over. I'm long out of the race. It's all different now.'

'How different, Ken?' I asked gently. He had become oddly naked.

'Envy and malice are impossible to sustain, I find, without a certain wastage of willpower. Come on, now; more whisky? In for a penny, in for a pound. Drink it up. There's a good fellow.'

The mask was up again, or almost.

'And besides,' he added, 'I'd sooner you didn't write anything bad or indifferent. It means you're something agreeable in my past. Livingstone might have been too. Pity. What the hell's that frown for?'

'I think we should eat, Ken, and sober up a little. Before this goes too far. What do you say?'

'I say after another drink. I don't suppose you know of a party tonight? No, of course not; you're just back in town. Never mind. There's my club.'

'We could always try Wiseman. Like we did the last time I saw you here. And like the old days, if it comes to that.'

Ken looked disgusted. 'Wiseman? You're joking. Or years out of date. Wiseman – our little Paul – is now growing fat and hideously rich on the frayed fringe of the art world. And successfully living down his derelict colonial past. And, if it comes to that, also his derelict old friends. We'll get short change there, or no change at all. Forget it.'

'So it looks like your club. Is Paul really so different?'

'Try him and see.'

'I might have to. Just in case.'

'Just in case what?'

'In case he has news.'

447

'Of Livingstone? You'll be wasting your time. Believe me. If he knows something about Livingstone, it's something he wouldn't want to know. On the other hand, he may just acknowledge you. They tell me he turns on some really swinging scenes. The sweet life; he's in the thick of it.'

'I don't see that as so great a change. Remember his bizarre parties? He always had a nose for them.'

'The mystery is, how did we survive? And not Livingstone?'

'Perhaps we didn't matter so much.'

'Perhaps,' he speculated. 'And perhaps Livingstone didn't matter so much either.'

'And perhaps,' I qualified, 'we'll never really know.'

For one dizzy moment I was on the edge of confessing the entire thing to Ken, telling him the whole story. Then I drew back; and was sure I'd had too much to drink. But I did retain enough sense to see that if I couldn't tell Ken, I couldn't tell anyone. And likely never would. The sound of that shattering glass was still distinct, and that cry; and the silence. Then the panic.

'One for the road,' Ken said, 'for the road grows longer.')

Ken said: 'Perhaps we ought to do something about Livingstone. Take him in hand. Make him think about an exhibition. This can't go on.'

'Probably not,' I agreed.

Later we sought Paul Wiseman, with bottles under our arms, to get more precise information about his bizarre party. Perhaps the wrong choice. It turned out not in the slightest bizarre. Ken found himself a tubercular-looking girl among the joss-sticks and I took a taxi home. As I paid off the driver, I saw light burning inside. Tim was there after all; and up late. If he had company he was slower than usual to darken the place.

But when I opened the door he was alone and at work. He didn't look up.

'A good night?' he asked.

'Reasonable,' I replied. 'With Ken, among others.'

'Ah,' he said. 'Ken.' He was watching his hand, which held a brush; and hand and brush seemed to be acting of their own volition, under his indifferent gaze.

'I seem to get along with Ken. More than with most.'

'Ken's all right,' he agreed. He still didn't look up. He seemed at some cold remove, both from me and his work; and calm in his chill.

Suddenly I wished to shake him.

'Ken and I have been talking about you,' I announced.

'I expect you have,' he said with irritating equanimity.

'We both think you ought to exhibit soon.'

'You do?'

'It's time, surely. And there's all this work besides.'

'One way of looking at it,' he said quietly. His hand appeared to be slowing.

'After all, it's something you've said yourself. Unless you get rid of something, we're going to be crowded out. We just haven't the space.'

'Well,' he said. 'That's that, then.' His hand came to life again, briefly; two swift movements and he stopped. And looked at me for the first time. 'Is that all you had to say?'

'The rest wouldn't interest you.'

'So,' he went on. 'My friends think I should do something about myself. That's no real news either. It can't go on – or can it? So all right, you and Ken go right ahead. And arrange something for me, if you like. I just haven't the energy left to move one way or the other. Or perhaps it's the willpower. Or the confidence. Christ knows.'

He limped across the room and slumped in a chair untidily, as if to demonstrate. Confidence struck me as a strange word for him to use; I'd never noticed him lacking it. And energy, and willpower? I couldn't imagine him not having those in abundance either.

'I'm going around in circles,' he claimed. 'Not getting anywhere at all. That's the truth of it.'

'You're tired,' I argued. 'That's all.'

I had to say something.

'It's all very well,' he added, 'telling Monty how he should paint his way out of his own trap. When I can't do anything about getting out of my own.'

'Your own what?'

'Trap. Or skin. Whatever you like.'

The paintings around seemed, for the first time, to be confessing; I might never have seen them before. The light, where it was, became more luminous; and the total of tones more haunting. Yet even my understanding would be approximate, at best.

He was still talking, it seemed.

'Thank Christ you're around anyway,' he finished suddenly and cryptically.

Soon afterwards he collapsed, still dressed, on his bed. By the time I'd made coffee he was asleep. I covered him with a rug. He didn't stir as I spread it over him.

Besides unwrapping his paintings Tim also, after a time, unpacked his books. I'd never thought him much of a reader, though he sometimes dipped and browsed and surfaced now and then with some brightly coloured idea or some unusually vivid information. Out of such bits and pieces, and out of things plucked from conversation, he made his nest in the city. Anyway his books were soon scattered among my own. On a Sunday morning, tidying the flat, I came across an old volume of Ben's poems. I expressed surprise.

'I didn't know you read verse,' I said. 'Does this interest you much?'

'Of course,' he replied. 'Of course it interests me. Or it has, on and off.' He retrieved the ragged book from my hands and considered it. 'Ken McAdam lent me this. Years ago. I made a point of not returning it.'

'What's so interesting about it?'

'The way the man looks at things. And the man too, I suppose. He could make sense. Listen to this.' He flipped through the book, hunting among dog-eared pages, and finally located some lines which he read aloud; there was affection in his tone. 'See what I mean?'

I wasn't sure. Meanings were obscure. A thick, rather incoherent chant of loneliness out of some dark place, possibly a stoic plea of faith. I hadn't looked at Ben's verse since I was very young, when I'd examined it without much comprehension, and more or less accepted my father's verdict: wordy nothings. And Ben had neither pressed his work upon me nor talked of it; it appeared to be all in the past anyway. This made Tim's evident enthusiasm the more surprising. Perhaps he contrived to create something for himself there, in the words Ben had scattered behind him, something he needed; and if it didn't actually exist, perhaps he invented it. How could I know?

'I met him once,' Tim went on. 'In the days when I was

Wiemken's disciple. I was still a bit tongue-tied then, so we didn't have much to say. Pleasant in his queer way.'

'Queer?'

'Quite a taste for young men. Perhaps he still has, though he's getting on. I wouldn't know. He didn't make a pass at me.'

Though I was shaken enough, it seemed in a way that I had always known; I just hadn't wanted to do simple addition of my different causes for wonder. Ben's company had been suffic-iently soothing.

'He's my uncle,' I managed to say.

'Your what?' Now it was Tim's turn for surprise.

'My uncle. I used to visit him quite a bit when I first came to the city. Not so much lately. But you might remember me saying, once or twice, that I was off to visit an uncle. Well, that was him. The same one.'

'Well, I'm damned,' he said. 'Your uncle. Why didn't you tell me?'

'Come to think, he mentioned you early on. That meeting with you. I didn't think to say.'

His expression changed. 'I hope,' he said quickly, 'I didn't say anything to upset you.'

'Nothing I shouldn't have guessed anyway. Ben's not the happiest of people.'

He considered that. After a time he said, 'You think I could help cheer him up? I'd like to tell him, sometime, how much I like his work. You think that would help?'

'It might.' I shrugged. 'He's glad of company anyhow. I'll take you along next time I visit.'

I did. Ben and Tim, despite their differences, and perhaps because of them, seemed pleased with each other; I was really a bystander.

Ken and I had at last committed him. He was going to exhibit. An art group had taken scruffy premises in the centre of the city, as a small gallery, and Ken had arranged hire of the place for a couple of weeks so that Tim could show. 'I think,' Ken predicted, 'you're going to make a big impression this time, old son. About time too. We'll shake this place up yet.'

I wished I could be as confident.

It was a mellow and summery Sunday morning. A gold light

on the old houses beyond our window, a glimpse of serene sea, and the smell of fresh coffee in the flat.

From time to time he roved restlessly about the table where two fresh paintings dried. Now and then I sensed him shoot a stare in my direction; I guessed him curious about my concentration. I sat tight in my corner, at my desk, and offered the room no more than the irregular sound of a scratching pen; I was at last attempting my promised piece for Ken. Ken had become too insistent for comfort. I could no longer escape with excuses; I had to produce something. And Tim's increasing industry was shaming to the point where I had to begin, if only to show that I could take something more than lightly. Actually I had begun to surprise myself.

'What is it you're up to, then?' he asked. 'An essay? I thought you'd quit university.'

'Nothing really,' I said. I couldn't afford to tell him; I had to have something to myself.

'A lot of time on nothing,' he observed. 'A bloody lot. I haven't heard a word out of you today.'

He left it there, clearly displeased.

I didn't take any of Ken McAdam's suggestions: court, prison, Tim himself. I tried them over in my mind and found them wanting; they refused to live in the only words I had, and it was difficult to find others. Where to begin, if I could? I lifted my eyes from the desk, the obstinately blank paper, and met a view of familiar hills; the painting became a window through which light could enter, perhaps just a silvering through bars. But sufficient for me. For what I needed to see was that foreground was lacking; foreground was my natural home, though perhaps Tim could live without. And such foreground as began to suggest itself, against those hills, was green and bright; there were dark shelter belts of pines and white football posts, and then two teams surging between, a mild explosion of colours upon the pitted grass. The winter sunlight was cool, the shadows already long, and probably there was frost in the evening ahead. Outside a dressing shed players champed, jogged, waiting for their game; a tight oval ball flicked from hand to hand; there was a smell of liniment and boot-black. Yet there were still the hills beyond, with corrugations of gathering shadow; I could ignore them only at risk. I remembered how

452

things were in mid-season, before a hard game, when all things were still possible, and found words in sudden and vivid abundance. Hard and shiny, rather metallic, and impossible to resist: they clicked into place, one after another, too easy to be true.

'Yes,' Ken said. 'Of course I'm going to use this. Just what I wanted. Something real. Nice atmosphere; you have an eye for the right detail. What does Tim think of this?'

'He hasn't seen it. He doesn't know about it.'

'He doesn't?'

'And I'd prefer that he didn't. Meantime.'

Ken looked at me quizzically.

'Anyway,' I added, with entire irrelevance, 'it's not something we share.'

Ken laughed and shrugged. 'Of course he's going to know about this, see this, sooner or later.'

'I'd rather it was later.'

'Please yourself. But don't you develop a temperament too. One Livingstone is enough.'

'Yes,' I said. 'I can see that.'

We finished hanging on a Sunday night. Through the weekend most of Tim's friends turned up, at some stage or other, to consider the scene and lend a hand. There was much distraction, often bottled, and progress was slow; Sandy West even had the inspiration of fetching along some giggling girls, to enliven things, which they did too well, and in the end we had to shut them out and lock the door. Paul Wiseman, of course, wanted joss-sticks; and Indian music playing softly for the duration of the exhibition. He was outvoted. Ken and Tim argued desperately about the arrangement of some of the paintings. Tim won most of the arguments; the best Ken could get was a compromise, reluctantly conceded. 'You don't know your own best work,' Ken said in mild fury, 'and you never will.' Tim remained impassive. Once, when Ken became particularly aggressive, Tim walked out for an hour; and returned when Ken had cooled. Ted Connolly made a point of turning up in the city for the occasion, and spent most of his time looking quietly over the paintings as they went up on the walls of the gallery; he had very little to say at all, but he was plainly pleased about something. Charlie Bates, clever with his hands,

453

proved the most useful visitor; he framed some paintings Tim wanted to show at the last minute. The only person missing, really, was Monty Nolan. And Stan Coates, of course. Impossible to fetch Monty, but I gave Stan a call and invited him to a preview. 'I must say,' he conceded, 'it's all very strong. Livingstone's full of surprises. How does he get away with it? I mean, what does this stuff have to do with him?' He shook his head. 'Still, I'd like to see a little more social content. What's this going to say to anyone? There's more to life than landscape. Where are all the people?' Yet Stan, I noticed, stayed far longer than he intended; I took it as a hopeful sign. If Stan could be impressed, for all his misgivings about Tim and his work, perhaps others would be too. So I felt reason for optimism by the time we finished hanging; the others also seemed to find reasons of their own. Ted Connolly had brought some potent black Dalmatian wine from a vineyard, and we settled down to our unofficial opening; the official opening was a day ahead, on the Monday night, and we saw no cause to wait for the polite pecking at sherry that would involve.

'Well,' Ken said. 'There it is. We've done it.'

There was a pause. He might have been waiting for the earth to tremble. A bus ground indifferently past the gallery window. There were drunken voices from a nearby piecart. Ken sighed and sat down; he looked tired, with reason. He had worked harder through the weekend than anyone. He had also composed a crisp introductory note for Tim's catalogue, which he'd cyclostyled with my help. Neither of us had found much sleep in the past forty-eight hours.

'It's all over to you, now,' Ken added, looking at Tim. 'Or your work. Here's hoping.' He lifted his huge glass of wine, and sucked it greedily. We joined in the toast.

As we sat there warm with optimism and wine, I remembered how we had been during the strike; it was well in the past now. The bleak basements had been exhanged for this shabby gallery, and we weren't exactly in danger of a police raid, however much we were still conscious of the weight of the world outside; a more indifferent world, possibly, but still as likely hostile. And peripheral people had changed: in place of seamen and watersiders we had Paul Wiseman, and whatever he represented. Instead of Stan we had Ken McAdam as the revolutionary, using Tim's work much as Stan had used the strike; Tim himself was largely indifferent to this, or seemed so. He had even allowed Ken to help devise or improve the titles of his paintings, to make his direction more explicit: *A Land with No Heroes* was one, *A Land with No Lovers* another, and *Can Anyone Save Us Here?* a third; a few, such as *And Did Those Feet in Ancient Time,* from Blake, had Biblical reference, to emphasize a certain pagan poignance in the work. Yet the titles, in the end, did no more than gently underline the despair; they seemed, these looming lumps of land around us, these blocks of basalt and towers of limestone and edges of earth, to join in one vast melancholy cry.

How could anyone fail to see? I was growing quickly drunk.

'Ken's right,' Sandy West was saying. 'Nothing like rubbing real mud in people's faces. That's what Tim's done.'

'No one's really looked before,' Ted Connolly insisted.

'Me,' said Paul Wiseman from a corner, introducing a lonely dissident note, 'I'd like a little less mud. Art's dead anyway; that's the only worthwhile statement an artist can make. All this kind of thing, it's so provincial. Who cares?'

'We care,' Charlie Bates said, surprisingly firm. 'We bloody care. We live here. And probably die here too.' He looked suddenly aggressive; Paul shrank back into his corner.

Perhaps we were all getting drunk quickly.

'All I was saying – ' Paul began.

'I heard what you were bloody saying, all right,' Charlie roared.

'Easy, now,' Ken said, putting a hand on Charlie's shoulder. 'Paul just may have a point.'

'All I was saying,' Paul stuttered, 'all I was saying . . .'

I looked around to see how Tim was taking it. He lay on the floor of the gallery, an empty glass beside him, a cushion behind his head, asleep.

The official opening came and went without excitement. There was much talk and sherry-sipping, but no buying and not even prospective purchasers visible; there were, on the other hand, a number of bewildered faces. And some distinct headshakes. 'Another joke,' I overheard someone say sourly. I almost made irritated interjection, but decided against it. There was no point in scenes : I'd already witnessed Ken in vehement dispute with a couple of the city's reputed art-lovers, and achieving nothing.

Tim arrived late and inconspicuously and stayed only briefly, sheltered by his friends, but while he was there a lean and tall man, with rather bleak face, pushed clear of the sherry-sippers, like a lonely vessel weighing anchor, and gave his hand to Tim. 'I cannot say,' this man observed, 'that I like what you do, but at least you do it well. And honestly, I think. So there is not much more to say. If you distress me, I can always console myself with the thought that your distress is greater. I cannot think you fool yourself, ever. But perhaps that is not for me to say.'

'No,' Tim said sharply. 'It isn't.' Yet he looked, to me, surprisingly vulnerable.

The rest of his reply, in the clashing conversation, was indistinct. I nudged Charlie Bates and asked him about the man. 'That,' said Charlie, 'is Hans Wiemken. This is the first time they've met since they fell out.'

They didn't have much to say to each other, even so. Tim spoke curtly, finally turning his back and leaving Hans Wiemken to carry on peripheral conversation with Ted Connolly and Sandy West; and a short time later Tim left the gallery altogether.

Others were leaving too. The sherry was finished, and the paintings entirely unbought.

Soon there seemed to be only Ken and I left, cleaning and closing up the place. Even Ted, Sandy, Charlie and the rest had fled the disaster; and we were left to stand our eroding ground. For a time we found it difficult to look at each other, still more difficult to speak.

'All right,' Ken said savagely, 'so we expected too much.'

'We did our best,' I suggested. I wondered about Tim, about what he was feeling. 'We couldn't have done much more.'

I thought not only of the work we had put into preparing the exhibition, the catalogue, everything, but also of the reviews we had both written; I had taken advantage of the absence of my newspaper's regular art critic to write mine, and Ken had composed one for the university newspaper. Perhaps Tim was grateful, but we couldn't expect him to say so; he was, after all, only receiving his due.

'Then our best isn't good enough,' he announced, shovelling empty glasses on to a tray.

I searched out other empty glasses beyond a partition. Then

I discovered we weren't left alone. A solitary figure sat there, slumped in a chair, possibly inhabiting some defeat of his own: Hans Wiemken. He looked up at me slowly. There was, of course, no recognition. Without speaking, he rose stiffly, handed me an empty glass, and then walked past me, out of the gallery, without a word to Ken either. He looked as if he had been weeping, but I couldn't be sure. He left me too shaken. I looked at Ken, who looked back at me, and we had even less to say.

There were a couple of days of calm after the opening. Tim appeared listless in the suddenly bare flat; he was more affected than I at first thought. Then my review appeared, and also a cruel attack in the columns of the rival city newspaper. Ken and I agreed this attack was laughable, and tried to persuade Tim to see it the same way. But he didn't laugh. He didn't react at all. He seemed quite numb.

'If he can just hold on,' Ken confided to me, his optimism regained, 'everything will be all right. People must begin to see.'

What people had in fact begun to see became clear to me the next day. Derek Martin called me to his desk. 'You've made a fine start as art critic,' he said. 'Look at this lot. We've never had anything like it before. The editor's sent down a please explain note.'

He indicated a heap of correspondence on his desk. I glimpsed phrases, words: 'rubbish' and 'modernist rubbish' and 'puerile daubs' frequently recurred. The surprising thing was that so many had been to see Tim's exhibition, if only to dislike it. And that so many felt strongly enough to write about it.

'Well,' Derek demanded, after giving me time to sample, 'can you explain?'

'Only,' I said, gathering breath, 'to the extent that it's obvious a fair number of people disagree with me.'

'You're bloody well right about that,' he said. 'A fair number? I'd say half the city. I might add that now includes the editor. He went down to see the show himself this morning, after reading this lot.'

'And I'm fired as art critic?'

'That's the general idea. I don't imagine you're too distressed. It was only temporary anyway. The editor wanted to know what the hell a court reporter was doing writing about art. You put me in the gun. I thought you knew what you were bloody well doing when you volunteered for the job.'

'I thought I did too.'

'This artist,' he went on, 'wouldn't be a mate of yours, by any chance?'

'As a matter of fact, yes.'

Derek looked relieved. 'Well, perhaps that explains it after all. And perhaps I can square off with the editor. And say friendship got the better of you. Meantime, you realize we're going to have to run some of this stuff?'

'Is it really necessary? It all looks pretty illiterate to me.'

'Freedom of the press, my boy. Of course we must.'

'You weren't talking too much about freedom of the press two or three years ago, as I recall. During the strike.'

'That,' he said, 'was different. And you know it.'

He began to look edgy. It was no use pushing Derek too far.

'At least,' I went on, 'I imagine I'll be given the right of reply.'

'I've just told you – I thought I made it perfectly clear – that you're fired as our temporary art critic and confined to courts again. On the editor's instruction.'

'All the same – '

'All the same, nothing. Since you're no longer art critic, you have no right of reply.'

'Freedom of the press?'

'Don't get too smart. And don't push your luck. In point of fact you're fortunate to get off so lightly. The editor seems to consider this exhibition blasphemous, one way or another. Or subversive; I'm not sure which. Hence his disgust with your review. He feels this newspaper compromised. Actually, I may as well tell you he's contemplating an editorial – on modern art in general, not just this show, and its corruption of society by stealth. He intends to argue, I gather, that we can't afford room for it in a healthy society.'

'Oh Christ,' was all I could say.

'What's that?' Derek said sharply.

I sighed; I felt extremely tired. 'Nothing. I don't suppose it's any good me telling you, or him, that there's nothing particularly modern about this exhibition. That actually it's rather traditional, even rather old-fashioned in some eyes.'

'No,' Derek agreed. 'I don't think you would do yourself any good.'

458

'That's that, then. And you're also telling me I have absolutely no right of reply?'

'We seem to understand each other at last,' he said.

'Then I'm telling you I no longer work here.'

'Look,' Derek said. 'Wait a minute.'

But I'd waited long enough; my arrival at this moment
appeared to have perfect logic. Derek could only spoil the
symmetry.

By the weekend the worst had more or less shown itself. Perhaps the city had been too short on sensation; something had
to be manufactured. Anyway the one thing we couldn't complain about now was public indifference to the exhibition; the
gallery was crowded whenever I looked in there, though most
of the comment I overheard didn't bear reporting to Tim. There
was, in our circumstances, a limit to the comfort I could offer.
I didn't even attempt to explain my absence from work, my
new idleness. I felt mildly paralysed and trapped with Tim's
silences. Most of the time he had his feet up on the bed, his face
hidden behind a book; he seemed determined to give nothing
away.

It was relief to escape for a furtive beer with Ken, and make
report.

'He's not suicidal or anything?' Ken asked anxiously.

'Not so you'd notice.'

'We're to blame,' he said. 'You realize that? We pushed
him into it. All too soon. I see that now. But we are to blame.
We can't escape it. And those provocative titles didn't help.
Or the things we wrote. We claimed too much, or made too
much. We should have taken it easier.'

I shrugged. 'It's done now. And I haven't got off lightly
either. I've lost my job.'

'But that,' protested Ken, 'wasn't really necessary.'

'I thought it was very necessary.'

Ken looked blank. 'What do you plan to do? Register as
unemployed? Join Comrade Coates on the Party press? If you
like, I could try to find you something in advertising. I'm
sure you'd make the grade.'

'No thanks. I think I may just drift for a week or two, and
let time make up my mind.'

'That sounds pretty vague.'

'And out of character.'

'The problem is whether I've a character to be out of.'

'Well,' he said, 'while I think of it, you'd better have a look at this.' He pushed a long brown envelope along the bar to me; I glimpsed something printed inside.

I felt a familiar tremor. 'Not another attack on Tim?'

Ken and I had already used the greater part of the week proposing, and composing, lines of defence; lines unlikely to be printed. Ted Connolly, Sandy West and Charlie Bates had all also written letters to the newspapers, trying to blunt philistine fury. Even Stan Coates had stood beside us, in what was likely to be the most widely unread review of Tim's exhibition, for the Party paper. He'd decided Tim's work must have some social content after all, since it was so disliked. The trouble was that this view had won him a reprimand from some cultural commissar who wished Tim denounced as formalist and subjective and escapist, whatever those things meant in total, or at all.

'No,' Ken said. 'Save your fire. Not another attack on Tim. It's yours. The proof of your story. That sketch you wrote for me. Remember?'

I did seem to have difficulty remembering.

'It's all set up in type now,' Ken went on. 'I'd like you to check the proof, and make any changes you want, before I shoot it back to the printer. If you don't mind me saying so, it still reads rather well. And I've shown the piece around to a few people – '

'Not to Tim?' I said quickly.

'No. Not to Livingstone, as it happens. I've respected your wishes there, though I still don't see the point. He's bound to see it anyway. But – '

'That's all right, then.' I picked up the envelope as if it had just come through quarantine.

'What I'm trying to say is that I've shown your piece around. And the reaction has been pretty favourable. People want to know where I dug you up. A good question. I rather like to think I dug you out of the mud of a Livingstone landscape.' He paused. 'Now,' he added briskly, 'let's get down to business. What else can we do to try and save the day? There must be some angle we haven't thought about.'

'Like a protest march on the press?'

Ken considered that, surprisingly serious. 'No,' he said finally. 'Not enough of us.'

'Then,' I suggested, 'there's probably nothing else to be done.'

'I'm glad you said it, then. I just don't like facing up to the fact. But nor do I like to think about Livingstone.'

We parted in defeat.

There was something else which could be done. And Tim, it turned out, did it himself.

On the Saturday several people arrived at the flat, with armloads of beer, and the intention of in some way distracting or consoling Tim; it was difficult to see precisely what each of them had in mind, but perhaps they hoped their collective noise would provide sufficient distraction from the city outside. Bottles clinked and glasses smashed more and more frequently; a record-player boomed; arguments spurted like sudden fires. I gave Stan Coates a call, since he also now seemed an ally, and might turn out slightly saner or at least more sober company, and he arrived to join us; he also presented a copy of his review to Tim, who hadn't seen it, and examined it with surprising care. They both in fact were unusually subdued, when I glimpsed them through the thickening haze, and quiet and earnest with each other; they sat rather leaden at the edge of things, on a bed, and I wondered what they were talking about. But some girls had arrived unexpectedly, in pleasing number, and I had my own distraction.

Then I saw Stan alone on the bed. I approached him.

'He was here a minute or two ago,' Stan explained. 'Then he just took off suddenly. As if he'd remembered something. Didn't say where.' He shrugged. 'Poor bugger. You know something? I actually feel sorry for him, for once. I've been doing my best to say the right things. About the nature of society, and the fate of the individual. I hope it helped.'

'I'm sure it did, Stan. Yes.' My speech sounded slovenly; I was, having a problem with focus on Stan's indefinite face. It struck me as always too bleak these days; Stan still wasn't himself at all. But then who was? I was drunk, all right. And to make sure of it I left Stan and fetched myself more beer. The party still flared.

Ten minutes later, perhaps more, I looked for Tim again. He seemed to have vanished.

'You sure,' I said to Stan, 'he didn't say where he was going?'

'I told you. He said nothing. He just shot through.'

461

'He doesn't seem to be here at all.'

'No. Look, why don't you sit down and relax? You look too hectic.'

But a tiny suspicion had just jigged into my untidy mind. Earlier that day Tim had asked me for my key to the gallery. He said he wanted a second look at something.

But now? It was midnight, or near enough. Impossible. Quite impossible.

'What's the matter now?' Stan asked, as I fled.

I didn't answer. I looked for Ken, and found him. He was, predictably, cornering a girl tightly, rather anonymous this time, with long hair and flushed face. 'No,' Ken said. 'I haven't seen him. We haven't spoken all evening.'

I was outside. The midnight air was cool. My feet snapped along the empty pavement.

There were other feet behind, following. Stan's. He grabbed my shoulder.

'For Christ's sake,' he said. 'What's eating you? Where are you going?'

'Looking for Livingstone,' I said cryptically.

'You think he might do himself in? That it?'

'Not exactly.'

'Well, it's too soon to drag the harbour. Give him a chance.'

He struggled to keep up with me, and panted. He was in poor physical condition.

'Just tell me,' he persisted, 'where in hell you're going.'

A few minutes later he found out, exactly; we arrived down town and climbed dark stairs to the gallery. There was a key in the door, and sound within.

I twisted the key, the door swung open, and I half-fell inside. The place was dimly lit. Yet there was still enough light to see the damage done. A third or half the paintings were already scraped, scratched, hacked or carved. And Tim, with the blade of a pocket knife, was still busy. Too busy, and possibly too drunk, to hear us enter. He seemed also to be singing or swearing; I couldn't tell which, and didn't have time to decide.

Perhaps I said, 'You can't.'

But of course he could, and had, and was.

Anyway I grabbed his shoulders. The knife dropped with almost no sound to the carpeted floor, and shone there. He swerved out of my grip, and faced me. His eyes were large and bright.

'Jesus,' he said, 'won't you buggers ever leave me alone?'

He snatched up the knife; and held it between us. A natural enough stance with a knife. I couldn't see it as a threatening gesture, or didn't wish to.

'Take it easy,' Stan said, from somewhere behind me. I'd forgotten for the moment that Stan was a spectator. 'Take it easy both of you. Someone might get hurt.'

'Someone is hurt, Stan,' I suggested. 'Can't you see?'

'Lay off,' Tim said, 'and let me finish. Go on. Lay off and fuck off.'

There was really no room for ambiguity in his gesture with the knife now. But he swayed. And I was also drunk enough, or fool enough, not to see the danger. I moved closer.

'You've made your point,' I argued. 'Why not just leave the rest?'

'None of your business,' he said. 'None of your fucking business.'

For emphasis he made a random stab at a painting already beyond repair.

'Mine,' he added, as if I'd contradicted him. 'This way, that way. Any way. Any way I bloody like. Right now I'm making some vast improvements in the public interest. Before I finish up altogether. Yes. So stand clear. None of your fucking business.'

'It is,' I said, my first and perhaps my only declaration of faith.

'Oh Christ,' I heard Stan sigh behind me, as I leapt; and gripped the arm with the knife; and fell together with Tim to the floor. I lost track of the knife. We were battering at each other with blunt fists, then trying to bend and shape each other into submission. I glimpsed his face, just the once, in our clumsy collisions. There was hate, perhaps, in his expression; but there was also, more certainly, relief. He was much stronger than I expected.

Stan stumbled around trying to separate us. He seemed to have a great deal of advice to offer. Sometimes we were upright; sometimes rolling on the floor again. Tim's head cracked against a wall, then mine. Clothing ripped, his or mine, it was hard to tell. Then it was quite definitely his. His shredding shirt peeled away altogether, and I felt his scarred back like blunt barbed wire under my hand. My shock gave him advantage; he butted me viciously in the face and I reeled back. A painting crashed from a wall, and was trampled. I managed to get above him briefly, as we fell again, and then astride him, so that I could slam my fist twice cleanly into his face; that was when I discovered relief of my own. Then I was tumbled, and myself blinded by a blow.

But it seemed, in the end, that neither could do the other sufficient damage. There was no dramatic finish, no real climax. We just grew weaker. Then we simply fell apart, as if by mutual consent, and lay limp.

'Stupid pair of bastards,' Stan offered by way of verdict. 'A wonder you didn't do for yourselves.'

He seemed far away.

'And,' he added, 'Tim's badly cut.'

I crawled towards Tim. He didn't appear more than barely conscious either. I hadn't realized we'd contrived to cover ourselves with so much blood. It was everywhere. At the beginning of our fight I'd evidently sliced his upper forearm with the knife. He still bled wildly. Stan bandaged the wound with a couple of handkerchiefs while I watched in daze. My body seemed one long bruise. Tim muttered incoherently. I tried to get to my feet; things lurched inside me, and I began vomiting, quite out of control. My face was too tender to touch. Yet, having saved half the paintings, I still managed to entertain some relief. And enough sense to say to Stan, 'We've got to shut up about this.'

'Quite,' Stan said coolly, knotting the bandage tight.

'And get out of here,' I added. 'Quick. And shut the place up again.'

'Yes,' he agreed.

My body might drag, but my mind continued to race. 'We could open a window. Leave the impression of forced entry.' I paused. 'At least,' I added, 'We've saved half the paintings. A good half.'

But Stan wasn't really with me; he was more concerned with Tim. He was trying to tidy his face now. 'I'll take him home to my place,' he said. 'No use taking him back to your shambles.'

'The knife,' I said, my mind beginning to clutter again. I retrieved it from the floor; to bend was cruel. 'The mess,' I went on. I found a cloth in a cupboard, and tried to soak up my vomit and such of the blood as I could see. I hoped the rest would be inconspicuous by Monday morning. 'We'll leave the rest,' I said. 'They'll probably think some maniac did it.'

'And they might,' said Stan, 'be right. Or two maniacs. Look, will you stop farting about, and give me a hand with him? We've got to get him out of here.'

'You realize,' I said, 'there wouldn't be a painting left if I hadn't stopped him? Nothing left at all.'

'Of course I bloody realize it. I wish you'd also realize there's bugger all left of Livingstone right now. So will you give me a hand? We've got to get him down those stairs, for a start. And then into a taxi. Stop trying to straighten those paintings. They can look after themselves. Come on. For Christ's sake come on.'

Stan was right, up to a point. The paintings, or such of them as remained reasonably intact, did look after themselves. And Tim?

He returned to the flat, from Stan's place, on the Sunday night, distinctly sobered and quiet. I'd just managed, by the time he arrived, to clear and clean away the last evidence of the party the night before. The stack of bottles outside was impressive. I hadn't told anyone what had happened at the gallery, not even Ken; the fewer who knew the better.

We shook hands. 'Sorry,' he said.

'That makes two of us.' There didn't seem much else to say; our bruises were not so prominent, or startling, after all. His bandaged arm was concealed by a long sleeve. Perhaps there wouldn't be much of a scar; anyway just one among many.

'I couldn't,' he explained, 'stand the idea of all that stuff landing back on me again.'

'I know. But we could always have tried that bonfire. Not that I ever thought you were serious.'

'Well,' he said, 'that's that, anyway.'

'Not altogether,' I observed. 'You didn't do them all in. Thank God. That was rather the point.'

'So Stan tells me. He also tells me you both want to shut up about it all.'

'Yes.'

'That's decent. But I don't really see why.'

'You might,' I said. 'Wait and see.'

'What do you mean?'

'I'm not sure yet.'

465

'Frankly,' he said, 'I couldn't give a stuff what anyone thinks. Not now. It's all finished.'

He began wandering around the flat, as if pleasantly surprised by its fresh appearance. 'And no hard feelings?' he added.

'None. I'd just like to see you get down to work again soon. It doesn't have to be all finished.'

'I appreciate your caring,' he said. 'I really do.'

I might have wished for a little more conviction; but perhaps that was expecting too much. In the circumstances.

'You and Ken both,' he went on, still wandering erratically. 'I'm grateful to you both. You tried.'

'Not hard enough. Obviously.' But my modesty, for once, seemed to stick in my throat: there was a limit. I began also to observe a limit to my patience.

'I can't think why you bother at all.'

I was tempted to tell him the truth: because he was worth it, or his work. Instead I replied, 'Because we've got to stick together. I might need you some day.'

As if I didn't already.

He stopped prowling; he seemed to be considering my suggestion seriously. Then I saw he was actually looking down at something on my desk, not paying me any attention at all. The proof of my story, left unwisely uncovered. I'd tried to look at it earlier in the day, in Tim's absence, but then, in a fit of mounting melancholy, had given myself to housework instead. And forgotten all about it.

'So what's this?' he asked abruptly.

'Nothing,' I said quickly. And then qualified, 'Just something I've written for Ken. To keep him quiet.'

'Oh?'

'Really nothing,' I insisted. I went to the desk and tried to cover the proof again. Too late, of course. Tim held my hand back.

'I'm just getting interested,' he said. 'Nothing to do with me?'

'No,' I lied. 'Nothing.'

'No? What is it, then?'

I wasn't up to explaining. Anyway he released my hand suddenly.

'Go ahead, then,' he said. 'Keep it, if that's the way you feel. Keep it to yourself.'

But I left the proof exposed, and turned away from the

466

desk. The whole thing began to seem absurd. As it was, in fact.
'It doesn't matter,' I said.
　'Look,' he said. 'What's the problem?'
　'The problem?'
　'Yes.'
　'Me,' I said. 'That's all.'

The damage done at the gallery was revealed to the public
when the place opened on Monday morning. I received an
agitated phone call from Ken, and affected the degree of dismay and bewilderment which seemed appropriate. 'It's going to
kill Tim,' he said. 'You'd better break it to him gently.' I
promised I would. 'God almighty,' he went on, despairingly, 'at
least we know things can't get any worse now. A lot of the
paintings are hurt in some way, and a good third are a total
write-off. One was smashed up all over the floor – and then
literally spewed upon, so far as I can see. The girl at the gallery
gave me a ring, and I called the police when I got down there.
Now the newspapers are on to it. I'm stalling; I don't know
quite what to tell them.' I advised him, in all seriousness, just
to convey the facts; and his own reaction to the outrage. And
to add that Tim wasn't available for comment. 'If you say so,'
he said miserably. 'I can see it's best to keep him out of it. You
try and hold the fort with him; I'll do my best here.'
　When I left the telephone, I didn't even trouble to wake
Tim, who was still sleeping heavily. Instead I sat at my desk,
with a fresh cup of coffee, and tried to give some attention
to the disrepair of my own life. A job, I supposed, was the
first thing : I felt remarkably cool about most things. Certainly
cooler than ever about the curious journey in proof on my desk.
　That afternoon's newspaper told about the vandalism at the
gallery, with photographs of the destruction, and cryptic comment from the police. There was a passionate denunciation of
the vandal, or vandals, by Ken (described as 'a young literary
associate of the painter's') and an equally emotional plea for
tolerance of adventurous young artists in the community. I was
glad I'd kept the truth from Ken; he possibly wouldn't have
sounded half so convincing, or distraught.
　But there was also a long and considered reply to Tim's
critics, written before the gallery trouble, from Ben. He was
identified editorially as a well-known writer and critic of an

older generation, which lent him some authority. Ben expressed alarm that so talented a young artist should be treated so cruelly, but added that it was really nothing new in the history of art. It was all remarkably reasonable, exactly the reply needed. The weekend sensation had lifted Ben's comment from the obscurity it would otherwise have been accorded, if it had been published at all.

I couldn't have been more delighted, altogether. I felt as if I'd almost done it all myself. Stan evidently thought so anyway, when he rang that evening.

'Congratulations,' he said. 'You pulled it off. But what does Tim think about it all?'

'I really,' I confessed, 'haven't asked him.'

('There's a story,' I said to Ken, one evening in Soho, 'I'm still thinking about. About a young artist who wants to quit. And attempts to destroy his own work in a gallery. In the dead of night, of course. But he's prevented from doing so by a friend, who drags him off. A friend who might, for argument's sake, care more for the work than the artist. But the highly visible damage done to the artist's work wins him all the sympathy he needs, and quite a reputation. So he doesn't quit. He goes on.'

Ken set down his drink slowly.

He was making quite an effort to take it all in.

'You bastard,' he pronounced finally. 'You bloody bastard.'

'That's not the point,' I said. 'The point is, do you think I could make a story like that work?'

'I rather think it is the point,' Ken said. 'Jesus Christ. What a bastard thing to do.' He shook his head. 'Don't worry. You've made the story work. All too bloody well. Why do you have to tell me now?'

'Because I've had too much to drink,' I said.)

That was the beginning, in a way. And possibly the end, in another. It was clear that for many people, and certainly the press, things had gone too far. Sympathy for Tim appeared suddenly substantial. Letters we had written to the newspapers the week before found print at last; Tim's critics were muted.

Tim himself was photographed, from several different angles, before his damaged work. 'I don't expect,' he was reported as saying, 'that I'll ever attempt to paint these again. It's best to forget them now.'

He was described as 'saddened but not particularly bitter'.

Elsewhere he was quoted: 'Everyone has the right to his opinion. The person who did this was only expressing his, after all. I'm pleased, in a way, that someone feels so strongly about my work. It's flattering.'

Evidently he managed it all with a straight face. And the words were more or less his own, though I'd made some suggestions.

But Charlie Bates and Sandy West, with no prompting from me, organized themselves and several art students into daily picketing of the gallery, with placards of protest about the outrage.

The police were said to be keeping close watch on the gallery, with regular checks day and night.

The rest of the paintings sold. This was only to small extent stage-managed. Ben happened to buy the first as a gesture of support, and to lend substance to his words. Ken and I ordered two for ourselves, and I ensured that these quick sales were reported. The remainder just went, even drawings and paintings partially damaged. Possibly Ben's influence; possibly the publicity. But certainly they weren't all bought by friends of the artist, though Hans Wiemken, I happened to learn, was among the early buyers; and, perhaps not altogether surprisingly, Stan Coates. Stan was the only one of our friends who didn't already own some of Tim's work, as gift from the artist.

But I didn't attempt to make up a list of patrons for Tim; in any case he no longer seemed to care much where his work went, who had bought it.

Because of the unusual public interest, Ken and I arranged for the exhibition to remain open an extra week. Then we closed it with some satisfaction.

We took down and stowed away the last of the paintings, and settled to a bottle of whisky.

'Well,' he said comfortably. 'We did it, after all. We really did it.'

469

'Not really,' I said.

'Oh?'

'Tim really did it,' I insisted, and hoped it true.

Twenty-two:

Documents

Avarua P.O.
Rarotonga etc.
February 2, 1967

Dear Max Kennedy,

Yes, I'm still here, though the end is in sight. I've really had to think about your new letter. I'm sure you'll find my answers as consistently evasive and unsatisfactory as always.

Yes, all the remaining paintings sold from that exhibition. Sorry I didn't make that clear; it seemed a huge success at the time. In retrospect? Never mind.

I don't know that I care for the new title you have for your project. A spoiled primitive? And a culture-hero too? A little too dramatic for my taste. I can see the historical point however. And you know your own business best.

So Ken McAdam thinks I can say all that needs to be said? I don't really like the responsibility. At least you heard from him. I'm glad I remembered Charlie Bates; I had no idea he'd actually become an architect, with all those buildings to his credit. I hope you find him approachable.

You ask if Margaret Saunders could be some local television personality. No, I'm sure you're wrong. Coincidence of name, almost certainly. And her name, besides, is bound to be different now. She would be thirty-six or thirty-seven years old at least. And I really can't imagine her as other than married, somewhere. The woman you describe sounds much younger. Also Margaret was never a city girl.

No, unless memory tricks me entirely, Livingstone never went home again – from the city, that is, to Te Ika and environs. And I think I can speak with some confidence of the period im-

471

mediately before the exhibition; I saw many of the paintings emerge.

Now for your leading question. I wish I knew what to make of it. What you really want me to do, I suppose, is confirm your own finding that he suffered loss of nerve consequent upon this exhibition. Yes, I can see that's one way of putting it. Perhaps it's just that it wasn't so apparent to me at the time. And perhaps it's just that your phrase irritates me. Anyway I find it difficult to accept. Whatever else he lacked, it never seemed to be nerve.

But it's true, all the same, that he never really painted landscape again. Or that never in the same way. There is that to be said for your argument. But couldn't this equally well be styled development – as much as, say, loss of nerve? I realize how difficult it is, often, for the critical intelligence to meet the creative in understanding. While both upon substantial ground.

Anyway you must see, by now, that you trouble me.

I also think I begin to see what you are driving towards. (Correct me if I'm wrong.) If you don't mind me saying so – and I'm sure you will mind me saying so – it seems rather conventional after all : the young artist of talent, possibly of genius, destroyed by his society. Please don't misunderstand me; I'm sure it *does* happen. And if you have a social point to make, by all means make it the way you see fit, and don't let me deter you. But don't mistake the social point for the whole point. Allow the cosmos something; and allow the artist something to himself. We aren't all our societies in miniature, not even the Walt Whitmans of the world. What I mean is, all our choices can't be illusory; not altogether. And God knows we do make choices, or seem to, now and then. Otherwise there is nothing to bring to judgement, and there must be judgement, somewhere; there must be, has to be.

Later : Sorry. I've lost myself somewhere. And lost track. The day is hot and heavy, the sky clear, and I've just tried my morning swim in the lagoon, in hope of clarifying my thought. Only to disperse it altogether. I can still see (or think I can) what you are driving at : what I can't recall is what I was. Perhaps I'd better leave the whole subject alone, leave it to you. Yes.

Did I really use that phrase 'hills as stark as prophecy' in writing of his work? Rather pretty; I must remember it. I imagine I must have meant something. It's so long, you see, since I have actually seen the paintings. What we felt about him at the time, and what he really was, are almost certainly two different things. Now. But it is conceivable, I agree, that he might not have known what he was doing: Certainly this would explain the rest, rather than 'loss of nerve' – sorry, that still sticks.

Is the work which follows so trivial by comparison? I recall some of it as most effective, in a social realist vein, not altogether worthless. And even his prison paintings, among his other glimpses of the city, are landscapes of a kind. What I mean is, I seem to remember the same concerns – and concern—being there. Or do I wish that upon the work? This was a period when he was close to Stan Coates. I'm sure he *could* help you more, if you persist with him. Try again.

I'm interested to hear that you find yourself more and more involved, but hope this doesn't lead to frustration.

Enough. It's noon and the sweat is pouring off me (I sit at the typewriter stripped to the waist). I hope you find something worthwhile in this rambling. Sorry this one has gone on so long. Lacking much real conversation here, I find my correspondence becomes increasingly garrulous.

Best wishes
Sincerely
Ian Freeman

Avarua P.O. etc.
February 2, 1967

Dear Ben,

Having today composed my (almost) monthly message to Max Kennedy – the fellow is remarkable – I feel almost duty bound to follow it up with a letter to you. Though it seems only a week or two since I last wrote.

It's late afternoon now. Picture me a moment. Grass shack, cool breeze off the sea (no windows, just openings in the walls), lovely late light on the palm fronds outside, and a steady thud of surf out on the reef. If my typewriter ceases to clack for a minute – and what an intrusion the sound is here – I can observe my nextdoor neighbours in Gauguinesque arrangement, mother, grandmother, and children scattered around in vague

473

blue smoke for their *umu,* or earth oven; or I can see Turepu, my fisherman friend, casting his net in the lagoon, where the fish have been running well. A day like any other; a day like most. Peace is sometimes the most inadequate word in the language.

And you think I should hurry home.

Because I've been away too long? Before it's too late? You don't say.

Well, yes. Perhaps I should. I don't doubt it; I mean doubt that you're right. I suppose it's a question of nerve.

I should add that I'm totally alone here at the moment. To express how fed up she is – or has been, with me – Ina has taken off again; she claims she is visiting relatives on a neighbouring island, an overnight boat trip. But I suspect her eye may be starting to rove again, perhaps in search of some new *papaa,* comfortably situated. If she isn't back today or tomorrow, then I can assume that she has found someone else. I won't blame her.

To get back to the point. I did walk from the village towards Avarua township yesterday, with the idea of making a booking on some southbound boat in the next month, in fact with every good intention. What happened was that on my way I paid a call at the house of a drunken *papaa* friend and, while sampling his latest issue of bush-beer, discovered that a passing plane had left behind some newspapers of recent date. (It's actually possible, here, to forget what newspapers look like, for a while.) The war in Vietnam seemed plastered on every page, with new highs in body counts, bombing raids, search and destroy missions (possible to forget that too) and other diverse detail. Is anything else happening in the world? Then I read of some modest rioting in your vicinity, the result of the visit of some swanky little Asian gangster who has bought and murdered his way into supposed leadership of the poor bloody Vietnamese, and whose name won't be remembered inside ten years: anyway it appears this gilded little fascist has been an honoured guest in your country – which you appear to think is mine too. So, anyway, I didn't quite reach Avarua and make that booking.

I suppose it *is* a question of nerve.

After all this correspondence with Kennedy, I'm looking forward, perhaps for perverse reasons, to looking over those paintings of Tim's you've been holding for me all this time. To see just what they *are* like, after all. He has me interested again.

Interested? I suppose that's only half of what I mean. It seems to me

February 9

Sorry; a slight distraction. Ina arrived back, with all-forgiving smile, in the middle of that sentence. And I don't quite know what has happened to it, let alone the week since.

The weather is still hot.

My brain remains reluctant to move.

I'd better mail this disaster, and try again next time.

Much love

Ian

P.S.: Do you ever watch television?

And if so, pay any attention to local television personalities?

I expect not. But I have to ask someone – or, rather, start somewhere. The question isn't as silly as it seems.

Kennedy thinks most of Tim's work, after that infamous exhibition, relatively trivial. Insists that he lost his nerve. What do you think? I just have a feeling you might agree, even that the idea might have been yours in the first place. And that you fed it to Kennedy.

I really must start thinking about that booking again. But *apopo* (tomorrow), the local equivalent of *manana*.

Must stop. Ina says she'll mail my silly letters down in the township. Hope this reaches you. Apopo. A lovely word.

It isn't much more than a year since this talented and vigorous young artist shook the complacent bourgeois of this sober city with an exhibition of landscapes. The total and vivid crudeness of this work, however intentional the impact, created more fuss than anything by a native artist within memory. Even on the left, by people who should have known better, his work was scorned as, among other things, formalist and escapist and even called totally reactionary. True, people were absent from his work – any hint of human society. Now, however, in this new exhibition, Livingstone sets out to fill the gap. Landscape has given way to cityscape. And the artist demonstrates that he does see people after all – the ordinary people of this country, working people, Polynesian and European. The people who have it in their hands to build a better, just and decent socialist

475

society. For those who care to use their eyes, the social comment is plain, particularly in his striking series of prison paintings.

— Review in Communist weekly, by Stan Coates

May I offer a few words of appreciation for the very fine art review written by Comrade Coates? It is good to see a genuine concern for art in your columns, and particularly a concern for the work of Tim Livingstone, surely the finest young painter this country has produced.

— Letter in Communist weekly, by Sandy West

Though his subjects are at least more recognizable, Mr Livingstone still hasn't lost his obsession with ugliness. A pity. We could do with less of the squalors of life, and more of its beauty. Is he altogether blind?

— Review in daily newspaper, author anonymous

Commentaries

I found a job finally. It came through Charlie Bates, who had joined a group of equally unqualified young architects in a construction firm of makeshift arrangement; his associates had also been expelled from architectural school, but for participation in a student strike against a conservative professor. They raised a small amount of capital between them and set to work as carpenters, bricklayers, anything to produce buildings of their own design. They would have taken pains even with fowlhouse or piggery, and some of their projects weren't much bigger. I was taken on, along with Sandy West, as builder's labourer; we usually, but not always, got paid a weekly wage. Sandy was the job delegate – representing some three or four labourers – to the trade union. We had no strikes. The other labourers were also recruited because of their tolerant nature. The money might have been erratic, and conditions unkempt, but we often had lengthened lunch-hours, and sometimes entire days, in bars or on beaches adjoining a job.

It suited me, with its absence of pressure; all decisions were made for me. And I was fitter physically, quickly brown in the sun. I couldn't see the job lasting, but that wasn't unusual.

I had lost my link with Te Ika. My parents shifted nearer the city when my father retired and I saw them more often, along with Diane. My father accepted my change in occupation with some satisfaction. 'I knew it wouldn't last,' he said. 'I knew you weren't cut out for some lying bloody newspaper. I could of told you that from the start.'

'Well – ' I began to explain.

'So they couldn't take your politics in the end, eh?' he went on. 'Or you theirs. Well, it was bound to come, the way I saw it.'

'Actually – '

'And now,' he finished, 'you've joined the ranks of the working class. You could do worse. Your hands might be dirty in one way, but they're clean in another. You've got the chance, the way I see it, to think again about your life. I'm proud of you walking out and telling those newspaper bastards where they could stick their lies.'

Finally I decided he was welcome to have it his own way, since he would anyhow. In any case how could I have explained, say, Tim Livingstone? Yet my life, in its new shape, didn't appear particularly perplexing.

My mother, though, seemed to feel I could find work more worthy. 'Is that the best you could get?' she asked.

'It suits me.'

'That's not the point.'

'I don't expect it is,' I agreed.

Diane was finishing off her last year at school, almost ready for university herself. She was already garlanded with prizes and honours; it seemed she couldn't touch anything without instant success. Willowy now, and still lovelier, she was no less nervously staccato in conversation. 'You're looking well,' she said. 'Better than I've seen you in years.'

'I'm glad someone thinks so.'

'Is it a girl friend, then?' she asked solemnly.

I laughed. 'Does it have to be?'

'No. I just wondered.'

I said, 'I'd sooner talk about you.'

'I've got nothing much to tell,' she said. 'Except that I miss my brother.'

'I don't see why.'

'Because he's the only one I've got,' she said. 'when I've got him. And today he's going to take me swimming. And afterwards for a long walk along the coast. And after that – '

'All right,' I said. 'You've got me.'

It seemed sufficiently true.

Stan Coates appeared at our flat more often. Loneliness appeared to drive him in our direction; he no longer seemed happy in his job, with his fellow comrades, or with his diverse left-wing projects. But he said his book on the strike, which he claimed to be expanding into a history of socialist and working class struggle in the country, was still moving along slowly. He also seemed no longer at loggerheads with Tim. I often arrived home from work to find them in intense conversation which I was seldom moved to join. I would be more interested in preparing a meal, and settling down to my desk. Tim, at this time, was hardly working, apart from odd jobs supplied by Ken; he scraped along from week to week. The excitement of his exhibition was almost forgotten, and I could sometimes marvel that there had been so much.

'I don't like it,' Ken confided.

But there was nothing obvious that either of us could do. Except wait, which we were doing anyway. I could wonder what Tim wanted, if anything, from Stan; or Stan from Tim. Such conversation as I overheard sounded remarkably general and political.

Paul Wiseman was another visitor, more irregular. Tim didn't display great patience with Paul. After a spell as a clerk, he was now refusing all employment and trying to make a life for himself as a poet on the fringe of society; he took François Villon as model, and brought his poems to me in hope that I might persuade Ken McAdam to publish. He also had the idea that he would find patrons. But the rare patrons he found were moody, it appeared, and mostly homosexual; they never lasted long. Or, rather, Paul never lasted long. His poems were obscene, necrophilic and unprintable. Nevertheless, Paul persisted in hope of both patrons and publication. Hunger frequently brought him to the flat; he would always make polite offer to leave when I prepared food, and I would have to insist that he stay to share, an offer accepted graciously in the end. Otherwise he borrowed money for food, when he could, and also slept where he could, mainly on park benches, and usually one bench ahead of the police. One winter night, taking pity, I brought Paul back to the flat for an evening's warmth; he was wet and miserable and near starvation. He stayed two weeks, sleeping on the floor. Then Tim grew tired of tumbling over him every morning and, in my absence, tipped him out the door, poems and all. It was a relief to me too, though I didn't say so. Something had to be done, as Tim observed; I was just glad that I hadn't had to do it. Anyway Paul didn't perish. The next time I saw him, he was speaking of a splendid new patron with a Japanese-style home among treeferns on the outskirts of the city.

Tim still made regular visits to Monty Nolan in prison, and took him material for his art work. One or two of Monty's austere prison paintings now decorated the flat. Stan often kept Tim company on these visits; I preferred to stay at home, with the flat to myself. For, after their prison visiting, Tim spent long periods walking through the city with Stan, and sometimes on his own.

I began to see that, whatever else was happening, Ken and I had been left bobbing in his wake. But the weeks had to add up to months, and the months to nearly a year, before I accepted it. Ken by that time had printed three of my stories.

Tim offered little comment. For that I had to depend on others. On Ken, or on Ted Connolly, when I saw him. 'Keep at it,' Ted urged. 'And how's Tim, by the way?'

And there was always, of course, retreat to Ben, in his garden. But he also, finally, appeared more interested in Tim. 'You're testing yourself,' he observed. 'That's the main thing. I hope, by the way, that you're setting an example to your flat-mate. Is he painting again yet?'

I had to say he wasn't really, though from time to time there were closed sketchbooks evident in the flat; I didn't pry. Perhaps because I'd sooner not know.

'Still,' Ben said, 'it will be interesting to see what he does next.'

If he does, I was tempted to add.

For if we talked now, it was never about Te Ika, or anything like it. He might have made a change of cell.

Yet we were still sometimes together outside the flat. On Saturday nights, for example, Tim often did lightning sketches of people in the coffee bar, or in dance halls, to pick up money; and I kept him company, unless otherwise involved. For it was also an effective way of picking up girls on unpromising nights, or learning about parties; at least it was better than sitting at home alone and listening to the sounds of the city, and chimes of the clocks. Not much better, on occasion, but better. Sunday could seem slow to come.

'Can you think of anything better to do?' Tim might ask.

'Not yet,' I replied, perhaps grimly.

It appeared everyone else in the city had somewhere to go. By eight-thirty the coffee bar was quite empty. Still, we had survived worse.

Worse, one evening, was Paul Wiseman arriving to find us sitting bleak. 'This poem here,' he said. 'What do you think of it?'

I read aloud. *'From foetal darkness/ The leaping leopards of my other dreams. . .'* I tried to consider it seriously. 'Not bad,' I said. 'Though there seems to be a certain confusion of ideas. And the poem doesn't really get anywhere.'

'But do you think Ken might be interested in taking it on?'

'He could be,' I allowed.

It was Saturday night, after all. Paul, like the rest of us, was allowed illusion. He beamed brightly in his canary-yellow sweater.

Better was Charlie Bates arriving. For Charlie had a car. And a car implied possibilities. He might have Sandy West and Ted Connolly with him, but there was still room for us all. Charlie's car was very flexible.

Better still was Ken McAdam appearing, having missed us at other watering places, with vague news of a party.

'But,' he explained, 'we are very definitely not invited. It's the place where all those windows got broken last time.'

'Leave it till late,' Charlie urged. 'When people are drunk enough, they never notice us at all.'

'Especially,' Sandy added, 'if we move in just one or two at a time.'

'So what do we do in the meantime?' Ken asked.

'The Polynesian Club,' Tim announced. 'I might pick up some money.'

'And a good place to pick up other things,' Charlie said, with obvious regret. 'The last time I – '

'You don't know for sure,' Sandy interjected. 'You could have collected that dose anywhere.'

The Polynesian Club was by reputation the roughest of the city's rougher dance halls. About the only thing to justify the title of the place were some paper-mache palm trees beside the brassy band. And, of course, the racial mixture on the floor. The music could be wild. And the dancers streamed with sweat. We found seats near a cool open window. Tim began work producing likenesses at a few shillings a time. Dancers swerved close to him as he worked, arms snapping and legs jerking, brown girls in brilliant frocks, dark boys in dark suits, but he seldom moved an inch. The rest of us danced when the mood allowed us. Drums boiled; feet thundered; colours clashed. It looked like life : perhaps it was, or some entirely convincing facsimile. Light flitted here and there among the dancers : here an ecstatic face, there a supplicant hand, or shiny shoulder. Everywhere flickering flesh and feet.

Tim, having delivered sufficient money into his pocket, watched the flow on the floor with interest, sketchbook still open on his knee, and his hand working. Waves of dancers beat up to him and ebbed, leaving him like driftwood high and dry, in impressive isolation.

Before long Charlie managed a fight; and was swiftly felled by a burly Maori. It was clearly time to leave : our departure from any situation was seldom less than spectacular. We swooped upon Charlie from our different parts of the hall and carried him off, lest he be hit again, or start hitting back; and tumbled noisily down the stairs into the street. Sandy, in this confusion, souvenired a couple of girls from the hall; they added to the accommodation problem in Charlies' car. This aged vehicle was really Charlie's home and world : cluttered with clothes, blankets, sleeping bag, a primus stove, pots and pans, cans of food, a draughting board, and plans for unlikely buildings. Almost entirely self-contained, but for a lavatory. For this Charlie had to depend on public installations, city parks and the goodwill of friends.

We all wedged ourselves in, with a crash of crockery. 'I think we're late enough for the party now,' Sandy announced.

Charlie, propped behind the wheel of the car, gave a faint groan. We examined him and found one eye bruised and swelling; otherwise he appeared intact and fit to drive. We allowed him a few minutes to recover.

'It was too good to last, back there,' Tim observed. 'I might have bloody known. Why don't we ever last the distance?'

'What's eating you now?' Ken asked.

'Nothing. Everything.' His silence became sullen.

The girls giggled nervously. Of indeterminate Polynesian blood, they otherwise appeared interestingly happy with themselves.

'Shall I tell you my new poem?' Paul asked irrelevantly and rather timidly.

'Christ save us,' Ken said. 'But go on. What is it this time?'

481

'Leaping leopards,' I muttered. 'The leaping leopards of his other dreams.'

'Spare us,' Sandy said. 'The night's bad enough.'

'Then I'll tell you another one,' Paul offered. 'This one's shorter, and it rhymes.'

'I like a good rhyme, myself,' Sandy said. 'All right, go on. We've nothing better at the moment.'

Paul recited squeakily. It sounded something like:

> *Does silence jettison now my soul's desire*
> *Wreathing film of fantasy round my funeral pyre?*
> *And has the fountain which pours out the light*
> *Grown dry, and left me lonely in the night?*

'It might rhyme,' Ken said critically, 'but I don't think it bloody scans.'

The two girls, however, in apparent panic, scrambled out of the car; they argued briefly between themselves on the pavement. We overheard scraps: 'Those boys are queer.' 'They said a party.' 'I don't want their parties.' Sandy's protest, and pleas to return, were ignored; the last we saw of them, they were running back to the hall.

'Well, that's stuffed it,' Sandy said savagely to Paul. 'You see what you've done? You and your bloody funeral pyre.'

Paul, unnerved entirely now, shrank into himself.

It was time to move on anyway. Charlie had recovered sufficiently to drive.

'Let's pick up Coates on the way,' Tim suggested.

'Do we have to?' Ken said. 'I don't need to hear about my petit-bourgeois mentality, or my lumpen-intellectual tendency.'

'He might,' Tim said, 'save us with some sanity.'

'Now I've heard everything,' Ken replied.

So had I, more or less. But I kept silence.

'At least Stan knows where he's going,' Tim argued, 'and what he's talking about. More than I can say for some.'

'All right,' Ken said. 'Loud and clear.'

A minute or two later Charlie parked in front of Stan's place. Tim went inside to fetch him; he was gone some time. Ted Connolly, who had been quietly listening most of the night, a patient observer of us all, began snoring in the back seat. Sandy whistled between his teeth. Charlie tapped the wheel impatiently. Ken tried to massage a cramp out of his leg. Paul fidgeted.

We could have been waiting upon a judgement.

And one of a kind came, eventually, when Stan emerged from his flat with Tim. He looked into the car, examined the chaos within, and was evidently satisfied to find no one he could not recognize. 'Is all this,' he asked, 'really necessary?'

But he climbed wearily into the vehicle, all the same, and joined the journey. Out of habit or hope.

Charlie slammed his car into low gear and began climbing. The house we sought was fastened high on a flank of one of the city's old volcanic cones; a last twist of steep road and we were there. House lights, flooding through doors and windows, made pale a wild green garden, where here and there odd pieces of statuary peered from behind shrubs. There was noise; there was music.

We unfurled ourselves from the car and flexed our stiffened limbs. 'Remember,' Ken said, 'one or two at a time. We don't invade; we infiltrate. And then circulate. We can meet up again later.'

But we didn't and possibly couldn't pass unnoticed. I had just poured myself a drink, at the bar, when I overheard someone say, 'I see the Livingstone gang is with us again.'

The place was crowded with people who seemed to have done something with their lives, or appeared happy to think so. There were university people, writers and journalists and others of modest repute; liberal lawyers and arty businessmen, and one or two leftist politicians. No wonder we appeared distinct, all the way down to Charlie's fresh bruises. We might sustain ourselves on sour grapes, but they feasted on sweet lemon. And we could, evidently, alarm.

'It seems,' said another, 'one can't escape the yahoos of our hobohemia these days. Are they the best we can produce? Typical of this country. The fact is we can never produce the genuine article, socially. Always something half-baked. Wouldn't you agree?'

'I suppose,' said the first, 'you're contemplating our lack of a genuine peasantry, among other things.'

'Among other things,' the second agreed. 'It seems we've acquired all the appurtenances of civilization, of a society, but we've only plugged half of them in. Or we forgot to have power laid on at all. One thing or the other.'

483

'Mind you,' said the first, 'one can't deny that some form of bohemia, however perverse, is often seedbed for the artist.'

'True. But what strange and curious plants we produce.'

'You mean Livingstone?'

'And his lot. Nothing to them. A poor sad crew with a colour-blind captain. Can you imagine worse?'

The atmosphere was as unpromising elsewhere. I saw Tim sheltering, conspicuously inconspicuous, in a corner of the room, with Paul beside him. Stan was arguing with one of the politicians, and becoming heated.

Sandy grabbed my shoulder. 'I think,' he confided, 'we ought to grab some grog and girls and go. Enough's enough. They don't like us here.'

'So we grab grog and girls and go,' I said.

'That's the idea.'

'Is that the best we can do, Sandy?'

'It's all we can do. What's the matter with you?'

'Nothing,' I said. 'Yet.'

I didn't have to see us as others saw us; but I could begin to see us as we were. We might all wish revelation or revolution but, in their absence, grabbed grog and girls and went. Perhaps Sandy was right : it was all we could do, together. And perhaps I wasn't drunk enough. That at least could find remedy.

Paul was performing on top of the piano, his trousers off again. Stan, his argument over, had collapsed drunkenly in a deep armchair. Sandy was trapped in an erotic dance with a blonde he had found. Ted Connolly was sitting thoughtful beside me; we both looked moodily into the middle distance. Tim was out of sight.

We weren't responsible for all the problems of the party. A woman was having hysterics in the kitchen because her husband had left her; there had been at least one scuffle in which we hadn't been involved at all.

Sandy danced, or staggered, past. His blonde was saying : 'Why don't you have your revolution tonight? I think it's a fantastic idea, the whole thing. What do you think I should wear?'

'Nothing,' Sandy growled.

Perhaps it was easy enough, after all, to make noise and call it conversation. I set out for an open door. I wished myself elsewhere. Where, though?

The open door, and cool air beyond, became another discarded ambition. For it filled abruptly with brawling figures. Among them I glimpsed Charlie, and Ken trying to rescue him. I was able to infer that Charlie had just been caught trying to carry a crate of beer to his car. I pushed into the fight, to help Ken, with some relief; at least things were clear now. Within moments we had Sandy as ally, then Ted. Behind us, Paul toppled from the piano in confusion.

Minutes later we were scrambling back into Charlie's car again. We found Tim in the back seat, occupied with a girl; but he didn't seem much happier with himself, less so for being disturbed. We deposited Stan beside him, making drowning motions with his arms; and then Paul, possibly concussed. Otherwise we were not in bad shape. We had fresh beer in the car, two or three girls, and still half the night.

We drove down to the sea. The beach we found was unpopulated, with the houses shut tight at two in the morning; street lights reached the sand only faintly. We arranged ourselves on the shore with blankets and beer. Navigation beacons flicked on and off across the gulf, spinning ephemeral threads of light on the dark water. The waves were dimly phosphorescent near our feet.

'We could still be dancing,' sighed Sandy's blonde. Her name was Ngaire; she was an actress of sorts.

But, one way or another, we made our best of the shore. Ted Connolly stripped off, and swam out into the dark. Others paddled; one or two sang. But most grew quieter, and fell asleep.

I dozed, and woke to find the sky grey with first light. Almost everyone was still asleep. Except Charlie, who sat tense, smoking. And, down by the receding tide, Tim skipped pebbles across the water. His silhouette was sharp in the growing light. With his characteristic jerky gait, he stalked the shore as if impatient with its limits.

I wished we could still talk, but there no longer seemed point in persisting. Instead I undressed, walked past him in silence, and gave my body to the sting of the sea. The night seemed to float behind : to become one with a hundred others. And I felt cleansed as I drifted back to shore.

Most had woken, or were trying to wake.

Ngaire said we should all go home to her flat for breakfast.

485

Sandy said we should wait for sunrise. Paul said the best place to see sunrise was from uptown, on the museum steps; he had watched it there often, when he hadn't anywhere else to sleep.

Charlie said he'd like people to remember it was his bloody car.

Sandy said, all right, it was Charlie's bloody car. We could walk, if that was the way Charlie felt.

Charlie said he felt like hell, that was all.

Ngaire said she felt like going to America, or somewhere.

Sandy said not at this time of night.

Tim, answering a question from one of the other girls, said the first thing an artist had to decide was how primary were the primary colours.

She said really.

Ken asked were we going anywhere at all.

Charlie said he would take us up town, if we insisted, but then we could bloody well walk.

Tim's girl said colour had always fascinated her, really, and what Tim thought was fascinating, really.

Paul said he thought he might go to London to make another start, if he could escape.

Sandy said escape what.

Paul said escape this police state.

Charlie asked would someone, anyone, make up their minds what we wanted to do. Because he was buggered.

It seemed we were agreed on the museum steps. We rose and blinked in the growing light of day. Sunrise was not too far off. The sea looked cold and grey; the distant lights had lost their lure.

Stan said, as we walked to the car, what a hell of a way to spend a Saturday night, and why didn't we ever learn.

Ken said look who was talking.

Sandy said he couldn't stand snarling before breakfast, and would they both shut up.

Ted Connolly remained remote, no longer quite with us at all.

Charlie's car, when we crammed into it, seemed to offer only diverse discomfort now. Elbows and knees, companionably pressing earlier, were now painfully locked.

Tim, still tenuously talking, said all he had was colour, and he didn't even have too much of that left. The girl he might have been trying to impress, perhaps out of habit, said that was a shame, really.

486

Charlie, starting the car, said the place he really ought to drive was the lunatic asylum.

His chariot bucked towards the centre of the city. Soon we were travelling between bleak warehouses and blackened railway yards, suburban gardens gone. Then there were shut shops, with street-lamps shining weakly in the grey morning; and idling breezes snatching litter off the pavements. The most colourless hour of the day, of the week. There wasn't even a policeman to be seen.

Ken said it was nice to have the feeling we were the only people alive in the whole damn country.

Stan said that too was a matter of opinion.

Sandy said for Christ's sake would they lay off each other.

We grew quiet in the bumping car. We drove out of the commercial area, and were suddenly among the grassy slopes, phoenix palms and giant trees of the city domain. The museum rose, pale and faintly luminous, on a height ahead : wide flights of steps and Grecian columns in the dawn, exact against the brightening sky.

Charlie parked the car at last. We untangled and escaped. And then, clutching our blankets, we made our way past the bulky war memorial with its stoic inscription to the glorious dead, up the flights of steps, to take shelter beneath tall columns. We might have looked like a tiny party of pilgrims, seen distant, if there were anyone to see.

It seemed at least we all were sober.

We arranged ourselves to see the sunrise, and soon were comfortable, within reason. The day was quiet, though there were birds noisy in the distance. Paul's head began to droop, and soon he slept against Charlie, who slipped an arm about him. Otherwise we were all separate, and silent.

Until Ken said it seemed a fair enough place for a last stand, the way things were.

I tried to trap some memory of the evening behind. All things seemed fugitive. Even the wave of dancers breaking and ebbing and Tim alone with his sketchbook or walking with jerky gait, skipping stones in silhouette against the sea.

Yet the night began to seem worthwhile after all. The sun began to rise, with comforting predictability, in the east. Faint mists clung to the old volcanic cones of the city. Islands floated in the golden glow; the city below grew bright, and the sea seemed solid with colour. And the classic columns which dwarfed us became alive with light. Gulls drifted here and there, or hung still, gliding without evident motion on such breeze as they found.

I wasn't surprised when Tim moved out of the flat. It put an end to the waiting. The obligation to communicate with him had become a strain. He said he was shifting in with Stan. 'I'm going to paint again,' he announced. 'This place has never been big enough for me. Stan has all the space I want.'

'That's all right,' I said. 'You don't have to explain.'

'But I do want to explain.'

'I'm just saying there's no real need.'

'If that's the way you feel,' he said, 'all right.'

So he said no more. The place seemed incredibly empty when he had gone; my relief was short-lived. But I did have a chance to get used to myself again. I avoided Stan's flat now, though Stan had always made me welcome there. I avoided other people too, with some success, though there was no escaping Charlie and Sandy on the job. And Ken called in sometimes, in the evenings.

'Have you heard what he's up to?' Ken asked. I confessed I had no idea.

'I don't like it,' Ken said.

'You've been saying that for months. There's nothing we can do about it. You must see that by now.'

'It's just,' he explained, 'that I can't help feeling we've let him down somewhere.'

'I know the feeling,' I admitted.

'He's never come right since that exhibition.'

'He did say, when he left, that he was going to paint again.'

'That's a relief, I admit. Though I still have my doubts.'

'About what?'

'Him. Us. I don't know.'

He looked extremely depressed. Nothing I could say would help. So I didn't try.

'I imagine you've heard,' he said, 'about Ted Connolly.'

'What about him?'

'He's quit the bush. And settled down at last in the city.'

'It's hard to believe,' I said. I had been so used to Ted coming and going.

488

'And no one ever sees him,' Ken added. 'A girl, I understand. Rather colourless and quiet. I saw Ted rush past in the
street yesterday. His beard has gone. And he was actually
wearing a tie, and a respectable white shirt. He's going back to
university, among other things.'

'No,' I said, surprised.

'He's always been around, easy to take for granted. You realize, I suppose, that he once took Tim under his wing? At the
beginning.'

'Yes,' I said. 'I knew that.'

'Anyway,' Ken said, 'we all have to live our lives. And look
at me; I'm the last one to talk. You notice I've always been
careful to have one foot on safe ground.'

'Yes, Ken. I've noticed.'

'Unlike Livingstone. He has the gambler's instinct. Go for
broke. He couldn't play it safe even if he knew how. And unlike
you, if it comes to that. You surprise me. Because, among other
things, you do know how.'

'Thanks,' I said. 'I should have guessed.'

'I imagine you have more time on your hands now. With
Livingstone gone.'

'That's one way of putting it.'

'Well,' he said, and rose to leave, 'I still can't help wondering
what he's up to. Don't you?'

Actually we didn't have long to wait for answer: a half dozen
months at most. It became clear that Tim was, as he said
in the first place, painting again. For another exhibition was
announced. I first learned of it through an invitation which
arrived in the mail. The venue was not a gallery this time, but a
trade union hall. Stan rang me the next day. 'You'll be along
to the opening of course,' he said.

'I'm thinking about it,' I replied, perhaps coolly.

'Of course you will be,' he said. 'We want everyone there. All
the old crowd. Everyone. You're due for a surprise.' He sounded
rather overwrought. 'A big surprise.'

'Really?'

'Wait and see. Tremendous stuff. Solid. Tremendous impact.
Tim's really got his feet on the ground now.'

'I always thought he had, when he had his feet anywhere.'

'But he's settled down. He's solid now. He knows where he's
going. And he knows who he's painting for.'

'Who for, Stan?'

'The people,' he said. 'Of course.'

'I see.'

'Nothing nebulous now. All solid, tight as a rock, really solid.'

He was oddly insistent on the word, as if the rest of the world might be melting, visibly.

'Well,' I said, 'That's certainly good to hear. And I'll try to get along.'

'Good. And pass the word. I'm doing my best. I'm not saying, mind you, that this show won't upset some people.'

I didn't ask who. Anyway Stan sounded far too excitable, unusually incoherent.

'So we'll see you there,' he finished.

'Yes, Stan. Very likely.'

'Of course we will,' he insisted.

Diane had arrived in the city to begin university; she stayed in a student hostel, but was a frequent visitor to my flat. I often arrived home dusty and tired to find her attractively in occupation, cooking me a meal; she insisted I sat down, and fetched me a cold bottle of beer before I cleaned up. But she was the real refreshment. I hadn't realized my life had grown so drab. Yet my situation as she saw it appealed to her. 'This is just the way I expected you to live,' she declared. 'Books and paintings and papers everywhere. I don't think I should tidy up too much. Just try and keep the dust down. And this place comfortable.'

'You shouldn't worry,' I argued.

'But I do worry. What's the point in your having a sister if I don't?'

'It's not the entire point.'

'Besides,' she said, 'if I don't worry about you, who will? You obviously don't – worry about yourself, I mean.'

'You'd be surprised.'

'Would I? I'd just like to see some sign of it, that's all. The job you've got, for example.'

'Not you too,' I sighed.

'There are other things.'

'Yes,' I agreed. 'Probably.'

'See?' she said. 'That's what I mean. You don't worry about yourself. So it's just as well I do. Finish that beer and wash yourself. Dinner's almost ready. At least I can see that you're fed properly, now and then, can't I?'

490

'Astonishingly,' I had to admit.

'So you agree you need me?'

I seemed to recall someone else once putting that question to me, or one very like it.

'But I don't want to be a bother to you,' she added. 'You only have to say. I'm just your kid sister. And you have friends.'

'One or two,' I conceded.

'And girl friends.'

'The odd one.' I tried to consider their faces, then their bodies : none seemed very real, though I had almost been able to convince myself, on occasion, that I loved someone or other and it was hard to say now which body, or whose face. At least I wasn't indifferent to Diane.

'I expect you'll have boy friends yourself soon,' I observed.

'More than enough. Then I won't see so much of you.'

'I expect I will. But I'm in no hurry.'

Sometimes we spent Sundays together, swimming and sunbathing at a beach; or travelling across the harbour, in a ferry, to visit Ben. Ben was much taken by Diane. 'Someone should have warned me,' he said, 'that my niece had grown so lovely. Come and see me any time.'

And Diane blushed quite prettily. 'He's a funny old thing,' she confided afterwards. 'And to think he once wrote all that poetry. It's hard to believe; he looks all dried up. I like him, do you?'

'Yes.'

'This artist he keeps talking about. Who is he?'

'A friend. The one who used to share my flat.' It appeared, from what Ben said, that Tim still visited him now and then.

'Oh, yes. Those paintings of yours. You don't ever mention him much.'

'Perhaps because I don't see him much now. Hardly at all.'

'Did you fall out, then?'

'Not exactly. We probably just grew tired of each other. We happened both to come from Te Ika. But then our lives grew different, I expect. Or perhaps too alike; I don't know. Anyway he left.'

'But you miss him,' she said shrewdly, 'don't you?'

'In a way. He was company.'

Saturday nights were easier to fill, if quietly, with Diane on my arm; I could arrive at Sunday morning without regret. She made the city fresh again, an innocent playground. And my need for her innocence, once identified, was a thirst I slaked with conscious care. Yet we couldn't, in other ways, have been closer. We had few reserves, or need for them.

I had, though, to face some questions. 'Don't tell me you're capitulating too,' Ken said. 'I never seem to see you much. And who, by the way, is that splendid little creature I glimpsed you with?'

'No one special,' I replied evasively.

'You're joking.'

'My sister, if you must know.'

'Well, now. You keep her well hidden, don't you?'

'Up to a point, yes, I suppose I do.'

'Never mind. I can see why. But I wouldn't mind an introduction sometime, if you can manage it.'

I didn't seem able to manage it, in the event. Or other introductions which would have been appreciated equally. My hours with Diane were time apart from the substance of my city existence. When with her, I avoided usual haunts. And, so long as luck lasted, my usual company. Yet it was inevitable that my two lives would touch. As they did at the point where Diane noticed my invitation to Tim's new opening, pinned on the kitchen wall. 'If you're going,' she asked, 'please take me. I've never been to anything like that before.'

'I'm not sure what this one will be like myself,' I explained. 'It's not the usual thing. I haven't made up my mind about going.' I'd begun to consider avoiding the occasion, and looking in on the exhibition later in the week; my reasons were diverse. And probably wouldn't stand much examination.

'Then I'll make up your mind for you,' she announced. 'You're going. And you're taking me, aren't you?'

I sighed. 'I'll think about it.'

'And anyway,' she persisted, 'won't your friend be disappointed if you don't go along?'

'I doubt it, really.'

'Please,' she said.

I hesitated.

'Please,' she repeated. 'Please go.' She smiled. 'And take me.'

If I refused, I would have to contend with her disappointment along with my own curiosity. 'All right,' I said. 'You have another date.'

The hall was off the edge of the commercial area of the city. A rather grim stone place from the outside; a bastion beside the marketplace, in which socialist hope had been invested, when hope was reasonable, and which still served to contain the smoke and drawled debate of trade union meetings. Inside, it was almost as bleak and cold, with glaring lights on drab wooden walls, and stacked benches and chairs; the paintings, as I first saw them from a distance, seemed small and lost. But faces were in the way, some recognizable, most not; were these others, the new faces, 'the people' of Stan's claim?

But the first person I saw was Monty Nolan, standing alone and rather apart from other people. I didn't know he was outside again, it was a shock to see him free, of prison grey, in a baggy dark suit, but he still had prison pallor. I led Diane up to him, and shook his hand. 'I got time off for good behaviour,' he explained wryly. 'The parole people seemed to think this art had done me good. They don't think I'll clobber too many cops with a paint-brush. The only thing I know for sure is I've still got a bed back at the jail, if I want it. I still don't know much about this art business, though. What do you think about our boy Tim and his new paintings?'

'I haven't had a chance to see yet.'

'They're pretty tough, I reckon. Pretty straight. But not my cup of tea. I like something to cheer me up. Still it takes all kinds.'

I observed Stan, in a wild sweat, racing about the hall, shaking hands, introducing people, talking rapidly, indicating the walls; he seemed all panic. 'Well,' I said, and nodded to Monty, 'we'd better see for ourselves, before the place fills up.'

'Sure,' Monty said. 'Nice to see you. And specially nice to meet your sister. It reminds me that it's worth being out.'

But Diane and I still found it difficult to get at the pictures: we were stopped by Ken. I was obliged to introduce them to each other. Ken gave an appreciative smile.

'Well,' he said to me, 'we might as well face it. The worst has happened. He's given up landscape. Just when he was starting to add up to something.'

Stan flashed past, guiding someone. 'Tremendous, isn't it?' he said over his shoulder. And then was gone, without waiting for reply.

493

I couldn't see Tim anywhere yet. There was a growing press of people.

When Diane and I eventually got at the paintings, I felt, like Ken, let down at first. He seemed to have settled, mystifyingly, for so many small things : mainly people and places in the city, sharply shaped; there was not the same anger in the paint, the same rush. It was possible, though, to look at the paintings with interest, almost as if I didn't know the artist.

But Diane, meanwhile, appeared pleased enough. 'I like this,' she said, racing me from one painting to the next. 'And this. And this too. I think they're marvellous. He makes everything so strange.'

Strange? He certainly, I began to see, made most things acidly real; and if real were strange, then Diane was right. She still rushed me along breathlessly. Yet possibly because of the rush, the swift accumulation of images, I thought I saw his stark intention : his people were almost all isolated in bleak and airless spaces, between brick and wood and stone and asphalt, under narrow skies. It became most explicit in his prison paintings, which we reached towards the end of the hall.

Then we bumped to a standstill. The crowd was too thick. From a distance I saw Tim enter the hall. He looked to right and left, as if trying to make up his mind which people to avoid; he could even, the way he hesitated, have been contemplating flight. 'Who are you looking at?' Diane asked. 'That blonde by the door?'

'No. The artist. He's just arrived. Alone over there. The tall one.'

'Well, shouldn't you go and cheer him up? It must be pretty awful for him. And he's supposed to be your friend, isn't he?'

'He'll survive,' I said abruptly. 'He always does. But yes, I expect you're right. I should say something. The problem is what to say.'

'Easy,' she said. 'Just say you like his paintings.'

'Well – '

'I'll say it, if you like. If it's too hard to say. Is that the problem?'

'In a way.' Her perception was quick.

'He looks,' she hurried on, 'just like an artist.'

'Then you're the first to think so.'

'His face,' she explained. 'And the way he stands.'

494

'He has a bad leg,' I said bluntly.

'That wasn't what I meant.'

Her romanticism was likely incurable. We pushed across the hall towards him. Tim, when he saw me coming, made no attempt to escape, as I half expected he might. Instead, he offered a reasonably warm smile. Still, there was a certain strain. We had hardly seen each other, and certainly not spoken, in months. He took my hand, as if pleased to see someone he knew after all, and I introduced him to Diane.

'Quite a crowd,' I observed.

He shrugged. 'Stan's doing. He arranged it all.'

'Yes,' I said. 'He's made quite a fist of it.'

There was a brief silence. Perhaps comparisons were made. Then Diane spoke up suddenly. 'If my brother hasn't any more to say,' she offered shyly, 'may I say how much I like your work?'

'You may.' There was life in his eyes; and his eyes were on Diane. He had begun to see her, and I wondered what he saw.

'I don't know what I like, exactly. And I'm not sure I know much, not about art.'

I could imagine his short and probably brutal reply in other circumstances. But, he said, 'I'm not sure I do either. Can't your brother help?'

'He looks after me. That's all. I almost had to blackmail him into bringing me here.'

'I can imagine he has to be careful,' Tim said, perhaps beginning to enjoy the conversation, 'if looking after you is his job.'

That was about the extent of our encounter. Stan arrived, and grabbed Tim's arm. 'Thank God you've come,' he said. 'There are some people I particularly want you to meet.'

'Now?' Tim said. 'Must I?'

'Now,' Stan insisted.

Tim was led away unwillingly, with a smile over his shoulder. I was surprised how easy we had been together. Perhaps the worst was past, and we were friends after all. It seemed possible. Anyway I felt relief.

I began to understand the nature of the crowd at last. Most, I gathered, were close to Stan politically : communists and other assorted left-wingers, a number from militant unions. I glimpsed Alex O'Leary, and one or two of his associates from the strike. I also began to sense their unease in this situation, all Stan's contrivance. They quickly retreated from the paintings

on the walls, and into their own familiar groups. I saw Sandy
trying to spread enthusiasm in one such group. He didn't appear
to be having much success. 'You've only got to look,' he was
saying. 'That's all. Look.'

They were looking at Sandy, perhaps. But not much more.
'What does this show offer the working man?' demanded a
lean and ascetic pipe-smoker. Possibly he was one of the cultural
commissars Stan complained about. He pointed his pipe like
a pistol at Sandy. 'It's all defeatist.'

Stan was obviously feeling the strain too; the sweat shone on
his brow now, whenever I saw him. He appeared to want to
spread Tim like a talisman through the crowd, and Tim was
no longer smiling.

Diane went for a last look at the paintings before we left; I
thought I would make another visit when the place was less
crowded. Ken approached me. 'At least we can say it's not
our fault this time,' he observed.

'I suppose we can,' I said. 'Or I'd like to think so.'

'What's the matter with you?'

'Nothing, yet.'

'Shall we clear out, then? The grog's cut.'

'If that's all we can do.'

I went to fetch Diane.

I did go back to the hall. The place was empty, apart from a
sleepy girl at the door. If the show was for the people, then the
people were staying away in their tens of thousands. None
of the paintings had been sold, despite the clamour of the opening; despite their modest prices.

I could imagine Stan in despair; I couldn't imagine Tim at
all.

But at least I saw the paintings. They no longer seemed quite
so random. My first impression, of suffocating space, was rein-
forced: this space was everywhere and possibly everything. And
objects, people, wandered into this space almost, but not quite,
by chance; they were at once haunting and haunted. And
tended to become other, or more. The Polynesian Club was
there, other dance halls, the coffee bar, pubs, streets, old houses,
the waterfront, parks, most things familiar in our city lives; all
offered the same eerie spaces. And the people within seemed all
too often to become as distinct and monumental as his past hills
and valleys. They could become, when he chose, as vivid as a

496

dead tree on an eroded ridge, with the same crisp edge. He left
light to tell the story, if there were story to tell.

Perhaps I didn't like the paintings, but I could see them.
Before I left I bought two. One for myself. One for Diane.

Tim began calling at my flat again.

Twenty-three:

Documents

Avarua P.O. etc.
June? '67

Dear Max,

Here we go again. I'm afraid the sequence of events, at least from my point of view, becomes rather confused about this point – that is, after that second disastrous exhibition. Is it really necessary for you to go any further? I should have thought that you had more than enough biographical material – virtually all that should concern your theme – by now. The rest, surely, is untidy postscript. What does it matter, for example, how or when or why he left the country? In any case I'm no authority. The fact is that he did.

Nevertheless, I promise to think about it, if I can.

Sorry about delay with this reply. My fault this time. I've been preoccupied.

Very best wishes
Ian Freeman

PS: I can understand why Stan Coates is still so evasive. But I don't think I should explain on his behalf. I'm glad you've found Charlie Bates helpful on points of detail. I'll write to Ken McAdam: I hope it helps.

Avarua P.O.
Rarotonga
Cook Islands
June, 1967

Dear Ken,

A long time etc. I'm really prompted (I may as well confess) to write this letter by one Max Kennedy from whom you've already heard – I understand – in connection with a once mutual friend. I must assure you, in the first place, that he appears really serious about his project, in fact rather too carried away by it. If you can give him any help on specific things, please do your best. 'm afraid I've almost come to a stop.

I'd better explain my present address. When I said goodbye to you in London, I had every intention of immediate return home. (That, it seems, was rather more than eighteen months ago now.) Instead, in some flutter of panic, I jumped ship here. Not an unfamiliar act in these islands, at least in times past, but more difficult of consummation these days. The beach-comber is a vanishing breed: there are a dozen forms to fill, diverse guarantees to be made, and at the end – with luck and sufficient Godliness on one's side – an entry permit. Initially I bluffed my way ashore, with some fast talk, as a working journalist. And have since actually written enough, in a left-handed and not entirely unprofitable way, to satisfy the authorities of my bona fides (titles: 'The World's Last Paradise', 'Swimming with Sharks in the Lonely Islands', 'In the Steps of Captain Cook'; need I go on?) Anyway the point seems to be that I'm here. Or still here. Christ knows how long. I keep thinking the end in sight, but it recedes every time I approach it. I have the consolation that my destination, my home or what passes for it, is a mere three days away by ship, or nine hours by antiquated aircraft. (We get a plane once a month, ships slightly more often.)

How is London? Still tolerable? I can sometimes conceive that the place actually exists. And not just London; most other places in the world. With effort, that is. With increasing effort.

I really must get hold of myself.

Very best

Ian

PS: Have recently heard, months late, about Sandy being killed in Vietnam. Please do help Max Kennedy, if you can. I think I've quit. Bloody terrible about Sandy.

Avarua etc.
Late June, '67

Dear Ben,

Well.

(Some hours or days later): I've been sitting here looking at the word, seeing what it may be trying to express. Perhaps nothing after all; I should delete it.

499

No, I didn't expect you would watch much television. It doesn't matter.

Fascinated to read of Diane's visit to you, with her growing family; and glad to hear she retains something of her old delicate charm. Relieved, rather. I have imagined her fattened and frayed slightly, in housewifely forms. I must try writing to her again. And, by the sound of it, I am likely to get more news of my father's health from her than through my mother's correspondence. The information you pass on, from Diane, isn't very encouraging.

Ina has gone. One day she was here, the next she wasn't. I've not been entirely alone since she left, but it's not the same. I realize I cared for the girl. Too late.

Max Kennedy has begun to get difficult, with his questions, and I really feel at the end of my tether. Can you call him off? I'm sure he has all he needs. He's become less scholar than inquisitor. If you can do something, exert some influence, I'd be grateful. Not to put too fine a point on it, I'd like the bugger to leave me alone.

My booking? All I can say, at the moment, is that I have every intention of getting out before the jet airport arrives. That is perhaps three years away, or four.

The tropic rain thunders down outside. I can't see the shore. It's been like this nearly a month, ever since a minor hurricane tumbled coconut palms and tossed blocks of coral around the house.

Trapped, I've begun to write again; and begun to write that book I promised not to write. *The Death of Polynesia*, that is. I find it difficult to say whether it's fiction or non-fiction. At present it's just a perplexing jumble, a personal anthology about the death of a dream. Does that sound credible? I can't organize any time-sequence; everything is happening at once. Captain Cook, nuclear weapons, me and Ina, everything. Perhaps it will never make sense, but I can try. I've only just arrived at the idea that all our forms, all our categories, were of and for a time now dead. Somewhere about 1950, allowing time for names like Hiroshima and Auschwitz to sink in, the dislocation began, and all certainties – and innocence – lost. Perhaps it was at that point that the conventional and omniscient novel began to perish. Past that point, all form is crippling by nature, and dishonest; only confession is honest. And then not always.

500

(Sorry. Must consider this more coherently sometime.)
Please tell Max Kennedy to leave me alone. Please.

Very best,

Ian

Commentaries

Tim was agreeable enough, always particularly pleasant to
Diane if she appeared. I could be surprised how agreeable, and
how much we found to talk about, after all. He didn't seem
dismayed by the failure of his new exhibition; he left the impression he expected it. I asked after Stan, but received no clear
answer. I also had the impression that I offered him some
relief, or my flat did. 'It's quiet here,' he observed. 'Now I've
gone. Just your sister dropping in now and again. It's a pleasant
place to visit. You don't mind?' I answered that of course I
didn't. He was welcome any time. 'Well,' he said, 'just tell me
when I'm unwelcome. I don't want to interrupt your work.' At
least he acknowledged, now, that I had something of my own.

He brought news that Monty Nolan, after several unsuccessful attempts to get back to sea, had settled for a job as manager
and bouncer of a beer house. 'A place for a drink after the
pubs have shut, if you're interested,' he added. 'Just knock
three times and ask for Monty. I look him up now and then.
He's always glad to see old friends.'

'What about his painting?' I asked. 'You still teaching him?'

'He's forgotten all he ever learned. Lucky bastard.'

'Lucky?'

'If Monty invests his ego in something, he wants quick return.
And the beer house is it, for the moment. He's a big man there.'

He was much less forthcoming about Stan.

Perhaps as well. My life had few demands. The rest of the
world could often cease to exist, though not, as it turned out,
forever.

After a while even Tim's visits to the flat became less frequent.
Perhaps he saw me as too self-sufficient. Or perhaps he had
simply wished to re-establish contact, and having done that
with some success, could drift away again. In any case the
Livingstone gang, if it had ever been real, more than just
apparent, had split into individuals who flew apart with gathering speed.

I also saw less of Diane. She appeared, at last, to be making
her own life in the city. I didn't ask questions.

501

Of course I had certain minor problems. I lost my job when Charlie's firm collapsed simultaneous with the collapse of a small factory it had contracted to build cheaply. Recriminations proliferated; it ended in bitter dissolution of the partnership. 'I told them,' Charlie sighed. 'I warned the bloody fools that the last place to cut costs was in the foundations. But they all knew better.'

In disgust, Charlie left the city and took a job as a draughtsman – something he would have rejected earlier – on a public works project in the country. He was seldom seen again.

I took one casual job, then another.

Then, after some months, Sandy arrived at my door. I hadn't seen him for some time, though I'd heard he was now in a position of some prominence in the trade union movement; he was reported to be a sober and forceful speaker. It seemed he also had a future somewhere. I'd never been able to take Sandy's politics, unlike Stan's, too seriously; but it seemed I was wrong. Nothing much surprised me any more. It was also true that I knew Sandy least well of all Tim's old, now scattering friends; he always seemed less engaged with us than in some vast, highly personal game of hit and run with society. But for all his perversity I'd never doubted his intelligence beneath. The question was what he would find to do with it.

'I've come about Stan,' he announced without preliminary, and pushed past me into the flat. 'You know about his breakdown, of course.'

'His what?'

'His breakdown. His crackup; whatever you like to call it.'

I found it hard to make reply. Then I understood I really wasn't so surprised. It was more the shock of having an intuition confirmed. 'No, Sandy. I don't. I'm pretty much out of touch with most people these days. What's happened?'

'What I say. A breakdown. He's just had more than he can take. That's all. He's been getting vague for quite a while. Then a couple of weeks ago he turned altogether queer. He stripped off in his office and took a walk in the street. He didn't get far, naturally. No police charge; he's been committed for psychiatric treatment.'

'Oh Christ.' I sat down weakly.

'Poor bastard,' Sandy said. 'But there we are. I've been to see

502

him in hospital. He's picked up a lot already. At times you would think he was almost normal. But he's not. At least not yet.'

'What can I do?' I said quickly. Perhaps too quickly; and certainly too late. I should have known; and did know, in my way, and didn't want to know.

'He's asking after you, for one thing. He'd like to see you. But that's not the whole point. There's more to it. He wants you to straighten out stuff in his flat, and pick up and look after his manuscript. He says he can trust you to do it.'

'But Tim's there, surely.'

'He was there. He buggered off, fast, as soon as Stan was committed. And has gone to stay with Monty Nolan, as I understand. The place is empty; and there's no point in Stan hanging on to it. I can look after some of his gear, if you can take care of the rest. And don't talk to me about Livingstone. Not at the moment. He's got one or two things to answer for. He must have known the way things were going to with Stan. And what did he do about it? Nothing. Not a bloody thing, so far as I can make out. He just leeched on Stan so long as the going was good. And then cleared out.'

'It mightn't have been quite like that,' I protested. 'We don't know.'

'No,' Sandy said. 'But I'm entitled to a reasonable guess. So don't talk to me about that bastard now.' He paused. 'When I think of what Stan's tried to do for Livingstone, I could spit.'

'Stan's not been alone in that, exactly,' I observed.

'Which doesn't make it any better,' Sandy replied. 'Stan has had more than enough on his plate for a long time now – finishing his book, and fighting to run a readable newspaper. When he took Livingstone on too, trying to boost him as some kind of socialist artist, that was probably the finish. It was his big mistake. He hasn't been the same since.'

'At least he got Tim painting again.'

'Much good that's done anyone. Stan least of all.'

'I don't know if that's the entire point.'

'Please yourself,' Sandy snorted. 'If you want to stick up for Livingstone, fair enough.'

'I'm talking about his work.'

'Or his fucking work.'

'You seemed to think highly of it yourself, as I recall.'

'That doesn't matter now.'

'Evidently not. But all the same – '

'All the same, hell. Stick up for Livingstone – or his bloody work – if you want to. The question is whether you're also going to stick by Stan. Are you?'

'Of course I am,' I said tamely. 'Of course I will.'

I made an effort not to tempt Sandy's fury to the surface again; and went out to the hospital with him the next day. Stan was brought to us in pyjamas and dressing gown; we sat together on uncomfortable chairs in a whitewashed visiting room. Stan's face, once plump and firm, was slack and colourless; he had lost a great deal of weight, and his hands trembled erratically. I was appalled: he looked a ruin. 'I'm really all right,' he kept insisting, and looked over his shoulder, where there was nothing but white wall. 'I'm really quite all right.'

'Sure,' Sandy said. 'But you've got to take it easy, old son.'

'You'll look after my manuscript?' Stan asked me anxiously.

'Of course I will. Sandy's explained it all. That's all right.'

'There's another thing,' he went on. 'My job.'

Sandy gave me a significant look.

'Yes?' I said.

'My job, you see. It's important. Important, you see. I can't let people down.'

'Don't worry about that now,' I urged.

'I have to worry about it,' he said. 'Important, you see. Too much at stake.'

I tried to imagine what might be at stake, what might be important: it was difficult. The country hardly waited upon Stan's words, lost in a weekly journal of tiny circulation.

'I can see that,' I lied. 'But you shouldn't worry yourself.'

'Sandy,' he said, 'has taken over some of my work, to keep it going. But he hasn't the background. The politics, but not the background – the journalistic background. He's groping. That right, Sandy?'

Sandy nodded.

'I wondered if you could help out a bit,' Stan said. 'You know the score. I know you're not a Party member, but you're the next best thing. You've got the right background. And people haven't forgotten you during the strike. If you could put Sandy on the rails, journalistically speaking. And give him a hand generally. Do you think you could?'

I could hardly promise not to try. In the circumstances. The white visiting room seemed to grow tight around us.

504

'Take it easy now,' Sandy said to Stan, and put a hand on his shoulder.

'I don't mind telling you,' Stan added, 'I've been having a bit of a battle in that office. About the principles of good journalism, among other things. It hasn't been easy. I've been up against people who don't understand or don't want to. I thought it was only a question of explaining to them, then they'd see. Like that show of Tim's. They didn't see that either. They didn't see it at all. Because it wasn't loaded with propaganda. You see. Jesus, what a mess of things I made there. I let Tim down badly. Really let him down badly.'

'You weren't to know,' I objected.

'Forget him,' Sandy snapped. 'He's not worth your worry. Anyhow he's gone.'

'Gone?' Stan looked up with dull expression.

'Cleared out, buggered off. He's shacked up at the back of a beer house, so far as I understand.'

'I hope he's all right,' Stan said. 'I don't like the sound of it.'

'He'll be all right,' Sandy replied. 'He's got the knack of looking out for number one. Don't worry about Livingstone.'

'But I do,' Stan insisted. 'He's had a rough spin. You don't understand him. He's not as wild as he looks. He only needs a little sympathy. Ian knows.'

'Have it your own way,' Sandy said harshly. 'But for Christ's sake stop worrying about everything. Just take it easy in here. The sooner you stop worrying, the sooner you'll be out. You can see that, can't you?'

Perhaps Stan did. Shortly afterwards he was taken away. There wasn't much left of him; his parting handshake was light.

'You see,' Sandy said, as we walked away from the hospital, 'Livingstone's got a bloody lot to answer for.'

'That's hardly fair,' I argued. 'Stan's obviously had other problems.'

'But it wasn't the other problems which pushed him over the edge. Let's face it.'

We journeyed to Stan's flat. The place was already dusty. Sandy set about packing : it was as if he were putting Stan's life into storage. And that feeling was more acute when I went to Stan's desk and began sorting through his papers. His manuscript was prominent. I did my best to avoid it, for a time. But then I could no longer. I riffled through the pages. The first chapters might have been politically excitable, but they were lucid enough; the ideas were at least vivid and his exposition clean. In later chapters an incoherence began to take root in the prose, and sprout in wild adjectives; he seemed to begin battering, in heightening hysteria, at some obstinate door. And the door, whatever it was, remained tight. He was left on the outside chanting gibberish. For gibberish was what the manuscript became. Chapters ceased to exist, then paragraphs, then sentences. There were just clouds of words, increasingly murky. They clutched at each other, fought each other, chased each other, rushing down each page and over to the next. Until at last, to my relief, they stopped : at the top of an almost blank page they bled away.

and surely it must be possible to see that no no no NO NO he wrote, and finished; but the pale paper beneath was even more expressive.

Perhaps the door had opened after all; perhaps he had got through to the other side, and seen. Was that the point?

I couldn't possibly know. Anyway it must have been going on for weeks, or months, while Stan presented an orderly front to his friends. While he talked art and politics in calm tone, he screamed rage and despair in his privacy, until the wall between his two selves became a thin shell, and cracked altogether. Then Stan, in pyjamas and dressing gown, trembled in a white visiting room.

He was the one among us who had some certainty. What was it Tim had said about Stan? 'He might save us with some sanity.' And, 'At least Stan knows where he's going, and what he's talking about.'

Which might have been true indeed, if I could read the message right. Doubtless Sandy, inheritor of certainty, and of Stan's job, would read it his own way.

For myself, though, I couldn't say that I hadn't been warned. It was possible to care too much.

I wondered what message Tim had read, if any. Was that why he'd fled?

'Are you getting on with the job?' Sandy called, as he fastened the lid of a suitcase.

'Yes,' I said. 'I'm getting on with it.'

That could have been true of us all.

I found Monty Nolan's beer house without much problem; it

was already well known in its sunken sector of the city. 'How's it going?' Monty said cheerfully. 'Drop in any night, and I'll buy you a drink. Yes, you'll find Tim down the back. Along with his mate.'

'His mate?'

'Sure. Young Paul. He's got himself in some scrape lately, and he's lying low. He tidies up for me in the morning, and does odd jobs. Funny little bugger. But he's all right.'

The backyard was broken concrete and trampled earth and a drooping clothes line; there was a small and decrepit outhouse on a lean, perhaps a converted laundry, with two entrances. I knocked at one of the doors. The right one: Tim appeared. In unravelling sweater and dirty jeans, he was clearly startled to see me.

'Well,' I said. 'Found you at last.'

More than just startled, perhaps. Unnerved. He didn't seem to know what to say.

'I thought I'd drop around,' I explained. 'I've only just heard about your move. And about Stan.'

There seemed a slight shift in his expression. Relief?

'I've been to see him,' I went on. 'He should come right, in time.'

'Yes,' he said. 'Terrible.'

'It was a shock to you, then?'

'I didn't expect him to go off the deep end, if that's what you mean.'

'But you had noticed something?'

'Not much. He was moody now and then. But who isn't? He was usually all right again after a couple of drinks. His job got him down. That was my impression.'

'I see. And now you're here.'

'Yes. Now I'm here. Why don't you take a seat in the sun?' He indicated a bench on the outside of the building; he appeared to be anxious that I didn't see the inside of his room. And I didn't.

'I might as well tell you,' I said, 'that one or two people blame you.'

'For what? For Stan? You're joking.'

'I just thought I'd mention it.'

'Look,' he said. 'Stan had his problems. I had mine. That's all there is to it. Monty offered me this room some time back. And I took him up on it when Stan went to hospital.

507

I'm not in a position to pay much rent. You know that.'

His coolness made Sandy's rage seem absurd.

'Well,' I said. 'You could have gone to see him since. For example.'

'All right,' he said, after hesitation, 'if you want the whole story, Stan and I hadn't been hitting it off. I mean, we weren't disagreeing violently, but we weren't agreeing at all.'

'What was the trouble?'

'He didn't think I felt enough responsibility towards myself. I said that was my business. He couldn't see it.'

'No,' I said. 'I don't expect Stan would.'

'He didn't see I can't afford to be owned. Not by him; or his friends. And not by – ' He hesitated.

'And not by Ken or me?' I suggested.

'All right. If you must know.'

'Fair enough,' I said. 'I think I knew that some time ago. I mean I came to terms with what it was all about.'

'Well, Stan didn't. One thing I'm sure about Monty here, he's not going to try to organize another bloody exhibition. Can you see what I mean?'

'Of course.' I paused. 'And you're painting again?'

'I might be,' he said. 'In my way.'

'What does that mean?'

'Just that it's in my way. I'm taking my time. That's all.'

'What about money? Ken tells me he doesn't see you any more.'

'I help Monty with the crowd in the evenings. Easy money. Enough to get by.'

'Well,' I said, 'so long as you're painting.'

'What does that mean?'

'So long as you're painting, that's the important thing. Isn't it? And it doesn't matter a damn how you get your money. I hear Wiseman's here too – in with the real underworld at last.'

'He's no bother,' Tim said quickly. 'And he can talk sense, when he feels like it.'

'Such as what?'

'Such as that there's no future for me anywhere here. Not that I need to be told.'

'But your real work's here,' I objected. 'You can't get away from that.'

'Well, perhaps that work doesn't matter a damn. And perhaps I've begun to see it.'

'You're not serious.'

'Of course I'm bloody serious.'

'Then I just hope you'll get back on the rails soon.' I felt depressed, and without enough conviction to argue the point. 'Never mind.'

'Look,' he said, 'does it really mean so much to you? My work?'

'It has. Yes. Why else – '

But I saw no point in continuing. I didn't feel my vehemence much impressed him.

'All right,' he said. 'We'll drop it. Is it just Stan you came to see me about?'

'More or less.' Stan had begun to seem remote, for some reason. 'But also to see how you are.'

'You sure that's all?'

'Yes.'

'That's all right, then,' he said, again with some slight but perceptible relief.

At this point Paul Wiseman emerged from the other door in the building. He yawned and stretched in the afternoon sun. Then he saw me and said hello. 'Why don't you fetch us a beer from the house, Paul?' Tim asked.

When Paul had gone, Tim said, 'I'll visit Stan, if you really think that would help. Though I doubt it myself; I might stir things up again.'

'All right, then. Let's leave it,' I agreed.

'And there's nothing else you want to talk about?'

'Not particularly. No.' I wondered, though, at his insistence that there might be.

'I suppose you're still wondering about Wiseman.'

'Well – '

'He's really just someone to talk to, now and then, in this situation. Monty hasn't got the widest range of conversation.'

'And how long will it last? This situation?'

'As long as it's comfortable,' he said shortly. 'Until I get myself sorted out again.'

Paul returned from the main building with bottles and glasses. He was followed by Monty and another man who was introduced to me as Reg Gilbert; he was clearly another employee of Monty's. He was thin, long-jawed, with curly hair and small shrewd eyes. He had a couple of faint, pale scars under one eye. It wasn't an easy face to forget, and he was quite good-looking in his bony way. He took an arrogant stance while he drank his beer, as if he had the rest of us summed up.

'Pretty neat set-up here, Ian,' Monty said. 'Don't you think?'

'No trouble from the police?' I asked.

'No. And we're not counting on any. We keep the place quiet and orderly. And the police know we're here anyway – at least the one we pay off. On the other hand we've got some very respectable customers. So we're not bothered.'

'Very neat,' I agreed.

'So drop around sometime. You know all the staff. And Reg here is usually on the door; he doesn't stand for any rough stuff.'

Looking at him, I didn't imagine Reg would.

'Reg and I were at sea together,' Monty explained. 'We've had our times. Isn't that right, Reg?'

Reg barely nodded acknowledgement. He seemed as indifferent to Monty as to anyone or anything else; his eyes were disconcertingly remote. I felt a small chill. Did no one else notice?

'We all rub along,' Monty went on. 'The place gives us a living. And we even get some fun out of it now and then. Isn't that right, boys?'

It was possible the boys agreed, but they made no very clear answer. Though I sensed Monty was about to offer me a job too, I felt very much the outsider in the group, for some reason; I couldn't define it. Shortly afterwards I made an excuse and left them over their beer in the sunny backyard. Tim walked with me to the front gate.

'It's only temporary,' he said. 'You understand that?'

'Of course,' I said. 'I expect everything is.'

As I walked away from the place, and back into my own ephemeral life, I found myself wishing for fresh sight of clean hills and clean sky. I made do with giving Diane a phone call, and met her that evening for coffee. That helped, as always, a great deal. She seemed as lively as ever. I asked after her study. Then after social life, and boy friends.

'Yes,' she conceded. 'I do have one or two.'

'I rather guessed it.'

'You did?' She looked surprised and uncertain.

'Well, I haven't seen so much of you lately, have I?'

'I suppose not.' She appeared suddenly reticent.

510

'It's all right,' I went on. 'You don't have to tell me about them. It's your life. Just be careful, that's all.'

'Careful?'

'You're young,' I added. 'I suppose that's what I mean. Besides, you mean a lot to me.'

'I'll be careful,' she promised.

She might have meant it too, if not entirely in the way I did. Possibly she meant careful about me.

There wasn't much I could do with Stan's manuscript, other than store it safely. I could visit him in hospital, though, and help Sandy with Stan's job. Sandy was quick to learn: he had the makings of a good journalist, with an eye for revealing detail and a gift for the vivid phrase. He also had the knack of skimming over surfaces, gathering up argument and atmosphere lucidly. And he had confidence in himself, seldom retreating from his own judgement. In time I saw that, because of this confidence, he would prove a far more considerable journalist than Stan, or myself.

I put aside my own work in the evenings, to help him in the Party office, when I had finished whatever daily job was providing sustenance; and I put it aside without much regret. For I was at standstill, and my work appeared to have less and less point. Or the same point, made too often: life wasn't what it seemed. That was hardly news; a platitude was a platitude, however decorative and precise the prose. Icing on the cake or, rather, icing without the cake: a shell, contrived in hope that something might take up residence inside. Truth, perhaps. But all I ever appeared to have, as guest, was doubt. I could envy those so evidently unafflicted, like Ken, or Sandy. And imagined I could understand others better, Stan, or Tim. But particularly Tim. Stan's shoes, though, were easier to fill.

So I moved again within the last innocence. I had something I could do with ease, because I was needed, and with reservations few and slender; I could see point where there had been none. I went to bed tired, most nights, and slept well. Such reservations as I had seldom got further than Sandy, when we relaxed over coffee in Stan's office late in the evening; he made them seem trivial.

'In this country,' he said, 'in this complacent little kingdom of little lives, it's just a question of keeping the light alive. That's all we're doing. Tending the lamp, if you like. Keeping the ideal visible, for those who care to see. Someone has to do it. Someone has to state the human possibility.'

I could, at times, be quite taken by his stoicism. Certainly I could go along with it, some of the way. Sandy himself changed; he had a new sense of responsibility. He laughed less, drank less. He even trimmed his untidy moustache as indication of his new austerity; he became more acceptable among dour puritans of the Party who affected alarm at bohemian flamboyance. Gone were corduroys and jeans; his trousers now possessed a crease more often than not. And there was sometimes even a woollen tie knotted, not always comfortably, about his neck.

While working beside him, I sometimes tried to recall him as he had been, careering around the city in Charlie's car, a bottle of beer tilted into his mouth. It was difficult to recall. I was impressed by the change.

'You know,' he once confided, in the quiet of night, 'I reckon Stan's breakdown is the best thing that's happened to me. Though I hate to say it.'

It wasn't hard to agree.

There soon came a point when Sandy was entirely self-sufficient, carrying on Stan's job with competence; he quit his trade union work, gave himself entirely to the paper, and received a small weekly wage from the Party. At that point I could very well have retired from his life, or Stan's, and looked for my own again. Instead I found excuses to continue calling on him in the office; there were always jobs I could do. And Stan, still in hospital, seemed easier in mind with the knowledge that I was working beside Sandy. He had improved, if shakily: his condition was still far short of healthy. 'What's all the news?' he asked, after hearing my praise of Sandy. 'What about other people? Do you see Tim?'

'Not often,' I understated. 'Hardly at all lately.'

'A pity,' he said. 'You should. What about other people?'

'What other people?' I asked.

But there was Ken McAdam, of course. He couldn't conceal his disgust. 'It's all right for Sandy West,' he said. 'He's got nothing better to do with himself. You have. You know your trouble? You're running away from the really hard work. You want something easy.'

512

'A matter of opinion,' I argued. 'It's not that easy. At least, not for me.'

'What I mean is,' he went on, 'you just don't like the hard work of being alone with yourself.'

'Don't be so romantic.'

'Give it a label, if you like. But it's true, just the same. No real sense of responsibility.'

'You're not talking about social responsibility, surely. Not you, Ken.'

'You've got to answer to yourself, in the end.'

'It still sounds romantic, Ken.'

'Well, don't tell me you're a fucking realist.'

Our encounters usually ended in wrangling, and stalemate. As if to shame me, he published a volume of verse; and then announced that he had finished a novel. His third; the others had been unpublishable. 'This one's got what it takes,' he insisted. 'I'm sure of myself now.'

I had never known Ken unsure of himself. But I let the point pass. 'So what's the next step?' I asked.

'I'm off to Europe. What else?'

I couldn't take him seriously yet. 'And fame and fortune?' I asked, probably smiling.

That enraged him. But it was possible, despite his incoherence, to gather that he was serious. 'I'm getting out,' he said. 'Out. That's all. This place just sucks up lives without anything to show for it. Everything depresses me. Things. People. You. Livingstone. Everyone. Bugger it. Why should I hang around?'

'But what's the real trouble, then? Have the good times all gone?'

That seemed to touch a nerve. 'There was a time,' he confessed, 'when I thought we might have added up to something. At least one or two of us.'

'And now there's only you?' I suggested.

'Well – ' Ken groped for some modest reply.

'I thought,' I observed, 'that you were rather keen on the hard work of being alone with yourself.'

'You know perfectly well what I mean.'

'I know we can't be young forever, Ken,' I said. 'And that's about all.'

It seemed more than he was prepared to accept. He didn't come near me for weeks. Then he rang to say goodbye. He was catching a ship to Europe the next day. 'I expect we might meet again,' he said, 'if ever you pull yourself together. Give my regards to anyone you happen to see; I'm not in the mood for farewells. And good luck.'

I could wish him the same.

Paul Wiseman, seen in the street: 'Yes, Tim's all right. And he's painting. Some quite stylish stuff now. None of the old nonsense. He's not really made for this country, you know.'

Stan Coates, seen in hospital: 'So Ken's gone. Well, you know, I didn't expect him to amount to much. A pretty bourgeois background there. I don't think it's much of a loss, do you? Incidentally, there's something much more important I've been meaning to talk about. About you and the Party, really. Isn't it time, all things considered, that you joined up?'

Sandy West, in his office: 'There's a job here for you, now, if you want to take it. No real money in it, of course, and never will be. But I don't think you're really looking for that.'

My father, seen on a visit home: 'I always thought you knew what you were doing. And it seems I was right. How is Alex O'Leary these days? Give him my best wishes. Alex was always a fighter.'

My mother: 'I'm sure I don't know. I thought Diane might set an example to you. I thought you might go back to university. But I suppose it's your own life.'

Ben: 'So you've made up your mind; you've picked up your father's torch after all. I must say you had me wondering for a while.'

Diane, visiting: 'Well, I don't suppose you'll ever be like other people anyway. No matter how hard you try. Now can we talk about something else? I mean, life isn't altogether politics, is it?'

Myself: Is it? And does it really matter what it is altogether? It seemed reasonable, at last, to take it on trust.

514

Twenty-four:

Documents

CHICAGO-TYPE SLAYING IN CITY SUBURB
POLICE INQUIRIES CONTINUE INTO
MACHINE-GUN MURDERS
– Newspaper headlines

New resignations from the Communist Party, following upon
last week's events in Hungary, include two staff members of the
Party's weekly newspaper. They are Mr Sandy West and Mr
Ian Freeman. In a joint statement they said their resignation was
the only way left to them to express their shame and dismay at
the brutal suppression of the Hungarian people by a supposedly
socialist Soviet Union. Support was given their statement by a
third Party journalist, Mr Stanley Coates, who is at present
convalescing after illness. Mr Coates said he also was resigning.
All three were denounced as 'confused liberals' and 'splitters'
in a statement prepared by Mr Alex O'Leary, present chairman
of the Communist Party's central committee. He added that the
departure of such people from the working class movement was
no loss and no cause for grief.

– Newspaper report

FRESH LEAD IN MACHINE-GUN MURDERS
ARRESTS EXPECTED
– Newspaper headlines

LOCAL WRITER EARNS LONDON PRAISE
Review pages in London this week give prominence to the
first novel of a New Zealand writer, Kenneth McAdam, formerly

515

of Auckland. 'A talented young man of some vitality and promise,' said a critic in *The Observer*. 'It will be interesting to see what this young Antipodean gives us next.'

– Newspaper report

ARRESTS END LONG POLICE HUNT
– Newspaper headline

Mr Coates, interviewed last night, said he had no present plans for his future; he did not anticipate either organizing or joining another political party. Mr Freeman was not available for comment. Mr West, the third of the trio, said that so far as he was concerned the fight was far from finished. He hoped, he added, to continue as a journalist, telling the truth as he saw it. Tomorrow this newspaper will begin a series of articles by Mr West telling of his life in the Communist Party, and of the many crises of conscience which led finally to his resignation.

– Newspaper report

The two men charged, Reginald Harold Gilbert, 28, unemployed, and Montagu Arthur Nolan, 27, seaman, both entered pleas of not guilty. They were remanded for trial.

– Newspaper report

The death occurred yesterday of a former Cabinet Minister, the Hon. Charles Higgins. A bachelor, Mr Higgins lived in virtually total seclusion after his departure from Parliament several years ago. He is remembered for ...

– Newspaper report

Relaxing in his small Earl's Court flat, Mr McAdam said he was naturally delighted by his book's success. 'Quite unexpected,' he confessed. 'I have a ton of plans now.' He added, 'Of course I don't forget my native country, though I have no present plans for return.'

– Feature article

When the trial entered its fourth day yesterday, Nolan, giving unsworn evidence on his own behalf, claimed there were people who could establish that he was in fact at some distance from the scene, at his own beer house, at the time of the murders. He

516

had, however, so far been unsuccessful in locating these witnesses.

– Newspaper report

Among the mourners were many connected, past and present, with the labour movement. Pallbearers included ... Mr William Freeman, an early colleague of Mr Higgins ...

– Newspaper report

Summing up, His Honour said the jury might consider that a clear case had not been established against the accused Nolan, as party to the crime. The fact was, however, that little weight should be given to Nolan's claim of missing witnesses to his alibi. Such witnesses had had every opportunity to come forward, in view of the widespread publicity given the trial, and they had not done so.

– Newspaper report

Avarua P.O.
September 7, '67

Dear Mr Kennedy,

I have received both your notes of inquiry. This is just to say that I *have* thought it over, and there is really nothing more I can say.

Forgive my long delay replying.

Yours sincerely,
Ian Freeman

Avarua etc.
October 17, 1967

Dear Ben,

Well, I seem to have Max Kennedy off my back at last. The relief is very real.

Yes, I'm still writing, though at the moment I'm taking a rest. I need it. I'm well into the manuscript of *The Death of Polynesia*, and have my fingers crossed that I will finish off soon.

Max Kennedy, I'm sorry to say, became too much altogether. I'm sure his intentions were the best.

I went to Ina's wedding last week. A pretty wild and lovely affair. She didn't marry an unskinned, four-layered *papaa* after

517

all – lucky girl – but quite a prosperous young Polynesian citrus farmer.

Just a note. Will write again. Not very articulate at present.

Very best

Ian

Commentaries

The afternoon began with Alex O'Leary, in a small and shabby Auckland office. It ended in Paris three years later.

Alex O'Leary was perhaps the least of it. He and Sandy were joined in weekly battle; it always seemed to flare up just before the paper went to press, which lent nervous tension to their encounters. The cause was usually something Sandy or I had written; and the complaint was mostly that we weren't tough enough, and hadn't finished our stories with conventional curtain-calls for the Party. Sandy was now sensitive enough to want accurate journalism; Alex O'Leary wanted blunt propaganda. And the issue was made sharper by dissent within the Party after the death and denunciation of Stalin. Alex refused to accept both the dissent and the denunciation. He appeared convinced that everything would burn itself out so long as we presented a solid face to the world. I tried to stand aside from their feuds; I was still a stranger to diverse doctrinal dispute. And besides, my feelings were ambiguous. I sided with Sandy superficially, or intellectually. But my sympathies were more with Alex, and his stubborn simplicities; his loyalty to his beliefs had survived a dozen fires which would have shrivelled lesser men. He might argue ponderously, and obtusely, but he made Sandy look too slick altogether, a man spendthrift with unearned convictions. Yet I was also aware, with increasing discomfort, that in other circumstances Alex might have had Sandy shot. But at the moment Sandy's energy, like mine, was useful.

Commitment, then, appeared easy only to the outsider; there were choices within choices, and evasions of choice. They could both become irritated with me, or my silence. And I was an inadequate referee. That afternoon, though, I made one of my rare attempts to reconcile their viewpoints. I began by trying to elucidate something Sandy argued, to show it really wasn't so far apart from Alex's own view. They both misunderstood me.

'Don't twist my words,' Sandy said.

518

I tried again, this time with gently implicit criticism of Alex's view.

He blazed. 'Just because you're your father's son,' he said, 'doesn't give you the right to be arrogant.'

I was involved before I knew it.

'I don't see what he has to do with it,' I replied sharply.

'A bloody lot.'

'If you want to be personal – ' I began. Then I saw that he had, perhaps, been waiting for this. My father had become a lonely legend. Alex O'Leary, who had never given up, might soon be forgotten. It seemed a likely cause of bitterness. And the thought effectively neutralized me.

'Your father,' he went on, taking advantage of my hesitation, 'didn't really amount to much, in the end. A pity his son doesn't amount to more. I thought you might. It seems I was wrong.'

It was no use; I gave up. And soon found excuse to escape the office, leaving Sandy and Alex to settle the issues without my help. Perhaps Sandy still felt he was stating a human possibility, somewhere beneath it all, but it was difficult to see. Or difficult for me to see it, and share; people got in my way.

When I arrived back at my flat late that afternoon, still dispirited, I found Diane in occupation, the place tidy and a meal cooking. 'I'm so glad to see you,' she said in a rush, kissing my cheek.

'I'm even more glad to see you,' I assured her.

She continued to cling to my arm. Without words.

'Something wrong?' I asked.

I searched her face. She also searched mine. We seemed to know each other too well. And, then again, not at all.

'Just let me get my breath,' I went on, 'and then you can tell me about it.'

For I had just observed a letter Diane had propped on my mantelpiece. An English stamp, a London postmark, and Ken McAdam's handwriting. Getting my breath amounted to opening this letter and reading it. Ken, it seemed, was prospering in London; the point of the letter was to tell me that his novel had been accepted for publication. His success sounded like a good clean game of football, or a triumphant hunting trip. 'Tell me about Livingstone,' he finished.

I was soon to have a great deal to tell him. I put the letter down and turned to Diane. 'Well, now,' I said, 'what's the trouble?'

519

'I don't know how to begin,' she said.

'Anywhere,' I said, advice Ken had once given me. He was still on my mind. 'Begin anywhere.'

I tried to give her my full attention. She came into focus again, rather limp. She was also, I noticed, pale.

Her distress was more and more evident. That made it easier to forget Ken.

'Here,' I said, helping her to a chair. 'Sit down. Tell me.'

'It's your friend,' she got out at last. 'Your friend Tim. I want to find him.'

'That's easy enough,' I said, 'But what's the point?'

'I don't know where he lives, exactly, you see. I've only ever had a phone number.'

'A phone number?' I repeated idiotically.

'That's all.'

'But what the hell did you have his phone number for?'

'We – ' She paused, and appeared to brace herself for huge effort. 'We've been seeing each other, you see.'

I couldn't believe it. 'Seeing each other? What do you mean?'

It should, of course, have been obvious. And at length was. I had to believe it. She was silent. I groped my way into a chair. The room we occupied, with its books and paintings, seemed to make no sense; the rush-hour sound of city traffic outside was equally meaningless. If there was meaning anywhere, it was in my sister's face, but I couldn't find it. I tried to concentrate, measure my words. They seemed momentarily trapped, dammed, building up pressure. But I didn't explode after all. I must have sounded remarkably cold.

'All right,' I went on. 'You'd better tell me about it.'

But I had already done simple addition. Diane had begun drifting out of my life at about the same time as Tim drifted back, for a while, into mine. There had been those pleasant evenings together, the three of us, in the flat. Then I hadn't seen much of either of them. Stan had collapsed, and I'd been preoccupied. Too preoccupied, evidently, for my own good; or, perhaps, Diane's. Yet the deception still staggered me.

'Come on,' I persisted, an edge of anger beginning to show. 'You've been seeing him. Is that all you've got to say? What else?'

As if I needed to be told. It didn't call for much imagination. I could see what Tim had doubtless found in Diane; I found it

520

there, up to a point, myself. He had naturally, gone beyond that point. He would, the bastard.

'Christ almighty,' I burst out. 'Are you going to say anything at all?'

'Yes,' she said in a small voice.

'Well, go on. Go on. Tell me.'

'I love him.'

The words were spoken in the same small voice. But more than I needed to hear.

There was still more, though. She was pregnant and thought she had been for some time. She just hadn't arrived at the point of telling Tim. She said she didn't want to disturb or distract him. And now she had reached the decision that she had to tell, she couldn't contact him. So she had turned to me. Perhaps my reaction was predictable. At least my anger didn't seem to surprise her.

'He's not to blame,' she insisted. 'You've got to understand that.'

She obviously didn't know what she was talking about. Still so absurdly young.

'It's all right,' I said. 'It's easily fixed. I'll find him. I'll find him tonight.'

'But I don't want you to find him. I want to do that myself. I just want you to tell me how.'

'You're not going around to that boozy den where he lives. That's definite. It's no place for you.'

At least Tim had kept her away from it; that was the only thing I could find to his credit, and it wasn't much.

'But – ' she began.

'Look, it's no use arguing. You're not going there. You're not even coming along with me.'

'Well,' she said meekly, 'what are you going to say to him?'

'What in bloody hell do you think I'm going to say?'

'I don't want you telling him,' she said with sudden firmness, 'that he has to marry me, or anything like that. You understand?'

That proposition hadn't passed through my mind. Not seriously. 'I'm just going to have a few words with him,' I said. 'A few words. That's all.'

I tried not to sound too vicious. It was difficult.

'And I don't want you hurting each other,' she added.

'So you think he can just run away from everything? Is that it? Is that what you think?'

'I don't know what I think,' she confessed, beginning to crack. 'I don't even know what I should think. I just want him to know. And I'd sooner tell him myself.'

'It's not the first time, you know.'

That stung her. Her eyes trembled.

'Not by any means,' I went on. 'The last time he got off lightly. Too lightly. The girl –' I saw no point in saying who '– went home. And let him get on with his life, or his work.'

'Perhaps I'd sooner do that too,' she said quietly.

'Like hell you will. He's going to face up to it this time.'

Face up to what, though, and how? I couldn't see beyond his facing up to my anger. And my contempt and disgust. That; and no more. My concern, I began to see, was for my own feelings; not for Diane, and her situation. That was something I'd hardly begun to contemplate.

She may have seen it too. She started to weep.

Later in the evening, much later, when Diane was more settled, I went around to the beer house to find Tim.

It was dark; there were no lights on in the house.

I walked to the back, across the yard. There were no lights in the outhouse either. And there was no response to my knock. Everything appeared deserted. A hungry cat rubbed around my legs.

I couldn't understand it. My anger, given new whip by frustration, began to erupt in my throat. Where the hell had they gone? I pushed open Tim's door, and switched on his light. It wasn't a large room. Peeling wallpaper, mould-darkened ceiling, bare floorboards. Most of his possessions were still there. Books, bedding, some clothing, paintbrushes, a few rather abstract sketches thumbtacked to the wall. And only the one painting. Large, a landscape, built up in brutal black, against a neutral sky. Larger than anything I had ever seen of his before; it took up almost one wall of the room. And not in the least stylish, more like his old work. Perhaps it *was* old work, just something I'd never seen. But I preferred not to think so; I preferred to imagine he might have painted his way back. For I could, even angry, take perverse pleasure in that. It seemed as if he might still be making up his mind about the sky. It looked unfinished. The whole thing looked unfinished. Too black to be true.

522

Where the hell was he?

I looked at the painting, nevertheless. As if I could find him there: it was certainly the only confrontation I would manage that evening. It offered nothing useful, of course, and couldn't. Nothing but itself, in the end. It was a painting of some satisfying power. If old, I could understand why he had hung on to it so long. If new, it was some compensation for his careless life. Not much. But something.

I disengaged myself, tried to give attention to other things in the room. I hoped for a note, something to indicate where he might have gone. But there was nothing. So I left the room, with a last look at the painting, and shut the door. As I walked back to the street, past the deserted house, I heard a telephone ringing inside.

I supposed I could try again in the morning. He surely couldn't have gone far.

Out on the street, I paused; and saw a car parked on the other side. Two men sat inside it. They were really too obvious. In the plainest of plain clothes.

As I walked away, the car moved too, behind me, very gently. It was never more than fifty yards behind me. It stopped only when I entered my door. I could imagine my address and description being scribbled.

Then there was Diane again. I tried to concentrate. 'He wasn't there,' I explained. 'No one was there.'

She looked relieved.

I decided not to explain my new unease. But I did go to a window, lift a curtain, and look out on to the street. The car had gone. I could wonder if it had been real.

'But he hasn't moved out,' I added. 'I'll go around again in the morning.'

I seemed, oddly, to have forgotten my anger. Something had grown very still inside me.

'I'm glad you didn't find him,' she said. 'Not tonight.'

'We still have your problem,' I observed. 'And we'd better think about it quickly.'

If I could think at all; it seemed impossibly difficult. I faced my sister. She appeared much more in control of herself now.

'I'm going to have the child, if that's what you mean,' she said. 'I'm certainly not going to have an abortion.'

She spoke with precision. And she seemed, with frightening

523

speed, to have become adult. But it was me, of course, or my illusion gone; I couldn't keep her young forever.

'I see,' I said. 'Well – '

'So don't try to talk me out of it,' she went on. 'It's no use. I've had time to think.'

'But have you thought it all out?' I asked. 'There's university, for one thing. You have examinations coming up. And there's next year.'

And our parents for another thing, I almost added. Could they stand another disastrous child?

'Examinations are no problem,' she said. 'Next year will have to look after itself.'

'Then perhaps he'd better bloody well marry you,' I said. 'If that's the way it is.'

'But I don't know that I want to marry him,' she replied coolly.

'You slept with him. You – ' I found myself at sudden loss.

'That,' she observed, very properly, 'is different. Isn't it? I thought you knew.'

She made me feel a fool, and innocent. Our roles reversed.

'Oh Christ,' I said. 'What's happened?'

The question was really more than rhetorical. I was tempted to go to the window again, to see if the place were being watched. That car. The empty house. God knew. What *had* happened? I felt chill, though it was spring, and warm.

'I'm sorry,' she said. 'I'm terribly sorry.'

'It's all right.' I tried to be gentle; I tried to forgive. And perhaps I would, in time. 'You can stay here tonight, if you like. If you'd rather not be alone.'

'I'd like that,' she said.

She had never stayed before. I prepared the couch for myself. I had the sense of things impending, or ending. I also felt unnervingly powerful need to protect Diane, as if she were the only thing worth while left in my world. She had become very quiet. 'If only you'd said,' I repeated. 'Or given me just some little warning.'

'And what good would that have done?' she answered, very reasonably. 'Would it have made you feel any better?'

Nevertheless, it seemed we had both very swiftly begun to accept things as they were. Perhaps, I began to concede, with first anger past, Tim had not been altogether at fault. He had to be understood. His work, besides, had obviously not been going well, if I could read that large painting right. And Diane? She could be understood too. Both of them could. Though that wouldn't do much towards repair.

I could see my life made useful, though, with Diane depending on me, and perhaps her child.

'We'll see how things are in the morning,' I said.

But morning, after I switched out the light, was slow to come. I twisted restless on my couch, and chain-smoked until the taste became unpleasant. Diane appeared to be finding sleep difficult too; I heard her stirring between the sheets. Once a car braked shrilly beyond the window; my nerves sang until it lurched noisily away. But there still seemed menace in the silence after. Something Diane evidently felt too, for she began to weep quietly. I was undecided whether to attempt consolation; she might, after all, have wished to weep alone. In the end I compromised: I rose and made hot drinks, and then sat beside her, without directly acknowledging her tears. 'It seems we're both pretty sleepless,' was all I said.

But it was enough. She reached clumsily for my hand and held tight, as if looking for a grip on the world. 'Don't go away,' she insisted, when I finally attempted a move back to the couch. 'Stay here. Stay with me.'

'You'll never sleep,' I objected. 'We'll never sleep.'

'It doesn't matter.'

She made me seem absurd. She gently pulled me down on the bed beside her.

'Just hold me,' she went on. 'Just hold me. That's all I want.'

I felt for her face in the dark. Her tears were almost dry. I submitted, and slid my arms around her. She was trembling, the length of her body. I could imagine new life soon beginning to move within it. I could imagine other things too: particularly the pleasure of possessing that body; and possibly it had never been more available.

She soon, in my arms, grew soft, and slept. I lay awake until daylight. While Diane still slept, I rose with relief, numb, or perhaps just hardened, but no more ready for the world. Everything, it seemed, was just a test for survival. And we continued, for some reason, to survive.

I did no more than approach the beer house that morning. The anonymous car still sat across the street.

I turned for home, where I told Diane that I again hadn't

been able to find Tim. She agreed to come back that evening, after I'd finished work.

At work, Sandy was agitated again about trouble in Poland and Hungary. I wasn't able to give him much attention. In the end he forced the morning newspaper upon me. 'See for yourself,' he said. 'How is O'Leary going to square off all this?' He paused. 'Worse still, what lies are we going to have to tell about it?'

But even with the newspaper in my hand revolt in the communist world became a minor distraction. Other headlines altogether took my interest: two men had been found shot in a suburban house with blinds drawn; they had apparently been dead several days. Their names meant nothing to me. But the fact that extensive police inquiries had begun – as the newspaper put it – conveyed a great deal.

'Well,' Sandy said, 'what do you think? Are we going to take a real stand this time? Or are we going to let O'Leary ride roughshod over us again? So far as I'm concerned, this is it.'

'Yes,' I said vaguely, and wondered how I might find out more.

'I had a yarn to Stan last night. He feels the same way.'

'The same way?'

'That we should take a stand. For Christ's sake, are you listening to me?'

'Of course,' I said. 'Sorry.'

'And you're with me?'

'Yes,' I said, impatient. I decided to telephone an ex-colleague, a crime reporter, and find out what he knew.

'And you agree,' Sandy went on, 'that we don't in any way allow ourselves to be used any longer as apologists for the political murder?'

'Fair enough,' I agreed.

I sat tight until he finished. Possibly I absorbed some of what he said; possibly I made the right replies. It was hard to judge. I found it difficult to lose Diane and her problem; and Tim and his situation, whatever it might be. I had to find out; I had to know.

I wished Sandy would get to the point.

'So now we know where we stand – or fall,' he announced finally, and left the office for the printery. I turned to the telephone, called my ex-colleague, and asked what he knew of the murders which had not been printed. 'The two dead men were criminals,' he said. 'And they were running a sly-grog house. The police suspect some underworld feud. That's about all I can say. Do you know anything?'

'Only,' I said, 'that another beer house is being watched. And that its occupants have all vanished. That's what made me curious.'

'Ah,' he said. 'A friend in need. Nothing else you know?'

'I wish there were,' I said.

I waited for the afternoon newspaper. It told only of fighting in Hungary, Russian tanks moving. There was little more about the murders. I hurried home to find Diane.

'You haven't found him,' she said, seeing my face.

'No,' I answered. 'And I'm wondering if we will.'

She stayed with me again that night.

She was there the next night too when Sandy arrived, with Stan, to discuss tactics in the office. Stan, after his recent release from hospital, had taken a quiet job as a postman; he looked fit again, and much less excitable. He and Sandy stayed until late. I didn't mention Tim's disappearance; it seemed, after all, rather trivial beside the world's large events. Possibly the news about the murders had passed them by anyway; they were too busy with their consciences. Everything they had to say was admirable and honourable, so far as I could see.

Which wasn't far. I was more concerned that they shouldn't stay too late, and that Diane got sleep. She was suffering morning sickness; and had examinations. I offered them my loyalty, for what that was worth: my agreement about most things. Anything to get the evening over quickly. I supposed my own conscience deficient in some way; it was true I had never felt excessively committed.

When they left, I had to consider Diane. I hadn't said anything to her.

'You sure you've really tried to find him?' she asked.

'Of course I've bloody well tried,' I snapped, and then was sorry. My nerves were ragged. The visit from Sandy and Stan hadn't dispersed anything. What had the bastard done this time? And why had he fled?

But Diane's distraught face was a more immediate problem. I apologized. 'Things,' I explained, 'are getting at me.'

'It's all right,' she said, though it wasn't.

527

He just couldn't walk out for no reason. Just wouldn't. And never, in his right mind, leave a painting like that behind.

I wished I could talk to someone. Ken McAdam, say. But the thought of Ken, out in the world, free, jubilant, didn't help at all. And if anything made my claustrophobia worse.

'Time for bed,' I told her. 'You need some rest.'

'We both do,' she observed. 'Sometimes I think you more than me. You don't look well.'

It was true that I had lost my tan. My life had lately been sunless. I was touched by her concern.

'After things have settled,' I said vaguely, 'and after your examinations are finished, perhaps we could take a quick holiday together.'

Her eyes brightened. 'You think we could? Really?'

'Of course.' Such a holiday was not difficult to imagine: Diane was made to dance again among hills, bright space, and sea.

'And just the two of us?'

'Just the two of us. Which reminds me. Tomorrow we'll go to the hostel to fetch the rest of your belongings. You might as well stay here with me now. Since you seem to be anyway. All right?'

She threw her arms around me. 'I don't,' she declared, 'care any more now.'

'About what?' I was puzzled.

'About whether we find him or not. I'm safe with you.'

I began to see that it was perhaps what she wanted in the first place. I gently disengaged myself.

'I gathered,' I said, 'that you loved him.'

'But I did,' she agreed, if uncertainly, 'I suppose.'

'You suppose?'

'Well, I suppose I had to, in a way. It would have been even more awful if I hadn't loved him, wouldn't it?'

I was confused; I seemed to be missing the point, if there were one. 'All I can see,' I explained, 'is that he took advantage of you.' I paused; her smile was ambiguous. 'Why,' I added, 'are you talking of love in the past tense?'

'Because I suppose it is in the past. He's cleared off, hasn't he? And you're afraid to tell me. He's cleared off.'

'Well – '

'You might as well tell me.'

528

'All right. He seems to be gone. But it's still something of a mystery.'

She looked relieved, to my immense surprise. 'At least I know, then.'

'Know what? I'm damned if I know anything.'

'At least I know it's over,' she said. 'And now I'm here, with you, I don't even feel much. And you really are serious about that holiday together?'

'Of course.'

'Then I even have something to look forward to. All through examinations.'

'Which you have in the morning,' I pointed out. 'Let's go to bed.'

I couldn't cope with her coolness. Would I really have preferred tears? My brain was too crowded. Everything, everyone, dragged at me; I fumbled my way out of my clothes and into the blankets on the couch. I left Diane to turn out the light. It was as if I were the one in need.

And certainly that night it was she who came to me, and placed her arms around me, to help me sleep; it was she who spoke consolation. I did sleep, in the end.

Diane, despite distraction, strolled through her examinations. The Russian tanks backed out of Budapest, though Sandy's agitation – and Stan's – was no less intense, and the atmosphere no less frosty whenever Alex O'Leary appeared in the office. The murder headlines shrank in size; inquiries, the public was informed, were still proceeding. There was no word of Tim, and I no longer especially sought it; or sought him. I certainly didn't look for him at the abandoned beer house again.

I managed, in the breathing space, to write a letter of congratulation to Ken, expressing my pleasure at his success. Perhaps I meant it.

I visited Ben in hope of unburdening. And in one respect my load was lightened. He suggested he might be better placed to look after Diane when her baby was born. That was, assuming we planned to keep our parents in ignorance of her pregnancy. I explained that we hadn't thought that far ahead.

'And you really think,' he said, 'that Tim's mixed up in this shooting?'

'I don't know what to think. I hate to think. I just know he's gone. Everyone has. The place is empty.'

'The bloody fool,' he said.

'He may surface,' I suggested. 'He usually does.'

Ben shook his head. 'Couldn't you have persuaded him not to live there?'

'Me?'

'You seemed to have had some influence with him.'

I assumed that Ben was joking. But he was serious.

'It was my impression,' he went on, 'that he was more relaxed with you than with anyone else in the city.'

'A half truth. He was just working better.'

'That may have been result. Not cause.'

'There was also a girl. Before he came to live with me. She seemed to have done him some good.'

'In any case,' Ben said, 'you should have had a word with him. He might have listened.'

'I doubt it. But I wouldn't mind a bloody word with him now. About Diane. That's more to the point. The bastard. To just walk out like that without a word.'

'There isn't,' Ben conceded, 'much excuse one can make. True. But he has had problems. He seemed, last time I saw him, more frustrated than ever. He said there was a lot he didn't believe in any more. Even reality had grown difficult to believe in. I put to him that that was a familiar experience. He argued that nothing easy could be worthwhile. And what he had wanted, he said, had become too easy.'

'Especially girls,' I suggested bitterly. 'Young ones.'

'Come now,' Ben said. 'Try to put things in perspective.'

'I've got all the perspective I need, thanks. And it isn't pretty.'

Nor, I recalled, was that large painting. Had that, perhaps, also been too easy? Or, for once, too difficult? It continued to disturb and irritate me. The answer wasn't in the paint. The paint only shaped a vast question into which the artist, and most things, vanished.

'I can understand how you feel,' Ben offered gently.

I thought this unlikely, but didn't argue. He meant well. It was just that his concern was unconfined. He saw us all, Diane, Tim, myself, with the same compassion. All young, confused, easily hurt.

He put his hand on my shoulder as I left. 'Come back soon,' he said. 'Diane too.'

Meantime, there was my job or what remained of it; and Sandy, and Alex O'Leary. I envied my father the substance of his vanished battlegrounds. In his time it must have been easier to find places on which to take a stand; places without crumbling edge. Now everything was confused, the enemy to right and left. No flank safe, no principle secure. And doubt was corrosive. Alex O'Leary, hanging on grimly to all he knew, had to be understood. Perhaps I was more troubled by my sympathy for him than by my stand with Sandy. It was no longer a question of who was right : it was a question of who was least wrong.

It seemed Sandy, now, was most interested in proving himself right. He was quick to draw blood. It pleased him to have Alex ranting in the office. 'The old shit,' he said. 'We've got him and them all on the run.'

'Take it easy,' I suggested. 'It's their life's work. All they've got. You can't take everything away from them.'

'Why not?' he said coolly. 'They've got it coming. All this garbage about their precious Soviet Union for years. They defended it while they murdered millions in the name of socialism. Christ, they perverted the whole bloody idea. And you tell me to take it easy? Use your head.'

It was more of a relief than ever to get home to Diane. And something, or someone, of my own. On that scale, at least, the world was not impossible.

Monty Nolan and Reg Gilbert were arrested in different parts of the city, and charged with murder, the day the Russian tanks rolled back though Hungary and began smashing the barricades of Budapest. They appeared handcuffed in court, the newspaper said; larger headlines told of communist slaying communist. 'This is it,' Sandy said. 'This is the end of the international communist movement, as we know it. As we've known it. It's all over.'

He seemed to feel it was all his own work.

'Don't you think so?' he added.

But I was considering Monty Nolan. I drew Sandy's attention to the other news.

'Well, yes,' he said. 'Nolan. He probably had something like that coming. You think he did it?'

I shrugged.

'Just a bloody anarchist anyway,' Sandy observed. 'Another no-hoper. He didn't have to bash those cops. And look where he is now. What's happened to Livingstone?'

'That's quite a question,' I said, tempted to tell more.

531

'He's lost his nest,' Sandy went on. 'That's for sure. I wonder who he'll suck up to now?'

I decided against telling more. Anyway Sandy was quick to lose patience with the subject. 'There's more to worry about in the world than Nolan,' he said, by way of dismissal, 'or Livingstone, for that matter.'

He was probably right, though it was hard to feel it. Perhaps Sandy sensed my inadequacy as a comrade. 'You ready for what's coming now?' he said.

'What *is* coming?' I asked.

The answer was Alex O'Leary. He arrived with a Party statement justifying Soviet intervention in Hungary as necessary for the health of world socialism, and a blow struck at imperialism and counter-revolutionaries. Its untruths were transparent. And saddening, like the desperate words of a collapsing love affair. Or saddening for me. Sandy appeared to feel only rage. 'You're serious about publishing this muck?' he roared.

At the end of the day Sandy and I were out of our jobs.

Next day, at home in the morning, I received a telephone call from Monty Nolan's lawyer. 'My client believes you can be of some assistance,' he said.

'I don't see how.'

'It's a matter of locating two witnesses, to establish his alibi. The names he has given me are Livingstone and Wiseman.'

'Then I can't help at all,' I told him.

'Are you sure about that?'

'Perfectly sure.'

'Well,' he said, 'I'll be in touch again.'

I imagined he would.

Sandy and Stan arrived with a lengthy statement on our resignations from the Party. 'Do I have to read it too?' I asked. 'Can't you just show me where to put my name?'

In any case I no longer felt I belonged to anything, if I ever had.

But they insisted; they had to have the full ritual. Then I signed. It was still too easy altogether; I couldn't believe I had squared my account with my father. Diane made coffee.

'What do you think about Nolan?' Stan said, relaxed and conversational. 'Tim's not mixed up in it anywhere, is he?'

I watched Diane's face. She didn't show much.

'I don't know where Tim is,' I said.

'But I mean,' Stan persisted, 'he's not mixed up anywhere in these murders, is he?'

I shrugged; I didn't dare look at Diane's face now. 'God knows,' I answered.

After they had gone, I made belated explanation. 'It's all right,' she said calmly. 'I knew there was something you didn't want to tell me. But you should have told me, you know. I mean, it might have been easier for you.'

'About that holiday,' I said evasively.

'Yes?' She brightened.

'I think it's time we took it. You've finished your examinations and I'm out of a job.'

'Is that the only reason?'

'Well,' I groped, 'I also think we both need it.'

I couldn't understand, for the moment, why she looked so disappointed. But she began packing, all the same. Then it was really just a question of finding the nearest route out of the city. North or south, east or west, the direction was a matter of indifference. The weather was fine.

The days dissolved swiftly into landscape and seascape; they were not worth counting anyway. We hitch-hiked, and camped, wherever roads took us. And when roads and rides gave out, we had our legs. And as much loneliness as we cared to take. There were warm bays where our campfire might have been the first; there were forgotten forests with a green sparkle of spring; there was surf shattering on long white beaches where we never found footprints not our own. The weather stayed fine, and we both grew brown.

'I suppose it has to have an end,' Diane observed.

I was as reluctant to suppose so. We lay under the hills, beside our fire, with the first stars in the evening sky.

I didn't find it hard to convince myself of love for lonely places, land still wild enough to shrug man off without trace. A long way from battles in Budapest and dusty arguments in a city office. Difficult to imagine that there was anything I wanted of other human beings. Except, possibly, Diane.

'Do we have to go back?' she asked.

I preferred to leave her without answer. Soon she slept. Within my own sleep I began to have a queerly recurrent dream of high mountains. I could not track its source: there were no

533

heights of great substance near us, and the days were hot. But there were icy slopes, silvery caverns, stark peaks and deep drifts of snow. And the distinct impression that someone had just been calling my name. Not that I ever heard sound; it was an echo left quivering silently on the thin sunlit air. And all I could ever find, as evidence that I had not been alone there, was a slender trail of fresh blood drops, vivid on the snow. No footprints; just blood, slowly freezing. And uncanny silence. And no one at all.

Of course we did go back. There was Diane's problem. And there were decisions. It was difficult to forget, for example, Monty Nolan in his cell. When we arrived back in the city I found a request to visit him. There were also urgent communications from his lawyer, and notes pushed under my door from Sandy and Stan, a dozen diverse demands. I replied to Monty, and contacted no one else.

My first decision was to give up my flat and move over the harbour to Ben's place with Diane. Ben had offered me a job labouring on his landscape gardens. It would see me through the months ahead, and keep me close to Diane.

It didn't take more than a day or two to empty my life from the flat: furniture, books, paintings, scruffy manuscripts, all the souvenirs of the city. And when the place at length was bare, I looked upon it without much regret before turning away; most memories already seemed to belong to someone else. The parties, the love affairs, the arguments, the tears, the people who had come and gone. Tim's painting; and my short-lived literary conceit. The people who stayed; the people who vanished. There was nothing left at all. Or no one.

I felt quite light, and rather dizzy, stepping out into the day. I wondered that so much could shrink so fast behind. Had it all been so unreal?

Only Tim, it seemed now, had been real. Or at least Diane and Monty Nolan might insist he had been. For that matter he had once made me seem plausible enough. Where was he?

Sandy, meanwhile, was prominent in the press, exposing his stricken socialist soul in daily instalments. It seemed I had never never appreciated the agony of his doubts, his long torment in the Party. 'Now I am free,' he wrote, 'to tell all.' But all was not, in the end, a great deal; unless the nature of Sandy West was a great deal.

I wondered how Stan felt about it, but made no point of looking him up. I began trundling wheelbarrows of black soil for Ben, and planting shrubs. There were still things I could do with reasonable success.

Then, when I could put it off no longer, I visited Monty Nolan. He was brought to me under heavy guard from the remand section of the prison, but didn't appear at all subdued. He came quickly to the point. 'First thing we better get straight,' he said, 'is I'm innocent, and I'm going to fight my way out of this. I swear to Christ I didn't have anything to do with the shooting. And there are some know that. So the second thing is I got to find them. I want to find Tim. I want to find young Paul. When the shit hit the fan, and we found what Reg had done, we all took off in different directions. Without stopping to think.'

'Well,' I said, 'what did happen?'

'Nothing much at the time. A party. Just a few of us at the house. A bit of booze, a bit of pot. Reg was the pothead, but young Paul and Tim were smoking too. I didn't let Reg push any hard stuff in the house; he's been a mainliner for years. Then Reg started raving about these two goons who ran the other beer house. They'd pinched his girl, among other things. Also they were trying to put us out of business with threats. Reg talked about the advantages of having them out of the way. I thought he meant just roughing them up. Then at a later stage, when I was pretty hazy, he produced a bloody machine gun he'd borrowed. I told him to stop clowning and put the bloody thing away before someone got hurt. It was all just a joke. I should of known. I should of grabbed the thing off him.'

He paused, shook his head.

'What about Tim?' I asked.

'He probably thought it was a joke too. Everyone was high. I think I passed out.'

'You think?'

'God knows. I'll never know. Next thing, there was a big bloody panic. Reg had gone out and done the job. Shot them both. And used my car. Christ. We all scattered that morning. Reg tossed the gun in the harbour. The police are still fishing for it.'

'Well,' I said, 'surely all you need to tell now is the truth. If you had nothing to do with it.'

535

'That's it. I can't. I can't tell the truth. I got a message from Reg. If I try shopping him, he says, then he'll shop me. He's pleading not guilty. And on top of that, it was my car seen outside the other house. The police have a witness. The worst thing is, I had more against those two goons than Reg. They were threatening me, not him. All he had to worry about, all he had to lose, was his girl. The police story is there was a feud between beer houses, and I was the master-mind. I should of known better than give a job to Reg. Jesus. You see how it looks.'

I tried to. 'But if you go in the witness box – ' I began.

'I can't. Can't you see? Then it's my word against his. And it'll look worse for me. I've just got to take my chance. Unless I can find someone to say I never left my place that night. Tim could say that. Or Paul. If I could find them.'

'But are you sure you didn't? What about your car?'

'Reg had a key too. But he can easily deny that.'

'You said the police had a witness. How much did he see?'

'My car, or one like it. Also he thinks he might have seen two people, not just one. That puts me in the gun either way. I can't win. If there were two people and not one, like the witness says, then the other one could of been Reg's girl. He could of picked her up from the other house after he put bullets through her boy friends. But she's in smoke too.'

'Look, Monty, are you absolutely sure you didn't go near the other house? Absolutely?'

'I told you, I passed out. You couldn't help me find that pair?'

'I'll try,' I promised. 'I want to find Tim anyway. For another reason.'

'Try everything,' he pleaded. 'Try every bloody thing. Anyone anywhere. Otherwise I'm for it. You know that? I'm for it. I'm for the big drop. I haven't a chance.'

I could believe that, all right.

'Meantime,' he added, 'I wonder could you go around to the house and fetch my clothes. A dark suit, some shoes, and a couple of white shirts. I'm going to need them in court. I just hope to Christ the place hasn't been ransacked. The lease was paid to the end of the year. If you see anything else there, take it. I don't think there's much there anyway.'

The visit ended abruptly; he was taken away.

I travelled by taxi around to his house and picked up his

clothing, after extracting a key from a neighbour. I also removed Tim's large painting from the outbuilding, since I doubted that anyone else had use for it, and arranged for a carrier to take it to Ben's place. Anyway Monty was right: there was nothing else worth taking.

It was all I ever found of Tim. There was nowhere to begin, and everywhere to end. Nor had anyone heard of Paul Wiseman, if there was anything to hear. Monty and Reg Gilbert came to trial early the next year. The evidence against Reg Gilbert was overwhelming: there was the witness who had lent him the machine gun; there were the witnesses who, after the event, had heard his drunken confession to the murders; his fingerprints were found in profusion in the house where the murders had taken place; Against Monty there was virtually nothing; but his lawyer's request for a separate trial was refused. So the bulk of evidence against Reg Gilbert told, in effect, against him too. Particularly since he, on evidence offered, had most to gain from the murders. Perhaps his rugged appearance also worked against him with the jury. All Monty had was his unsworn plea of innocence, his claim that he was still seeking witnesses. It was too little to offer, and too late.

I was in court through most of the trial, hopeless in the public gallery. On the last day, at my bleakest, and alone, I received a nudge. Stan had slid into the space beside me. We sat in silence through the judge's summing up, then left the court upon the jury's retirement. 'He's had it, hasn't he?' Stan said.

I nodded. 'Not a chance. Not now.'

'And Tim's the missing witness?'

'Along with Wiseman. Yes.'

'What a bastard of a situation. Is there nothing we can do?'

'I can't see it.'

Nor could I see the jury's retirement being long.

'Well,' said Stan, trying to be cheerful, 'you are a stranger. I haven't seen you since the big bust up. For a while there, Sandy and I were desperate to get in touch with you. But you'd vanished. What the hell are you doing now?'

'Minding my own garden. For once. What about you?'

'Well,' he said, 'a man has to live.'

'What does that mean?'

'Advertising, actually.'

'And Sandy? What's happened to him?'

Stan looked unhappy. 'We fell out. Over all his breast-beating in the press. Too much was too much. He certainly had his eye to the main chance. He didn't miss a trick. When I told him so, he didn't like it. Anyway he's gone off into the world free-lancing. Latin America for a start. Who knows. He may find a clean cause. One, that is, which coincides with the advancement of Sandy West.' He shook his head sadly. 'Christ,' he went on, 'what's happened to us all? Where are we? Who's left? And what's happened to Tim?'

'You tell me. Perhaps he's used us all up. Monty Nolan too. Poor bloody Monty too.'

The jury was returning. We went back to the courtroom to hear the verdicts of guilty, and see the donning of the black cap for the death sentences.

'We have to do something,' Stan insisted.

Once we'd contrived to save a world; now our ambition went no further than salvaging a single life. In the weeks afterward we again tried every track which might lead to Tim – or Paul Wiseman. It was useless. 'I'm beginning to think,' Stan confessed, 'that neither of them exist. Do you think Livingstone was just a figment of our imagination?'

'His painting wasn't,' I observed.

'True. But what good is that going to do Monty?'

'Possibly as much good as he would.'

'What do you mean?'

'I mean Livingstone and Wiseman – both – might make a pretty unimpressive pair of witnesses anyway.'

It was something I had hardly dared admit to myself. But it was also thin consolation.

'Odd you should say that,' Stan said. 'I've had a similar thought.'

'Oh?'

'That police witness said he saw two people in the car near the scene of the shooting. Obviously one was Reg Gilbert. If Monty wasn't the other, who was it?'

'Gilbert's girl. One theory.'

'Or?'

'Well,' I shrugged, 'someone else.'

'Exactly. Who else?'

I had to think about that.

538

'You must admit the range is limited,' Stan pushed. 'Only one or two people.'

'You're not saying Tim?'

'Not necessarily. I'd rather opt for Wiseman. He liked a little excitement and drama. And unusual kicks. He doubtless got the kick – and fright – of his life.'

'So what does that mean?' I felt confused, solid ground crumbling again.

'Please yourself. All I know is that they took off together, fast. You might say that Tim, perhaps, had a choice somewhere along the line. And obviously it was to help Wiseman out of trouble, which he did. Monty was left to look after himself.'

'We don't know,' I argued.

'No,' Stan agreed. 'I also prefer not to.'

'What are you implying?'

'I'm just telling you that I prefer not to think about it. And about why, for example, Tim might have chosen Wiseman rather than Monty.'

'If he did,' I said.

'All right,' Stan sighed. 'If he did.'

When Monty's case came to appeal, and failed, we worked on a petition of clemency alongside his lawyer. It was a small enough hope. Our argument was too technical : there was insufficient direct evidence against Monty to convict, we claimed; and he would never have been convicted if he had been granted separate trial from Reg Gilbert. Apart from that, we could muster only routine argument against capital punishment. But public sympathy was missing. We gathered few names to our petition. 'Who the hell cares,' said one journalist we approached, 'if there's one Nolan more or less in the world?'

A few days before the date for execution, when things seemed at their most hopeless, Reg Gilbert made full confession to the murders; he claimed he had acted alone, under influence of drink and drugs. A police spokesman shed doubt upon the confession's entire credibility, but there was enough confusion for our petition to succeed. Monty was granted clemency, but no immediate retrial. Reg Gilbert died alone.

'While there's life there's hope,' Monty insisted cheerfully, when we visited him afterwards. 'I'll get out of this place yet.'

We should, perhaps, have taken this at face value. A week or two later, after knocking down a warder, he escaped prison. At once he changed from a possible victim of a miscarriage of justice to a man of violence, a convicted murderer, on the loose. He was free just twenty-four hours, more than enough. All hope of retrial or pardon was gone. In court again he pleaded that he had escaped in an attempt to establish his innocence, and locate missing witnesses.

In return the judge said Nolan was already fortunate to have his life. In his considered view, such an individual would never be fit for release; he hoped Nolan would be kept under the strictest possible confinement for the remainder of his life sentence.

Stan and I had shared our last lost cause. Perhaps we had something to say to each other when we separated. But it seems, in retrospect, unlikely.

I went back to Ben's gardens.

Charlie Higgins died. I went to the funeral with my father. 'We never gave up until we had to, Charlie and I,' he said. 'Will you ever be able to say that for yourself?'

Diane miscarried. Her pregnancy hadn't become apparent. We didn't even have that much left.

Ken wrote from England after publication of his book. 'Guess who I saw in Regent Street the other day,' he said. 'None other than our old friend Wiseman amiably on the make in London. Perhaps a degree more sober, and a shade less vivid, but rather lovably much the same. He says Livingstone's around too, though he's pretty vague about the location. But claims he's painting well, and will exhibit soon here if he (Wiseman) can organize it. Wiseman, among other cheerful chat, claims contacts in the art world who will help Tim along. Yet I suppose it could be true.'

And some months later : 'By Christ it *was* true. I don't know how Wiseman managed it, but he has himself a job fronting in a small gallery here. And he's got Tim an exhibition. I'm still rubbing my eyes. My invitation, exactly as promised by Wiseman, arrived in today's mail. I can't, by the way, understand your last letter – it isn't entirely your scrawl, I'm sure. Just bloody incoherent. What's all this about Monty Nolan and murder charges and Tim?'

And a little later still : 'To think I was hoping (secretly) for something to make me nostalgic for the hills of home. I had a sick feeling as soon as I walked into the gallery – my first wild thought (or hope) was that I'd walked into the wrong place. But no such luck. It was Livingstone's exhibition, all right. At least the catalogue – with a note by Wiseman – said so. And there was dear old personable Paul himself near the door, a fluttering butterfly with an endearing line of patter for old ladies. The paintings? All slick and sure and safe in the authorized international style. He must certainly have worked hard at it. He deserves colossal success. Wiseman's still vague on Tim's whereabouts. Says he is probably in Spain. You still haven't written to tell me about that Monty Nolan business. What other news? What about yourself?'

Indeed.

Twenty-five:

Documents

The latest New Zealand expatriate to win recognition in London is a young artist, Timothy Livingstone, formerly of Auckland, whose one-man exhibition opened in a small Soho gallery last week. Though not so far widely noticed, the exhibition was described as 'interestingly vital' by one well-known London art critic, who then went on to say: 'Promise is plainly there in abundance; there is a certain refreshing alien ferocity in his handling of colour. One naturally hopes that Livingstone's antipodean fire will not sputter out for lack of oxygen in the rarified European air.' The manager of the gallery, another young man recently arrived from New Zealand, Mr Paul Wiseman, said: 'We have great hopes for Tim, though no one is actually buying his work here yet.'

– News item

A man perished in a farmhouse fire several miles from Te Ika late last night. The man was Edward Livingstone, aged 64, a pioneer resident of the district. He lived alone. A police spokesman said there appeared to be no suspicious circumstances. His next of kin are at present being sought.

– News item

Commentaries

None.

542

Part Four

Fathers

Twenty-six:

HE MADE NO MOVE. HE HAD STILL TO REMIND HIMSELF HE was in Paris, and not half a world away. He sat there, in the American Bar, considering Tim Livingstone. The Spanish conversation of his neighbours flowed steadily against the beat of the music. A hostess arrived at his table, but was largely unseen. She shrugged, laughed and left. Presently he was aware that his hand held a drink. He finished it, rose, and moved ten yards to Tim Livingstone's table. He was completing a drawing of a companion, or customer. Ian stood for a while at his shoulder, ignored. Then Tim scribbled a signature, ripped the drawing free, and handed it to its subject, a rather pudgy middle-aged man with a girl in tow. Money was exchanged, the man laughed at his likeness, and handed it to his girl. The girl giggled. The transaction was complete. The man waved for more drinks.

At length Tim was aware of the fresh presence. 'Yes?' he said, looking up.

'So we're back,' Ian said, 'to lightning sketches again.'

Was there fright? He couldn't be sure. He would, of course, like to think there had been. But the voice which came was bland.

'Well,' Tim said. 'I should have known.'

'Yes. Perhaps.'

'Not even here.'

'No. Not even here.'

There was a silence. Tim had time to recover.

'I have a feeling we first met on some muddy riverbank,' he said.

'As I recall. Yes.'

'I also have a feeling you're still trailing some of that mud around.'

Ian shrugged. 'Possibly.'

'Well, sit down.' He spoke in rough French to his previous client. 'Another customer,' he explained. The pudgy man and his girl left for another table.

'You must have gone to some trouble to find me here.'

'Only up to a point. It's not such a large world outside, after all.'

'If you insist. And what are you doing here, anyway?'

'I think that's my question. If you don't mind.'

'But I do mind. Beyond a certain point one place is as good as another. I'm past that point now. And what do you want?'

'Want?'

'You must want something.'

'I shouldn't have thought that obvious.'

'If you want a likeness, I can provide you with that for a certain number of francs. I could even, come to think, allow a discount.'

'For old times' sake?'

'I have room to bargain.'

'I see.

'The management here, in any case, likes to see me working. Not to speak of the expensive drinks their clients are obliged to buy for me. I'm like another hostess, you might say, with a not dissimilar sideline. They, in their way, do their best to provide flattering likenesses too.'

'Go ahead then. Point taken.' Ian gestured towards a waiter at the bar.

'Odd,' Tim said, as he began, 'I never drew you before.'

'Perhaps there wasn't occasion.'

'Or need. After all, I lived with your face long enough.'

'And others.'

'True. And others.'

'A long way from here. Well, not quite. I saw Wiseman in London.'

'You did?' Tim did not seem much interested.

'I thought you were close.'

Tim made no comment. His thick pencil moved quickly.

'He seemed to be doing spectacularly well for himself.'

Again no comment.

'It was Wiseman, initially, who put me on your trail. He told

546

me you were last heard of in Spain. On Ibiza. While I was there, incidentally, I wrote to Wiseman to see if he'd heard anything about you in the meantime. Just on the off chance. I got no reply.'

'The little bastard,' Tim said at last.

'Why? Because he didn't reply? I had the impression that he might have been trying to keep you in quarantine.'

'Wiseman and I finished up some time ago.'

'A fight?'

'We no longer had use for each other.'

'That sounds familiar.' Ian, setting this picture straight, could now walk back the length of the gallery, past other pictures which still hung askew. And straighten those, too, in passing. But he could take his time.

'He thought, you see, he might use me as a small stepping stone in London. But he found others more promising, other discoveries. And that was that.'

'And now you're here.'

'Obviously.' Tim's pencil worked vigorously, shading.

'And he's there, prospering.'

'If you say so.'

'I'd say he's just found his milieu at last. He's plausible enough.'

'Look,' Tim said abruptly, 'can't we find something better to talk about?'

'Well, at least you have your own life again.'

Tim said nothing. Their drinks arrived. The urgency of the confrontation seemed to be diminishing by the minute. Somewhere, surely, there was a point to begin. Ian struggled to find it. Tim was engrossed in his drawing; he appeared to be taking pains.

'You might,' he said at length, 'tell me how you got here.'

'The usual route. Through Panama.' Ian did not mean to be so cryptic. But there were other things on his mind, and they did not altogether concern himself.

'Another local boy trying to make good.' There was only the slight suggestion of a sneer.

'Not really. I just came to see what it was all about over here. Ken McAdam was very persuasive. So I came.'

'Having nothing better to do with yourself?'

'Possibly.'

'Come now, how's the literary life?'

547

'Ken had hopes for me. I can't say I had. Ken's agent was inclined to agree with me. So I've been free-lancing here and there, in the meantime. I imagine it's likely I'll go home soon. I've seen enough; I've got the drift.'

Ian was suddenly irritated at having to make a defensive account. It was not he, after all, who should be obliged to make account.

'And how's McAdam flourishing?'

'His bubble's burst. He's having trouble with another book. But he claims London has consolations. He tells me he's hoped for sight of you.'

'Someone else I've avoided with success, then.'

'If you need isolation, that's understandable. I mean, for your work.'

When Tim looked up from the drawing, it was just to consider Ian's face, no more.

'I hope it's going well,' Ian added. 'Particularly now you're away from Wiseman.'

'Well?'

'Your work.'

'Yes,' Tim said vaguely. 'I should have this finished any minute now.'

'I mean your real work. Your painting.'

'Oh yes,' Tim said ambiguously.

It was unlike him to give such concentration to so trivial a task. Unless he chose distraction; in this instance he evidently chose.

'You used, in the old days, to have these finished in half the time,' Ian said lightly.

'This is rather special.' Tim looked up from the drawing for a moment, no longer vague. 'You can take it home with you. Your personal souvenir of Paris. If anyone asks, you can say it was done by some cranky artist you encountered in a bar off Pigalle. With very little effort, you should be able to concoct quite a neat little anecdote to account for it.'

'I was hoping for a signature. That might give it rather more value.'

'Then the price is another round of drinks.'

'Fair enough.' Ian waved again to the waiter. He would likely feel frustrated soon. Not yet, but soon. At least his anger was gone; nearly three years ebbed. He was surprised how cool he found himself now, how cool and reasonable, considering how long he had sought to manufacture this meeting. Perhaps it was too remote in time and space from occasions which once made it seem necessary. Necessary? Of course it was, still. Why else was he here?

There was another silence. Ian was tempted to send names rattling, like stones, across the table: Margaret, Stan, Monty, Diane. Any number of damaged lives. Including, of course, his own.

Then, quite suddenly, he had a place to begin.

'I was sorry,' he said, 'to hear about your father.'

Tim, who had evidently been preoccupied with some finishing touch to Ian's likeness, perceptibly stiffened. 'About my father?' he said, the pencil paused.

'About his death.'

Perhaps it was news. Perhaps Tim hadn't known. But if so he was not going to concede this or anything else. There was no way of telling. After a time he found something more for his pencil to do.

'It couldn't have been long before I left,' Ian went on. 'The report of the fire, and his death. Very brief. Just the police verdict that there were no suspicious circumstances.'

The pencil hesitated, hovered. 'Why did they have to say that?' he asked at length.

'I imagine they felt obliged to. With a man living alone there's always a possibility, I suppose, of his being murdered. And of his place being set alight, afterwards, to conceal the murder.'

'Oh, yes. Murder. I see.'

'Anyway he wasn't, they thought. He wasn't murdered.'

'Kind of them, in that case, to say so.'

'To think so.' Ian, having discovered advantage, could not afford to lose it now.

'To think so, then.' The voice was cool.

'I know you were pretty distant from him, in more ways than one,' Ian continued. 'All the same, the news must have hit you.'

He could offer pretence too. Tim offered nothing.

'And hurt you,' Ian added. 'At times like that we must all have our regrets. And guilts.'

'True.' He uttered the word without tremble.

'Even, say, here. In a place so different. So remote.'

'Surely.' Tim was growing glib in reply again, almost himself. Whatever Ian's advantage had been, it was gone. Casually, still conceding nothing, he put his signature to the likeness. And hesitated over it again, evading Ian's outstretched hand.

'It's quite a thought,' Tim said, 'that I have that land back there now.'

'Oh yes. The farm.'

'For what it's worth. The place was pretty run down when I last saw it. But still, it's there, isn't it? My inheritance. My patch of earth. The only one I'm likely to have. Something to think about.'

'I imagine it is.' Ian was surprised by the sudden sentiment.

'You sure you wouldn't like it?' Tim said abruptly.

'You're not serious.'

'Why not? You tell me you're going back there.'

'And you're not.'

'Not foreseeably, as they say.'

'The best thing you can do is get the farm sold up. Obviously you could do with the money. Even if it's only to pay your fare back.'

'The idea of selling it up doesn't appeal to me. Or going back. You have it. All yours, for the asking. Not even for the asking. Here. I'll make it formal. I don't know about legal, but never mind.' Tim began to scribble quickly on the drawing, under the still unseen likeness. He spoke the words aloud as he wrote them. 'I, Timothy Livingstone, being sound of body and mind – does that have the right ring? – hereby transfer title of all such land as is mine by right of inheritance from my deceased father, Edward Livingstone, to Ian Freeman, wherever and whoever he may be, as pictured above. There. You think that will do? Morally the place becomes yours anyway. And who would argue with the evidence?'

'This is ridiculous,' Ian said. 'A joke's a joke, but there's no point spoiling what might be a good drawing.'

'You haven't seen the drawing yet. The words beneath are small compensation, let's say, for a rather shoddy piece of work. The trouble with your features, Freeman, is that there's nothing for me to catch on to. Nothing at all. So I improvise, and pretend to see something I don't even begin to see. Your character, that is. I can only see you as an idea, an idea of my own, and not a very visual one at that.'

'What idea, exactly?'

'A forlorn form of conscience, I suppose. Sorry if I'm vague. I'd prefer something, some idea, more blatant – more dramatic.

An avenging angel, say. But it's not your style. So I have to make do with a careful face belonging to a careful person. Sad.'

He again held the drawing back when Ian reached for it. 'Why don't you,' he suggested, 'say what you want to say? Why don't you just call me a bastard and have done with it?'

'Perhaps because that would be too easy.'

'Oh?'

'Perhaps even because it might give you some satisfaction.'

'Some relief anyway. You seem determined to prolong your agony. So say it, why not?'

'Insufficient evidence, I suppose. I'd like to understand more. And that's always a risk. I might forgive more.'

'Christ. You see what I mean. What can I do with you?'

'I'd say, for example, that you're perfectly reconciled to being a bastard. That you revel in it. As a way of protecting yourself, probably. To make it less easy for people to get at you.'

'And you're trying to get at me a different way?'

'I didn't say that.'

'No, of course, you wouldn't. You wouldn't.' Tim showed, for the first time, a distinct twitch of irritation. 'So what in hell is the point of this meeting?'

'I'm just finding out myself.'

'Look,' said Tim, 'it's over. All over. Whatever it is you want, you're not going to find it here.'

'If I wanted anything, I wanted to know what you were doing with yourself.'

'I'm doing nothing with myself. And it gives me great pleasure.'

'I don't believe that.'

'Then that's your problem.'

'Perhaps,' Ian agreed. 'But still.'

'I'd like to tell you to bugger off. But I can't, quite.'

'That's a start, then.'

'And you wouldn't anyway.'

'Probably not.'

'Jesus,' Tim said heavily. 'Just like a dog, when I was a kid, always snapping at my ankles. A neighbour's dog. They shot it finally. So don't push me too far. Better still, don't push me at all.'

'I still don't see harm in asking what you're on about.'

'And I gave you the answer. Nothing. Because I don't need to.'

'Need to?' Ian repeated.

'Need to be on about anything. Do I? I've even got myself rid of that land now. I often wondered what I'd do with that problem. And now there's only you to be rid of. I should have known you'd arrive, sooner or later.'

'You could look happier in your situation.'

'Now you're talking like a management consultant. And anyway this is a hell of a place to discuss happiness. Look around, and you'll see people trying to buy it, or something that passes for it.'

'You don't belong here.'

'Just what I said in the first place. You're tracking that mud in here, in your inimitable style. Why don't you just follow the trail back and leave me alone?'

'I probably will, given time.'

'And I think I've given you enough time.'

'Not quite,' Ian insisted.

'And, besides, this place is near closing,' Tim added.

It was true the crowd had thinned. A drunken couple lurched in dance to the sound of a faint piano. The girls had almost all gone.

'We could go elsewhere,' Ian said. 'And anyway you must live somewhere.'

'I'm a two-time loser. First you cut my income for the night, and now you invite yourself home.'

'Just a suggestion.'

'All right. Come on back, then. I might still have something drinkable under the bed.'

They rose from the table. Tim snapped the sketchbook shut and arranged it firmly under his arm; Ian still hadn't seen the likeness. But there was, perhaps, no hurry. Tim said goodnight to the barman, and a hostess alone and smoking near the door. Then they were out in the narrow street. There had been another shower; the air was fresh and pleasantly cool.

'Is it far?' Ian asked. 'I could get a cab.'

'Save your money.'

They walked. The streets grew tighter. Most buildings were dark. There was the irregular scrape of Tim's feet beside him. Yet his pace was brisk enough.

'Easy to lose yourself here,' Ian observed conversationally.

'Are you being literal or existential?'

'Take your pick.'

'You're so bloody heavy-handed with your cues.'

They moved off the street, around a building, and climbed a narrow flight of steps. Tim unlocked a door, and they were climbing more steps, to the top of the building. Another door, and Tim switched on a light.

They were, evidently, in his room. Or someone's room. It could, really, have been anyone's: the evidence of occupation was negligible and anonymous. A bed, a table, a chair; a few books, and some unwashed plates. And empty space. The room was long and high, with a large window at one end. Their footsteps echoed emptily off the walls. For the walls, coloured or discoloured faint yellow, were quite bare.

All things considered, incredibly bare.

Ian needed time to take it in. It was conceivable, of course, that Tim had only just taken over the place. Anything else, for the moment, was inconceivable.

Tim went across the room, groped under his bed, and produced a bottle of wine. 'So we drink,' he observed. The cork was already loosened; he slopped the wine into two glasses.

'You just live here,' Ian said at length, allowing himself to speak. His voice seemed small in the space.

'Just live?' Tim said, puzzled. 'If you mean exist, yes. I exist here.'

'I mean – ' Ian hesitated uncomfortably. 'I should have thought a room this size would have made a good studio too.'

'True.' Tim pushed one of the glasses at him.

'It even looks as if it might have been meant as a studio.'

'Possibly,' Tim agreed.

'So where do you work? Where do you paint?'

'Oh,' Tim said, 'so that's it. I'd forgotten you were so bloody slow on the uptake. Because I'm holed up in Paris I have to be painting?'

'I don't see that as unreasonable.'

'Just reasonably romantic?'

'Well – '

'I imagined I'd got the idea across to you at least once tonight. That I wasn't. That I wasn't painting. Now are you going to drink this or am I going to drink it for you?'

Ian took the glass. And something, perhaps sufficient, of what was said. 'You mean,' he suggested, 'for the time being? You aren't painting for the time being?'

'I said I'm not painting, full stop. And I mean full stop.'

'Why here? Why Paris?'

'Why not? As good a place as any for a final cure. Better than any, if you like.'

'You're not serious.'

'Then look around.'

'I've done that, thanks.'

'And you're still not satisfied?'

'No. Not really.'

'Then the best thing you can do is help me finish this bottle. And then, for preference, leave me alone. But you won't, will you?'

'You can't have done nothing for the past three years.'

'Unless you count the show for Wiseman, and a few dribs and drabs after. He's probably junked the paintings.'

'And you've been here since?'

'More or less. Look, let's strike a bargain. If I convince you, you leave me alone. How does that sound?'

'A poor bargain.'

'Oh?'

'I don't need any more convincing. All of a sudden.' He might have begun to accept the bare walls, the space about them. What he could not accept yet was the person before him. Accept or forgive. But the walls were blank. As blank, say, as the anger he thought forgotten, if not as blinding.

'I just want to hear you say it's all been for nothing. For this, for nothing.' His voice, he imagined, was still reasonably level.

'All what?' Tim's smile was odd and crooked; his expression was uncertain for the first time.

'Everything.' It had now become intense effort to say anything.

'Jesus. Easy on. What do you think – '

For he had grabbed Tim's shirt. Wine spilt. His own glass dropped and smashed, then Tim's. Tim tried to pull away, then push Ian off. They reeled against the table, which shifted with sharp sound.

There was enough pause for Tim to say, 'So what's it all about?' He was hardly terrified; he had a bemused, perhaps amused smile.

When it came to a point Ian could not say; he could not even speak names which might make partial explanation. But would hardly explain himself. When it came to a point he could only lurch at Tim with a fist and, when that failed, grab at a wine

554

bottle in frustration. They seemed, as they wrestled, to have
inhabited the scene before. And they had, of course, though in a
different place, within other walls. Then he managed to bring
the bottle down on Tim's skull. The blow was deflected and light,
not really stunning.

'Jesus. You – '

The impact of his second blow jarred his arm; it was a
wonder the bottle survived. Tim, freed of protest, drifted for a
moment on his heel, on his weak leg, and staggered back through
the large window. There was a sound of breaking glass. And a
falling cry, and silence.

A few splinters of glass tinkled down from the giant gap in
the window.

He let the bottle drop and then, so far as it was safe, stepped
to the window and looked out. It seemed there was a courtyard,
two or three floors down, into which Tim had fallen. There was
just sufficient light to show the scene. Tim's pale shirt, vaguely
luminous in the gloom, marked the end of his fall; the rest was
obscure. But a broken body was easy enough to imagine. Dead?
He could not imagine otherwise. The silence was incredible.
There was soon much more illumination, as lights in neighbouring buildings flicked on. And voices, sudden and loud.
Whatever was left of Tim would be easy enough to rescue.

Then he felt only panic.

He backed away from his conspicuous place at the window,
thus leaving the scene entirely to his imagination. He looked
quickly over the debris in the room, lest something of himself
remain. And there was, after all, only Tim's sketchbook, which
he remembered in time. He riffled through the book to his likeness and jerked it, trembling, from the wire loops which bound
the page. It seemed, in his haste, reluctant to come free. A tear
raced across the page, and through the lean mocking caricature
Tim had finally and predictably made. His first impulse was to
crumple the page into a ball and throw it away. But he folded it
quickly and placed it in his pocket.

He was shutting the door, hurrying down steps, and out in
the street. He circled for a time, in confusing alleys, before he
found the fringe of Pigalle again. At one stage he encountered
a speeding ambulance, and he stepped into a doorway, alarmed
to know that so much time had passed already; he could not tell
whether it was going to, or coming from, the scene. Then again,

it may have had no connection with Tim at all; it may have been too soon.

He found Clichy, and lights; and was back where he began that night. The crowds were gone. Just a little traffic, a few late strollers. A streetwalker or two, and a corner bar prominently open. Most places were shuttered, including the cafe with the negro band, above which an uncaged canary had so briefly sung.

Trying to summon sanity, or something to pass for it, he crossed to the open bar. He could have a quick cognac and call a cab back to Odeon, the sooner the better. He might yet convince himself it hadn't happened.

He took fright, of course, at the touch on his shoulder almost as soon as he had ordered his cognac; he lived an entire sequence of arrest and interrogation before he turned to see the girl smiling behind him. He should have known the night unfinished.

'Did you,' asked Yvette from Toulouse, 'find the friend you were sad for?'

'It wasn't like that, exactly,' he insisted, resuming where they had left off.

'No matter. Did you find him? This one from almost nowhere?'

'Not really. No.'

'And not even the love?'

'Not even the love,' he agreed.

'So,' she said, and paused, her smile dimpling, 'at this hour even my price for the love is small.'

'Whatever it is,' he said, 'I sometimes think it is always too much.'

'Pardon?'

'It doesn't matter.'

'I can promise more than enough for the price. I am new, you must understand, and try hard to please.'

'I understand.'

And he could wonder if he trembled perceptibly. The cognac was warming. She might mistake the nature of his trembling, and imagine turning it to her advantage. And perhaps, after all, she wasn't so wrong about her advantage.

'For that,' she said, 'I have a bed. The bed alone is free. It is just the rest for which so small a price must be paid.'

'The trimmings?' he suggested.

556

'The trimmings, yes. For that there is the small price. And the bed, afterward, is yours. There will be no one to disturb. That you will sleep well, I promise.'

'You're very persistent.'

'It is my business, yes. To be so.'

He imagined his ride back across the city and Seine to his small room and narrow bed in Odeon; he was, to say the least, unlikely to sleep well there. Yvette's bed was suddenly much to be preferred. It was extraordinarily simple, really; there was no decision to be made at all. He rose from his stool at the bar, and Yvette took his arm.

'It is sad, all the same,' Yvette said, as they left, 'that you could not find your friend tonight.'

'Perhaps,' he suggested, 'he was unwilling to be found.'

She laughed, uncertainty, and held his arm tight. He was not so greatly unsteady.

('And when I had no luck in Paris,' he told Margaret ten years later, 'I gave up the exercise. Or, rather, when it became obvious that I was going to have no luck, I just took off suddenly.'

'And he could still be there?'

'Possibly,' Ian agreed.

'You make it sound very sad.'

'It is damn sad. In retrospect.'

'He mightn't have amounted to much anyway.'

'I don't know if that's the whole point.'

'And perhaps just as well you didn't find him. At least, by the sound of it, you began to do something with yourself then.'

'There was chance too,' he insisted. 'In Paris, when I decided to take off suddenly, probably back to London, there just happened to be a fellow, an American research student, staying in the room next door. He was on his way down to Yugoslavia. He had a car; and I went along for the ride. I finished up in a cheap place down on the Dalmatian coast, writing my head off for a month or two. Until my money was almost gone and I had something recognisable as a manuscript. It turned out to be my first book. Or the first published.'

'*No Angels Sing,*' Margaret said. 'I still think it your best.'

'So people keep telling me,' he said, irritated. 'Sometimes I'd sooner forget it.'

'It had this vivid quality,' Margaret persisted. 'Everything seemed luminous. The land, the people. It wasn't as if there was even much of a story, yet I remember scene after scene. Strange. It seemed to be painted rather than written. Your other books were just written, I'm sorry to say. I didn't have the feeling that you needed to write them. But that one, the first one, was different.'

Ian didn't disagree. He didn't say anything.

'Sorry if it upsets you.'

'It doesn't upset me. I was just remembering how the wind off the sea turned bitter when I finished the manuscript. I had an unheated stone cottage and I sat there shivering. I persuaded myself that I'd done my dash. That I wouldn't write anything again. Anyway I said goodbye to a lot there. It was like discharging a debt, or buying my own likeness.'

'I don't quite follow.'

'It doesn't matter. The point I'm making is just that I felt free.'

'You just said something about buying your own likeness.'

'A figure of speech,' Ian said quickly.

'I know. But how did you see yourself?'

'As hungry to do something with life again.'

'After writing *No Angels Sing*? You're joking.'

'That was too passive. I mean, in an active way. To live a little more while I had the time.'

'So what happened?'

'Nothing spectacular. I went up to Belgrade to find my American friend and hitch a ride back to London. I encountered a cultural conference at which there was a fair representation from communist countries. And hitched a ride with that instead. Some surprising information came my way. Also I could talk enough of the Marxist language to detect what might really be going on the other side of the jargon. An editor or two thought my articles readable and asked for more. The rest is routine. For a while I was in and out of Eastern Europe trying to make sense of what I saw. But that was how it started. In Belgrade. Chance again. Oh yes, I also first met Katya there.'

'The girl you don't like to talk about.'

'No,' Ian conceded. 'Not much.'

'Well,' she said. 'Please yourself. There's plenty of time. So long as you don't object to my company for the time being.'

'It's better than I deserve.'

'Thank you.' She paused. 'Anyway you're telling me, I take it, that you never got back to Paris again.'

'Only briefly, passing through. I never looked for Tim again, if that's what you mean. Before I left Europe, though, I checked with one or two people in London who just might have heard of him. They hadn't. So far as I can tell, no one has, anywhere. He's gone as if he's never been.'

'You were saying something about his work earlier.'

'Well, yes. Except for his work. True. Which reminds me, I still have to do something about this Kennedy fellow who seems so interested in the paintings. And perhaps invent some more information for him; God knows.' He paused. 'Except for his work, yes.'

'And *No Angels Sing*?' Margaret suggested quietly.

'What do you mean?' He was suddenly tense.

'Well, it seems fairly obvious to me, the way you tell it, that if you hadn't gone looking for Tim in Paris, you might never have finished up on the Dalmatian coast writing the book. You mightn't have written it at all.'

'Possibly,' Ian agreed with caution.

'I was tempted to say, when I suggested the book was painted rather than written, that it could have been like something he might have painted, if he'd had the time. Only you did it instead. Or do I carry the thought too far? Tell me if I've said the wrong thing.'

'Well –'

'Have I? Please say.'

'No,' he said finally. 'Not altogether.'

'Which leaves me to consider whether I'm not altogether right, or not altogether wrong. Never mind; it doesn't matter. *No Angels Sing* looks after itself quite admirably. I still taste the book now and again. Just to get the flavour of the mist off the land, the frost on the grass, the cattle under the trees – and the river running near. It touches me close to home. That's all.'

'I'm grateful then.'

'And that old farmer. The one who lives alone. Was there an original? Someone from Te Ika, perhaps?'

Ian sighed. 'Yes; in a way.'

'Who?'

'Tim's father. A wonder you didn't guess. Cranky old Livingstone up the gorge.'

'You knew him?'

'Not really; no. I never met him anyway. But I suppose I knew just enough about him. The precious particle.'

'There's that beautiful scene, towards the end, where he finds this young girl picking flowers in the bush at the edge of his farm. Like some sprite. Or like some vision of his past, when he and the land were younger. Then she just melts away, as if he'd dreamed her, and everything's too solid around him again; too solid altogether. That was wonderfully imagined.'

'Imagined? Yes, I expect it was.'

'Obviously it must have been.'

'Perhaps it just seemed very real to me at the time. I made my own little world and crawled into it.'

'Afraid of something outside?'

'Possibly. Or of a great many things.'

'So,' she said. 'Tim's father. I might have known. The more we talk about it, the bigger your debt seems.'

'One way and another,' he allowed. 'But still, I'm beginning to wish we could empty him out of our conversation for good.'

'Any time you're ready,' she said crisply.

He had the urgent impulse to tell Margaret everything; and have done with it all. The story was safe enough with her, so why not? He might even make it credible, if not explicable. He could wonder why he didn't. Still, he had time for that too. Besides, the end, or such as he had, was still too unsatisfying. His confession would hardly leave Tim, as a subject of conversation, for dead. No more than he had, for all he knew.)

In Paris, while packing and otherwise preparing departure, he bought morning and afternoon newspapers in hope that they might tell him what he wanted to know. He traced his way down columns of fine print, through obscure headings and cross-headings, really just in search of a name. The newspapers, however, told him nothing at all. The woman who cleaned his room might have wondered at his enthusiasm for the French press, in all political shades. Likewise the American next door, Steve Becker, who looked in to remind Ian of his offered trip to Yugoslavia.

Such evidence as existed in Tim's room, the broken glass, the spilt wine, the empty bottle, was probably read as residue of a drunken accident, or suicide. He didn't know whether the French press recorded such trivial fatalities. Possibly not. There was, really, only one thing more chilling than the thought that

560

he had killed Tim; and that was the thought that he might never know. He was tempted to cross the Seine again, to make discreet inquiry, if he could find that part of Paris in which he had lost himself. He didn't. And besides, Becker's Renault, fuelled and ready for the journey south, was waiting at the hotel door.

The last thing he packed, not quite forgotten, was Tim's drawing: the likeness. It might not have been gratifying but he was careful, after all, not to crush it; it was already sufficiently damaged. And also the words beneath apparently gave him title to something. Land? Hardly. Something less, or something more. In any case only his imagination was free to claim it.

On the way down to Yugoslavia, still frustrated, still short of certainty, he remembered the report of Ned Livingstone's death. That at least had been clear enough. Hadn't it? Suddenly he was no longer very sure of that either. In dreamy doze, with Becker comfortingly steady at the wheel of the car, through southern France and then Italy, his mind made too many intricate resurrections for him to be sure of much at all. Anyway he seemed at times to have all of the answers and none of the questions. He could, at least, ask one.

'Your turn at the wheel,' said Becker.

(Years later, having just said goodnight to Margaret, he searched among the debris of his unpacked possessions and at length found the likeness Tim had made in Paris; and considered whether to show it to her, as preliminary to the truth. And, while considering this, wondered that he had ever thought it a caricature.)

Twenty-seven:

THE MIRROR IN HIS CABIN WAS STILL HUNG ABOUT WITH SOME of the floral garlands which smothered him when he boarded the ship and farewelled friends at Rarotonga. The frangipani, hibiscus and tiare maori were wilted and withering now, but their scent remained sweet in the cabin. He shaved, made swift examination of his face, and brushed his thinning hair. He was as ready as he was likely to be. He went up on deck.

It was early morning, with land at last in sight. Possibly he could allow himself, now, some small excitement; he had lived this often enough in imagination. The sea was calm. The night had tugged tall blue hills and lean limbs of land from the Pacific; and verdant islands and rocky islets, among which the ship now cruised. The entire horizon, after two days of blindingly empty ocean, was crammed with terrain of diverse formation. Gulls flew in thick drifts across the brightening sky. The sunrise had begun to paint the sea.

He held tight to the rail. He couldn't understand why death should be so immediate and vivid a presence. Suddenly he had no doubt. He was proposing not just to live here, but also to die. It was not really so unique a prospect, when considered. And not so large a discovery that he had to die, here or elsewhere. Yet in a sense, looking out upon the silver-grey land, he was contemplating his coffin. And it looked solid enough, as it floated out of the dawn, frighteningly solid, with just a faint shroud of inland mist.

Soon he was quite ready. The sunlight was touching the land now, rippling across the sea, and maritime suburbs became visible, a thin dusting of pale houses at the foot of hills along the coast; there was evidence of human occupation. The ship, engines gently beating, moved toward harbour and city.

Other passengers began to join him at the rail. Tourists mainly, earnestly discovering the South Pacific, equipped with cameras and maps, leaflets and books. Voices, some pleasant, some strident, floated around him.

'Sheep,' said a woman. 'I read they have sixty million here.'

'And Maoris,' said another. 'Friendly dark people, who used to be cannibals, in grass skirts.'

They examined the nearing shore with binoculars, perhaps for first sight of both.

When he moved away, it wasn't so much because his mood had shattered. It was because he had just seen, held in a well manicured hand, a copy of *The Death of Polynesia*, with dull shock of recognition; his own name, upon the dustjacket, seemed singularly alien. As if it, and he, had no business here. Perhaps he should have examined himself more carefully in the mirror, among those garlands.

The ship swung out of the long coastal channel and into the harbour. The seaside suburbs, now close each side, had lost some of their mystery, and become regiments of red rooftops above the bright sea. All clean and shiny, as if daily painted and polished. Like toys; a city of dolls' houses. There were phoenix palms, explosions of glinting green fronds, along the shore; and Norfolk Island pines rising spikily beyond. Further up the harbour, a large new steel bridge stalked from shore to shore; it seemed he was obliged to cope with the unfamiliar too, when the familiar was demanding enough. At least the early sunlight was soft. The city, or such as showed itself to the approaching voyager, was distinctly taller. Soon he had seen sufficient. He left the deck and went down to his cabin.

The garlands were gone. His steward had taken them in tidying his cabin. Possibly something to do with health regulations, agricultural hazards; anyway they were gone and probably floating somewhere in the ship's wake. And the mirror, in which he could consider himself again if he wished, was strangely naked. Still, the scent remained, if faintly; he could take a last breath, untypically and unfairly sweet, of a world outside his own. He avoided the mirror. *Papaa*: four layers. He didn't need the mirror to tell him that he was down to the last layer now. And it wasn't skin from which he could easily wriggle free.

Still, he could make an effort. He tried, for example, with the

563

journalist who arrived off the pilot's launch to interview him.

'And why are you back with us, Mr Freeman?' he asked, amiable enough.

'Family reasons.'

'And that's all?'

'A certain amount of curiosity. That too.'

'Your new book, *The Death of Polynesia,* appears to be something of a best-seller. Have you something new on the way?'

'Nothing. I finished that some time ago.'

'Would it be fair to suggest, then, that you're back here to recharge your batteries?'

'As long as it's your suggestion. Not mine.'

'It's difficult to imagine that you don't have some large intention in mind. Do you think you'll be staying home long?'

'I prefer to leave that open.'

'Do you think you might find it too quiet here? I mean, you appear to have had an adventurous life – correspondent in Eastern Europe, sailing among remote Pacific islands.'

'In that case this might be another adventure.'

'As an author?'

'As a human being.'

'I see.' The journalist seemed rather baffled. So far he hadn't taken a note. Ian felt obliged, after all, not to disappoint him.

'You could say,' he suggested, 'that I'm back here only because I failed to make a successful escape. Or is that too obvious?'

If he expected a smile of gratitude, he was wrong. 'Perhaps you might explain,' the journalist said.

Later that day, driving out of Auckland with Ben beside him in the rental car, he watched familiar hills drift up from the summery haze ahead; perhaps they explained, better than most. 'Livingstone landscape,' he heard himself say suddenly to Ben.

'What's that?' Ben had begun to doze in the hot car. He was showing his age, if not altogether ungracefully. He had begun to look, at last, the part of the elderly and distinguished man of literature; his verse had lately been discovered, published in collected edition, and studied in universities. And Ben, in turn, had almost come to life again; he wrote and lectured.

'I said Livingstone landscape. Those hills ahead.'

'True. Though I don't see why you need to be so exclusive. There are other painters.

'All the same – '

'Yes?'

'All the same, they're still his. Those shapes. Abrupt and angular, quite rigid; like waves frozen at the point of breaking. And queer calm. Perhaps it was his innocent eye. He just saw where the light fell. There was no one to suggest a softer line.'

'Careful,' Ben said.

'It was a shock to me, seeing that work again at your place this morning. After not seeing it in ten years. I should have avoided it, perhaps. It's rather taken the edge off things. I didn't want to come back to look through his eyes. I actually looked because I wanted to believe it bad. Preferably quite worthless. Instead – '

He paused to overtake a car. Ben was silent.

'Instead,' he went on, 'I seem back where I began. Of course I should be noticing the other things. The changes. And surprised, possibly, at the overblown city back there – the motorways, the flyovers, the new skyline, those elephantine suburbs. Instead I'm snatching again at what I know.'

'Well,' Ben said, 'take comfort where you can, then.'

'It's not,' he replied, 'comfort I'm finding.'

'Oh?'

'On the ship this morning,' he confessed, 'I had the sensation I'd come back here to die. Until I saw your face down on the wharf, waiting for me, I could quite easily have gone sailing on.'

'You're exaggerating now.'

'A little. But not much. When I saw you I was able to remind myself, quite efficiently, that I was back here to see my father before he died. And make believe that was all.'

'Then stop making believe. You might find it painless after all.'

'I'll consider it. Experimentally.'

The hills were nearer now.

'You mean you might leave again soon?'

'It's not impossible.' He paused. 'Absurd, of course. My first day back and already – ' He shook his head.

'Already you're confused,' Ben suggested. 'That's natural enough.'

The hills ahead began to shift and part, sufficient to admit the highway. There was a narrow gorge, with a swift river beating upon rocks below the road; the highway needed

565

patience here. Already much of the gorge was in shadow. The afternoon light fell mellow on the ridges.

'You seemed fairly determined to find him, when you left,' Ben said. 'Why didn't you?'

'I told you when I wrote. He wasn't to be found; at least not by me.'

'I wondered, at the time, whether there might be more to it.'

'More?' he said casually. Too casually. He took a new, firmer grip on the wheel of the car.

'More than you told me.'

'Not much. I don't see how there could be, if I didn't find him.'

'Agreed. But the sudden loss of interest intrigued me. After Paris, wasn't it? You just never mentioned him.'

'I'd become busy with my own life.'

'Admirably too. You mean, surely, with *No Angels Sing.*'

'Same thing.'

'But you will concede the sudden loss of interest. In finding Livingstone in the flesh, I mean.'

'I expect it's true,' he said. 'It's hard to recall.'

Or only too easy. As the narrow highway curled around corners, the hills arranged themselves in diverse perspectives. Alien pines grew darkly, here and there, out of the dense native treefern. Possibly they would take over the steep slopes soon.

'Years later, before I left London, I did ask around again,' he added evasively. 'But the scent, if any, had gone quite cold; there wasn't a trail to follow. Nothing.'

'But the scent,' Ben persisted, 'was quite warm at the beginning. Or so I gathered.'

'Let's forget it,' Ian said abruptly.

'If you can,' Ben observed.

'I've no cause to care whether he's alive or dead. It's much the same, all things considered.'

'Oh?'

'Bugger this Max Kennedy. Damn and blast him.'

They were quiet. In the heart of the gorge, with hills shadowy and sharp, they passed crumbled cottages; all that was left of a once large gold-mining town. The river ran more sluggishly here.

'What intrigues me, at the moment,' Ben said, 'is what you'll find to start running away from now.'

He thought about that.

566

'If I'm allowed a choice,' he said, 'I suppose I'd most like to escape this sudden awful feeling that I belong somewhere. Or is that predictable?'

'Fairly,' Ben allowed.

'I'll be fairly predictable then. Still, I'm nearing forty. I ought, by now, to be married and settled, shouldn't I? With a child or two, at least.'

'I'll admit I expected that, or something like it. I always saw you as choosing safety. What went wrong?'

He shrugged. 'When it came to a point, something always seemed to happen. I always fell on my face, never on my feet. I don't mean that to sound like self-pity. Because the worst of it is, it always seemed to have been the best thing in the long run. Except once.'

'In Paris?'

'No. In Berlin. I'm talking about Katya.'

'Another hole in your life; I didn't understand much of that either.'

'Perhaps I didn't want you to understand too much. I don't remember.'

'I just had this incoherent cry of despair from Berlin. With no preliminary, and damn little explanation afterward. Of course I could put two and two together; but I wasn't sure I'd come up with four.'

'I imagine I told you about meeting Katya at a cultural conference in Yugoslavia.'

'Indeed you did. At some length.'

'Afterwards, travelling, I used to look her up in Prague often. At first largely as a useful contact; then something more. But at that point, because of an article I'd published, the Czech government decided to deprive me of a visa. Katya was in trouble too, purely because she knew me. That should have put an end to it.'

'But it didn't?'

'No. Since she was off to East Berlin on another cultural jaunt that summer, that August, we arranged a rendezvous there. A time and place in West Berlin. I wasn't to go East so as not to arouse suspicion. She was to take the subway West and there, in short order, we were to marry and fly out. Only one thing went wrong with the plan: that was the bloody August the wall went up. I walked up and down the obscene thing for three days, hoping for some weak spot, before I

567

understood she wasn't going to make it across.'

'So that's it. I thought of it as some spiritual crisis, some sickness in your socialist soul.'

'There was that too, probably. Until then I was trying not to take the world very personally; it was just good copy. And highly edible. Then suddenly it stuck in my throat. I've been trying to cough it out ever since.'

'So I've noticed.'

'I don't complain. It's been reasonably rewarding.'

'I've noticed the sales of *The Death of Polynesia*.'

'It wasn't that I meant, entirely.'

'No?'

'But never mind. I'll let it stand.'

'It was obvious you changed somewhere along the line. It seems I got the location wrong, that's all. It was Berlin, not Paris after all.'

'I don't see why you should harp on Paris. I wasn't even there long.'

'And you weren't in Berlin long either.'

'True.'

'And you were pretty incoherent, and evasive, from both places.'

'Perhaps.' Ian's tone was tight. 'Look, is there something you're trying to say, some point you're trying to make?'

'No. I'm just setting it all straight in my mind. I've followed your career, you must remember, with more than mild interest. And still do.'

'Despite *The Death of Polynesia*?'

'Well, perhaps not because of it, I admit. I'm just saying I have a few adjustments to make.'

'I'd sooner you said what you've avoided saying. About that book, I mean.'

'Well.' Ben sighed. 'A lazy idea, cheaply executed. If you hadn't been on your way home anyway, I should have been tempted to write and say it was time you did come back.'

'I see.'

'Quite aside from the fact that you ought to see your father.'

'Well, I'm back at last. And on my way to see him. That should satisfy you.'

They were out of the gorge now, travelling through easier coastal country. The hills were gentle rises among bright pasture-land. Now and then they were allowed glimpses of distant sea, a vivid blue. They weren't far, now, from the township where his parents lived in retirement.

'As for the therapeutic value,' Ben said, 'I won't know, unless you stay. As for the other, my real hope is that your father is satisfied, seeing you again.'

'Oh?'

'He's built a lot on your return. He's been waiting years. I hope he's not disappointed.'

'You think he might be?'

'That's up to you.'

The car was cruelly hot. He was aware of the sweat growing uncomfortably on his body. The highway ran wide and straight now, delivering him swiftly to his destination; he had, with Ben as company, been preferring not to think about it. He would sooner the luminous day had no end. Or at least an end less precise in its priorities.

'It's a lot to take at this stage,' he observed. 'Perhaps I should have waited a day or two.'

'I don't think you have that much time to play with,' Ben said. 'Not really.'

'I understood he'd made an impressive recovery, after that last heart attack.'

'True. Willpower, possibly; at least I'd like to think so. Sometimes I think now his heart will be the last thing to go. That it will still be pumping when the rest is gone. He's quite a man.'

'So people have been telling me all my life.'

'You're not still bitter about it?'

'Not really. I've even begun to think it's very likely true. What I don't understand is why he should want so much to see me again.'

'Just something for himself, probably. After all, you were never much more than a disappointment to him, with your shift-less life; and he doubtless showed it. He could conceivably wish to make amends.' Ben shrugged. 'Or just quietly satisfy himself that he was wrong. That's all.' The second, the man considered, seems more likely.

'I still feel there's something you haven't told me.'

'True,' Ben admitted. 'I've been getting around to it all day.'

'You just said I haven't much time to play with. What is it, then?'

'Cancer,' Ben answered with difficulty.

'Christ. Not his heart?'

569

'No. Sorry.'

'Why wasn't I told before?'

'It was diagnosed, late, just a month or two ago. When it was well on its way. And he crumbled enough to see a doctor again. It's been a swift slide since. Your mother and I agreed there was no point telling you sooner, since you were on your way in any case, packing up and waiting for the first ship home. We left you to think it was still his heart.'

'And there's not much time left?'

'No. Not much at all.'

He was quiet for a time. 'And that's why Diane is down there too, I take it. I was expecting to see her on the wharf this morning.'

'She's been helping your mother nurse him. Since he left hospital. He insisted on going home again. I gather he wanted to be there, not in hospital, when you arrived. But he's going fast.'

So was the car. Ian's foot had become urgent on the accelerator.

There was little left of his father. A restless shadow between sheets. Ian had to draw his chair close to the bed to hear his father speak. 'You been a long time coming,' Bill Freeman said; each word was an effort. But there was still a shrewd flicker in his eyes, under the glaze.

'I should have come sooner,' Ian apologized.

'Never mind. You're here.'

The others, Ben, Diane, his mother, had all retreated from the bedroom; the doctor had just been, with morphine.

'You're here,' the old man persisted, 'and I can take a look at you. It's all I wanted, another look at you.'

Ian felt uneasy. And perhaps useless. 'Are you comfortable?' he asked. 'Can I straighten your pillows?'

'It's all right. Everything's all right. I'm glad you got here. I suppose they told you I haven't got much longer.'

'Well –'

'It's all right; I know it too. I done my dash. I been done with it a long time now. A man dies when he knows – well, when he knows there's nothing more he can do with the bloody world. Then it's only a question of what more the world can do to him. That's the first death, the one that hurts. The second, this one, is just routine. It's just a matter of getting

570

the stupid business over. I closed my account with the world; now the world is closing down on me. Of course there's a lot in my life I would of liked different. Shall I tell you one of them?'

'Go on,' Ian said gently.

'It seems to be the only one that matters now. Funny, all those regrets; and now I only got one left. Just one. I suppose you could say I'm getting off light. What do you think?'

'I don't know till you tell me.'

'Well, the one I got left is that I was in jail when you was born. Not that I was in jail; that was just part of the game. But because I was shut in there when you was born. My first child, you see; my son. And I was shut in there.' He closed his eyes, as if subduing something. Perhaps just the desire to sleep. In a few moments he appeared renewed: at least his eyes opened again.

'It's all right,' Ian said. 'You don't have to go on.'

'I have to,' his father said. 'Otherwise you miss the point. The point of what I'm trying to say. I was shut in there, and you was born.' He was groping now.

'Yes,' Ian said.

'Charlie Higgins, he was all right. Walking the streets, and in Parliament. But he never had a son. He had nothing, in the end.'

'No,' Ian said.

'But that's not the bloody point either. No; that's not it. The point is – '

'Look, Dad, perhaps you could tell me tomorrow. You need some rest.'

'The way things are, I don't count on too many tomorrows. I don't even like to think of them. Can you see the sea out that window?'

'Yes. It's a nice sunset. The estuary's just taking on colour. And the cottages, the other side. The tide's coming in.'

'Good.' Bill Freeman closed his eyes again. Then, as they trembled open, he added, 'Perhaps the point doesn't amount to much anyway. I was only trying to say I was shut in there when you was born. And when I got out, you was grown into a child; I never seen you as a baby. You was a boy already, growing fast. And I couldn't catch up with you. Yo see what I mean?'

'Well; not altogether.'

571

There was a flash of irritation on his father's face. 'All I'm saying, boy, if you want me to say it, is I never caught up with you. I never did. I tried more than once, and never did.'

'It's all right.' Ian's tone was soothing.

'That's where you're dead wrong. It never bloody well can be all right for me. Not now. Not unless – '

'Yes?'

'Not unless I catch up with you now. I suppose that's all I wanted, one last try.'

Ian took his father's hand, which lay limp upon the sheet. The hand was bony, and the skin coarse and loose.

'One last try,' Bill Freeman went on. 'But I don't know whether I got the heart for it now, or the guts. There's bugger all left of my heart, and my guts are almost burnt out with this other. I don't know what I got left functioning inside. The doctor would know, but that bastard's not going to tell me.' There was a painful pause. 'Here I am, I got my chance with you, and I'm not up to it any more. Not that I'm complaining about death. It's just I never got my life finished. Or squared off: same thing.' Another pause; his breath had become wheezy. 'Just sit there for a while, boy. That will have to do. We never got the strength of each other, did we? Or maybe it's just me. Maybe it's just I never got the strength of you, because I never caught up.'

'If I had a son,' Ian suggested, 'I might have a job catching up with him too, the way things are. I hate to think, anyway. I'm glad I don't have the problem.'

'Perhaps time you did.'

'Perhaps.' Ian was not convinced.

'You could do worse than settle down. And worse than this country, since you're home.'

'I'll see,' Ian promised.

'I had to try myself out against this country. But I can see now that wasn't enough for you. What did you find out there?'

Ian considered the question. 'A black shark,' he answered finally. This seemed to puzzle his father, so he added, 'Also a wall. Among other things. A wall to butt against.'

'Like I did,' his father suggested.

'True.'

'Mind you, there was a time, a moment, when I thought the wall might crumble. There seemed a chance.'

'You were lucky, then. I never had any illusion.'

572

'I can see that. I mean, I've tried to read you right, boy. Not just you; those books too. What I mean is, I done my best to catch up. I wouldn't say I understood all you're on about, but I think I understood enough. I understood that you had a fight too. Not my fight. Your own. I didn't understand that easy. It took time. But I had the time.'

Ian began to understand something of his own. He began to understand that, in a left-handed way, his father was trying to set him free.

'It's just there's not much left now,' Bill Freeman said. 'Bugger all.'

'At least,' his son suggested, 'you're making the best of it.'

Bill Freeman didn't say anything for a time : his eyes were closed. Ian wondered if he heard. Then there was movement in the hand he held. Evidence of life : some, not much. The eyelids lifted too, with effort.

'Why did you take so long coming back?' the old man asked. 'We might of got it all straight. Did you think you was going to get some rest up in the islands?'

'I didn't find much.'

'I could see that. The book you wrote, the one people have been talking about. My memory's going, like everything else. I can't remember the name of the damn thing.'

'It doesn't matter.'

'What I was wanting to ask you about, anyway, wasn't that one. It was the first. About the old farmer, with the word angels in the title. Or no angels, that's it. Never mind, you know the one I mean. That's the one I wanted to ask you about.'

'Yes?' Ian said.

'Well, what I was wanting to ask you about, it might sound strange . . .'

'Go on,' Ian said.

'I wanted to ask whether you had me in mind, when you wrote that. I just wondered. I know I wasn't like that old farmer, strictly speaking, lonely on his land. I never was a farmer, never. All the same, when I read that book, I had this queer feeling it was me walking round in his boots. Even me losing his son. You know what I mean?' A pause. 'I had this queer feeling it was me all the time, not him. I couldn't shake it off, for a long time after, that feeling. How do you account for it?'

'You just identified with him,' Ian suggested. 'That would be the easy thing for me to say.'

'And what's the hard thing for you to say?'

'To admit it's possibly true. Or partly. Of course I imagined I was writing about someone else. Someone I didn't know. I expect I had to imagine I was.'

'You're telling me, then, I mightn't be so stupid after all.'

'If you like. Yes.'

'It's a hell of a time to ask you. If you're frightened of hurting my feelings, forget it. The only feeling I got now, if they let me feel it, is just a kind of slow fire inside. A slow fire. That's all. I mean – where was I? No, you don't need to worry about my feelings, not now. If you wanted to write about me, and disguise me as that old farmer, well that's all right. That's all right by me. You understand? I might even be proud of it. That you thought I was worth all that trouble. You see.'

'Yes,' Ian said quietly. 'I see.'

'Ben reckoned that book was a good one. I know I never had much use for his opinions in the past, one way and another. Maybe because I never had much use for him until lately. I heard him say it, once, over a bottle of brandy.'

'I'd better buy him another bottle then.'

'So,' Bill Freeman said, 'are you going to put it on the line, then? Are you going to tell me whether I'm right, whether it was me?'

'Obviously it's for you to decide. I mean, you know best.'

There was a short silence. 'Then it was me,' his father said finally. 'Yes. That was me, all right. I don't know why, come to think, I needed to ask you. I knew all along.'

Bill Freeman closed his eyes: his thin face began to relax. Perhaps the morphine was claiming him now, and his son could safely leave him to sleep. But when he moved slightly, just shifting in his chair, his father's hand came to life again, and gripped his with surprising pressure. 'Don't go,' he said. 'Not yet.'

'All right.'

'I can dream something terrible now. I get in a panic.'

'I'll stay here,' his son promised.

'It's always the same dream. Of a huge Swedish bastard. Someone I knew once. And he always has the same thing to

574

say. Chaos, he talks about. He says chaos is our kingdom. That's all. Never anything more.'

'It's all right,' his son said. 'Take it easy. I'm here.'

'I mightn't of caught up with you, but at least I been making a fair enough try, haven't I?'

'Yes,' his son agreed. 'You have.'

'So just sit there for a while, boy. Like I said, that will have to do.'

After a while Bill Freeman's hand became loose again; his faltering grip was gone. The old man slept, his breath just faintly wheezing. Beyond the window the estuary was darkening, slipping from sight. There was just a fading line of light above the hills. Even the gulls had become quiet. The distant surf had a pleasantly regular beat. A star or two appeared in the sky, and soon vast clusters, doubtless somewhere among them the Southern Cross; he looked for it alone now. Ian, in the dark with his dying father, had sense of land crowding around him again; he had been back twelve hours, and might never have gone.

A day or two later the doctor insisted that his father return to hospital. Within a week Bill Freeman was dead. He died quite easily, between one moment and the next, or between one sagging breath and the next, which never came. His family, his son, daughter, wife and brother-in-law, were all at the bedside; they were slow, each of them, to accept the silence at their centre. When they filed from the room, Ian looked back and saw a nurse covering his father's face with a sheet. It was all over, though his instinct still told him otherwise. Ben comforted his mother; he comforted Diane. They walked out of the hospital into the chill, before dawn, of a summer morning; the light was grey and misty. Their feet made oddly distinct sound on the gravel pathway. His eyes were tired and twitching; Ben's looked red and lifeless after the long night. The grief of the women, mother and daughter, was quiet; there had been ample preliminary. When they had been helped into the car, Ben turned to Ian for a moment; he seemed obliged to make some summary. Ian wished it unnecessary. Words for once were distasteful to him : even at their best they might cheapen.

'It wasn't a little thing,' Ben said. 'It wasn't ignoble or unimportant, whatever it was died with him.'

'No,' Ian agreed, reluctantly.

575

'I loved him, of course.'

But Ian was still too numb to consider the substance of this confession. 'Of course,' was all he said. 'As we all did, I expect, in our different ways.'

Then he persuaded Ben into the car, and they drove from the hospital into the brightening day.

There was so much to manage. It wasn't just a question of handling the funeral arrangements, and answering the telephone. There was his mother, for example. He had found too little time to get to know her again. Or Diane, for that matter. And in the vacuum afterwards, it still wasn't easy. They seemed to remain as appendages of the man. Perhaps they would become distinct again with first grief gone. Some decisions had been made already. That his mother would sell up the seaside cottage; that she would go to live with Diane. In any case he had no alternatives to propose. He had to do his best with small things; and, otherwise, the token of his presence at the end. His mother appeared satisfied with that, at least.

'It made a difference to us all,' she said, 'that you got here in time.'

It was no real surprise to find her so small and limp and grey a woman. She had almost used up her life too. The last months had drained her; she trembled fitfully. And Ben, her brother, seemed to know best how to console her. Ian often felt futile.

Yet it was still startling to find Diane such a substantial woman. A coolly attractive mother of four, with a lively interest in the world. The day after the death, and the day before the funeral, with the house quiet, Ian and Diane at last had a chance to walk together, past the estuary and tidal mangrove flats and down to the open ocean. 'So you're home,' she said. 'It's still hard to believe. You think you'll stay?'

Ian shrugged; the surf had slight sound. 'I haven't had time to think. Perhaps you can give me a reason.'

'Because we all want you to,' she said impulsively. 'That's the best reason I can think of, at the moment. I'd rather like a brother around again.'

She pushed her arm in his as they walked along the sand. Ian imagined he knew what was coming next; it always did.

'It seems a lifetime since you left,' she went on. 'And of course it is, in a way. Most of my adult life, at least.'

It came, then.

576

'Did you ever,' she asked, 'catch up with your friend? Did you ever catch up with Tim Livingstone?'

'No,' he said. 'Not really.'

'What happened to him, then?'

'No one seems to know.'

He did not explain. And Diane, rather oddly, didn't persist with questions; he had expected she would. Perhaps she had rather more urgent interest in the present. They walked together back to the cottage. Her husband, a young doctor, was due to arrive for the funeral; her children were being looked after by in-laws, and she appeared anxious for news of them.

'Don't you miss,' she asked, 'never having been a father?'

'Not particularly. Or not yet.'

'I'd hate to think of you old and lonely like Ben. While you've been away, hasn't there been someone? Someone you might have married?'

'Once. Yes. But I wasn't up to it. Or she wasn't.'

The rest of the day was largely spent with Ben and, later, his mother. Between the death and funeral, time was slow to shift; they seemed trapped in some limbo of life. Until, that night, alone with his mother in the kitchen, helping her clean and tidy away dishes, a name arrived out of his past. It should, really, have been no surprise; she had been recalling things of his childhood and youth. But his mother said, 'Margaret Saunders now, she seems to have done well with herself after all.'

'What's that?'

'I was just saying, Margaret Saunders seems to have done well with herself after all. After that bad beginning.'

'In what way?'

'I'm sorry; I thought you might have known. She's on television almost every night.'

'Well; yes. I did hear something vague. I'd forgotten.'

'She's become quite a personality. Everyone seems to think they know her now. Of course you haven't had time to catch up on television yet.'

'On a great many things,' Ian agreed.

'She has a very fresh and friendly manner. I expect that's why people like her. There's talk, of course. She's been divorced once or twice, so people say. But as far as I can gather, she still has only the one child. A boy, that baby she kept. She must have been a very determined girl.'

'She was,' Ian said. 'When she put her mind to it.'

577

'I expect you would know,' his mother said quietly. 'Your father used to enjoy her on television; I think he was a bit struck on her. Is that, he used to say, that skinny Saunders girl Ian used to know? Anyway he was quite taken with the thought that she was an old girl friend of yours. Ian, he'd say, could have done a lot worse for himself; what went wrong with the boy?'

At the memory, she smiled; it was the first time Ian had seen her smile since he arrived home.

'It was a long time ago,' he said.

'Go into the living room,' she insisted, 'and switch on our set. She should be on any time now.'

'I think I'd prefer to get used to the idea first.'

'Please yourself,' his mother said.

'I'd like to catch up with one thing at a time.'

'Of course. You know best.'

But when at length he went into the living room, he found the television set switched on, by Diane or her personable husband. And Margaret Saunders, with shoulder length hair, public smile, and high-collared silvery gown, was looking into his life again.

Before the funeral newspapers appeared with obituaries. Bill Freeman's name had become quaintly distant, almost respectable. They recalled his roll in the depression riots, and his consequent imprisonment. In later years, one obituary said, he had been content with political obscurity; another suggested that he had repudiated his past beliefs, particularly those he had held as founder of the Communist Party. It was like a gentle defusing. Otherwise the obituaries were not greatly inaccurate; there was nothing to be gained from irritation with them.

At the funeral itself he should not, perhaps, have been surprised at so large a gathering of strangers; there were few familiar faces. A great many had evidently driven down from the city. Ian often found his hand clutched passionately by these strangers, while incoherent things were said, as he farewelled mourners by the cemetery gate. He wondered who they were, and what his father meant to them, as their departing cars made the countryside dusty. Even his mother was vague. 'I expect they all knew Bill at some time or other,' she said.

Anyway they were gone, with most of their mystery; the coastal countryside grew quiet again; the dust subsided. A light breeze fluttered the flowers which covered the heaped clay of

Bill Freeman's grave. Beyond the cemetery were hills and valleys of the country his father once wished to tame, and which in the end tamed him. Ian, despite Ben at his shoulder, could not really believe that the grave held anything larger than the man himself. That surely was enough.

Twenty-eight:

BACK IN THE CITY HE HESITATED FOR SOME TIME OVER THE telephone before he dialled the number he wanted. It was still too strange. The drab and dour post-colonial city of his youth was almost gone; and in its place, with high-rise buildings and banks of bright glass, was a brisk and modern city of struggling sophistication. He wasn't sure he cared for the change; it robbed him of his past. Yet he felt fearful of the familiar. How could he manage, for example, some face he knew in the street? He preferred to walk anonymous, ghostly, through the city. But here he was, at length, experimenting with the past. Or with himself.

There was an impatient knock on the glass of the telephone booth : someone else was waiting to use it. He dialled swiftly, and asked for a name. When Margaret's voice came on to the line, though, he almost replaced the receiver. It seemed too soon to become solid. But he held on to say, 'Ian here. Ian Freeman.'

'My God,' she said. 'There's magic for you.'

'What do you mean?'

'I've been trying to track you down since yesterday. Not just for personal reasons. Also for an interview. But no one seemed to know where you were. So I tried willing you to call me. And see? It's worked.'

'Brilliantly.'

'Seriously, though, I saw that your father had died. So I decided to leave off getting in touch until you felt more up to it, perhaps. Now you've saved me the trouble. But I really did try willing you to call. I'm sorry to hear about your father, by the way.'

'It's all right.'

'Is it, really?'

'He had a large enough life. And death didn't altogether take him by surprise.'

'Anyway you're still here.'

'Just,' he allowed.

'When can we see each other?' A pause. 'I don't mind admitting I'm nervous.'

'Then it seems I have the advantage for once. I've already seen you. In black and white, true; but that was impressive enough.'

'Thank you. Well, when can we?'

'Soon, if you like.'

'Now,' she insisted.

They met in a coffee shop near the television studio. It would have been difficult not to recognize her, since most of the customers in the shop did; their eyes tracked her to his table. She was smartly dressed, with faint flamboyance; she still had a good figure, and might have turned eyes anyway. He tried to see in her face a girl who had vanished into rain half a life before, and wasn't sure who he found. He certainly had this brisk urban woman who seemed too vivid a summary of change.

'To be continued,' she said. 'Here we are, then.'

She smiled winningly as she sat at the table.

'I can't seem to find my place in the script,' he confessed. 'All I can find is a legend saying, here be dragons.'

'Am I that frightening?'

'Almost.'

'I think the script calls for a certain amount of surprised fascination,' Margaret observed. 'To be expressed in dialogue as, You've changed – or, You haven't changed a bit. Take your choice. I think I'll reserve my opinion, if you don't mind. It's all right; you don't have to say anything at all. If you like, in fact, we can get right down to business. You can pretend to be the arrogant author of *The Death of Polynesia*, and I can pretend to be a tart television interviewer. How's that?'

'Well – '

'And then, with all that over, we might pretend to be ourselves. Can you think of a better idea?'

'Not really,' Ian admitted.

That evening, when finished at the studio, Margaret took him home to her flat, with promise of dinner. Her son, she said, was involved with something at university; he was a first-year student. The flat was airy and comfortable, just out of the central city, overlooking harbour and waterfront lights.

'I've done better interviews,' Margaret said, passing him a drink. 'I blame past involvement with the subject. Besides, you weren't very forthcoming; I had to prod you every inch of the way.' She paused. 'Come to think of it, you're the most bloody exhausting subject I've ever had.'

'I thought we were going to pretend to be ourselves now.'

'True.'

'You still haven't told me just how all this happened. What happened, for example, after you went home to Te Ika?'

She examined her drink. 'I had my baby.'

He thought it best not to pursue this. 'And then?'

'After a year or two back on the farm I took off again. Clem wasn't very happy with me around the farm any more; he was planning marriage. And Fred and Judy were taking off too. So I travelled with David, from place to place, taking jobs which allowed me to look after him. Finally I took a job, in a town which otherwise I'd prefer not to remember, as typist and general dogsbody in a radio station. A girl announcer fell ill, and they gave my voice a trial. I seemed to suit; and one thing led to another, including a marriage or two I'd also prefer not to remember. And so here I am again.'

'It sounds so painless.'

'It was meant to.'

'But it wasn't, of course.'

'Well, what do you think?'

Ian, for the moment, preferred not to think. 'How has it worked out for David?' he asked. 'Does he ever wonder about his father?'

'If he does, he keeps agreeably quiet about it. But he's had, of course, a few substitutes in the meantime. He's managed; we've managed. Oh, I don't doubt he's curious. About his father, I mean. I've wondered myself, at times.'

'What do you mean?'

'It looks as if I'd better pour you another drink.' She took Ian's empty glass. 'I need one too.'

'I just took it for granted Tim was the father,' Ian observed.

Margaret was quiet. She poured the drinks.

'Well?' Ian persisted.

'Well what?'

'Wasn't he the father?'

582

'I don't know how this happened,' she said. 'You must have started talking about it. I certainly didn't mean to.'

Ian was baffled. 'What is it?' he asked.

She handed him his drink. 'Let's just sit and look at the lights for a while,' she suggested; she took a chair and crossed her legs comfortably. 'I'll do something about dinner soon.'

'I think it would be easier on both of us if you just told me what you're trying not to tell me.'

'It was all so long ago. And we were very young. And things were so innocent. Doesn't that strike you now? We just had babies. We didn't die on drugs.'

'I don't see how that makes an answer.'

'I didn't intend it as one. I'm just saying it doesn't matter now, either way.'

'Either way?'

'David was, is, the only relevant fact. You see.'

'I don't see. Sorry.'

'Well,' she said finally. And sat silent for a time. 'All right, then. I lived roughly three months with Tim; I was also roughly three months pregnant when I left him. Does that make an answer?'

He watched as his life shook itself into new shape, new possibility; he seemed a passive, stunned spectator. Yet the surprise left his mouth dry. 'You mean I'm the father?' he said at length.

'I should have thought you faster on figures.'

'But is that what you're saying? That I'm the father?'

'Not really; no. If you would like me to phrase it gently, let's just say that I can't exclude the possibility. It was one or the other of you; either you or Tim. Let's say a fifty per cent chance either way. It almost cancels itself out. So, does it matter?'

'I think it does,' Ian insisted.

'How, then?'

He found himself unable to say.

'Obviously you need another drink,' she observed. 'We both do.' She took his empty glass. 'If you want to forget it, please go ahead. I've just told you David's the only relevant fact. And he's long past the stage of needing a father. It's too late to matter, too late to care.'

'You must have cared.'

'Well,' she said, 'yes. I suppose I did, in a perverse way.'

'And what does that mean?'

'Just that, at first, I thought of David as Tim's child. And then, as he grew, I tended to think of him as yours, for some reason. Equally illogical. You see, even my feelings tended to cancel themselves out, in the end. So I didn't think of anyone at all. All that mattered, really, was that I was his mother. But I can't pretend entirely that I didn't care, or haven't cared. Yet it would have made no difference, would it, if I'd known anything for certain.'

'I don't know.'

'It seems rather more likely to me that, as possible fathers, you both had the perfect out. You would have preferred to consider the child as Tim's and vice versa.'

'What if I said, now, that I'd like to think of your child as mine?'

'I'd say you were bloody sentimental. And that I've very likely given you too much to drink already. But take this one, all the same, and try changing the subject. For one thing, the child isn't a child any more; he's a young man. For another, you're almost a total stranger. Almost to me. Certainly to him. I can conceive of more useful concerns for your conscience. If that's what it is at work.'

'I wouldn't call it conscience.'

'Whatever it is, then. It's all the same. So what else can we talk about?'

Ian was quiet. He observed that his right hand, which held his replenished glass, still trembled. There didn't seem, for the moment, anything else to talk about. He lifted his glass presently and drank.

'Has it really shot the evening down in flames?' Margaret asked. 'I didn't mean to talk about it. I blame you. There's no reason you should ever have known, I suppose. But now you do, what difference can it possibly make to us? Be realistic. And relevant, if you can.'

'I'll be all right soón,' he promised.

'That's more like it. Now I'll get dinner. Oh, there's the door. David's home.'

There was, it seemed, no escaping relevance now : David arrived quietly in the room. A slight figure, inconspicuously clad in the international uniform of his generation. Tight jeans, sweat shirt, a string of beads and casual corduroy jacket; and duffel-bag slung on a shoulder. His light brown hair was long and his face young, lean and open. Ian tried to see more in it, and failed.

'Hello, Mum,' he said, tossing his bag into a chair. Then he noticed Ian, and looked in appeal to his mother. Ian rose, nursing his drink.

'This is Ian Freeman,' Margaret said. 'You remember me talking about him.'

'Oh,' David said. 'Yes. Often. She's often talked about you.' He gave Ian a frankly curious stare. Then he crossed the room to shake Ian's hand. 'She's even force-fed me a couple of your books.'

'I hope that isn't to be held against me,' Ian observed. Rather too stuffily, he thought. He also thought the boy had, perhaps, Margaret's eyes. Otherwise the boy was himself, no other resemblance to be seen. They were quick intelligent eyes which probably didn't miss much.

'I survived them,' David said. 'I think I might even have liked them, in places. It was just that, at the time, she was big on improving my mind, and I wasn't in the mood to be improved. Consumer resistance. You're back here now?'

'For a while,' Ian said. 'At least.'

'Well,' the boy said, 'I hope I'm not breaking up a big reunion scene. Tell me if I'm in the way.' He looked toward his mother.

'Not at all,' she said. 'We were only just talking about you.'

'I can easily go out again. Or lock myself sullenly in my room. I'd like it better, though, if you fed me first. You might get by on alcohol, but I'm still a growing boy. You're inclined to forget.' He looked cheerfully at Ian.

'Every inch the neglected child,' Margaret observed before picking up her drink and disappearing into the kitchen. 'Perhaps you can entertain Mr Freeman, for a while, with tales of teen-age misery. Excuse me, Ian.'

'I'll horrify the hell out of him,' David promised.

It was some time before his paralysis dispersed. A large enough task to accommodate the shock, without the substance of the shock becoming tangible too. Yet the years assumed pleasing shape in David. He was likeable company, if not entirely relaxing; he disconcerted Ian, doubtless deliberately, with rapid switches of subject. Perhaps he was nervous too.

'There was someone else, wasn't there?' the boy asked eventually. 'Someone both you and my mother used to know. She's mentioned you in the same breath, sometimes. An artist.'

'Yes,' he said.

'You all came from the same place anyway; you all came from Te Ika.'

'That's right.'

'And she went back there while you, the way she tells it, went off to make your mark in the world. In the fashionable way. What happened to him?'

'He went off too.'

'Did he do any good for himself?'

'I wouldn't know. I never saw him again.'

'He was a failure, then.'

'It depends.' Ian paused. 'He might have made a success of getting out. Arguably more than I did. Since I'm back.'

'That's what I can't understand about you people,' the boy said. 'Why you have to make countries such a big deal, I mean. Why does a place to live have to be such a big deal? You could get along with what you've got; most people do. A place to live is just a place to live, so why go on about it?'

'There must have been a reason,' Ian suggested.

'All right. Like what?'

'Like people not quite feeling at home in a country.'

'Well, people are used to it now. Perhaps they've had more practice. You've been away too long. Is this place so very different from any other place now?'

'Not much,' Ian allowed.

'There you are,' the boy said. 'So what was the point of it all, the point of clearing out?'

'I've forgotten,' Ian said. 'But I seem to remember there was one, at the time.'

'Oh?'

'I was never very strong on the ideology of the thing anyway. Perhaps the point of the thing, after all, was just success. They thought this country wasn't made for success; it was made for comfortable kinds of failure. So young people went looking for dangerous kinds of success.'

'And what did they find?'

'I expect they found the danger, on the whole.'

'While people like you drifted around the world, other people got on with the business of living here.' The boy paused. 'Without any damn fuss about it.'

586

'True.' Ian found himself considering Margaret; possibly the boy was too. Margaret tracking through the years and raising her child. Perhaps his too; or Tim's. The same, in a sense, either way. He could see that now, if not really in the way Margaret meant it.

For all it seemed coloured by this cool-eyed, aggressive youth before him: this youth determined to let nothing pass easily. He certainly didn't intend to allow Ian comfort.

'Probably,' the boy went on, relentless, 'that's why you've got nothing much to say to me. Your books, they're all so defeated. If you don't mind me saying so, they're a pretty miserable experience. And if this country's so sad, I don't understand why you should have bothered coming back here.'

'I'm not sure I understand either,' Ian said.

'As for the rest,' the boy persisted, 'if the human race is really such a disaster, I don't understand why you haven't written out your resignation.'

'Perhaps I was trying to,' Ian suggested. 'Or something like it. You might put it down to a certain loss of faith – not just in things as they are, but also in things as they might be. I've also, you see, been intimate with things as they might be.'

'You're talking about communism now?'

'Or, if you like, in a kind of hope. Yes.'

'It's all pretty old rubbish now, isn't it?'

'I was under the impression that Che Guevara, and even Ho Chi Minh, rank rather large with the young lately. Tell me if I'm wrong.'

'I mean your argument with it is pretty old rubbish. Besides, Che and Ho don't stand for communism; they just stand for possibilities. Strictly speaking, neither of them should have been possible, everything should have been against them. But they did what they could; they didn't give up.'

'I see.'

'We don't have to be under illusion otherwise.'

'Or trust anyone over thirty?'

'Unless there's reason to. You must admit no one over thirty offers much hope. You don't. We have to take it where we can.'

'Or make it where you can.'

'That's the cynical kind of thing I might have expected you to say. Haven't you anything worthwhile to offer?'

'Well –'

Ian was tiring under the assault. Margaret saved him; she

587

returned from the kitchen to measure out new drinks. 'I hope,' she said, 'you two are getting to know each other.'

'In a sense,' Ian said.

Later, after dinner, and after David had gone to his room, Margaret and Ian sat together for a time; the evening became peaceful enough, though not undemanding.

'I made my own little world and crawled into it,' he confessed at length.

'Afraid of something outside?'

'Possibly. Or of a great many things.'

'So,' she said. 'Tim's father. I might have known. The more we talk about it, the bigger your debt seems.'

'One way and another,' he allowed. 'But still, I'm beginning to wish we could empty him out of our conversation for good.'

'Any time you're ready,' she said crisply.

He rose to his feet, briefly restless, and walked to a window. The city lights shone beneath.

'I suppose there's more to tell,' he admitted.

'I'm always here,' she said. 'You know where to find me.'

'Up to a point, yes. Beyond that I'm not so sure.' He did not elaborate, and she did not ask him to. He turned from the window, and looked back into the room; it had begun to seem comfortable again. 'I notice you don't have one of his paintings. You must be the only person who ever knew him not to have made off with one or two, at least.'

'Short sighted of me, I expect. But then, unlike you, I didn't know whether they were up to much. I just tried to make allowances. Also I could argue that I made off with something weightier.'

He wasn't inclined to dispute this; he avoided it. 'I seem to find an impressive collection of his work on my hands, now I'm back here. You're welcome to pick yourself out something you like.'

'I might take you up on that.'

'You don't have to think about it, surely.'

'Probably not,' she agreed.

'Since you're fond of *No Angels Sing* it strikes me, in light of what you've been saying, that you might like something more original. Or the real thing, perhaps.'

'You're being unkind now. Not to me. To yourself.'

'It's necessary, sometimes.'

'I don't see that you have anything to be depressed about.'

'A certain amount of failure is always depressing.'

'Failure?' She laughed and shook back her hair.

'Ask your son. He seems to have me summed up.'

'He's young.'

'I don't see that as a disqualification. The reverse, really.'

'Also one of these student rebels. The kind that wants to rubbish everything. So help me, it's not my doing. I come from a long line of placid peasants. Anyway I don't see why you should be put out by anything he has to say. You should hear him trying to put me in my place as a corrupt appendage of the system. He's like that.'

'I do have other cause.'

'Oh?'

'It doesn't matter.'

'You still go under your shell. That doesn't change. Come on, now. Please don't go away.'

'You put it rather well yourself earlier. You said you thought *No Angels Sing* the best thing I'd done.'

'Aren't I allowed a preference?'

'It's just that it's true enough. The rest is just so much profitable journalistic junk.'

'You said it. Not me.'

'And even the price of that may have been too high,' he finished. 'One way and another.'

'I don't understand.'

'Let's just say the price of art, middling or more; it's always a certain sum of life.'

'That's not a wonderfully original thought.'

'I don't mean just that of the artist. That might even be the least of it. He wades into the untidiness other lives have left behind and tries to shape sense, some neat artifact, from it all. Too neat, usually. The point is just that those other lives, those other people, have bought whatever success he makes of the job. And sometimes the price is too high. That's all I mean.'

'And it sounds to me as if you have a pretty precious conscience about it all.'

'Not really.'

'In that book, obviously, you just made use of what little you knew about Tim's father.'

'And probably my own father,' he added.

'I still don't see reason to be guilt-stricken. If you made some

589

sense of their lives here it may even be better than they deserve. Who knows? You certainly don't; you're too close to judge. So what's all this queer nonsense about a price?' She paused. 'Or must you soar away on your own metaphors?'

'Perhaps,' he replied evasively, 'I just mean that the price is literal too. And sometimes more literal than others.'

'Sorry,' she said. 'Now you've lost me.'

'Never mind. I'm getting hazy too. I've had too much to drink, and it's late.'

'I feel you're getting off the hook,' she observed. 'Just at the point when I'm hauling you in. Do you think I'll ever have another chance?'

'I imagine it likely. Don't you?'

'It would hurt, I admit, to imagine it unlikely.' She hesitated. 'You could stay the night here, of course. There's a spare bed, if you like, and no complications. You're welcome anyway.'

'Thanks all the same. But my uncle's expecting me back.'

'Well, remember you're welcome to make use of this place.'

'I will,' he promised, and rose; he began to feel awkward in his flight from the flat. But Margaret gracefully eased his journey to the door.

'It hasn't exactly been a surprise,' she summed up. 'But it's been quite a night.'

'True.' It would be hard to put behind him. He preferred not to risk a step beyond that thought. And his steps were in any case difficult enough away from Margaret's flat that night. He walked through quiet streets for a time, looking for a taxi, identifying the crisp sound of his own shod feet with surprise; it seemed the only thing familiar. He could recall another city on another night.

Later, in the spare room of Ben's cottage, he unpacked sufficient belongings to see him through the next few days, then paused and picked out his one souvenir of Paris. The damaged drawing had been repaired with transparent tape; the likeness, after all, seemed reasonably accurate. He had quite forgotten the inscription beneath. As a document it was, no doubt, altogether worthless. Nevertheless he sat on the edge of the bed, with Ben murmuring in his sleep the other side of the wall, and considered the thing for some time.

Still later, still sleepless, searching for comfort on a lumpy bed, another search became brisk and brutal in its detail. Possibly because it was safe now. Guilt was almost gone, dispersed across the years. There were some things, though, he would prefer to do without. He could still flinch at memory of the moment he struck; he would sooner not remember Tim's falling cry. Or, for that matter, his rush to depart. Up to that point all was understandable, and guilt elsewhere. Yet what would he have earned by staying? He might, true, have become familiar with a French prison for a year or two. But he might also have known whether Tim was alive or dead; he might have known whether to expect him again at this or any time in his life. He might have been free. Free for what, though? To do more with his life?

It narrowed to the challenge and indifference in the face of Margaret's son.

Perhaps also Tim's, or his own. Half a father, then, at best. But failure could not be apportioned so precisely; there was no such beast as half a failure. That was something he had on his own. And this likeness, this joke scribbled beneath. The real joke had flesh; it also had very cool eyes.

Ben groaned in his sleep, the other side of the wall. There was light on the bedroom window. Early morning. Soon he heard birds.

Sleep was still impossible; he finally rose from the bed in defeat. He dressed quietly and left the cottage, moving through Ben's gripping greenery down a narrow track to the sea. There was a long pale crescent of sand under his feet. Houses along the suburban shore were without lights. The city, the country, still slept; he had it to himself in the quiet before dawn. The waves which rose with faint flash up the sand were small; there was just a thin flicker of foam. At each end of the beach stood headlands where the sea had hammered the land down to bare bone, yellow rock, with twisted trees poised perilously above; another storm or two would doubtless bite more away, and leave them starker still. He could make what he liked of their melancholy message.

He took a stick and scratched a design on the damp sand for the tide to take; and another, and another, until he was absorbed in the effort. From a distance he might have appeared lunatic at that time, in that place. Soon the tide was higher, the sun risen, the night entirely gone. He threw the stick away; it spun high and fell soundless to the sea. He looked landward again, across and beyond safely settled shore, perhaps in search of hills of satisfying symmetry.

Margaret couldn't telephone him at the cottage; Ben had no telephone. He had to call her. And he put it off. His excuses to himself became more intricate. Perhaps the most effective was that he had to make up his mind whether he was home to stay. But he did see others. Stan Coates, for example, in his shiny public relations office high above the city. Stan had fattened. He had a fixed, flashing smile. He confessed his fresh political ambition; he was hoping to take a seat in Parliament in a coming election. 'Of course,' he said, 'my past is sometimes used against me. But I think I'm well clear of that now. My past, I mean.'

Ian was inclined to agree.

'Sometimes it all seems pretty unreal,' Stan insisted. 'The old days. Or our old days. I have to see a face like yours again to remind myself it really happened. That I was once a card-carrying menace to this society. Mind you, I still get the odd twinge. Things were so clear-cut then. But I see you've made the best of it too. So my wife tells me anyway; she's a fan of yours, always with-it in these things. I suppose I thought I was pretty with-it myself once. Remember when we thought Livingstone the best artist in the world?'

'I do,' Ian said.

'I still have a couple of his paintings hung in a back bedroom. There was some fellow asking about them recently. Someone who mentioned your name. Kennedy, that's it. I got the impression that the paintings might be worth a dollar or two, in the end. So just as well I haven't junked them after all.' Stan paused. 'And you've really no idea what happened to him?'

'No, Stan. None.'

'You don't think,' Stan asked cautiously, 'that he might have sold out somewhere along the line?'

'I've no idea. But it's difficult to imagine.'

Stan seemed disappointed.

'It looks to me,' he went on, 'as if you still have a pretty inflated idea of his integrity. He sold other people out, in his time.'

'But not himself, perhaps. That may have been his version of integrity.'

'Well, you may know best. I don't know at all. All I know is that we were well rid of him, when we finished picking up the

592

pieces. Monty Nolan, say. At least we can say we saved his life, if not much else.'

'He's still inside?'

'To the best of my knowledge; he's certainly never made a break again. Poor bastard. He might have been better off dead. Of course we don't hang them any more. We put them alive into concrete coffins.'

'You've never visited him, I suppose?'

'To tell the truth, I always found Monty difficult to manage. An unruly personality, if you know what I mean. A natural anarchist, or troublemaker. Not my style. It's possible, of course, that he's different now. He very likely is. All these years. Anyway the answer is no, I've never visited him.'

Stan was plainly irritated with the subject, besides.

'It's all right, Stan. I just wondered.'

'I suppose you're thinking it's my position in the community. And that I can't afford association with a convicted murderer of some notoriety.'

'I wasn't thinking anything of the kind.'

'Well, it might be true, up to a point,' Stan sighed suddenly. 'I'm not as free as I'd like. With someone like you, it's different; you can get away with anything. Even if you were actually a murderer yourself, say, people would still go on buying your books. Probably even more so.'

'True,' Ian agreed. He paused. 'Perhaps too true.'

Stan looked puzzled briefly, then concentrated on himself again. 'So it's unfair, anyway, for someone like yourself to sit in judgement.'

'I'm not sitting in judgement, Stan. I wish you'd get that out of your head. And just relax.'

'Sorry. That's something I find difficult. Relaxing, I mean. Some of my best friends give me ulcers.' He was, in unconscious demonstration, starting to fidget. But it might, of course, just have been the pressure of work on his desk. It was clearly time for Ian to leave. He stood up; they shook hands again.

'It's not the end, is it?' Stan said anxiously. 'What I mean is, we will see each other again, won't we?'

'Of course. If you like.'

'That's all right, then.' His relief was visible. 'Seeing you again — it's like, well, like walking into myself around a corner.'

'I think I know the feeling.'

'Do you? I wonder.'

'And good luck with the election,' Ian said.

He left the office, walking swiftly past Stan's cool secretary and industrious staff, and took an elevator down to the freedom of the city street again. He had the same feeling of relief, a few days later, after he visited Monty Nolan in prison. But without the same dismay.

Keeping guessing, Monty said. Keep them guessing, and yourself. The only way to stay alive.

And, perhaps, watch for the black shark.

Otherwise the visit was inconsequential, until almost the end. Then, with doors crashing open, warders arriving to take Monty away, he asked the question. 'All that time you was gone,' Monty said 'did you ever come across our old mate? Did you ever come across Tim Livingstone?'

'No, Monty. Not really.'

'You looked for him, though?'

'Up to a point. Yes.'

He shrugged. 'Well, it doesn't matter now anyway. Does it? If they didn't have me inside on one thing, they'd probably have me in on another.'

The warders were waiting, and listening. Monty ignored them.

'And it could be worse,' he added. 'If I behave, I could be out inside of two or three years. The trouble is, if I behave, I might as well be dead. Like I said.'

'Yes.'

'It's a problem. Like a bargain with the devil. I admit one thing, though. I wouldn't mind getting out to see these miniskirts while they're still going. So I might weaken, in the end. I'm only human.'

The warders were impatient now. Monty rose.

'You don't have to come again,' he finished. 'It's a pretty miserable experience.'

'But I'd like to. I've enjoyed it, in a way.'

'Seeing me here?' Monty looked incredulous.

'Seeing you.'

'If you say so.' Monty was plainly puzzled. 'I'm only sorry we couldn't of shaken hands. I mustn't keep my nursemaids waiting.'

Then, on the other side of the bars and bulletproof glass, he was led away. He looked back once, over his shoulder, between the warders, and winked at Ian, as if with a secret shared.

A day or two later Ian found cause to call Margaret again.

Twenty-nine:

IT WASN'T SO DIFFICULT TO TELL MARGARET. 'YES,' HE SAID.
'I found him in Paris, all right; I've never told anyone that
before.' He swallowed, and paused. 'I found him in some dive,
and he took me home with him. That was the mistake, I expect
– going home with him. And realizing what a miserable bargain
he'd settled for. The trouble was I couldn't believe it, not until I
had to. I couldn't believe it had all been for nothing.'

'You still sound angry enough.'

'People had sheltered him, protected him, made allowances,
done all they could. And he'd fed off them all. And for what?
For that. For nothing. Do you really wonder why I was bitter?'

'He had the right, though. Surely. He had the right to that
choice.'

'Well, I couldn't see it that way. Not then. Even now. I only
have to look at his paintings again. Perhaps you've a more
forgiving nature.'

'And perhaps I just see him as another human being.'

'All right. You have it your own way.'

'Well, we do seem to have scrambled up to this point before.
What happened then?'

'We had a fight. Not a verbal one, a real one. And not our first,
but our last. In the course of which I hit him over the head. He
went out a window. And I took off in fright, without waiting
to see how much injury I'd done. I might have killed him; I
don't know. I still don't know.'

'I see.'

'You're welcome to think less of me.'

'Is that what you want?'

He shrugged, and was silent.

'Because,' she went on, 'I'm the last person to judge, God

596

knows. My life's been as messy as most. And there are one or two people I've as good as left for dead, without looking back. Because I couldn't afford to. It just seems to me that you may have made a more efficient job of the same thing.' She paused. 'Unless, of course, you meant to kill him; did you?'

He shook his head. 'I don't think so. No. At least not at first – but later, when I struck him, I felt pretty murderous then; that's true. But at first, no. That's the odd thing. Things were much as they had been before; the aggression was on his side, not mine. He even seemed disappointed that I wasn't, as he put it, an avenging angel.'

'But you turned into one.'

'Apparently.'

'Then that, possibly, was what he wanted.'

'I admit that has occurred to me. Yes.'

'He could go free then. Perhaps he was just sitting there waiting for someone to catch up with him. And you did it. After that, he could walk away without any conscience at all.'

'If he was alive, perhaps.'

'Well, I'm still not convinced, as I told you, that I didn't see him in the street one day. From a distance, true. But if it wasn't him, it was someone very like. Uncannily like. Even the same stiff walk.'

'I often think I recognize people from a distance. And turn out to be wrong.'

'This was different. I can't explain.'

'In any case, what would he be doing back here? I can't imagine it.'

'Why not? He could be living some quiet ordinary life, some-where here. Perhaps within a few hundred yards.'

'I can't imagine that either. Sorry.'

'For an author, you're remarkably deficient in imagination. It seems I have it all.'

'I need more to go on. You have a fancied sighting. I just have the memory of him before he went out that window. And the fact of his going out. From that point my imagination ceases to function. And as for him living some quiet ordinary life here – '

'It's what most people do, after all. It's what people mostly came here for in the first place, and still do.'

'Tim wasn't most people.'

'Possibly because people like you had to make him more.

597

And still do, evidently. You shouldn't protest anyway; you got your pound of flesh from him in the end.'

'What do you mean?'

'You got his work. And some of your own. That seems clear from the way you've told it. You can't complain.'

'I'm not complaining.'

'Well, you're certainly not using your imagination. The same thing.'

'If he wanted to be quiet and ordinary he had his father's land. And we'd know if he was back there, wouldn't we?'

'Would we? It's true I go back to Te Ika now and then, to see Clem on the farm. But I haven't made a point of inquiring; it's never occurred to me.'

'Well, it's not likely. In any case he gave me title to his father's land, for what it's worth.'

'He what?' Margaret was puzzled.

'Gave me title to his father's land. He scribbled it on a likeness he drew of me when we met in Paris. A joke, in a way; a sad joke. He seemed to think he was well rid of it. Which doubtless he was. No, he's not back there, wherever he is – and if he is, if he exists at all.'

'You'd prefer him not to. Obviously.'

Ian hesitated. 'In a way,' he confessed. 'Yes. I'd like to know there was an end to it somewhere.'

'All the strings tied up.'

'Yes; I expect so.'

'A pity life's not so neat.'

It seemed there wasn't much more to be said. They were in Margaret's room, on her bed. It had been a long evening. Her windows were open to the mild summer night. The lights of the harbour, ships at anchor, winking buoys, were visible from where they lay.

'I don't mind surprises,' he argued at length. 'This, for example, loose ends and all.'

'I wasn't too sure what to expect myself. Until you rang again today; I'd begun to think you wouldn't ring again. Was it just stage fright?'

'I had things on my mind; and one or two people. Also I had to consider the possibility you were involved elsewhere.'

'Not me. Not again. A lover or two, yes. Involvements, no. But then it's always been like that. Well, almost always.'

He did not care to inquire when or how.

'I've only myself to blame for my rotten marriages,' she went on. 'Which were one result. On my credit side, though, I managed to keep my head above water for David's sake, and give him a chance.'

Her finger moved lightly down his chest. He was slow to relax.

'He doesn't, I suppose, have any suspicion about me?' he asked.

'That you might be his father?'

'Yes.'

'Well, it's probably not beyond him. Certainly he knows you figure obscurely in my early past. He could put two and two together. And come up with one.'

'When the answer is two.'

'On the contrary, the answer is one. The problem is which one. But it's no longer a question I find interesting. But if the problem interests you, there's another way of looking at it. If Tim Livingstone no longer exists, as you wish to believe, then the answer is still one. You disposed, in your way, of the other possibility.'

'That has struck me.'

'Good. So that's settled. You can go right ahead and imagine yourself his father, if it makes you happy.'

'It doesn't make me happy.'

'In that case, then, if it's unhappiness you want. That doesn't change. This girl you knew in Eastern Europe, the one the other side of the wall. This Katya. Didn't she give you enough to get along with?'

'Probably. I may have started coming home then. Though I prolonged the journey as long as I could.'

'And finished up here.'

'It could be worse.'

'Thank you,' she said.

'It didn't mean in your bed. This is something unexpected. And hardly earned.'

'Anything to make you feel at home again.'

'You do,' he insisted.

'Good. It's nice to know I'm some use.'

'I can't think of a better place to start again.'

'You mean that?'

'Of course.'

'Then show me.'

So he did, again. Her arms were as strong as he remembered, and her body no less demanding; he emptied himself upon it without reserve.

Margaret asked sleepily, 'You're not going home tonight?'

'Not much point now. If it's all right with you.'

'It's all right with me.'

'What about David, in the morning?'

'No problem there. You notice how quickly he vanished from the living room when he found us there tonight.'

'I thought he might have been avoiding me.'

'He was being discreet. He'd be disappointed not to find you here in the morning; he'd feel his discretion had been a waste.'

'Is he always so obliging?'

'It depends, rather. On whether he approves of the company I keep. He's a reasonable chaperone. Also I don't complain about some of the scruffy little girls he trails home with, at times, to introduce to his infamous mother. I can't help it if sometimes they find me intimidating. But the point is that he seems prepared to make the best of you. Tonight and in the future.'

There was a pause. 'Yes,' he said. 'The future.'

'I was getting round to that,' she confessed.

'And I suppose I've been avoiding it.'

'It would be nice to think there is one. When you've got things out of your system. And you haven't been making a bad job of that tonight.'

'True,' he allowed.

'So it would be nice to think there is a future. So long as you let me think so, for a while, perhaps I won't mind so much if there isn't.'

'I'll do my best,' he promised.

'I certainly couldn't ask you to do more. It might be good enough. And if it isn't, that's my bad luck.'

'Mine too.'

'You should find it reasonable here. You'll have a quiet flat to work in during the day. What else? Expenses we can work out later. And –'

'David? What about him?'

'I think he can be left to me. If it comes to the point, he's willing to be won over. Apart from the fact that he might belatedly find someone around worth his anger. I noticed, the other day, a couple of your books missing from their usual

600

shelf, and found them in his bedroom. It seemed he'd been trying them again. He allowed that *No Angels Sing* wasn't too bad, so far as it went. It was grudging, of course.' She paused. 'Oh yes, he also said that at least you hadn't got too fat and square; you weren't altogether on the other side, at least not yet.'

She moved lightly into his arms again; her skin was still surprisingly soft. He had time to harvest its surprise.

'It's not love I'm asking for,' she said. 'But we can make do, can't we?'

'I don't see why not,' he said.

She went on, 'I have a sudden urge to see Te Ika again.'

'Something of the sort passed through my mind too.'

'Perhaps we could take David with us,' she said.

Not long after Ian moved in with Margaret the newspapers recorded that Stan Coates had won his seat in Parliament. Though his party failed to make great gains elsewhere, Stan's majority was impressive. Political commentators seemed to consider him future ministerial material as a man of proven managerial capacity, and wide connection with the problems of industry. Ian, after a day of doubt, telephoned his congratulations. Stan still had his victory-night ebullience; the newspapers had shown him, celebratory drink in hand, with huge smile. 'So you're still around,' Stan said at length. 'I thought you'd gone into smoke. If you can come out of hiding for a night, you might have that drink with me. What about tonight?'

'Well – '

'I want a pretty convincing excuse.'

Ian had none. He telephoned Margaret; she was working late at the studio anyway. So he had Stan for the night, his expansive home, his shy wife. Stan still seemed to be talking from a platform.

'Automation, imagination and education,' he said, as they sat together on the terrace beside his heated swimming pool. 'They're the keys to the country's future.'

'And what,' Ian asked gently, 'is the end of it all?'

Stan didn't need to pause for thought. 'A vigorous economy, of course.'

'If that's the end, then, what are the means?'

He hesitated only fractionally this time. 'Well,' he replied. 'I suppose you could say people.'

601

'I suppose you could.'

'The best raw material we have. Any nation's greatest asset. People.'

'And you see that as a fair bargain all round?'

'Of course. Increased productivity, rising living standards and –' A pause; Stan showed slow suspicion. 'Now, wait a moment. You're not trying to draw me on the old ends-and-means thing?'

'Not really. I'm just wondering where life fits into your scheme of things.'

'Life? A better life for all; of course that's my aim.'

'But if people exist only to fit the needs of this efficient machine –'

'Look,' Stan said abruptly, 'You've got to live in the real world. I'm beginning to think you've been up in the islands too long.'

'Perhaps,' Ian conceded.

'There's no escape. We have to be in the race. It's the same everywhere. Look at statistics. That's the world as it is. We've been living leanly off the technological revolution, not exploiting it. We seem to think the land's enough. We've been half-asleep too long. We have to make things move again. We can't dream here forever.'

'It would be pleasant to think, though,' Ian said, having had more than sufficient to drink, 'that there might be one country in the world to turn a back on the whole miserable business. And live a life not conducted on the principles of accountancy.'

'So help me,' Stan said, 'you have been in the islands too long.'

'Don't worry. The world's there too.'

'Well, at the least you don't sound too different from these young anarchists who go yodelling through the streets and parks about the system. God knows we're getting enough of that lately; I have to watch my own kids.'

'I seem to remember we had our turn at bucking things.'

'These kids, though, they want to scrap everything, and start again. And you know as well as I do it can't be done.'

'Probably not,' Ian allowed. 'But still –'

'The secret is to ride the system, not fight it. Use it constructively.'

'But what if it's only using you?'

'My God,' Stan said, 'you do sound like those kids.'

602

'I'd like to hear you try to tell someone else that,' Ian said. 'But never mind.'

'Someone else?'

'One of these kids you've been talking about.'

'You mean,' Stan said, 'you know another parent with problems too?'

Ian thought about that. 'I'm getting to know him,' he answered.

Their trip down to Te Ika was delayed. David and like-minded friends, were campaigning to liberate some of the city's parkland for free speech; his weekends were occupied with organizing and demonstrating. The grey elderly men of the city council promised police protection of the parkland, and widespread arrest of all who dared set foot there on Sundays to disturb the museum-like quiet; their argument appeared to be that parks, as expensive enclaves in the city, were too precious for people. David and his friends were answering with dance bands, folk singers, a dozen free-speakers, and lolly scrambles for children. It was less a revolutionary situation than comic opera. Ian was entertained, but short of enthusiastic. Nevertheless he tried to offer intelligent interest. 'What it could come to,' David said hopefully, 'is that they put up watch towers and barbed wire to keep us out. That way, the issue will be made even more clear.'

'What issue is that?' Ian asked gently.

'Whether cities are for people, or people are for cities. And countries too.'

'I see. And you think this will help decide it.'

'You just have to do what you can. Either you buckle under, or you don't. And if you don't, you might as well get some fun out of it while it lasts.'

'Well,' Ian conceded, 'I can see you're enjoying it.'

'Come along on Sunday,' David said. 'You might even enjoy it too.'

He was reasonably relaxed with David now; and David less wary of him. Standing aside, Margaret watched them both with cool interest. He felt himself on probation. If he couldn't manage David, then the best thing would be to pack up and leave. But where? He felt at home with Margaret. In the mornings, with the flat quiet, he worked fitfully, trying to find his way into an article or two. Then he climbed the old volcanic cones above the narrow isthmus on which the city had grown, and where bright new suburbs sprawled under dark green hills. The clear sky and bright light, moody clouds and violent rains, the bays and beaches, estuaries and islands, spoke with Pacific accent. So did the streets, with Polynesian faces, casual dress, and pleasant pace. Man no longer seemed quite so crass here, or so unworthy. It was just another country. He could no longer be impatient.

The paintings he had given Margaret now hung prominently in her flat. David was surprisingly impressed.

'This is the fellow you talked about?' he said. 'The one who cleared out and vanished?'

'Yes,' Ian said.

Margaret was watching David's face too.

'He wasn't too bad, then, was he?' David said.

'Unsophisticated, perhaps,' Ian said. 'He was only just beginning, you see.'

'All the same,' David insisted, 'he had something good going there. He had something real to say.'

'I thought you might find them pretty tame,' Ian observed. 'Or too obvious.'

'I don't know what's supposed to be tame about them. Or obvious. They're cool. He knew where he was at. Do you mind if I take one away for my room?'

'Go ahead. Take two if you like. There are plenty more.'

'What I'd like to know is what you people did with him. If he could paint like this. Why didn't you appreciate him, give him a chance here?'

'You're asking the wrong person,' Margaret interjected.

'I bought his paintings,' Ian explained. 'I even saved some he wanted to destroy. And I've had them looked after since.'

'I don't give a stuff about the paintings,' David replied. 'They're all right, but they're not the point.'

'No?'

'No. I'm talking about the person who painted them.'

'Well, that,' Ian agreed, 'is slightly different.'

'How different?'

Ian shrugged.

'You mean he was too much trouble, himself?' David suggested. 'You could only be bothered with his paintings?'

'Up to a point,' Ian allowed. 'Yes. People tried to help him as much as they could while he was painting; perhaps too much.'

'So long as you got what you wanted out of him, you couldn't give a damn?'

'I didn't say that.'

'Well, then you just forgot him.'

'I didn't say that either.'

'Well, so far as I'm concerned, you're not saying anything.'

'I'm just trying to give you the facts of the case.'

'I'm not interested in the facts of the case; I'm interested in the person who painted these pictures. And he's gone missing somewhere, the way you tell it.'

'Well, he did go missing,' Ian said patiently. 'Literally.'

'Before then, though.'

'He existed, yes. These paintings prove it.'

'And nothing else?'

Ian sought Margaret's eye, found it, and then lost it again; he was left with his own reply.

'Your mother and I, perhaps,' he suggested. 'He touched our lives.'

'Well,' David said, 'I'll leave the pair of you to sort that one out. It looks as if I'll just have to take the paintings, thanks, and see if they tell me any more.' He paused, then, and switched direction; he looked from Ian to his mother. 'By the way,' he added, in a voice casually controlled, 'the point of all this wouldn't be, I suppose, that this fellow was my father?'

There was an extremely brief silence. 'You've never,' she observed, 'displayed passionate interest in that subject before.'

'I'm interested now. And I'd like some kind of answer to get along with.'

'Then my best answer is no.'

'Your best answer?'

'My only available answer.'

'Mother dear,' David said, surprisingly amiable again, 'I've always known you want only the best for me.' His smile was wide; he winked at Ian. 'I don't really give a damn,' he confessed. 'I just liked seeing you both jump.' He began to leave the room with the paintings he had selected. 'It was,' he added, over his shoulder, 'a fascinating sight to see.'

Margaret and Ian were left looking at each other. Margaret's expression was faintly dazed, then amused. 'End of round one,' she said finally, and poured Ian a drink.

The next Sunday they went to witness the invasion of the forbidden parkland. There was no barbed wire, after all, and no watch towers; and incredibly few police. But there were some thousands of people, mainly young, and brightly dressed, strolling and sitting, speaking from stepladders, or dancing to music with heavy beat. The old men of the city had quietly capitulated; the park was free. With the warm sunshine on the grass, the colour spun among the huge old tropical trees, it seemed more than some lilliputian liberation. They looked for David among the crowds but failed to find him among the garlanded hippies, the lines of dancers, the wandering folksingers, the leaping children. His spirit might have been evident everywhere, but his substance was more difficult to locate. In the end they gave up, and retreated to a part of the park at small distance from the festivity; the grass was dry and the flowers scented with summer.

The rest would doubtless happen with Margaret. They might find land somewhere, trees, fruit, animals, and a new start; somewhere to keep guessing beyond the black shark.

He took his moment, turned to Margaret, and touched her hand; she smiled. 'I expect we ought to get married soon,' he said.

'If you like,' she agreed casually, and then rose. 'I think perhaps we should look for David again.'

'Did you hear what I said?'

'Of course. You said we ought to get married soon. And I said, if you like. Because I don't see why not, do you?'

'No.'

'So let's see if we can find David,' she said.

He rose from the grass too, and she put her arm through his. They walked across the sunlit park into the noisy crowds again.

A face in the crowd, not quite familiar, no longer haunted and starved. And he was, suddenly, shaking Charlie Bates' hand. Queer, lonely, simple Charlie who only wanted to build. And now did, evidently. For he wanted Ian to look over some of the buildings on which he had lately been working: a new hospital, a university department. Promises were made, telephone numbers exchanged. With a brown, confident Charlie.

'These kids,' Charlie said, 'they know how to enjoy themselves. More than we did.'

'Yes,' Ian said. 'Possibly.'

'Unless we were miserable,' Charlie observed, 'we didn't feel we had the world properly on our shoulders. Still, we did our best.'

'Very likely,' Ian said.

It was only afterwards that Ian realized that Charlie, this new Charlie, hadn't once asked about Tim Livingstone, unlike others. Perhaps some were too busy building. On the last day of the world there would doubtless be someone like Charlie, some- where, still building as if life depended on it, as if tomorrow would come.

Stan kept in touch. If not to convert Ian any longer, it was perhaps to seek reassurance. On the other hand he still seemed to believe that Ian might be used at some point, and he was seldom subtle. 'I'm thinking of doing some publishing on the side,' he confided, in the course of a telephone conversation. 'For example, I'd like a book on the state of this country now. Telling it like it is, and implying the demands of the future in the modern world. You might be just the person to do the job. Don't say yes or no now. Just think about it for a while. I'm in a position to see that you'd do very well on it indeed.'

'You seem to have all the ideas,' Ian said. 'Why don't you write it yourself?'

'That would be too obvious, surely.'

'Would it?'

'Of course. In politics I'm a sitting duck, even in my own party. Too many old-time doctrinaire socialists, not enough modern men. I have to play it carefully. I can't risk committing too much to print, at least in my own name. Not yet. I have to prepare the ground a little.'

'And you'd like me to be groundsman.'

'That's putting it too crudely. I recognize that you have a professional integrity. I'd just like you to do an objective job. And, if you did that, my ideas would emerge among others; they would emerge in their right perspective. Naturally.'

'Well, Stan – '

'Don't say yes or no. Anyway that's not what I'm really calling you about. It's about tomorrow night. You may have noticed that we have a certain prominent American visitor in the country at the moment.'

'It's difficult not to notice.' The bland features of the Ameri- can president's current right-hand man had been displayed on front pages for the past three days. So had his bland utterances.

607

'There's a reception for him, and I'm entitled to take along a guest. It was to have been my wife, naturally, but she caught a chill on the yacht last weekend. So I was wondering if you might like – '

'It hardly sounds my style.'

'If you could face up to the Stalinists in Eastern Europe, I don't see why you can't face up to the Americans here. We have to live in the same world, and one country's getting like another anyway. It wouldn't do you any harm to see a slice of life. You'll get too cosy. And damn it, aren't you supposed to be a man of the world?' Stan began to sound impatient.

'Look, Stan – '

'Chicken out if you like. All the same to me.'

'It's just I can think of more interesting challenges.'

'Then look at it as a challenge to see how much free booze you can put away. Your old style; our old style. Come on.'

In the end he allowed himself to be persuaded, rather than reject Stan. With Ian at his side – perhaps he even hoped Ian would behave aggressively – Stan might feel less compromised by his company. It was possible that Stan needed Ian beside him only to measure how far he had come.

When he dressed for the occasion, Ian didn't confess his destination to Margaret or David; he just mentioned an evening with Stan Coates. 'Some dinner,' he said vaguely. David was not within earshot anyway.

The reception was almost as dull as he expected. The tailor-made American with the switch-on smile swung elegantly among parliamentarians and other dour dignitaries, always charming, earnest, and saying nothing with profound precision. War and death would have been dirty words. It was, in its way, a triumph of style. And the style of the emperor's representative moving among the emperor's provinces, receiving tribute; in this case, in return for some modest bargain struck, a certain additional package of lives for imperial conquest. It was a scene as old as civilization. He would, after all, have been sorry not to have seen it. But that didn't stop him drinking, if still not as much as he should have liked.

Afterwards, as they teetered tenderly downstairs in the tall new hotel where the reception had been held, Stan observed, 'Well, you must admit it wasn't so bad after all. He had a certain aura.'

There were black limousines drawn up outside the hotel; and

thick ranks of police. Beyond the police were the demonstrators. And above the demonstrators, on crude placards and banners, the unmentionable words rippled and flashed.

There were possibly a thousand of them out there now, mostly young, contained by the police; there had been no more than a dozen or two when they went into the reception. And as the guests left impatience and anger found new expression. There was a contemptuous roar, and then surges against the police lines, and scuffles.

When Ian paused, Stan took his arm. 'Come on,' he said. 'You've got to expect this kind of thing these days. It gets them nowhere; it gets us nowhere. God knows we both know that.' He began to tug at Ian, irritated. 'And if you stop and stare, we'll finish up a target for something.'

Other guests were hurrying past, into the limousines, or to the police-protected parking lot.

The scuffles had now become open fights. The police ranks were churning, thickening in places, thinning in others. Placards swayed and vanished under the impact of a police charge. But in another place, as a result of the pressure, a wedge of demonstrators crashed through the confused defence, towards the hotel. The police were drawing their batons, running to head them off.

'I warned you,' Stan said. 'This is becoming bloody dangerous.'

Some guests were now retreating to take sanctuary in the hotel, rather than risk the street; it was true that he and Stan, stationary, were becoming more conspicuous.

'And bloody pointless,' Stan added. 'So bloody pointless.'

The wedge obstinately held its new ground, and took fresh stance with its banners; the police circled warily. A truce seemed likely. But then, to crisp command, the attack began. Batons began to isolate, then split the wedge. And as it opened, with screams and tumbling bodies, David came into sight. Just for a moment; he was raising his arms to fend off a blow. Then he was lost again.

'Where the hell are you going?' Stan cried. And made vain clutch at Ian's sleeve.

It was a short if bruising run from one side of the street to the other. But perhaps he wasn't fit; it seemed as long as any in his life. And by the time he burst through the police and arrived at the scene it was almost all over anyway. The brutality had been brisk. There were only the remnants. A girl, long hair trailing, weeping in the gutter; another girl bending to her. Both were being arrested. The others were pushed into police vans. He couldn't see David among them.

A police sergeant tapped his shoulder with surprising deference, evidently impressed by his dress. 'Excuse me, sir,' he said, 'but you really shouldn't be here.'

'Where are you taking them?'

'Up to the cells for the night. They'll be charged in the morning. I wouldn't waste your sympathy on them. These young scum have been trying to buy it; and they bought it, with interest.' He spoke with some satisfaction.

'You have some pretty willing salesmen.'

'I can't expect my boys to stand here all night without itching to get stuck in. They're only human. I'd go back to the hotel if I were you, sir. We should have the street safe again soon.'

He looked back toward the hotel: Stan no longer stood on the front steps; Stan wasn't to be seen at all. He hadn't even said goodnight, though he had as good as said goodbye. He hoped Stan hadn't been too embarrassed.

The police were now systematically driving the rest of the demonstrators away from the hotel, off the street; there was charge after charge. So it took Ian, in the end, some time to get across the city to the central police station; and there, because of pressure of work, he had to wait an hour or two for information. Others were making inquiries too. It turned out that, yes, a youth named David Saunders had been one of those arrested.

'I'd like to get him out,' Ian told the constable across the desk.

'He's being processed.'

'When he's processed, then.'

'It takes time.'

'No doubt. But I'd still like to get him out.'

'A night in the cells never hurt anyone.'

'Nor did a small working over, I expect.'

'I don't know what you mean, sir.'

'I want bail. That's all I mean.'

The constable went away to confer with a senior colleague. He returned with a form. 'You'll have to give me your full name, sir.' Ian gave it.

'And your relationship to the prisoner? Friend, is it?'

'Father,' Ian said.

'But your names,' objected the constable, 'they're different.'

610

'Father,' Ian insisted. 'He's my son.'

Later he took the boy home by taxi to his mother. 'Funny thing,' David said, 'when they came down to the cells, they told me my father was getting me out. I thought there was some mix-up; I almost told them I didn't have one. And when I came out, there you were. My father, they said. Obviously they got the thing wrong, didn't they?'

Ian was silent, considering his reply.

'Or did you tell them that yourself?' David persisted.

'Yes,' Ian confessed. 'I did.'

'Why?'

'Because it's probably true.'

David thought about this for a moment; he became very still. 'Well,' he said finally, 'you might have told me first. It's a hell of a way to learn. To have the fuzz unlock a cell and tell me my father's waiting, after all these years. What am I supposed to say now? "Gee, thanks, Dad"? That doesn't sound right, does it?'

'No,' Ian agreed.

'Well, thanks anyway,' David said.

Postscripts

Waiatarua 1958

AT FIRST IT WAS A DAY LIKE OTHERS. IF ANYTHING DIS-
tinguished it from the day just past, it was the stiffer chill of
autumn in the morning, when he crossed the paddocks to chase
his last cows into the shed for milking; they would soon be
dried off. Certainly his morning was as mechanical as most : he
jerked from task to task.

There were no surprises left. And he had ceased puzzling at
the point. The mail van never called. What could it bring? News
was alien in his life. There was no longer even demand for
mortgage payments. There was no mortgage. The land was his,
if there were someone to notice.

For the boy was gone. He didn't often doubt it now. Gone, it
didn't matter where. Once, twice, he might have thought
different; he might have imagined the boy back again. But
his imagination, of course, raced beyond reason. Reason always
told him no. Then again, reason generally said no, to most
things. It said no, when he listened, most of his life. It didn't pay,
all things considered, to listen to reason. A man would do
nothing; a man would never hang on. This land under the
hills, for example, would still be fern and scrub, and tall
timber. Reason had told him he wouldn't walk off the slopes
of Gallipoli, or the mud of the Somme. But he had; he had hung
on. So much for reason, then. It should have fled away. Instead
it always returned and settled on his shoulder like a dark bird
with unpleasant smell, perhaps graveyard seepage, anyway not
to his liking; and insisted on another hearing. It was imagination
which began to flee away, the idea that things would come right,
that there was some sense to it all. That dark bird said there
was no sense. Reason was Nick Bell haunted by horrors within
his wandering mind and bucking body. Reason was Nance, a

mad dying thing. Reason was his boy going, Christ knew why. Reason was himself alone, with no one to trust, on this land which once seemed harbour in hell. And reason perhaps was also the spanner he once used to dispatch an old bull dying. Reason said the rest was nonsense, a hundred times nothing. Yet he hung on. That was the real miracle, if he wanted one.

He fried himself mutton chops for breakfast; the kitchen filled with fatty smoke and smell. He spread clean newspaper over the kitchen table and, when the chops were done, sat down to eat. His teeth were still vigorous enough : they demolished the meat without mercy, and then he picked them clean with a split match, ready for the next meal. Thus occupied, and also involving himself with a mug of tea, he examined the month-old newspaper spread under his elbows with no particular concentration. Until it seemed to him, incredibly, that he had just read his son's name. He read that portion of print again. It was true; the boy's name was there. His heart thudded in his empty chest, as if seeking a way out, as he read the boy's name for a third time. The problem was gathering in the other words, all around; gathering in all the words about the boy, to see how they added up, or if they did. At first it was difficult. His wits were scattered and his sight shaky; he might have just been delivered a blow.

But the words did add up, in the end. That was the second blow, not to the head, to the stomach. His senses sang; he felt sick, and could have thrown up the food he had just eaten. The boy, the way this newspaper told it, was so far gone it didn't matter. The boy was in London, or somewhere near, according to these words about him. And still trying to fool himself, and other people.

He might have known, should have known. The boy was a write-off, and Ned should never have doubted otherwise. He was probably there with that newspaper for an hour, until the print had done its worst. Then he pushed himself out from the table.

Timothy; that was the first and worst mistake. The boy's name, taken from an idiot. Nance, of course, having her way even now. He had been weak when she wanted the name; he had been soft about her and the kid. She had her way too easy, and always did. He could still, it seemed, blister with bitterness; he could spit on her grave, if there were one to find. He had never put up a stone to mark it. She was under weeds somewhere,

and long grass, he had never gone back to see. Nick too, somewhere, the world away.

He hadn't teased himself with Nance's taunt about Nick in
years. But he discovered he could, again.

Last year or the year before, for example, he imagined he
had seen his son. A year or two anyway. The boy just arrived at
the place one day, like he had before, without warning, as if he
had the right. This time, though, he didn't vanish in the night;
he stayed on a day or two. And he had a friend with him, of
sorts. Ned never properly caught the name. A small strange
fellow, with a line of fast talk, who seemed never to have seen
a farm before. And who looked nervous about something. The
boy never looked easy either. He went into whispers with this
friend at a distance from the house. Not until near the end was
it plain, and perhaps too late. Ned took the boy aside and at
length suggested that if he was in trouble he had at least done
the right thing, come to the right place; he still had a home. He
looked into the boy's face with care, and anticipation, hoping for
something to display itself. But nothing did; the face remained
empty. Ned persisted, though. He had always, he went on, known
things might finish up badly in the city, the way things were
there; it was no more than he, Ned, had expected. He wasn't,
however, going to say he had told the boy so. He didn't even
want to know what the trouble was. He was just saying the farm
was still here, and he was, the boy had a home and a father; and
he wasn't sitting in judgement, not now. He just wanted to put
things straight, the best way he could, and if his best wasn't good
enough, he added, he hoped the boy would make allowances for
him not having the gift of the gab.

Something seemed to flicker in the boy's face then. Ned
thought he might have got across to him after all. 'I don't care
what the trouble is,' Ned told him again, pushing the possible
advantage. 'So long as you know where to come, in the end.
That's the main thing.' Perhaps he pushed it too far. For then
the boy stiffened.

'You think I'm beaten,' the boy said.

'I didn't say that,' Ned replied. 'But you look as though you
been living rough.'

'Well, I'm not beaten.'

'Have it your own way, son. You usually do.' He paused. 'You
can still have it your own way, and take a good long rest back

here, to sort yourself out. I don't know about your mate, though; he don't look likely to take.'

'We can't stay. We're shooting through.'

'To where?'

'A long way from here. We have an arrangement.' He went on, 'And if anyone comes asking questions, you've never seen us.'

But after they left, towards dusk on a mild evening, no one came asking questions; Ned was not obliged to say he hadn't seen them. The lie, if it was, would not have been difficult to tell. Ned could easily enough imagine that he had not seen his son again.

In another year, another season, it was still easier. He could have just dreamed the boy, and most things in his life.

The day, once he sighted that newspaper, seemed blasted at its centre; he wandered into the vacuum. He found himself, eventually, in the front room of the house. He could not remember having been there in years; this chilly, sunless place was still filled with Nance's knick-knacks. There were still those chintzy chairs, discoloured and rotted with mould, and a dusty glass china cabinet with painted plates and plaster ducks; on the wall was a painting of swans in flight against a sunset sky. Like things in a forgotten museum. There were other things, among them a photograph of Ned and Nance on their wedding day. He picked it up. The young awkward man in the photograph, with stiff smile, seemed to belong to someone else's life. And the girl there, on his arm, blinking against the bright sun; who was she? Christ knew she didn't have much to do with that thin arrangement of flesh and bone Ned had boxed and buried. He replaced it on the shelf quickly, as if fearing contamination. Then there was another photograph. This one was coloured. The boy, perhaps four years old, taken and tinted by a travelling salesman in the depression; the kid sat rigid with fright before the lens. The colour had grown even more unnatural over the years; the boy's eyes looked feverish in a painted mask. He did not touch that one at all. The photographs, after all, told him nothing. They could not account for his shortness of breath when he worked too long outside, nor for the familiar ache in his side now. He did not need to be told that some things had got away. He ought by rights to have made a clean sweep of this room years ago. He arrived, finally, at a small doll dressed like a gypsy, which sat lonely at the centre of the mantelpiece; a tiny tambourine tinkled when he touched her.

618

Then, for a moment, he was quite numb with recognition. He was careering through the countryside again, in his high wild Ford. He was throwing balls, or tossing hoops, to win the prize at the annual show. He was pushing the doll into the hands of a girl who laughed. And he was astride a crashing beast, for as long as he could last. And he had lasted, all right. There was no one could say different. He held the doll in his big hands to hear the tambourine tinkle again, but carefully, lest it should come apart. It was such a small, tinny sound. The doll had a cheeky, pouting face: that face, or perhaps the sound, seemed to puncture his day. As the light shrivelled, the corner of the mantelpiece kicked forward to meet him; the face and the sound receded down a roaring tunnel.

Some time later that day Ned Livingstone lifted himself off the floor of his house, in a room which was strange to him. The right side of his head was bruised, though not seriously, where it had struck the mantelpiece. The stiffness in his left side was another thing, however; that part of his body seemed fixed in a clamp. He had to tell his arm to move, and his leg, without much success. He could, in the end, persuade himself to stand upright, but he held trembling to a chair for support. The doll now lay half crushed on the floor; it must have taken his full weight. He bent to retrieve it. But he had another slight dizzy rush and his left hand, besides, seemed unwilling to act. He took a large breath, then, and after a time groped back through the house to the sunlit kitchen, where he took a chair at the table. And sat breathless.

So he had waited; he had hung on. For what? For this. It was only too plain now. Even his own body turned traitor; he could consider its weakness with disgust. It had nothing to do with him, really. Nothing. And should never have been trusted. His mind raged in its prison. For it was still vivid enough, and active, perhaps never more so. That was the queer thing. Possibly his flesh had been the trap of his life. It had demanded Nance, and got the boy, if the boy were his. Its need had kept him going, and it had never answered back before. And now it was saying, with no warning, that it had had enough. Before he had a chance to argue.

Argue? He couldn't. There was, after all, nothing to negotiate. He wasn't going to trade the house he built, the land he walked, for a hospital bed and antiseptic corridors. He wasn't going to shift. For he wouldn't see it through to the end otherwise.

619

In that way, then, his back was to the wall. He had no ground to bargain at all.

He could still hang on, of course; it was always possible. He began to roll himself a cigarette, but had trouble with the makings. His left hand again. But, largely with his right, he managed to make a reasonable facsimile of a cigarette, and licked the paper down. He fixed the matchbox firm under his right hand, struck an awkward light, and raised the shaky flame. It was difficult to join the flame to the untidy end of the cigarette; the complexity of the task seemed, for a time, to hypnotize him. Finally the flame leapt up the straggling ends of tobacco, and caught at the paper. And the cigarette began to function.

Jesus, he thought, sweating with relief, and what about the rest of the day?

There was not really much left of the rest of the day. Before dusk, though, Ned Livingstone managed another smoke, and a cup of tea, and using a broom as support steered himself out on to the back porch, to see the last of the day, the thinning ripples of light as sunset ebbed from the hills. He sat short of breath on the steps. The cows were already murmuring in confusion, past their milking time. Well, the buggers were due to dry off anyway. The nip of coming winter was sharper in the air tonight. Another month and frost would whiten the mornings.

He started to understand, then, that he couldn't reckon on another month, not without everything going to pieces. He hadn't thought the thing through. He had to listen to reason, which he did.

So later in the evening, when he felt up to it, he dragged outside and fetched a gallon can of petrol; he had to rest several times before he got back to the house. The steps up to the back porch were vast effort. He knew he couldn't do that again. He was listening to reason now, all right, and for once it was less enemy than ally, almost a friend. Then, after another rest, he was inside the house. It was really just a question of where to make a start, or finish. He arrived, as he should have expected, in the front room again. The petrol had a clean smell in that musty place; he had no regret about his business there. He uncapped the can, trembling and short of breath again, and then, jerking it back and forward with his right hand, slopped the petrol around the room. Over the lacy curtains and frilly chairs, the glassy cabinet, everything; he blundered against sharp

620

corners in the dark. Until the can was empty, or near enough. All the room needed now was a match to put it right. His pocket, though, was empty; he had to drag back to the kitchen table to fetch his matches. And, since he had gone that distance, he manufactured another cigarette. The cows sounded loud now, out there in the night, poor bastards. Otherwise the world was perfectly still, twisted finally to the shape of a question. Or perhaps it had never been anything else. Perhaps, no matter how hard a man tried to make it an answer, it always sprang back to its true shape in the end, and always would.

Satisfied on that account, he had the matches in his hand, and his smoke was almost finished; he still had enough life to square the deal. He could only give back, after all, what he had taken, at no interest and hellish small profit. It was time, everything considered, for the front room.

When he arrived back there, he leaned against the doorway for support, and persuaded a match to strike. The tiny flame leapt into a pool of petrol; he tossed the glowing butt of his cigarette in another direction. Fire flashed from two sides of the room, quite spectacular. It flicked across the floor and danced up the curtains. Perhaps the place had never been seen to better effect. The windows, and pictures on the wall, trapped red reflections. Across the room he looked out stiffly from his wedding day, with shy girl beside him. And the boy, framed with peeling gilt, looked even more feverish in the light. The flames were noisy now, roaring to the roof, and the heat immense.

Then Ned saw, the other side of the fire, the crushed doll on the floor, with arms outflung and legs askew. He had forgotten it. The fire snapped all around, quite near. The sequins on the gypsy dress had a red shine.

He did not stop to think. He did not stop at all, though the heat did its best to dissuade him, and flame scorched his trouser-legs. But he beat the fire to the doll, and clumsily gathered it up as he fell; and the tambourine gave a last tiny tinkle.

621

1970

IT WAS A HIGH HOT SUMMER BEFORE THEY GOT DOWN TO TE IKA.
They stayed on the Saunders farm with Clem, who was reasonably
agreeable, and articulate about his problems. The drought was
the worst in most memories: the countryside was brown, the
rivers thin, and the roads dusty. 'If this keeps up,' Clem
predicted, 'there'll be a few farmers going down the drain.
Perhaps more than a few.' He paused. 'I think the powers
that be rather like the idea. It would speed up bigger farms,
land incorporations and the like. More efficient, they reckon.
The day of the small farm is over. If I hang on here I'll
probably finish up an antique before I die. It seems to me there's
not much room in this country for the little man any more. It'll
soon be the same as anywhere else.'

'Hardly,' Ian said. 'At least I hope not.'

'What would you know about it?' Clem challenged. 'You're
almost a foreigner.'

'It wouldn't be worth coming back otherwise. Don't disillu-
sion me yet.'

Clem snorted. 'You please yourself. So far as I can see, we've
got the same troubles as everyone else. Even,' and he paused,
looking significantly at David, 'the same young fools making a
noise in the cities. Perhaps you can tell me what it's all about;
I'm damned if I know.'

They were sitting in the front room of the Saunders farmhouse; the place had changed little in twenty years. The same
dull furnishings, the same family photographs. And much the
same Clem, two decades on. But he had a wife now, and three
large sons.

'You wouldn't pack it in here and go anywhere else, would
you?' Ian asked.

'Why should I?' Clem said, aggressive. 'This is my bloody country.'

'I suppose,' Ian replied, 'that was more or less the answer I wanted.'

'Besides,' Clem continued, 'where could I go? The world's used up. There are no blank spaces left. This was pretty near the last, it seems to me.'

At least Ian had saved David from his uncle's inquisition. The boy looked more comfortable. They had arrived just before dinner, an hour or two earlier, and Clem appeared to welcome the distraction they made in his life. 'About time I had another look at my television sister in the flesh,' he said to Margaret. 'People around here keep quizzing me about your private life, and get irritated when I can't tell them anything. I'm supposed to know, you see. Now I can tell them you've got married for a third time – or is it the fourth? Anyway that should keep them happy.'

To Ian, later in the evening, he just said, 'So you finally made it, after all, you and Marg.'

'Yes.'

'Well, congratulations. You took long enough about it. Pity it wasn't sooner.'

'Sometimes I think so too.'

'She's had a pretty ropey life. Christ knows how she's come out on top of it all. But she has. We breed them tough around Te Ika. You back here for any special reason?'

'Just to look around for a day or two.'

'You don't really expect to find anything interesting here, do you? The way I understand it, you've travelled most of the world. What's Te Ika got to give you?'

Ian shrugged. 'Hard to say yet.'

'Not Marg anyway. You found her first. That boy of hers, by the way, wouldn't be your child?'

'Very likely.'

'Then you did leave it bloody late in the piece. Well, better a reasonable brother-in-law late than never. I couldn't wear the other bastards she married. She seemed to have a taste for slobs.'

'Thanks.'

'I don't mean to be back-handed. It's just the way things are.'

'Of course.'

'What are you planning to do with yourself tomorrow?'

'Not much. I'm hoping to look at some land.'

623

'Don't tell me you're thinking of buying in back here?'

'I doubt it. No. I'm just hoping to bring myself up to date with some history.'

'History?'

'Yes.'

'That's news to me,' Clem said. 'I didn't know we had any.'

The next morning Ian rose at first light to help Clem and his sons with milking. And after an early breakfast he drove into Te Ika, leaving Margaret and David behind, to make an inquiry at the county council office. The town, though more substantial, was not really so different: a large new hotel with potted trees outside, a couple of hamburger bars, a brassy new supermarket; otherwise much the same line of unlovely buildings teetering at the edge of the railway track and a vanished frontier. The county clerk, a gentle grey-haired man, was helpful enough. He hunted through records. 'Ah, yes,' he said, 'the Livingstone land. Of course I remember it well. Here we are. The occupier died quite a few years ago.'

'That's right.'

'In unfortunate circumstances.'

'Yes.'

'And the land's been held in trust, since. The next of kin, the son, has never claimed it. The land was debt-free, so there was no claim elsewhere. The chances are that it will have to be put up for sale soon, to cover unpaid back rates. Though I see a note here from our valuer saying it's a pretty poor proposition now, hardly an economic unit at all the way things are. Like a lot of this marginal land now. Also it would require pretty intensive clearing; it's all gone back. The question is whether it would be worth anyone's trouble.'

'I see.'

'Do you have,' asked the county clerk hopefully, 'any special interest in the land? You could always put in a bid.'

Ian shook his head. 'Not really; I'm just interested in knowing what happened to it, in the end. A mildly personal interest.'

The old man gave him a shrewd look. 'You wouldn't by any chance, be the errant son?'

Ian did his best to laugh.

'It's just, you see, that you'd be about the same age, as I remember it. And also I seem to remember hearing that he'd been seen about here, once or twice. There was talk at the time.

624

Some kind of artist, wasn't he? Anyway there was scandal, quite apart from the circumstances of his father's death. You're bringing it back to me. Almost, not quite. Perhaps you know more.'

'Possibly,' Ian agreed. 'When was he seen?'

'The son? Hard to say. I just remember hearing something.'

'Before his father's death, or after?'

'Now you have me. I think after, but I can't swear to it. Now let me think; someone must know. His nearest neighbour up there would have been Fletcher. Jock Fletcher. Jock died a couple of years back, but his wife's still in the town. You might try her. She has a cottage by the river on South Road; the farm's been sold up.'

'Of course I know your name,' said Mrs Fletcher. 'What I never knew until now was that you had ever lived in this town.'

They sat in garden seats, among rose bushes, above the river. An impeccable lawn sloped down to the bank. The river ran slow and swirling here, in a lazy bend; on the other side was steep pastureland sprinkled with sheep and then, abruptly, craggy hills. Mrs Fletcher was a pleasant, precise old lady. She put him at ease with gentle manner and dry sherry.

'And you wish to know about Timothy Livingstone,' she went on. 'May I ask the reason for your interest?'

'I knew him once.'

'I see.'

'And I'm interested in knowing what's happened to him, if that's possible.'

'Quite understandable. I should be interested in knowing myself. He had, I always thought, a remarkable talent.'

'I thought so too.'

'I should confess, perhaps, that I gave him his first lessons in art. Or, rather, I gave him something to unlearn, when it suited him. I was an art teacher once, you see.'

'I seem to remember him talking about you.'

'Then you must have known him well.'

'Up to a point. Yes. But a long time ago now. The last I knew of him, he was in Paris. Ten years or more ago. But I heard something this morning which seems to suggest that he has been around here since.'

'Jock swore to it.'

'Jock?'

'My husband. Late husband. He swore to having seen Timothy once. Perhaps four or five years ago, not long before he died; otherwise it's hard to be exact. He was driving into town one evening, just after dark, when this figure rose up in his headlights. Someone walking on the verge of the road. It was rare to see anyone walking up there at the top of the Waiatarua valley. And whoever it was could have been going only towards two places. Our farm, or the Livingstone land. And whoever it was never turned up at our place, so it must have been the Livingstone land. You see.'

He didn't, altogether. 'But your husband didn't actually recognize him?'

'Well, not immediately. No. Or he would have stopped his car. He just thought there was something familiar about the face, and figure; he couldn't place it immediately. But by the time he reached town he was sure who it was. He rang me to say we might be having a visitor. But we never did; he never turned up at our place.'

She trailed off sadly.

'He could have been wrong,' Ian suggested. 'Just someone in his headlights for a moment; it can be deceptive.'

'There was more to it than that,' she said.

'Oh?'

'That was on a Friday evening. The next day, Saturday, we decided to go up to the Livingstone land ourselves, to see who was up there. But we had visitors; it was difficult to get away. In the end we didn't get up there until Sunday. We didn't find anyone; we were too late. But we did find, near where the farmhouse had stood, the remains of a freshly lit campfire. The ashes were still warm. Whoever it was had gone early in the morning.'

'You say whoever it was,' Ian observed. 'You don't appear entirely convinced yourself.'

'But who else could it have been?' she asked. 'Only Timothy, surely.'

It was, true, difficult to argue. 'And what,' he asked gently, 'do you suppose he might have been doing there?'

'Settling something to his own satisfaction, I imagine,' she answered. 'Between himself and the land, himself and his father; or himself and his creator. I rather think you're not without imagination yourself, Mr Freeman. Perhaps you could be more exact.'

'No,' Ian said.

'Imagination is a gift and a curse. In war, I believe, the least imaginative men are usually the most brave, because they cannot see consequences. Therefore an imaginative man who is also brave must be doubly so. I confess I have always found it taxing, myself. Yet I should sooner not be without it. Imagination, I mean. I hope I have not wandered from the point. It is just that, in connection with Timothy, I have always had much opportunity to use it. I never, really, knew him as other than a child. Can I offer you another sherry?'

'Thank you,' Ian said, 'but I'm expected elsewhere.' He rose.

'I am afraid I have been little help to you.'

'Not at all. You've told me a great deal.'

'That he once returned to spend a night or two on his father's land? I cannot see that as a great deal, however much I try; I cannot see anything extraordinary about it at all.'

'It means a great deal to me. It means that he is still alive, for example. And very likely alive in this country somewhere.'

'I see. And is that enough?'

'I'm sorry; I don't understand.' Ian, for a moment, was honestly perplexed.

'What of this rare talent he had? Doesn't it concern you whether that is alive too?'

'I think,' Ian said, 'that is another story.'

'I prefer to see it as all one. I wonder, you see, whether his talent, or his desire to make use of it, might not have died with his father. Surely that idea doesn't puzzle you.'

'I never knew his father. So – '

'One had the substance of the land, the other the shadow. In that way, then, there was a contest between the two. That is what I felt, many years ago, when I visited the city to see Timothy's paintings on public display.'

'Did you see him?'

'No. I preferred not to. I felt I might have been an embarrassment to him.' She paused. 'But the nature of their context seemed clear to me then, if less so now. When Ned Livingstone died there was, of course, no longer a contest; and Tim, it would appear, no longer painted. At least not that I heard. The arrangement of circumstances seems, to me, significant. And why should he never have returned to claim his father's land? At the least he might have sold it, at some gain to himself.

Guilt, some might say. I prefer to imagine something other, and more. Never mind; it's all over now.'

'Yes,' Ian agreed.

'Except in my imagination,' she qualified. 'I hope the wanderings of an old woman have not been too great a strain on your patience.'

'Not at all,' he insisted. 'I just wish there was something I could give you in exchange; I seem to have done nothing but take.'

'It is in the nature of the artist to take,' she observed. 'As it was in Timothy's, for example. So you are forgiven.'

'I have a number of his paintings. Perhaps you would accept one.'

'Indeed,' she said. 'I should be delighted.'

He left her, then, in her immaculate garden, beside the slowly turning river.

The road gave out half way through the gorge; it became increasingly eroded and overgrown and then simply ceased to exist, where it had collapsed into the river. There was, of course, no need for it now : no repair had been attempted. Ian parked the car on the last safe ground, and then they clambered carefully around the edge of the subsidence, and continued through the gorge on foot. David appeared more cheerful, away from Clem and the Saunders farm; his walk into the country became a casual browse. Margaret, in jeans and a dilapidated farm shirt, a floppy yellow sunhat shading her face, appeared jaunty enough too, but kept pace with Ian, while David dawdled behind. Eventually the limestone walls of the gorge drifted away, and the road, now little more than track, wandered through scrubby lowland, with the hills still crowding close. The afternoon sun burned down the western sky; dust lifted under their feet. The scrub, where touched by light breeze, gave off a dry crackle. The cicadas were subdued; the birds were soundless. There was, apart from the remnant of road, thin evidence of man : a rotted fence-post here, some rusted strands of barbed wire there. It was difficult to imagine that where they walked pastures had once shone in the sun, like something polished. Or that cattle had grazed, like tiny toys in the distance. Creeper involved itself untidily in the scrub and fern. There would soon be forest of substance again. The hills, though in a way strangely smaller than he expected, continued to command, the further they pushed across the land. All too familiar, and then unreal.

The scrub and other second growth opened upon a grassy clearing. Pines and poplars grew at the perimeter. At the centre, stark and moss-grown, like some natural element, stood an old brick chimney. There was creepered debris at its foot, skeletal stumps of charred timber, corrugated roofing iron. Honeysuckle grew wild, and potatoes in uncultivated tangle. Off to one side were a couple of collapsing outbuildings, a garage perhaps, and a cowshed. Sunken in long grass was an antique vehicle, almost stripped down to its chassis. The clearing was quiet, apart from their feet moving through the dry grass, and the sound of the creek running near. 'Here we are, then,' Margaret said. 'Satisfied?'

Ian made no answer. He shrugged.

'I don't expect you ever will be,' she observed. 'He's not here, is he?'

'Who?'

'Tim, of course.'

'No,' he said shortly. 'But then I didn't expect he would be.'

'Then what's the point?'

'The point?' he repeated vaguely.

'There must have been one,' she suggested.

'Probably,' he agreed. 'Yes. I've forgotten now.'

'Perhaps you just had to see there was an end to the trail.'

'Something like that.'

'At least you don't have to make your peace with the dead any more. Because he's not, evidently.'

'No.'

'And you're not interested in the land?'

'No.'

'If you don't want to talk, that's all right. Just say so. I'm going down to the creek. At least I can get something to drink.'

There was still a rudimentary track towards the creek. Fern grew down to the water's edge. Sunlight trickled through the dense fronds, patchily colouring the surface of the water; tiny stones were distinct upon the sandy bottom. David, who had just caught up, followed them down. They all knelt and drank. The water had a pleasing chill.

'So,' David said. 'Where have we got to?'

'We were just considering that,' his mother replied. 'The end of the trail, it seems agreed.'

'A pretty godforsaken place.'

'The end of the trail usually is.'

'If this is it, then, I might try a swim and cool off. If you've no better suggestion.'

'And I think I might just dangle my feet in the water for a while,' Margaret said, and rolled up her jeans. She looked at Ian. 'And what about you?'

'I'm easy. I think I'll wander for a bit.'

'In case you've missed something?'

He walked back towards the clearing again, brushing fern free of his face. There was a splash and shout behind him as David dived. It seemed to make the quiet of the clearing even more unnatural. He was not really looking for anything, other than the certainty that there was nothing to find, as he circled the ruin of the house. So there was dismay in his discovery.

Off to one side was some distinctly crushed grass where someone appeared to have pitched a tent. And there was a circle of cinders where a campfire had been. Plainly not the campfire the Fletchers had seen; that would have been years overgrown. One much more recent, perhaps only a month or two old. Whose? Possibly some hunter or tramper : some stranger. Otherwise it was only too easy to imagine. He would have preferred not.

He had only himself to blame. Cicadas had begun to drum louder in the late afternoon.

He wandered the clearing again in vague daze. Then his arm was taken from behind; his nerves flashed. Margaret had come to stand quietly beside him.

'So there's nothing,' she said at last.

'No.'

'But you had to see.'

'Yes.'

'It's all right. It's been a pleasant walk. David seems to think so too.'

They moved around the remains of the farmhouse until they were in the lengthening shadow cast by the chimney. Debris, broken glass, nails, crunched under their feet; there were shards of shattered chinaware. Margaret took a stick and poked at a pile of it. 'I might as well have a turn at raking through ashes too,' she observed. 'Perhaps I'll have more luck.'

She did. Something dislodged with small sound; he bent to retrieve it. It appeared at first to be an old coin, rather thick, and encrusted. 'Here,' he said, and pushed it into her hand.

'It's hollow,' she said, 'and makes a sound when you shake it. Listen.'

He listened. The sound was faint in the afternoon.

'It's like,' she went on, 'a little tambourine. That little frilled edge. What else could it be?'

She shook it again.

'I can't for the life of me imagine,' she added. 'How odd. A kind of toy-size tambourine. What would it be doing here?'

'I can't imagine either.'

She rubbed at its blackened surface, until a shine showed through.

'Keep it,' he suggested, 'for luck.'

Ian, with this distraction, felt almost calm again. Shadows had moved across the hills in bold corrugation. The breeze was brisker, and temperature cooler. There wasn't much of the afternoon left.

'Well,' she said, 'what do you really make of it now?'

'Of what?'

'This place.'

'You mean this land in particular, or the country in general?'

'Either, if you like. Or both.'

He shrugged.

'Come on. You must have something to say.'

'I don't know that anyone can make much of it. Except paint pictures, perhaps, and tell stories. To show that we've been here. It mightn't be good for much else in the long run. And, then again, that might be true of anywhere.'

She laughed. 'So I should have known better than to ask.'

'Yes.'

'Tell me,' she said suddenly, 'how does God fit into your scheme of things?'

'He doesn't.'

'No?'

'He never quite made the voyage out. Too much pressing business elsewhere, no doubt. Or because of doubt. He would know. I don't.'

'So no angels sing.'

'No,' he agreed. 'None I can hear.'

'Well,' she said, 'time to fetch David. If we're to get home before dark.'

'Does he realize?' Ian asked.

631

'What?'

'That his other possible relatives lived here.'

'It might interest him to know. But I doubt it. I think he'd sooner leave possibilities to us. Besides, I'd sooner not confuse him now. He seems to think you're a reasonable, if rather belated proposition as a father. I think I should leave it at that. You too.'

'I'll try,' he promised.

'And leave Tim Livingstone unfound.'

'It seems to me I've already done that with some success.'

'True,' she said. 'So let's get home before dark.'

Later, with David young and cool between them, they walked away from the land. Before they entered the gorge, though, Ian looked back. Most of the valley was in evening shadow, and the sky was taking the first colour of sunset. Despite himself he wondered how a campfire might look, down there, in the distance, under the hills. But there were, in the end, only the hills to see.

It was no effort, then, to meet Margaret's inquiring eyes; they hurried together to catch up with David.

1971

THE TRACK INTO THE VALLEY WAS STILL DRYING OUT AFTER heavy summer rain. The man and the boy walked it with care. They both carried packs. The boy also carried a fishing rod, and the man a rifle. The boy was possibly ten years old, and the man at least forty. The boy walked lightly, slowing now and then to keep in step with the man; the man limped. They both appeared familiar with the way. The afternoon air was crisp.

'Do you think many other people ever come up here?' the boy asked.

'I shouldn't think so,' replied the man. 'Not now.'

'Then it's almost all ours,' the boy said.

'Yes,' the man agreed. 'Almost.'

'That's good.'

'Why is it good?'

'Because it is,' said the boy. 'I don't like to think of other people coming here. I like to think it's ours.'

'I see.'

'Why do you like coming back here?' asked the boy. 'We could go to other places.'

The man shrugged. 'Perhaps other places aren't the same.'

'It doesn't matter. I don't really want to go to other places anyway. I was just wondering.'

They walked in silence for a time. It was only an hour or two away from dark; the birds were loud.

'I expect I was just wondering,' the boy went on, 'why you like it so much. And I expect it's because you know it.'

'Yes. I expect it is.'

'And because you like getting away from things.'

'Yes.'

'I like getting away from things too,' the boy said. 'But most of all I like getting away with you.'

'That's good,' his father said. 'I'm glad about that.'

'It's the only time we do.'

'That's true.'

'At home you're always so busy with things.'

'Never mind,' his father said. 'We're here, aren't we?'

'Almost,' the boy agreed. 'Are we going to camp in the same place as last year?'

'We might as well. It's sheltered. And there's water near.'

'I used to think it was spooky, by the chimney of the old house. I don't think I mind so much now.'

'That's good, then.'

Another hundred yards and they arrived in the clearing. They boy went across the clearing first. His father followed slowly. 'Here,' the boy called. 'You can still see the place where we had our last fire.'

'Time to get another one lit, then.'

The boy unshouldered his pack and propped his fishing rod against a branch. 'I'll collect wood,' he said, 'and get it started.'

'You do that,' the man said. 'And I'll get my breath.' He removed his own pack, stood the rifle against it, and found a place to sit near their last campfire. It seemed much less than a year since they had doused it. But the boy was undeniably a year older. Otherwise there was not much change. There never was much change, unless in the size of the clearing, as it shrank. The hills were certainly the same. He took a large breath. The hills had not changed at all.

'I'll get water,' he said presently.

The boy had firewood stacked neatly and almost ready to light. They had their rituals now; his father always fetched the water.

The man carried a billy down to the creek. When he arrived, he bent, drank, and then slowly sank his face into the water. He was there on the edge of the creek for some time. Finally he dipped the billy into the fast current and carried the water back to the boy. The fire was lit. Smoke drifted across the clearing; it had the sweet smell of dry manuka. The boy was now struggling to erect their tent. His father helped him finish the job. Soon they were almost ready for the night, with their food cooking. They could sit for a while.

'Were you happy here?' asked the boy.

'Sometimes,' the man said.

'I supposed you must have been.'

'Why?'

'Otherwise you wouldn't keep coming back.'

'It's not quite as easy as that. I did leave, you know.'

'I know; you told me.'

'It's true I sometimes wonder why. The point of it all, I mean. Some day I might try to explain. When you're old enough, perhaps. Or when I am.'

'What did you do when you went away?'

'A great deal, or nothing at all. I'm not sure which. It doesn't matter now.'

'What about when you lived in France? You told me you lived there once.'

'Yes, once. But no, I'm not talking about that. Not really. That was before I came back here.'

'And before you met my mother.'

'Yes. And before you were born. Then I had to settle down. I wasn't sorry. It was time I settled down, you see.'

The boy didn't see. He looked puzzled.

'Is it true that you used to paint pictures? Mum says so.'

'Your mother has a vivid imagination.'

'But you did, didn't you?'

'Well, now and then. Yes. Not any more.'

'Why not?'

'Because I don't need to. Besides, I think I only ever wanted to paint one.'

'And what happened to it? The one you wanted to paint?'

'I expect I lost it somewhere. Anyway I've never seen it again. And, besides, other things happened.'

'What things?'

'You, for example. You were one of the better things.' He paused; the boy still looked uncertain. 'But let's forget it,' he insisted. 'What will we do tomorrow?'

'Fishing,' the boy said. 'Please.'

'You think that big trout might still be there from last year?'

'We could see.'

'All right. We'll see.'

Soon the hills shouldered the last of the light; the valley grew dark. They ate, then, in the glow of their campfire. A large moon rose, drenching the forest trees, the scrub and tall fern with vivid light. Their fire sank low, no rival at all. When

635

its warmth went, the boy announced himself sleepy, crawled into the tent, and climbed into his sleeping bag. The man saw that the boy was comfortable and then, outside the tent again, seated on a log beside the ebbing fire, resumed his watch on the valley. He was slower to admit himself tired. But he did in the end. The night was rich in particulars; too rich. He could not begin to select. And perhaps he no longer had wish to. The even sound of his son's breathing came from the tent, quite reassuring, one particular he could never escape. He would need to be fresh to keep pace with the boy in the morning. He rose, flexing his stiffened limbs. There was little left of their camp-fire : a fading ember or two. He thought he could sleep now, and safely leave the land until morning. For it would still be there tomorrow, of course. It would still be there when all the fires had burned.